THE BAT
THE HAUNTED LADY
THE YELLOW ROOM

MARY ROBERTS RINEHART

Three Complete Novels by America's Mistress of Mystery

THE BAT
THE HAUNTED LADY
THE YELLOW ROOM

Kensington Books

KENSINGTON BOOKS are published by

Kensington Publishing Corp.
850 Third Avenue
New York, NY 10022

ISBN 1-57566-114-4

First Kensington Trade Paperback Printing: October, 1995

10 9 8 7 6 5 4 3 2

Printed in the United States of America

Contents

THE BAT
1

THE HAUNTED LADY
175

THE YELLOW ROOM
357

THE BAT

1

The Shadow
of the Bat

"You've *got* to get him, boys—get him or bust!" said a tired police chief, pounding a heavy fist on a table. The detectives he bellowed the words at looked at the floor. They had done their best and failed. Failure meant "resignation" for the police chief, return to the hated work of pounding the pavements for them—they knew it, and, knowing it, could summon no gesture of bravado to answer their chief's. Gunmen, thugs, hi-jackers, loft-robbers, murderers, they could get them all in time—but they could not get the man he wanted.

"Get him—to hell with expense—I'll give you carte blanche—but get him!" said a haggard millionaire in the sedate inner offices of the best private detective firm in the country. The man on the other side of the desk, man hunter extraordinary, old servant of Government and State, sleuthhound without a peer, threw up his hands in a gesture of odd hopelessness. "It isn't the money, Mr. De Courcy—I'd give every cent I've made to get the man you want—but I can't promise you results—for the first time in my life." The conversation was ended.

"Get him? Huh! I'll get him, watch my smoke!" It was young ambition speaking in a certain set of rooms in Washington. Three days later young ambition lay in a New York gutter with a bullet in his heart and a look of such horror and surprise on his dead face that even the ambulance-doctor who found him felt shaken. "We've lost the most promising man I've had in ten years," said his chief when the news came in. He swore helplessly, "Damn the luck!"

"Get him—get him—get him—*get* him!" From a thousand sources now the clamor arose—press, police, and public alike crying out for the capture of the master criminal of a century—lost voices hounding a specter down the alleyways of the wind. And still the meshes broke and the quarry slipped away before the hounds were well on the scent—leaving behind a trail of shattered safes and rifled jewel cases— while ever the clamor rose higher to "Get him—get him—get—"

Get whom, in God's name—get what? Beast, man, or devil? A specter—a flying shadow—the shadow of a Bat.

From thieves' hangout to thieves' hangout the word passed along stirring the underworld like the passage of an electric spark. "There's a bigger guy than Pete Flynn shooting the works, a guy that could have Jim Gunderson for breakfast and not notice he'd et." The underworld heard and waited to be shown; after a little while the underworld began to whisper to itself in tones of awed respect. There were bright stars and flashing comets in the sky of the world of crime—but this new planet rose with the portent of an evil moon.

The Bat—they called him the Bat. Like a bat he chose the night hours for his work of rapine; like a bat he struck and vanished, pouncingly, noiselessly; like a bat he never showed himself to the face of the day. He'd never been in stir, the bulls had never mugged him, he didn't run with a mob, he played a lone hand, and fenced his stuff so that even the Fence couldn't swear he knew his face. Most lone wolves had a moll at any rate—women were their ruin—but if the Bat had a moll, not even the grapevine telegraph could locate her.

Rat-faced gunmen in the dingy back rooms of saloons muttered over his exploits with bated breath. In tawdrily gorgeous apartments, where gathered the larger figures, the proconsuls of the world of crime, cold, conscienceless brains dissected the work of a colder and swifter brain than theirs, with suave and bitter envy. Evil's Four Hundred chattered, discussed, debated—sent out a thousand invisible tentacles to clutch at a shadow—to turn this shadow and its distorted genius to their own ends. The tentacles recoiled, baffled—the Bat worked alone—not even Evil's Four Hundred could bend him into a willing instrument to execute another's plan.

The men higher up waited. They had dealt with lone wolves before and broken them. Some day the Bat would slip and falter; then they would have him. But the weeks passed into months and still the Bat flew free, solitary, untamed, and deadly. At last even his own kind turned upon him; the underworld is like the upper in its fear and distrust of genius that flies alone. But when they turned against him, they turned against a spook—a shadow. A cold and bodiless laughter from a pit of darkness answered and mocked at their bungling gestures of hate—and went on, flouting Law and Lawless alike.

Where official trailer and private sleuth had failed, the newspapers might succeed—or so thought the disillusioned young men of the Fourth Estate—the tireless foxes, nose-down on the trail of news—the trackers, who never gave up until that news was run to earth. Star reporter, leg-man, cub, veteran gray in the trade—one and all they tried to pin the Bat like a caught butterfly to the front page of their respective journals—soon or late each gave up, beaten. He was news— bigger news each week—a thousand ticking typewriters clicked his adventures—the brief, staccato recital of his career in the morgues of the great dailies grew longer and more incredible each day. But the big news—the scoop of the century—the yearned-for headline, *Bat Nabbed Red-Handed, Bat Slain in Gun Duel with Police*—still eluded the ravenous maw of the Linotypes. And meanwhile, the red-scored list of his felonies lengthened and the rewards offered from various sources for any clue which might lead to his apprehension mounted and mounted till they totaled a small fortune.

Columnists took him up, played with the name and the terror, used the name and the terror as a starting point from which to exhibit their own particular opinions on everything and anything. Ministers mentioned him in sermons; cranks wrote fanatic letters denouncing him as one of the seven-headed beasts of the Apocalypse and a forerunner of the end of the world; a popular revue put on a special Bat number wherein eighteen beautiful chorus girls appeared masked and black-winged in costumes of Brazilian bat fur; there were Bat club sandwiches, Bat cigarettes, and a new shade of hosiery called simply and succinctly *Bat*. He became a fad—a catchword—a national figure. And yet—he was walking Death—cold—remorseless. But Death itself had become a toy of publicity.

A city editor, at lunch with a colleague, pulled at his cigarette and talked. "See that Sunday story we had on the Bat?" he asked. "Pretty tidy—huh—and yet we didn't have to play it up. It's an amazing list— the Marshall jewels—the Allison murder—the mail truck thing—two hundred thousand he got out of that, all negotiable, and two men dead. I wonder how many people he's really killed. We made it six murders and nearly a million in loot—didn't even have room for the small stuff—but there must be more—"

His companion whistled.

"And when is the Universe's Finest Newspaper going to burst forth with *Bat Captured by* BLADE *Reporter?*" he queried sardonically.

"Oh, for—lay off it, will you?" said the city editor peevishly. "The Old Man's been hopping around about it for two months till everybody's plumb cuckoo. Even offered a bonus—a big one—and that shows how crazy he is—he doesn't love a nickel any better than his right eye—for any sort of exclusive story. Bonus—huh!" and he crushed out his cigarette. "It won't be a *Blade* reporter that gets that bonus—or any reporter. It'll be Sherlock Holmes from the spirit world!"

"Well, can't you dig up a Sherlock?"

The editor spread out his hands. "Now, look here," he said. "We've got the best staff of any paper in the country, if I do say it. We've got boys that could get a personal signed story from Delilah on how she barbered Samson—and find out who struck Billy Patterson and who was the Man in the Iron Mask. But the Bat's something else again. Oh, of course, we've panned the police for not getting him; that's always the game. But, personally, I won't pan them; they've done their damnedest. They're up against something new. Scotland Yard wouldn't do any better—or any other bunch of cops that I know about."

"But look here, Bill, you don't mean to tell me he'll keep on getting away with it indefinitely?"

The editor frowned. "Confidentially—I don't know," he said with a chuckle. "The situation's this: for the first time the super-crook—the super-crook of fiction—the kind that never makes a mistake—has come to life—real life. And it'll take a cleverer man than any Central Office dick I've ever met to catch him!"

"Then you don't think he's just an ordinary crook with a lot of luck?"

"I do not." The editor was emphatic. "He's much brainier. Got a ghastly sense of humor, too. Look at the way he leaves his calling card after every job—a black paper bat inside the Marshall safe—a bat drawn on the wall with a burnt match where he'd jimmied the Cedarburg Bank—a real bat, dead, tacked to the mantelpiece over poor old Allison's body. Oh, he's in a class by himself—and I very much doubt if he was a crook at all for most of his life."

"You mean?"

"I mean this. The police have been combing the underworld for him; I don't think he comes from there. I think they've got to look higher, up in our world, for a brilliant man with a kink in the brain. He may be a doctor, a lawyer, a merchant, honored in his community by day—good line that, I'll use it some time—and at night, a bloodthirsty assassin. Deacon Brodie—ever hear of him—the Scotch deacon that burgled his parishioners' houses on the quiet? Well—that's our man."

"But my Lord, Bill—"

"I know. I've been going around the last month, looking at everybody I knew and thinking—*are you the Bat?* Try it for a while. You'll want to sleep with a light in your room after a few days of it. Look around the University Club—that white-haired man over there—dignified—respectable—is he the Bat? Your own lawyer—your own doctor—your own best friend. Can happen you know."

"Bill! You're giving me the shivers!"

"Am I?" The editor laughed grimly. "Think it over. No, it isn't so pleasant. But that's my theory—and I swear I think I'm right." He rose.

His companion laughed uncertainly.

"How about you, Bill—are you the Bat?"

The editor smiled. "See," he said, "it's got you already. No, I can prove an alibi. The Bat's been laying off the city recently—taking a fling at some of the swell suburbs. Besides I haven't the brains—I'm free to admit it." He struggled into his coat. "Well, let's talk about something else. I'm sick of the Bat and his murders."

His companion rose as well, but it was evident that the editor's theory had taken firm hold on his mind. As they went out the door together he recurred to the subject.

"Honestly, though, Bill—were you serious, really serious—when you said you didn't know of a single detective with brains enough to trap this devil?"

The editor paused in the doorway. "Serious enough," he said. "And yet there's one man—I don't know him myself but from what I have heard of him, he might be able—but what's the use of speculating?"

"I'd like to know all the same," insisted the other, and laughed nervously. "We're moving out to the country next week ourselves—right in the Bat's new territory."

"We-el," said the editor, "you won't let it go any further? Of course it's just an idea of mine, but if the Bat ever came prowling around our place, the detective I'd try to get in touch with would be—" He put his lips close to his companions's ear and whispered a name.

The man whose name he whispered, oddly enough, was at that moment standing before his official superior in a quiet room not very far away. Tall, reticently good-looking and well, if inconspicuously, clothed and groomed, he by no means seemed the typical detective that the editor had spoken of so scornfully. He looked something like a college athlete who had kept up his training, something like a pillar of one of the more sedate financial houses. He could assume and discard a dozen manners in as many minutes, but, to the casual observer, the one thing certain about him would probably seem his utter lack of connection with the seamier side of existence. The key to his real secret of life, however, lay in his eyes. When in repose, as now, they were veiled and without unusual quality—but they were the eyes of a man who can wait and a man who can strike.

He stood perfectly easy before his chief for several moments before the latter looked up from his papers.

"Well, Anderson," he said at last, looking up, "I got your report on the Wilhenry burglary this morning. I'll tell you this about it—if you do a neater and quicker job in the next ten years, you can take this desk away from me. I'll give it to you. As it is, your name's gone up for promotion today; you deserved it long ago."

"Thank you, sir," replied the tall man quietly, "but I had luck with that case."

"Of course you had luck," said the chief. "Sit down, won't you, and have a cigar—if you can stand my brand. Of course you had luck, Anderson, but that isn't the point. It takes a man with brains to use a piece of luck as you used it. I've waited a long time here for a man with your sort of brains and, by Judas, for a while I thought they were all as dead as Pinkerton. But now I know there's one of them alive at any rate—and it's a hell of a relief."

"Thank you, sir," said the tall man, smiling and sitting down. He took a cigar and lit it. "That makes it easier, sir—your telling me that. Because—I've come to ask a favor."

"All right," responded the chief promptly. "Whatever it is, it's granted."

Anderson smiled again. "You'd better hear what it is first, sir. I don't want to put anything over on you. I want to be assigned to a certain case—that's all."

The chief's look grew searching. "H'm," he said. "Well, as I say, anything within reason. What case do you want to be assigned to?"

The muscles of Anderson's left hand tensed on the arm of his chair. He looked squarely at the chief. "I want a chance at the Bat!" he replied slowly.

The chief's face became expressionless. "I said—anything within reason," he responded softly, regarding Anderson keenly.

"I want a chance at the Bat!" repeated Anderson stubbornly. "If I've done good work so far—I want a chance at the Bat!"

The chief drummed on the desk. Annoyance and surprise were in his voice when he spoke.

"But look here, Anderson," he burst out finally. "Anything else and I'll—but what's the use? I said a minute ago, you had brains—but now, by Judas, I doubt it! If anyone else wanted a chance at the Bat, I'd give it to them and gladly—I'm hard-boiled. But you're too valuable a man to be thrown away!"

"I'm no more valuable than Wentworth would have been."

"Maybe not—and look what happened to him! A bullet hole in his heart—and thirty years of work that he might have done thrown away! No, Anderson, I've found two first-class men since I've been at this desk—Wentworth and you. He asked for his chance; I gave it to him—turned him over to the Government—and lost him. Good detectives aren't so plentiful that I can afford to lose you both."

"Wentworth was a friend of mine," said Anderson softly. His knuckles were white dints in the hand that gripped the chair. "Ever since the Bat got him I've wanted my chance. Now my other work's cleaned up—and I still want it."

"But I tell you—" began the chief in tones of high exasperation. Then he stopped and looked at his protégé. There was a silence for a time.

"Oh, well—" said the chief finally in a hopeless voice. "Go ahead—commit suicide—I'll send you a 'Gates Ajar' and a card, 'Here lies a damn fool who would have been a great detective if he hadn't been so pigheaded.' Go ahead!"

Anderson rose. "Thank you, sir," he said in a deep voice. His eyes had light in them now. "I can't thank you enough, sir."

"Don't try," grumbled the chief. "If I weren't as much of a damned fool as you are I wouldn't let you do it. And if I weren't so damned old, I'd go after the slippery devil myself and let you sit here and watch *me* get brought in with an infernal paper bat pinned where my shield ought to be. The Bat's supernatural, Anderson. You haven't a chance in the world but it does me good all the same to shake hands with a man with brains *and* nerve," and he solemnly wrung Anderson's hand in an iron grip.

Anderson smiled. "The cagiest bat flies once too often," he said. "I'm not promising anything, chief, but—"

"Maybe," said the chief. "Now wait a minute, keep your shirt on, you're not going bat hunting this minute, you know—"

"Sir? I thought I—"

"Well, you're not," said the chief decidedly. "I've still some little respect for my own intelligence and it tells me to get all the work out of you I can, before you start wild-goose chasing after this—this bat out of hell. The first time he's heard of again—and it shouldn't be long from the fast way he works—you're assigned to the case. That's understood. Till then, you do what *I* tell you—and it'll be *work*, believe me!''

''All right, sir,'' Anderson laughed and turned to the door. ''And— thank you again.''

He went out. The door closed. The chief remained for some minutes looking at the door and shaking his head. ''The best man I've had in years—except Wentworth,'' he murmured to himself. ''And throwing himself away—to be killed by a cold-blooded devil that nothing human can catch—you're getting old, John Grogan—but, by Judas, you can't blame him, can you? If you were a man in the prime like him, by Judas, you'd be doing it yourself. And yet it'll go hard—losing him—''

He turned back to his desk and his papers. But for some minutes he could not pay attention to the papers. There was a shadow on them—a shadow that blurred the typed letters—the shadow of bat's wings.

2

The Indomitable
Miss Van Gorder

Miss Cornelia Van Gorder, indomitable spinster, last bearer of a name which has been great in New York when New York was a red-roofed Nieuw Amsterdam and Peter Stuyvesant a parvenu, sat propped up in bed in the green room of her newly rented country house reading the morning newspaper. Thus seen, with an old soft Paisley shawl tucked in about her thin shoulders and without the stately gray transformation that adorned her on less intimate occasions, she looked much less formidable and more innocently placid than those could ever have imagined who had only felt the bite of her tart wit at such functions as the state Van Gorder dinners. Patrician to her finger tips, independent to the roots of her hair, she preserved, at 65, a humorous and quenchless curiosity in regard to every side of life, which even the full and crowded years that already lay behind her had not entirely satisfied. She was an Age and an Attitude, but she was more than that; she had grown old without growing dull or losing touch with youth—her face had the delicate strength of a fine cameo and her mild and youthful heart preserved an innocent zest for adventure.

Wide travel, social leadership, the world of art and books, a dozen charities, an existence rich with diverse experience—all these she had enjoyed energetically and to the full—but she felt, with ingenious vanity, that there were still sides to her character which even these had not brought to light. As a little girl she had hesitated between wishing to be a locomotive engineer or a famous bandit—and when she had found, at seven, that the accident of sex would probably debar her from either occupation, she had resolved fiercely that some time before she died she would show the world in general and the Van Gorder clan in particular that a woman was quite as capable of dangerous exploits as a man. So far her life, while exciting enough at moments, had never actually been dangerous and time was slipping away without giving her an opportunity to prove her hardiness of heart. Whenever she thought of this the fact annoyed her extremely—and she thought of it now.

She threw down the morning paper disgustedly. Here she was at 65—rich, safe, settled for the summer in a delightful country place with a good cook, excellent servants, beautiful gardens and grounds— everything as respectable and comfortable as—as a limousine! And out in the world people were murdering and robbing each other, floating over Niagara Falls in barrels, rescuing children from burning houses, taming tigers, going to Africa to hunt gorillas, doing all sorts of exciting things! She could not float over Niagara Falls in a barrel; Lizzie Allen, her faithful old maid, would never let her! She could not go to Africa to hunt gorillas; Sally Ogden, her sister, would never let her hear the last of it. She could not even, as she certainly would if she were a man, try and track down this terrible creature, the Bat!

She sniffed disgruntledly. Things came to her much too easily. Take this very house she was living in. Ten days ago she had decided on the spur of the moment—a decision suddenly crystallized by a weariness of charitable committees and the noise and heat of New York—to take a place in the country for the summer. It was late in the renting season—even the ordinary difficulties of finding a suitable spot would have added some spice to the quest—but this ideal place had practically fallen into her lap, with no trouble or search at all. Courtleigh Fleming, president of the Union Bank, who had built the house on a scale of comfortable magnificence—Courtleigh Fleming had died suddenly in the West when Miss Van Gorder was beginning her house hunting. The day after his death her agent had called her up. Richard Fleming, Courtleigh Fleming's nephew and heir, was anxious to rent the Fleming house at once. If she made a quick decision it was hers for the summer, at a bargain. Miss Van Gorder had decided at once; she took an innocent pleasure in bargains.

And yet she could not really say that her move to the country had brought her no adventures at all. There had been—things. Last night the lights had gone off unexpectedly and Billy, the Japanese butler and handy man, had said that he had seen a face at one of the kitchen windows—a face that vanished when he went to the window. Servants' nonsense, probably, but the servants seemed unusually nervous for people who were used to the country. And Lizzie, of course, had sworn that she had seen a man trying to get up the stairs but Lizzie could grow hysterical over a creaking door. Still—it was queer! And what had that affable Doctor Wells said to her—"I respect your courage, Miss Van Gorder—moving out into the Bat's home country, you know!" She picked up the paper again. There was a map of the scene of the Bat's most recent exploits and, yes, three of his recent crimes had been within a twenty-mile radius of this spot. She thought it over and gave a little shudder of pleasurable fear. Then she dismissed the thought with a shrug. No chance! She might live in a lonely house, two miles from the railroad station, all summer long—and the Bat would never disturb her. Nothing ever did.

She had skimmed through the paper hurriedly; now a headline caught her eye. *Failure of Union Bank*—wasn't that the bank of which Courtleigh Fleming had been president? She settled down to read the article but it was disappointingly brief. The Union Bank had closed its doors; the cashier, a young man named Bailey, was apparently under suspicion; the article mentioned Coutleigh Fleming's recent and tragic death in the best vein of newspaperese. She laid down the paper and thought—*Bailey—Bailey*—she seemed to have a vague recollection of hearing about a young man named Bailey who worked in a bank—but she could not remember where or by whom his name had been mentioned.

Well, it didn't matter. She had other things to think about. She must ring for Lizzie, get up and dress. The bright morning sun, streaming in through the long window, made lying in bed an old woman's luxury and she refused to be an old woman.

Though the worst old woman I ever knew was a man, she thought with a satiric twinkle. She was glad Sally's daughter, young Dale Ogden, was here in the house with her. The companionship of Dale's bright youth would keep her from getting old-womanish if anything could.

She smiled, thinking of Dale. Dale was a nice child, her favorite niece. Sally didn't understand her, of course—but Sally wouldn't. Sally read magazine articles on the younger generation and its wild ways. *Sally doesn't remember when she was a younger generation herself,* thought Miss Cornelia. *But I do—and if we didn't have automobiles, we had buggies—and youth doesn't change its ways just because it has cut its hair.* Before Mr. and Mrs. Ogden left for Europe, Sally had talked to her sister Cornelia, long and weightily, on the problem of Dale. *Problem of Dale, indeed!* thought Miss Cornelia scornfully. *Dale's the nicest thing I've seen in some time. She'd be ten times happier if Sally wasn't always trying to marry her off to some young snip with more of what fools call "eligibility" than brains! But there, Cornelia Van Gorder, Sally's given you your innings of ram-*

paging off to Europe and leaving Dale with you all summer. You've a lot less sense than I flatter myself you have, if you can't give your favorite niece a happy vacation from all her immediate family and maybe find her someone who'll make her happy for good and all. Miss Cornelia was an incorrigible matchmaker.

Nevertheless, she was more concerned with "the problem of Dale" than she would have admitted. Dale, at her age, with her charm and beauty—*why, she ought to behave as if she were walking on air,* thought her aunt worriedly. *And instead she acts more as if she were walking on pins and needles. She seems to like being here, I know she likes me, I'm pretty sure she's just as pleased to get a little holiday from Sally and Harry. She amuses herself, she falls in with any plan I want to make, and yet*—And yet Dale was not happy; Miss Cornelia felt sure of it. *It isn't natural for a girl to seem so lackluster and—and quiet—at her age and she's nervous, too—as if something were preying on her mind, particularly these last few days. If she were in love with somebody, somebody Sally didn't approve of particularly—well, that would account for it, of course. But Sally didn't say anything that would make me think that—or Dale either—though I don't suppose Dale would, yet, even to me. I haven't seen so much of her in these last two years*—

Then Miss Cornelia's mind seized upon a sentence in a hurried flow of her sister's last instructions, a sentence that had passed almost unnoticed at the time, something about Dale and "an unfortunate attachment—but of course, Cornelia, dear she's so young—and I'm sure it will come to nothing now her father and I have made our attitude *plain!*"

Pshaw, I bet that's it, thought Miss Cornelia shrewdly. *Dale's fallen in love, or thinks she has, with some decent young man without a penny or an "eligibility" to his name—and now she's unhappy because her parents don't approve—or because she's trying to give him up and finds she can't. Well*—and Miss Cornelia's tight little gray curls trembled with the vehemence of her decision, *if the young thing ever comes to me for advice I'll give her a piece of my mind that will surprise her and scandalize Sally Van Gorder Ogden out of her seven senses. Sally thinks nobody's worth looking at if they didn't come over to America when our family did.*

She was just stretching out her hand to ring for Lizzie when a knock came at the door. She gathered her Paisley shawl more tightly about her shoulders. "Who is it—oh, it's only you, Lizzie," as a pleasant Irish face, crowned by an old-fashioned pompadour of graying hair, peeped in at the door. "Good morning, Lizzie. I was just going to ring for you. Has Miss Dale had breakfast—I know it's shamefully late."

"Good morning, Miss Neily," said Lizzie, "and a lovely morning it is, too—if that was all of it," she added somewhat tartly as she came into the room with a little silver tray whereupon the morning mail reposed.

We have not yet described Lizzie Allen—and she deserves description. A fixture in the Van Gorder household since her sixteenth year, she had long ere now attained the dignity of a Tradition. The slip of a colleen fresh from Kerry had grown old with her mistress, until the casual bond between mistress and servant had changed into something deeper; more in keeping with a better-mannered age than ours. One could not imagine Miss Cornelia without a Lizzie to grumble at and cherish—or Lizzie without a Miss Cornelia to baby and scold with the privileged frankness of such old family servitors. The two were at once a contrast and a complement. Fifty years of American ways had not shaken Lizzie's firm belief in banshees and leprechauns or tamed her wild Irish tongue; fifty years of Lizzie had not altered Miss Cornelia's attitude of fond exasperation with some of Lizzie's more startling eccentricities. Together they may have been, as one of the younger Van Gorder cousins had irreverently put it, "a scream," but apart each would have felt lost without the other.

"Now what do you mean—if that were all of it, Lizzie?" queried Miss Cornelia sharply as she took her letters from the tray.

Lizzie's face assumed an expression of doleful reticence.

"It's not my place to speak," she said with a grim shake of her head, "but I saw my grandmother last night, God rest her—plain as life she was, the way she looked when they waked her, and if it was *my* doing we'd be leaving this house this hour!"

"Cheese-pudding for supper—of course you saw your grandmother!" said Miss Cornelia crisply, slitting open the first of her letters with a paper knife. "Nonsense, Lizzie, I'm not going to be scared away from an ideal country place because you happen to have a bad dream!"

"Was it a bad dream I saw on the stairs last night when the lights went out and I was looking for the candles?" said Lizzie heatedly. "Was it a bad dream that ran away from me and out the back door, as fast as Paddy's pig? No, Miss Neily, it was a man. Seven feet tall he was, and eyes that shone in the dark and—"

"Lizzie Allen!"

"Well, it's true for all that," insisted Lizzie stubbornly. "And why did the lights go out—tell me that, Miss Neily? They never go out in the city."

"Well, this isn't the city," said Miss Cornelia decisively. "It's the country, and very nice it is, and we're staying here all summer. I suppose I may be thankful," she went on ironically, "that it was only your grandmother you saw last night. It might have been the Bat—and then where would you be this morning?"

"I'd be stiff and stark with candles at me head and feet," said Lizzie gloomily. "Oh, Miss Neily, don't talk of that terrible creature, the Bat!" She came nearer to her mistress. *"There's bats in this house, too— real bats,"* she whispered impressively. "I saw one yesterday in the trunk room—the creature! It flew in the window and nearly had the switch off me before I could get away!"

Miss Cornelia chuckled. "Of course there are bats," she said. "There are always bats in the country. They're perfectly harmless, except to switches."

"And the Bat ye were talking of just then—he's harmless, too, I suppose?" said Lizzie with mournful satire. "Oh, Miss Neily, Miss Neily— do let's go back to the city before he flies away with us all!"

"Nonsense, Lizzie," said Miss Cornelia again, but this time less firmly. Her face grew serious. "If I thought for an instant that there was any real possibility of our being in danger here—" she said slowly. "But—oh, look at the map, Lizzie! The Bat has been—flying in this district—that's true enough but he hasn't come within ten miles of us yet!"

"What's ten miles to the Bat?" the obdurate Lizzie sighed. "And what of the letter ye had when ye first moved in here? *the Fleming house is unhealthy for strangers,* it said. *Leave it while ye can.*"

"Some silly boy or some crank." Miss Cornelia's voice was firm. "I never pay any attention to anonymous letters."

"And there's a funny-lookin' letter this mornin', down at the bottom of the pile—" persisted Lizzie. "It looked like the other one. I'd half a mind to throw it away before you saw it!"

"Now, Lizzie, that's quite enough!" Miss Cornelia had the Van Gorder manner on now. "I don't care to discuss your ridiculous fears any further. Where is Miss Dale?"

Lizzie assumed an attitude of prim rebuff. "Miss Dale's gone into the city, ma'am."

"Gone into the city?"

"Yes, ma'am. She got a telephone call this morning, early—long distance it was. I don't know who it was called her."

"Lizzie! You didn't listen?"

"Of course not, Miss Neily." Lizzie's face was a study in injured virtue. "Miss Dale took the call in her own room and shut the door."

"And you were outside the door?"

"Where else would I be dustin' that time in the mornin'?" said Lizzie fiercely. "But it's yourself knows well enough the doors in this house is thick and not a sound goes past them."

"I should hope not," said Miss Cornelia rebukingly. "But tell me, Lizzie, did Miss Dale seem—well—this morning?"

"That she did not," said Lizzie promptly. "When she came down to breakfast, after the call, she looked like a ghost. I made her the eggs she likes, too—but she wouldn't eat 'em."

"H'm," Miss Cornelia pondered. "I'm sorry if—well, Lizzie, we mustn't meddle in Miss Dale's affairs."

"No, ma'am."

"But—did she say when she would be back?"

"Yes, Miss Neily. On the two o'clock train. Oh, and I was almost forgettin'—she told me to tell you particular—she said while she was in the city she'd be after engagin' the gardener you spoke of."

"The gardener? Oh, yes, I spoke to her about that the other night. The place is beginning to look run down—so many flowers to attend to. Well, that's very kind of Miss Dale."

"Yes, Miss Neily." Lizzie hesitated, obviously with some weighty news on her mind which she wished to impart. Finally she took the plunge. "I might have told Miss Dale she could have been lookin' for a cook as well—and a housemaid—" she muttered at last, "but they hadn't spoken to me then."

Miss Cornelia sat bolt upright in bed. "A cook—and a housemaid? But we have a cook and a housemaid, Lizzie! You don't mean to tell me—"

Lizzie nodded her head. "Yes'm. They're leaving. Both of 'em. Today."

"But good heav— Lizzie, why on earth didn't you tell me before?"

Lizzie spoke soothingly, all the blarney of Kerry in her voice. "Now, Miss Neily, as if I'd wake you first thing in the morning with bad news like that! And thinks I, well, maybe 'tis all for the best after all, for when Miss Neily hears they're leavin' and her so particular, maybe she'll go back to the city for just a little and leave this house to its haunts and its bats and—"

"Go back to the city? I shall do nothing of the sort. I rented this house to live in and live in it I will, with servants or without them. You should have told me at once, Lizzie. I'm really very much annoyed with you because you didn't. I shall get up immediately; I want to give those two a piece of my mind. Is Billy leaving too?"

"Not that I know of," said Lizzie sorrowfully, "And yet he'd be better riddance than cook or housemaid."

"Now, Lizzie, how many times have I told you that you must conquer your prejudices? Billy is an excellent butler. He'd been with Mr. Fleming ten years and has the very highest recommendations. I am very glad that he is staying, if he is. With you to help him, we shall do very well until I can get other servants." Miss Cornelia had risen now and Lizzie was helping her with the intricacies of her toilet. "But it's too annoying," she went on, in the pauses of Lizzie's deft ministrations. "What did they say to you, Lizzie—did they give any reason? It isn't as if they were new to the country like you. They'd been with Mr. Fleming for some time, though not as long as Billy."

"Oh, yes, Miss Neily, they had reasons you could choke a goat with," said Lizzie viciously as she arranged Miss Cornelia's transformation. "Cook was the first of them—she was up late—I think they'd been talking it over together. She comes into the kitchen with her hat on and her bag in her hand. 'Good morning,' says I, pleasant enough, 'you've got your hat on,' says I. 'I'm leaving,' says she. 'Leaving, are you?' says I. 'Leaving,' says she. 'My sister has twins,' says she. 'I just got word, I must go to her right away.' 'What?' says I, all struck in a heap. 'Twins,' says she, 'you've heard of such things as twins.' 'That I have,' says I, 'and I know a lie on a face when I see it, too.' "

"Lizzie!"

"Well, it made me sick at heart, Miss Neily. Her with her hat and her bag and her talk about twins and no consideration for you. Well, I'll go on. 'You're a clever woman, aren't you?' says she—the impudence! 'I can see through a millstone as far as most,' says I. I wouldn't put up with her sauce. 'Well!' says she, 'you can see that Annie the housemaid's leaving, too.' 'Has her sister got twins as well?' says I and looked at her. 'No,' says she as bold as brass, 'but Annie's got a pain in her side and she's feared it's appendycitis—so she's leaving to go back to her family.' 'Oh,' says I, 'and what about Miss Van Gorder?' 'I'm sorry for Miss Van Gorder,' says she—the falseness of her!—'But she'll have to do the best she can for twins and appendycitis is acts of God and not to be put aside for even the best of wages.' 'Is that so?' says I and with that I left her, for I knew if I listened to her a minute longer I'd be giving her bonnet a shake and that wouldn't be respectable. So there you are, Miss Neily, and that's the gist of the matter."

Miss Cornelia laughed. "Lizzie, you're unique," she said. "But I'm glad you didn't give her bonnet a shake, though I've no doubt you could."

"Humph!" said Lizzie snorting, the fire of battle in her eye. "And is it any Black Irish from Ulster would play impudence to a Kerrywoman without getting the flat of a hand in, but that's neither here nor there. The truth of it is, Miss Neily," her voice grew solemn, "it's my belief they're scared, both of them, by the haunts and the banshees here—and that's all."

"If they are they're very silly," said Miss Cornelia practically. "No, they may have heard of a better place, though it would seem as if when one pays the present extortionate wages and asks as little as we do here—but it doesn't matter. If they want to go, they may. Am I ready, Lizzie?"

"You look like an angel, ma'am," said Lizzie, clasping her hands.

"Well, I feel very little like one," said Miss Cornelia, rising. "As cook and housemaid may discover before I'm through with them. Send them into the livingroom, Lizzie, when I've gone down. I'll talk to them there."

An hour or so later, Miss Cornelia sat in a deep chintz chair in the comfortable living-room of the Fleming house going through the pile of letters which Lizzie's news of domestic revolt had prevented her reading earlier. Cook and housemaid had come and gone—civil enough, but so obviously determined upon leaving the house at once that Miss Cornelia had sighed and let them go, though not without caustic comment. Since then, she had devoted herself to calling up various employment agencies without entirely satisfactory results. A new cook and housemaid were promised for the end of the week but for the next three days the Japanese butler, Billy, and Lizzie between them would have to bear the brunt of the service. *Oh, yes and then there's Dale's gardner, if she gets one,* thought Miss Cornelia. *I wish he could cook but I don't suppose gardeners can—and Billy's a treasure.*

She had reached the bottom of her pile of letters—these to be thrown away, these to be answered—ah, here was the one she had overlooked somehow. She took it up. It must be the one Lizzie had wanted to throw away; she smiled at Lizzie's fears. The address was badly typed, on cheap paper; she tore the envelope open and drew out a single unsigned sheet.

If you stay in this house any longer—DEATH. Go back to the city at once and save your life.

Her fingers trembled a little as she turned the missive over but her face remained calm. She looked at the envelope, at the postmark, while her heart thudded uncomfortably for a moment and then resumed its normal beat. It had come at last—the adventure—and she was not afraid!

3

Pistol Practice

She knew who it was, of course. The Bat! No doubt of it. And yet—did the Bat ever threaten before he struck? She could not remember. But it didn't matter. The Bat was unprecedented—unique. At any rate, Bat or no Bat, she must think out a course of action. The defection of cook and housemaid left her alone in the house with Lizzie and Billy—and Dale, of course, if Dale returned. *Two old women, a young girl, and a Japanese butler to face the most dangerous criminal in America,* she thought grimly. And yet, one couldn't be sure. The threatening letter might be only a joke—a letter from a crank—after all. Still, she must take precautions; look for aid somewhere. But where could she look for aid?

She ran over in her mind the new acquaintances she had made since she moved to the country. There was Doctor Wells, the local physician, who had joked with her about moving into the Bat's home territory. He seemed an intelligent man but she knew him only slightly and she couldn't call a busy doctor away from his patients to investigate something which might only prove to be a mare's-nest. The boys Dale had met at the country club—"Humph!" she sniffed, "I'd rather trust my gumption than any of theirs." The logical person to call on, of course, was Richard Fleming, Courtleigh Fleming's nephew and heir, who had rented her the house. He lived at the country club; she could probably reach him now. She was just on the point of doing so when she decided against it—partly from delicacy, partly from an indefinable feeling that he would not be of much help. *Besides,* she thought sturdily, *it's my house now, not his. He didn't guarantee burglar protection in the lease.*

As for the local police—her independence revolted at summoning them. They would bombard her with ponderous questions and undoubtedly think she was merely a nervous old spinster. *If it was just me,* she thought, *I swear I wouldn't say a word to anybody—and if the Bat flew in he mightn't find it so easy to fly out again, if I am sixty-five and never shot a burglar in my life! But there's Dale and Lizzie. I've got to be fair to them.*

For a moment she felt very helpless, very much alone. Then her courage returned.

"Pshaw, Cornelia, if you have got to get help—get the help *you* want and hang the consequences!" she adjured herself. "You've always hankered to see a first-class detective do his detecting—well, *get one*—or decide to do the job yourself. I'll bet you could at that."

She tiptoed to the main door of the living-room and closed it cautiously, smiling as she did so. Lizzie might be about and Lizzie would promptly go into hysterics if she got an inkling of her mistress's present intentions. Then she went to the city telephone and asked for long distance.

When she had finished her telephoning, she looked at once relieved and a little naughty—like a demure child who has carried out some piece of innocent mischief unobserved. "My stars!" she muttered to herself. "You never can tell what you can do till you try." Then she sat down again and tried to think of other measures of defense.

Now if I were the Bat, or any criminal, she mused, *how would I get into this house? Well, that's it—I might get in 'most any way—it's so big and rambling. All the grounds you want to lurk in, too; it'd take a company of police to shut them off. Then there's the house itself. Let's see—third floor—trunk room, servants' rooms—couldn't get in there very well except with a pretty long ladder—that's all right. Second floor—well, I suppose a man could get into my bedroom from the porch if I were an acrobat, but he'd need to be a very good acrobat and there's no use borrowing trouble. Downstairs is the problem, Cornelia, downstairs is the problem.*

"Take this room now." She rose and examined it carefully. "There's the door over there on the right that leads into the billiard room. There's this door over here that leads into the hall. Then there's that other door by the alcove, and all those French windows—whew!" She shook her head.

It was true. The room in which she stood, while comfortable and charming, seemed unusually accessible to the night prowler. A row of French windows at the rear gave upon a little terrace; below the terrace, the drive curved about and beneath the billiard-room windows in a hairpin loop, drawing up again at the main entrance on the other side of the house. At the left of the French windows (if one faced the terrace as Miss Cornelia was doing) was the alcove door of which she spoke. When open, it disclosed a little alcove, almost entirely devoted to the foot of a flight of stairs that gave direct access to the upper regions of the house. The alcove itself opened on one side upon the terrace and upon the other into a large butler's pantry. The arrangement was obviously designed so that, if necessary, one could pass directly from the terrace to the downstairs service quarters or the second floor of the house without going through the living-room, and so that trays could be carried up from the pantry by the side stairs without using the main staircase.

The middle pair of French windows were open, forming a double door. Miss Cornelia went over to them, shut them, tried the locks. *Humph! Flimsy enough!* she thought. Then she turned toward the billiard room.

The billiard room, as has been said, was the last room to the right in the main wing of the house. A single door led to it from the living-room. Miss Cornelia passed through this door, glanced about the billiard room, noting that most of its windows were too high from the ground to greatly encourage a marauder. She locked the only one that seemed to her particularly tempting—the billiard-room window on the terrace side of the house. Then she returned to the living-room and again considered her defenses.

Three points of access from the terrace to the house: the door that led into the alcove, the French windows of the living-room, the billiard-room window. On the other side of the house there was the main entrance, the porch, the library and dining-room windows. The main entrance led into a hall. The main door of the living-room was on the right as one entered, the dining-room and library on the left, the main staircase in front.

"My mind is starting to go round like a pinwheel, thinking of all those windows and doors," she murmured to herself. She sat down once more, and taking a pencil and a piece of paper drew a plan of the lower floor of the house.

And now I've studied it, she thought for a while, *I'm no further than if I hadn't. As far as I can figure out, there are so many ways for a clever man to get into this house that I'd have to be a couple of Siamese twins to watch it properly. The next house I rent in the country,* she decided, *just isn't going to have any windows and doors—or I'll know the reason why.*

But of course she was not entirely shut off from the world, even if the worst developed. She considered the telephone instruments on a table near the wall, one the general phone, the other connecting a house line which also connected with the garage and the greenhouses. The garage would not be helpful, since Slocum, her chauffeur for many years, had gone back to England for a visit. Dale had been driving the car. But with an able-bodied man in the gardener's house—

She pulled herself together with a jerk.

"Cornelia Van Gorder, you're going to go crazy before nightfall if you don't take hold of yourself. What you need is lunch and a nap in the afternoon if you can make yourself take it. You'd better look up that revolver of yours, too, that you bought when you thought you were going to take a trip to China. You've never fired it off yet, but you've got to sometime today; there's no other way of telling if it will work. You can shut your eyes when you do it—no, you can't either—that's silly.

"Call you a spirited old lady, do they? Well, you never had a better time to show your spirit than now!"

And Miss Van Gorder, sighing, left the living-room to reach the kitchen just in time to calm a heated argument between Lizzie and Billy on the relative merits of Japanese and Irish-American cooking.

Dale Ogden, taxiing up from the two o'clock train some time later, to her surprise discovered the front door locked and rang for some time before she could get an answer. At last, Billy appeared, white-coated, with an inscrutable expression on his face.

"Will you take my bag, Billy—thanks. Where is Miss Van Gorder—taking a nap?"

"No," said Billy succinctly. "She take no nap. She out in srubbery shotting."

Dale stared at him incredulously. "Shooting, Billy?"

"Yes, ma'am. At least—she not shott yet but she say she going to soon."

"But, good heavens, Billy—shooting what?"

"Shotting pistol," said Billy, his yellow mask of a face preserving its impish repose. He waved his hand. "You go srubbery. You see."

The scene that met Dale's eyes when she finally found the "srubbery" was indeed a singular one. Miss Van Gorder, her back firmly planted against the trunk of a large elm tree and an expression of ineffable distaste on her features, was holding out a blunt, deadly looking revolver at arm's length. Its muzzle wavered, now pointing at the ground, now at the sky. Behind the tree Lizzie sat in a heap, moaning quietly to herself, and now and then appealing to the saints to avert a visioned calamity.

As Dale approached, unseen, the climax came. The revolver steadied, pointed ferociously at an inoffensive grass-blade some 10 yards from Miss Van Gorder and went off. Lizzie promptly gave vent to a shrill Irish scream. Miss Van Gorder dropped the revolver like a hot potato and opened her mouth to tell Lizzie not to be such a fool. Then she saw Dale; her mouth went into a round O of horror and her hand clutched weakly at her heart.

"Good heavens, child!" she gasped. "Didn't Billy tell you what I was doing? I might have shot you like a rabbit!" and, overcome with emotion, she sat down on the ground and started to fan herself mechanically with a cartridge.

Dale couldn't help laughing, and the longer she looked at her aunt the more she laughed, until that dignified lady joined in the mirth herself.

"Aunt Cornelia, Aunt Cornelia!" said Dale when she could get her breath. "That I've lived to see the day! Why on earth were you having pistol practice, darling—has Billy turned into a spy or what?"

Miss Van Gorder rose from the ground with as much stateliness as she could muster under the circumstances.

"No, my dear, but there's no fool like an old fool, that's all," she stated. "I've wanted to fire that infernal revolver off ever since I bought it two years ago, and now I have and I'm satisfied. Still," she went on thoughtfully, picking up the weapon, "it seems a very good revolver—and shooting people must be much easier than I supposed. All you have to do is to point the—the front of it—like this and—"

"Oh, Miss Dale, dear Miss Dale!" came the woebegone accents from the other side of the tree. "For the love of heaven, Miss Dale, say no more but take it away from her. She'll have herself all riddled through with bullets like a kitchen sieve, and me too, if she's let to have it again."

"Lizzie, I'm ashamed of you!" said Lizzie's mistress. "Come out from behind that tree and stop wailing like a siren. This weapon is perfectly safe in competent hands and—" She seemed on the verge of another demonstration of its powers.

"Miss Dale, for the dear love o' God, will you make her put it away?"

Dale laughed again. "I really think you'd better, Aunt Cornelia. Or both of us will have to put Lizzie to bed with a case of acute hysteria."

"Well," said Miss Van Gorder, "perhaps you're right, dear." Her eyes gleamed. "I *should* have liked to try it just once more though," she confided. "I feel certain that I could hit that tree over there if my eye wouldn't *wink* so when the thing goes off."

"Now, it's winking eyes," said Lizzie on a note of tragic chant, "but next time it'll be bleeding corpses and—"

Dale added her own protestations to Lizzie's. "Please, darling, if you really want to practice, Billy can fix up some sort of target range but I don't want my favorite aunt assassinated by a ricocheted bullet before my eyes!"

"Well, perhaps it would be best to try again another time," admitted Miss Van Gorder. But there was a wistful look in her eyes as she gave the revolver to Dale and the three started back to the house.

"I should *never* have allowed Lizzie to know what I was doing," she confided in a whisper, on the way. "A woman is perfectly capable of managing firearms—but Lizzie is really too nervous to live, sometimes."

"I know just how you feel, darling," Dale agreed, suppressed mirth shaking her as the little procession reached the terrace. "But—oh," she could keep it no longer, "oh—you did look funny, darling—sitting under that tree, with Lizzie on the other side of it making banshee noises and—"

Miss Van Gorder laughed too, a little shamefacedly.

"I must have," she said. "But—oh, you needn't shake your head, Lizzie Allen—I *am* going to practice with it. There's no reason I shouldn't and you never can tell when things like that might be useful," she ended rather vaguely. She did not wish to alarm Dale with her suspicions yet.

"There, Dale—yes, put it in the drawer of the table—that will reassure Lizzie. Lizzie, you might make us some lemonade, I think—Miss Dale must be thirsty after her long, hot ride."

"Yes, Miss Cornelia," said Lizzie, recovering her normal calm as the revolver was shut away in the drawer of the large table in the living-room. But she could not resist one parting shot. "And thank God it's lemonade I'll be making—and not bandages for bullet wounds!" she muttered darkly as she went toward the service quarters.

Miss Van Gorder glared after her departing back. "Lizzie is really impossible sometimes!" she said with stately ire. Then her voice softened. "Though of course I couldn't do without her," she added.

Dale stretched out on the settee opposite her aunt's chair. "I know you couldn't, darling. Thanks for thinking of the lemonade." She passed her hand over her forehead in a gesture of fatigue. "I *am* hot—and tired."

Miss Van Gorder looked at her keenly. The young face seemed curiously worn and haggard in the clear afternoon light.

"You—you don't really feel very well, do you, Dale?"

"Oh—it's nothing. I feel all right—really."

"I could send for Doctor Wells if—"

"Oh, heavens, no, Aunt Cornelia." She managed a wan smile. "It isn't as bad as all that. I'm just tired and the city was terribly hot and noisy and—" She stole a glance at her aunt from between lowered lids. "I got your gardener, by the way," she said casually.

"Did you, dear? That's splendid, though—but I'll tell you about that later. Where did you get him?"

"That good agency, I can't remember its name." Dale's hand moved restlessly over her eyes, as if remembering details were too great an effort. "But I'm sure he'll be satisfactory. He'll be out here this evening—he—he couldn't get away before, I believe. What have you been doing all day, darling?"

Miss Cornelia hesitated. Now that Dale had returned she suddenly wanted very much to talk over the various odd happenings of the day with her—get the support of her youth and her common sense. Then that independence which was so firmly rooted a characteristic of hers restrained her. No use worrying the child unnecessarily; they all might have to worry enough before tomorrow morning.

She compromised. "We have had a domestic upheaval," she said. "The cook and the housemaid have left; if you'd only waited till the next train you could have had the pleasure of their company into town."

"Aunt Cornelia, how exciting! I'm so sorry! Why did they leave?"

"Why do servants ever leave a good place?" asked Miss Cornelia grimly. "Because if they had sense enough to know when they were well off, they wouldn't be servants. Anyhow, they've gone; we'll have to depend on Lizzie and Billy the rest of this week. I telephoned—but they couldn't promise me any others before Monday."

"And I was in town and could have seen people for you—if I'd only known!" said Dale remorsefully. "Only," she hesitated, "I mightn't have had time—at least I mean there were some other things I had to do, besides getting the gardener and—" She rose. "I think I will go and lie down for a little if you don't mind, darling."

Miss Van Gorder was concerned. "Of course I don't mind—but won't you even have your lemonade?"

"Oh, I'll get some from Lizzie in the pantry before I go up," Dale managed to laugh. "I think I must have a headache after all," she said. "Maybe I'll take an aspirin. Don't worry, darling."

"I shan't. I only wish there were something I could do for you, my dear."

Dale stopped in the alcove doorway. "There's nothing anybody can do for me, really," she said soberly. "At least—oh, I don't know what I'm saying! But don't worry. I'm quite all right. I may go over to the country club after dinner—and dance. Won't you come with me, Aunt Cornelia?"

"Depends on your escort," said Miss Cornelia tartly. "If our landlord, Mr. Richard Fleming, is taking you I certainly shall—I don't like his looks and never did!"

Dale laughed. "Oh, he's all right," she said. "Drinks a good deal and wastes a lot of money, but harmless enough. No, this is a very sedate party; I'll be home early."

"Well, in that case," said her aunt, "I shall stay here with my Lizzie and my ouija-board. Lizzie deserves *some* punishment for the *very* cowardly way she behaved this afternoon—and the ouija-board will furnish it. She's scared to death to touch the thing. I think she believes it's alive."

"Well, maybe I'll send you a message on it from the country club," said Dale lightly. She had paused, halfway up the flight of side stairs in the alcove, and her aunt noticed how her shoulders drooped, belying the lightness of her voice. "Oh," she went on, "by the way—have the afternoon papers come yet? I didn't have time to get one when I was rushing for the train."

"I don't think so, dear, but I'll ask Lizzie." Miss Cornelia moved toward a bell push.

"Oh, don't bother; it doesn't matter. Only if they have, would you ask Lizzie to bring me one when she brings up the lemonade? I want to read about—about the Bat—he fascinates me."

"There was something else in the paper this morning," said Miss Cornelia idly. "Oh, yes—the Union Bank—the bank Mr. Fleming, Senior, was president of has failed. They seem to think the cashier robbed it. Did you see that, Dale?"

The shoulders of the girl on the staircase straightened suddenly. Then they drooped again. "Yes—I saw it," she said in a queerly colorless voice. "Too bad. It must be terrible to—to have everyone suspect you—and hunt you—as I suppose they're hunting that poor cashier."

"Well," said Miss Cornelia, "a man who wrecks a bank deserves very little sympathy to my way of thinking. But then I'm old-fashioned. Well, dear, I won't keep you. Run along and if you want an aspirin, there's a box in my top bureau-drawer."

"Thanks, darling. Maybe I'll take one and maybe I won't—all I really need is to lie down for a while."

She moved on up the staircase and disappeared from the range of Miss Cornelia's vision, leaving Miss Cornelia to ponder many things. Her trip to the city had done Dale no good, of a certainty. If not actually ill, she was obviously under some considerable mental strain. And why this sudden interest, first in the Bat, then in the failure of the Union Bank? Was it possible that Dale, too, had been receiving threatening letters?

I'll be glad when that gardener comes, she thought to herself. *He'll make a man in the house at any rate.*

When Lizzie at last came in with the lemonade she found her mistress shaking her head.

"Cornelia, Cornelia," she was murmuring to herself, "you should have taken to pistol practice when you were younger; it just shows how children waste their opportunities."

4

The Storm Gathers

The long summer afternoon wore away, sunset came, red and angry, a sunset presaging storm. A chill crept into the air with the twilight. When night fell, it was not a night of silver patterns enskied, but a dark and cloudy cloak where a few stars glittered fitfully. Miss Cornelia, at dinner, saw a bat swoop past the window of the dining-room in its scurrying flight, and narrowly escaped oversetting her glass of water with a nervous start. The tension of waiting—waiting—for some vague menace which might not materialize after all—had begun to prey on her nerves. She saw Dale off to the country club with relief; the girl looked a little better after her nap but she was still not her normal self. When Dale was gone, she wandered restlessly for some time between living-room and library, now giving an unnecessary dusting to a piece of bric-a-brac with her handkerchief, now taking a book from one of the shelves in the library only to throw it down before she read a page.

This house was queer. She would not have admitted it to Lizzie, for her soul's salvation—but, for the first time in her sensible life, she listened for creakings of woodwork, rustling of leaves, stealthy steps outside, beyond the safe, bright squares of the windows—for anything that was actual, tangible, not merely formless fear.

"There's too much *room* in the country for things to happen to you!" she confided to herself with a shiver. "Even the night—whenever I look out, it seems to me as if the night were ten times bigger and blacker than it ever is in New York!"

To comfort herself she mentally rehearsed her telephone conversation of the morning, the conversation she had not mentioned to her household. At the time it had seemed to her most reassuring—the plans she had based upon it adequate and sensible in the normal light of day. But now the light of day had been blotted out and with it her security. Her plans seemed weapons of paper against the sinister might of the darkness beyond her windows.

She made herself sit down in the chair beside her favorite lamp on the center table and take up her knitting with stiff fingers. Knit two—purl two—Her hands fell into the accustomed rhythm mechanically. A spy, peering in through the French windows, would have deemed her the picture of calm. But she had never felt less calm in all the long years of her life.

She wouldn't ring for Lizzie to come and sit with her, she simply wouldn't. But she was very glad, nevertheless, when Lizzie appeared at the door.

"Miss Neily."

"Yes, Lizzie?" Miss Cornelia's voice was composed but her heart felt a throb of relief.

"Can I—can I sit in here with you, Miss Neily, just a minute?" Lizzie's voice was plaintive. "I've been sitting out in the kitchen watching that Jap read his funny newspaper the wrong way and listening for ghosts till I'm nearly crazy!"

"Why, certainly, Lizzie," said Miss Cornelia primly. "Though," she added doubtfully, "I really shouldn't pamper your absurd fears, I suppose, but—"

"Oh, please, Miss Neily!"

"Very well," said Miss Cornelia brightly. "You can sit here, Lizzie—and help me work the ouija-board. That will take your mind off listening for things!"

Lizzie groaned. "You know I'd rather be shot than touch that uncanny ouijie!" she said dolefully. "It gives me the creeps every time I put my hands on it!"

"Well, of course, if you'd rather sit in the kitchen, Lizzie—"

"Oh, give me the ouijie!" said Lizzie in tones of heartbreak. "I'd rather be shot *and* stabbed than stay in the kitchen any more."

"Very well," said Miss Cornelia, "it's your own decision, Lizzie—remember that." Her needles clicked on. "I'll just finish this row before we start," she said. "You might call up the light company in the meantime, Lizzie. There seems to be a storm coming up and I want to find out if they intend to turn out the lights tonight as they did last night. Tell them I find it most inconvenient to be left without light that way."

"It's worse than inconvenient," muttered Lizzie, "it's criminal, that's what it is, turning off all the lights in a haunted house like this one. As if spooks wasn't bad enough with the lights *on*—"

"Lizzie!"

"Yes, Miss Neily, I wasn't going to say another word." She went to the telephone. Miss Cornelia knitted on—knit two—purl two— In spite of her experiments with the ouija-board she didn't believe in ghosts, and yet, there were things one couldn't explain by logic. Was there something like that in this house—a shadow walking the corridors—a vague shape of evil, drifting like mist from room to room, till its cold breath whispered on one's back and—there! She had ruined her knitting, the last two rows would have to be ripped out. That came of mooning about ghosts like a ninny.

She put down the knitting with an exasperated little gesture. Lizzie had just finished her telephoning and was hanging up the receiver.

"Well, Lizzie?"

"Yes'm," said the latter, glaring at the phone. "That's what he says—they turned off the lights last night because there was a storm threatening. He says it burns out their fuses if they leave 'em on in a storm."

A louder roll of thunder punctuated her words.

"There!" said Lizzie. "They'll be going off again tonight." She took an uncertain step toward the French windows.

"Humph!" said Miss Cornelia, "I hope it will be a dry summer." Her hands tightened on each other. Darkness—darkness inside this house of whispers to match with the darkness outside! She forced herself to speak in a normal voice.

"Ask Billy to bring some candles, Lizzie—and have them ready."

Lizzie had been staring fixedly at the French windows. At Miss Cornelia's command she gave a little jump of terror and moved closer to her mistress.

"You're not going to ask me to go out in that hall alone?" she said in a hurt voice.

It was too much. Miss Cornelia found vent for her feelings in crisp exasperation.

"What's the matter with you anyhow, Lizzie Allen?"

The nervousness in her own tones infected Lizzie's. She shivered frankly.

"Oh, Miss Neily—Miss Neily!" she pleaded. "I don't like it! I want to go back to the city!"

Miss Cornelia braced herself. "I have rented this house for four months and I am going to stay," she said firmly. Her eyes sought Lizzie's, striving to pour some of her own inflexible courage into the latter's quaking form. But Lizzie would not look at her. Suddenly she started and gave a low scream.

"There's somebody on the terrace!" she breathed in a ghastly whisper, clutching at Miss Cornelia's arm.

For a second Miss Cornelia sat frozen. Then, "Don't do that!" she said sharply. "What nonsense!" but she looked over her shoulder as she said it and Lizzie saw the look. Both waited, in pulsing stillness—one second—two.

"I guess it was the wind," said Lizzie at last, relieved, her grip on Miss Cornelia's relaxing. She began to look a trifle ashamed of herself and Miss Cornelia seized the opportunity.

"You were born on a brick pavement," she said crushingly. "You get nervous out here at night whenever a cricket begins to sing—or scrape his legs—or whatever it is they do!"

Lizzie bowed before the blast of her mistress's scorn and began to move gingerly toward the alcove door. But obviously she was not entirely convinced.

"Oh, it's more than that, Miss Neily," she mumbled. "I—"

Miss Cornelia turned to her fiercely. If Lizzie was going to behave like this, they might as well have it out now between them—before Dale came home.

"What did you *really* see last night?" she said in a minatory voice.

The instant relief on Lizzie's face was ludicrous; she so obviously preferred discussing any subject at any length to braving the dangers of the other part of the house unaccompanied.

"I was standing right there at the top of that there staircase," she began, gesticulating toward the alcove stairs in the manner of one who embarks upon the narration of an epic. "Standing there with your switch in my hand, Miss Neily—and then I looked down and," her voice dropped. "I saw a *gleaming eye!* It looked at me and *winked!* I tell you this house is haunted!"

"A flirtatious ghost?" queried Miss Cornelia skeptically. She snorted. "Humph! Why didn't you yell?"

"I was too scared to yell! And I'm not the only one." She started to back away from the alcove, her eyes still fixed upon its haunted stairs. "Why do you think the servants left so sudden this morning?" she went on. "Do you really believe the housemaid had appendicitis? Or the cook's sister had twins?"

She turned and gestured at her mistress with a long, pointed forefinger. Her voice had a note of doom.

"I bet a cent the cook never had any sister—and the sister never had any twins," she said impressively. "No, Miss Neily, they couldn't put it over on me like that! They were scared away. They saw—It!"

She concluded her epic and stood nodding her head, an Irish Cassandra who had prophesied the evil to come.

"Fiddlesticks!" said Miss Cornelia briskly, more shaken by the recital than she would have admitted. She tried to think of another topic of conversation.

"What time is it?" she asked.

Lizzie glanced at the mantel clock. "Half-past ten, Miss Neily."

Miss Cornelia yawned, a little dismally. She felt as if the last two hours had not been hours but years.

"Miss Dale won't be home for half an hour," she said reflectively. *And if I have to spend another thirty minutes listening to Lizzie shiver,* she thought, *Dale will find me a nervous wreck when she does come home.* She rolled up her knitting and put it back in her knitting-bag; it was no use going on, doing work that would have to be ripped out again and yet she must do something to occupy her thoughts. She raised her head and discovered Lizzie returning toward the alcove stairs with the stealthy tread of a panther. The sight exasperated her.

"Now, Lizzie Allen!" she said sharply, "you forget all that superstitious nonsense and stop looking for ghosts! There's nothing in that sort of thing." She smiled—she would punish Lizzie for her obdurate timorousness. "Where's that ouija-board?" she questioned, rising, with determination in her eye.

Lizzie shuddered violently. "It's up there—with a prayer book on it to keep it quiet!" she groaned, jerking her thumb in the direction of the farther bookcase.

"Bring it here!" said Miss Cornelia implacably; then as Lizzie still hesitated, "Lizzie!"

Shivering, every movement of her body a conscious protest, Lizzie slowly went over to the bookcase, lifted off the prayer book, and took down the ouija-board. Even then she would not carry it normally but bore it over to Miss Cornelia at arms'-length, as if any closer contact would blast her with lightning, her face a comic mask of loathing and repulsion.

She placed the lettered board in Miss Cornelia's lap with a sigh of relief. "You can do it yourself! I'll have none of it!" she said firmly.

"It takes two people and you know it, Lizzie Allen!" Miss Cornelia's voice was stern but it was also amused.

Lizzie groaned, but she knew her mistress. She obeyed. She carefully chose the farthest chair in the room and took a long time bringing it over to where her mistress sat waiting.

"I've been working for you for twenty years," she muttered. "I've been your goat for twenty years and I've got a right to speak my mind—"

Miss Cornelia cut her off. "You haven't got a mind. Sit down," she commanded.

Lizzie sat, her hands at her sides. With a sigh of tried patience, Miss Cornelia put her unwilling fingers on the little moving table that is used to point to the letters on the board itself. Then she placed her own hands on it, too, the tips of the fingers just touching Lizzie's.

"Now make your mind a blank!" she commanded her factotum.

"You just said I haven't got any mind," complained the latter.

"Well," said Miss Cornelia magnificently, "make what you haven't got a blank."

The repartee silenced Lizzie for the moment, but only for the moment. As soon as Miss Cornelia had settled herself comfortably and tried to make her mind a suitable receiving station for ouija messages, Lizzie began to mumble the sorrows of her heart.

"I've stood by you through thick and thin," she mourned in a low voice. "I stood by you when you were a vegetarian, I stood by you when you were a theosophist, and I seen you through socialism, Fletcherism and rheumatism—but when it comes to carrying on with ghosts—"

"Be still!" ordered Miss Cornelia. "Nothing will come if you keep chattering!"

"That's *why* I'm chattering!" said Lizzie, driven to the wall. "My teeth are, too," she added. "I can hardly keep my upper set in," and a desolate clicking of artificial molars attested the truth of the remark. Then, to Miss Cornelia's relief, she was silent for nearly two minutes, only to start so violently at the end of the time that she nearly upset the ouija-board on her mistress's toes.

"I've got a queer feeling in my fingers—all the way up my arms," she whispered in awed accents, wriggling the arms she spoke of violently.

"Hush!" said Miss Cornelia indignantly. Lizzie always exaggerated, of course—yet now her own fingers felt prickly, uncanny. There was a little pause while both sat tense, staring at the board.

"Now, Ouija," said Miss Cornelia defiantly, "is Lizzie Allen right about this house or is it all stuff and nonsense?"

For one second—two—the ouija remained anchored to its resting place in the center of the board. Then—

"My Gawd! It's moving!" said Lizzie in tones of pure horror as the little pointer began to wander among the letters.

"You shoved it!"

"I did not. Cross my heart, Miss Neily—I—" Lizzie's eyes were round, her fingers glued rigidly and awkwardly to the ouija. As the movements of the pointer grew more rapid her mouth dropped open, wider and wider, prepared for an ear-piercing scream.

"Keep quiet!" said Miss Cornelia tensely. There was a pause of a few seconds while the pointer darted from one letter to another wildly.

"B—M—C—X—P—R—S—K—Z—" murmured Miss Cornelia trying to follow the spelled letters.

"It's Russian!" gasped Lizzie breathlessly and Miss Cornelia nearly disgraced herself in the eyes of any spirits that might be present by inappropriate laughter. The ouija continued to move—more letters—what was it spelling?—it couldn't be—good heavens—

"B—A—T—Bat!" said Miss Cornelia with a tiny catch in her voice.

The pointer stopped moving. She took her hands from the board.

"That's queer," she said with a forced laugh. She glanced at Lizzie to see how Lizzie was taking it. But the latter seemed too relieved to have her hands off the ouija-board to make the mental connection that her mistress had feared.

All she said was, "Bats indeed! That shows it's spirits. There's been a bat flying around this house all evening."

She got up from her chair tentatively, obviously hoping that the séance was over.

"Oh, Miss Neily," she burst out. "Please let me sleep in your room tonight! It's only when my jaw drops that I snore, I can tie it up with a handkerchief!"

"I wish you'd tie it up with a handkerchief now," said her mistress absent-mindedly, still pondering the message that the pointer had spelled. "B—A—T—Bat!" she murmured. Thought transference— warning—accident? Whatever it was, it was—nerve shaking. She put the ouija-board aside. Accident or not, she was done with it for the evening. But she could not so easily dispose of the Bat. Sending a protesting Lizzie off for her reading glasses, Miss Cornelia got the evening paper and settled down to what by now had become her obsession. She had not far to search for a long black streamer ran across the front page—*Bat Baffles Police Again.*

She skimmed through the article with eerie fascination, reading bits of it aloud for Lizzie's benefit.

" 'Unique criminal—long baffled the police—record of his crimes shows him to be endowed with an almost diabolical ingenuity—so far there is no clue to his identity—' " *Pleasant reading for an old woman who's just received a threatening letter,* she thought ironically—ah, here was something new in a black-bordered box on the front page—a statement by the paper.

She read it aloud. " 'We must cease combing the criminal world for the Bat and look higher. He may be a merchant—a lawyer—a doctor—honored in his community by day and at night a bloodthirsty assassin—' " The print blurred before her eyes, she could read no more for the moment. She thought of the revolver in the drawer of the table close at hand and felt glad that it was there, loaded.

"I'm going to take the butcher knife to bed with me!" Lizzie was saying.

Miss Cornelia touched the ouija-board. "That thing certainly spelled Bat," she remarked. "I wish I were a man. I'd like to see any lawyer, doctor, or merchant of my acquaintance leading a double life without my suspecting it."

"Every man leads a double life and some more than that," Lizzie observed. "I guess it rests them, like it does me to take off my corset."

Miss Cornelia opened her mouth to rebuke her but just at that moment there was a clink of ice from the hall, and Billy, the Japanese, entered carrying a tray with a pitcher of water and some glasses on it. Miss Cornelia watched his impassive progress, wondering if the Oriental races ever felt terror; she could not imagine all Lizzie's banshees and kelpies producing a single shiver from Billy. He set down the tray and was about to go as silently as he had come when Miss Cornelia spoke to him on impulse.

"Billy, what's all this about the cook's sister not having twins?" she said in an offhand voice. She had not really discussed the departure of the other servants with Billy before. "Did you happen to know that this interesting event was anticipated?"

Billy drew in his breath with a polite hiss. "Maybe she have twins," he admitted. "It happen sometime. Mostly not expected."

"Do you think there was any other reason for her leaving?"

"Maybe," said Billy blandly.

"Well, what was the reason?"

"All say the same thing—house haunted." Billy's reply was prompt as it was calm.

Miss Cornelia gave a slight laugh. "You know better than that, though, don't you?"

Billy's Oriental placidity remained unruffled. He neither admitted nor denied. He shrugged his shoulders.

"Funny house," he said laconically. "Find window open—nobody there. Door slam—nobody there!"

On the heels of his words came a single, startling bang from the kitchen quarters—the bang of a slammed door!

5

Alopecia and Rubeola

Miss Cornelia dropped her newspaper. Lizzie, frankly frightened, gave a little squeal and moved closer to her mistress. Only Billy remained impassive but even he looked sharply in the direction whence the sound had come.

Miss Cornelia was the first of the others to recover her poise.

"Stop that! It was the wind!" she said, a little irritably—the "Stop that!" addressed to Lizzie who seemed on the point of squealing again.

"I think not wind," said Billy. His very lack of perturbation added weight to the statement. It made Miss Cornelia uneasy. She took out her knitting again.

"How long have you lived in this house, Billy?"

"Since Mr. Fleming built."

"H'm." Miss Cornelia spondered. "And this is the first time you have been disturbed?"

"Last two days only." Billy would have made an ideal witness in a courtroom. He restricted himself so precisely to answering what was asked of him in as few words as possible.

"What about that face Lizzie said you saw last night at the window?" she asked in a steady voice.

Billy grinned, as if slightly embarrassed.

"Just face—that's all."

"A—man's face?"

He shrugged again.

"Don't know—maybe. It there! It gone!"

Miss Cornelia did not want to believe him—but she did. "Did you go out after it?" she persisted.

Billy's yellow grin grew wider. "No thanks," he said cheerfully with ideal succinctness.

Lizzie, meanwhile, had stood first on one foot and then on the other during the interrogation, terror and morbid interest fighting in her for mastery. Now she could hold herself in no longer.

"Oh, Miss Neily!" she exploded in a graveyard moan, "last night when the lights went out I had a token! My oil lamp was full of oil but, do what I would, it kept going out, too—the minute I shut my eyes, out that lamp would go. There ain't a surer token of death! The Bible says, 'Let your light shine'—and when a hand you can't see puts your lights out—good night!"

She ended in a hushed whisper and even Billy looked a trifle uncomfortable after her climax.

"Well, now that you've cheered us up," began Miss Cornelia undauntedly, but a long, ominous roll of thunder that rattled the panes in the French windows drowned out the end of her sentence. Nevertheless she welcomed the thunder as a diversion. At least its menace was a physical one, to be guarded against by physical means.

She rose and went over to the French windows. That flimsy bolt! She parted the curtains, and looked out; a flicker of lightning stabbed the night, the storm must be almost upon them.

"Bring some candles, Billy," she said. "The lights may be going out any moment—and Billy," as he started to leave, "there's a gentleman arriving on the last train. After he comes you may go to bed. I'll wait up for Miss Dale—oh, and Billy," arresting him at the door, "see that all the outer doors on this floor are locked and bring the keys here."

Billy nodded and departed. Miss Cornelia took a long breath. Now that the moment for waiting had passed, the moment for action come—she felt suddenly indomitable, prepared to face a dozen Bats!

Her feelings were not shared by her maid. "I know what all this means," moaned Lizzie. "I tell you there's going to be a death, sure!"

"There certainly will be if you don't keep quiet," said her mistress acidly. "Lock the billiard-room windows and go to bed."

But this was the last straw for Lizzie. A picture of the two long, dark flights of stairs up which she had to pass to reach her bedchamber rose before her—and she spoke her mind.

"I am not going to bed!" she said wildly. "I'm going to pack up tomorrow and leave this house." That such a threat would never be carried out while she lived made little difference to her, she was beyond the need of Truth's consolations. "I asked you on my bended knees not to take this place two miles from a railroad," she went on heatedly. "For mercy's sake, Miss Neily, let's go back to the city before it's too late!"

Miss Cornelia was inflexible.

"I'm not going. You can make up your mind to that. I'm going to find out what's wrong with this place if it takes all summer. I came out to the country for a rest and I'm going to *get* it."

"You'll get your heavenly rest!" mourned Lizzie, giving it up. She looked pitifully at her mistress's face for a sign that the latter might be weakening but no such sign came. Instead, Miss Cornelia seemed to grow more determined.

"Besides," she said, suddenly deciding to share the secret she had hugged to herself all day, "I might as well tell you, Lizzie. I'm having a detective sent down tonight from police headquarters in the city."

"A detective?" Lizzie's face was horrified. "Miss Neily, you're keeping something from me! You know something I don't know."

"I hope so. I daresay he will be stupid enough. Most of them are. But at least we can have one proper night's sleep."

"Not I. I trust no man," said Lizzie. But Miss Cornelia had picked up the paper again.

" 'The Bat's last crime was a particularly atrocious one,' " she read. " 'The body of the murdered man—' "

But Lizzie could bear no more.

"Why don't you read the funny page once in a while?" she wailed and hurried to close the windows in the billiard room. The door leading into the billiard room shut behind her.

Miss Cornelia remained reading for a moment. Then—was that a sound from the alcove? She dropped the paper, went into the alcove and stood for a moment at the foot of the stairs, listening. No—it must have been imagination. But, while she was here, she might as well put on the spring lock that bolted the door from the alcove to the terrace. She did so, returned to the living-room and switched off the lights for a moment to look out at the coming storm. It was closer now—the lightning flashes more continuous. She turned on the lights again as Billy re-entered with three candles and a box of matches.

He put them down on a side table.

"New gardener come," he said briefly to Miss Cornelia's back.

Miss Cornelia turned. "Nice hour for him to get here. What's his name?"

"Say his name Brook," said Billy, a little doubtful. English names still bothered him—he was never quite sure of them at first.

Miss Cornelia thought. "Ask him to come in," she said. "And Billy—where are the keys?"

Billy silently took two keys from his pocket and laid them on the table. Then he pointed to the terrace door which Miss Cornelia had just bolted.

"Door up there—spring lock," he said.

"Yes." She nodded. "And the new bolt you put on today makes it fairly secure. One thing is fairly sure, Billy. If anyone tries to get in tonight, he will have to break a window and make a certain amount of noise."

But he only smiled his curious enigmatic smile and went out. And no sooner had Miss Cornelia seated herself when the door of the billiard room slammed open suddenly and Lizzie burst into the room as if she had been shot from a gun—her hair wild—her face stricken with fear.

"I heard somebody yell out in the grounds—away down by the gate!" she informed her mistress in a loud stage whisper which had a curious note of pride in it, as if she were not too displeased at seeing her doleful predictions so swiftly coming to pass.

Miss Cornelia took her by the shoulder—half-startled, half-dubious.

"What did they yell?"

"Just yelled a yell!"

"Lizzie!"

"I heard them!"

But she had cried "Wolf!" too often.

"You take a liver pill," said her mistress disgustedly, "and go to bed."

Lizzie was about to protest both the verdict on her story and the judgment on herself when the door in the hall was opened by Billy to admit the new gardener. A handsome young fellow, in his late twenties, he came two steps into the the room and then stood there respectfully with his cap in his hand, waiting for Miss Cornelia to speak to him.

After a swift glance of observation that gave her food for thought she did so.

"You are Brooks, the new gardener?"

The young man inclined his head.

"Yes, madam. The butler said you wanted to speak to me."

Miss Cornelia regarded him anew. *His hands look soft—for a gardener's,* she thought. *And his manners seem much too good for one—still—*

"Come in," she said briskly. The young man advanced another two steps. "You're the man my niece engaged in the city this afternoon?"

"Yes, madam." He seemed a little uneasy under her searching scrutiny. She dropped her eyes.

"I could not verify your references as the Brays are in Canada—" she proceeded.

The young man took an eager step forward. "I am sure if Mrs. Bray were here—" he began, then flushed and stopped, twisting his cap.

"Were here?" said Miss Cornelia in a curious voice. "Are you a *professional* gardener?"

"Yes." The young man's manner had grown a trifle defiant but Miss Cornelia's next question followed remorselessly.

"Know anything about hardy perennials?" she said in a soothing voice, while Lizzie regarded the interview with wondering eyes.

"Oh, yes," but the young man seemed curiously lacking in confidence. "They—they're the ones that keep their leaves during the winter, aren't they?"

"Come over here—closer—" said Miss Cornelia imperiously. Once more she scrutinized him and this time there was no doubt of his discomfort under her stare.

"Have you had any experience with ruboela?" she queried finally.

"Oh, yes—yes—yes, indeed," the gardener stammered. "Yes."

"And—alopecia?" pursued Miss Cornelia.

The young man seemed to fumble in his mind for the characteristics of such a flower or shrub.

"The dry weather is very hard on alopecia," he asserted finally, and was evidently relieved to see Miss Cornelia receive the statement with a pleasant smile.

"What do you think is the best treatment for urticaria?" she propounded with a highly professional manner.

It appeared to be a catch-question. The young man knotted his brows. Finally a gleam of light seemed to come to him.

"Urticaria frequently needs—er—thinning," he announced decisively.

"Needs scratching you mean!" Miss Cornelia rose with a snort of disdain and faced him. "Young man, urticaria is *hives,* rubeola is *measles,* and alopecia is *baldness!*" she thundered. She waited a moment for his defense. None came.

"Why did you tell me you were a professional gardener?" she went on accusingly. "Why have you come here at this hour of night pretending to be something you're not?"

By all standards of drama the young man should have wilted before her wrath. Instead he suddenly smiled at her, boyishly, and threw up his hands in a gesture of defeat.

"I know I shouldn't have done it!" he confessed with appealing frankness. "You'd have found me out anyhow! I don't know anything about gardening. The truth is," his tone grew somber, "I was desperate! I *had* to have work!"

The candor of his smile would have disarmed a stonier-hearted person than Miss Cornelia. But her suspicions were still awake.

"That's all, is it?"

"That's enough when you're down and out." His words had an unmistakable accent of finality. She couldn't help wanting to believe him, and yet, he wasn't what he had pretended to be—and this night of all nights was no time to take people on trust!

"How do I know you won't steal the spoons?" she queried, her voice still gruff.

"Are they nice spoons?" he asked with absurd seriousness.

She couldn't help smiling at his tone. "Beautiful spoons."

Again that engaging, boyish manner of his touched something in her heart.

"Spoons are a great temptation to me, Miss Van Gorder, but if you'll take me, I'll promise to leave them alone."

"That's extremely kind of you," she answered with grim humor, knowing herself beaten. She went over to ring for Billy.

Lizzie took the opportunity to gain her ear.

"I don't trust him, Miss Neily! He's too smooth!" she whispered warningly.

Miss Cornelia stiffened. "I haven't asked for your opinion, Lizzie," she said.

But Lizzie was not to be put off by the Van Gorder manner.

"Oh," she whispered, "you're just as bad as all the rest of 'em. A good-looking man comes in the door and your brains fly out the window!"

Miss Cornelia quelled her with a gesture and turned back to the young man. He was standing just where she had left him, his cap in his hands—but, while her back had been turned, his eyes had made a stealthy survey of the living-room—a survey that would have made it plain to Miss Cornelia, if she had seen him, that his interest in the Fleming establishment was not merely the casual interest of a servant and his new place of abode. But she had not seen and she could have told nothing from his present expression.

"Have you had anything to eat lately?" she asked in a kindly voice.

He looked down at his cap. "Not since this morning," he admitted as Billy answered the bell.

Miss Cornelia turned to the impassive Japanese.

"Billy, give this man something to eat and then show him where he is to sleep."

She hesitated. The gardener's house was some distance from the main building, and with the night and the approaching storm she felt her own courage weakening. Into the bargain, whether this stranger had lied about his gardening or not, she was curiously attracted to him.

"I think," she said slowly, "that I'll have you sleep in the house here, at least for tonight. Tomorrow we can—the housemaid's room, Billy," she told the butler. And before their departure she held out a candle and a box of matches.

"Better take these with you, Brooks," she said. "The local light company crawls under its bed every time there is a thunderstorm. Good night, Brooks."

"Good night, ma'am," said the young man smiling. Following Billy to the door, he paused. "You're being mighty good to me," he said diffidently, smiled again, and disappeared after Billy.

As the door closed behind them, Miss Cornelia found herself smiling too. "That's a pleasant young fellow—no matter what he is," she said to herself decidedly, and not even Lizzie's feverish "Haven't you any sense taking strange men into the house? How do you know he isn't the Bat?" could draw a reply from her.

Again the thunder rolled as she straightened the papers and magazines on the table and Lizzie gingerly took up the ouija-board to replace it on the bookcase with the prayer book firmly on top of it. And this time, with the roll of the thunder, the lights in the living-room blinked uncertainly for an instant before they recovered their normal brilliance.

"There go the lights!" grumbled Lizzie, her fingers still touching the prayer book, as if for protection. Miss Cornelia did not answer her directly.

"We'll put the detective in the blue room when he comes," she said. "You'd better go up and see if it's all ready."

Lizzie started to obey, going toward the alcove to ascend to the second floor by the alcove stairs. But Miss Cornelia stopped her.

"Lizzie—you know that stair rail's just been varnished. Miss Dale got a stain on her sleeve there this afternoon—and Lizzie—"

"Yes'm?"

"No one is to know that he is a detective. Not even Billy." Miss Cornelia was very firm.

"Well, what'll I *say* he is?"

"It's nobody's business."

"A detective," moaned Lizzie, opening the hall door to go by the main staircase. "Tiptoeing around with his eye to all the keyholes. A body won't be safe in the bathtub." She shut the door with a little slap and disappeared. Miss Cornelia sat down—she had many things to think over. *If I ever get time really to think of anything again,* she thought, *because with gardeners coming who aren't gardeners—and Lizzie hearing yells in the grounds and—*

She started slightly. The front door bell was ringing—a long trill, uncannily loud in the quiet house.

She sat rigid in her chair, waiting. Billy came in.

"Front door key, please?" he asked urbanely. She gave him the key.

"Find out who it is before you unlock the door," she said. He nodded. She heard him at the door, then a murmur of voices—Dale's voice and another's—"Won't you come in for a few minutes?" "Oh, thank you." She relaxed.

The door opened; it was Dale. *How lovely she looks in that evening wrap!* thought Miss Cornelia. *But how tired, too. I wish I knew what was worrying her.*

She smiled. "Aren't you back early, Dale?"

Dale threw off her wrap and stood for a moment patting back into its becoming coiffure, hair ruffled by the wind.

"I was tired," she said, sinking into a chair.

"Not worried about anything?" Miss Cornelia's eyes were sharp.

"No," said Dale without conviction, "but I've come here to be company for you and I don't want to run away all the time." She picked up the evening paper and looked at it without apparently seeing it. Miss Cornelia heard voices in the hall—a man's voice—affable—"How have you been, Billy?"—Billy's voice in answer, "Very well, sir."

"Who's out there, Dale?" she queried.

Dale looked up from the paper. "Doctor Wells, darling," she said in a listless voice. "He brought me over from the club; I asked him to come in for a few minutes. Billy's just taking his coat." She rose, threw the paper aside, came over and kissed Miss Cornelia suddenly and passionately—then, before Miss Cornelia, a little startled, could return the kiss, went over and sat on the settee by the fireplace near the door of the billiard room.

Miss Cornelia turned to her with a thousand questions on her tongue, but before she could ask any of them, Billy was ushering in Doctor Wells.

As she shook hands with the doctor, Miss Cornelia observed him with casual interest—wondering why such a good-looking man, in his early forties, apparently built for success, should be content with the comparative rustication of his local practice. That shrewd, rather aquiline face, with its keen gray eyes, would have found itself more at home in a wider sphere of action, she thought—there was just that touch of ruthlessness about it which makes or mars a captain in the world's affairs. She found herself murmuring the usual conventionalities of greeting.

"Oh, I'm very well, Doctor, thank you. Well, many people at the country club?"

"Not very many," he said, with a shake of his head. "This failure of the Union Bank has knocked a good many of the club members sky high."

"Just how did it happen?" Miss Cornelia was making conversation.

"Oh, the usual thing." The doctor took out his cigarette case. "The cashier, a young chap named Bailey, looted the bank to the tune of over a million."

Dale turned sharply toward them from her seat by the fireplace.

"How do you *know* the cashier did it?" she said in a low voice.

The doctor laughed. "Well—he's run away, for one thing. The bank examiners found the deficit. Bailey, the cashier, went out on an errand and didn't come back. The method was simple enough— worthless bonds substituted for good ones—with a good bond on the top and bottom of each package, so the packages would pass a casual inspection. Probably been going on for some time."

The fingers of Dale's right hand drummed restlessly on the edge of her settee.

"Couldn't somebody else have done it?" she queried tensely.

The doctor smiled, a trifle patronizingly.

"Of course the president of the bank had access to the vaults," he said. "But, as you know, Mr. Courtleigh Fleming, the late president, was buried last Monday."

Miss Cornelia had seen her niece's face light up oddly at the beginning of the doctor's statement—to relapse into lassitude again at its conclusion. Bailey—Bailey—she was sure she remembered that name—on Dale's lips.

"Dale, dear, did you know this young Bailey?" she asked point-blank.

The girl had started to light a cigarette. The flame wavered in her fingers, the match went out.

"Yes—slightly," she said. She bent to strike another match, averting her face. Miss Cornelia did not press her.

"What with bank robberies and communism and the income tax," she said, turning the subject, "the only way to keep your money these days is to spend it."

"Or not to have any—like myself!" the doctor agreed.

"It seems strange," Miss Cornelia went on, "living in Courtleigh Fleming's house. A month ago I'd never even heard of Mr. Fleming, though I suppose I should have, and now—why, I'm as interested in the failure of his bank as if I were a depositor!"

The doctor regarded the end of his cigarette.

"As a matter of fact," he said pleasantly, "Dick Fleming had no right to rent you the property before the estate was settled. He must have done it the moment he received my telegram announcing his uncle's death."

"Were you with him when he died?"

"Yes, in Colorado. He had angina pectoris and took me with him for that reason. But with care he might have lived a considerable time. The trouble was that he wouldn't use ordinary care. He ate and drank more than he should, and so—"

"I suppose," pursued Miss Cornelia, watching Dale out of the corner of her eye, "that there is no suspicion that Courtleigh Fleming robbed his own bank?"

"Well, if he did," said the doctor amicably, "I can testify that he didn't have the loot with him." His tone grew more serious. "No! He had his faults—but not that."

Miss Cornelia made up her mind. She had resolved before not to summon the doctor for aid in her difficulties, but now that chance had brought him here the opportunity seemed too good a one to let slip.

"Doctor," she said, "I think I ought to tell you something. Last night and the night before, attempts were made to enter this house. Once an intruder actually got in and was frightened away by Lizzie at the top of that staircase." She indicated the alcove stairs. "And twice I have received anonymous communications threatening my life if I did not leave the house and go back to the city."

Dale rose from her settee, startled.

"I didn't know that, Auntie! How dreadful!" she gasped.

Instantly Miss Cornelia regretted her impulse of confidence. She tried to pass the matter off with tart humor.

"Don't tell Lizzie," she said. "She'd yell like a siren. It's the only thing she does like a siren, but she does it superbly!"

For a moment it seemed as if Miss Cornelia had succeeded. The doctor smiled; Dale sat down again, her expression altering from one of anxiety to one of amusement. Miss Cornelia opened her lips to dilate further upon Lizzie's eccentricities.

But just then there was a splintering crash of glass from one of the French windows behind her!

6

Detective Anderson Takes Charge

"What's that?"

"Somebody smashed a windowpane!"

"And threw in a stone!"

"Wait a minute, I'll—" The doctor, all alert at once, ran into the alcove and jerked at the terrace door.

"It's bolted at the top, too," called Miss Cornelia. He nodded, without wasting words on a reply, unbolted the door and dashed out into the darkness of the terrace. Miss Cornelia saw him run past the French windows and disappear into blackness. Meanwhile Dale, her listlessness vanished before the shock of the strange occurrence, had gone to the broken window and picked up the stone. It was wrapped in paper; there seemed to be writing on the paper. She closed the terrace door and brought the stone to her aunt.

Miss Cornelia unwrapped the paper and smoothed out the sheet.

Two lines of course, round handwriting sprawled across it: *Take warning! Leave this house at once! It is threatened with disaster which will involve you if you remain!*

There was no signature.

"Who do you think wrote it?" asked Dale breathlessly.

Miss Cornelia straightened up like a ramrod—indomitable.

"A fool—that's who! If anything was calculated to make me stay here forever, this sort of thing would do it!"

She twitched the sheet of paper angrily.

"But—something may happen, darling!"

"I hope so! That's the reason I—"

She stopped. The doorbell was ringing again—thrilling, insistent. Her niece started at the sound.

"Oh, don't let anybody in!" she besought Miss Cornelia as Billy came in from the hall with his usual air of walking on velvet.

"Key, front door please—bell ring," he explained tersely, taking the key from the table.

Miss Cornelia issued instructions.

"See that the chain is on the door, Billy. Don't open it all the way. And get the visitor's name before you let him in."

She lowered her voice.

"If he says he is Mr. Anderson, let him in and take him to the library."

Billy nodded and disappeared. Dale turned to her aunt, the color out of her cheeks.

"Anderson? Who is Mr.—"

Miss Cornelia did not answer. She thought for a moment. Then she put her hand on Dale's shoulder in a gesture of protective affection.

"Dale, dear, you know how I love having you here, but it might be better if you went back to the city."

"Tonight, darling?" Dale managed a wan smile. But Miss Cornelia seemed serious.

"There's something *behind* all this disturbance—something I don't understand. But I mean to."

She glanced about to see if the doctor was returning. She lowered her voice. She drew Dale closer to her.

"The man in the library is a detective from police headquarters," she said.

She had expected Dale to show surprise—excitement—but the white mask of horror which the girl turned toward her appalled her. The young body trembled under her hand for a moment like a leaf in the storm.

"Not—the police!" breathed Dale in tones of utter consternation. Miss Cornelia could not understand why the news had stirred her niece so deeply. But there was no time to puzzle it out, she heard crunching steps on the terrace, the doctor was returning.

"Ssh!" she whispered. "It isn't necessary to tell the doctor. I think he's a sort of perambulating bedside gossip and once it's known the police are here we'll *never* catch the criminals!"

When the doctor entered from the terrace, brushing drops of rain from his no longer immaculate evening clothes, Dale was back on her favorite settee and Miss Cornelia was poring over the mysterious missive that had been wrapped about the stone.

"He got away in the shrubbery," said the doctor disgustedly, taking out a handkerchief to fleck the spots of mud from his shoes.

Miss Cornelia gave him the letter of warning. "Read this," she said.

The doctor adjusted a pair of prince-nez—read the two crude sentences over—once—twice. Then he looked shrewdly at Miss Cornelia.

"Were the others like this?" he queried.

She nodded. "Practically."

He hesitated for a moment like a man with an unpleasant social duty to face.

"Miss Van Gorder, may I speak frankly?"

"Generally speaking, I detest frankness," said that lady grimly. "But—go on!"

The doctor tapped the letter. His face was wholly serious.

"I think you *ought* to leave this house," he said bluntly.

"Because of that letter? Humph!" His very seriousness, perversely enough, made her suddenly wish to treat the whole matter as lightly as possible.

The doctor repressed the obvious annoyance of a man who sees a warning, given in all sobriety, unexpectedly taken as a quip.

"There is some deviltry afoot," he persisted. "You are not safe here, Miss Van Gorder."

But if he was persistent in his attitude, so was she in hers.

"I've been safe in all kinds of houses for sixty-odd years," she said lightly. "It's time I had a bit of a change. Besides," she gestured toward her defenses, "this house is as nearly impregnable as I can make it. The window locks are sound enough, the doors are locked, and the keys are there," she pointed to the keys lying on the table. "As for the terrace door you just used," she went on, "I had Billy put an extra bolt on it today. By the way, did you bolt that door again?" She moved toward the alcove.

"Yes, I did," said the doctor quickly, still seeming unconvinced of the wisdom of her attitude.

"Miss Van Gorder, I confess—I'm very anxious for you," he continued. "This letter is—ominous. Have you any enemies?"

"Don't insult me! Of course I have. Enemies are an indication of character."

The doctor's smile held both masculine pity and equally masculine exasperation. He went on more gently.

"Why not accept my hospitality in the village tonight?" he proposed reasonably. "It's a little house but I'll make you comfortable.

Or," he threw out his hands in the gesture of one who reasons with a willful child, "if you won't come to me, let me stay here!"

Miss Cornelia hesitated for an instant. The proposition seemed logical enough—more than that—sensible, safe. And yet, some indefinable feeling—hardly strong enough to be called a premonition—kept her from accepting it. Besides, she knew what the doctor did not, that help was waiting across the hall in the library.

"Thank you, no, Doctor," she said briskly, before she had time to change her mind. "I'm not easily frightened. And tomorrow I intend to equip this entire house with burglar alarms on doors and windows!" she went on defiantly. The incident, as far as she was concerned, was closed. She moved on into the alcove.

She tried the terrace door. "There, I knew it!" she said triumphantly. "Doctor—you *didn't* fasten that bolt!"

The doctor seemed a little taken aback. "Oh—I'm sorry—" he said.

"You only pushed it part of the way," she explained. She completed the task and stepped back into the living-room. "The only thing that worries me now is that broken French window," she said thoughtfully. "Anyone can reach a hand through it and open the latch." She came down toward the settee where Dale was sitting. "Please, Doctor!"

"Oh, what are you going to do?" said the doctor, coming out of a brown study.

"I'm going to barricade that window!" said Miss Cornelia firmly, already struggling to lift one end of the settee. But now Dale came to her rescue.

"Oh, darling, you'll hurt yourself. Let me—" and between them, the doctor and Dale moved the heavy settee along until it stood in front of the window in question.

The doctor stood up when the dusty task was finished, wiping his hands.

"It would take a furniture mover to get in there now!" he said airily.

Miss Cornelia smiled.

"Well, Doctor, I'll say good night now—and thank you very much," she said, extending her hand to the doctor, who bowed over it silently. "Don't keep this young lady up too late; she looks tired." She flashed a look at Dale who stood staring out at the night.

"I'll only smoke a cigarette," promised the doctor. Once again his voice had a note of plea in it. "You won't change your mind?" he asked anew.

Miss Van Gorder's smile was obdurate. "I have a great deal of mind," she said. "It takes a long time to change it."

Then, having exercised her feminine privilege of the last word, she sailed out of the room, still smiling, and closed the door behind her.

The doctor seemed a little nettled by her abrupt departure.

"It may be mind," he said, turning back toward Dale, "but forgive me if I say I think it seems more like foolhardy stubbornness!"

Dale turned away from the window. "Then you think there is really danger?"

The doctor's eyes were grave.

"Well, those letters—" he dropped the letter on the table. "They mean *something*. Here you are—isolated—the village two miles away—and enough shrubbery around the place to hide a dozen assassins—"

If his manner had been in the slightest degree melodramatic, Dale would have found the ominous sentences more easy to discount. But this calm, intent statement of fact was a chill touch at her heart. And yet—

"But what enemies can Aunt Cornelia have?" she asked helplessly.

"Any man will tell you what I do," said the doctor with increasing seriousness. He took a cigarette from his case and tapped it on the case to emphasize his words. "This is no place for two women, practically alone."

Dale moved away from him restlessly, to warm her hands at the fire. The doctor gave a quick glance around the room. Then, unseen by her, he stepped noiselessly over to the table, took the matchbox there off its holder and slipped it into his pocket. It seemed a curiously useless and meaningless gesture, but his next words envinced that the action had been deliberate.

"I don't seem to be able to find any matches—" he said with assumed carelessness, fiddling with the matchbox holder.

Dale turned away from the fire. "Oh, aren't there any? I'll get you some," she said with automatic politeness, and departed to search for them.

The doctor watched her go, saw the door close behind her. Instantly his face set into tense and wary lines. He glanced about—then ran lightly into the alcove and noiselessly unfastened the bolt on the terrace door which he had pretented to fasten after his search of the shrubbery. When Dale returned with the matches, he was back where he had been when she had left him, glancing at a magazine on the table.

He thanked her urbanely as she offered him the box.

"So sorry to trouble you—but tobacco is the one drug every doctor forbids his patients and prescribes for himself."

Dale smiled at the little joke. He lit his cigarette and drew in the fragrant smoke with apparent gusto. But a moment later he had crushed out the glowing end in an ash tray.

"By the way, has Miss Van Gorder a revolver?" he queried casually, glancing at his wrist watch.

"Yes. She fired it off this afternoon to see if it would work." Dale smiled at the memory.

The doctor, too, seemed amused. "If she tries to shoot anything— for goodness' sake stand behind her!" he advised. He glanced at the wrist watch again. "Well—I must be going—"

"If anything happens," said Dale slowly, "I shall telephone you at once."

Her words seemed to disturb the doctor slightly—but only for a second. He grew even more urbane.

"I'll be home shortly after midnight," he said. "I'm stopping at the Johnsons' on my way. One of their children is ill—or supposed to be." He took a step toward the door, then he turned toward Dale again.

"Take a parting word of advice," he said. "The thing to do with a midnight prowler is—let him alone. Lock your bedroom doors and don't let anything bring you out till morning." He glanced at Dale to see how she took the advice, his hand on the knob of the door.

"Thank you," said Dale seriously. "Good night, Doctor—Billy will let you out, he has the key."

"By Jove!" laughed the doctor, "you *are* careful, aren't you! The place is like a fortress! Well—good night, Miss Dale—"

"Good night." The door closed behind him. Dale was left alone. Suddenly her composure left her, the fixed smile died. She stood gazing ahead at nothing, her face a mask of terror and apprehension. But it was like a curtain that had lifted for a moment on some secret tragedy and then fallen again. When Billy returned with the front door key she was as impassive as he was.

"Has the new gardener come yet?"

"He here," said Billy stolidly. "Name Brook."

She was entirely herself once more when Billy, departing, held the door open wide—to admit Miss Cornelia Van Gorder and a tall, strong-featured man, quietly dressed, with reticent, piercing eyes— the detective!

Dale's first conscious emotion was one of complete surprise. She had expected a heavy-set, blue-jowled vulgarian with a black cigar, a battered derby, and stubby policemen's shoes. *Why this man's a gentleman!* she thought. *At least he looks like one—and yet—you can tell from his face he'd have as little mercy as a steel trap for anyone he had to—catch—* She shuddered uncontrollably.

"Dale, dear," said Miss Cornelia with triumph in her voice. "This is Mr. Anderson."

The newcomer bowed politely, glancing at her casually and then looking away. Miss Cornelia, however, was obviously a fine feather and relishing to the utmost the presence of a real detective in the house.

"This is the room I spoke of," she said briskly. "All the disturbances have taken place around that terrace door."

The detective took three swift steps into the alcove, glanced about it searchingly. He indicated the stairs.

"That is not the main staircase?"

"No, the main staircase is out there." Miss Cornelia waved her hand in the direction of the hall.

The detective came out of the alcove and paused by the French windows.

"I think there must be a conspiracy between the Architects' Association and the Housebreakers' Union these days," he said grimly. "Look at all that glass. All a burglar needs is a piece of putty and a diamond-cutter to break in."

"But the curious thing is," continued Miss Cornelia, "that whoever got into the house evidently had a key to that door." Again she indicated the terrace door, but Anderson did not seem to be listening to her.

"Hello—what's this?" he said sharply, his eye lighting on the broken glass below the shattered French window. He picked up a piece of glass and examined it.

Dale cleared her throat. "It was broken from the outside a few minutes ago," she said.

"The outside?" Instantly the detective had pulled aside a blind and was staring out into the darkness.

"Yes. And then that letter was thrown in." She pointed to the threatening missive on the center table.

Anderson picked it up, glanced through it, laid it down. All his movements were quick and sure—each executed with the minimum expense of effort.

"H'm," he said in a calm voice that held a glint of humor. "Curious, the anonymous letter complex! Apparently someone considers you an undesirable tenant!"

Miss Cornelia took up the tale.

"There are some things I haven't told you yet," she said. "This house belonged to the late Courtleigh Fleming." He glanced at her sharply.

"The Union Bank?"

"Yes. I rented it for the summer and moved in last Monday. We have not had a really quiet night since I came. The very first night I saw a man with an electric flashlight making his way through the shrubbery!"

"You poor dear!" from Dale sympathetically. "And you were here alone!"

"Well, I had Lizzie. And," said Miss Cornelia with enormous importance, opening the drawer of the center table, "I had my revolver. I know so little about these things, Mr. Anderson, that if I didn't hit a burglar, I knew I'd hit somebody or something!" and she gazed with innocent awe directly down the muzzle of her beloved weapon, then waved it with an airy gesture beneath the detective's nose.

Anderson gave an involuntary start, then his eyes lit up with grim mirth.

"Would you mind putting that away?" he said suavely. "I like to get in the papers as much as anybody, but I don't want to have them say— *omit flowers.*"

Miss Cornelia gave him a glare of offended pride, but he endured it with such quiet equanimity that she merely replaced the revolver in the drawer, with a hurt expression, and waited for him to open the next topic of conversation.

He finished his preliminary survey of the room and returned to her.

"Now you say you don't think anybody has got upstairs yet?" he queried.

Miss Cornelia regarded the alcove stairs.

"I think not. I'm a very light sleeper, especially since the papers have been so full of the exploits of this criminal they call the Bat. He's in them again tonight." She nodded toward the evening paper.

The detective smiled faintly.

"Yes, he's contrived to surround himself with such an air of mystery that it verges on the supernatural—or seems that way to newspapermen."

"I confess," admitted Miss Cornelia, "I've thought of him in this connection." She looked at Anderson to see how he would take the suggestion but the latter merely smiled again, this time more broadly.

"That's going rather a long way for a theory," he said. "And the Bat is not in the habit of giving warnings."

"Nevertheless," she insisted, "somebody has been trying to get into this house, night after night."

The detective smiled ruefully. He picked up the evening paper, glanced at it, shook his head. "I'd forget the Bat in all this. You can always tell when the Bat has had anything to do with a crime. When he's through, he signs his name to it."

Miss Cornelia sat upright. "His name? I thought nobody knew his name?"

The detective made a little gesture of apology. "That was a figure of speech. The newspapers named him the Bat because he moved with incredible rapidity, always at night, and by signing his name I mean he leaves the symbol of his identity—the Bat, which can see in the dark."

"I wish I could," Miss Cornelia, striving to seem unimpressed. "These country lights are always going out."

Anderson's face grew stern. "Sometimes he draws the outline of a bat at the scene of the crime. Once, in some way, he got hold of a real bat, and nailed it to the wall."

Dale, listening, could not repress a shudder at the gruesome picture and Miss Cornelia's hands gave an involuntary twitch as her knitting needles clicked together. Anderson seemed by no means unconscious of the effect he had created.

"How many people in this house, Miss Van Gorder?"

"My niece and myself." Miss Cornelia indicated Dale, who had picked up her wrap and was starting to leave the room. "Lizzie Allen, who has been my personal maid ever since I was a child, the Japanese butler, and the gardener. The cook and the housemaid left this morning—frightened away."

She smiled as she finished her description. Dale reached the door and passed slowly out into the hall. The detective gave her a single, sharp glance as she made her exit. He seemed to think over the factors Miss Cornelia had mentioned.

"Well," he said, after a slight pause, "you can have a good night's sleep tonight. I'll stay right here in the dark and watch."

"Would you like some coffee to keep you awake?"

Anderson nodded. "Thank you." His voice sank lower. "Do the servants know who I am?"

"Only Lizzie, my maid."

His eyes fixed hers. "I wouldn't tell anyone I'm remaining up all night," he said.

A formless fear rose in Miss Cornelia's mind. "You don't suspect my household?" she said in a low voice.

He spoke with emphasis—all the more pronounced because of the quietude of his tone.

"I'm not taking any chances," he said determinedly.

7

Cross-Questions and Crooked Answers

All unconscious of the slur just cast upon her forty years of single-minded devotion to the Van Gorder family, Lizzie chose that particular moment to open the door and make a little bob at her mistress and the detective.

"The gentleman's room is ready," she said meekly. In her mind she was already beseeching her patron saint that she would not have to show the gentleman to his room. Her ideas of detectives were entirely drawn from sensational magazines and her private opinion was that Anderson might have anything in his pocket from a set of terrifying false whiskers to a bomb!

Miss Cornelia, obedient to the detective's instructions, promptly told the whitest of fibs for Lizzie's benefit.

"The maid will show you to your room now and you can make yourself comfortable for the night." There—that would mislead Lizzie, without being quite a lie.

"My toilet is made for an occasion like this when I've got my gun loaded," answered Anderson carelessly. The allusion to the gun made Lizzie start nervously, unhappily for her, for it drew his attention to her and he now transfixed her with a stare.

"This is the maid you referred to?" he inquired. Miss Cornelia assented. He drew nearer to the unhappy Lizzie.

"What's your name?" he asked, turning to her.

"E-Elizabeth Allen," stammered Lizzie, feeling like a small and distrustful sparrow in the toils of an officious python.

Anderson seemed to run through a mental rogues' gallery of other criminals named Elizabeth Allen that he had known.

"How old are you?" he proceeded.

Lizzie looked at her mistress despairingly. "Have I got to answer that?" she wailed. Miss Cornelia nodded inexorably.

Lizzie braced herself. "Thirty-two," she said, with an arch toss of her head.

The detective looked surprised and slightly amused.

"She's fifty if she's a day," said Miss Cornelia treacherously in spite of a look from Lizzie that would have melted a stone.

The trace of a smile appeared and vanished on the detective's face.

"Now, Lizzie," he said sternly, "do you ever walk in your sleep?"

"I do not," said Lizzie indignantly.

"Don't care for the country, I suppose?"

"I do not!"

"Or detectives?" Anderson deigned to be facetious.

"*I do not!*" There could be no doubt as to the sincerity of Lizzie's answer.

"All right, Lizzie. Be calm. I can stand it," said the detective with treacherous suavity. But he favored her with a long and careful scrutiny before he moved to the table and picked up the note that had been thrown through the windows. Quietly he extended it beneath Lizzie's nose.

"Ever see this before?" he said crisply, watching her face.

Lizzie read the note with bulging eyes, her face horror-stricken. When she had finished, she made a gesture of wild disclaimer that nearly removed a portion of Anderson's left ear.

"Mercy on us!" she moaned, mentally invoking not only her patron saint but all the rosary of heaven to protect herself and her mistress.

But the detective still kept his eyes on her.

"Didn't write it yourself, did you?" he queried curtly.

"I did not!" said Lizzie angrily. "I did *not!*"

"And—you're sure you don't walk in your sleep?"

The bare idea strained Lizzie's nerves to the breaking point.

"When I get into bed in this house I wouldn't put my feet out for a million dollars!" she said with heartfelt candor. Even Anderson was compelled to grin at this.

"Then I won't ask you to," he said, relaxing considerably. "That's more money than I'm worth, Lizzie."

"Well, *I'll say it is!*" quoth Lizzie, now thoroughly aroused, and flounced out of the room in high dudgeon, her pompadour bristling, before he had time to interrogate her further.

He replaced the note on the table and turned back to Miss Cornelia. If he had found any clue to the mystery in Lizzie's demeanor, she could not read it in his manner.

"Now, what about the butler?" he said.

"Nothing about him—except that he was Courtleigh Fleming's servant."

Anderson paused. "Do you consider that significant?"

A shadow appeared behind him deep in the alcove—a vague, listening figure—Dale, on tiptoe, conspiratorial, taking pains not to draw the attention of the others to her prescence. But both Miss Cornelia and Anderson were too engrossed in their conversation to notice her.

Miss Cornelia hesitated.

"Isn't it possible that there is a connection between the colossal theft at the Union Bank and *these* disturbances?" she said.

Anderson seemed to think over the question.

"What do you mean?" he asked as Dale slowly moved into the room from the alcove, silently closing the alcove doors behind her, and still unobserved.

"Suppose," said Miss Cornelia slowly, "that Courtleigh Fleming took that money from his own bank and concealed it in this house?" The eavesdropper grew rigid.

"That's the theory you gave headquarters, isn't it?" said Anderson. "But I'll tell you how headquarters figures it out. In the first place, the cashier is missing. In the second place, if Courtleigh Fleming did it and got as far as Colorado, he had it with him when he died, and the facts apparently don't bear that out. In the third place, suppose he had hidden the money in or around the house. Why did he rent it to you?"

"But he didn't," said Miss Cornelia obstinately, "I leased this house from his nephew, his heir."

The detective smiled tolerantly.

"Well, I wouldn't struggle like that for a theory," he said, the professional note coming back to his voice. "The cashier's *missing*—that's the answer."

Miss Cornelia resented his offhand demolition of the mental cardcastle she had erected with such pride.

"I have read a great deal on the detection of crime," she said hotly, "and—"

"Well, we all have our little hobbies," he said tolerantly. "A good many people rather fancy themselves as detectives and run around looking for clues under the impression that a clue is a big and vital factor that sticks up like—well, like a sore thumb. The fact is that the criminal takes care of the big and important factors. It's only the little ones he may overlook. To go back to your friend the Bat, it's because of his skill in little things that he's still at large."

"Then *you* don't think there's a chance that the money from the Union Bank is in this house?" persisted Miss Cornelia.

"I think it is very unlikely."

Miss Cornelia put her knitting away and rose. She still clung tenaciously to her own theories but her belief in them had been badly shaken.

"If you'll come with me, I'll show you to your room," she said a little stiffly. The detective stepped back to let her pass.

"Sorry to spoil your little theory," he said, and followed her to the door. If either had noticed the unobtrusive listener to their conversation, neither made a sign.

The moment the door had closed on them Dale sprang into action. She seemed a different girl from the one who had left the room so inconspicuously such a short time before. There were two bright spots of color in her cheeks and she was obviously laboring under great excitement. She went quickly to the alcove doors—they opened softly— disclosing the young man who had said that he was Brooks the new gardener—and yet not the same young man—for his assumed air of servitude had dropped from him like a cloak, revealing him as a young fellow at least of the same general social class as Dale's if not a fellow-inhabitant of the select circle where Van Gorders revolved about Van Gorders, and a man's greatgrandfather was more important than the man himself.

Dale cautioned him with a warning finger as he advanced into the room.

"Sh! Sh!" she whispered. "Be careful! That man's a detective!"

Brooks gave a hunted glance at the door into the hall.

"Then they've traced me here," he said in a dejected voice.

"I don't think so."

He made a gesture of helplessness.

"I couldn't get back to my rooms," he said in a whisper. "If they've searched them," he paused, "as they're sure to—they'll find your letters to me." He paused again. "Your aunt doesn't suspect anything?"

"No, I told her I'd engaged a gardener—and that's all there was about it."

He came nearer to her. "Dale!" he murmured in a tense voice. "You *know* I didn't take that money!" he said with boyish simplicity.

All the loyalty of first-love was in her answer.

"Of course! I believe in you absolutely!" she said. He caught her in his arms and kissed her—gratefully, passionately. Then the galling memory of the predicament in which he stood, the hunt already on his trail, came back to him. He released her gently, still holding one of her hands.

"But—the police here!" he stammered, turning away. "What does that mean?"

Dale swiftly informed him of the situation.

"Aunt Cornelia says people have been trying to break into the house for days—at night."

Brooks ran his hand through his hair in a gesture of bewilderment. Then he seemed to catch at a hope.

"What sort of people?" he queried sharply.

Dale was puzzled. "She doesn't know."

The excitement in her lover's manner came to a head. "That proves exactly what I've contended right along," he said, thudding one fist softly in the palm of the other. "Through some underneath channel old Fleming had been selling those securities for months, turning them into cash. And somebody knows about it, and knows that that money is hidden here. Don't you see? Your Aunt Cornelia has crabbed the game by coming here."

"Why didn't you tell the police that? Now they think, because you ran away—"

"Ran away! The only chance I had was a few hours to myself to try to prove what actually happened."

"Why don't you tell the detective what you think?" said Dale at her wits' end. "That Courtleigh Fleming took the money and that it is still here?"

Her lover's face grew somber.

"He'd take me into custody at once and I'd have no chance to search."

He was searching now. His eyes roved about the living-room— walls—ceiling—hopefully—desperately—looking for a clue—the tiniest clue to support his theory.

"Why are you so sure it is here?" queried Dale.

Brooks explained. "You must remember Fleming was no ordinary defaulter and *he* had no intention of being exiled to a foreign country. He wanted to come back here and take his place in the community while I was in the pen."

"But even then—"

He interrupted her. "Listen, dear—" He crossed to the billiard-room door, closed it firmly, returned.

"The architect that built this house was an old friend of mine," he said in hushed accents. "We were together in France and you know the way fellows get to talking when they're far away and cut off—" He paused, seeing the cruel gleam of the flame throwers—two figures huddled in a foxhole, whiling away the terrible hours of waiting by muttered talk.

"Just an hour or two before—a shell got this friend of mine," he resumed, "he told me he had built a hidden room in this house."

"Where?" gasped Dale.

Brooks shook his head. "I don't know. We never got to finish that conversation. But I remember what he said. He said, 'You watch old Fleming. If I get mine over here it won't break his heart. He didn't want any living being to know about that room.' "

Now Dale was as excited as he.

"Then you think the money is in this hidden room?"

"I do," said Brooks decidedly. "I don't think Fleming took it away with him. He was too shrewd for that. No, he meant to come back all right, the minute he got the word the bank had been looted. And he'd fixed things so I'd be railroaded to prison—you wouldn't understand, but it was pretty neat. And then the fool nephew rents this house the minute he's dead, and whoever knows about the money—"

"Jack! Why isn't it the nephew who is trying to break in?"

"He wouldn't *have* to break in. He could make an excuse and come in any time."

He clenched his hands despairingly.

"If I could only get hold of a blueprint of this place!" he muttered.

Dale's face fell. It was sickening to be so close to the secret—and yet not find it. "Oh, Jack, I'm so confused and worried!" she confessed, with a little sob.

Brooks put his hands on her shoulders in an effort to cheer her spirits.

"Now listen, dear," he said firmly, "this isn't as hard as it sounds. I've got a clear night to work in—and as true as I'm standing here, that money's in this house. Listen, honey—it's like this." He pantomimed the old nursery rhyme of *The House that Jack Built.* "Here's the house that Courtleigh Fleming built—here, somewhere, is the Hidden Room in the house that Courtleigh Fleming built—and here—somewhere—pray heaven—is the money—in the Hidden Room—in the house that Courtleigh Fleming built. When you're low in your mind, just say that over!"

She managed a faint smile. "I've forgotten it already," she said, drooping.

He still strove for an offhand gaiety that he did not feel.

"Why, look here!" and she followed the play of his hands obediently, like a tired child "it's a sort of game, dearest. 'Money, money—who's got the money?' You know!" For the dozenth time he stared at the unrevealing walls of the room. "For that matter," he added, "the Hidden Room may be behind these very walls."

He looked about for a tool, a poker, anything that would sound the walls and test them for hollow spaces. Ah, he had it—that driver in the bag of golf clubs over in the corner. He got the driver and stood wondering where he had best begin. That blank wall above the fireplace looked as promising as any. He tapped it gently with the golf club—afraid to make too much noise and yet anxious to test the wall as thoroughly as possible. A dull, heavy reverberation answered his stroke—nothing hollow there apparently.

As he tried another spot, again thunder beat the long roll on its iron drum outside, in the night. The lights blinked—wavered—recovered.

"The lights are going out again," said Dale dully, her excitement sunk into a stupefied calm.

"Let them go! The less light the better for me. The only thing to do is to go over this house room by room." He pointed to the billiard-room door. "What's in there?"

"The billiard room." She was thinking hard. "Jack! Perhaps Courtleigh Fleming's nephew would know where the blueprints are!"

He looked dubious. "It's a chance, but not a very good one," he said. "Well—" He led the way into the billiard room and began to rap at random upon its walls while Dale listened intently for any echo that might betray the presence of a hidden chamber of sliding panel.

Thus it happened that Lizzie received the first real thrill of what was to prove to her—and to others—a sensational and hideous night. For, coming into the living-room to lay a cloth for Mr. Anderson's night supper, not only did the lights blink threateningly and the thunder roll, but a series of spirit raps was certainly to be heard coming from the region of the billiard room.

"Oh, my God!" she wailed, and the next instant the lights went out, leaving her in inky darkness. With a loud shriek she bolted out of the room.

Thunder—lightning—dashing of rain on the streaming glass of the windows—the storm hallooing its hounds. Dale huddled close to her lover as they groped their way back to the living-room, cautiously, doing their best to keep from stumbling against some heavy piece of furniture whose fall would arouse the house.

"There's a candle on the table, Jack, if I can find the table." Her outstretched hands touched a familiar object. "Here it is." She fumbled for a moment. "Have you any matches?"

"Yes." He struck one—another—lit the candle—set it down on the table. In the weak glow of the little taper, whose tiny flame illuminated but a portion of the living-room, his face looked tense and strained.

"It's pretty nearly hopeless," he said, "if all the walls are paneled like that."

As if in mockery of his words and his quest, a muffled knocking that seemed to come from the ceiling of the very room he stood in answered his despair.

"What's that?" gasped Dale.

They listened. The knocking was repeated—knock—knock—knock—knock.

"Someone else is looking for the Hidden Room!" muttered Brooks, gazing up at the ceiling intently, as if he could tear from it the secret of this new mystery by sheer strength of will.

8

The Gleaming Eye

"It's upstairs!" Dale took a step toward the alcove stairs. Brooks halted her.

"Who's in this house besides ourselves?" he queried.

"Only the detective, Aunt Cornelia, Lizzie, and Billy."

"Billy's the Jap?"

"Yes." Brooks paused an instant. "Does he belong to your aunt?"

"No. He was Courtleigh Fleming's butler."

Knock—knock—knock—knock—the dull, methodical rapping on the ceiling of the living-room began again.

"Courtleigh Fleming's butler, eh?" muttered Brooks. He put down his candle and stole noiselessly into the alcove. "It may be the Jap!" he whispered.

Knock—knock—knock—knock! This time the mysterious rapping seemed to come from the upper hall.

"If it is the Jap, I'll get him!" Brooks's voice was tense with resolution. He hesitated—made for the hall door—tiptoed out into the darkness around the main staircase, leaving Dale alone in the living-room beset by shadowy terrors.

Utter silence succeeded his noiseless departure. Even the storm lulled for a moment. Dale stood thinking, wondering, searching desperately for some way to help her lover.

At last a resolution formed in her mind. She went to the city telephone.

"Hello," she said in a low voice, glancing over her shoulder now and then to make sure she was not overheard. "1—2—4—please—yes, that's right. Hello—is that the country club? Is Mr. Richard Fleming there? Yes, I'll hold the wire."

She looked about nervously. Had something moved in that corner of blackness where her candle did not pierce? No! How silly of her!

Buzz-buzz on the telephone. She picked up the receiver again.

"Hello—is this Mr. Fleming? This is Miss Ogden—Dale Ogden. I know it must seem odd my calling you this late, but—I wonder if you could come over here for a few minutes. Yes—tonight." Her voice grew stronger. "I wouldn't trouble you but—it's awfully important. Hold the wire a moment." She put down the phone and made another swift survey of the room, listened furtively at the door—all clear! She returned to the phone.

"Hello—Mr. Fleming—I'll wait outside the house on the drive. It— it's a confidential matter. Thank you so much."

She hung up the phone, relieved—not an instant too soon, for, as she crossed toward the fireplace to add a new log to the dying glow of the fire, the hall door opened and Anderson, the detective, came softly in with an unlighted candle in his hand.

Her composure almost deserted her. How much had he heard? What deduction would he draw if he had heard? An assignation, perhaps! Well, she could stand that; she could stand anything to secure the next few hours of liberty for Jack. For that length of time she and the law were at war; she and this man were at war.

But his first words relieved her fears.

"Spooky sort of place in the dark, isn't it?" he said casually.

"Yes, rather." If he would only go away before Brooks came back or Richard Fleming arrived! But he seemed in a distressingly chatty frame of mind.

"Left me upstairs without a match," continued Anderson. "I found my way down by walking part of the way and falling the rest. Don't suppose I'll ever find the room I left my toothbrush in!" He laughed, lighting the candle in his hand from the candle on the table.

"You're not going to stay up all night, are you?" said Dale nervously, hoping he would take the hint. But he seemed entirely oblivious of such minor considerations as sleep. He took out a cigar.

"Oh, I may doze a bit," he said. He eyed her with a certain approval. She was a darned pretty girl and she looked intelligent. "I suppose you have a theory of your own about these intrusions you've been having here? Or apparently having."

"I knew nothing about them until tonight."

"Still," he persisted conversationally, "you know about them now." But when she remained silent, "Is Miss Van Gorder usually—of a nervous temperament? Imagines she sees things, and all that?"

"I don't think so." Dale's voice was strained. Where was Brooks? What had happened to him?

Anderson puffed on his cigar, pondering. "Know the Flemings?" he asked.

"I've met Mr. Richard Fleming once or twice."

Something in her tone caused him to glance at her. "Nice fellow?"

"I don't know him at all well."

"Know the cashier of the Union Bank?" he shot at her suddenly.

"No!" She strove desperately to make the denial convincing but she could not hide the little tremor in her voice.

The detective mused.

"Fellow of good family, I understand," he said, eyeing her. "Very popular. That's what's behind most of these bank embezzlements; men getting into society and spending more than they make."

Dale hailed the tinkle of the city telephone with an inward sigh of relief. The detective moved to answer the house phone on the wall by the alcove, mistaking the direction of the ring.

Dale corrected him quickly.

"No, the other one. That's the house phone."

Anderson looked the apparatus over.

"No connection with the outside, eh?"

"No," Dale said absent-mindedly. "Just from room to room in the house."

He accepted her explanation and answered the other telephone.

"Hello—hello—what the—" He moved the receiver hook up and down, without result, and gave it up. "This line sounds dead," he said.

"It was all right a few minutes ago," said Dale without thinking.

"You were using it a few minutes ago?"

She hesitated—what use to deny what she had already admitted, for all practical purposes.

"Yes."

The city telephone rang again. The detective pounced upon it.

"Hello—yes—yes—this is Anderson—go ahead." He paused, while the tiny voice in the receiver buzzed for some seconds. Then he interrupted it impatiently.

"You're sure of that, are you? I see. All right. 'By."

He hung up the receiver and turned swiftly on Dale.

"Did I understand you to say that you were not acquainted with the cashier of the Union Bank?" he said to her with a new note in his voice.

Dale stared ahead of her blankly. It had come! She did not reply.

Anderson went on ruthlessly.

"That was headquarters, Miss Ogden. They have found some letters in Bailey's room which seem to indicate that you were not telling the entire truth just now."

He paused, waiting for her answer. "What letters?" she said wearily.

"From you to Jack Bailey—showing that you had recently become engaged to him."

Dale decided to make a clean breast of it, or as clean a one as she dared.

"Very well," she said in an even voice, "that's true."

"Why didn't you say so before?" There was menace beneath his suavity.

She thought swiftly. Apparent frankness seemed to be the only resource left her. She gave him a candid smile.

"It's been a secret. I haven't even told my aunt yet." Now she let indignation color her tones. "How can the police be so stupid as to accuse Jack Bailey, a young man and about to be married? Do you think he would wreck his future like that?"

"Some people wouldn't call it wrecking a future to lay away a million dollars," said Anderson ominously. He came closer to Dale, fixing her with his eyes. "Do you know *where* Bailey is now?" He spoke slowly and menacingly.

She did not flinch.

"No."

The detective paused.

"Miss Ogden," he said, still with that hidden threat in his voice, "in the last minute or so the Union Bank case and certain things in this house have begun to tie up pretty close together. Bailey disappeared this morning. Have you heard from him since?"

Her eyes met his without weakening, her voice was cool and composed.

"No."

The detective did not comment on her answer. She could not tell from his face whether he thought she had told the truth or lied. He turned away from her brusquely.

"I'll ask you to bring Miss Van Gorder here," he said in his professional voice.

"Why do you want her?" Dale blazed at him rebelliously.

He was quiet. "Because this case is taking on a new phase."

"You don't think I know anything about that money?" she said, a little wildly, hoping that a display of sham anger might throw him off the trail he seemed to be following.

He seemed to accept her words, cynically, at their face value.

"No," he said, "but you know somebody who does."

Dale hesitated, sought for a biting retort, found none. It did not matter; any respite, no matter how momentary, from these probing questions, would be a relief. She silently took one of the lighted candles and left the living-room to search for her aunt.

Left alone, the detective reflected for a moment, then picking up the one lighted candle that remained, commenced a systematic examination of the living-room. His methods were thorough, but it, when he came to the end of his quest, he had made any new discoveries, the reticent composure of his face did not betray the fact. When he had finished he turned patiently toward the billiard room—the little flame of his candle was swallowed up in its dark recesses—he closed the door of the living-room behind him. The storm was dying away now, but a few flashes of lightning still flickered, lighting up the darkness of the deserted living-room now and then with a harsh, brief glare.

A lightning flash—a shadow cast abruptly on the shade of one of the French windows, to disappear as abruptly as the flash was blotted out—the shadow of a man—a prowler—feeling his way through the lightning-slashed darkness to the terrace door. The detective? Brooks? The Bat? The lightning flash was too brief for any observer to have recognized the stealing shape—if any observer had been there.

But the lack of an observer was promptly remedied. Just as the shadowy shape reached the terrace door and its shadow-fingers closed over the knob, Lizzie entered the deserted living-room on stumbling feet. She was carrying a tray of dishes and food—some cold meat on a platter, a cup and saucer, a roll, a butter pat—and she walked slowly, with terror only one leap behind her and blank darkness ahead.

She had only reached the table and was preparing to deposit her tray and beat a shameful retreat, when a sound behind her made her turn. The key in the door from the terrace to the alcove had clicked. Paralyzed with fright she stared and waited, and the next moment a formless thing, a blacker shadow in a world of shadows, passed swiftly in and up the small staircase.

But not only a shadow. To Lizzie's terrified eyes it bore an eye, a single gleaming eye, just above the level of the stair rail, and this eye was turned on her.

It was too much. She dropped the tray on the table with a crash and gave vent to a piercing shriek that would have shamed the siren of a fire engine.

Miss Cornelia and Anderson, rushing in from the hall and the billiard room respectively, each with a lighted candle, found her gasping and clutching at the table for support.

"For the love of heaven, what's wrong?" cried Miss Cornelia irritatedly. The coffeepot she was carrying in her other hand spilled a portion of its boiling contents on Lizzie's shoe and Lizzie screamed anew and began to dance up and down on the uninjured foot.

"Oh, my foot—my foot!" she squealed hysterically. "My foot!"

Miss Cornelia tried to shake her back to her senses.

"My patience! Did you yell like that because you stubbed your toe?"

"You scalded it!" cried Lizzie wildly. "It went up the staircase!"

"Your *toe* went up the staircase?"

"No, no! An eye—an eye as big as a saucer! It ran right up that staircase—" She indicated the alcove with a trembling forefinger. Miss Cornelia put her coffeepot and her candle down on the table and opened her mouth to express her frank opinion of her factotum's sanity. But here the detective took charge.

"Now see here," he said with some sternness to the quaking Lizzie, "stop this racket and tell me what you saw!"

"A ghost!" persisted Lizzie, still hopping around on one leg. "It came right through that door and ran up the stairs—oh—" and she seemed prepared to scream again as Dale, white-faced, came in from the hall, followed by Billy and Brooks, the latter holding still another candle.

"Who screamed?" said Dale tensely.

"I did!" Lizzie wailed, "I saw a ghost!" She turned to Miss Cornelia. "I begged you not to come here," she vociferated. "I begged you on my bended knees. There's a graveyard not a quarter of a mile away."

"Yes, and one more scare like that, Lizzie Allen, and you'll have me lying in it," said her mistress unsympathetically. She moved up to examine the scene of Lizzie's ghostly misadventure, while Anderson began to interrogate its heroine.

"Now, Lizzie," he said, forcing himself to urbanity, "what did you really see?"

"I told you what I saw."

His manner grew somewhat threatening.

"You're not trying to frighten Miss Van Gorder into leaving this house and going back to the city?"

"Well, if I am," said Lizzie with grim, unconscious humor, "I'm giving myself an awful good scare, too, ain't I?"

The two glared at each other as Miss Cornelia returned from her survey of the alcove.

"Somebody who had a key could have got in here, Mr. Anderson," she said annoyedly. "That terrace door's been unbolted from the inside."

Lizzie groaned. "I told you so," she wailed. "I knew something was going to happen tonight. I heard rappings all over the house today, and the ouija-board spelled Bat!"

The detective recovered his poise. "I think I see the answer to your puzzle, Miss Van Gorder," he said, with a scornful glance at Lizzie. "A hysterical and not very reliable woman, anxious to go back to the city and terrified over and over by the shutting off of the electric lights."

If looks could slay, his characterization of Lizzie would have laid him dead at her feet at that instant. Miss Van Gorder considered his theory.

"I wonder," she said.

The detective rubbed his hands together more cheerfully.

"A good night's sleep and—" he began, but the irrepressible Lizzie interrupted him.

"My God, we're not going to bed, are we?" she said, with her eyes as big as saucers.

He gave her a kindly pat on the shoulder, which she obviously resented.

"You'll feel better in the morning," he said. "Lock your door and say your prayers, and leave the rest to me."

Lizzie muttered something inaudible and rebellious, but now Miss Cornelia added her protestations to his.

"That's very good advice," she said decisively. "You take her, Dale."

Reluctantly, with a dragging of feet and scared glances cast back over her shoulder, Lizzie allowed herself to be drawn toward the door and the main staircase by Dale. But she did not depart without one Parthian shot.

"I'm not going to bed!" she wailed as Dale's strong young arm helped her out into the hall. "Do you think I want to wake up in the morning with my throat cut?" Then the creaking of the stairs, and Dale's soothing voice reassuring her as she painfully clambered toward the third floor, announced that Lizzie, for some time at least, had been removed as an active factor from the puzzling equation of Cedarcrest.

Anderson confronted Miss Cornelia with certain relief.

"There are certain things I want to discuss with you, Miss Van Gorder," he said. "But they can wait until tomorrow morning."

Miss Cornelia glanced about the room. His manner was reassuring.

"Do you think all this—pure imagination?" she said.

"Don't you?"

She hesitated, "I'm not sure."

He laughed. "I'll tell you what I'll do. You go upstairs and go to bed comfortably. I'll make a careful search of the house before I settle down, and if I find anything at all suspicious, I'll promise to let you know."

She agreed to that, and after sending the Jap out for more coffee prepared to go upstairs.

Never had the thought of her own comfortable bed appealed to her so much. But, in spite of her weariness, she could not quite resign herself to take Lizzie's story as lightly as the detective seemed to.

"If what Lizzie says is true," she said, taking her candle, "the upper floors of the house are even less safe than this one."

"I imagine Lizzie's account just now is about as reliable as her previous one as to her age," Anderson assured her. "I'm certain you need not worry. Just go on up and get your beauty sleep; I'm sure you need it."

On which ambiguous remark Miss Van Gorder took her leave, rather grimly smiling.

It was after she had gone that Anderson's glance fell on Brooks, standing warily in the doorway.

"What are you? The gardener?"

But Brooks was prepared for him.

"Ordinarily I drive a car," he said. "Just now I'm working on the place here."

Anderson was observing him closely, with the eyes of a man ransacking his memory for a name—a picture. "I've seen you somewhere—" he went on slowly. "And I'll place you before long." There was a little threat in his shrewd scrutiny. He took a step toward Brooks.

"Not in the portrait gallery at headquarters, are you?"

"Not yet." Brooks's voice was resentful. Then he remembered his pose and his back grew supple, his whole attitude that of the respectful servant.

"Well, we slip up now and then," said the detective slowly. Then, apparently, he gave up his search for the name—the pictured face. But his manner was still suspicious.

"All right, Brooks," he said tersely. "if you're needed in the night, you'll be *called!*"

Brooks bowed, "Very well, sir." He closed the door softly behind him, glad to have escaped as well as he had.

But that he had not entirely lulled the detective's watchfullness to rest was evident as soon as he had gone. Anderson waited a few seconds, then moved noiselessly over to the hall door—listened— opened it suddenly—closed it again. Then he proceeded to examine the alcove—the stairs, where the gleaming eye had wavered like a corpse-candle before Lizzie's affrighted vision. He tested the terrace door and bolted it. How much truth had there been in her story? He could not decide, but he drew out his revolver nevertheless and gave it a quick inspection to see if it was in working order. A smile crept over his face—the smile of a man who has dangerous work to do and does not shrink from the prospect. He put the revolver back in his pocket and, taking the one lighted candle remaining, went out by the hall door.

For a moment, in the living-room, except for the thunder, all was silence. Then the creak of surreptitious footsteps broke the stillness— light footsteps descending the alcove stairs where the gleaming eye had passed.

It was Dale slipping out of the house to keep her appointment with Richard Fleming. She carried a raincoat over her arm and a pair of rubbers in one hand. Her other hand held a candle. By the terrace door she paused, unbolted it, glanced out into the streaming night with a shiver. Then she came into the living-room and sat down to put on her rubbers.

Hardly had she begun to do so when she started up again. A muffled knocking sounded at the terrace door. It was ominous and determined, and in a panic of terror she rose to her feet. If it was the law, come after Jack, what should she do? Or again, suppose it was the Unknown who had threatened them with death? Not coherent thoughts these, but chaotic, bringing panic with them. Almost unconscious of what she was doing, she reached into the drawer beside her, secured the revolver there and leveled it at the door.

9

A Shot in the Dark

A key clicked in the terrace door—a voice swore muffledly at the rain. Dale lowered her revolver slowly. It was Richard Fleming—come to meet her here, instead of down by the drive.

She had telephoned him on an impulse. But now, as she looked at him in the light of her single candle, she wondered if this rather dissipated, rather foppish young man about town, in his early thirties, could possibly understand and appreciate the motives that had driven her to seek his aid. Still, it was for Jack! She clenched her teeth and resolved to go through with the plan mapped out in her mind. It might be a desperate expedient but she had nowhere else to turn!

Fleming shut the terrace door behind him and moved down from the alcove, trying to shake the rain from his coat.

"Did I frighten you?"

"Oh, Mr. Fleming—yes!" Dale laid her aunt's revolver down on the table. Fleming perceived her nervousness and made a gesture of apology.

"I'm sorry," he said, "I rapped but nobody seemed to hear me, so I used my key."

"You're wet through—I'm sorry," said Dale with mechanical politeness.

He smiled. "Oh, no." He stripped off his cap and raincoat and placed them on a chair, brushing himself off as he did so with finicky little movements of his hands.

"Reggie Beresford brought me over in his car," he said. "He's waiting down the drive."

Dale decided not to waste words in the usual commonplaces of social greeting.

"Mr. Fleming, I'm in dreadful trouble!" she said, facing him squarely, with a courageous appeal in her eyes.

He made a polite movement. "Oh, I say! That's too bad."

She plunged on. "You know the Union Bank closed today."

He laughed lightly.

"Yes, I know it! I didn't have anything in it—or any other bank for that matter," he admitted ruefully, "but I hate to see the old thing go to smash."

Dale wondered which angle was best from which to present her appeal.

"Well, even if you haven't lost anything in this bank failure, a lot of your friends have—surely?" she went on.

"I'll say so!" said Fleming, debonairly. "Beresford is sitting down the road in his Packard now writhing with pain!"

Dale hesitated; Fleming's lightness seemed so incorrigible that, for a moment, she was on the verge of giving her project up entirely. Then, *Waster or not—he's the only man who can help us!* she told herself and continued.

"Lots of awfully poor people are going to suffer, too," she said wistfully.

Fleming chuckled, dismissing the poor with a wave of his hand.

"Oh, well, the poor are always in trouble," he said with airy heartlessness. "They specialize in suffering."

He extracted a monogrammed cigarette from a thin gold case.

"But look here," he went on, moving closer to Dale, "you didn't send for me to discuss this hypothetical poor depositor, did you? Mind if I smoke?"

"No." He lit his cigarette and puffed at it with enjoyment while Dale paused, summoning up her courage. Finally the words came in a rush.

"Mr. Fleming, I'm going to say something rather brutal. Please don't mind. I'm merely—desperate! You see, I happen to be engaged to the cashier, Jack Bailey—"

Fleming whistled. "I *see!* And he's beat it!"

Dale blazed with indignation.

"He has not! I'm going to tell you something. He's here, now, in this house—" she continued fierily, all her defenses thrown aside. "My aunt thinks he's a new gardener. He is here, Mr. Fleming, because he knows he didn't take the money, and the only person who could have done it was—your uncle!"

Dick Fleming dropped his cigarette in a convenient ash tray and crushed it out there, absently, not seeming to notice whether it

scorched his fingers or no. He rose and took a turn about the room.
Then he came back to Dale.

"That's a pretty strong indictment to bring against a dead man," he
said slowly, seriously.

"It's true!" Dale insisted stubbornly, giving him glance for glance.
Fleming nodded. "All right."

He smiled—a smile that Dale didn't like.

"Suppose it's true—where do I come in?" he said. "You don't think
I know where the money is?"

"No," admitted Dale, "but I think you might help to find it."

She went swiftly over to the hall door and listened tensely for an
instant. Then she came back to Fleming.

"If anybody comes in—you've just come to get something of
yours," she said in a low voice. He nodded understandingly. She
dropped her voice still lower.

"Do you know anything about a Hidden Room in this house?" she
asked.

Dick Fleming stared at her for a moment. Then he burst into laughter.

"A Hidden Room—that's rich!" he said, still laughing. "Never
heard of it! Now, let me get this straight. The idea is—a Hidden
Room—and the money is in it—is that it?"

Dale nodded a "Yes."

"The architect who built this house told Jack Bailey that he had
built a Hidden Room in it," she persisted.

For a moment Dick Fleming stared at her as if he could not believe
his ears. Then, slowly, his expression changed. Beneath the well-fed,
debonair mask of the clubman about town, other lines appeared—
lines of avarice and calculation—wolf-marks, betokening the craft
and petty ruthlessness of the small soul within the gentlemanly shell.
His eyes took on a shifty, uncertain stare—they no longer looked at
Dale—their gaze seemed turned inward, beholding a visioned treasure, a glittering pile of gold. And yet, the change in his look was not
so pronounced as to give Dale pause—she felt a vague uneasiness steal
over her, true—but it would have taken a shrewd and long-
experienced woman of the world to read the secret behind Fleming's
eyes at first glance—and Dale, for all her courage and common sense,
was a young and headstrong girl.

She watched him, puzzled, wondering why he made no comment
on her last statement.

"Do you know where there are any blueprints of the house?" she asked at last.

An odd light glittered in Fleming's eyes for a moment. Then it vanished—he held himself in check—the casual idler again.

"Blueprints?" He seemed to think it over. "Why—there may be some. Have you looked in the old secretary in the library? My uncle used to keep all sorts of papers there," he said with apparent helpfulness.

"Why, don't you remember—you locked it when we took the house."

"So I did." Fleming took out his key ring, selected a key. "Suppose you go and look," he said. "Don't you think I better stay here?"

"Oh, yes—" said Dale, blinded to everything else by the rising hope in her heart. "Oh, I can hardly thank you enough!" and before he could even reply, she had taken the key and was hurrying toward the hall door.

He watched her leave the room, a bleak smile on his face. As soon as she had closed the door behind her, his languor dropped from him. He became a hound—a ferret—questing for its prey. He ran lightly over to the bookcase by the hall door—a moment's inspection—he shook his head. Perhaps the other bookcase near the French windows—no—it wasn't there. Ah, the bookcase over the fireplace! He remembered now! He made for it, hastily swept the books from the top shelf, reached groping fingers into the space behind the second row of books. There! A dusty roll of three blueprints! He unrolled them hurriedly and tried to make out the white tracings by the light of the fire—no—better take them over to the candle on the table.

He peered at them hungrily in the little spot of light thrown by the candle. The first one—no—nor the second—but the third—the bottom one—good heavens! He took in the significance of the blurred white lines with greedy eyes, his lips opening in a silent exclamation of triumph. Then he pondered for an instant, the blueprint itself was an awkward size—bulky—good, he had it! He carefully tore a small portion from the third blueprint and was about to stuff it in the inside pocket of his dinner jacket when Dale, returning, caught him before he had time to conceal his find. She took in the situation at once.

"Oh, you found it!" she said in tones of rejoicing, giving him back the key to the secretary. Then, as he still made no move to transfer the scrap of blue paper to her, "Please let me have it, Mr. Fleming. I *know* that's it."

Dick Fleming's lips set in a thin line. "Just a moment," he said, putting the table between them with a swift movement. Once more he stole a glance at the scrap of paper in his hand by the flickering light of the candle. Then he faced Dale boldly.

"Do you suppose, if that money is actually here, that I can simply turn this over to you and let you give it to Bailey?" he said. "Every man has his price. How do I know that Bailey's isn't a million dollars?"

Dale felt as if he had dashed cold water in her face.

"What do you mean to do with it then?" she said.

Fleming turned the blueprint over in his hand.

"I don't know," he said. "What is it you want me to do?"

But by now Dale's vague distrust in him had grown very definite.

"Aren't you going to give it to me?"

He put her off. "I'll have to think about that." He looked at the blueprint again. "So the missing cashier is in this house posing as a gardener?" he said with a sneer in his tones.

Dale's temper was rising.

"If you won't give it to me—there's a detective in this house," she said, with a stamp of her foot. She made a movement as if to call Anderson—then, remembering Jack, turned back to Fleming.

"Give it to the detective and let him search," she pleaded.

"A detective?" said Fleming startled. "What's a detective doing here?"

"People have been trying to break in."

"What people?"

"I don't know."

Fleming stared out beyond Dale, into the night.

"Then it *is* here," he muttered to himself.

Behind his back—was it a gust of air that moved them?—the double doors of the alcove swung open just a crack. Was a listener crouched behind those doors—or was it only a trick of carpentry—a gesture of chance?

The mask of the clubman dropped from Fleming completely. His lips drew back from his teeth in the snarl of a predatory animal that clings to its prey at the cost of life or death.

Before Dale could stop him, he picked up the discarded blueprints and threw them on the fire, retaining only the precious scrap in his hand. The roll blackened and burst into flame. He watched it, smiling.

"I'm not going to give this to any detective," he said quietly, tapping the piece of paper in his hand.

Dale's heart pounded sickeningly but she kept her courage up.

"What do you mean?" she said fiercely. "What are you going to do?"

He faced her across the fireplace, his airy manner coming back to him just enough to add an additional touch of the sinister to the cold self-revelation of his words.

"Let us suppose a few things, Miss Ogden." he said. "Suppose *my* price is a million dollars. Suppose I need money very badly and my uncle has left me a house containing that amount in cash. Suppose I choose to consider that that money is mine—then it wouldn't be hard to suppose, would it, that I'd make a pretty sincere attempt to get away with it?"

Dale summoned all of her fortitude.

"If you go out of this room with that paper I'll scream for help!" she said defiantly.

Fleming made a little mock-bow of courtesy. He smiled.

"To carry on our little game of supposing," he said easily, "suppose there is a detective in this house—and that, if I were concerned, I should tell him where to lay his hands on *Jack Bailey*. Do you suppose you would scream?"

Dale's hands dropped, powerless, at her sides. If only she hadn't told him—too late!—she was helpless. She could not call the detective without ruining Jack—and yet, if Fleming escaped with the money—how could Jack ever prove his innocence?

Fleming watched her for an instant, smiling. Then, seeing she made no move, he darted hastily toward the double doors of the alcove, flung them open, seemed about to dash up the alcove stairs. The sight of him escaping with the only existing clue to the hidden room galvanized Dale into action. She followed him, hurriedly snatching up Miss Cornelia's revolver from the table as she did so, in a last gesture of desperation.

"No! No! Give it to me! Give it to me!" and she sprang after him, clutching the revolver. He waited for her on the bottom step of the stairs, the slight smile on his face.

Panting breaths in the darkness of the alcove—a short, furious scuffle—he had wrested the revolver away from her, but in doing so had unguarded the precious blueprint. She snatched at it desperately, tearing most of it away, leaving only a corner in his hand. He swore— tried to get it back; she jerked away.

Then suddenly a bright shaft of light split the darkness of the alcove stairs like a sword, a spot of brilliance centered on Fleming's face like the glare of a flashlight focused from above by an invisible hand. For an instant it revealed him, his features distorted with fury, about to rush down the stairs again and attack the trembling girl at their foot.

A single shot rang out. For a second, the fury on Fleming's face seemed to change to a strange look of bewilderment and surprise.

Then the shaft of light was extinguished as suddenly as the snuffing of a candle, and he crumpled forward to the foot of the stairs—struck —lay on his face in the darkness, just inside the double doors.

Dale gave a little whimpering cry of horror.

"Oh, no, no, no," she whispered from a dry throat, automatically stuffing her portion of the precious scrap of blueprint into the bosom of her dress. She stood frozen, not daring to move, not daring even to reach down with her hand and touch the body of Fleming to see if he was dead or alive.

A murmur of excited voices sounded from the hall. The door flew open, feet stumbled through the darkness—"The noise came from this room!" that was Anderson's voice—"Holy Virgin!" that must be Lizzie—

Even as Dale turned to face the assembled household, the house lights, extinguished since the storm, came on in full brilliance— revealing her to them, standing beside Fleming's body with Miss Cornelia's revolver between them.

She shuddered, seeing Fleming's arm flung out awkwardly by his side. No living man could lie in such a posture.

"I didn't do it! I didn't do it!" she stammered, after a tense silence that followed the sudden reillumining of the lights. Her eyes wandered from figure to figure idly, noting unimportant details. Billy was still in his white coat and his face, impassive as ever, showed not the slightest surprise. Brooks and Anderson were likewise completely dressed, but Miss Cornelia had evidently begun to retire for the night when she had heard the shot—her transformation was askew and she wore a dressing-gown. As for Lizzie, that worthy shivered in a gaudy wrapper adorned with incredible orange flowers, with her hair done up in curlers. Dale saw it all and was never after to forget one single detail of it.

The detective was beside her now, examining Fleming's body with professional thoroughness. At last he rose.

"He's dead," he said quietly. A shiver ran through the watching group. Dale felt a stifling hand constrict about her heart.

There was a pause. Anderson picked up the revolver beside Fleming's body and examined it swiftly, careful not to confuse his own fingerprints with any that might already be on the polished steel. Then he looked at Dale. "Who is he?" he said bluntly.

Dale fought hysteria for some seconds before she could speak.

"Richard Fleming—somebody shot him!" she managed to whisper at last.

Anderson took a step toward her.

"What do you mean by somebody?" he said.

The world to Dale turned into a crowd of threatening, accusing eyes—a multitude of shadowy voices, shouting, *Guilty! Guilty! Prove that you're innocent—you can't!*

"I don't know," she said wildly. "Somebody on the staircase."

"Did you see anybody?" Anderson's voice was as passionless and cold as a bar of steel.

"No—but there was a light from somewhere—like a pocket-flash—" She could not go on. She saw Fleming's face before her, furious at first, then changing to that strange look of bewildered, surprise. She put her hands over her eyes to shut the vision out.

Lizzie made a welcome interruption.

"I *told* you I saw a man go up that staircase!" she wailed, jabbing her forefinger in the direction of the alcove stairs.

Miss Cornelia, now recovered from the first shock of the discovery, supported her gallantly.

"That's the only explanation, Mr. Anderson," she said decidedly.

The detective looked at the stairs—at the terrace door. His eyes made a circuit of the room and came back to Fleming's body. "I've been all over the house," he said. "There's nobody there."

A pause followed. Dale found herself helplessly looking toward her lover for comfort—comfort he could not give without revealing his own secret.

Eerily, through the tense silence, a sudden tinkling sounded—the sharp, persistent ringing of a telephone bell.

Miss Cornelia rose to answer it automatically. "The house phone!" she said. Then she stopped. "But we're all *here!*"

They looked at each other aghast. It was true. And yet, somehow—somewhere—one of the other phones on the circuit was calling the living-room.

Miss Cornelia summoned every ounce of inherited Van Gorder pride she possessed and went to the phone. She took off the receiver. The ringing stopped.

"Hello—hello—" she said, while the others stood rigid, listening. Then she gasped. An expression of wondering horror came over her face.

10

The Phone Call From Nowhere

"Somebody groaning!" gasped Miss Cornelia. "It's horrible!"

The detective stepped up and took the receiver from her. He listened anxiously for a moment.

"I don't hear anything," he said.

"*I* heard it! I couldn't *imagine* such a dreadful sound! I tell you—somebody in this house is in terrible distress."

"Where does this phone connect?" queried Anderson practically.

Miss Cornelia made a hopeless little gesture. "Practically every room in this house!"

The detective put the receiver to his ear again.

"Just what did you hear?" he said stolidly.

Miss Cornelia's voice shook.

"Dreadful groans—and what seemed to be an inarticulate effort to speak!"

Lizzie drew her gaudy wrapper closer about her shuddering form.

"I'd go somewhere," she wailed in the voice of a lost soul, "if only I had somewhere to go!"

Miss Cornelia quelled her with a glare and turned back to the detective.

"Won't you send these men to investigate—or go yourself?" she said, indicating Brooks and Billy.

The detective thought swiftly.

"My place is here," he said. "You two men," Brooks and Billy moved forward to take his orders, "take another look through the house. Don't leave the building, I'll want you pretty soon."

Brooks—or Jack Bailey, as we may as well call him through the remainder of this narrative—started to obey. Then his eye fell on Miss

Cornelia's revolver which Anderson had taken from beside Fleming's body and still held clasped in his hand.

"If you'll give me that revolver—" he began in an offhand tone, hoping Anderson would not see through his little ruse. Once wiped clean of fingerprints, the revolver would not be such telling evidence against Dale Ogden.

But Anderson was not to be caught napping.

"That revolver will stay where it is," he said with a grim smile.

Jack Bailey knew better than to try and argue the point. He followed Billy reluctantly out of the door, giving Dale a surreptitious glance of encouragement and faith as he did so. The Japanese and he mounted to the second floor as stealthily as possible, prying into dark corners and searching unused rooms for any clue that might betray the source of the startling phone call from nowhere. But Bailey's heart was not in the search. His mind kept going back to the figure of Dale—nervous, shaken, undergoing the terrors of the third degree at Anderson's hands. She *couldn't* have shot Fleming of course, and yet, unless he and Billy found something to substantiate her story of how the killing had happened, it was her own, unsupported word against a damning mass of circumstantial evidence. He plunged with renewed vigor into his quest.

Back in the living-room, as he had feared, Anderson was subjecting Dale to a merciless interrogation.

"Now I want the *real* story!" he began with calculated brutality. "You lied before!"

"That's no tone to use! You'll only terrify her," cried Miss Cornelia indignantly. The detective paid no attention, his face had hardened, he seemed every inch the remorseless sleuthhound of the law. He turned on Miss Cornelia for a moment.

"Where were you when this happened?" he said.

"Upstairs in my room." Miss Cornelia's tones were icy.

"And you?" badgeringly, to Lizzie.

"In *my* room," said the latter pertly, "brushing Miss Cornelia's hair."

Anderson broke open the revolver and gave a swift glance at the bullet chambers.

"One shot has been fired from this revolver!"

Miss Cornelia sprang to her niece's defense.

"I fired it myself this afternoon," she said.

The detective regarded her with grudging admiration.

"You're a quick thinker," he said with obvious unbelief in his voice. He put the revolver down on the table.

Miss Cornelia followed up her advantage.

"I demand that you get the coroner here," she said.

"Doctor Wells is the coroner," offerred Lizzie eagerly. Anderson brushed their suggestions aside.

"I'm going to ask you some questions!" he said menacingly to Dale. But Miss Cornelia stuck to her guns. Dale was not going to be bullied into any sort of confession, true or false, if she could help it—and from the way that the girl's eyes returned with fascinated horror to the ghastly heap on the floor that had been Fleming, she knew that Dale was on the edge of violent hysteria.

"Do you mind covering that body first?" she asked crisply. The detective eyed her for a moment in a rather ugly fashion, then grunted ungraciously and, taking Fleming's raincoat from the chair, threw it over the body. Dale's eyes telegraphed her aunt a silent message of gratitude.

"Now, shall *I* telephone for the coroner?" persisted Miss Cornelia. The detective obviously resented her interference with his methods but he could not well refuse such a customary request.

"I'll do it," he said with a snort, going over to the city telephone. "What's his number?"

"He's not at his office; he's at the Johnsons'," murmured Dale.

Miss Cornelia took the telephone from Anderson's hands.

"I'll get the Johnsons', Mr. Anderson," she said firmly. The detective seemed about to rebuke her. Then his manner recovered some of its former suavity. He relinquished the telephone and turned back toward his prey.

"Now, what was Fleming doing here?" he asked Dale in a gentler voice.

Should she tell him the truth? No—Jack Bailey's safety was too inextricably bound up with the whole sinister business. She must lie, and lie again, while there was any chance of a lie's being believed.

"I don't know," she said weakly, trying to avoid the detective's eyes. Anderson took thought.

"Well, I'll ask that question another way," he said. "How did he get into the house?"

Dale brightened—no need for a lie here.

"He had a key."

"Key to what door?"

"That door over there." Dale indicated the terrace door of the alcove.

The detective was about to ask another question—then he paused. Miss Cornelia was talking on the phone.

"Hello—is that Mr. Johnson's residence? Is Doctor Wells there? No?" Her expression was puzzled. "Oh—all right—thank you—good night—"

Meanwhile Anderson had been listening—but thinking as well. Dale saw his sharp glance travel over to the fireplace—rest for a moment, with an air of discovery, on the fragments of the roll of blueprints that remained unburned among ashes—return. She shut her eyes for a moment, trying tensely to summon every atom of shrewdness she possessed to aid her.

He was hammering her with questions again.

"When did you take the revolver out of the table drawer?"

"When I heard him outside on the terrace," said Dale promptly and truthfully. "I was frightened."

Lizzie tiptoed over to Miss Cornelia.

"You wanted a detective!" she said in an ironic whisper. "I hope you're happy now you've got one!"

Miss Cornelia gave her a look that sent her scuttling back to her former post by the door. But nevertheless, internally, she felt thoroughly in accord with Lizzie.

Again Anderson's questions pounded at the rigid Dale, striving to pierce her armor of mingled truth and falsehood.

"When Fleming came in, what did he say to you?"

"Just—something about the weather," said Dale weakly. The whole scene was still too horribly vivid before her eyes for her to furnish a more convincing alibi.

"You didn't have any quarrel with him?"

Dale hesitated.

"No."

"He just came in that door, said something about the weather, and was shot from that staircase. Is that it?" said the detective in tones of utter incredulity.

Dale hesitated again. Thus baldly put, her story seemed too flimsy for words; she could not even blame Anderson for disbelieving it. And yet—what other story could she tell that would not bring ruin on Jack?

Her face whitened. She put her hand on the back of a chair for support.

"Yes—that's it," she said at last, and swayed where she stood.

Again Miss Cornelia tried to come to the rescue.

"Are all these questions necessary?" she queried sharply. "You can't for a moment believe that Miss Ogden shot that man!'' But by now, though she did not show it, she too began to realize the strength of the appalling net of circumstances that drew with each minute tighter around the unhappy girl. Dale gratefully seized the momentary respite and sank into a chair. The detective looked at her.

"I think she knows more than she's telling. She's concealing something!'' he said with deadly intentness. ''The nephew of the president of the Union Bank—shot in his own house the day the bank has failed—that's queer enough—'' Now he turned back to Miss Cornelia. ''But when the only person present at his murder is the girl who's engaged to the guilty cashier,'' he continued, watching Miss Cornelia's face as the full force of his words sank into her mind, ''I want to know more about it!''

He stopped. His right hand moved idly over the edge of the table, halted beside an ash tray, closed upon something.

Miss Cornelia rose.

"Is that true, Dale?'' she said sorrowfully.

Dale nodded. ''Yes.'' She could not trust herself to explain at greater length.

Then Miss Cornelia made one of the most magnificent gestures of her life.

"Well, even if it is—what has *that* got to do with it?'' she said, turning upon Anderson fiercely, all her protective instinct for those whom she loved aroused.

Anderson seemed somewhat impressed by the fierceness of her query. When he went on it was with less harshness in his manner.

"I'm not accusing this girl,'' he said more gently. ''But behind every crime there is a motive. When we've found the motive for *this* crime, we'll have found the criminal.''

Unobserved, Dale's hand instinctively went to her bosom. There it lay—the motive—the precious fragment of blueprint which she had torn from Fleming's grasp but an instant before he was shot down. Once Anderson found it in her possession the case was closed, the evidence against her overwhelming. She could not destroy it—it was the only clue to the Hidden Room and the truth that might clear Jack Bailey. But, somehow, she must hide it—get it out of her hands—before Anderson's third-degree methods broke her down or he insisted on a search of her person. Her eyes roved wildly about the room, looking for a hiding place.

The rain of Anderson's questions began anew.

"What papers did Fleming burn in that grate?" he asked abruptly, turning back to Dale.

"Papers!" she faltered.

"Papers! The ashes are still there."

Miss Cornelia made an unavailing interruption.

"Miss Ogden has said he didn't come into this room."

The detective smiled.

"I hold in my hand proof that he was in this room for some time," he said coldly, displaying the half-burned cigarette he had taken from the ash tray a moment before.

"His cigarette—with his monogram on it." He put the fragment of tobacco and paper carefully away in an envelope and marched over to the fireplace. There he rummaged among the ashes for a moment, like a dog uncovering a bone. He returned to the center of the room with a fragment of blackened blue paper fluttering between his fingers.

"A fragment of what is technically known as a blueprint," he announced. "What were you and Richard Fleming doing with a blueprint?" His eyes bored into Dale's.

Dale hesitated—shut her lips.

"Now think it over!" he warned. "The truth will come out, sooner or later! Better to be frank *now!*

If he only knew how I wanted to be, he wouldn't be so cruel, thought Dale wearily. *But I can't—I can't!* Then her heart gave a throb of relief. Jack had come back into the room—Jack and Billy—Jack would protect her! But even as she thought of this her heart sank again. Protect her, indeed! Poor Jack! He would find it hard enough to protect himself if once this terrible man with the cold smile and steely eyes started questioning him. She looked up anxiously.

Bailey made his report breathlessly.

"Nothing in the house, sir."

Billy's impassive lips confirmed him.

"We go all over house—nobody!"

Nobody—nobody in the house! And yet—the mysterious ringing of the phone—the groans Miss Cornelia had heard! Were old wives' tales and witches' fables true after all? Did a power—merciless—evil—exist, outside the barriers of the flesh—blasting that trembling flesh with a cold breath from beyond the portals of the grave? There seemed to be no other explanation.

"You men stay here!" said the detective. "I want to ask you some questions." He doggedly returned to his third-degreeing of Dale.

"Now what about this blueprint?" he queried sharply.

Dale stiffened in her chair. Her lies had failed. Now she would tell a portion of the truth, as much of it as she could without menacing Jack.

"I'll tell you just what happened," she began. "I sent for Richard Fleming—and when he came, I asked him if he knew where there were any blueprints of the house."

The detective pounced eagerly upon her admission.

"*Why* did you want blueprints?" he thundered.

"Because," Dale took a long breath, "I believe old Mr. Fleming took the money himself from the Union Bank and hid it here."

"Where did you get that idea?"

Dale's jaw set. "I won't tell you."

"What had the blueprints to do with it?"

She could think of no plausible explanation but the true one.

"Because I'd heard there was a Hidden Room in this house."

The detective leaned forward intently.

"Did you locate that room?"

Dale hesitated. "No."

"Then why did you burn the blueprints?"

Dale's nerve was crumbling—breaking—under the repeated, monotonous impact of his questions.

"*He* burned them!" she cried wildly. "I don't *know* why!"

The detective paused an instant, then returned to a previous query.

"Then you *didn't* locate this Hidden Room?"

Dale's lips formed a pale "No."

"Did he?" went on Anderson inexorably.

Dale stared at him, dully—the breaking point had come. Another question—another—and she would no longer be able to control herself. She would sob out the truth hysterically—that Brooks, the gardener, was Jack Bailey, the missing cashier—that the scrap of blueprint hidden in the bosom of her dress might unravel the secret of the Hidden Room—that—

But just as she felt herself, sucked of strength, beginning to slide toward a black, tingling pit of merciful oblivion, Miss Cornelia provided a diversion.

"What's that?" she said in a startled voice.

The detective turned away from his quarry for an instant.

"What's what?"

"I heard something," averred Miss Cornelia, staring toward the French windows.

All eyes followed the direction of her stare. There was an instant of silence.

Then, suddenly, traveling swiftly from right to left across the shades of the French windows, there appeared a glowing circle of brilliant white light. Inside the circle was a black, distorted shadow—a shadow like the shadow of a gigantic black Bat! It was there—then a second later, it was gone!

"Oh, my God!" wailed Lizzie from her corner. "It's the Bat—that's his sign!"

Jack Bailey made a dash for the terrace door. But Miss Cornelia halted him peremptorily.

"Wait, Brooks!" She turned to the detective. "Mr. Anderson, you are familiar with the sign of the Bat. Did that look like it?"

The detective seemed both puzzled and disturbed.

"Well, it looked like the shadow of a bat. I'll say that for it," he said finally.

On the heels of his words the front door bell began to ring. All turned in the direction of the hall.

"I'll answer that!" said Jack Bailey eagerly.

Miss Cornelia gave him the key to the front door.

"Don't admit anyone till you know who it is," she said. Bailey nodded and disappeared into the hall. The others waited tensely. Miss Cornelia's hand crept toward the revolver lying on the table where Anderson had put it down.

There was the click of an opening door, the noise of a little scuffle, then men's voices raised in an angry dispute. "What do I know about a flashlight?" cried an irritated voice. "I haven't got a pocket-flash. Take your hands off me!" Bailey's voice answered the other voice, grim, threatening. The scuffle resumed.

Then Doctor Wells burst suddenly into the room, closely followed by Bailey. The doctor's tie was askew, he looked ruffled and enraged. Bailey followed him vigilantly, seeming not quite sure whether to allow him to enter or not.

"My dear Miss Van Gorder," began the doctor in tones of high dudgeon, "won't you instruct your servants that even if I do make a late call, I am not to be received with violence?"

"I asked you if you had a pocket-flash about you!" answered Bailey indignantly. "If you call a question like that violence—" He seemed about to restrain the doctor by physical force.

Miss Cornelia quelled the teapot-tempest.

"It's all right, Brooks," she said, taking the front door key from his hand and putting it back on the table. She turned to Doctor Wells.

"You see, Doctor Wells," she explained, "just a moment before you rang the doorbell a circle of white light was thrown on those window shades."

The doctor laughed with a certain relief.

"Why, that was probably the searchlight from my car!" he said. "I noticed as I drove up that it fell directly on that window."

His explanation seemed to satisfy all present but Lizzie. She regarded him with a deep suspicion. *He may be a lawyer, a merchant, a* DOCTOR, she chanted ominously to herself.

Miss Cornelia, too, was not entirely at ease.

"In the center of this ring of light," she proceeded, her eyes on the doctor's calm countenance, "was an almost perfect silhouette of a bat."

"A bat!" The doctor seemed at sea. "Ah, I see—the symbol of the criminal of that name." He laughed again.

"I think I can explain what you saw. Quite often my headlights collect insects at night and a large moth, spread on the glass, would give precisely the effect you speak of. Just to satisfy you, I'll go out and take a look."

He turned to do so. Then he caught sight of the raincoat-covered huddle on the floor.

"Why—" he said in a voice that mingled astonishment with horror. He paused. His glance slowly traversed the circle of silent faces.

11

Billy Practices Jiu-Jitsu

"We have had a very sad occurrence here, Doctor," said Miss Cornelia gently.

The doctor braced himself.

"Who?"

"Richard Fleming."

"Richard Fleming?" gasped the doctor in tones of incredulous horror.

"Shot and killed from that staircase," said Miss Cornelia tonelessly.

The detective demurred.

"Shot and killed, anyhow," he said in accents of significant omission.

The doctor knelt beside the huddle on the floor. He removed the fold of the raincoat that covered the face of the corpse and stared at the dead, blank mask. Till a moment ago, even at the height of his irritation with Bailey, he had been blithe and offhand—a man who seemed comparatively young for his years. Now Age seemed to fall upon him, suddenly, like a gray, clinging dust—he looked stricken and feeble under the impact of this unexpected shock.

"Shot and killed from that stairway," he repeated dully. He rose from his knees and glanced at the fatal stairs.

"What was Richard Fleming doing in this house at this hour?" he said.

He spoke to Miss Cornelia but Anderson answered the question.

"That's what *I'm* trying to find out," he said with a saturnine smile.

The doctor gave him a look of astonished inquiry. Miss Cornelia remembered her manners.

"Doctor, this is Mr. Anderson."

"Headquarters," said Anderson tersely, shaking hands.

It was Lizzie's turn to play her part in the tangled game of mutual suspicion that by now made each member of the party at Cedarcrest watch every other member with nervous distrust. She crossed to her mistress on tiptoe.

"Don't you let him fool you with any of that moth business!" she said in a thrilling whisper, jerking her thumb in the direction of the doctor. "He's the Bat."

Ordinarily Miss Cornelia would have dismissed her words with a smile. But by now her brain felt as if it had begun to revolve like a pinwheel in her efforts to fathom the uncanny mystery of the various events of the night.

She addressed Doctor Wells.

"I didn't tell you, Doctor. I sent for a detective this afternoon." Then, with mounting suspicion, "You happened in very opportunely!"

"After I left the Johnsons' I felt very uneasy," he explained. "I determined to make one more effort to get you away from this house. As this shows, my fears were justified!"

He shook his head sadly. Miss Cornelia sat down. His last words had given her food for thought. She wanted to mull them over for a moment.

The doctor removed muffler and topcoat, stuffed the former in his topcoat pocket and threw the latter on the settee. He took out his handkerchief and began to mop his face, as if to wipe away some strain of mental excitement under which he was laboring. His breath came quickly, the muscles of his jaw stood out.

"Died instantly, I suppose?" he said, looking over at the body. "Didn't have time to say anything?"

"Ask the young lady," said Anderson, with a jerk of his head. "She was here when it happened."

The doctor gave Dale a feverish glance of inquiry.

"He just fell over," said the latter pitifully. Her answer seemed to relieve the doctor of some unseen weight on his mind. He drew a long breath and turned back toward Fleming's body with comparative calm.

"Poor Dick has proved my case for me better than I expected," he said, regarding the still, unbreathing heap beneath the raincoat. He swerved toward the detective.

"Mr. Anderson," he said with dignified pleading, "I ask you to use your influence to see that these two ladies find some safer spot than this for the night."

Lizzie bounced up from her chair, instanter.

"Two?" she wailed. "If you know any safe spot, lead me to it!"

The doctor overlooked her sudden eruption into the scene. He wandered back again toward the huddle under the raincoat, as if still unable to believe that it was—or rather had been—Richard Fleming.

Miss Cornelia spoke suddenly in a low voice, without moving a muscle of her body.

"I have a strange feeling that I'm being watched by unfriendly eyes," she said.

Lizzie clutched at her across the table.

"I wish the light would go out again!" she pattered. "No, I don't neither!" as Miss Cornelia gave the clutching hand a nervous little slap.

During the little interlude of comedy, Billy, the Japanese, unwatched by the others, had stolen into the French windows, pulled aside a blind, looked out. When he turned back to the room his face had lost a portion of its Oriental calm—there was suspicion in his eyes. Softly, under cover of pretending to arrange the tray of food that lay untouched on the table, he possessed himself of the key to the front door, unperceived by the rest, and slipped out of the room like a ghost.

Meanwhile the detective confronted Doctor Wells.

"You say, Doctor, that you came back to take these women away from the house. Why?"

The doctor gave him a dignified stare.

"Miss Van Gorder has already explained."

Miss Cornelia elucidated. "Mr. Anderson has already formed a theory of the crime," she said with a trace of sarcasm in her tones.

The detective turned on her quickly. "I haven't said that." He started.

It had come again—tinkling—persistent—the phone call from nowhere—the ringing of the bell of the house telephone!

"The house telephone—again!" breathed Dale. Miss Cornelia made a movement to answer the tinkling, inexplicable bell. But Anderson was before her.

"I'll answer that!" he barked. He sprang to the phone.

"Hello—hello—"

All eyes were bent on him nervously—the doctor's face, in particular, seemed a very study in fear and amazement. He clutched the back of a chair to support himself, his hand was the trembling hand of a sick, old man.

"Hello—hello—" Anderson swore impatiently. He hung up the phone.

"There's nobody there!"

Again a chill breath from another world than ours seemed to brush across the faces of the little group in the living-room. Dale, sensitive, impressionable, felt a cold, uncanny prickling at the roots of her hair.

A light came into Anderson's eyes. "Where's that Jap?" he almost shouted.

"He just went out," said Miss Cornelia. The cold fear, the fear of the unearthly, subsided from around Dale's heart, leaving her shaken but more at peace.

The detective turned swiftly to the doctor, as if to put his case before the eyes of an unprejudiced witness.

"That Jap rang the phone," he said decisively. "Miss Van Gorder believes that this murder is the culmination of the series of mysterious happenings that caused her to send for me. I do not."

"Then what is the significance of the anonymous letters?" broke in Miss Cornelia heatedly. "Of the man Lizzie saw going up the stairs, of the attempt to break into this house—of the ringing of that telephone bell?"

Anderson replied with one deliberate word.

"Terrorization," he said.

The doctor moistened his dry lips in an effort to speak.

"By whom?" he asked.

Anderson's voice was an icicle.

"I imagine by Miss Van Gorder's servants. By that woman there—" he pointed at Lizzie, who rose indignantly to deny the charge. But he gave her no time for denial. He rushed on, "—who probably writes the letters," he continued. "By the gardener—" his pointing finger found Bailey "—who may have been the man Lizzie saw slipping up the stairs. By the Jap, who goes out and rings the telephone," he concluded triumphantly.

Miss Cornelia seemed unimpressed by his fervor.

"With what object?" she queried smoothly.

"That's what I'm going to find out!" There was determination in Anderson's reply.

Miss Cornelia sniffed. "Absurd! The butler was in this room when the telephone rang for the first time."

The thrust pierced Anderson's armor. For once he seemed at a loss. Here was something he had omitted from his calculations. But he did not give up. He was about to retort when—crash! thud!—the noise of a violent struggle in the hall outside drew all eyes to the hall door.

An instant later the door slammed open and a disheveled young man in evening clothes was catapulted into the living-room as if slung there by a giant's arm. He tripped and fell to the floor in the center of the room. Billy stood in the doorway behind him, inscrutable, arms folded, on his face an expression of mild satisfaction as if he were demurely pleased with a neat piece of housework, neatly carried out.

The young man picked himself up, brushed off his clothes, sought for his hat, which had rolled under the table. Then he turned on Billy furiously.

"Damn you—what do you mean by this?"

"Jiu-jitsu," said Billy, his yellow face quite untroubled. "Pretty good stuff. Found on terrace with searchlight," he added.

"With searchlight?" barked Anderson.

The young man turned to face this new enemy.

"Well, why shouldn't I be on the terrace with a searchlight?" he demanded.

The detective moved toward him menacingly.

"Who *are* you?"

"Who are you?" said the young man with cool impertinence, giving him stare for stare.

Anderson did not deign to reply, in so many words. Instead he displayed the police badge which glittered on the inside of the right lapel of his coat.

The young man examined it coolly.

"H'm," he said. "Very pretty—nice neat design—very chaste!" He took out a cigarette case and opened it, seemingly entirely unimpressed by both the badge and Anderson. The detective chafed.

"If you've finished admiring my badge," he said with heavy sarcasm, "I'd like to know what you were doing on the terrace."

The young man hesitated—shot an odd, swift glance at Dale who, ever since his abrupt entrance into the room, had been sitting rigid in her chair with her hands clenched tightly together.

"I've had some trouble with my car down the road," he said finally. He glanced at Dale again. "I came to ask if I might telephone."

"Did it require a flashlight to find the house?" Miss Cornelia asked suspiciously.

"Look here," the young man blustered, "why are you asking me all these questions?" He tapped his cigarette case with an irritated air.

Miss Cornelia stepped closer to him.

"Do you mind letting me see that flashlight?" she said.

The young man gave it to her with a little, mocking bow. She turned it over, examined it, passed it to Anderson, who examined it also, seeming to devote particular attention to the lens. The young man stood puffing his cigarette a little nervously while the examination was in progress. He did not look at Dale again.

Anderson handed back the flashlight to its owner.

"Now—what's your name?" he said sternly.

"Beresford—Reginald Beresford," said the young man sulkily. "If you doubt it I've probably got a card somewhere—" He began to search through his pockets.

"What's your business?" went on the detective.

"What's my business here?" queried the young man, obviously fending with his interrogator.

"No, how do you earn your living?" said Anderson sharply.

"I don't," said the young man flippantly. "I may have to begin now, if that is any interest to you. As a matter of fact, I've studied law but—"

The one word was enough to start Lizzie off on another trail of distrust. *He may be a* LAWYER—she quoted to herself sepulchrally from the evening newspaper article that had dealt with the mysterious identity of the Bat.

"And you came here to telephone about your car?" persisted the detective.

Dale rose from her chair with a hopeless little sigh.

"Oh, don't you see—he's trying to protect me," she said wearily. She turned to the young man. "It's no use, Mr. Beresford."

Beresford's air of flippancy vanished.

"I see," he said. He turned to the other, frankly. "Well, the plain truth is—I didn't know the situation and I thought I'd play safe for Miss Ogden's sake."

Miss Cornelia moved over to her niece protectingly. She put a hand on Dale's shoulder to reassure her. But Dale was quite composed now. She had gone through so many shocks already that one more or less seemed to make very little difference to her overwearied nerves. She turned to Anderson calmly.

"He doesn't know anything about—this," she said, indicating Beresford. "He brought Mr. Fleming here in his car—that's all."

Anderson looked to Beresford for confirmation.

"Is that true?"

"Yes," said Beresford. He started to explain. "I got tired of waiting and so I—"

The detective broke in curtly.

"All right."

He took a step toward the alcove.

"Now, Doctor." He nodded at the huddle beneath the raincoat. Beresford followed his glance—and saw the ominous heap for the first time.

"What's that?" he said tensely. No one answered him. The doctor was already on his knees beside the body, drawing the raincoat gently aside. Beresford stared at the shape thus revealed with frightened eyes. The color left his face.

"That's not—Dick Fleming—is it?" he said thickly. Anderson slowly nodded his head. Beresford seemed unable to believe his eyes.

"If you've looked over the ground," said the doctor in a low voice to Anderson, "I'll move the body where we can have a better light." His right hand fluttered swiftly over Fleming's still, clenched fist—extracted from it a torn corner of paper.

Still Beresford did not seem to be able to take in what had happened. He took another step toward the body.

"Do you mean to say that Dick Fleming—" he began. Anderson silenced him with an uplifted hand.

"What have you got there, Doctor?" he said in a still voice.

The doctor, still on his knees beside the corpse, lifted his head.

"What do you mean?"

"You took something, just then, out of Fleming's hand," said the detective.

"I took nothing out of his hand," said the doctor firmly.

Anderson's manner grew peremptory.

"I warn you not to obstruct the course of justice!" he said forcibly. "Give it here!"

The doctor rose slowly, dusting off his knees. His eyes tried to meet Anderson's and failed. He produced a torn corner of blueprint.

"Why, it's only a scrap of paper, nothing at all," he said evasively.

Anderson looked at him meaningly.

"Scraps of paper are sometimes very important," he said with a side glance at Dale.

Beresford approached the two angrily.

"Look here!" he burst out, "I've got a right to know about this thing. I brought Fleming over here and I want to know what happened to him!"

"You don't have to be a mind reader to know that!" moaned Lizzie, overcome.

As usual, her comment went unanswered. Beresford persisted in his questions.

"Who killed him? That's what *I* want to know!" he continued, nervously puffing his cigarette.

"Well, you're not alone in that," said Anderson in his grimly humorous vein.

The doctor motioned nervously to them both.

"As the coroner, if Mr. Anderson is satisfied, I suggest that the body be taken where I can make a thorough examination," he said haltingly.

Once more Anderson bent over the shell that had been Richard Fleming. He turned the body halfover—let it sink back on its face. For a moment he glanced at the corner of the blueprint in his hand, then at the doctor. Then he stood aside.

"All right," he said laconically.

So Richard Fleming left the room where he had been struck down so suddenly and strangely—borne out by Beresford, the doctor, and Jack Bailey. The little procession moved as swiftly and softly as circumstances would permit; Anderson followed its passage with watchful eyes. Billy went mechanically to pick up the stained rug which the detective had kicked aside and carried it off after the body. When the burden and its bearers, with Anderson in the rear, reached the doorway into the hall, Lizzie shrank before the sight, affrighted, and turned toward the alcove while Miss Cornelia stared unseeingly out toward the front windows. So, for perhaps a dozen ticks of time Dale was left unwatched; she made the most of her opportunity.

Her fingers fumbled at the bosom of her dress—she took out the precious, dangerous fragment of blueprint that Anderson must not find in her possession—but where to hide it, before her chance had passed? Her eyes fell on the bread roll that had fallen from the detective's supper tray to the floor when Lizzie had seen the gleaming eye on the stairs and had lain there unnoticed ever since. She bent over swiftly and secreted the tantalizing scrap of blue paper in the body of the roll, smoothing the crust back above it with trembling fingers. Then she replaced the roll where it had fallen originally and straightened up just as Billy and the detective returned.

Billy went immediately to the tray, picked it up, and started to go out again. Then he noticed the roll on the floor, stooped for it, and replaced it upon the tray. He looked at Miss Cornelia for instructions.

"Take that tray out to the dining-room," she said mechanically. But Anderson's attention had already been drawn to the tiny incident.

"Wait, I'll look at that tray," he said briskly. Dale, her heart in her mouth, watched him examine the knives, the plates, even shake out the napkin to see that nothing was hidden in its folds. At last he seemed satisfied.

"All right, take it away," he commanded. Billy nodded and vanished toward the dining-room with tray and roll. Dale breathed again.

The sight of the tray had made Miss Cornelia's thoughts return to practical affairs.

"Lizzie," she commanded now, "go out in the kitchen and make some coffee. I'm sure we all need it," she sighed.

Lizzie bristled at once.

"Go out in that kitchen alone?"

"Billy's there," said Miss Cornelia wearily.

The thought of Billy seemed to bring little solace to Lizzie's heart.

"That Jap and his jooy-jitsu," she muttered viciously. "One twist and I'd be folded up like a pretzel."

But Miss Cornelia's manner was imperative, and Lizzie slowly dragged herself kitchenward, yawning and promising the saints repentance of every sin she had or had not committed if she were allowed to get there without something grabbing at her ankles in the dark corner of the hall.

When the door had shut behind her, Anderson turned to Dale, the corner of blueprint which he had taken from the doctor in his hand.

"Now, Miss Ogden," he said tensely, "I have here a scrap of blueprint which was in Dick Fleming's hand when he was killed. I'll trouble you for the rest of it, if you please!"

12

"I Didn't Kill Him."

"The rest of it?" queried Dale with a show of bewilderment, silently thanking her stars that, for the moment at least, the incriminating fragment had passed out of her possession.

Her reply seemed only to infuriate the detective.

"Don't tell me Fleming started to go out of this house with a blank scrap of paper in his hand," he threatened. "He didn't start to go out at all!"

Dale rose. Was Anderson trying a chance shot in the dark—or had he stumbled upon some fresh evidence against her? She could not tell from his manner.

"Why do you say that?" she feinted.

"His cap's there on the table," said the detective with crushing terseness. Dale started. She had not remembered the cap—why hadn't she burned it, concealed it—as she had concealed the blueprint? She passed a hand over her forehead wearily.

Miss Cornelia watched her niece.

"If you're keeping anything back, Dale—tell him," she said.

"She's keeping something back all right," he said. "She's told part of the truth, but not all." He hammered at Dale again. "You and Fleming located that room by means of a blueprint of the house. He started—*not* to go out—but, probably, to go up that staircase. And he had in his hand the rest of this!" Again he displayed the blank corner of blue paper.

Dale knew herself cornered at last. The detective's deductions were too shrewd; do what she would, she could keep him away from the truth no longer.

"He was going to take the money and go away with it!" she said rather pitifully, feeling a certain relief of despair steal over her, now that she no longer needed to go on lying—lying—involving herself in an inextricable web of falsehood.

"Dale!" gasped Miss Cornelia, alarmed. But Dale went on, reckless of consequences to herself, though still warily shielding Jack.

"He changed the minute he heard about it. He was all kindness before that—but afterward—" She shuddered, closing her eyes. Fleming's face rose before her again, furious, distorted with passion and greed—then, suddenly, quenched of life.

Anderson turned to Miss Cornelia triumphantly.

"She started to find the money—and save Bailey," he explained, building up his theory of the crime. "But to do it she had to take Fleming into her confidence—and he turned yellow. Rather than let him get away with it, she—" He made an expressive gesture toward his hip pocket.

Dale trembled, feeling herself already in the toils. She had not quite realized, until now, how damningly plausible such an explanation of Fleming's death could sound. It fitted the evidence perfectly, it took account of every factor but one—the factor left unaccounted for was one which even she herself could not explain.

"Isn't that true?" demanded Anderson. Dale already felt the cold clasp of handcuffs on her slim wrists. What use of denial when every tiny circumstance was so leagued against her? And yet she must deny.

"I didn't kill him," she repeated perplexedly, weakly.

"Why didn't you call for help? You—you knew I was here."

Dale hesitated. "I—I couldn't." The moment the words were out of her mouth she knew from his expression that they had only cemented his growing certainty of her guilt.

"Dale! Be careful what you say!" warned Miss Cornelia agitatedly. Dale looked dumbly at her aunt. Her answers must seem the height of reckless folly to Miss Cornelia—oh, if there were only someone who understood!

Anderson resumed his grilling.

"Now I mean to find out two things," he said, advancing upon Dale. *"Why* you did not call for help—and *what* you have done with that blueprint."

"Suppose I could find that piece of blueprint for you?" said Dale desperately. "Would that establish Jack Bailey's innocence?"

The detective stared at her keenly for a moment.

"If the money's there—yes."

Dale opened her lips to reveal the secret, reckless of what might follow. As long as Jack was cleared—what matter what happened to herself? But Miss Cornelia nipped the heroic attempt at self-sacrifice in the bud.

She put herself between her niece and the detective, shielding Dale from his eager gaze.

"But her own guilt!" she said in tones of great dignity. "No, Mr. Anderson, granting that she knows where that paper is—and she has not said that she does, I shall want more time and much legal advice before I allow her to turn it over to you."

All the unconscious note of command that long-inherited wealth and the pride of a great name can give was in her voice, and the detective, for the moment, bowed before it, defeated. Perhaps he thought of men who had been broken from the Force for injudicious arrests, perhaps he merely bided his time. At any rate, he gave up his grilling of Dale for the present and turned to question the doctor and Beresford who had just returned, with Jack Bailey, from their grim task of placing Fleming's body in a temporary resting place in the library.

"Well, Doctor?" he grunted.

The doctor shook his head.

"Poor fellow—straight through the heart."

"Were there any powder marks?" queried Miss Cornelia.

"No—and the clothing was not burned. He was apparently shot from some little distance—and I should say from above."

The detective received this information without the change of a muscle in his face. He turned to Beresford—resuming his attack on Dale from another angle.

"Beresford, did Fleming tell you why he came here tonight?"

Beresford considered the question.

"No. He seemed in a great hurry, said Miss Ogden had telephoned him, and asked me to drive him over."

"Why did you come up to the house?"

"We-el," said Beresford with seeming candor, "I thought it was putting rather a premium on friendship to keep me sitting out in the rain all night, so I came up the drive—and, by the way!" He snapped his fingers irritatedly, as if recalling some significant incident that had slipped his memory, and drew a battered object from his pocket. "I picked this up, about a hundred feet from the house," he explained. "A man's watch. It was partly crushed into the ground, and, as you see, it's stopped running."

The detective took the object and examined it carefully. A man's open-faced gold watch, crushed and battered in as if it had been trampled upon by a heavy heel.

"Yes," he said thoughtfully. "Stopped running at ten-thirty."
Beresford went on, with mounting excitement.

"I was using my pocket-flash to find my way and what first attracted
my attention was the ground—torn up, you know, all around it. Then
I saw the watch itself. Anybody here recognize it?"

The detective silently held up the watch so that all present could
examine it. He waited. But if anyone in the party recognized the
watch—no one moved forward to claim it.

"You didn't hear any evidence of a struggle, did you?" went on
Beresford. "The ground looked as if a fight had taken place. Of
course it might have been a dozen other things."

Miss Cornelia started.

"Just about ten-thirty Lizzie heard somebody cry out, in the
grounds," she said.

The detective looked Beresford over till the latter grew a little uncomfortable.

"I don't suppose it has any bearing on the case," admitted the latter
uneasily. "But it's interesting."

The detective seemed to agree. At least he slipped the watch in his
pocket.

"Do you always carry a flashlight, Mr. Beresford?" asked Miss Cornelia a trifle suspiciously.

"Always at night, in the car." His reply was prompt and certain.

"This is all you found?" queried the detective, a curious note in his
voice.

"Yes." Beresford sat down, relieved. Miss Cornelia followed his ex-
ample. Another clue had led into a blind alley, leaving the mystery of
the night's affairs as impenetrable as ever.

"Some day I hope to meet the real estate agent who promised me
that I would sleep here as I never slept before!" she murmured
acridly. "He's right! I've slept with my clothes on every night since I
came!"

As she ended, Billy darted in from the hall, his beady little black
eyes gleaming with excitement, a long, wicked-looking butcher knife
in his hand.

"Key, kitchen door, please!" he said, addressing his mistress.

"Key?" said Miss Cornelia, startled. "What for?"

For once Billy's polite little grin was absent from his countenance.

"Somebody outside trying to get in," he chattered. "I see knob
turn, so," he illustrated with the butcher knife, "and so—three
times."

The detective's hand went at once to his revolver.

"You're sure of that, are you?" he said roughly to Billy.

"Sure, I sure!"

"Where's that hysterical woman Lizzie?" queried Anderson. "She may get a bullet in her if she's not careful."

"She see too. She shut in closet—say prayers, maybe," said Billy, without a smile.

The picture was a ludicrous one but not one of the little group laughed.

"Doctor, have you a revolver?" Anderson seemed to be going over the possible means of defense against this new peril.

"No."

"How about you, Beresford?"

Beresford hesitated.

"Yes," he admitted finally. "Always carry one at night in the country." The statement seemed reasonable enough but Miss Cornelia gave him a sharp glance of mistrust, nevertheless.

The detective seemed to have more confidence in the young idler.

"Beresford, will you go with this Jap to the kitchen?" as Billy, grimly clutching his butcher knife, retraced his steps toward the hall. "If anyone's working at the knob—shoot through the door. I'm going round to take a look outside."

Beresford started to obey. Then he paused.

"I advise you not to turn the doorknob yourself, then," he said flippantly.

The detective nodded. "Much obliged," he said, with a grin. He ran lightly into the alcove and tiptoed out of the terrace door, closing the door behind him. Beresford and Billy departed to take up their posts in the kitchen. "I'll go with you, if you don't mind—" and Jack Bailey had followed them, leaving Miss Cornelia and Dale alone with the doctor. Miss Cornelia, glad of the opportunity to get the doctor's theories on the mystery without Anderson's interference, started to question him at once.

"Doctor."

"Yes." The doctor turned, politely.

"Have *you* any theory about this occurrence tonight?" She watched him eagerly as she asked the question.

He made a gesture of bafflement.

"None whatever, it's beyond me," he confessed.

"And yet you warned me to leave this house," said Miss Cornelia cannily. "You didn't have any reason to believe that the situation was even as serious as it has proved to be?"

"I did the perfectly obvious thing when I warned you," said the doctor easily. "Those letters made a distinct threat."

Miss Cornelia could not deny the truth in his words. And yet she felt decidedly unsatisfied with the way things were progressing.

"You said Fleming had probably been shot from above?" she queried, thinking hard.

The doctor nodded. "Yes."

"Have you a pocket-flash, Doctor?" she asked him suddenly.

"Why—yes—" The doctor did not seem to perceive the significance of the query. "A flashlight is more important to a country doctor than—castor oil," he added, with a little smile.

Miss Cornelia decided upon an experiment. She turned to Dale.

"Dale, you said you saw a white light shining down from above?"

"Yes," said Dale in a minor voice.

Miss Cornelia rose.

"May I borrow your flashlight, Doctor? Now that fool detective is out of the way," she continued somewhat acidly, "I want to do something."

The doctor gave her his flashlight with a stare of bewilderment. She took it and moved into the alcove.

"Doctor, I shall ask you to stand at the foot of the small staircase, facing up."

"Now?" queried the doctor with some reluctance.

"Now, please."

The doctor slowly followed her into the alcove and took up the position she assigned him at the foot of the stairs.

"Now, Dale," said Miss Cornelia briskly, "when I give the word, you put out the lights here—and then tell me when I have reached the point on the staircase from which the flashlight seemed to come. All ready?"

Two silent nods gave assent. Miss Cornelia left the room to seek the second floor by the main staircase and then slowly return by the alcove stairs, her flashlight poised, in her reconstruction of the events of the crime. At the foot of the alcove stairs the doctor waited uneasily for her arrival. He glanced up the stairs—were those her footsteps now? He peered more closely into the darkness.

An expression of surprise and apprehension came over his face.

He glanced swiftly at Dale—was she watching him? No—she sat in her chair, musing. He turned back toward the stairs and made a frantic, insistent gesture—"Go back, go back!" it said, plainer than words, to—Something—in the darkness by the head of the stairs. Then his face relaxed, he gave a noiseless sigh of relief.

Dale, rousing from her brown study, turned out the floor lamp by the table and went over to the main light switch, awaiting Miss Cornelia's signal to plunge the room in darkness. The doctor stole another glance at her—had his gestures been observed?—apparently not.

Unobserved by either, as both waited tensely for Miss Cornelia's signal, a Hand stole through the broken pane of the shattered French window behind their backs and fumbled for the knob which unlocked the window-door. It found the catch—unlocked it—the window-door swung open, noiselessly—just enough to admit a crouching figure that cramped itself uncomfortably behind the settee which Dale and the doctor had placed to barricade those very doors. When it had settled itself, unperceived, in its lurking place—the Hand stole out again—closed the window-door, relocked it.

Hand or claw? Hand of man or woman or paw of beast? In the name of God—*whose hand?*

Miss Cornelia's voice from the head of the stairs broke the silence.

"All right! Put out the lights!"

Dale pressed the switch. Heavy darkness. The sound of her own breathing. A mutter from the doctor. Then, abruptly, a white, piercing shaft of light cut the darkness of the stairs—horribly reminiscent of that other light-shaft that had signaled Fleming's doom.

"Was it here?" Miss Cornelia's voice came muffledly from the head of the stairs.

Dale considered. "Come down a little," she said. The white spot of light wavered, settled on the doctor's face.

"I hope you haven't a weapon," the doctor called up the stairs with an unsuccessful attempt at jocularity.

Miss Cornelia descended another step.

"How's this?"

"That's about right," said Dale uncertainly. Miss Cornelia was satisfied.

"Lights, please." She went up the stairs again to see if she could puzzle out what course of escape the man who had shot Fleming had taken after his crime—if it had been a man.

Dale switched on the living-room lights with a sense of relief. The reconstruction of the crime had tried her sorely. She sat down to recover her poise.

"Doctor! I'm so frightened!" she confessed.

The doctor at once assumed his best manner of professional reassurance.

"Why, my dear child?" he asked lightly. "Because you happened to be in the room when a crime was committed?"

"But he has a perfect case against me," sighed Dale.

"That's absurd!"

"No."

"You don't mean?" said the doctor aghast.

Dale looked at him with horror in her face.

"I didn't kill him!" she insisted anew. "But, you know the piece of blueprint you found in his hand?"

"Yes," from the doctor tensely.

Dale's nerves, too bitterly tested, gave way at last under the strain of keeping her secret. She felt that she must confide in someone or perish. The doctor was kind and thoughtful—more than that, he was an experienced man of the world—if he could not advise her, who could? Besides, a doctor was in many ways like a priest—both sworn to keep inviolate the secrets of their respective confessionals.

"There was another piece of blueprint, a larger piece—" said Dale slowly, "I tore it from him just before—"

The doctor seemed greatly excited by her words. But he controlled himself swiftly.

"Why did you do such a thing?"

"Oh, I'll explain that later," said Dale tiredly, only too glad to be talking the matter out at last, to pay attention to the logic of her sentences. "It's not safe where it is," she went on, as if the doctor already knew the whole story. "Billy may throw it out or burn it without knowing—"

"Let me understand this," said the doctor. "The butler has the paper now?"

"He doesn't know he has it. It was in one of the rolls that went out on the tray."

The doctor's eyes gleamed. He gave Dale's shoulder a sympathetic pat.

"Now don't you worry about it, I'll get it," he said. Then, on the point of going toward the dining-room, he turned.

"But you oughtn't to have it in your possession," he said thoughtfully. "Why not let it be burned?"

Dale was on the defensive at once.

"Oh, no! It's important, it's vital!" she said decidedly.

The doctor seemed to consider ways and means of getting the paper.

"The tray is in the dining-room?" he asked.

"Yes," said Dale.

He thought a moment, then left the room by the hall door. Dale sank back in her chair and felt a sense of overpowering relief steal over her whole body, as if new life had been poured into her veins. The doctor had been so helpful—why had she not confided in him before? He would know what to do with the paper; she would have the benefit of his counsel through the rest of this troubled time. For a moment she saw herself and Jack, exonerated, their worries at an end, wandering hand in hand over the green lawns of Cedarcrest in the cheerful sunlight of morning.

Behind her, mockingly, the head of the Unknown concealed behind the settee lifted cautiously until, if she had turned, she would have just been able to perceive the top of its skull.

13

The Blackened Bag

As it chanced, she did not turn. The hall door opened—the head behind the settee sank down again. Jack Bailey entered, carrying a couple of logs of firewood.

Dale moved toward him as soon as he had shut the door.

"Oh, things have gone awfully wrong, haven't they?" she said with a little break in her voice.

He put his fingers to his lips.

"Be careful!" he whispered. He glanced about the room cautiously.

"I don't trust even the furniture in this house tonight!" he said. He took Dale hungrily in his arms and kissed her once, swiftly, on the lips. Then they parted, his voice changed to the formal voice of a servant.

"Miss Van Gorder wishes the fire kept burning," he announced, with a whispered *"Play up!"* to Dale.

Dale caught his meaning at once.

"Put some logs on the fire, please," she said loudly for the benefit of any listening ears. Then in an undertone to Bailey, "Jack—I'm nearly distracted!"

Bailey threw his wood on the fire, which received it with appreciative crackles and sputterings. Then again, for a moment, he clasped his sweetheart closely to him.

"Dale, pull yourself together!" he whispered warningly. "We've got a fight ahead of us!"

He released her and turned back toward the fire.

"These old-fashioned fireplaces eat up a lot of wood," he said in casual tones, pretending to arrange the logs with the poker so the fire would draw more cleanly.

But Dale felt that she must settle one point between them before they took up their game of pretense again.

"You know why I sent for Richard Fleming, don't you?" she said, her eyes fixed beseechingly on her lover. The rest of the world might interpret her action as it pleased but she couldn't bear to have Jack misunderstand.

But there was no danger of that. His faith in her was too complete.

"Yes, of course—" he said, with a look of gratitude. Then his mind reverted to the ever-present problem before them. "But who in God's name killed him?" he muttered, kneeling before the fire.

"You don't think it was—Billy?" Dale saw Billy's face before her for a moment, calm, impassive. But he was an Oriental, an alien; his face might be just as calm, just as impassive while his hands were still red with blood. She shuddered at the thought.

Bailey considered the matter.

"More likely the man Lizzie saw going upstairs," he said finally. "But—I've been all over the upper floors."

"And—nothing?" breathed Dale.

"Nothing." Bailey's voice had an accent of dour finality. "Dale, do you think that—" he began.

Some instinct warned the girl that they were not to continue their conversation uninterrupted. "Be careful!" she breathed, as footsteps sounded in the hall. Bailey nodded and turned back to his pretense of mending the fire. Dale moved away from him slowly.

The door opened and Miss Cornelia entered, her black knitting-bag in her hand, on her face a demure little smile of triumph. She closed the door carefully behind her and began to speak at once.

"Well, Mr. Alopecia—Urticaria—Rubeola—otherwise *Bailey!*" she said in tones of the greatest satisfaction, addressing herself to Bailey's rigid back. Bailey jumped to his feet mechanically at her mention of his name. He and Dale exchanged one swift and hopeless glance of utter defeat.

"I wish," proceeded Miss Cornelia, obviously enjoying the situation to the full, "I wish you young people would remember that even if hair and teeth have fallen out at sixty the mind still functions."

She pulled out a cabinet photograph from the depths of her knitting-bag.

"His photograph—sitting on your dresser!" she chided Dale. "Burn it and be quick about it!"

Dale took the photograph but continued to stare at her aunt with incredulous eyes.

"Then—you knew?" she stammered.

Miss Cornelia, the effective little tableau she had planned now accomplished to her most humorous satisfaction, relapsed into a chair.

"My dear child," said the indomitable lady, with a sharp glance at Bailey's bewildered face, "I have employed many gardeners in my time and never before had one who manicured his fingernails, wore silk socks, and regarded baldness as a plant instead of a calamity."

An unwilling smile began to break on the faces of both Dale and her lover. The former crossed to the fireplace and threw the damning photograph of Bailey on the flames. She watched it shrivel, curl up, be reduced to ash. She stirred the ashes with a poker till they were well scattered.

Bailey, recovering from the shock of finding that Miss Cornelia's sharp eyes had pierced his disguise without his even suspecting it, now threw himself on her mercy.

"Then you know why I'm here?" he stammered.

"I still have a certain amount of imagination! I may think you are a fool for taking the risk, but I can see what that idiot of a detective might not—that if you had looted the Union Bank you wouldn't be trying to discover if the money is in this house. You would at least presumably know where it is."

The knowledge that he had an ally in this brisk and indomitable spinster lady cheered him greatly. But she did not wait for any comment from him. She turned abruptly to Dale.

"Now I want to ask *you* something," she said more gravely. "Was there a blueprint, and did you get it from Richard Fleming?"

It was Dale's turn now to bow her head.

"Yes," she confessed.

Bailey felt a thrill of horror run through him. She hadn't told him this!

"Dale!" he said uncomprehendingly, "don't you see where this places you? If you had it, why didn't you give it to Anderson when he asked for it?"

"Because," said Miss Cornelia uncompromisingly, "she had sense enough to see that Mr. Anderson considered that piece of paper the final link in the evidence against *her!*"

"But she could have no *motive!*" stammered Bailey, distraught, still failing to grasp the significance of Dale's refusal.

"Couldn't she?" queried Miss Cornelia pityingly. "The detective thinks she could—to save you!"

Now the full light of revelation broke upon Bailey. He took a step back.

"Good God!" he said.

Miss Cornelia would have liked to comment tartly upon the singular lack of intelligence displayed by even the nicest young men in trying circumstances. But there was no time. They might be interrupted at any moment and before they were, there were things she must find out.

"Where is that paper, now?" she asked Dale sharply.

"Why—the doctor is getting it for me." Dale seemed puzzled by the intensity of her aunt's manner.

"What?" almost shouted Miss Cornelia. Dale explained.

"It was on the tray Billy took out," she said, still wondering why so simple an answer should disturb Miss Cornelia so greatly.

"Then I'm afraid everything's over," Miss Cornelia said despairingly, and made her first gesture of defeat. She turned away. Dale followed her, still unable to fathom her course of reasoning.

"I didn't know what else to do," she said rather plaintively, wondering if again, as with Fleming, she had misplaced her confidence at a moment critical for them all.

But Miss Cornelia seemed to have no great patience with her dejection.

"One of two things will happen now," she said, with acrid logic. "Either the doctor's an honest man—in which case, as coroner, he will hand that paper to the detective." Dale gasped. "Or he is *not* an honest man," went on Miss Cornelia, "and he will keep it for himself. *I* don't think he's an honest man."

The frank expression of her distrust seemed to calm her a little. She resumed her interrogation of Dale more gently.

"Now, let's be clear about this. Had Richard Fleming ascertained that there was a concealed room in this house?"

"He was starting up to it!" said Dale in the voice of a ghost, remembering.

"Just what did you tell him?"

"That I believed there was a Hidden Room in the house and that the money from the Union Bank might be in it."

Again, for the millionth time, indeed it seemed to her, she reviewed the circumstances of the crime.

"Could anyone have overheard?" asked Miss Cornelia.

The question had rung in Dale's ears ever since she had come to her senses after the firing of the shot and seen Fleming's body stark on the floor of the alcove.

"I don't know," she said. "We were very cautious."

"You don't know where this room is?"

"No, I never saw the print. Upstairs somewhere, for he—"

"Upstairs! Then the thing to do, if we can get that paper from the doctor, is to locate the room at once."

Jack Bailey did not recognize the direction where her thoughts were tending. It seemed terrible to him that anyone should devote a thought to the money while Dale was still in danger.

"What does the money matter now?" he broke in somewhat irritably. "We've got to save *her!*" and his eyes went to Dale.

Miss Cornelia gave him an ineffable look of weary patience.

"The money matters a great deal," she said, sensibly. "Someone was in this house on the same errand as Richard Fleming. After all," she went on with a tinge of irony, "the course of reasoning that you followed, Mr. Bailey, is not necessarily unique."

She rose.

"Somebody else may have suspected that Courtleigh Fleming robbed his own bank," she said thoughtfully. Her eye fell on the doctor's professional bag. She seemed to consider it as if it were a strange sort of animal.

"Find the man who followed *your* course of reasoning," she ended, with a stare at Bailey, "and you have found the murderer."

"With that reasoning you might suspect *me!*" said the latter a trifle touchily.

Miss Cornelia did not give an inch.

"I have," she said. Dale shot a swift, sympathetic glance at her lover, another less sympathetic and more indignant at her aunt. Miss Cornelia smiled.

"However, I now suspect somebody else," she said. They waited for her to reveal the name of the suspect but she kept her own counsel. By now she had entirely given up confidence if not in the probity at least in the intelligence of all persons, male or female, under the age of sixty-five.

She rang the bell for Billy. But Dale was still worrying over the possible effects of the confidence she had given Doctor Wells.

"Then you think the doctor may give this paper to Mr. Anderson?" she asked.

"He may or he may not. It is entirely possible that he may elect to search for this room himself! He may even already have gone upstairs!"

She moved quickly to the door and glanced across toward the dining-room, but so far apparently all was safe. The doctor was at the table making a pretense of drinking a cup of coffee and Billy was in close attendance. That the doctor already had the paper she was certain; it was the use he intended to make of it that was her concern.

She signaled to the Jap and he came out into the hall. Beresford, she learned, was still in the kitchen with his revolver, waiting for another attempt on the door and the detective was still outside in his search. To Billy she gave her order in a low voice.

"If the doctor attempts to go upstairs," she said, "let me know at once. Don't seem to be watching. You can be in the pantry. But let me know instantly."

Once back in the living-room the vague outlines of a plan, a test, formed slowly in Miss Cornelia's mind, grew more definite.

"Dale, watch that door and warn me if anyone is coming!" she commanded, indicating the door into the hall. Dale obeyed, marveling silently at her aunt's extraordinary force of character. Most of Miss Cornelia's contemporaries would have called for a quiet ambulance to take them to a sanatorium some hours ere this. But Miss Cornelia was not merely, comparatively speaking, as fresh as a daisy; her manner bore every evidence of a firm intention to play Sherlock Holmes to the mysteries that surrounded her, in spite of doctors, detectives, dubious noises, or even the Bat himself.

The last of the Van Gorder spinsters turned to Bailey now.

"Get some soot from that fireplace," she ordered. "Be quick. Scrape it off with a knife or a piece of paper. Anything."

Bailey wondered and obeyed. As he was engaged in his grimy task, Miss Cornelia got out a piece of writing paper from a drawer and placed it on the center table, with a lead pencil beside it.

Bailey emerged from the fireplace with a handful of sooty flakes.

"Is this all right?"

"Yes. Now rub it on the handle of that bag." She indicated the little black bag in which Doctor Wells carried the usual paraphernalia of a country doctor.

A private suspicion grew in Bailey's mind as to whether Miss Cornelia's fine but eccentric brain had not suffered too sorely under the shocks of the night. But he did not dare disobey. He blackened the handle of the doctor's bag with painstaking thoroughness and awaited further instructions.

"Somebody's coming!" Dale whispered, warning from her post by the door.

Bailey quickly went to the fireplace and resumed his pretended labors with the fire. Miss Cornelia moved away from the doctor's bag and spoke for the benefit of whoever might be coming.

"We all need sleep," she began, as if ending a conversation with Dale, "and I think—"

The door opened, admitting Billy.

"Doctor just go upstairs," he said, and went out again leaving the door open.

A flash passed across Miss Cornelia's face. She stepped to the door. She called.

"Doctor! Oh, Doctor!"

"Yes?" answered the doctor's voice from the main staircase. His steps clattered down the stairs; he entered the room. Perhaps he read something in Miss Cornelia's manner that demanded an explanation of his action. At any rate, he forestalled her, just as she was about to question him.

"I was about to look around above," he said. "I don't like to leave if there is the possibility of some assassin still hidden in the house."

"That is very considerate of you. But we are well protected now. And besides, why should this person remain in the house? The murder is done, the police are here."

"True," he said. "I only thought—"

But a knocking at the terrace door interrupted him. While the attention of the others was turned in that direction Dale, less cynical than her aunt, made a small plea to him and realized before she had finished with it that the doctor too had his price.

"Doctor—*did you get it?*" she repeated, drawing the doctor aside.

The doctor gave her a look of apparent bewilderment.

"My dear child," he said softly, "are you *sure* that you put it there?"

Dale felt as if she had received a blow in the face.

"Why, yes—I—" she began in tones of utter dismay. Then she stopped. The doctor's seeming bewilderment was too pat, too plausible. Of course she was sure—and, though possible, it seemed extremely unlikely that anyone else could have discovered the hiding-place of the blueprint in the few moments that had elapsed between the time when Billy took the tray from the room and the time when the doctor ostensibly went to find it. A cold wave of distrust swept over her; she turned away from the doctor silently.

Meanwhile Anderson had entered, slamming the terrace-door behind him.

"I couldn't find anybody!" he said in an irritated voice. "I think that Jap's crazy."

The doctor began to struggle into his topcoat, avoiding any look at Dale.

"Well," he said, "I believe I've fulfilled all the legal requirements. I think I must be going." He turned toward the door but the detective halted him.

"Doctor," he said, "did you ever hear Courtleigh Fleming mention a Hidden Room in this house?"

If the doctor started, the movement passed apparently unnoted by Anderson. And his reply was coolly made.

"No—and I knew him rather well."

"You don't think then," persisted the detective, "that such a room and the money in it could be the motive for this crime?"

The doctor's voice grew a little curt.

"I don't believe Courtleigh Fleming robbed his own bank, if that's what you mean," he said with nicely calculated emphasis, real or feigned. He crossed over to get his bag and spoke to Miss Cornelia.

"Well, Miss Van Gorder," he said, picking up the bag by its blackened handle, "I can't wish you a comfortable night but I can wish you a quiet one."

Miss Cornelia watched him silently. As he turned to go, she spoke.

"We're all of us a little upset, naturally," she confessed. "Perhaps you could write a prescription—a sleeping-powder or a bromide of some sort."

"Why, certainly," agreed the doctor at once. He turned back. Miss Cornelia seemed pleased.

"I hoped you would," she said with a little tremble in her voice such as might easily occur in the voice of a nervous old lady. "Oh, yes, here's paper and a pencil," as the doctor fumbled in a pocket.

The doctor took the sheet of paper she proffered and, using the side of his bag as a pad, began to write out the prescription.

"I don't generally advise these drugs," he said, looking up for a moment. "Still—"

He paused. "What time is it?"

Miss Cornelia glanced at the clock. "Half-past eleven."

"Then I'd better bring you the powders myself," decided the doctor. "The pharmacy closes at eleven. I shall have to make them up myself."

"That seems a lot of trouble."

"Nothing is any trouble if I can be helpful," he assured her, smilingly. And Miss Cornelia also smiled, took the piece of paper from his hand, glanced at it once, as if out of idle curiosity about the unfinished prescription, and then laid it down on the table with a careless little gesture. Dale gave her aunt a glance of dumb entreaty. Miss Cornelia read her wish for another moment alone with the doctor.

"Dale will let you out, Doctor," said she, giving the girl the key to the front door.

The doctor approved her watchfulness.

"That's right," he said smilingly. "Keep things locked up. Discretion is the better part of valor!"

But Miss Cornelia failed to agree with him.

"I've been discreet for sixty-five years," she said with a sniff, "and sometimes I think it was a mistake!"

The doctor laughed easily and followed Dale out of the room, with a nod of farewell to the others in passing. The detective, seeking for some object upon whom to vent the growing irritation which seemed to possess him, made Bailey the scapegoat of his wrath.

"I guess we can do without you for the present!" he said, with an angry frown at the latter. Bailey flushed, then remembered himself, and left the room submissively, with the air of a well-trained servant accepting an unmerited rebuke. The detective turned at once to Miss Cornelia.

"Now I want a few words with you!"

"Which means that you mean to do all the talking!" said Miss Cornelia acidly. "Very well! But first I want to show you something. Will you come here, please, Mr. Anderson?"

She started for the alcove.

"I've examined that staircase," said the detective.

"Not with me!" insisted Miss Cornelia. "I have something to show you."

He followed her unwillingly up the stairs, his whole manner seeming to betray a complete lack of confidence in the theories of all amateur sleuths in general and spinster detectives of sixty-five in particular. Their footsteps died away up the alcove stairs. The living-room was left vacant for an instant.

Vacant? Only in seeming. The moment that Miss Cornelia and the detective had passed up the stairs, the croutching, mysterious Unknown, behind the settee, began to move. The French window-door opened, a stealthy figure passed through it silently to be swallowed up in the darkness of the terrace.

And poor Lizzie, entering the room at that moment, saw a hand covered with blood reach back and gropingly, horribly, through the broken pane, refasten the lock.

She shrieked madly.

14

Handcuffs

Dale had failed with the doctor. When Lizzie's screams once more had called the startled household to the living-room, she knew she had failed. She followed in mechanically, watched an irritated Anderson send the Pride of Kerry to bed and threaten to lock her up, and listened vaguely to the conversation between her aunt and the detective that followed it, without more than casual interest.

Nevertheless, that conversation was to have vital results later on.

"Your point about the thumbprint on the stair rail is very interesting," Anderson said with a certain respect. "But just what does it prove?"

"It points down," said Miss Cornelia, still glowing with the memory of the whistle of surprise the detective had given when she had shown him the strange thumbprint on the rail of the alcove stairs.

"It does," he admitted. "But what then?"

Miss Cornelia tried to put her case as clearly and tersely as possible.

"It shows that somebody stood there for some time, listening to my niece and Richard Fleming in this room below," she said.

"All right, I'll grant that to save argument," retorted the detective. "But the moment that shot was fired the lights came on. If somebody on that staircase shot him, and then came down and took the blueprint, Miss Ogden would have seen him."

He turned upon Dale.

"Did you?"

She hesitated. Why hadn't she thought of such an explanation before? But now—it would sound too flimsy!

"No, nobody came down," she admitted candidly.

The detective's face altered, grew menacing. Miss Cornelia once more had put herself between him and Dale.

"Now, Mr. Anderson—" she warned.

The detective was obviously trying to keep his temper.

"I'm not hounding this girl!" he said doggedly. "I haven't said yet that she committed the murder but she took that blueprint and I want it!"

"You want it to connect her with the murder," parried Miss Cornelia.

The detective threw up his hands.

"It's rather reasonable to suppose that I might want to return the funds to the Union Bank, isn't it?" he queried in tones of heavy sarcasm. "Provided they're here," he added doubtfully.

Miss Cornelia resolved upon comparative frankness.

"I see," she said. "Well, I'll tell you this much, Mr. Anderson, and I'll ask you to believe me as a lady. Granting that at one time my niece knew something of that blueprint—at this moment we do not know where it is or who has it."

Her words had the unmistakable ring of truth. The very oath from the detective that succeeded them showed his recognition of the fact.

"Damnation," he muttered. "That's true, is it?"

"That's true," said Miss Cornelia firmly. A silence of troubled thoughts fell upon the three. Miss Cornelia took out her knitting.

"Did you ever try knitting when you wanted to think?" she queried sweetly, after a pause in which the detective trampled from one side of the room to the other, brows knotted, eyes bent on the floor.

"No," grunted the detective. He took out a cigar, bit off the end with a savage snap of teeth, lit it, resumed his pacing.

"You should, sometimes," continued Miss Cornelia, watching his troubled movements with a faint light of mockery in her eyes. "I find it very helpful."

"I don't need knitting to think straight," rasped Anderson indignantly. Miss Cornelia's eyes danced.

"I wonder!" she said with caustic affability. "You seem to have so much evidence left over."

The detective paused and glared at her helplessly.

"Did you ever hear of the man who took a clock apart and when he put it together again, he had enough left over to make another clock?" she twitted.

The detective, ignoring the taunt, crossed quickly to Dale.

"What do you mean by saying that paper isn't where you put it?" he demanded in tones of extreme severity.

Miss Cornelia replied for her niece.

"She hasn't said that."

The detective made an impatient movement of his hand and walked away, as if to get out of the reach of the indefatigable spinster's tongue. But Miss Cornelia had not finished with him yet, by any means.

"Do you believe in circumstantial evidence?" she asked him with seeming ingenuousness.

"It's my business," said the detective stolidly. Miss Cornelia smiled.

"While you have been investigating," she announced, "I, too, have not been idle."

The detective gave a barking laugh. She let it pass.

"To me," she continued, "it is perfectly obvious that *one* intelligence has been at work behind many of the things that have occurred in this house."

Now Anderson observed her with a new respect.

"Who?" he grunted tersely.

Her eyes flashed.

"I'll ask you that! Some one person who, knowing Courtleigh Fleming well, probably knows of the existence of a Hidden Room in this house and who, finding us in occupation of the house, has tried to get rid of me in two ways. First, by frightening me with anonymous threats and, second, by urging me to leave. Someone, who very possibly entered this house tonight shortly before the murder and slipped up that staircase!"

The detective had listened to her outburst with unusual thoughtfulness. A certain wonder—perhaps at her shrewdness, perhaps at an unexpected confirmation of certain ideas of his own—grew upon his face. Now he jerked out two words.

"The doctor?"

Miss Cornelia knitted on as if every movement of her needles added one more link to the strong chain of probabilities she was piecing together.

"When Doctor Wells said he was leaving here earlier in the evening for the Johnsons' he did not go there," she observed. "He was not expected to go there. I found that out when I telephoned."

"The doctor!" repeated the detective, his eyes narrowing, his head beginning to sway from side to side like the head of some great cat just before a spring.

"As you know," Miss Cornelia went on, "I had a supplementary bolt placed on that terrace door today." She nodded toward the door that gave access into the alcove from the terrace. "Earlier this evening

Doctor Wells said that he had *bolted* it, when he had left it *open*—
purposely, as I now realize, in order that he might return later. You
may also recall that Doctor Wells took a scrap of paper from Richard
Fleming's hand and tried to conceal it. Why did he do *that?*"

She paused for a second. Then she changed her tone a little.

"May I ask you to look at this?"

She displayed the piece of paper on which Doctor Wells had started
to write the prescription for her sleeping-powders—and now her strategy with the doctor's bag and the soot Jack Bailey had got from the
fireplace stood revealed. A sharp, black imprint of a man's right
thumb, the doctor's, stood out on the paper below the broken line of
writing. The doctor had not noticed the staining of his hand by the
blackened bag handle, or, noticing, had thought nothing of it. But the
blackened bag handle had been a trap and he had left an indelible
piece of evidence behind him. It now remained to test the value of this
evidence.

Miss Cornelia handed the paper to Anderson silently. But her eyes
were bright with pardonable vanity at the success of her little piece of
strategy.

"A thumbprint," muttered Anderson. "Whose is it?"

"Doctor Wells," said Miss Cornelia with what might have been a
little crow of triumph in anyone not a Van Gorder.

Anderson looked thoughtful. Then he felt in his pocket for a mag-
nifying glass, failed to find it, muttered, and took the reading glass
Miss Cornelia offered him.

"Try this," she said. "My whole case hangs on my conviction that
that print and the one out there on the stair rail are the same."

He put down the paper and smiled at her ironically.

"Your case!" he said. "You don't really believe you need a detective
at all, do you?"

"I will only say that so far your views and mine have failed to coin-
cide. If I am right about that fingerprint, then you may be right about
my private opinion."

And on that he went out, rather grimly, paper and reading glass in
hand, to make his comparison.

It was then that Beresford came in, a new and slightly rigid Beresford, and crossed to her at once.

"Miss Van Gorder," he said, all the flippancy gone from his voice,
"may I ask you to make an excuse and call your gardener here?"

Dale started uncontrollably at the ominous words, but Miss Cornelia betrayed no emotion except in the increased rapidity of her knitting.

"The gardener? Certainly, if you'll touch that bell," she said pleasantly.

Beresford stalked to the bell and rang it. The three waited—Dale in an agony of suspense.

The detective re-entered the room by the alcove stairs, his mien unfathomable by any of the anxious glances that sought him out at once.

"It's no good, Miss Van Gorder," he said quietly. "The prints are not the same."

"Not the same!" gasped Miss Cornelia, unwilling to believe her ears.

Anderson laid down the paper and the reading glass with a little gesture of dismissal.

"If you think I'm mistaken, I'll leave it to any unprejudiced person or your own eyesight. Thumbprints never lie," he said in a flat, convincing voice. Miss Cornelia stared at him, disappointment written large on her features. He allowed himself a little ironic smile.

"Did you ever try a good cigar when you wanted to think?" he queried suavely, puffing upon his own.

But Miss Cornelia's spirit was too broken by the collapse of her dearly loved and adroitly managed scheme for her to take up the gauge of battle he offered.

"I still believe it was the doctor," she said stubbornly. But her tones were not the tones of utter conviction which she had used before.

"And yet," said the detective, ruthlessly demolishing another link in her broken chain of evidence, "the doctor was in this room tonight, according to your own statement, when the anonymous letter came through the window."

Miss Cornelia gazed at him blankly, for the first time in her life at a loss for an appropriately sharp retort. It was true. The doctor had been here in the room beside her when the stone bearing the last anonymous warning had crashed through the windowpane. And yet—

Billy's entrance in answer to Beresford's ring made her mind turn to other matters for the moment. Why had Beresford's manner changed so, and what was he saying to Billy now?

"Tell the gardener Miss Van Gorder wants him and don't say we're all here," the young lawyer commanded the butler sharply. Billy nodded and disappeared. Miss Cornelia's back began to stiffen; she didn't like other people ordering her servants around like that.

The detective, apparently, had somewhat of the same feeling.

"I seem to have plenty of *help* in this case!" he said with obvious sarcasm, turning to Beresford.

The latter made no reply. Dale rose anxiously from her chair, her lips quivering.

"Why have you sent for the gardener?" she inquired haltingly.

Beresford deigned to answer at last.

"I'll tell you that in a moment," he said with a grim tightening of his lips.

There was a fateful pause, for an instant, while Dale roved nervously from one side of the room to the other. Then Jack Bailey came into the room—alone.

He seemed to sense danger in the air. His hands clenched at his sides, but except for that tiny betrayal of emotion, he still kept his servant's pose.

"You sent for me?" he queried Miss Cornelia submissively, ignoring the glowering Beresford.

But Beresford would be ignored no longer. He came between them before Miss Cornelia had time to answer.

"How long has this man been in your employ?" he asked brusquely, manner tense.

Miss Cornelia made one final attempt at evasion.

"Why should that interest you?" she parried, answering his question with an icy question of her own.

It was too late. Already Bailey had read the truth in Beresford's eyes.

"I came this evening," he admitted, still hoping against hope that his cringing posture of the servitor might give Beresford pause for the moment.

But the promptness of his answer only crystallized Beresford's suspicions.

"Exactly," he said with terse finality. He turned to the detective.

"I've been trying to recall this man's face ever since I came in tonight—" he said with grim triumph. "Now, I know who he is."

"Who is he?"

Bailey straightened up. He had lost his game with Chance. And the loss, coming when it did, seemed bitterer than even he had thought it could be, but before they took him away he would speak his mind.

"It's all right, Beresford," he said with a fatigue so deep that it colored his voice like flakes of iron-rust. "I know you think you're doing your duty but I wish to God you could have *restrained* your sense of duty for about three hours more!"

"To let you get away?" the young lawyer sneered, unconvinced.

"No," said Bailey with quiet defiance. "To let me finish what I came here to do."

"Don't you think you have done enough?" Beresford's voice flicked him with righteous scorn, no less telling because of its youthfulness. He turned back to the detective soberly enough.

"This man has imposed upon the credulity of these women, I am quite sure without their knowledge," he said with a trace of his former gallantry. "He is Bailey of the Union Bank, the missing cashier."

The detective slowly put down his cigar on an ash tray.

"That's the truth, is it?" he demanded.

Dale's hand flew to her breast. If Jack would only deny it—even now! But even as she thought this, she realized the uselessness of any such denial.

Bailey realized it, too.

"It's true, all right," he admitted hopelessly. He closed his eyes for a moment. Let them come with the handcuffs now and get it over. Every moment the scene dragged out was a moment of unnecessary torture for Dale.

But Beresford had not finished with his indictment.

"I accuse him not only of the thing he is wanted for, but of the murder of Richard Fleming!" he said fiercely, glaring at Bailey as if only a youthful horror of making a scene before Dale and Miss Cornelia held him back from striking the latter down where he stood.

Bailey's eyes snapped open. He took a threatening step toward his accuser. "You lie!" he said in a hoarse, violent voice.

Anderson crossed between them, just as conflict seemed inevitable.

"*You* knew this?" he queried sharply in Dale's direction.

Dale set her lips in a line. She did not answer.

He turned to Miss Cornelia.

"Did you?"

"Yes," admitted the latter quietly, her knitting needles at last at rest. "I knew he was Mr. Bailey if that is all you mean."

The quietness of her answer seemed to infuriate the detective.

"Quite a pretty little conspiracy," he said. "How in the name of God do you expect me to do anything with the entire household united against me? Tell me that."

"Exactly," said Miss Cornelia. "And if we are united against you, why should I have sent for you? You might tell me that, too."

He turned on Bailey savagely.

"What did you mean by that 'three hours more'?" he demanded.

"I could have cleared myself in three hours," said Bailey with calm despair.

Beresford laughed mockingly—a laugh that seemed to sear into Bailey's consciousness like the touch of a hot iron. Again he turned frenziedly upon the young lawyer and Anderson was just preparing to hold them away from each other, by force if necessary, when the door-bell rang.

For an instant the ringing of the bell held the various figures of the little scene in the rigid postures of a waxworks tableau—Bailey, one foot advanced toward Beresford, his hand balled up into fists—Beresford already in an attitude of defense—the detective about to step in between them—Miss Cornelia stiff in her chair—Dale over by the fire-place, her hand at her heart. Then they relaxed, but not, at least on the part of Bailey and Beresford, to resume their interrupted conflict. Too many nerveshaking things had already happened that night for either of the young men not to drop their mutual squabble in the face of a common danger.

"Probably the doctor," murmured Miss Cornelia uncertainly as the doorbell rang again. "He was to come back with some sleeping-powders."

Billy appeared for the key of the front door.

"If that's Doctor Wells," warned the detective, "admit him. If it's anybody else, call me."

Billy grinned acquiescently and departed. The detective moved nearer to Bailey.

"Have you got a gun on you?"

"No." Bailey bowed his head.

"Well, I'll just make sure of that." The detective's hands ran swiftly and expertly over Bailey's form, through his pockets, probing for concealed weapons. Then, slowly drawing a pair of handcuffs from his pockets, he prepared to put them on Bailey's wrists.

15

The Sign of the Bat

But Dale could bear it no longer. The sight of her lover, beaten, submissive, his head bowed, waiting obediently like a common criminal for the detective to lock his wrists in steel broke down her last defenses. She rushed into the center of the room, between Bailey and the detective, her eyes wild with terror, her words stumbling over each other in her eagerness to get them out.

"Oh, no! I can't stand it! I'll tell you everything!" she cried frenziedly. "He got to the foot of the staircase—Richard Fleming, I mean," she was facing the detective now, "and he had the blueprint you've been talking about. I had told him Jack Bailey was here as the gardener and he said if I screamed he would tell that. I was desperate. I threatened him with the revolver but he took it from me. Then when I tore the blueprint from him—he was shot—from the stairs—"

"By Bailey!" interjected Beresford angrily.

"I didn't even know he was in the house!" Bailey's answer was as instant as it was hot. Meanwhile, the doctor had entered the room, hardly noticed, in the middle of Dale's confession, and now stood watching the scene intently from a post by the door.

"What did you do with the blueprint?" The detective's voice beat at Dale like a whip.

"I put it first in the neck of my dress—" she faltered. "Then, when I found you were watching me, I hid it somewhere else."

Her eyes fell on the doctor. She saw his hand steal out toward the knob of the door. Was he going to run away on some pretext before she could finish her story? She gave a sigh of relief when Billy, reentering with the key to the front door, blocked any such attempt at escape.

Mechanically she watched Billy cross to the table, lay the key upon it, and return to the hall without so much as a glance at the tense, suspicious circle of faces focused upon herself and her lover.

"I put it—somewhere else," she repeated, her eyes going back to the doctor.

"Did you give it to Bailey?"

"No—I hid it—and then I told where it was—to the doctor—" Dale swayed on her feet. All turned surprisedly toward the doctor. Miss Cornelia rose from her chair.

The doctor bore the battery of eyes unflinchingly.

"That's rather inaccurate," he said, with a tight little smile. "You told me where you had placed it, but when I went to look for it, it was gone."

"Are you quite sure of that?" queried Miss Cornelia acidly.

"Absolutely," he said. He ignored the rest of the party, addressing himself directly to Anderson.

"She said she had hidden it inside one of the rolls that were on the tray on that table," he continued in tones of easy explanation, approaching the table as he did so, and tapping it with the box of sleeping-powders he had brought for Miss Cornelia.

"She was in such distress that I finally went to look for it. It wasn't there."

"Do you realize the significance of this paper?" Anderson boomed at once.

"Nothing, beyond the fact that Miss Ogden was afraid it linked her with the crime." The doctor's voice was very clear and firm.

Anderson pondered an instant. Then—

"I'd like to have a few minutes with the doctor alone," he said somberly.

The group about him dissolved at once. Miss Cornelia, her arm around her niece's waist, led the latter gently to the door. As the two lovers passed each other a glance flashed between them—a glance, pathetically brief, of longing and love. Dale's finger tips brushed Bailey's hand gently in passing.

"Beresford," commanded the detective, "take Bailey to the library and see that he stays there."

Beresford tapped his pocket with a significant gesture and motioned Bailey to the door. Then they, too, left the room. The door closed. The doctor and the detective were alone.

The detective spoke at once—and surprisingly.

"Doctor, I'll have that blueprint!" he said sternly, his eyes the color of steel.

The doctor gave him a wary little glance.

"But I've just made the statement that I didn't find the blueprint," he affirmed flatly.

"I heard you!" Anderson's voice was very dry. "Now this situation is between you and me, Doctor Wells." His forefinger sought the doctor's chest. "It has nothing to do with that poor fool of a cashier. He hasn't got either those securities or the money from them and you know it. It's in this house and you know that, too!"

"In this house?" repeated the doctor as if stalling for time.

"In this house! Tonight, when you claimed to be making a professional call, you were in this house and I think you were on that staircase when Richard Fleming was killed!"

"No, Anderson, I'll swear I was not!" The doctor might be acting, but if he was, it was incomparable acting. The terror in his voice seemed too real to be feigned.

But Anderson was remorseless.

"I'll tell you this," he continued. "Miss Van Gorder very cleverly got a thumbprint of yours tonight. Does that mean anything to you?"

His eyes bored into the doctor, the eyes of a poker player bluffing on a hidden card. But the doctor did not flinch.

"Nothing," he said firmly. "I have not been upstairs in this house in three months."

The accent of truth in his voice seemed so unmistakable that even Anderson's shrewd brain was puzzled by it. But he persisted in his attempt to wring a confession from this latest suspect.

"Before Courtleigh Fleming died—did he tell you anything about a Hidden Room in this house?" he queried cannily.

The doctor's confident air of honesty lessened, a furtive look appeared in his eyes.

"No," he insisted, but not as convincingly as he had made his previous denial.

The detective hammered at the point again.

"You haven't been trying to frighten these women out of here with anonymous letters so you could get in?"

"No. Certainly not." But again the doctor's air had that odd mixture of truth and falsehood in it.

The detective paused for an instant.

"Let me see your key ring!" he ordered. The doctor passed it over silently. The detective glanced at the keys—then, suddenly, his revolver glittered in his other hand.

The doctor watched him anxiously. A puff of wind rattled the panes of the French windows. The storm, quieted for a while, was gathering its strength for a fresh unleashing of its dogs of thunder.

The detective stepped to the terrace door, opened it, and then quietly proceeded to try the doctor's keys in the lock. Thus located he was out of visual range, and Wells took advantage of it at once. He moved swiftly toward the fireplace, extracting the missing piece of blueprint from an inside pocket as he did so. The secret the blueprint guarded was already graven on his mind in indelible characters. Now he would destroy all evidence that it had ever been in his possession and bluff through the rest of the situation as best he might.

He threw the paper toward the flames with a nervous gesture of relief. But for once his cunning failed; the throw was too hurried to be sure and the light scrap of paper wavered and settled to the floor just outside the fireplace. The doctor swore noiselessly and stooped to pick it up and make sure of its destruction. But he was not quick enough. Through the window the detective had seen the incident, and the next moment the doctor heard his voice bark behind him. He turned, and stared at the leveled muzzle of Anderson's revolver.

"Hands up and stand back!" he commanded.

As he did so Anderson picked up the paper and a sardonic smile crossed his face as his eyes took in the significance of the print. He laid his revolver down on the table where he could snatch it up again at a moment's notice.

"Behind a fireplace, eh?" he muttered. "What fireplace? In what room?"

"I won't tell you!" The doctor's voice was sullen. He inched, gingerly, cautiously, toward the other side of the table.

"All right—I'll find it, you know." The detective's eyes turned swiftly back to the blueprint. Experience should have taught him never to underrate an adversary, even of the doctor's caliber, but long familiarity with danger can make the shrewdest careless. For a moment, as he bent over the paper again, he was off guard.

The doctor seized the moment with a savage promptitude and sprang. There followed a silent, furious struggle between the two. Under normal circumstances Anderson would have been the stronger and quicker, but the doctor fought with an added strength of despair and his initial leap had pinioned the detective's arms behind him. Now the detective shook one hand free and snatched at the revolver— in vain—for the doctor, with a groan of desperation, struck at his hand as its fingers were about to close on the smooth butt and the revolver skidded from the table to the floor. With a sudden terrible movement he pinioned both the detective's arms behind him again and reached for the telephone. Its heavy base descended on the back of the detective's head with stunning force. The next moment the battle was ended and the doctor, panting with exhaustion, held the limp form of an unconscious man in his arms.

He lowered the detective to the floor and straightened up again, listening tensely. So brief and intense had been the struggle that even now he could hardly believe in its reality. It seemed impossible, too, that the struggle had not been heard. Then he realized dully, as a louder roll of thunder smote on his ears, that the elements themselves had played into his hand. The storm, with its wind and fury, had returned just in time to save him and drown out all sounds of conflict from the rest of the house with its giant clamor.

He bent swiftly over Anderson, listening to his heart. Good—the man still breathed; he had enough on his conscience without adding the murder of a detective to the black weight. Now he pocketed the revolver and the blueprint, gagged Anderson rapidly with a knotted handkerchief and proceeded to wrap his own muffler around the detective's head as an additional silencer. Anderson gave a faint sigh.

The doctor thought rapidly. Soon or late the detective would return to consciousness; with his hands free he could easily tear out the gag. He looked wildly around the room for a rope, a curtain—ah, he had it—the detective's own handcuffs! He snapped the cuffs on Anderson's wrists, then realized that, in his hurry, he had bound the detective's hands in front of him instead of behind him. Well, it would do for the moment; he did not need much time to carry out his plans. He dragged the limp body, its head lolling, into the billiard room where he deposited it on the floor in the corner farthest from the door.

So far, so good. Now to lock the door of the billiard room. Fortunately, the key was there on the inside of the door. He quickly transferred it, locked the billiard-room door from the outside, and pocketed the key. For a second he stood by the center table in the living-room, recovering his breath and trying to straighten his rumpled clothing. Then he crossed cautiously into the alcove and started to pad up the alcove stairs, his face white and strained with excitement and hope.

And it was then that there happened one of the most dramatic events of the night. One which was to remain, for the next hour or so, as bewildering as the murder and which, had it come a few moments sooner or a few moments later, would have entirely changed the course of events.

It was preceded by a desperate hammering on the door of the terrace. It halted the doctor on his way upstairs, drew Beresford on a run into the living-room, and even reached the bedrooms of the women up above.

"My God! What's that?" Beresford panted.

The doctor indicated the door. It was too late now. Already he could hear Miss Cornelia's voice above; it was only a question of a short time until Anderson in the billiard room revived and would try to make his plight known. And in the brief moment of that résumé of his position the knocking came again. But feebler, as though the suppliant outside had exhausted his strength.

As Beresford drew his revolver and moved to the door, Miss Cornelia came in, followed by Lizzie.

"It's the Bat," Lizzie announced mournfully. "Good-by, Miss Neily. Good-by, everybody. I saw his hand, all covered with blood. He's had a good night for sure!"

But they ignored her. And Beresford flung open the door.

Just what they had expected, what figure of horror or of fear they waited for, no one can say. But there was no horror and no fear; only unutterable amazement as an unknown man, in torn and muddied garments, with a streak of dried blood seaming his forehead like a scar, fell through the open doorway into Beresford's arms.

"Good God!" muttered Beresford, dropping his revolver to catch the strange burden. For a moment the Unknown lay in his arms like a corpse. Then he straighted dizzily, staggered into the room, took a few steps toward the table, and fell prostrate upon his face—at the end of his strength.

"Doctor!" gasped Miss Cornelia dazedly and the doctor, whatever guilt lay on his conscience, responded at once to the call of his profession.

He bent over the Unknown Man—the physician once more—and made a brief examination.

"He's fainted!" he said, rising. "Struck on the head, too."

"But *who is he?*" faltered Miss Cornelia.

"I never saw him before," said the doctor. It was obvious that he spoke the truth. "Does anyone recognize him?"

All crowded about the Unknown, trying to read the riddle of his identity. Miss Cornelia rapidly revised her first impressions of the stranger. When he had first fallen through the doorway into Beresford's arms she had not known what to think. Now, in the brighter light of the living-room she saw that the still face, beneath its mask of dirt and dried blood, was strong and fairly youthful; if the man were a criminal, he belonged, like the Bat, to the upper fringes of the world of crime. She noted mechanically that his hands and feet had been tied, ends of frayed rope still dangled from his wrists and ankles. And that terrible injury on his head! She shuddered and closed her eyes.

"Does anyone recognize him?" repeated the doctor but one by one the others shook their heads. Crook, casual tramp, or honest laborer unexpectedly caught in the sinister toils of the Cedarcrest affair—his identity seemed a mystery to one and all.

"Is he badly hurt?" asked Miss Cornelia, shuddering again.

"It's hard to say," answered the doctor. "I think not."

The Unknown stirred feebly, made an effort to sit up. Beresford and the doctor caught him under the arms and helped him to his feet. He stood there swaying, a blank expression on his face.

"A chair!" said the doctor quickly. "Ah—" He helped the strange figure to sit down and bent over him again.

"You're all right now, my friend," he said in his best tones of professional cheeriness. "Dizzy a bit, aren't you?"

The Unknown rubbed his wrists where his bonds had cut them. He made an effort to speak.

"Water!" he said in a low voice.

The doctor gestured to Billy. "Get some water—or whisky—if there is any—that'd be better."

"There's a flask of whisky in my room, Billy," added Miss Cornelia helpfully.

"Now, my man," continued the doctor to the Unknown. "You're in the hands of friends. Brace up and tell us what happened!"

Beresford had been looking about for the detective, puzzled not to find him, as usual, in charge of affairs. Now, "Where's Anderson? This is a police matter!" he said, making a movement as if to go in search of him.

The doctor stopped him quickly.

"He was here a minute ago, he'll be back presently," he said, praying to whatever gods he served that Anderson, bound and gagged in the billiard room, had not yet returned to consciousness.

Unobserved by all except Miss Cornelia, the mention of the detective's name had caused a strange reaction in the Unknown. His eyes had opened—he had started—the haze in his mind had seemed to clear away for a moment. Then, for some reason, his shoulders had slumped again and the look of apathy come back to his face. But, stunned or not, it now seemed possible that he was not quite as dazed as he appeared.

The doctor gave the slumped shoulders a little shake.

"Rouse yourself, man!" he said. "What has happened to you?"

"I'm dazed!" said the Unknown thickly and slowly. "I can't remember." He passed a hand weakly over his forehead.

"What a night!" sighed Miss Cornelia, sinking into a chair. "Richard Fleming murdered in this house—and now—this!"

The Unknown shot her a stealthy glance from beneath lowered eyelids. But when she looked at him, his face was blank again.

"Why doesn't somebody ask his name?" queried Dale, and "Where the devil is that detective?" muttered Beresford, almost in the same instant.

Neither question was answered, and Beresford, increasingly uneasy at the continued absence of Anderson, turned toward the hall.

The doctor took Dale's suggestion.

"What's your name?"

Silence from the Unknown—and that blank stare of stupefaction.

"Look at his papers." It was Miss Cornelia's voice. The doctor and Bailey searched the torn trouser pockets, the pockets of the muddied shirt, while the Unknown submitted passively, not seeming to care what happened to him. But search him as they would—it was in vain.

"Not a paper on him," said Jack Bailey at last, straightening up.

A crash of breaking glass from the head of the alcove stairs put a period to his sentence. All turned toward the stairs—or all except the Unknown, who, for a moment, half-rose in his chair, his eyes gleaming, his face alert, the mask of bewildered apathy gone from his face.

As they watched, a rigid little figure of horror backed slowly down the alcove stairs and into the room—Billy, the Japanese, his Oriental placidity disturbed at last, incomprehensible terror written in every line of his face.

"Billy!"

"Billy, what is it?"

The diminutive butler made a pitiful attempt at his usual grin.

"It—nothing," he gasped. The Unknown relapsed in his chair— again the dazed stranger from nowhere.

Beresford took the Japanese by the shoulders.

"Now see here!" he said sharply. "You've seen something! What was it!"

Billy trembled like a leaf.

"Ghost! Ghost!" he muttered frantically, his face working.

"He's concealing something. Look at him!" Miss Cornelia stared at her servant.

"No, no!" insisted Billy in an ague of fright. "No, no!"

But Miss Cornelia was sure of it.

"Brooks, close that door!" she said, pointing at the terrace door in the alcove which still stood ajar after the entrance of the Unknown.

Bailey moved to obey. But just as he reached the alcove the terrace door slammed shut in his face. At the same moment every light in Cedarcrest blinked and went out again.

Bailey fumbled for the doorknob in the sudden darkness.

"The door's *locked!*" he said incredulously. "The key's gone too. Where's your revolver, Beresford?"

"I dropped it in the alcove when I caught that man," called Beresford, cursing himself for his carelessness.

The illuminated dial of Bailey's wrist watch flickered in the darkness as he searched for the revolver—a round, glowing spot of phosphorescence.

Lizzie screamed. "The eye! The gleaming eye I saw on the stairs!" she shrieked, pointing at it frenziedly.

"Quick—there's a candle on the table—light it somebody. Never mind the revolver, I have one!" called Miss Cornelia.

"Righto!" called Beresford in reply. He found the candle, lit it—

The group blinked at each other for a moment, still unable to co-ordinate their thoughts.

Bailey ratted the knob of the door into the hall.

"This door's locked, too!" he said with increasing puzzlement. A gasp went over the group. They were locked in the room while some devilment was going on in the rest of the house. That they knew. But what it might be, what form it might take, they had not the remotest idea. They were too distracted to notice the injured man, now alert in his chair, or the doctor's odd attitude of listening, above the rattle and banging of the storm.

But it was not until Miss Cornelia took the candle and proceeded toward the hall door to examine it that the full horror of the situation burst upon them.

Neatly fastened to the white panel of the door, chest high and hardly more than just dead, was the body of a bat.

Of what happened thereafter no one afterward remembered the details. To be shut in there at the mercy of one who knew no mercy was intolerable. It was left for Miss Cornelia to remember her own revolver, lying unnoticed on the table since the crime earlier in the evening, and to suggest its use in shattering the lock.

Just what they had expected when the door was finally opened they did not know. But the house was quiet and in order; no new horror faced them in the hall; their candle revealed no bloody figure, their ears heard no unearthly sound.

Slowly they began to breathe normally once more.

After that they began to search the house. Since no room was apparently immune from danger, the men made no protest when the women insisted on accompanying them. And as time went on and chamber after chamber was discovered empty and undisturbed, gradually the courage of the party began to rise. Lizzie, still whimpering, stuck closely to Miss Cornelia's heels, but that spirited lady began to make small side excursions of her own.

Of the men, only Bailey, Beresford, and the doctor could really be said to search at all. Billy had remained below, impassive of face but rolling of eye; the Unknown, after an attempt to depart with them, had sunk back weakly into his chair again, and the detective, Anderson, was still unaccountably missing.

While no one could be said to be grieving over this, still the belief that somehow, somewhere, he had met the Bat and suffered at his hands was strong in all of them except the doctor. As each door was opened they expected to find him, probably foully murdered; as each door was closed again they breathed with relief.

And as time went on and the silence and peace remained unbroken, the conviction grew on them that the Bat had in this manner achieved his object and departed; had done his work, signed it after his usual fashion, and gone.

And thus were matters when Miss Cornelia, happening on the attic staircase with Lizzie at her heels, decided to look about her up there. And went up.

16

The Hidden Room

A few moments later Jack Bailey, seeing a thin glow of candlelight from the attic above and hearing Lizzie's protesting voice, made his way up there. He found them in the trunk room, a dusty, dingy apartment lined with high closets along the walls—the floor littered with an incongruous assortment of attic objects—two battered trunks, a clothes hamper, an old sewing machine, a broken-backed kitchen chair, two dilapidated suitcases and a shabby satchel that might once have been a woman's dressing case—in one corner a grimy fireplace in which, obviously, no fire had been lighted for years.

But he also found Miss Cornelia holding her candle to the floor and staring at something there.

"Candle grease!" she said sharply, staring at a line of white spots by the window. She stooped and touched the spots with an exploratory finger.

"Fresh candle grease! Now who do you suppose did that? Do you remember how Mr. Gillette, in Sherlock Holmes, when he—"

Her voice trailed off. She stooped and followed the trail of the candle grease away from the window, ingeniously trying to copy the shrewd, piercing gaze of Mr. Gillette as she remembered him in his most famous role.

"It leads straight to the fireplace!" she murmured in tones of Sherlockian gravity. Bailey repressed an involuntary smile. But her next words gave him genuine food for thought.

She stared at the mantel of the fireplace accusingly.

"It's been going through my mind for the last few minutes that no chimney flue runs up this side of the house!" she said.

Bailey stared. "Then why the fireplace?"

"That's what I'm going to find out!" said the spinster grimly. She started to rap the mantel, testing it for secret springs.

"Jack! Jack!" It was Dale's voice, low and cautious, coming from the landing of the stairs.

Bailey stepped to the door of the trunk room.

"Come in," he called in reply. "And shut the door behind you."

Dale entered, closing the door behind her.

"Where are the others?"

"They're still searching the house. There's no sign of anybody."

"They haven't found—Mr. Anderson?"

Dale shook her head. "Not yet."

She turned toward her aunt. Miss Cornelia had begun to enjoy herself once more.

Rapping on the mantelpiece, poking and pressing various corners and sections of the mantel itself, she remembered all the detective stories she had ever read and thought, with a sniff of scorn, that she could better them. There were always sliding panels and hidden drawers in detective stories and the detective discovered them by rapping just as she was doing, and listening for a hollow sound in answer. She rapped on the wall above the mantel—exactly—there was the hollow echo she wanted.

"Hollow as Lizzie's head!" she said triumphantly. The fireplace was obviously not what it seemed, there must be a space behind it unaccounted for in the building plans. Now what was the next step detectives always took? Oh, yes—they looked for panels; panels that moved. And when one shoved them away there was a button or something. She pushed and pressed and finally something did move. It was the mantelpiece itself, false grate and all, which began to swing out into the room, revealing behind a dark, hollow cubbyhole, some six feet by six—the Hidden Room at last!

"Oh, Jack, be careful!" breathed Dale as her lover took Miss Cornelia's candle and moved toward the dark hiding-place. But her eyes had already caught the outlines of a tall iron safe in the gloom and in spite of her fears, her lips formed a wordless cry of victory.

But Jack Bailey said nothing at all. One glance had shown him that the safe was empty.

The tragic collapse of all their hopes was almost more than they could bear. Coming on top of the nerve-racking events of the night, it left them dazed and directionless. It was, of course, Miss Cornelia who recovered first.

"Even without the money," she said, "the mere presence of this safe here, hidden away, tells the story. The fact that someone else knew and got here first cannot alter that.''

But she could not cheer them. It was Lizzie who created a diversion. Lizzie who had bolted into the hall at the first motion of the mantelpiece outward and who now, with equal precipitation, came bolting back. She rushed into the room, slamming the door behind her, and collapsed into a heap of moaning terror at her mistress's feet. At first she was completely inarticulate, but after a time she muttered that she had seen "him" and then fell to groaning again.

The same thought was in all their minds, that in some corner of the upper floor she had come across the body of Anderson. But when Miss Cornelia finally quieted her and asked this, she shook her head.

"It was the Bat I saw," was her astounding statement. "He dropped through the skylight out there and ran along the hall. I *saw* him I tell you. He went right by me!"

"Nonsense," said Miss Cornelia briskly. "How can you say such a thing?"

But Bailey pushed forward and took Lizzie by the shoulder.

"What did he look like?"

"He hadn't any face. He was all black where his face ought to be."

"Do you mean he wore a mask?"

"Maybe. I don't know."

She collapsed again but when Bailey, followed by Miss Cornelia, made a move toward the door she broke into frantic wailing.

"Don't go out there!" she shrieked. "He's there I tell you. I'm not crazy. If you open that door, he'll shoot."

But the door was already open and no shot came. With the departure of Bailey and Miss Cornelia, and the resulting darkness due to their taking the candle, Lizzie and Dale were left alone. The girl was faint with disappointment and strain; she sat huddled on a trunk, saying nothing, and after a moment or so Lizzie roused to her condition.

"Not feeling sick, are you?" she asked.

"I feel a little queer."

"Who wouldn't in the dark here with that monster loose somewhere near by?" But she stirred herself and got up. "I'd better get the smelling salts," she said heavily. "God knows I hate to move, but if there's one place safer in this house than another, I've yet to find it."

She went out, leaving Dale alone. The trunk room was dark, save that now and then as the candle appeared and reappeared the doorway was faintly outlined. On this outline she kept her eyes fixed, by way of comfort, and thus passed the next few moments. She felt weak and dizzy and entirely despairing.

Then—the outline was not so clear. She had heard nothing but there was something in the doorway. It stood there, formless, diabolical, and then she saw what was happening. It was closing the door. Afterward she was mercifully not to remember what came next; the figure was perhaps intent on what was going on outside, or her own movements may have been as silent as its own. That she got into the mantel-room and even partially closed it behind her is certain, and that her description of what followed is fairly accurate is borne out by the facts as known.

The Bat was working rapidly. She heard his quick, nervous movements; apparently he had come back for something and secured it, for now he moved again toward the door. But he was too late; they were returning that way. She heard him mutter something and quickly turn the key in the lock. Then he seemed to run toward the window, and for some reason to recoil from it.

The next instant she realized that he was coming toward the mantel-room, that he intended to hide in it. There was no doubt in her mind as to his identity. It was the Bat, and in a moment more he would be shut in there with her.

She tried to scream and could not, and the next instant, when the Bat leaped into concealment beside her, she was in a dead faint on the floor.

Bailey meanwhile had crawled out on the roof and was carefully searching it. But other things were happening also. A disinterested observer could have seen very soon why the Bat had abandoned the window as a means of egress.

Almost before the mantel had swung to behind the archcriminal, the top of a tall pruning ladder had appeared at the window and by its quivering showed that someone was climbing up, rung by rung. Unsuspiciously enough he came on, pausing at the top to flash a light into the room, and then cautiously swinging a leg over the sill. It was the doctor. He gave a low whistle but there was no reply, save that, had he seen it, the mantel swung out an inch or two. Perhaps he was never so near death as that movement but that instant of irresolution on his part saved him, for by coming into the room he had taken himself out of range.

Even then he was very close to destruction, for after a brief pause and a second rather puzzled survey of the room, he started toward the mantel itself. Only the rattle of the doorknob stopped him, and a call from outside.

"Dale!" called Bailey's voice from the corridor. "Dale!"

"Dale! Dale! The door's locked!" cried Miss Cornelia. The doctor hesitated. The call came again.

"Dale! Dale!" and Bailey pounded on the door as if he meant to break it down.

The doctor made up his mind.

"Wait a moment!" he called. He stepped to the door and unlocked it. Bailey hurled himself into the room, followed by Miss Cornelia with her candle. Lizzie stood in the doorway, timidly, ready to leap for safety at a moment's notice.

"Why did you lock that door?" said Bailey angrily, threatening the doctor.

"But I didn't," said the latter, truthfully enough. Bailey made a movement of irritation. Then a glance about the room informed him of the amazing, the incredible fact. Dale was not there! She had disappeared!

"You—you," he stammered at the doctor. "Where's Miss Ogden? What have you done with her?"

The doctor was equally baffled.

"Done with her?" he said indignantly. "I don't know what you're talking about, I haven't seen her!"

"Then you didn't lock that door?" Bailey menaced him.

The doctor's denial was firm.

"Absolutely not. I was coming through the window when I heard your voice at the door!"

Bailey's eyes leaped to the window—yes—a ladder was there. The doctor might be speaking the truth after all. But if so, how and why had Dale disappeared?

The doctor's admission of his manner of entrance did not make Lizzie any the happier.

"In at the window—just like a bat!" she muttered in shaking tones. She would not have stayed in the doorway if she had not been afraid to move anywhere else.

"I saw lights up here from outside," continued the doctor easily. "And I thought—"

Miss Cornelia interrupted him. She had set down her candle and laid the revolver on the top of the clothes hamper and now stood gazing at the mantel-fireplace.

"The mantel's—closed!" she said.

The doctor stared. So the secret of the Hidden Room was a secret no longer. He saw ruin gaping before him—a bottomless abyss. "Damnation!" he cursed impotently under his breath.

Bailey turned on him savagely.

"Did you shut that mantel?"

"No!"

"I'll see whether you shut it or not!" Bailey leaped toward the fireplace. "Dale! Dale!" he called desperately, leaning against the mantel. His fingers groped for the knob that worked the mechanism of the hidden entrance.

The doctor picked up the single lighted candle from the hamper, as if to throw more light on Bailey's task. Bailey's fingers found the knob. He turned it. The mantel began to swing out into the room.

As it did so the doctor deliberately snuffed out the light of the candle he held, leaving the room in abrupt and obliterating darkness.

17

Anderson Makes
An Arrest

"Doctor, why did you put out that candle?" Miss Cornelia's voice cut the blackness like a knife.

"I didn't—I—"

"You did. I saw you do it."

The brief exchange of accusation and denial took but an instant of time, as the mantel swung wide open. The next instant there was a rush of feet across the floor, from the fireplace—the shock of a collision between two bodies—the sound of a heavy fall.

"What was that?" queried Bailey dazedly, with a feeling as if some great winged creature had brushed at him and passed.

Lizzie answered from the doorway.

"Oh, oh!" she groaned in stricken accents. "Somebody knocked me down and tramped on me!"

"Matches, quick!" commanded Miss Cornelia. "Where's the candle?"

The doctor was still trying to explain his curious action of a moment before.

"Awfully sorry, I assure you. It dropped out of the holder—ah, here it is!"

He held it up triumphantly. Bailey struck a match and lighted it. The wavering little flame showed Lizzie prostrate but vocal, in the doorway—and Dale lying on the floor of the Hidden Room, her eyes shut, and her face as drained of color as the face of a marble statue. For one horrible instant Bailey thought she must be dead.

He rushed to her wildly and picked her up in his arms. No—still breathing—thank God! He carried her tenderly to the only chair in the room.

"Doctor!"

The doctor, once more the physician, knelt at her side and felt for her pulse. And Lizzie, picking herself up from where the collision with some violent body had throw her, retrieved the smelling salts from the floor. It was onto this picture—the candlelight shining on strained faces, the dramatic figure of Dale, now semi-conscious, the desperate rage of Bailey—that a new actor appeared on the scene.

Anderson, the detective, stood in the doorway, holding a candle—as grim and menacing a figure as a man just arisen from the dead.

"That's right!" said Lizzie, unappalled for once. "Come in when everything's over!"

The doctor glanced up and met the detective's eyes, cold and menacing.

"You took my revolver from me downstairs," he said. "I'll trouble you for it."

The doctor got heavily to his feet. The others, their suspicions confirmed at last, looked at him with startled eyes. The detective seemed to enjoy the universal confusion his words had brought.

Slowly, with sullen reluctance, the doctor yielded up the stolen weapon. The detective examined it casually and replaced it in his hip pocket.

"I've something to settle with you pretty soon," he said through clenched teeth, addressing the doctor. "And I'll settle it properly. Now, what's this?"

He indicated Dale, her face still and waxen, her breath coming so faintly she seemed hardly to breathe at all as Miss Cornelia and Bailey tried to revive her.

"She's coming to—" said Miss Cornelia triumphantly, as a first faint flush of color reappeared in the girl's cheeks. "We found her shut in there, Mr. Anderson," the spinster added, pointing toward the gaping entrance of the Hidden Room.

A gleam crossed the detective's face. He went up to examine the secret chamber. As he did so, Doctor Wells, who had been inching surreptitiously toward the door, sought the opportunity of slipping out unobserved.

But Anderson was not to be caught napping again.

"Wells!" he barked. The doctor stopped and turned.

"Where were you when she was locked in this room?"

The doctor's eyes sought the floor—the walls—wildly—for any possible loophole of escape.

"I didn't shut her in if that's what you mean!" he said defiantly.

"There was *someone* shut in there with her!" He gestured at the Hidden Room. "Ask these people here."

Miss Cornelia caught him up at once.

"The fact remains, Doctor," she said, her voice cold with anger, "that we left her here alone. When we came back you were here. The corridor door was locked, and she was in that room—unconscious!"

She moved forward to throw the light of her candle on the Hidden Room as the detective passed into it, gave it a swift professional glance, and stepped out again. But she had not finished her story by any means.

"As we opened that door," she continued to the detective, tapping the false mantel, "the doctor deliberately extinguished our only candle!"

"Do you know who was in that room?" queried the detective fiercely, wheeling on the doctor.

But the latter had evidently made up his mind to cling stubbornly to a policy of complete denial.

"No," he said sullenly. "I didn't put out the candle. It fell. And I didn't lock that door into the hall. I found it locked!"

A sigh of relief from Bailey now centered everyone's attention on himself and Dale. At last the girl was recovering from the shock of her terrible experience and regaining consciousness. Her eyelids fluttered, closed again, opened once more. She tried to sit up, weakly, clinging to Bailey's shoulder. The color returned to her cheeks, the stupor left her eyes.

She gave the Hidden Room a hunted little glance and then shuddered violently.

"Please close that awful door," she said in a tremulous voice. "I don't want to see it again."

The detective went silently to close the iron doors.

"What happened to you? Can't you remember?" faltered Bailey, on his knees at her side.

The shadow of an old terror lay on the girl's face.

"I was in here alone in the dark," she began slowly—"Then, as I looked at the doorway there, I saw there was somebody there. He came in and closed the door. I didn't know what to do, so I slipped in—there, and after a while I knew he was coming in too, for he couldn't get out. Then I must have fainted."

"There was nothing about the figure that you recognized?"

"No. Nothing."

"But we know it was the Bat," put in Miss Cornelia.

The detective laughed sardonically. The old duel of opposing theories between the two seemed about to recommence.

"Still harping on the Bat!" he said, with a little sneer.

Miss Cornelia stuck to her guns.

"I have every reason to believe that the Bat is in this house," she said.

The detective gave another jarring, mirthless laugh.

"And that he took the Union Bank money out of the safe, I suppose?" he jeered. "No, Miss Van Gorder."

He wheeled on the doctor now.

"Ask the doctor who took the Union Bank money out of that safe!" he thundered. "Ask the doctor who attacked me downstairs in the living-room, knocked me senseless, and locked me in the billiard room!"

There was an astounded silence. The detective added a parting shot to his indictment of the doctor.

"The next time you put handcuffs on a man be sure to take the key out of his vest pocket," he said, biting off the words.

Rage and consternation mingled on the doctor's countenance; on the faces of the others astonishment was followed by a growing certainty. Only Miss Cornelia clung stubbornly to her original theory.

"Perhaps I'm an obstinate old woman," she said in tones which obviously showed that if so she was rather proud of it, "but the doctor and all the rest of us were locked in the living-room not ten minutes ago!"

"By the Bat, I suppose!" mocked Anderson.

"By the Bat!" insisted Miss Cornelia inflexibly. "Who else would have fastened a dead bat to the door downstairs? Who else would have the bravado to do that? Or what you call the imagination?"

In spite of himself Anderson seemed to be impressed.

"The Bat, eh?" he muttered, then, changing his tone, "You knew about this hidden room, Wells?" he shot at the doctor.

"Yes." The doctor bowed his head.

"And you knew the money was in the room?"

"Well, I was wrong, wasn't I?" parried the doctor. "You can look for yourself. That safe is empty."

The detective brushed his evasive answer aside.

"You were up in this room earlier tonight," he said in tones of apparent certainty.

"No, I couldn't *get* up!" the doctor still insisted, with strange violence for a man who had already admitted such damning knowledge.

The detective's face was a study in disbelief.

"You know where that money is, Wells, and I'm going to find it!"

This last taunt seemed to goad the doctor beyond endurance.

"Good God!" he shouted recklessly. "Do you suppose if I knew where it is, I'd be here? I've had plenty of chances to get away! No, you can't pin anything on me, Anderson! It isn't criminal to have known that room is here."

He paused, trembling with anger and, curiously enough, with an anger that seemed at least half sincere.

"Oh, don't be so damned virtuous!" said the detective brutally. "Maybe you haven't been upstairs but, unless I miss my guess, you know who was!"

The doctor's face changed a little.

"What about Richard Fleming?" persisted the detective scornfully.

The doctor drew himself up.

"I never killed him!" he said so impressively that even Bailey's faith in his guilt was shaken. "I don't even own a revolver!"

The detective alone maintained his attitude unchanged.

"You come with me, Wells," he ordered, with a jerk of his thumb toward the door. "This time I'll do the locking up."

The doctor, head bowed, prepared to obey. The detective took up a candle to light their path. Then he turned to the others for a moment.

"Better get the young lady to bed," he said with a gruff kindliness of manner. "I think that I can promise you a quiet night from now on."

"I'm glad you think so, Mr. Anderson!" Miss Cornelia insisted on the last word. The detective ignored the satiric twist of her speech, motioned the doctor out ahead of him, and followed. The faint glow of his candle flickered a moment and vanished toward the stairs.

It was Bailey who broke the silence.

"I can believe a good bit about Wells," he said, "but not that he stood on that staircase and killed Dick Fleming."

Miss Cornelia roused from deep thought.

"Of course not," she said briskly. "Go down and fix Miss Dale's bed, Lizzie. And then bring up some wine."

"Down there, where the Bat is?" Lizzie demanded.

"The Bat has gone."

"Don't you believe it. He's just got his hand in!"

But at last Lizzie went, and, closing the door behind her, Miss Cornelia proceeded more or less to think out loud.

"Suppose," she said, "that the Bat, or whoever it was shut in there with you, killed Richard Fleming. Say that he is the one Lizzie saw coming in by the terrace door. Then he knew where the money was for he went directly up the stairs. But that is two hours ago or more. Why didn't he get the money, if it was here, and get away?"

"He may have had trouble with the combination."

"Perhaps. Anyhow, he was on the small staircase when Dick Fleming started up, and of course he shot him. That's clear enough. Then he finally got the safe open, after locking us in below, and my coming up interrupted him. How on earth did he get out on the roof?"

Bailey glanced out the window.

"It would be possible from here. Possible, but not easy."

"But, if he could do that," she persisted, "he could have got away, too. There are trellises and porches. Instead of that he came back here to this room." She stared at the window. "Could a man have done that with one hand?"

"Never in the world."

Saying nothing, but deeply thoughtful, Miss Cornelia made a fresh progress around the room.

"I know very little about bank-currency," she said finally. "Could such a sum as was looted from the Union Bank be carried away in a man's pocket?"

Bailey considered the question.

"Even in bills of large denomination it would make a pretty sizeable bundle," he said.

But that Miss Cornelia's deductions were correct, whatever they were, was in question when Lizzie returned with the elderberry wine. Apparently Miss Cornelia was to be like the man who repaired the clock: she still had certain things left over.

For Lizzie announced that the Unknown was ranging the second floor hall. From the time they had escaped from the living-room this man had not been seen or thought of, but that he was a part of the mystery there could by no doubt. It flashed over Miss Cornelia, that, although he could not possibly have locked them in, in the darkness that followed he could easily have fastened the bat to the door. For the first time it occurred to her that the archcriminal might not be working alone, and that the entrance of the Unknown might have been a carefully devised ruse to draw them all together and hold them there.

Nor was Beresford's arrival with the statement that the Unknown was moving through the house below particularly comforting.

"He may be dazed, or he may not," he said. "Personally, this is not a time to trust anybody."

Beresford knew nothing of what had just occurred, and now seeing Bailey he favored him with an ugly glance.

"In the absence of Anderson, Bailey," he added, "I don't propose to trust you too far. I'm making it my business from now on to see that you don't try to get away. Get that?"

But Bailey heard him without particular resentment.

"All right," he said. "But I'll tell you this. Anderson is here and has arrested the doctor. Keep your eye on me, if you think it's your duty, but don't talk to me as if I were a criminal. You don't know that yet."

"The doctor!" Beresford gasped.

But Miss Cornelia's keen ears had heard a sound outside and her eyes were focused on the door.

"The doorknob is moving," she said in a hushed voice.

Beresford moved to the door and jerked it violently open.

The butler, Billy, almost pitched into the room.

18

The Bat Still Flies

He stepped back in the doorway, looked out, then turned to them again.

"I come in, please?" he said pathetically, his hands quivering. "I not like to stay in dark."

Miss Cornelia took pity on him.

"Come in, Billy, of course. What is it? Anything the matter?"

Billy glanced about nervously.

"Man with sore head."

"What about him?"

"Act very strange." Again Billy's slim hands trembled.

Beresford broke in. "The man who fell into the room downstairs?"

Billy nodded.

"Yes. On second floor, walking around."

Beresford smiled, a bit smugly.

"I told you!" he said to Miss Cornelia. "I didn't think he was as dazed as he pretended to be."

Miss Cornelia, too, had been pondering the problem of the Unknown. She reached a swift decision. If he were what he pretended to be, a dazed wanderer, he could do them no harm. If he were not, a little strategy properly employed might unravel the whole mystery.

"Bring him up here, Billy," she said, turning to the butler.

Billy started to obey. But the darkness of the corridor seemed to appall him anew the moment he took a step toward it.

"You give candle, please?" he asked with a pleading expression. "Don't like dark."

Miss Cornelia handed him one of the two precious candles. Then his present terror reminded her of that one other occasion when she had seen him lose completely his stoic Oriental calm.

"Billy," she queried, "what did you see when you came running down the stairs before we were locked in, down below?"

The candle shook like a reed in Billy's grasp.

"Nothing!" he gasped with obvious untruth, though it did not seem so much as if he wished to conceal what he had seen as that he was trying to convince himself he had seen nothing.

"Nothing!" said Lizzie scornfully. "It was some nothing that would make him drop a bottle of whiskey!"

But Billy only backed toward the door, smiling apologetically.

"Thought I saw ghost," he said, and went out and down the stairs, the candlelight flickering, growing fainter, and finally disappearing. Silence and eerie darkness enveloped them all as they waited. And suddenly out of the blackness came a sound.

Something was flapping and thumping around the room.

"That's damned odd," muttered Beresford uneasily. "There *is* something moving around the room."

"It's up near the ceiling!" cried Bailey as the sound began again.

Lizzie began a slow wail of doom and disaster.

"Oh—h—h—h—"

"Good God!" cried Beresford abruptly. "It hit me in the face!" He slapped his hands together in a vain attempt to capture the flying intruder.

Lizzie rose.

"I'm going!" she announced. "I don't know where, but I'm going!"

She took a wild step in the direction of the door. Then the flapping noise was all about her, her nose was bumped by an invisible object and she gave a horrified shriek.

"It's in my hair!" she screamed madly. "It's in my hair!"

The next instant Baily gave a triumphant cry.

"I've got it! It's a bat!"

Lizzie sank to her knees, still moaning, and Bailey carried the cause of the trouble over to the window and threw it out.

But the result of the absurd incident was a further destruction of their morale. Even Beresford, so far calm with the quiet of the virtuous onlooker, was now pallid in the light of the matches they successively lighted. And onto this strained situation came at last Billy and the Unknown.

The Unknown still wore his air of dazed bewilderment, true or feigned, but at least he was not able to walk without support. They stared at him, at his tattered, muddy garments, at the threads of rope still clinging to his ankles—and wondered. He returned their stares vacantly.

"Come in," began Miss Cornelia. "Sit down." He obeyed both commands docilely enough.

"Are you better now?"

"Somewhat." His words still came very slowly.

"Billy, you can go."

"I stay, please!" said Billy wistfully, making no movement to leave. His gesture toward the darkness of the corridor spoke louder than words.

Bailey watched him, suspicion dawning in his eyes. He could not account for the butler's inexplicable terror of being left alone.

"Anderson intimated that the doctor had an accomplice in this house," he said, crossing to Billy and taking him by the arm. "Why isn't this the man?" Billy cringed away. "Please, no," he begged pitifully.

Bailey turned him around so that he faced the Hidden Room.

"Did you know that room was there?" he questioned, his doubts still unquieted.

Billy shook his head.

"No."

"He couldn't have locked us in," said Miss Cornelia. "He was *with* us."

Bailey demurred, not to her remark itself, but to its implication of Billy's entire innocence.

"He may *know* who did it. Do you?"

Billy shook his head.

Bailey remained unconvinced.

"Who did you see at the head of the small staircase?" he queried imperatively. "Now we're through with nonsense; I want the truth!"

Billy shivered.

"See face—that's all," he brought out at last.

"Whose face?"

Again it was evident that Billy knew or thought he knew more than he was willing to tell.

"Don't know," he said with obvious untruth, looking down at the floor.

"Never mind, Billy," cut in Miss Cornelia. To her mind questioning Billy was wasting time. She looked at the Unknown.

"Solve the mystery of *this* man and we may get at the facts," she said in accents of conviction.

As Bailey turned toward her questioningly, Billy attempted to steal silently out of the door, apparently preferring any fears that might lurk in the darkness of the corridor to a further grilling on the subject of whom or what he had seen on the alcove stairs. But Bailey caught the movement out of the tail of his eye.

"You stay here," he commanded. Billy stood frozen.

Beresford raised the candle so that it cast its light full in the Unknown's face.

"This chap claims to have lost his memory," he said dubiously. "I suppose a blow on the head might do that, I don't know."

"I wish somebody would knock *me* on the head! *I'd* like to forget a few things!" moaned Lizzie, but the interruption went unregarded.

"Don't you even know your name?" queried Miss Cornelia of the Unknown.

The Unknown shook his head with a slow, laborious gesture.

"Not—yet."

"Or where you came from?"

Once more the battered head made its movement of negation.

"Do you remember how you got in this house?"

The Unknown made an effort.

"Yes—I—remember—that—all—right—" he said, apparently undergoing an enormous strain in order to make himself speak at all. He put his hand to his head.

"My—head—aches—to—beat—the—band," he continued slowly.

Miss Cornelia was at a loss. If this were acting, it was at least fine acting.

"How did you happen to come to this house?" she persisted, her voice unconsciously tuning itself to the slow, laborious speech of the Unknown.

"Saw—the—lights."

Bailey broke in with a question.

"Where were you when you saw the lights?"

The Unknown wet his lips with his tongue, painfully.

"I—broke—out—of—the—garage," he said at length.

This was unexpected. A general movement of interest ran over the group.

"How did you get there?" Beresford took his turn as questioner.

The Unknown shook his head, so slowly and deliberately that Miss Cornelia's fingers itched to shake him in spite of his injuries.

"I—don't—know."

"Have you been robbed?" queried Bailey with keen suspicion.

The Unknown mumbled something unintelligible. Then he seemed to get command of his tongue again.

"Everything gone—out of—my pockets," he said.

"Including your watch?" pursued Bailey, remembering the watch that Beresford had found in the grounds.

The Unknown would neither affirm nor deny.

"If—I—had—a—watch—it's gone," he said with maddening deliberation. "All my—papers—are gone."

Miss Cornelia pounced upon this last statement like a cat upon a mouse.

"How do you know you *had* papers?" she asked sharply.

For the first time the faintest flicker of a smile seemed to appear for a moment on the Unknown's features. Then it vanished as abruptly as it had come.

"Most men—carry papers—don't they?" he asked, staring blindly in front of him. "I'm dazed—but—my mind's—all—right. If you—ask me—I—think—I'm—d-damned funny!"

He gave the ghost of a chuckle. Bailey and Beresford exchanged glances.

"Did you ring the house phone?" insisted Miss Cornelia.

The Unknown nodded.

"Yes."

Miss Cornelia and Bailey gave each other a look of wonderment.

"I—leaned against—the button—in the garage—" he went on. "Then—I think—maybe I—fainted. That's not clear."

His eyelids drooped. He seemed about to faint again.

Dale rose, and came over to him, with a sympathetic movement of her hand.

"You don't remember how you were hurt?" she asked gently.

The Unknown stared ahead of him, his eyes filming, as if he were trying to puzzle it out.

"No," he said at last. "The first thing I remember—I was in the garage—tied." He moved his lips. "I was—gagged—too—that's—what's the matter—with my tongue—now—Then—I got myself—free—and—got out—of a window—"

Miss Cornelia made a movement to question him further. Beresford stopped her with his hand uplifted.

"Just a moment, Miss Van Gorder. Anderson ought to know of this."

He started for the door without perceiving the flash of keen intelligence and alertness that had lit the Unknown's countenance for an instant, as once before, at the mention of the detective's name. But just as he reached the door the detective entered.

He halted for a moment, staring at the strange figure of the Unknown.

"A new element in our mystery, Mr. Anderson," said Miss Cornelia, remembering that the detective might not have heard of the mysterious stranger before—as he had been locked in the billiard room when the latter had made his queer entrance.

The detective and the Unknown gazed at each other for a moment—the Unknown with his old expression of vacant stupidity.

"Quite dazed, poor fellow," Miss Cornelia went on.

Beresford added other words of explanation.

"He doesn't remember what happened to him. Curious, isn't it?"

The detective still seemed puzzled.

"How did he get into the house?"

"He came through the terrace door some time ago," answered Miss Cornelia. "Just before we were locked in."

Her answer seemed to solve the problem to Anderson's satisfaction.

"Doesn't remember anything, eh?" he said dryly. He crossed over to the mysterious stranger and put his hand under the Unknown's chin, jerking his head up roughly.

"Look up here!" he commanded.

The Unknown stared at him for an instant with blank, vacuous eyes. Then his head dropped back upon his breast again.

"Look up, you—" muttered the detective, jerking his head again. "This losing your memory stuff doesn't go down with me!" His eyes bored into the Unknown's.

"It doesn't—go down—very well—with me—either," said the Unknown weakly, making no movement of protest against Anderson's rough handling.

"Did you ever see me before?" demanded the latter. Beresford held the candle closer so that he might watch the Unknown's face for any involuntary movement of betrayal.

But the Unknown made no such movement. He gazed at Anderson, apparently with the greatest bewilderment, then his eyes cleared, he seemed to be about to remember who the detective was.

"You're—the—doctor—I—saw—downstairs—aren't you?" he said innocently. The detective set his jaw. He started off on a new tack.

"Does this belong to you?" he said suddenly, plucking from his pocket the battered gold watch that Beresford had found and waving it before the Unknown's blank face.

The Unknown stared at it a moment, as a child might stare at a new toy, with no gleam of recognition. Then—

"Maybe," he admitted. "I—don't—know."

His voice trailed off. He fell back against Bailey's arm.

Miss Cornelia gave a little shiver. The third degree in reality was less pleasant to watch than it had been to read about in the pages of her favorite detective stories.

"He's evidently been attacked," she said, turning to Anderson. "He claims to have recovered consciousness in the garage where he was tied hand and foot!"

"He does, eh?" said the detective heavily. He glared at the Unknown. "If you'll give me five minutes alone with him, I'll get the *truth out of him!*" he promised.

A look of swift alarm swept over the Unknown's face at the words, unperceived by any except Miss Cornelia. The others started obediently to yield to the detective's behest and leave him alone with his prisoner. Miss Cornelia was the first to move toward the door. On her way, she turned.

"Do you believe that money is irrevocably gone?" she asked of Anderson.

The detective smiled.

"There's no such word as 'irrevocable' in my vocabulary," he answered. "But I believe it's out of the house, if that's what you mean."

Miss Cornelia still hesitated, on the verge of departure.

"Suppose I tell you that there are certain facts that you have overlooked?" she said slowly.

"Still on the trail!" muttered the detective sardonically. He did not even glance at her. He seemed only anxious that the other members of the group would get out of his way for once and leave him a clear field for his work.

"I was right about the doctor, wasn't I?" she insisted.

"Just fifty per cent right," said Anderson crushingly. "And the doctor didn't turn that trick alone. Now—" he went on with weary patience, "if you'll *all* go out and close that door—"

Miss Cornelia, defeated, took a candle from Bailey and stepped into the corridor. Her figure stiffened. She gave an audible gasp of dismayed surprise.

"Quick!" she cried, turning back to the others and gesturing toward corridor. "A man just went through that skylight and out onto the roof!"

19

Murder on Murder

"Out on the roof!"

"Come on Beresford!"

"Hustle—you men! He may be armed!"

"Righto—coming!"

And following Miss Cornelia's lead, Jack Bailey, Anderson, Beresford, and Billy dashed out into the corridor, leaving Dale and the frightened Lizzie alone with the Unknown.

"And *I'd* run if my legs would!" Lizzie despaired.

"Hush!" said Dale, her ears strained for sounds of conflict. Lizzie, creeping closer to her for comfort, stumbled over one of the Unknown's feet and promptly set up a new wail.

"How do we know this fellow right here isn't *the Bat?*" she asked in a blood-chilling whisper, nearly stabbing the unfortunate Unknown in the eye with her thumb as she pointed at him. The Unknown was either too dazed or too crafty to make any answer. His silence confirmed Lizzie's worst suspicions. She fairly hugged the floor and began to pray in a whisper.

Miss Cornelia re-entered cautiously with her candle, closing the door gently behind her as she came.

"What did you see?" gasped Dale.

Miss Cornelia smiled broadly.

"I didn't see anything," she admitted with the greatest calm. "I had to get that dratted detective out of the room before I assassinated him."

"Nobody went through the skylight?" said Dale incredulously.

"They have now," answered Miss Cornelia with obvious satisfaction. "The whole outfit of them."

She stole a glance at the veiled eyes of the Unknown. He was lying limply back in his chair, as if the excitement had been too much for him, and yet she could have sworn she had seen him leap to his feet, like a man in full possession of his faculties, when she had given her false cry of alarm.

"Then why did you—" began Dale dazedly, unable to fathom her aunt's reasons for her trick.

"Because," interrupted Miss Cornelia decidedly, "that money's in this room. If the man who took it out of the safe got away with it, why did he come back and hide there?"

Her forefinger jabbed at the hidden chamber wherein the masked intruder had terrified Dale with threats of instant death.

"He got it out of the safe—and that's as far as he *did* get with it," she persisted inexorably. "There's a *hat* behind that safe, a man's felt hat!"

So this was the discovery she had hinted of to Anderson before he rebuffed her proffer of assistance!

"Oh, I wish he'd take his hat and go home!" groaned Lizzie inattentive to all but her own fears.

Miss Cornelia did not even bother to rebuke her. She crossed behind the wicker clothes hamper and picked up something from the floor.

"A half-burned candle," she mused. "Another thing the detective overlooked."

She stepped back to the center of the room, looking knowingly from the candle to the Hidden Room and back again.

"Oh, my God—another one!" shrieked Lizzie as the dark shape of a man appeared suddenly outside the window, as if materialized from the air.

Miss Cornelia snatched up the revolver from the top of the hamper.

"Don't shoot, it's Jack!" came a warning cry from Dale as she recognized the figure of her lover.

Miss Cornelia laid her revolver down on the hamper again. The vacant eyes of the Unknown caught the movement.

Bailey swung in through the window, panting a little from his exertions.

"The man Lizzie saw drop from the skylight undoubtedly got to the roof from this window," he said. "It's quite easy."

"But not with one hand," said Miss Cornelia, with her gaze now directed at the row of tall closets around the walls of the room. "When that detective comes back I may have a surprise party for him," she muttered, with a gleam of hope in her eye.

Dale explained the situation to Jack.

"Aunt Cornelia thinks the money's still here."

Miss Cornelia snorted.

"I *know* it's here." She started to open the closets, one after the other, beginning at the left. Bailey saw what she was doing and began to help her.

Not so Lizzie. She sat on the floor in a heap, her eyes riveted on the Unknown, who in his turn was gazing at Miss Cornelia's revolver on the hamper with the intent stare of a baby or an idiot fascinated by a glittering piece of glass.

Dale noticed the curious tableau.

"Lizzie, what are you looking at?" she said with a nervous shake in her voice.

"What's *he* looking at?" asked Lizzie sepulchrally, pointing at the Unknown. Her pointed forefinger drew his eyes away from the revolver; he sank back into his former apathy, listless, drooping.

Miss Cornelia rattled the knob of a high closet by the other wall.

"This one is locked and the key's gone," she announced. A new flicker of interest grew in the eyes of the Unknown. Lizzie glanced away from him, terrified.

"If there's anything locked up in that closet," she whimpered, "you'd better let it stay! There's enough running loose in this house as it is!"

Unfortunately for her, her whimper drew Miss Cornelia's attention upon her.

"Lizzie, did you ever take that key?" the latter queried sternly.

"No'm," said Lizzie, too scared to dissimulate if she had wished. She wagged her head violently a dozen times, like a china figure on a mantelpiece.

Miss Cornelia pondered.

"It may be locked from the inside; I'll soon find out." She took a wire hairpin from her hair and pushed it through the keyhole. But there was no key on the other side; the hairpin went through without obstruction. Repeated efforts to jerk the door open failed. And finally Miss Cornelia bethought herself of a key from the other closet doors.

Dale and Lizzie on one side, Bailey on the other, collected the keys of the other closets from their locks while Miss Cornelia stared at the one whose doors were closed as if she would force its secret from it with her eyes. The Unknown had been so quiet during the last few minutes, that, unconsciously, the others had ceased to pay much attention to him, except the casual attention one devotes to a piece of furniture. Even Lizzie's eyes were now fixed on the locked closet. And the Unknown himself was the first to notice this.

At once his expression altered to one of cunning—cautiously, with infinite patience, he began to inch his chair over toward the wicker clothes hamper. The noise of the others, moving about the room, drowned out what little he made in moving his chair.

At last he was within reach of the revolver. His hand shot out in one swift sinuous thrust, clutched the weapon, withdrew. He then concealed the revolver among his tattered garments as best he could and, cautiously as before, inched his chair back again to its original position. When the others noticed him again, the mask of lifelessness was back on his face and one could have sworn he had not changed his position by the breadth of an inch.

"There, that unlocked it!" cried Miss Cornelia triumphantly at last, as the key to one of the other closet doors slid smoothly into the lock and she heard the click that meant victory.

She was about to throw open the closet door. But Bailey motioned her back.

"I'd keep *back* a little," he cautioned. "You don't know what may be inside."

"Mercy sakes, who wants to know?" shivered Lizzie. Dale and Miss Cornelia, too, stepped aside involuntarily as Bailey took the candle and prepared, with a good deal of caution, to open the closet door.

The door swung open at last. He could look in. He did so—and stared appalled at what he saw, while goose flesh crawled on his spine and the hairs of his head stood up.

After a moment he closed the door of the closet and turned back, white-faced, to the others.

"What is it?" said Dale aghast. "What did you see?"

Bailey found himself unable to answer for a moment. Then he pulled himself together. He turned to Miss Van Gorder.

"Miss Cornelia, I think we have found the ghost the Jap butler saw," he said slowly. "How are your nerves?"

Miss Cornelia extended a hand that did not tremble.

"Give me the candle."

He did so. She went to the closet and opened the door.

Whatever faults Miss Cornelia may have had, lack of courage was not one of them—or the ability to withstand a stunning mental shock. Had it been otherwise she might well have crumpled to the floor, as if struck down by an invisible hammer, the moment the closet door swung open before her.

Huddled on the floor of the closet was the body of a man. So crudely had he been crammed into this hiding-place that he lay twisted and bent. And as if to add to the horror of the moment one arm, released from its confinement, now slipped and slid out into the floor of the room.

Miss Cornelia's voice sounded strange to her own ears when finally she spoke.

"But who is it?"

"It is—or was—Courtleigh Flemming," said Bailey dully.

"But how can it be? Mr. Fleming died two weeks ago. I—"

"He died in this house sometime tonight. The body is still warm."

"But who killed him? The Bat?"

"Isn't it likely that the doctor did it? The man who has been his accomplice all along? Who probably bought a cadaver out West and buried it with honors here not long ago?"

He spoke without bitterness. Whatever resentment he might have felt died in that awful presence.

"He got into the house early tonight," he said, "probably with the doctor's connivance. That wrist watch there is probably the luminous eye Lizzie thought she saw."

But Miss Cornelia's face was still thoughtful, and he went on:

"Isn't it clear, Miss Van Gorder?" he queried, with a smile. "The doctor and old Mr. Fleming formed a conspiracy, both needed money, lots of it. Fleming was to rob the bank and hide the money here. Well's part was to issue a false death certificate in the West, and bury a substitute body, secured God knows how. It was easy; it kept the name of the president of the Union Bank free from suspicion—and it put the blame on me."

He paused, thinking it out.

"Only they slipped up in one place. Dick Fleming leased the house to you and they couldn't get it back."

"Then you are sure," said Miss Cornelia quickly, "that tonight Courtleigh Fleming broke in, with the doctor's assistance—and that he killed Dick, his own nephew, from the staircase?"

"Aren't you?" asked Bailey surprised. The more he thought of it the less clearly could he visualize it any other way.

Miss Cornelia shook her head decidedly.

"No."

Bailey thought her merely obstinate—unwilling to give up, for pride's sake, her own pet theory of the activities of the Bat.

"Wells tried to get out of the house tonight with that blueprint.

Why? Because he knew the moment we got it, we'd come up here—and Fleming was here.''

"Perfectly true," nodded Miss Cornelia. "And then?"

"Old Fleming killed Dick and Wells killed Fleming," said Bailey succinctly. "You can't get away from it!"

But Miss Cornelia still shook her head. The explanation was too mechanical. It laid too little emphasis on the characters of those most concerned.

"No," she said. "No. The doctor isn't a murderer. He's as puzzled as we are about some things. He and Courtleigh Fleming were working together but remember this—Doctor Wells was locked in the living-room with us. He'd been trying to get up the stairs all evening and failed every time."

But Bailey was as convinced of the truth of his theory as she of hers.

"He was here ten minutes ago, locked in this room," he said with a glance at the ladder up which the doctor had ascended.

"I'll grant you that," said Miss Cornelia. "But—" She thought back swiftly. "But at the same time an Unknown Masked Man was locked in that mantelroom with Dale. The doctor put out the candle when you opened that Hidden Room. *Why? Because he thought Courtleigh Fleming was hiding there?*" Now the missing pieces of her puzzle were falling into their places with a vengeance. "But at this moment," she continued, "the doctor believes that Fleming has made his escape! No, we haven't solved the mystery yet. There's another element—an *unknown* element," her eyes rested for a moment upon the , "and that element is—the Bat!"

She paused, impressively. The others stared at her, no longer able to deny the sinister plausibility of her theory. But this new tangling of the mystery, just when the black threads seemed raveled out at last, was almost too much for Dale.

"Oh, call the detective!" she stammered, on the verge of hysterical tears. "Let's get through with this thing! I can't bear any more!"

But Miss Cornelia did not even hear her. Her mind, strung now to concert pitch, had harked back to the point it had reached some time ago, and which all recent distractions had momentarily obliterated.

Had the money been taken out of the house or had it not? In that mad rush for escape had the man hidden with Dale in the recess back of the mantel carried his booty with him, or left it behind? It was not in the Hidden Room, that was certain.

Yet she was so hopeless by that time that her first search was purely perfunctory.

During her progress about the room the Unknown's eyes followed her, but so still had he sat, so amazing had been the discovery of the body, that no one any longer observed him. Now and then his head drooped forward as if actual weakness was almost overpowering him, but his eyes were keen and observant, and he was no longer taking the trouble to act—if he had been acting.

It was when Bailey finally opened the lid of a clothes hamper that they stumbled on their first clue.

"Nothing here but some clothes and books," he said, glancing inside.

"Books?" said Miss Cornelia dubiously. "I left no books in that hamper."

Bailey picked up one of the cheap paper novels and read its title aloud, with a wry smile.

"*Little Rosebud's Lover, Or The Cruel Revenge,*" by Laura Jean—"

"That's mine!" said Lizzie promptly. "Oh, Miss Neily, I tell you this house *is* haunted. I left that book in my satchel along with *Wedded But No Wife* and now—"

"Where's your satchel?" snapped Miss Cornelia, her eyes gleaming.

"Where's my satchel?" mumbled Lizzie, staring about as best she could. "I don't see it. If that wretch has stolen my satchel—!"

"Where did you leave it?"

"Up here. Right in this room. It was a new satchel too. I'll have the law on him, that's what I'll do."

"Isn't that your satchel, Lizzie?" asked Miss Cornelia, indicating a battered bag in a dark corner of shadows above the window.

Lizzie approached it gingerly.

"Yes'm," she admitted. But she did not dare approach very close to the recovered bag. It might bite her!

"Put it there on the hamper," ordered Miss Cornelia.

"I'm scared to touch it!" moaned Lizzie. "It may have a bomb in it!"

She took up the bag between finger and thumb and, holding it with the care she would have bestowed upon a bottle of nitroglycerin, carried it over to the hamper and set it down. Then she backed away from it, ready to leap for the door at a moment's warning.

Miss Cornelia started for the satchel. Then she remembered. She turned to Bailey.

"You open it," she said graciously. "If the money's there you're the one who ought to find it."

Bailey gave her a look of gratitude. Then, smiling at Dale encouragingly, he crossed over to the satchel, Dale at his heels. Miss Cornelia watched him fumble at the catch of the bag—even Lizzie drew closer. For a moment even the Unknown was forgotten.

Bailey gave a triumphant cry.

"The money's here!"

"Oh, thank God!" sobbed Dale.

It was an emotional moment. It seemed to have penetrated even through the haze enveloping the injured man in his chair. Slowly he got up, like a man who has been waiting for his moment, and now that it had come was in no hurry about it. With equal deliberation he drew the revolver and took a step forward. And at that instant a red glare appeared outside the open window and overhead could be heard the feet of the searchers, running.

"Fire!" screamed Lizzie, pointing to the window, even as Beresford's voice from the roof rang out in a shout. "The garage is burning!"

They turned toward the door to escape, but a strange and menacing figure blocked their way.

It was the Unknown, no longer the bewildered stranger who had stumbled in through the living-room door but a man with every faculty of mind and body alert and the light of a deadly purpose in his eyes. He covered the group with Miss Cornelia's revolver.

"This door is locked and the key is in my pocket!" he said in a savage voice as the red light at the window grew yet more vivid and muffled cries and tramplings from overhead betokened universal confusion and alarm.

20

"He Is—The Bat!"

Lizzie opened her mouth to scream. But for once she did not carry out her purpose.

"Not a sound out of *you!*" warned the Unknown brutally, almost jabbing the revolver into her ribs. He wheeled on Bailey.

"Close that satchel," he commanded, "and put it back where you found it!"

Bailey's fist closed. He took a step toward his captor.

"You—" he began in a furious voice. But the steely glint in the eyes of the Unknown was enough to give any man pause.

"Jack!" pleaded Dale. Bailey halted.

"Do what he tells you!" Miss Cornelia insisted, her voice shaking.

A brave man may be willing to fight with odds a hundred to one but only a fool will rush on certain death. Reluctantly, dejectedly, Bailey obeyed—stuffed the money back in the satchel and replaced the latter in its corner of shadows near the window.

"It's the Bat—it's the Bat!" whispered Lizzie eerily, and, for once her gloomy prophecies seemed to be in a fair way of justification, for "Blow out that candle!" commanded the Unknown sternly, and, after a moment of hesitation as Miss Cornelia's part, the room was again plunged in darkness except for the red glow at the window.

This finished Lizzie for the evening. She spoke from a dry throat.

"I'm going to scream!" she sobbed hysterically. "I can't keep it back!"

But at last she had encountered someone who had no patience with her vagaries.

"Put that woman in the mantel-room and shut her up!" ordered the Unknown, the muzzle of his revolver emphasizing his words with a savage little movement.

Bailey took Lizzie under the arms and started to execute the order. But the sometime colleen from Kerry did not depart without one Parthian arrow.

"Don't shove," she said in tones of the greatest dignity as she stumbled into the Hidden Room. "I'm damn glad to go!"

The iron doors shut behind her. Bailey watched the Unknown intently. One moment of relaxed vigilance and—

But though the Unknown was unlocking the door with his left hand the revolver in his right hand was as steady as a rock. He seemed to listen for a moment at the crack of the door.

"Not a sound if you value your lives!" he warned again. He shepherded them away from the direction of the window with his revolver.

"In a moment or two," he said in a hushed, taut voice, "a man will come into this room, either through the door or by that window—the man who started the fire to draw you out of this house."

Bailey threw aside all pride in his concern for Dale's safety.

"For God's sake, don't keep these women here!" he pleaded in low, tense tones.

The Unknown seemed to tower above him like a destroying angel.

"Keep them here where we can watch them!" he whispered with fierce impatience. "Don't you understand? There's a *killer* loose!"

And so for a moment they stood there, waiting for they knew not what. So swift had been the transition from joy to deadly terror, and now to suspense, that only Miss Cornelia's agile brain seemed able to respond.

"I begin to understand," she said in a low tone. "The man who struck you down and tied you in the garage—the man who killed Dick Fleming and stabbed that poor wretch in the closet—the man who locked us in downstairs and removed the money from that safe—the man who started the fire outside—is—"

"Sssh!" warned the Unknown imperatively as a sound from the direction of the window seemed to reach his ears. He ran quickly back to the corridor door and locked it.

"Stand back out of that light! The ladder!"

Miss Cornelia and Dale shrank back against the mantel. Bailey took up a post beside the window, the Unknown flattening himself against the wall beside him. There was a breathless pause.

The top of the extension ladder began to tremble. A black bulk stood clearly outlined against the diminishing red glow—the Bat, masked and sinister, on his last foray!

There was no sound as the killer stepped into the room. He waited for a second that seemed a year—still no sound. Then he turned cautiously toward the place where he had left the satchel—the beam of his flashlight picked it out.

In an instant the Unknown and Bailey were upon him. There was a short, ferocious struggle in the darkness, a gasp of laboring lungs, the thud of fighting bodies clenched in a death grapple.

"Get his gun!" muttered the Unknown hoarsely to Bailey as he tore the Bat's lean hands away from his throat. "Got it?"

"Yes," gasped Bailey. He jabbed the muzzle against a straining back. The Bat ceased to struggle. Bailey stepped a little away.

"I've still got you covered!" he said fiercely. The Bat made no sound.

"Hold out your hands, Bat, while I put on the bracelets," commanded the Unknown in tones of terse triumph. He snapped the steel cuffs on the wrists of the murderous prowler. "Sometimes even the cleverest Bat comes through a window at night and is caught. Double murder—burglary—and arson! That's a good night's work even for you, Bat!"

He switched his flashlight on the Bat's masked face. As he did so the house lights came on; the electric light company had at last remembered its duties. All blinked for an instant in the sudden illumination.

"Take off that handkerchief!" barked the Unknown, motioning at the black silk handkerchief that still hid the face of the Bat from recognition. Bailey stripped it from the haggard, desperate features with a quick movement—and stood appalled.

A simultaneous gasp went up from Dale and Miss Cornelia.

It was Anderson, the detective! And he was—the Bat!

"It's Mr. Anderson!" stuttered Dale, aghast at the discovery.

The Unknown gloated over his captive.

"*I'm* Anderson," he said. "This man has been impersonating me. You're a good actor, Bat, for a fellow that's such a *bad* actor!" he taunted. "How did you get the dope on this case? Did you tap the wires to headquarters?"

The Bat allowed himself a little sardonic smile.

"I'll tell you that when I—" he began, then, suddenly, made his last bid for freedom. With one swift, desperate movement, in spite of his handcuffs, he jerked the real Anderson's revolver from him by the barrel, then wheeling with lightning rapidity on Bailey, brought the butt of Anderson's revolver down on his wrist. Bailey's revolver fell to the floor with a clatter. The Bat swung toward the door. Again the tables were turned!

"Hands up, everybody!" he ordered, menacing the group with the stolen pistol. "Hands up—you!" as Miss Cornelia kept her hands at her sides.

It was the greatest moment of Miss Cornelia's life.

She smiled sweetly and came toward the Bat as if the pistol aimed at her heart were as innocuous as a toothbrush.

"Why?" she queried mildly. "I took the bullets out of that revolver two hours ago."

The Bat flung the revolver toward her with a curse. The real Anderson instantly snatched up the gun that Bailey had dropped and covered the Bat.

"Don't move!" he warned, "or I'll fill you full of lead!" He smiled out of the corner of his mouth at Miss Cornelia who was primly picking up the revolver that the Bat had flung at her—her own revolver.

"You see—you never know what a woman will do," he continued.

Miss Cornelia smiled. She broken open the revolver, five loaded shells fell from it to the floor. The Bat stared at her, then stared incredulously at the bullets.

"You see," she said, "I, too, have a little imagination!"

21

Quite A Collection

An hour or so later, in a living-room whose terrors had departed, Miss Cornelia, her niece, and Jack Bailey were gathered before a roaring fire. The local police had come and gone; the bodies of Courtleigh Fleming and his nephew had been removed to the mortuary; Beresford had returned to his home, though under summons as a material witness; the Bat, under heavy guard, had gone off under charge of the detective. As for Doctor Wells, he too was under arrest, and a broken man, though, considering the fact that Courtleigh Fleming had been throughout the prime mover in the conspiracy, he might escape with a comparatively light sentence. In a little while the newspapermen of all the great journals would be at the door—but for a moment the sorely tried group at Cedarcrest enjoyed a temporary respite and they made the best of it while they could.

The fire burned brightly and the lovers, hand in hand, sat before it. But Miss Cornelia, birdlike and brisk, sat upright on a chair near by and relived the greatest triumph of her life while she knitted with automatic precision.

"Knit two, purl two," she would say, and then would wander once more back to the subject in hand. Out behind the flower garden the ruins of the garage and her beloved car were still smoldering; a cool night wind came through the broken windowpane where not so long before the bloody hand of the injured detective had intruded itself. On the door to the hall, still fastened as the Bat had left it, was the pathetic little creature with which the Bat had signed a job—for once, before he had completed it.

But calmly and dispassionately Miss Cornelia worked out the cross-word puzzle of the evening and announced her results.

"It is all clear," she said. "Of course the doctor had the blueprint. And the Bat tried to get it from him. Then when the doctor had stunned him and locked him in the billiard room, the Bat still had the key and unlocked his own handcuffs. After that he had only to get out of a window and shut us in here."

And again:

"He had probably trailed the real detective all the way from town and attacked him where Mr. Beresford found the watch."

Once, too, she harkened back to the anonymous letters.

"It must have been a blow to the doctor and Courtleigh Fleming when they found me settled in the house!" She smiled grimly. "And when their letters failed to dislodge me."

But it was the Bat who held her interest; his daring assumption of the detective's identity, his searching of the house ostensibly for their safety but in reality for the treasure, and that one moment of irresolution when he did not shoot the doctor at the top of the ladder. And thereafter lost his chance.

It somehow weakened her terrified admiration for him, but she had nothing but acclaim for the escape he had made from the Hidden Room itself.

"That took brains," she said. "Cold, hard brains. To dash out of that room and down the stairs, pull off his mask and pick up a candle, and then to come calmly back to the trunk room again and accuse the doctor. That took real ability. But I dread to think what would have happened when he asked us all to go out and leave him alone with the real Anderson!"

It was after two o'clock when she finally sent the young people off to get some needed sleep but she herself was still bright-eyed and wide-awake.

When Lizzie came at last to coax and scold her into bed, she was sitting happily at the table surrounded by divers small articles which she was handling with an almost childlike zest. A clipping about the Bat from the evening newspaper; a piece of paper on which was a well-defined fingerprint; a revolver and a heap of five shells; a small very dead bat; the anonymous warnings, including the stone in which the last one had been wrapped; a battered and broken watch, somehow left behind; a dried and broken dinner roll; and the box of sedative powders brought by Doctor Wells.

Lizzie came over to the table and surveyed her grimly.

"You see, Lizzie, it's quite a collection. I'm going to take them and—"

But Lizzie bent over the table and picked up the box of powders.

"No, ma'am," she said with extreme finality. "You are not. You are going to take these and go to bed."

And Miss Cornelia did.

THE
HAUNTED LADY

1

Hilda Adams was going through her usual routine after coming off a case. She had taken a long bath, using plenty of bath salts, shampooed her short, slightly graying hair, examined her feet and cut her toenails, and was now carefully rubbing hand lotion into her small but capable hands.

Sitting there in her nightgown she looked rather like a thirty-eight-year-old cherub. Her skin was rosy, her eyes clear, almost childish. That appearance of hers was her stock in trade, as Inspector Fuller had said to the new commissioner that same day.

"She looks as though she still thought the stork brought babies," he said. "That's something for a woman who has been a trained nurse for fifteen years. But she can see more with those blue eyes of hers than most of us could with a microscope. What's more, people confide in her. She's not the talking sort, so they think she's safe. She sits and knits and tells them about her canary bird at home, and pretty soon they're pouring out all they know. It's a gift."

"Pretty useful, eh?"

"Useful! I'll say. What's the first thing the first families think of when there's trouble? A trained nurse. Somebody cracks, and there you are. Or there she is."

"I shouldn't think the first families would have that kind of trouble."

The inspector looked at the new commissioner with a faintly patronizing smile.

"You'd be surprised," he said. "They have money, and money breeds trouble. Not only that. Sometimes they have bats."

He grinned. The new commissioner stared at him suspiciously.

"Fact," said the inspector. "Had an old woman in this afternoon who says she gets bats in her bedroom. Everything closed up, but bats just the same. Also a rat now and then, and a sparrow or two."

The commissioner raised his eyebrows.

"No giant panda?" he inquired. "No elephants?"

"Not so far. Hears queer noises, too."

"Sounds haunted," said the commissioner. "Old women get funny sometimes. My wife's mother used to think she saw her dead husband. She'd never liked him. Threw things at him."

The inspector smiled politely.

"Maybe. Maybe not. She had her granddaughter with her. The girl said it was true. I gathered that the granddaughter made her come."

"What was the general idea?"

"The girl wanted an officer in the grounds at night. It's the Fairbanks place. Maybe you know it. She seemed to think somebody gets in the house at night and lets in the menagerie. The old lady said that was nonsense; that the trouble was in the house itself."

The commissioner looked astounded.

"You're not talking about Eliza Fairbanks?"

"We're not on first-name terms yet. It's Mrs. Fairbanks, relict of one Henry Fairbanks, if that means anything to you."

"Good God," said the commissioner feebly. "What about it? What did you tell her?"

The inspector got up and shook down the legs of his trousers.

"I suggested a good reliable companion; a woman to keep her comfortable as well as safe." He smiled. "Preferably a trained nurse. The old lady said she'd talk to her doctor. I'm waiting to hear from him."

"And you'll send the Adams woman?"

"I'll send Miss Adams, if she's free," said the inspector, with a slight emphasis on the "Miss." "And if Hilda Adams says the house is haunted, or that the entire city zoo has moved into the Fairbanks place, I'll believe her."

He went out then, grinning, and the commissioner leaned back in the chair behind his big desk and grunted. He had enough to do without worrying about senile old women, even if the woman was Eliza Fairbanks. Or was the word "anile"? He wasn't sure.

The message did not reach the inspector until eight o'clock that night. Then it was not the doctor who called. It was the granddaughter.

"Is that Inspector Fuller?" she said.

"It is."

The girl seemed slightly breathless.

"I'm calling for my grandmother. She said to tell you she has caught another bat."

"Has she?"

"Has she what?"

"Caught another bat."

"Yes. She has it in a towel. I slipped out to telephone. She doesn't trust the servants or any of us. She wants you to send somebody. You spoke about a nurse today. I think she should have someone tonight. She's pretty nervous."

The inspector considered that.

"What about the doctor?"

"I've told him. He'll call you soon. Doctor Brooke. Courtney Brooke."

"Fine," said the inspector, and hung up.

Which was why, as Hilda Adams finished rubbing in the hand lotion that night, covered her canary, and was about to crawl into her tidy bed, her telephone rang.

She looked at it with distaste. She liked an interval between her cases, to go over her uniforms and caps, to darn her stockings— although the way stockings went today they were usually beyond darning—and to see a movie or two. For a moment she was tempted to let it ring. Then she lifted the receiver.

"Hello," she said.

"Fuller speaking. That Miss Pinkerton?"

"This is Hilda Adams," she said coldly. "I wish you'd stop that nonsense."

"Gone to bed?"

"Yes."

"Well, that's too bad. I've got a case for you."

"Not tonight you haven't," said Hilda flatly.

"This will interest you, Hilda. Old lady has just caught a bat in her room. Has it in a towel."

"Really? Not in her hair? Or a butterfly net?"

"When I say towel I mean towel," said the inspector firmly. "She seems to have visits from a sort of traveling menagerie—birds, bats, and rats."

"I don't take mental cases, and you know it, inspector. Besides, I've just come off duty."

The inspector was exasperated.

"See here, Hilda," he said. "This may be something or it may be nothing. But it looks damned queer to me. Her granddaughter was with her, and she says it's true. She'll call you pretty soon. I want you to take the case. Be a sport.''

Hilda looked desperately about her, at the covered birdcage, at her soft bed, and through the door to her small sitting-room with its chintz-covered chairs, its soft blue curtains, and its piles of unread magazines. She even felt her hair, which was still slightly damp.

"There are plenty of bats around this time of year," she said. "Why shouldn't she catch one?"

"Because there is no possible way for it to get in," said the inspector. Be a good girl, Hilda, and keep those blue eyes of yours open."

She agreed finally, but without enthusiasm, and when a few minutes later a young and troubled voice called her over the telephone, she was already packing her suitcase. The girl was evidently following instructions.

"I'm telephoning for Doctor Brooke," she said. "My grandmother isn't well. I'm terribly sorry to call you so late, but I don't think she ought to be alone tonight. Can you possibly come?"

"Is this the case Inspector Fuller telephoned about?"

The girl's voice sounded constrained.

"Yes," she said.

"All right. I'll be there in an hour. Maybe less."

Hilda thought she heard a sigh of relief.

"That's splendid. It's Mrs. Henry Fairbanks. The address is Ten Grove Avenue. I'll be waiting for you."

Hilda hung up and sat back on the edge of her bed. The name had startled her. So old Eliza Fairbanks was catching bats in towels, after years of dominating the social life of the city. Lady Fairbanks, they had called her in Hilda's childhood, when the Henry Fairbanks place still had the last iron deer on its front lawn, and an iron fence around it to keep out *hoi polloi*. The deer was gone now, and so was Henry. Even the neighborhood had changed. It was filled with bleak boarding-houses, and a neighborhood market was on the opposite corner. But the big square house still stood in its own grounds surrounded by its fence, as though defiant of a changing neighborhood and a changing world.

She got up and began to dress. Perhaps in deference to her memories she put on her best suit and a new hat. Then, canary cage in one hand and suitcase in the other, she went down the stairs. At her land-lady's door she uncovered the cage. The bird was excited. He was hopping from perch to perch, but when he saw her he was quiet, looking at her with sharp, beadlike eyes.

"Be good, Dicky," she said. "And mind you take your bath every day."

The bird chirped and she re-covered him. She thought rather drearily that she lived vicariously a good many lives, but very little of her own, including Dicky's. She left the cage, after her usual custom, with a card saying where she had gone. Then, letting herself quietly out of the house, she walked to the taxi stand at the corner. Jim Smith, who often drove her, touched his cap and took her suitcase.

"Thought you just came in," he said conversationally.

"So I did, Jim. Take me to Ten Grove Avenue, will you?"

He looked at her quickly.

"Somebody sick at the Fairbanks?"

"Old Mrs. Fairbanks isn't well."

Jim laughed.

"Been seeing more bats, has she?"

"Bats? Where did you hear that?"

"Things get around," said Jim cheerfully.

Hilda sat forward on the edge of the seat. Without her nightgown and with her short hair covered she had lost the look of a thirty-eight-year-old cherub and become a calm and efficient spinster, the sort who could knit and talk about her canary at home, while people poured out their secrets to her. She stared at Jim's back.

"What *is* all this talk about Mrs. Fairbanks, Jim?"

"Well, she's had a lot of trouble, the old lady. And she ain't so young nowadays. The talk is that she's got softening of the brain; thinks she's haunted. Sees bats in her room, and all sorts of things. What I say is if she wants to see bats, let her see them. I've known 'em to see worse."

He turned neatly into the Fairbanks driveway and stopped with a flourish under the porte-cochere at the side of the house. Hilda glanced about her. The building looked quiet and normal; just a big red brick block with a light in the side hall and one or two scattered above. Jim carried her suitcase up to the door and put it down there.

"Well, good luck to you," he said. "Don't let that talk bother you any. It sounds screwy to me."

"I'm not easy to scare," said Hilda grimly.

She paid him and saw him off before she rang the bell, but she felt rather lonely as the taxi disappeared. There was something wrong if the inspector wanted her on the case. And he definitely did not believe in ghosts. Standing there in the darkness she remembered the day Mrs. Fairbanks's daughter Marian had been married almost twenty years ago. She had been a probationer at the hospital then, and she had walked past the place on her off-duty. There had been a red carpet over these steps then, and a crowd kept outside the iron fence by a policeman was looking in excitedly. She had stopped and looked, too.

The cars were coming back from the church, and press photographers were waiting. When the bride and groom arrived they had stopped on the steps, and now, years later, Hilda still remembered that picture—Marian in white satin and veil, with a long train caught up in one hand, while the other held her bouquet of white orchids; and the groom, tall and handsome, a gardenia in the lapel of his morning coat, smiling down at her.

To the little probationer outside on the pavement it had been pure romance, Marian and Frank Garrison, clad in youth and beauty that day. And it had ended in a divorce.

She turned abruptly and rang the doorbell.

2

S he was surprised when a girl opened the door. She had expected a
butler, or at least a parlormaid. It was the girl who had telephoned
her, as she knew when she spoke.

"I suppose you are Miss Adams?"

Hilda was aware that the girl was inspecting her. She smiled reassuringly.

"Yes."

"I'm Janice Garrison. I'm so glad you came." She looked around, as
if she was afraid of being overheard. "I've been frightfully worried."

She led the way along the side passage to the main hall, and there
paused uncertainly. There were low voices from what Hilda later
learned was the library, and after a moment's indecision she threw
open the doors across from it into what had once been the front and
back parlors of the house. Now they were united into one huge
drawing-room, a Victorian room of yellow brocaded furniture, crystal
chandeliers, and what looked in the semidarkness to be extremely bad
oil paintings. Only one lamp was lit, but it gave Hilda a chance to see
the girl clearly.

She was a lovely creature, she thought. Perhaps eighteen; it was
hard to tell these days. But certainly young and certainly troubled. She
closed the double doors behind her, after a hurried glance into the
hall.

"I had to speak to you alone," she said breathlessly. "It's about my
grandmother. Don't—please don't think she is queer, or anything
like that. If she acts strangely it's because she has reason to."

Hilda felt sorry for the girl. She looked on the verge of tears. But
her voice was matter-of-fact.

"I'm accustomed to old ladies who do odd things," she said, smiling. "What do you mean by a reason?"

Janice, however, did not hear her. Across the hall a door had opened, and the girl was listening. She said, "Excuse me for a minute, will you?" and darted out, closing the doors behind her. There followed a low exchange of voices in the hall. Then the doors were opened again, and a man stepped into the room. He was a big man, with a tired face and a mop of heavy dark hair, prematurely gray over the ears. Hilda felt a sudden sense of shock. It was Frank Garrison, but he was far removed from the bridegroom of almost twenty years ago. He was still handsome, but he looked his age, and more. Nevertheless, he had an attractive smile as he took her hand.

"I'm glad you're here," he said. "My daughter told me you were coming. My name is Garrison. I hope you'll see that she gets some rest, Miss Adams. She's been carrying a pretty heavy load."

"That's what I'm here for," said Hilda cheerfully.

"Thank you. I've been worried. Jan is far too thin. She doesn't get enough sleep. Her grandmother—"

He did not finish. He passed a hand over his hair, and Hilda saw that he had not only aged. He looked worn, and his suit could have stood a pressing. As if she realized this the girl slid an arm through his and held it tight. She looked up at him with soft brown eyes.

"You're not to worry, Father. I'll be all right."

"I don't like what's going on, Jan darling."

"Would you like to see Granny?"

He looked at his watch and shook his head.

"I'd better get Eileen out of here. She wanted to come, but— Give Granny my love, Jan, and get some sleep tonight."

As he opened the door Hilda saw a small blond woman in the hall. She was drawing on her gloves and gazing at the door with interest. She had a sort of faded prettiness, and a slightly petulant look. Janice seemed embarrassed.

"This is Miss Adams, Eileen," she said. "Granny is nervous, so she's going to look after her."

Eileen acknowledged Hilda with a nod, and turned to the girl.

"If you want my opinion, Jan," she said coolly, "Granny ought to be in an institution. All this stuff about bats and so on! It's ridiculous."

Janice flushed but said nothing. Frank Garrison opened the front door, his face set.

"I wish you would keep your ideas to yourself, Eileen," he said. "Let's get out of here. 'Night Jan."

With the closing of the door Hilda turned to the girl. To her surprise Jan's eyes were filled with tears.

"I'm sorry," she said, fumbling in her sleeve for a handkerchief. "I never get used to his going away like that. You know they are divorced, my father and mother. Eileen is his second wife." She wiped her eyes and put the handkerchief away. "He can come only when Mother's out. She—they're not very friendly."

"I see," said Hilda cautiously.

"I was devoted to my father, but when the court asked me what I wanted to do, I said I would stay here. My grandmother had taken it very hard. The divorce, I mean. She loved my father. Then, too"—she hesitated—"he married Eileen very soon after, and I—well, it seemed best to stay. I thought I'd better tell you," she added. "Eileen doesn't come often, but since you've seen her—"

She broke off, and Hilda saw that she was trembling.

"See here," she said. "You're tired. Suppose you tell me all this tomorrow? Just now you need your bed and a good sleep. Why not take me up to my patient and forget about it until then?"

Janice shook her head. She was quieter now. Evidently the emotional part of her story was over.

"I'm all right," she said. "You have to know before you see my grandmother. I was telling you why I am here, wasn't I? It wasn't only because of Grandmother. My mother was terribly unhappy, too. She's never been the same since. They both seemed to need me. But of course Granny needed me most."

Hilda said nothing, but her usually bland face was stiff. The complete selfishness of the aged, she thought. This girl who should have been out in her young world of sport and pleasure, living in this mortuary of a house with two dismal women. For how long? Six or seven years, she thought.

"I see," she said dryly. "They were all right. What about you?"

"I haven't minded it. I drive out with Granny, and read to her at night. It hasn't been bad."

"What about your mother? I suppose she can read."

Janice looked shocked, then embarrassed.

"She and my grandmother haven't got along very well since the divorce. My grandmother has never quite forgiven her. I'm afraid I've given you a very bad idea of us," she went on valiantly. "Actually everything was all right until lately. My father comes in every now and then. When Mother's out, of course. And when I can I go to his house. He married my governess, so, of course, I knew her."

Hilda sensed a reserve at this point. She did what was an unusual thing for her. She reached over and patted the girl's shoulder.

"Try to forget it," she said. "I'm here, and I can read aloud. I read rather well, as a matter of fact. It's my one vanity. Also I like to drive in the afternoons. I don't get much of it."

She smiled, but the girl did not respond. Her young face was grave and intent. Hilda thought she was listening again. When the house remained quiet she looked relieved.

"I'm sorry," she said. "I guess I *am* tired. I've been watching my grandmother as best I could for the last month or two. I want to say this again before you see her, Miss Adams. She isn't crazy. She is as sane as I am. If anybody says anything different, don't believe it."

The hall was still empty when they started up the stairs. The girl insisted on carrying the suitcase, and Hilda looked around her curiously. She felt vaguely disappointed. The house had interested her ever since the day of the wedding so long ago. She had visualized it as a must have been then, gay with flowers and music, and filled with people. But if there had ever been any glamour it was definitely gone.

Not that it was shabby. The long main hall, with doors right and left, was well carpeted, the dark paneling was waxed, the furniture old-fashioned but handsome. Like the big drawing-room, however, it was badly lighted, and Hilda, following the young figure ahead of her, wondered if it was always like that; if Janice Garrison lived out her young life in that half-darkness.

Outside the door of a front room upstairs the girl paused. She gave a quick look at Hilda before she tapped at the door, a look that was like a warning.

"It's Jan, Granny," she said brightly. "May I come in?"

Somebody stirred in the room. There were footsteps, and then a voice.

"Are you alone, Jan?"

"I brought the nurse Doctor Brooke suggested. You'll like her, Grandmother. I do."

Very slowly a key turned in a lock. The door was opened a few inches, and a little old woman looked out. Hilda was startled. She had remembered Mrs. Fairbanks as a dominant woman, handsome in a stately way, whose visits to the hospital as a member of the board had been known to send the nurses into acute attacks of jitters. Now she was incredibly shrunken. Her eyes, however, were still bright. They rested on Hilda shrewdly. Then, as though her inspection had satisfied her, she took off what was evidently a chain and opened the door.

"I've still got it," she said triumphantly.

"That's fine. This is Miss Adams, Granny."

The old lady nodded. She did not shake hands.

"I don't want to be nursed," she said, peering up at Hilda. "I want to be watched. I want to know who is trying to scare me, and why. But I don't want anyone hanging over me. I'm not sick."

"That's all right," Hilda said. "I won't bother you."

"It's the nights." The old voice was suddenly pathetic. "I'm all right in the daytime. You can sleep then. Jan has a room for you. I want somebody by me at night. You could sit in the hall, couldn't you. Outside my door, I mean. If there's a draft, Jan can get you a screen. You won't go to sleep, will you? Jan's been doing it, but she dozes. I'm sure she dozes."

Janice looked guilty. She picked up the suitcase.

"I'll show you your room," she said to Hilda. "I suppose you'll want to change."

She did not speak again until the old lady's door had been closed and locked behind them.

"You see what I mean," she said as they went down the hall. "She's perfectly sane, and something *is* going on. She'll tell you about it. I don't understand it. I can't. I'm nearly crazy."

"You're nearly dead from loss of sleep," said Hilda grimly. "What is it she says she still has?"

"I'd rather she'd tell you herself, Miss Adams. You don't mind, do you?"

Hilda did not mind. Left alone, she went about her preparations with businesslike movements, unpacked her suitcase, hung up her fresh uniforms, laid out her knitting bag, her flashlight, her hypodermic case, thermometer, and various charts. After that she dressed methodically, white uniform, white rubber-soled shoes, stiff white cap. But she stood for some time, looking down at the 38-caliber automatic which still lay in the bottom of the case. It had been a gift from the inspector.

"When I send you somewhere it's because there's trouble," he had said. "Learn to use it, Hilda. You may never need it. Then again you may."

Well, she had learned to use it. She could even take it apart, clean it, and put it together again, and once or twice just knowing she had it had been important. But now she left it locked in the suitcase. Whatever this case promised, she thought—and it seemed to promise quite a bit—there was no violence indicated. She was wrong, of course, but she was definitely cheerful when, after surveying her neat reflection in the mirror, she stopped for a moment to survey what lay outside her window.

Her room, like Janice's behind it, faced toward the side street. Some two hundred feet away was the old brick stable with its white-painted cupola where Henry Fairbanks had once kept his horses, and which was now probably used as a garage. And not far behind it was the fence again, and the side street. A stream of light from Joe's Market at the corner helped the street lamps to illuminate the fringes of the property. But the house itself withstood these intrusions. It stood withdrawn and still, as if it resented the bourgeois life about it.

Hilda's cheerfulness suffered a setback. She picked up what she had laid out, tucked under her arm the five-pound *Practice of Nursing*—a book which on night duty induced a gentle somnolence which was not sleep—and went back to Janice's door.

The girl also was standing by her window, staring out. So absorbed was she that she did not hear Hilda. She rapped twice on the doorframe before she heard and turned, looking startled.

"Oh!" she said, flushing. "I'm sorry. Are you ready?"

Hilda surveyed the room. Janice had evidently made an attempt to make it cheerful. The old mahogany bed had a bright patchwork quilt on it, there were yellow curtains at the window, and a low chair by the fireplace looked as if she had upholstered it herself in a blue-and-gray chintz. But there was little sign of Janice's personal life, no photographs, no letters or invitations. The small desk was bare, except for a few books and a package of cigarettes.

"All ready," Hilda said composedly. "Did the doctor leave any orders?"

For some reason Janice flushed.

"No. She's not really sick. Just a sedative if she can't sleep. Her heart's weak, of course. That's why it all seems—so fiendish."

She did not explain. She led the way forward, and Hilda took her bearings carefully, as she always did in a strange house. The layout, so far as she could see, was simple. The narrow hall into which her room and Jan's opened had two rooms also on the other side. But in the front of the house the hall widened, at the top of the stairs, into a large square landing, lighted in daytime by a window over the staircase, and furnished as an informal sitting-room. Two bedrooms occupied the front corners of the house, with what had once been a third smaller room between them now apparently converted into bathrooms.

Janice explained as they went forward.

"My uncle, Carlton Fairbanks, and his wife have these rooms across from yours and mine," she said. "They're out of town just now. And Mother has the other corner in front, over the library."

Unexpectedly she yawned. Then she smiled. The smile changed her completely. She looked younger, as if she had recaptured her youth.

"You go straight to bed," Hilda said sternly.

"You'll call me if anything goes wrong?"

"Nothing will go wrong."

She watched the girl as she went back along the hall. In her short skirt and green pullover sweater she looked like a child. Hilda grunted with disapproval, put down her impedimenta—including *Practice of Nursing*—on a marble topped table, looked around for a comfortable chair in which to spend the night and saw none, and then finally rapped at her patient's door.

3

Her first real view was not prepossessing. Mrs. Fairbanks was dressed in an ancient quilted dressing-gown, and she looked less like an alert but uneasy terrier, and more like a frightened and rather dowdy old woman. Nor was her manner reassuring.

"Come in," she said shortly, "and lock the door. I have something to show you. And don't tell me it came down the chimney or through a window. The windows are barred and screened and the chimney flue is closed. Not only that. There is a wad of newspaper above the flue. I put it there myself."

Hilda stepped inside and closed the door behind her. The room was large and square. It had two windows facing the front of the house and two at the side. A large four-poster bed with a tester top occupied the wall opposite the side windows, with a door to a bathroom beside it. The other wall contained a fireplace flanked, as she discovered later, by two closets.

Save for a radio by the bed the room was probably as it had been since the old lady had come there as a bride. The heavy walnut bureau, the cane-seated rocking chair by the empty fireplace, even the faded photograph of Henry Fairbanks on the mantel, a Henry wearing a high choker collar and a heavy mustache, dated from before the turn of the century.

Mrs. Fairbanks saw her glance at it.

"I keep that there to remind myself of an early mistake," she said dryly. "And I don't want my back rubbed, young woman. What I want to know is how this got into my room."

She led the way to the bed, which had been neatly turned down for the night. On the blanket cover lay a bath towel with something undeniably alive in it. Hilda reached over and touched it.

"What is it?" she asked.

Mrs. Fairbanks jerked her hand away.

"Don't touch it," she said irritably. "I had a hard enough time catching it. What do you think it is?"

"Perhaps you'd better tell me."

"It's a bat," said the old lady. "They think I'm crazy. My own daughter thinks I'm crazy. I keep on telling them that things get into my room, but nobody believes me. Yes, Miss Adams, it's a bat."

There was hard triumph in her voice.

"Three bats, two sparrows, and a rat," she went on. "All in the last month or two. A rat!" she said scornfully. "I've lived in this house fifty years, and there has never been a rat in it."

Hilda felt uncomfortable. She did not like rats. She resisted an impulse to look at the floor.

"How do they get in?" she inquired. "After all, there must be some way."

"That's why you're here. You find that out and I'll pay you an extra week's salary. And I want that bat kept. When I saw that police officer today he said to keep anything I found, if I could get it."

"I don't take extra pay," said Hilda mildly. "What am I to do with the thing?"

"Take it back to the storeroom. The last door on the right. There's a shoe box there. Put it inside and tie it up. And don't let it get away, young woman. I want it."

Hilda picked up the towel gingerly. Under her hands something small and warm squirmed. She felt a horrible distaste for the whole business. But Mrs. Fairbanks's eyes were on her, intellectual and wary and somehow pathetic. She started on her errand, to hear the key turn behind her, and all at once she had the feeling of something sinister about the whole business—the gloomy house, the old woman locked in her room, the wretched little creature in her hands. The inspector had been right when he said it all looked damned queer to him.

The storeroom was, as Mrs. Fairbanks had said, at the back of the hall. She held her towel carefully in one hand and opened the door with the other. She had stepped inside and was feeling for the light switch when there was a sudden noise overhead. The next moment something soft and furry had landed on her shoulder and dropped with a plop to the floor.

"Oh, my God!" she said feebly.

But the rat—she was sure it was a rat—had disappeared when at last she found the light switch and turned it on. She was still shaken, however. Her hands trembled when she found the shoe box and dumped the bat into it. It lay there, stunned and helpless, and before she carried it back to the old lady she stopped at the table and cut a small air hole with her surgical scissors. But she was irritable when, after the usual unlocking, she was again admitted to the room.

"How am I to look after you," she inquired, "if you keep me locked out all the time?"

"I haven't asked you to look after me."

"But surely—"

"Listen, young woman. I want you to examine this room. Maybe you can find out how these creatures get in. If you can't, then I'll know that somebody in this house is trying to scare me to death."

"That's dreadful, Mrs. Fairbanks. You can't believe it."

"Of course it's dreadful. But not so dreadful as poison."

"Poison!"

"Poison," repeated Mrs. Fairbanks. "Ask the doctor, if you don't believe me. It was in the sugar on my tray. Arsenic."

She sat in the rocking chair by the fireplace, looking wizened but complacent. As though, having set out to startle the nurse, she had happily succeeded. She had indeed. Hilda was thoroughly startled. She stood looking down, her face set and unsmiling. Quite definitely she did not like this case. But equally definitely the old woman believed what she was saying.

"When was all this?" she asked.

"Three months ago. It was in the sugar on my breakfast tray."

"You are sure you didn't imagine it?"

"I didn't imagine that bat, did I?"

She went on. She had strawberries the morning it happened. She always had her breakfast in her room. The arsenic was in the powdered sugar, and she had almost died.

"But I didn't," she said. "I fooled them all. And I didn't imagine it. The doctor took samples of everything. It was in the sugar. That's the advantage of having a young man," she said. "This boy is smart. He knows all the new things. If I'd had old Smythe I'd have died. Jan got young Brooke. She'd met him somewhere. And he was close. He lives across from the stable on Huston Street. It was arsenic, all right."

Hilda looked—and felt—horrified.

"What about the servants?" she said sharply.

"Had them for years. Trust them more than I trust my family."

"Who brought up the tray?"

"Janice."

"But you can't suspect her, Mrs. Fairbanks."

"I suspect everybody," said Mrs. Fairbanks grimly.

Hilda sat down. All at once the whole situation seemed incredible—the deadly quiet of the house, the barred and screened windows, the thick atmosphere of an unaired room, this talk of attempted murder, and the old woman in the rocking chair, telling calmly of an attempt to murder her.

"Of course you notified the police," she said.

"Of course I did nothing of the kind."

"But the doctor—"

Mrs. Fairbanks smiled, showing a pair of excellent dentures.

"I told him I took it myself by mistake," she said. "He didn't believe me, but what could he do? For a good many years I have kept this family out of the newspapers. We have had our troubles, like other people. My daughter's divorce, for one thing." Her face hardened. "A most tragic and unnecessary thing. It lost me Frank Garrison, the one person I trusted. And my son Carlton's unhappy marriage to a girl far beneath him. Could I tell the police that a member of my family was trying to kill me?"

"But you don't know that it is a member of your family, Mrs. Fairbanks."

"Who else? I have had my servants for years. They get a little by my will, but they don't know it. Not enough anyhow to justify their trying to kill me. Amos, my old coachman, drives my car when I go out, and I usually take Janice with me. He may not be fond of me. I don't suppose he is, but he won't let anything happen to Jan. He used to drive her around in her pony cart."

Hilda was puzzled. Mrs. Fairbank's own attitude was bewildering. It was as though she were playing a game with death, and so far had been victorious.

"Have there been any attempts since?" she asked.

"I've seen to that. When I eat downstairs I see that everybody eats what I do, and before I do. And I get my breakfasts up here. I squeeze my own orange juice, and I make my coffee in a percolator in the bathroom. And I don't take sugar in it! Now you'd better look around. I've told you what you're here for."

Hilda got up, her uniform rustling starchily. She was convinced now that something was wrong, unless Mrs. Fairbanks was not rational, and that she did not believe. There was the hard ring of truth in her voice. Of course she could check the poison story with Dr. Brooke. And there was the bat. Even supposing that the old lady was playing a game of some sort for her own purposes, how, living the life she did, could she have obtained a bat? Hilda had no idea how anyone got possession of such a creature. Now and then one saw them at night in the country. Once in her childhood one had got into the house, and they had all covered their heads for fear it would get in their hair. But here, in the city—

"Was your door open tonight?" she said.

"My door is never open."

That seemed to be that. Hilda began to search the room; without result, however. The windows, including the bathroom, were as Mrs. Fairbanks had said both barred and screened, and the screens were screwed into place. The closets which flanked the fireplace revealed themselves as unbroken stretches of painted plaster, and gave forth the musty odor of old garments long used. Only in one was a break. In the closet nearest the door was a small safe, built in at one side, and looking modern and substantial.

As she backed out she found Mrs. Fairbanks watching her.

"What about the safe?" she asked. "Could anything be put in it, so that when you open it it could get out?"

"Nobody can open it but myself. And I don't. There is nothing in it."

But once more the crafty look was on her face, and Hilda did not believe her. When, after crawling under the bed, examining the chimney in a rain of soot and replacing the paper which closed it, and peering behind the old-fashioned bathtub, she agreed that the room was as tight as a drum, the old woman gave her a sardonic grin.

"I told that policeman that," she said. "But he as much as said I was a liar."

It was after eleven at night when at last she agreed to go to bed. She refused the sleeping tablet the doctor had left, and she did not let Hilda undress her. She sent her away rather promptly, with orders to sit outside the door and not to shut her eyes for a minute. And Hilda went, to hear the door being locked behind her, and to find that a metamorphosis had taken place in the hall outside. A large comfortable chair had been brought and placed by the table near the old lady's door. There was a reading lamp beside it, and the table itself was piled high with books and magazines. In addition there was a screen to cut off drafts, and as she looked Janice came up the front stairs carrying a heavy tray.

She was slightly breathless.

"I hope you don't mind," she said. "There's coffee in a Thermos. I
had Maggie make it when I knew you were coming. Maggie's the cook.
You see, Grandmother doesn't want to be left. If you went downstairs
for supper—"

Hilda took the tray from her.

"I ought to scold you," she said severely. "I thought I sent you to
bed."

"I know. I'm sorry. I'm going now." She looked at Hilda shyly. "I'm
so glad you're here," she said. "Now nothing can happen, can it?"

Days later Hilda was to remember the girl's face, too thin but now
confident and relieved, the sounds of Mrs. Fairbanks moving about in
her looked room, the shoe box with the captive bat on the table, and
her own confident voice.

"Of course nothing can happen. Go to bed and forget all about it."

Janice did not go at once, however. She picked up Hilda's textbook
and opened it at random.

"I suppose it's pretty hard, studying to be a nurse."

"It's a good bit more than study."

"I would like to go into a hospital. But, of course, the way things
are— It must be wonderful to—well, to know what a doctor means
when he says things. I feel so ignorant."

Hilda looked at her. Was it a desire to escape from this house? Or
was she perhaps interested in young Brooke? She thought back over
the long line of interns she had known. She did not like interns. They
were too cocky. They grinned at the young nurses and ignored the
older ones. Once one of them had grabbed her as she came around a
corner, and his face had been funny when he saw who it was. But
Brooke must have interned long after she left Mount Hope Hospital.

She changed the subject.

"Tell me a little about the household," she suggested. "Your
mother, your uncle and aunt live here. What about the servants?"

Jan sat down and lit a cigarette.

"There are only three in the house now," she said, "and Amos outside. There used to be more, but lately Granny—well, you know how it
is. I think Granny is scared. She's cut down on them. We even save on
light. Maybe you've noticed!"

She smiled and curled up in the chair, looking relaxed and comfortable.

"How long have they been here, Miss Janice?"

"Oh, please call me Jan. Everybody does. Well, William's been here
thirty years. Maggie, the cook, has been here for twenty. Ida"—Jan

smiled—"Ida's a newcomer. Only ten. And, of course, Amos. He lives over the stable. The others live upstairs, at the rear."

"I suppose you trust them all?"

"Absolutely."

"Any others? Any regular visitors?"

Janice looked slightly defiant.

"Only my father. Granny doesn't like callers, and Mother—well, she sees her friends outside. At the country club or at restaurants. Since the—since the trouble Granny hasn't liked her to have them here."

She put out her cigarette and got up. The box containing the bat was on the table. She looked at it.

"I suppose you'll show that to the police?" she asked.

"That seems to be your grandmother's idea."

Janice drew a long breath.

"I had to do it," she said. "I was afraid they would say she was crazy. Have her committed. I had to, Miss Adams."

"Who are 'they'?"

But Janice had already gone. She was walking down the hall toward her bedroom, and she was fumbling in her sleeve for her handkerchief.

Hilda was thoughtful after the girl had gone. She got out her knitting, but after a few minutes she put it down and opened her textbook. What she found was far from satisfactory. Arsenic was disposed of in a brief paragraph:

Many drugs, such as dilute acids, iron, arsenic, and so on, are irritating to mucous lining of the stomach and may cause pain, nausea, and vomiting.

And death, she thought. Death to an old woman who, whatever her peculiarities, was helpless and pathetic.

She put the book away and picking up the chart wrote on it in her neat hand: *11:30 P.M. Patient excitable. Pulse small and rapid. Refuses to take sedative.*

She was still writing when the radio was turned on in Mrs. Fairbanks's room. It made her jump. It was loud, and it blatted on her eardrums like a thousand shrieking devils. She stood it for ten minutes. Then she banged on the door.

"Are you all right?" she shouted.

To her surprise the old lady answered at once from just inside the door.

"Of course I'm all right," she said sharply. "Mind you, stay out there. No running around the house."

Quite definitely, Hilda decided, she did not like the case. She was accustomed to finding herself at night in unknown houses, with no knowledge of what went on within them; to being dumped among strangers, plunged into their lives, and for a time to live those lives with them. But quite definitely she did not like this case, or this house.

The house was not ghostly. She did not believe in ghosts. It was merely, as she said to herself with unusual vigor, damned unpleasant; too dark, too queer, too detached. And the old lady didn't need a nurse. What she needed was a keeper, or a policeman.

4

The radio went on until after midnight. Then it ceased abruptly, leaving a beating silence behind it, and in that silence Hilda suddenly heard stealthy footsteps on the stairs. She stiffened. But the figure which eventually came into view was the tragic rather than alarming.

It was a woman in a black dinner dress, and she seemed shocked to see Hilda. She stood on the landing, staring.

"Has anything happened to Mother?" she half whispered.

Hilda knew her then. It was Marian Garrison, Janice's mother, but changed beyond belief. She was painfully thin and her careful make-up only accentuated the haggard lines of her face. But she still had beauty, of a sort. The fine lines of her face, the dark eyes—so like Jan's—had not altered. Given happiness, Hilda thought, she would be lovely.

She stood still, fingering the heavy rope of pearls around her neck, and Hilda saw that she was carrying her slippers in the other hand.

"It isn't—she hasn't had another—"

She seemed unable to go on, and Hilda shook her head. She picked up a pad from the table and wrote on it: *Only nervous. She caught a bat in her room tonight.*

Marian read it. Under the rouge her face lost what color it had had.

"Then it's true!" she said, still whispering. "I can't believe it."

"It's in that box."

Marian shivered.

"I never believed it," she said. "I thought she imagined it. Where on earth do they come from?" Then she apparently recognized the strangeness of Hilda in her uniform, settled outside her mother's door. "I suppose the shock—she's not really sick, is she?"

Hilda smiled.

"No. The doctor thought she needed someone for a night or two. Naturally she's nervous."

"I suppose she would be," said Marian vaguely, and after a momentary hesitation went into her own room and closed the door behind her. Hilda watched her go. She was trusting no one in the house that night, or any night. But she felt uncomfortable. So that was what divorce did to some women! Sent them home to arbitrary old mothers, made them slip in and out of their houses, lost them their looks and their health and their zest for living. She thought of Frank Garrison with his faded little blond second wife. He had not looked happy, either. And the girl Janice, torn among them all, the old woman, Marian, and her father.

The bat was moving around in the box, making small scraping noises. She cut another hole for air, and tried to look inside. But all she could see was a black mass, now inert, and she put down the box again.

She had a curious feeling that the old lady was still awake. There was no transom over the door, but she seemed still to be moving around. Once a closet door apparently creaked. Then the radio came on again, and Hilda, who abominated radio in all its forms, wondered if she was to endure it all night. She was still wondering when the door to Marian's room opened, and Marian came into the hall.

"Can't you stop it?" she asked feverishly. "It's driving me crazy."

"The door's locked."

"Well, bang on it. Do something."

"Does she always do it?"

"Not always. For the past month or two. Sometimes she goes to sleep and it goes on all night. It's sickening."

She had not bothered to put on a dressing-gown. She stood shivering in the June night, her silk nightgown outlining her thin body, with its small high breasts, and her eyes desperate.

"Sometimes I wonder if she really is—"

What she wondered was lost. From the bedroom came a thin high shriek. It dominated the radio, and was succeeded by another even louder one. Marian, panic-stricken, flung herself against the door and hammered on it.

"Mother," she called, "let me in. What is it? What's wrong?"

Abruptly the radio ceased, and Mrs. Fairbanks's thin old voice could be heard.

"There's a rat in here," she quavered.

Out of sheer relief Marian leaned against the door.

"A rat won't hurt you," she said. "Let me in. Unlock the door, Mother."

But Mrs. Fairbanks did not want to unlock the door. She did not want to get out of her bed. After she had finally turned the key she scurried back to it, and sitting upright in it surveyed them both with hard, triumphant eyes.

"He's under the bureau," she said. "I saw him. Perhaps now you'll believe me."

"Don't get excited, Mother," Marian said. "It's bad for you. If it's here we'll get William to kill it."

Mrs. Fairbanks regarded her daughter coldly.

"Maybe you know it's here," she said.

"That's idiotic, Mother. I hate the things. How could I know?"

Hilda's bland eyes watched them both, the suspicion in the old lady's face, the hurt astonishment in the daughter's. It was Marian who recovered first. She stood by the bed, looking down at her mother.

"I'll get William to kill it," she said. "Where were you, Mother, when you saw it?"

"I was in bed. Where would I be?"

"With all the lights on?"

There was a quick exchange of looks between the two, both suspicious and wary. Hilda was puzzled.

"Don't stand there like a fool," said Mrs. Fairbanks. "Get William and tell him to bring a poker."

Marian went out, closing the door behind her, and Hilda, getting down on her knees not too happily, reported that the rat was still under the bureau, and apparently also not too happy about it. She got up and beat a hasty retreat to the door, from which she inspected the room.

It was much as she had left it, except that the old lady's clothes were neatly laid on a chair. The windows were all closed, however, and the bed was hardly disturbed. It looked indeed as though she had just got into it. There was another difference, too. A card table with a padded cover had been set up in front of the empty fireplace, and on it lay a pack of cards.

The old lady was watching her.

"I lied to Marian," she said cheerfully. "I hadn't gone to bed. I was playing solitaire."

"Why shouldn't you play solitaire? Especially if you can't sleep."

"And have the doctor give me stuff to make me sleep? I need my wits, Miss Adams. Nobody is going to dope me in this house, especially at night."

The rest of the night was quiet. William, an elderly man in a worn bathrobe with "old family servant" written all over him, finally cornered the rat, dispatched it, and carried it out in a dustpan. Marian went back to her room and closed and locked the door. Janice had slept through it all, and Hilda, after an hour on her knees, discovered no holes in the floor or baseboard and finally gave up, to see Mrs. Fairbanks's eyes on her, filled with suspicion.

"Who sent you here?" she said abruptly. "How do I know you're not in with them?"

Hilda stiffened.

"You know exactly why I'm here, Mrs. Fairbanks. Inspector Fuller—"

"Does he know you?"

"Very well. I have worked for him before. But I can't help you if you keep me locked out. You will have to trust me better than that."

To her dismay the old lady began to whimper, the tearless crying of age. Her face was twisted, her chin quivered.

"I can't trust anybody," she said brokenly. "Not even my own children. Not even Carlton. My own son. My own boy."

Hilda felt a wave of pity for her.

"But he's not here tonight," she said. "He couldn't have done it. Don't you see that?"

The whimpering ceased. Mrs. Fairbanks looked up at her.

"Then it was Marian," she said. "She blames me for bringing that woman Frank married into the house. She was crazy about Frank. She still is. When that woman got him she nearly lost her mind."

"She couldn't possibly have done it," Hilda told her sharply. "Try to be reasonable, Mrs. Fairbanks. Even if she had come into this room she couldn't have brought it with her. People don't carry rats around in their pockets. Or bats, either."

It was over an hour before she could leave her. She utilized it to make a more careful examination of the room. The bathroom, which was tiled, did not connect with Marian's room, and its screen was, like the others, screwed into place. The closets revealed nothing except the safe and the rows of clothing old women collect. Hanging on the door of the one where the safe stood was a shoe bag, filled with shoes. She smiled at it, but days later she was to realize the importance of that bag; to see its place in the picture.

One thing was certain. No rat or bat could have entered the room by any normal means. The old-fashioned floor register was closed. Not entirely. There were, she saw with the aid of a match, small spaces where the iron blades beneath did not entirely meet. The grating over them, however, was tightly screwed to the floor and its openings less than a square inch in size.

Mrs. Fairbanks lay in her bed, watching her every move. She had taken out her teeth, and now she yawned, showing her pale gums.

"Now you know what I'm talking about," she said. "Put out the light, and maybe you'd better leave the door unlocked. But don't you go away. I wake up now and then, and if I find you're not there—"

Outside in the hall Hilda's face was no longer bland. Inspector Fuller would have called it her fighting face. She waited until she heard her patient snoring. Then she tiptoed back to her room, and from what she called her emergency case she removed several things—a spool of thread, a pair of rubber gloves, and a card of thumbtacks. These she carried forward and, after a look to see that all was quiet, went to work. Near the floor she set two of the tacks, one in the doorframe and one in the door itself. She tied a piece of the black thread from one to the other and, cutting off the ends with her surgical scissors, stood up and surveyed her work. Against the dark woodwork it was invisible.

After that she put the screen around her chair so as to shield it, picked up the flashlight, the gloves, and a newspaper Janice had left for her, and very deliberately went down the stairs.

The lower floor was dark. She stopped and listened in the hall. Somewhere a clock was ticking loudly. Otherwise everything was quiet, and she made her way back to the kitchen premises without having to use her light. Here, however, she turned it on. She was in a long old-fashioned pantry, the floor covered with worn linoleum, the shelves filled with china and glassware. A glance told her that what she was looking for was not there, and she went on to the kitchen.

It was a huge bleak room, long unpainted. On one side was a coal range, long enough to feed a hotel. There was a fire going, but it had been carefully banked. Nevertheless, she took off the lids, one by one. There was nothing there, and she gave a sigh of relief. After that she inspected a small garbage can under the sink, without result.

It was in the yard outside the kitchen porch that she finally found what she was looking for. It lay on top of a barrel of ashes, and she drew on her gloves before she touched it. When she went upstairs again it was to place and lock in her suitcase the neatly wrapped body of a dead rat.

Then, having found that the door had not been opened, she calmly moved her chair against it and picking up the *Practice of Nursing* opened it at random. *The physician, the nurse, and others should report what they see, hear, smell, or feel, rather than what they deduce.* She read on, feeling pleasantly somnolent.

5

Things looked better the next morning. The old house in the June sunlight looked shabby but not sinister. Mrs. Fairbanks wakened early and allowed Hilda to bring her a breakfast tray. But she took her grapefruit without sugar, and insisted on opening her egg herself.

In the kitchen waiting for her tray, Hilda inspected the servants—Maggie, stout and middle-aged, over the stove, Amos outside on the porch smoking a corncob pipe, William, taciturn and elderly, and Ida, a pallid listless creature in her late thirties, drinking a cup of tea at the table. They were watching her, too, although they ignored her. She was familiar with the resentment of house servants toward all trained nurses; resentment and suspicion. But it seemed to her that these four were not only suspicious of her. They were suspicious of each other. They did not talk among themselves. Save for the clattering of Maggie's pans and stove lids the room was too quiet.

She was in the pantry when she heard William speaking.

"I tell you I put it there," he was saying. "I'm not likely to forget a thing like that."

"You'd forget your head if it wasn't fastened on." This was Maggie.

"Someone's taken it," said William stubbornly. "And don't tell me it wasn't dead. It was."

When she went back to the kitchen conversation ceased, but on the porch Amos was grinning.

Janice slept late that morning, but Marian was at the table when Hilda went down for her own breakfast. She looked as though she had not slept at all. The green housecoat she wore brought out the pallor of her skin and her thinness, and beside her Hilda looked once more like a fresh, slightly plump cherub. Marian had already eaten, but after William had served the nurse and gone, she stayed on, nervously fingering her coffee cup.

"I suppose," she said, "that Mother has been telling you how we have tried to murder her."

Hilda looked unruffled.

"I wouldn't say that, Mrs. Garrison. She did say there was an incident some time ago. Something about arsenic in the sugar."

Marian smiled grimly. She got a cigarette from a side table and lit it before she spoke.

"As it happens, that's true," she said. "That was when Doctor Brooke had the contents of her tray analyzed. It was there, all right. Only I ask you—" she smiled again, her tight-lipped smile—"would we have left it there if we had done it? Everybody handled that tray. My daughter Janice had taken it up to her. I took it out of the room. My brother Carlton carried it to the head of the back stairs and later his wife carried it down. If the servants were guilty they could have got rid of it. But nobody did." She put down her cigarette. "We may be an unpleasant family, but we are not fools, Miss Adams. We wanted to call the police, but Mother refused."

She shrugged her thin shoulders.

"What could we do? If she wanted to think we did it, that was all right with us; but life hasn't been very pleasant since."

"Was there arsenic in the house?"

"We never found any. Of course she suspects us all."

"Why should she?"

"She has the money," Marian said dryly. "She has it and she keeps it. I could leave, of course. I have my alimony." She flushed. "And I have a little place in the country. But Mother wants Janice here, and Jan thinks we ought to stay. That rat last night was merely an accident. As for the bats and all the rest of it—"

She shrugged again. Hilda's expression did not change.

"Have you thought that she might be doing some of this herself?" she inquired. "Old women do strange things sometimes. They crave attention and don't get it, so they resort to all sorts of devices."

"How could she?"

"Through one of the servants, possibly. Or, she drives out every day or so, doesn't she? She might have an arrangement—somebody handing her a package of some sort."

Marian laughed, without particular mirth.

"Such as arsenic, I suppose!"

"I gather that she didn't take enough to kill her," said Hilda dryly.

"She may resent some member of the family and want to make trouble."

"She resents us all," said Marian. "All but Jan, and she uses her until I'm frantic. The child has no life of her own at all." She lit another cigarette, and Hilda saw her hands were shaking. "Don't judge us too soon," she went on. "I'd get out and take Jan, but she doesn't want to leave her grandmother. And my brother has no place to go. His business is shot to pieces. He was a broker, but that's all over. He doesn't make enough to buy shoes these days. And he has a wife to support."

She got up.

"We're not a bad lot," she said. "Even Susie has her points." She smiled thinly. "None of us would try to kill Mother, or even scare her to death. Now I suppose you'll need some sleep. I'll stay within call, if she wants anything."

Hilda, however, did not go to bed that morning. She saw that Mrs. Fairbanks was bathed and partly dressed, and made up her bed with fresh linen. Then, leaving Ida to clean the room and finish, she changed into street clothing and took a bus at the corner for police headquarters. The inspector was alone in his bare little office, and when Hilda walked in in her neat tailored suit and small hat he eyed her with appreciation.

"Hello," he said. "How's the haunted lady today?" She smiled and deposited the box and the parcel on the desk in front of him. He looked faintly alarmed.

"What's this?" he inquired. "Don't tell me you've brought me cigars."

She sat down and pulled off her gloves.

"The box," she said smugly, "contains one bat. It's alive, so don't open it while I'm here. The other is a dead rat. I got it out of a trash can, at three o'clock in the morning—if that interests you."

"Great Scott! The place sounds like Noah's ark. What do you mean, you got the rat out of a trash can?"

She told him then, sitting across the desk, her hands primly folded in her lap. She began with the arsenic in March, and went on to the events of the night before. He looked bewildered. He stared at the body of the rat, neatly wrapped in its newspaper.

"I see. And this thing couldn't get into the room, but it did. That's the idea?"

"It may not be the same one I saw in the linen closet."

"But you think it is, eh?"

"I think it is. Yes."

"What am I to do with it?" he inquired rather helplessly. "What about rats, anyhow? Don't the best houses have them?"

"They carry bubonic plague sometimes."

"Good God," said the inspector. "What did you bring it to me for?"

"I don't suppose it has any fleas on it now. It's the fleas that are dangerous. I just thought it had better be examined. Certainly somebody is trying to kill Mrs. Fairbanks."

"Just like that?"

"Just like that."

He leaned back and lit a cigarette.

"I suppose you haven't any ideas?"

She smiled faintly.

"All of them have motives. I haven't seen Carlton and Susie, the son and his wife. They're out of town. But Mrs. Fairbanks has the money and apparently holds on to it. Her ex-son-in-law, Frank Garrison, sees her now and then, but I doubt if he gains by her death. The doctor might have a reason, but she was poisoned before any of them knew him, except the granddaughter. She'd met him somewhere. He was called because he lives close by. I haven't seen him yet."

"Why the doctor?"

"I think the girl may be in love with him. And I suppose he could carry more than babies in his bag."

The inspector laughed. He had a considerable affection for her, and an even greater respect.

"You're a great girl, Hilda," he said, as she got up. "All right. Go back to your menagerie. And, for God's sake, don't get any fleas."

She took a bus back to her corner, but she did not go directly to the house. Instead she turned at Joe's Market into Huston Street and passing a row of once handsome houses, now largely given over to roomers and showing neglect, found Dr. Brooke's office in one of them. It was almost directly across from the Fairbanks stable, and a small brass plate, marked *C. A. Brooke, M.D.* and needing polishing, told her where she was.

On the steps she turned and surveyed the outlook. The stable and its cupola concealed the service wing of the house, but the rest was in full view. She could see the porte-cochere, and as far back as Jan's room. So that was why Jan had been gazing out her window the night before!

It was some time before an untidy girl answered her ring. Then she jerked the door open and stuck her head out.

"Is the doctor in?" Hilda asked.

The girl surveyed her, looking astonished.

"I'll see," she said, and ducked back.

Hilda followed her into the house. To the left was a waiting room. It was sparsely furnished with a center table, a row of chairs around the wall, and a bookcase which had seen better days. Double doors opened into the consulting room behind, where a young man, with his coat off, was sound asleep behind a desk.

The girl made a gesture.

"That's him," she said, and disappeared.

The young man opened his eyes, looked bewildered, then jumped to his feet and grabbed his coat.

"Terribly sorry," he said. "Up all night. Please come in."

He was not particularly handsome. He had, however, a nice smile and good teeth. Hilda rather hated disappointing him.

"I'm afraid I'm not a patient," she said.

"No? Well, I didn't really expect one. Sit down, anyhow. It's hot, isn't it?"

Hilda was not interested in the weather. She looked at him and said, "I'm the nurse at Mrs. Fairbanks's. I'd like to ask some questions, doctor."

She thought he stiffened. Nevertheless, he smiled.

"I can't violate any professional confidences, even to you, you know, Miss—"

"Adams is my name."

"I see. In a way I'm responsible for your being there Miss Adams. I was worried about Jan. But I didn't expect her to get a police nurse."

"I'm not a police nurse, doctor. When there is trouble I report to the police. That's all."

"I see," he said again. "Well, Miss Adams, if you want to know whether or not I think Mrs. Fairbanks is haunted, the answer is no. She's an old woman, and she was always eccentric. Lately she has developed some fixed ideas. One is that her family is trying to do away with her. Scare her to death, as she puts it. I don't believe it. When you know them—"

"The arsenic wasn't a fixed idea, doctor."

He looked unhappy and annoyed.

"Who told you about that? The family and she herself have insisted on keeping it to themselves. I argued against it, but it was no good."

"It was arsenic, wasn't it?"

"It was. Arsenious acid. She didn't get a lot, but she got it on an empty stomach. Luckily I got there in an hour. Even at that she was in poor shape—cyanosed, pulse feeble, and so on. I washed her out, but she was pretty well collapsed."

"There was no doubt what it was?"

"No. I used Reinsch's test. She'd had it, all right."

He went on. He had wanted to call the police, but look at it! Nobody there but the family and servants who had been there a lifetime. Impossible to blame it on any of them. Impossible to have a scandal, too. And there had been no repetition. All that had happened had been a change in the old lady herself. She had been imagining things ever since. This story of things in her room, bats, rats, sparrows or what have you—

When he heard about the night before he got up and took a turn about the room.

"Well, I'll be damned," he said. "I'll be eternally everlastingly damned! Of course," he added, "things like that won't necessarily kill her. It's not murder. The other time—"

"You thought it was an attempt at murder?"

"She didn't take white arsenic for her complexion," he said grimly.

He went to the door with her, a tall, lanky young man who towered over her and who as she started out put a hand on her shoulder.

"Look here," he said. "Keep an eye on Janice, will you? She's been under a terrific strain. They're a decent lot over there, but there isn't anything to hold them together. They fight like cats and dogs. If anything happens to her—"

He did not finish.

He stood still, gazing across the street to where, beyond the fence and the brick stable, the dark rectangle of the Fairbanks house stood in all the dignity of past grandeur.

"Funny, isn't it?" he said. "When I was a kid I used to stand outside that fence to see the old lady drive out in her carriage!"

Except that she was trusting nobody just then, Hilda would have liked him that day. He had a boyish quality which appealed to her. But she hardened herself against him.

"I suppose you know," she said coolly, "that you are on the list of suspects?"

"Suspects! What on earth have I done?"

"You might have carried a few vermin into Mrs. Fairbanks's room in that bag of yours."

He looked astounded. Then he laughed, long and heartily.

"And tried to scare my best and almost only patient to death!" he said. "Come and look, Miss Adams. If ever you've seen a bag of pristine purity you'll see one now."

She did not go back, however. He showed her a break in the fence near the stable and she took that short cut to the house. Amos was washing a muddy car as she passed him, but he did not look up. He was a short, surly-looking man, and she felt that he was staring after her as she went toward the house. She had an unpleasant feeling, too, that he was grinning again, as he had grinned that morning on the kitchen porch.

She did not go to the front door; instead, she walked to the rear of the house. It was twelve o'clock by that time and the servants—with the exception of Amos—were already eating their midday dinner in a small room off the kitchen. She stopped in the doorway, and William got up.

"I was wondering," she said blandly, "whether you have a rattrap in the house. If there are rats here—"

"There are no rats in this house," said Maggie shortly. "One was caught last night."

"You ask Amos about that. He's got them in the stable, if you ask me."

But Amos, arriving and overhearing, grouchily affirmed that there were no rats in the stable. Hilda surveyed them. They were the usual lot, she thought; loyal rather than intelligent, and just now definitely uneasy. Ida glared at Amos.

"What about that arsenic? Maybe there's arsenic in the stable."

Her voice was high and shrill. Amos glared back at her.

"You'd better keep your mouth shut, if you know what's good for you."

They were all close to hysteria, but it was left to Maggie, matter-of-fact Maggie, to put the keystone on the arch of their terror.

"If you ask me," she said, "the place is haunted. I've sat with the old lady when Ida and Miss Jan were out, and I've heard plenty."

"What have you heard?" Hilda asked.

"Raps all over the room. Queer scraping noises. And once the closet door opened. The one with the safe. I was looking right at it, and only me and Mrs. Fairbanks in the room—and her asleep."

Ida screamed, and William pounded on the table.

"Stop that kind of talk," he ordered sharply. "All old houses creak. Do you want to scare the nurse away?"

Maggie subsided, looking flushed. Ida was pale and plainly terrified. Only Amos went on eating. And Hilda, on her way upstairs, was convinced of two things, that they were all badly scared, and that they were all equally innocent.

6

The old lady's room when she reached it bore no resemblance to the eerie chamber of the night before. Someone—Jan, she thought—had been at work in it.

The sun was pouring in, there were lilacs on a table, the bed had a silk cover over it, and a number of small pillows gave it an almost frivolous look. Even Jan looked better, rested and smiling, and Mrs. Fairbanks herself, dressed now in black silk and sitting in her rocker, was a different creature from the untidy old woman of the previous evening.

Not that she was entirely changed. She was still domineering, even suspicious. Her small eyes were fixed on one of the closets, which contained the safe, and she ignored Hilda in the doorway.

"Come out of that closet, Carlton," she said. "I told you there was nothing there."

Carlton Fairbanks emerged reluctantly. He backed out, dusting his knees as he came, a small, dapper man in his forties, his thin face ruffled, his expression stubborn.

"They have to get in somehow, Mother. Why don't you let me look?"

"They're brought in," said Mrs. Fairbanks tartly.

"I've told you that. Someone in this house brings them in."

Carlton tried to smile.

"If you mean that I did it, I was out of town last night. So was Susie. Anyhow, she's afraid of rats."

"I imagine Susie has seen rats before, and plenty of them," said Mrs. Fairbanks coldly.

This for some reason caused a blank silence in the room. Carlton's mouth tightened, and Janice looked uneasy. The silence was broken only by the old lady's tardy recognition of Hilda in the doorway. She looked at her with small, malicious eyes.

"You see me surrounded by my loving family, Miss Adams," she said. "This is my son. He was out of town last night when you came. Or so he says."

Carlton stiffened. He nodded at Hilda and then confronted his mother.

"Just what do you mean by that?" he demanded. "I'm doing the best I know how. If things go on the way they are you must make some plans. As to last night—"

"I'm perfectly capable of making my own plans."

"All right. All right," he said irritably. "As to last night, if you think I need an alibi I have one. So has Susie. But the whole thing's ridiculous. Why in God's name would anybody carry these things into this room?"

"To scare me to death," said the old lady placidly. "Only I'm pretty hard to scare, Carlton. I'm pretty hard to scare."

Later Hilda tried to recall in order the events of the next few days, beginning with the lunch that followed this scene. Marian, she remembered, had been silent. In daylight she looked even more ravaged than the night before. Janice had seemed uneasy and distracted. Carlton was irritated and showed it. And Mrs. Fairbanks, at the head of the table, watched it all, touching no food until the others had taken it, and pointedly refusing the sugar for her strawberries.

Only Carlton's wife, Susie, seemed to be herself. Hilda was to find that Susie was always herself. She was a big blond girl, and she sauntered into the room as casually as though an aged Nemesis was not fixing her with a most unpleasant eye.

"Put out that cigarette," said Mrs. Fairbanks. "I've told you again and again I won't have smoking at the table."

Susie grinned. She extinguished the cigarette on the edge of her butter dish, a gesture evidently intended to annoy the old lady, and sat down. She was heavily made up, but she was a handsome creature, and she wore a bright purple house gown which revealed a shapely body. Hilda suspected that there was little or nothing beneath it.

"Well, here's the happy family," she said ironically. "Anybody bitten anybody else while we were away?"

Janice spoke up quickly.

"Did you have a nice trip?" she asked. "Oh, I forgot. This is Miss Adams, Susie. She's taking care of Granny."

"And about time," said Susie, smiling across the table at the nurse.

But Hilda was aware that Susie's sharp blue eyes were taking stock of her, appraising her. "Time you got a rest, kid. You've looked like hell lately."

She spoke as though Mrs. Fairbanks was not there, and soon Hilda was to discover that Susie practically never spoke to her mother-in-law. She spoke at her, the more annoyingly the better. She did that now.

"As to having a nice trip. No. My feet hurt, and I'll yell my head off if I have to inspect another chicken house. I'm practically covered with lice—if that's what chickens have. Anyhow, Carl can't buy a farm. What's the use?"

"Are you sure you would like a farm?" Janice persisted.

"I'd like it better than starving to death, honey. Or going on living here."

"Susie!" said Carlton. "I wish you'd control your tongue. We ought to be very grateful to be here. I'm sure Mother—"

"I'm sure Mother hates my guts," said Susie smoothly. "All right, Carl. I'll be good. What's all this about last night?"

Hilda studied them, Marian vaguely picking at what was on her plate, Janice looking anxious, Carlton scowling, Susie eating and evidently enjoying both the food and the bickering, and at the head of the table Mrs. Fairbanks stiff in her black silk and watching them all.

"I wonder, Carlton," she said coldly, "if your wife has any theories about some of the things which have been happening here?"

Carlton looked indignant. Susie, however, only looked amused.

"I might explain that I've spent the last three days alternating between chicken houses and pigpens," she said to her husband. "I rather enjoyed it. At least it was a change. I *like* pigs."

All in all it was an unpleasant meal. Yet, remembering it later, she could not believe that there had been murder in the air. Differences of all sorts, acute dislikes and resentments; even Susie—she could see Susie figuratively thumbing her nose at her mother-in-law. But she could not see her stealthily putting poison in her food. There was apparently nothing stealthy about Susie.

Marian she dismissed. She was too ineffectual, too detached, too absorbed in her own personal unhappiness. She wondered if Mrs. Fairbanks was right and Marian was still in love with Frank Garrison, and what was the story behind the divorce. But over Carlton Fairbanks she hesitated. Men did kill their mothers, she thought. Not often, but now and then. And his position in the house was unhappy enough; dependent on a suspicious old woman who was both jealous and possessive, and who loathed his wife.

He was talking now, his face slightly flushed.

"I'm not trying to force your hand, Mother," he said. "It's a good offer. I think you ought to take it. This neighborhood is gone as residential property. A good apartment building here—well, what I say is that, with war and God knows what, a farm somewhere would be an ace in the hole. We could raise enough to live on, at least."

"Don't talk nonsense. What do you know about farming?"

"I could learn. And I like the country."

There was enthusiasm in his voice. He even looked hopeful for a moment. But his mother shook her head. "This place will never be an apartment," she said, putting down her napkin. "Not so long as I am alive, anyhow," she added, and gave Susie a long, hard look.

Hilda watched her as she got up. Old she was, bitter and suspicious she might be, but there was nothing childish about her standing there, with her family about her. Even Susie, who had lit another cigarette and grinned at her mother-in-law's hard stare, rose when the others did.

Hilda slept a few hours that afternoon. The house was quiet. Susie had gone to bed with a novel. Carlton had driven out in the car Amos had washed. Marian had—not too cheerfully—offered to drive with her mother. And Hilda, looking out her window, saw Janice cross the street to the doctor's office and come out with him a few minutes later, to enter a shabby Ford and drive away.

When she had wakened and dressed she telephoned the inspector from the empty library.

"Any news?" she asked.

"I've got the report. Nothing doing. Your Noah's ark is as pure as lilies. Anything new there?"

"No. Nothing."

She hung up. There was a telephone extention in the pantry, and she did not want to commit herself. But she was uneasy. She did not think Maggie's story had been pure hysteria. She put on her hat and went across the street to a small electrical shop. There she ordered a bell and batteries, with a long cord attached and a push button. It took some time to put together, and the electrician talked as he worked.

"You come from the Fairbankses', don't you?" he said. "I saw you coming out the driveway."

"Yes. I'm looking after Mrs. Fairbanks."

He grinned up at her.

"Seen the ghost yet?"

"I don't believe in ghosts."

"You're lucky," he said. "The help over there—they're scared to death. Say all sorts of things are going on."

"They would," said Hilda shortly.

She took her package and went back to the house. It was still quiet. The door to Mrs. Fairbanks's room was open, but the closet containing the safe was locked. She shrugged and tried out her experiment. The push button she placed on the old lady's bedside table. Then she carried the battery and bell out into the hall. To her relief the door closed over the cord.

After that she made a more careful inspection of the room than she had been able to make before. She examined the walls behind the pictures, lifted as much of the rug as she could move, tested the screens and bars at the windows again, even examined the tiles in the walls of the bathroom and the baseboards everywhere. In the end she gave up. The room was as impregnable as a fortress.

She was still there when the door opened and Carlton came in. He had a highball in his hand, and his eyes were bloodshot. He seemed startled when he saw her.

"Sorry," he said, backing out. "I didn't know—I thought my mother was here."

He was looking at her suspiciously. Hilda smiled, her small demure smile.

"She hasn't come back, Mr. Fairbanks. I was installing a bell for her."

"A bell? What for?"

"So if anything bothers her in the night she can ring it. I might not hear her call. Or she might not be able to."

He had recovered, however.

"All damn nonsense, if you ask me," he said, swaying slightly. "Who would want to bother her?"

"Or want to poison her, Mr. Fairbanks?"

He colored. The veins on his forehead swelled.

"We've only got young Brooke's word for that. I don't believe it."

"He seems pretty positive."

"Sure he does," he said violently. "Look what he gets out of it! An important patient, grateful because he saved her life! If I had my way—"

He did not finish. He turned and left her, slamming the door behind him.

Hilda went downstairs. Ida was out, and Maggie was alone in the kitchen. She was drinking a cup of tea, and she eyed Hilda without expression.

"I want to try an experiment," Hilda said. "Maybe you'll help me. It's about those raps you heard."

"What about them? I heard them, no matter who says what."

"Exactly. I'm sure you did. Only I think I know how they happened. If you'll go up to Mrs. Fairbanks's room—"

"I'm not going there alone," said Maggie stolidly.

Hilda was exasperated.

"Don't be an idiot. It's broad daylight, and anything you hear I'll be doing. All I want to know is if the noise is the same."

In the end an unwilling Maggie was installed in the room, but with the door open and giving every indication of immediate flight. The house was very quiet. Only a faint rumble of the traffic on Grove Avenue penetrated its thick walls, and Hilda, making her way to the basement on rubber-heeled shoes, might have been a small and dauntless ghost herself.

She found the furnace without difficulty. She could hardly have missed it. It stood Medusa-like in the center of a large room, with its huge hot-air pipes extending in every direction. She opened the door, and reaching inside rapped the iron wall of the firebox, at first softly, then louder. After that she tried the pipes but, as they were covered with asbestos, with less hope.

There were no sounds from above, however. No Maggie shrieked. The quiet of the house was unbroken. Finally she took the poker and tapped on the furnace itself, with unexpected results. Susie's voice came from the top of the basement stairs.

"For God's sake, stop that racket Amos," she called. "Don't tell me you're building a fire in weather like this."

Hilda stood still, and after a moment Susie banged the door and went away. When at last Hilda went upstairs to Mrs. Fairbanks's room it was to find Maggie smiling dourly in the hall.

"That hammering on the furnace wouldn't fool anybody," she said. "You take it from me, miss. Those noises were in this room. And there were no bats flying around, either."

7

That Night, Tuesday, June the tenth, Hilda had a baffling experience of her own.

Rather to her surprise Mrs. Fairbanks had accepted the bell without protest. "Provided you keep out unless I ring it," she said. "I don't want you running in and out. Once I've settled for the night you stay out. But don't you leave that door. Not for a minute."

She was tired, however, after her drive. Hilda, taking her pulse, was not satisfied with it. She coaxed her to have her dinner in bed, and that evening she called the doctor.

"I think she's overdone, and I know she's frightened," she said. "Can you come?"

"Try to keep me away," he said. "I use the short cut. One minute and thirty seconds!"

He was highly professional, however, when he stood beside Mrs. Fairbanks's bed and smiled down at her.

"Just thought I'd look you over tonight," he said. "Can't have a nurse reporting that I neglect a patient. How's everything?"

"She's not a nurse. She's a policeman," said the old lady surprisingly. "I'm not easy to fool, doctor. That officer I talked to suggested a companion, and *she* comes. Maybe it's just as well. I don't intend to be murdered in my bed."

He pretended immense surprise.

"Well, well," he said. "A policewoman! We'll have to be careful, won't we? And I've had an eye on the spoons for weeks!"

He ordered her some digitalis and sat with her for a while. But some of his boyishness was gone. Hilda, following him out of the room as he went down the stairs, heard him speaking to Jan in the hall below. Their voices, though guarded, carried up clearly.

"We're not so smart, are we, darling?" he said. "Miss Gimlet-Eyes up there isn't missing a trick."

"I don't want her to miss anything, Court."

"Are you sure of that?"

His tone was quizzical, but there was anxiety in it too.

"Certainly I am." Jan's voice was defiant. "So are you. But if the police—"

"Look, sweet," he said. "If and when your grandmother dies, it will be a natural death. The police won't come into it at all. Only, for God's sake, don't tell the family that the Adams woman is on the watch. If there's any funny business going on—"

"You can't suspect them, Court."

"Can't I?" he said grimly. "You'd be surprised what I can suspect."

He went out the side door under the porte-cochere, his head down, his face moody and unhappy. Near the stable, however, he roused. A figure had slid stealthily into the door leading up to Amos's rooms, and he dropped his bag and plunged it after it. To his dismay it was a woman. She was cowering against the wall at the foot of the stairs and softly moaning.

He let go of her and lit a match, to find Ida gazing at him with horrified eyes. She looked ready to faint, and he caught hold of her.

"Here, here," he said, "none of that! I'm damned sorry, Ida. I didn't know it was you."

He eased her down on the steps. Her color came back slowly, although she was still breathless.

"I was scared," she said. "I saw someone coming at me in the dark, and I thought—" She stopped and picked up a parcel she had dropped. "It's my day out, sir. I was just coming home."

"Better use the driveway after this," he told her. "I'll watch you to the house."

She went on slowly, while he retrieved his bag. But his own nerves were badly shaken. He let himself into the house across the street, to find the slatternly girl in his back office avidly studying the plates in one of his medical books. He strode in and jerked the book out of her hands.

"Keep that filthy nose of yours out of my books and out of my office," he snapped. "Not that I think you have anything to learn, at that. Now get out and keep out."

The girl went out sniveling. He felt ashamed of his anger. And he was tired. He yawned. But he did not go to bed. He picked up a cap from the hall and, after a brief survey of the Fairbanks property across the street, went cautiously back there and moved toward the house.

Back at the Fairbanks house the evening was following what Hilda gathered was its usual pattern. In the small morning room behind the library Susie and Carlton bickered over a game of gin-rummy. Jan, after seeing that Hilda was fixed for the night, went to bed. And Marian, having read for an hour or two in the library, came up to bed. Apparently none of them outside of Jan suspected Hilda's dual role. But Marian paused for a time in the upper hall.

"It isn't serious, is it? Mother's heart, I mean."

"No. Her pulse was weak. It's better now."

Marian stood still, looking at her mother's door. She looked better now, dressed and made up for the evening. Jan's resemblance to her was stronger. On apparently an impulse she drew up a chair and sat down.

"I suppose she has talked about me? My divorce, I mean."

"She mentioned it. That's all."

Marian's face hardened.

"I begged her not to bring that woman here as Jan's governess," she said. "I knew her type. When she had been here a month I almost went on my knees to Mother to have her sent away. But she wouldn't. She said Jan was fond of her."

Hilda picked up her knitting. She kept her head bent over it, the picture of impersonal interest.

"All divorces are sad," she said. "Especially when there are children."

"I stood it for years. I could see her, day after day, undermining me. I wanted to go away and live somewhere else, but my—but my husband didn't want to leave Mother alone. At least that's what he said. I know better now. Carlton had got out, but I had to stay."

If anyone was to be murdered, Hilda considered, it would probably be Eileen, the second Mrs. Garrison. It was obvious that Marian was bitterly jealous of her successor. She changed the subject tactfully.

"Tell me, Mrs. Garrison," she said, "when did all this begin? I mean, the arsenic and the bats and so on."

Marian's flush subsided. She pulled herself together with an effort.

"I don't know exactly," she said. "Mother wanted a safe in her room, God knows why. It was installed while I took her to Florida in February. We got home on the ninth of March, and a day or two later she got the poison. If it was poison."

"And the bats?"

"I don't know. She didn't tell us about them at first. She said she opened the screens, and let them out. That was before she had her screens fastened. None of us believed her, I'm afraid. After all, bats and birds and rats do get into houses, don't they?"

She smiled faintly, and Hilda smiled back at her.

"I suppose the raps come under the same category," she said mildly.

Marian looked startled.

"Raps? What raps?"

"The servants say there are noises at night in your mother's room. I talked to Maggie. She doesn't strike me as a neurotic type."

But Marian only shrugged.

"Oh, Maggie!" she said. "She's at a bad time of life. She can imagine anything. And you know servants. They like to raise a fuss. Their lives are pretty drab, I imagine. Anything for excitement."

She got up and put out her cigarette. She was slightly flushed.

"We have trouble enough without inviting any, Miss Adams," she said. "I don't give the orders in this house, but I'd be glad if you didn't take the servants into your confidence."

She went on into her room, her head high and the short train of her black dress trailing behind her. Hilda, watching her, felt that something like the furies of hell were bottled up in her thin body; hatred for the woman who had supplanted her, resentment toward her mother, scorn and contempt for Susie, indignation at her brother. She put down her knitting—she loathed having to knit—and considered one by one the occupants of the house. Marian, frustrated and bitterly unhappy; Carlton, timid toward his mother, slightly pompous otherwise, certainly discontented; Susie, shrewd, indifferent, and indolent. Jan she left out, but she considered Courtney Brooke for some time.

The girl would probably be an heiress when Mrs. Fairbanks died, and he had known her before the poisoning incident. If he was earning more than his rent she would be surprised. And he had been very glib about the arsenious acid, very sure of what it was. Perhaps she had not been meant to have it at breakfast? Suppose she had had it at night, with her door locked and unable to call for help? One thing was certain. He was afraid of her, Hilda. That remark about Miss Gimlet-Eyes had left her rather annoyed. On the other hand—

By midnight the house had settled down. In his room next to his mother's Carlton was snoring comfortably. Janice was apparently asleep. From the transom over Susie's door came a light and the odor of a burning cigarette, and Marian had not reappeared. Hilda went cautiously into the old lady's room and stood listening. She was asleep, breathing quietly, but the air in the room was close and hot. Mrs. Fairbanks had refused to have a window open. She stood in the darkness, worrying. There should be air. Heart cases needed oxygen. She tiptoed to a window and suddenly stopped.

There was a sound behind her, a faint scraping sound as though something had been moved. She turned sharply, but the room was as it had been. The old lady had not stirred. Then she saw it. The door to the closet which held the safe was slowly moving. In the light from the hall it edged out six inches or more, creaking as it came.

She stared at it incredulously. Then she took a quick step forward, and as carefully as it had opened it began to close again. Not entirely. The latch did not click. But close it did, and she found herself staring at it, the very hair on her scalp lifting with horror. She did not dare give herself time to think. She walked over with buckling knees and stood outside of it.

"Come out," she said in a low voice. "Whoever is in there, come out or I'll raise an alarm."

There was no reply, and when she tried the door it swung open easily in her hand. The closet was empty. The shoebag hung undisturbed, the safe was closed, the row of dresses harbored no lurking figure. She felt deflated, as though all the breath had gone out of her. *It's a trick,* she thought furiously. *A part of the campaign to terrify the old lady. A trick! A dirty trick! And it's been tried tonight because her heart hasn't been too strong. If she had wakened and seen it—*

She hurried out into the hall. Nothing there had changed, however. Carlton was still snoring, and when she went back along the hall to Susie's open door that lady put down a magazine with a lurid cover and stared at her.

"Hello!" she said. "Anything wrong?"

Hilda studied her, the gleam of cold cream on her face, the half-smoked cigarette in her fingers.

"Somebody's playing tricks around this house," she said. "And don't tell me I imagine it, or that it's done with mirrors. It's got to stop. I've got a patient to consider."

Susie sat up in bed.

"What sort of tricks?" she inquired with interest.

"Were you in your husband's room just now, Mrs. Fairbanks?"

Susie raised her eyebrows and grinned. The connecting door into Carlton's room was open, and through it came the unmistakable snoring of a sleeping man, which begins softly and rises gradually to an ear-splitting snort.

"Listen to that," she said. "If you think Carl is in any mood for amorous dalliance—"

Hilda left her abruptly, the amused smile still on her face, and went on. Jan was in bed, sleeping like a tired child. Marian's door was locked. And there was nobody else. In a cold rage she got her gun from the suitcase and took it forward. In the same rage she folded back the screen, so that it gave her an unimpeded view of the hall. And still in the implacable anger of a woman who has been the victim of a cheap trick she crept into Mrs. Fairbanks's room and examined the closet again, this time with her flashlight. There was no break in the plaster, no place where anything could have been introduced to open the door and close it again.

She spent the remainder of the night in baffled indignation. Her patient slept. No sounds came from the door. At seven she heard the servants going down the back staircase, and shortly after Ida brought her a cup of coffee. She asked the girl to take her place for a few minutes.

"I want to go up to the third floor," she said. "I thought I heard somebody up there last night."

Ida looked surprised.

"There was nobody up there, miss. Not in the front of the house."

"Well, I'll look at it anyhow," she said, and climbed the stairs.

The upper floor was much like the second. Two large rooms across the front and a smaller one above Carlton's were evidently guest rooms. They were long unused, however. Dustcloths covered the furniture and beds, and a faint film of dust showed that rooms and baths were given only periodical cleanings. Hilda paid particular attention to the one over Mrs. Fairbanks. It had a fireplace, like the room below, but it had evidently been long unused. The dust on the hearth was undisturbed, and the flue in the chimney was closed.

There was a closet there, similar to the one below, and this she examined minutely, going over the sides and floor boards. But she discovered nothing out of the way. She thought dejectedly that she would have to come to the theory of a ghost after all.

8

Young Brooke looked tired that morning. Jan was sleeping late, and she was still not around when he made his morning call. He stood over the old lady's bed, and protested her intention of getting up.

"You're not as young as you used to be," he said, smiling down at her. "If you won't take care of yourself we have to do it for you, Mrs. Fairbanks."

"I've got the Adams woman to do that," she retorted dryly. "I don't trust any of the rest of you. And I've noticed that she doesn't bring any bats in with her. I can't say that of anybody else."

Very gravely he offered to let her look into his bag, and the bit of foolery seemed to amuse her.

"Get on with you," she said. "If you'd wanted to kill me why would you have pumped the poison out of me?"

It was rather grisly, but she seemed to enjoy it. Outside the door, however, young Brooke lost his professional cheerfulness. He glanced about and lowered his voice.

"I wish you'd tell Jan something for me," he said. "Just tell her it's all right. She will understand."

"I'm not so sure it's all right, doctor."

Then and there she reported the incident of the closet door. He was puzzled rather than alarmed.

"Of course, a house as old as this—"

"It had nothing to do with the age of the house," she said tartly. "Something opened it and then closed it. I was there. I saw it."

He did not answer. He picked up his bag and glanced back toward Jan's room.

"Don't forget to tell her," he said. "Nobody was around the place.

She's got a fool idea somebody gets in at night. Well, tell her that nobody did. Or tried to."

"You mean you watched all night?"

"You and me both, Miss Adams," he said, with a return of his old
manner. "You and me both."

She had a strong feeling that she should report the door incident to
the inspector. There was some sort of pernicious activity going on.
When she went back to Mrs. Fairbanks's room she took the first opportunity to examine the door. It could be opened, she thought; a
string tied to the knob and carried out into the hall might do it. But
she could see no way by which it could be closed again.

Jan relieved her for sleep, but she did not go to bed. The June day
was bright and warm, so she wandered into the grounds. Outside the
garage Amos was tinkering with one of the three cars, and she wandered over in that direction.

"Good morning," she said. "I can remember this place when they
kept horses."

"Pity they ever changed," said Amos grumpily.

"Mind if I look around a bit?"

He muttered something, and she went inside.

Behind the former carriage house was the tack room, and then
came seven or eight fine old box stalls, now empty save for Amos's
gardening implements and two or three long pieces of rubber hose.

Amos had stopped work and was watching her. She was aware of his
hard, intent stare. But her eyes were fixed on the hose. A motor going
in the garage at night, a long hose leading into the house, perhaps to
the furnace, and Mrs. Fairbanks's windows closed. All the other windows open where people slept, but the old lady—

Amos was still watching her. She smiled at him blandly.

"Mind if I go upstairs?" she said. "I've always longed to see out of
that cupola."

"I live up there."

"You don't live in the cupola, do you?"

She had a strong impression that he did not want her to go up.
Then he shrugged and gave her a faint grin.

"All right," he granted. "But you won't find anything."

So Amos knew why she was there! She felt uneasy as she started up
the stairs, and even more so when she discovered that he was behind
her. He did not speak, however. He merely followed her. But at the
top he ostentatiously reached inside for the key of the door leading to
his own quarters and locked it. What was left was only the old hayloft,

and over it the cupola, dusty and evidently unused for years. There was a ladder lying on the floor, but Amos made no move to lift it.

"What's up there?" she asked.

"Nothing. Used to be pigeons. I've boarded it up. None there now."

She abandoned the idea of the cupola, and took a brief look at the loft itself. It was dark, but she could see that it was filled with cast-offs of the house itself. She could make out broken chairs, a pile of dusty books, an ancient butterfly net, a half-dozen or so battered trunks, and a table with a leg missing. Days later she was to wish that she had examined the place thoroughly that morning. But Amos was there, surly and watchful. She gave it up, and another event that afternoon drove it entirely from her mind.

Marian, looking bored, had taken her mother for a drive, and Janice after seeing them off had slipped out of the house on some mysterious errand of her own. Hilda, undressing for bed, heard her rap at the door.

"I'm going out," she said. "If they get back before I do please don't say I'm not here. I'll get in somehow."

Hilda watched from the window. The girl did not go to young Brooke's office, however. She took a bus at the corner, and Hilda finally went to bed. She slept until five o'clock. Then, having missed her luncheon, she dressed and went down the back stairs for a cup of tea, to find the kitchen in a state of excitement, Maggie flushed with anger, William on the defensive, and Ida pale but quiet.

"Why did you let her in?" Maggie was demanding.

"What else could I do?" William said. "The child brought her in and asked for her grandmother. When I said she was still out in the car she took her into the library. She looks sick."

"She has no business in this," Maggie said furiously. "After the trouble she made! She has a nerve, that's all I've got to say."

They saw Hilda then, and the three faces became impassive.

A few minutes later Hilda carried her cup of tea to the front of the house. Everything was quiet there, however, and she was puzzled. Then she saw what had happened. A woman was lying on the couch in the library. Her hat was off, lying on the floor, and her eyes were closed. But Hilda knew at once who it was.

She went in, putting down her tea, and picked up a limp hand.

"Feeling faint?" she asked.

Eileen opened her eyes and seeing who it was jerked her hand away.

"You startled me," she said. "I thought you were Jan."

Hilda inspected her. She was pale, and her lips, without lipstick, were colorless. Seen now in the strong daylight she looked faded and drab. Resentful, too. There was a tight look to her mouth.

"Jan's getting me some brandy," she said in her flat voice. "We were—we were walking near here, and all at once I felt faint. I'll get out as soon as I can. Marian would have a fit if she found me here."

She tried to sit up, but just then Jan came in, carrying a small glass of brandy and some water. She looked worried, but her small head was high and defiant.

"You're not getting out until you're able to go," she said. "Here, drink this. It will help."

Eileen drank, taking small ladylike sips, and Jan looked at Hilda.

"I'm sorry, but you'd better let me handle this," she said. "I was taking her to see Doctor Brooke, but he was out and she got faint. That's all."

Thus dismissed Hilda went up the stairs. She prayed devoutly that Eileen would be out of the house before Marian and her mother got back. But the family would have to work out its own problems. She had one of her own. If, as she now fully believed, someone was trying to get rid of Mrs. Fairbanks, either directly or by indirection, it was up to her to shut off every possible method. As she expected, the closet door was locked, and a careful examination of Carlton's behind it revealed nothing but his clothes in orderly rows and his shoes lined neatly on the floor. The register in the floor in Mrs. Fairbanks's room, however, did not close entirely. She found a screwdriver in the storeroom as well as a piece of pasteboard, and was in the act of fitting the latter into place when she heard the car drive in. After that there was a moment or two of quiet below. Then she heard Marian coming up the stairs and a moment later she slammed and locked her door.

Hilda shrugged. It was trouble, but it was not hers. She was screwing down the grille over the register when she heard Jan in the hall outside.

"I must speak to you, Mother. I must."

There was no immediate answer. Then Marian's door flew open, and her voice shook with rage when she spoke.

"How dare you, Jan? How dare you do a thing like this to me?"

"I couldn't help it, Mother. She was sick."

"Sick! I don't believe it."

"She was. Ask Miss Adams. Ask Grandmother."

"She can put anything over on your grandmother. As for you, forever hanging around her—"

"Listen, Mother. She telephoned me. She doesn't want Father to know yet, but—she's going to have a baby."

There was a brief stunned silence. Then Marian began to laugh. It was a terrifying laugh, and Hilda got quickly to her feet. Before she reached the door, however, Marian had vanished into her room and the laughter, wild and hysterical, was still going on.

Jan was standing in the hall. She was trembling, and Hilda put an arm around her.

"Never mind," she said. "Don't worry, child. She'll get over it."

"I didn't think she'd care," said Jan blankly, and went down the stairs again.

That evening, Wednesday, June the eleventh, Marian left the house, bag and baggage. Nobody saw her go except Ida, who carried down her luggage. She left while the family was at dinner, and she told nobody where she was going. And only a few nights later her mother was murdered as she lay asleep in her bed.

9

Jan took her mother's departure very hard. She found the room empty after dinner, and Hilda, seeing her as she came out, realized that she was badly shocked.

"She's gone," she said. "Mother's gone. I don't understand. Why would she do a thing like that?"

"I wouldn't worry. She'll come back."

"You don't know her," said Jan. "She hates Eileen. She's made life pretty hard for her, and for my father, too. I'm—" She steadied herself by a chair. "I guess I'm frightened, Miss Adams."

Hilda tried to send her to bed. She refused, however. She spent the evening trying to locate Marian at the hotels in town and at the place she owned in the country. But there was no sign of her. She had not registered anywhere, and the caretaker on the small farm had had no word from her. Jan, giving up finally, looked wan and despairing.

"You don't think she would do anything dreadful?" she asked Hilda. "She's been so terribly unhappy."

"I doubt it," said Hilda briskly. "She's had a shock. She'll get over it."

The old lady took Marian's departure rather philosophically.

"What did she expect? They're married, aren't they? If they want a child—"

On the whole, Hilda thought, she was pleased rather than resentful. As though Marian was getting the punishment she deserved. But she carried through her usual routine that night, an hour or so with her door locked, the radio on, and her game of solitaire.

During that interval Hilda found Carlton in the library and told him about the night before, the noises and the moving closet door.

His reaction rather surprised her. He was alone, the evening paper on his knee but his eyes fixed on the empty fireplace. He stared at her when she had finished without replying. Then he walked to the portable bar and poured himself a drink. When he came back he looked more normal.

"I wouldn't listen to servants' gossip, Miss Adams."

"I heard the sounds myself. And I saw the door move, Mr. Fairbanks."

In the end he went upstairs to his mother's room. It was some time, however, before she admitted him. The room was as usual, the card table set out in front of the hearth and the cards lying on it, but she looked annoyed.

"Really, Carlton, at this time of night."

"It isn't late, Mother."

"It's my time for bed."

"Miss Adams heard something in here last night. I want to find out what it was."

She was quiet after that, although she watched him grimly. Reluctantly she allowed him in the closet with the safe, but he found nothing there. After that he concentrated on the fireplace. At Hilda's suggestion he tore the paper wadding out of the chimney. Nothing resulted but a shower of soot, however. No bricks were loose, and when at last he turned a grimy face to his mother it was to find her coldly indignant.

"Now that you have ruined my room perhaps you'll get out."

"If somebody is trying to scare you—"

"Who would be trying to scare me out of this house? Who wants to sell this place? Who wants to live on a farm? Not Marian. Not Janice. Certainly not the servants. Then who?"

He looked at her, soot and all, with a queer sort of dignity.

"I'm sorry, Mother," he said. "I'm trying to protect you, that's all. As to the farm, I've given that up. Don't worry about it."

He went out, carrying his coat, and Hilda watched him go. It was impossible to think of him, mild and ineffectual as he was, in connection with poison, or even with a mild form of terrorism. It was indeed impossible to think it of any of them—of Jan, young and evidently in love with Courtney Brooke; of Susie, cheerful and irresponsible; of Marian, involved in her own troubles. Even Frank Garrison and Eileen—what had they to gain by the old lady's death?

As it happened, it was Susie who told her about Frank and Eileen that same Wednesday night. Told it with considerable gusto, too, while smoking an endless chain of cigarettes. She came wandering along the hall at one in the morning, in a pale-blue negligee over a chiffon nightdress, and wearing an outrageous pair of old knitted bed-room slippers.

She pulled up a chair and took a chicken sandwich from the supper tray.

"God, how my feet hurt!" she said. "Try walking over farm fields in spike heels and see how you like it."

"I don't think I would try," said Hilda, picking up her knitting. "I have to take care of my feet."

Susie looked at Marian's door.

"Funny about her running off," she said. "Look here, you look like a regular person. What do you make of Eileen Garrison coming here today? Why did the old"—here Susie caught herself and grinned—"witch see her, anyhow?"

"I don't know the circumstances, Mrs. Fairbanks. Of course she was feeling faint."

"Yeah. She's in a chronic state of feeling faint. Can't do any house-work. You ought to see the way they live!" She finished the sandwich and lit another cigarette. "Well, if you ask me it's damned queer. First Mrs. Fairbanks drives her out with curses—same like me, only I don't go. For years she doesn't speak her name or let us speak it. Then Jan brings her here and she talks to her for an hour. No wonder Marian screamed. She's still crazy about Frank. I could be myself, without half trying."

Hilda glanced at her.

"I thought you knew. Mrs. Garrison is going to have a baby."

"Oh, my God!" said Susie. "That spills it. That certainly spills it—for Marian."

It was some time before Hilda got Susie back to where she had left off. She sat grinning to herself over another sandwich until a question brought her back.

"If she was crazy about Mr. Garrison, why did she divorce him?"

Susie finished her sandwich.

"Why? Well, the Fairbankses have got their pride, or haven't you noticed? She'd caught him in Eileen's room, I guess. Maybe nothing to it, but there it was. So she goes off to Reno, and Frank, the poor sap, thinks he's got to marry the girl."

There was much more, of course. Susie, according to herself, might be from the wrong side of the tracks. She was, she said. Her father was a contractor in a small way, who liked to eat in his shirt sleeves. But Eileen was worse.

"Not her family," she said. "They're all right, I suppose. They live
in the country. But they managed to get Eileen an education. However, she couldn't get a job, so she went back to the farm. And believe
you me," Susie added, "there's nothing like a country girl who once
gets to town. The one thing she won't do is go back to the farm. She'll
grab a man if she can, and if she can't she will grab some other
woman's. She tried for Carl, but I slapped her face for her. After that
she let him alone. But Frank, the big softie—"

She put out her cigarette.

"I don't know just how she came in the first place. The old lady
wanted a nice country girl, I guess. Anyhow, Marian was jealous of her
from the start. She soft-soaped everybody. The servants liked her, and
she was the nearest to a mother Jan ever had. Marian was pretty much
the society girl in those days. But Eileen was on the make all the time.
Well, I'd better go by-by."

She rose and stretched.

"Good heavens," she said. "I've eaten all your supper! I'll go down
and get some more."

Hilda protested, but she went down, padding up the stairs, a few
minutes later with a laden tray. She looked indignant.

"That William ought to be fired," she said. "He left the kitchen
door unlocked. I'll tell him plenty in the morning."

Hilda ate her supper, but she was uneasy. She got up and went to
the window which lighted the stairs. Outside a faint illumination from
the street lamps showed the trees which bordered the place, and the
garage. Joe's Market on its corner was closed and dark, but there was a
small light in the house where young Brooke had his office. Below her
was the roof of the porte-cochere, and beyond it the vague outline of
the stable.

Then she stiffened. A figure was moving stealthily from the stable
toward the house. It seemed to be carrying something bulky, and whoever it was knew its way about. It kept off the driveway and on the grass,
and as she watched it ducked around the rear of the building toward
the service wing.

She hesitated. The thought of the huge dark rooms below was almost too much for her. But this was why she was here and, after locking Mrs. Fairbanks's door and taking the key with her, she picked up
her flashlight and went swiftly back to her room. There she got the
automatic and as quietly as she could made her way down the back
stairs.

There was no question about it. Someone was trying the kitchen

door. She did not turn on her light. She listened, and the footseps
moved on to the pantry. Here whoever it was was trying to pry up a
window and—with her gun ready—she threw the light of her flashlight full in his face.

It was Carlton Fairbanks, and at first he seemed too startled for
speech. Then he recovered somewhat.

"Get that damned light out of my face," he shouted furiously. "And
who locked the kitchen door?"

Hilda, too, had recovered.

"Your wife found it open. If you'll go around I'll let you in. I
thought you were a burglar."

She turned on the kitchen lights and admitted him. He was in a
dressing-gown and slippers, and whatever he had been carrying was
not in sight. His anger was gone. He looked embarrassed and uneasy,
especially when he saw the automatic in her hand.

"Always carry a thing like that?"

"I got it out of my suitcase when I saw you coming from the garage."

He relaxed somewhat.

"Sorry if I scared you," he said. "I ran out of cigarettes, and I'd left
some in the car. What on earth," he added suspiciously, "was my wife
doing down here?"

Hilda explained. He seemed satisfied, but he did not leave her
there. He watched her up the stairs and then went back, ostensibly to
get some matches. Wherever they were he was a long time finding
them. When he came up he said a curt good night. But he did not
close his door entirely, and she sat in the hall through the rest of the
night convinced that he was still awake, listening and watching her.

She reported to Inspector Fuller the next morning. He looked relieved when she laid no parcel on his desk.

"What? No livestock?"

She shook her head. She looked very pretty, he thought, but also
she looked devilishly tired.

"No. No livestock. But I'm worried."

"You look it. What's going on there?"

"Everything, from a ghost that opens and closes doors to a family
row. Also breaking and entering. And, of course, a love affair." She
smiled faintly. "That makes it perfect, I suppose."

"Just so long as it isn't yours. I—we can't afford to lose you, you
know."

He was grave enough, however, when she told her story.

"Any idea what Carlton as carrying last night?"

"No. I looked around this morning. I couldn't find anything. Whatever it was, he hid it before he came upstairs."

"Bulky, eh?"

"Maybe two feet high and a foot or so across. That's merely a guess."

"Seem heavy?"

"I don't think so, no. He's a small man. If it had been—"

"And you think it centers about the safe? Is that it?"

"She has something in it," Hilda said stubbornly. "She gets me out of the room, sets up a card table and pretends to play solitaire. I don't believe she does."

"What does she do?"

"She gets something out of the safe and looks at it. She locks me out of the room and turns on the radio. But I have pretty good ears. She goes to the closet and opens it. I can hear it creak. Then she moves back and forward, to the card table, I think. It takes about an hour."

The inspector whistled.

"Hoarded money!" he said. "That's the first time anything has made any sense. And it's the money you're to guard, not the old lady."

"It might be both," said Hilda, and got up.

He did not let her go at once, however.

"You talk about family rows, and so on. Why? I mean—why does Marian Garrison stay there? She could live on her alimony, couldn't she? She gets ten thousand a year, tax free. I've been in touch with Garrison's lawyer. Says the poor devil's business is gone—he's an architect—and it's about all he has."

"Ten thousand a year!" Hilda looked shocked.

"That's right. She takes her pound of flesh every month, and these are hard times on the alimony boys. The damned fool could probably get it reduced by court order. It seems he refuses. But if you want a motive for a murder, there it is, Miss Pinkerton. Maybe that arsenic was meant for Marian, after all."

"And the bats?"

"Oh, come, come, Hilda," he said impatiently. "Carlton wants to sell the place for an apartment. He wants to live on a farm. If he tries to scare his mother into moving, what has that to do with murder?"

"I'd like to know," said Hilda quietly, and went home.

It was that night that Susie fainted.

The day had gone much as usual. No word had come from Marian, and Jan, looking pale and tired, went with her grandmother for her drive that afternoon. On her return she came back to Hilda's room as she was getting into her uniform, but at first she had little to say. She stood gazing out the window, to where across Huston Street young Brooke had his shabby offices. When she turned, her young face looked determined.

"We must seem a queer lot to you, Miss Adams," she said. "Maybe we are. Everyone pulling in a different direction. But we're fond of one another, and we're all fond of Granny. That is, none of us would hurt her. You must believe that."

Hilda was pinning on her cap. She took a moment before she replied.

"I would certainly hope so."

"My father is devoted to her. He always was."

"So I understand," said Hilda quietly.

Jan lit a cigarette, and Hilda saw her hands were trembling. She took a puff or two before she went on.

"Then what was he doing outside our fence last night? On Huston Street? He was there. Courtney Brooke saw him."

She went on feverishly. Brooke had had a late call. When he came back he had seen a figure lurking across the way. He had gone inside and without turning on the light had watched from his window. It was Frank Garrison. His big body was unmistakable. Now and then a car had lighted it, and he had moved a bit. But he had stayed there from midnight until two o'clock in the morning. Then at last he had gone.

Hilda thought quickly. That was when Carlton had come from the stable. Had he been watching Carlton? Or had he some other reason? What on earth could take a man out of bed and put him outside the Fairbanks fence for two hours? But Jan had not finished.

"There is something else, too," she said. "Court says someone with a flashlight was in the stable loft at that same time. It might have been Amos, of course. He's a bad sleeper."

"Did you ask Amos?"

"Yes. He says nobody was there. He'd have heard whoever it was. And I've been to the loft. It's just the same as usual."

"There's probably some perfectly simple explanation for it all," Hilda said, with her mental fingers crossed. "Ask your father when you see him."

Jan looked at her wistfully.

"You don't think he wanted to see Mother? He might have thought she was out, and waited for her to come in. If Eileen told him she had been here—"

"That's something I wouldn't know about," said Hilda firmly, and went forward to her patient.

These people, she thought resentfully, with their interlocking relationships, their loves and hates, what had they to do with the safety of a little old woman, domineering but at least providing a home for them? They only cluttered up the situation. There was Carlton, annoyed with Susie about something and hardly speaking to her all day. And Marian, alone somewhere with her furious jealousy and resentment. And now Frank Garrison, probably hearing of Eileen's visit and trying to make his peace in the small hours of the night.

It was eleven o'clock that night when Susie fainted.

There had been no gin-rummy. Carlton had come up early and gone to bed. Jan had gone out with young Brooke. Even Mrs. Fairbanks had settled down early, and the quiet was broken only by Carlton's regular snoring. Hilda had picked up the *Practice of Nursing* and opened it at random.

When an emergency arises, she read, *a nurse must be able to recognize what has happened, think clearly, act promptly, know what to do and how to do it.*

That was when Susie screamed and fell. Hilda, running back, found her lying on the floor, in the doorway between her room and that of her husband. She was totally unconscious. As Hilda bent over her she heard Carlton getting out of bed.

"What is it?" he said thickly. "Who yelled?" Then he saw his wife and stared at her incredulously. "Susie!" he said. "Good God, what's happened to her?"

"She's only fainted."

"Get some water," he yelped distractedly. "Get a pillow. Get the doctor. Do something."

"Oh, for heaven's sake, keep quiet." Hilda's voice was taut. "She's all right. Keep her flat and let her alone. She's all right."

He got down on his knees, however, and tried to gather her big body to him.

"I'm sorry, old girl," he said hoarsely. "It's all right, isn't it? You know I love you. I'm crazy about you. It's all right, darling."

Susie opened her eyes. She seemed puzzled.

"What's happened to me?"

"You fainted," said Hilda practically. "You screamed and then you fainted. What scared you?"

Susie, however, had closed her eyes.

"I don't remember," she said, and shivered.

10

Mrs. Fairbanks was murdered on Saturday night, the fourteenth of June; or rather early on Sunday morning. Marian had been gone since Wednesday evening, and no word whatever had come from her. The intervening period had been quiet. There were no alarms in the house. On Friday Hilda caught up with her sleep, and Carlton was once more the loving husband, spending long hours beside Susie's bed. He had insisted that she stay in bed.

But Susie was not talking, at least not to Hilda. She eyed her dinner tray Friday evening sulkily.

"Take that pap away and get me an honest-to-God meal," she said. "I'm not sick. Just because I banged my head—"

"What made you do it, Mrs. Fairbanks? Why did you faint?"

"Why does anybody faint?"

"I thought possibly something had frightened you. You shrieked like a fire engine."

"Did I?" said Susie. "You ought to hear me when I really let go."

But her eyes were wary, and Hilda, bringing back the piece of roast beef and so on that she had demanded, was to discover Carlton on his hands and knees poking a golf club under her bed. He got up, looking sheepish, when Hilda came in.

"My wife thinks there is a rat in the room," he explained carefully.

"A rat!" said Susie. "I've told you over and over—"

She did not finish, and Hilda was left with the baffled feeling that the entire household had entered into a conspiracy of silence.

By Saturday, save for Marian's absence, the house had settled down to normal again. Susie was up and about. At dinner that night she persuaded Carlton to take her to the movies, and they left at eight o'clock. At eight-thirty Courtney Brooke came in, announcing to all

and sundry that he had made three dollars in the office and was good
for anything from a Coca-Cola to a ham on rye and a glass of beer.
Mrs. Fairbanks chuckled.

"If that's the way you intend to nourish my granddaughter—" she
began.

"I?" he said. "I am to nourish your granddaughter? What will *you*
be doing while she starves to death?"

She was more cheerful than Hilda had ever seen her when at last he
left her and went downstairs to where Jan waited for him in the library.

Looking back later over the evening, Hilda could find nothing significant in it. Mrs. Fairbanks had locked her door at ten o'clock and
pursued her usual mysterious activities until eleven. Hilda took advantage of part of that hour of leisure and of Carlton's absence to examine both his and Susie's rooms carefully. She found nothing
suspicious, however, and save for Jan's and young Brooke's voices
coming faintly from below the house was quiet except for the distant
rumble of thunder. It was appallingly hot, and when she was at last
allowed to put Mrs. Fairbanks to bed she opened a window."

"You need the air," she said, "and I'll be just outside."

She drew a sheet over the thin old body, feeling a sense of pity for it,
that age had brought it neither serenity nor beauty, nor even love.

"Sleep well," she said gently, and going out closed the door behind
her.

It was a quarter after eleven when the doorbell rang, and Jan answered it. Immediately there were voices below, Jan's and another,
high-pitched and hysterical. It was a moment before Hilda realized
that it was Eileen's.

"So I came here, Jan. I didn't know where else to go. I can leave
tomorrow," she added feverishly. "I can go back home. But tonight—"

Hilda started down the stairs. Eileen, white-faced and trembling,
was in the front hall, a suitcase beside her on the floor. Jan was staring
at her.

"I can't believe it," she said slowly. "Why would he leave you, Eileen?"

"He was furious because I came here the other day. He's hardly
spoken to me since."

"But even then—"

"He's gone, I tell you. He packed a bag and left. He didn't even say
good-by."

Jan looked bewildered. Eileen sat down on a hall chair and took off

her gloves. Her hysteria was gone now. She looked stubbornly determined.

"I can't go to a hotel," she said. "I have no money. Anyhow, your
grandmother told me to let her know if I was in trouble. She said that
the other day. You heard her, Jan."

Hilda inspected her. She looked sick. Her color was high, and she
was breathing fast. And that was the moment when Carlton and Susie
arrived. They stopped and stared at the scene before them. Susie
spoke first.

"What's wrong, Eileen? Frank left you for another woman?"

And then Eileen threw her bombshell.

"If you care to know," she said, "I think he's somewhere with
Marian."

Jan looked suddenly young and rather sick.

"You know that's a lie, Eileen," she said, and turning went stiffly up
the stairs.

After that what? Hilda tried to sort it out in her mind. Carlton went
up to consult his mother, and there were loud voices from the old
lady's room. Eileen leaned back in her chair, her eyes closed. Susie
smoked, casually dropping her ashes into a vase on the hall table, and
young Brooke came out of the library, felt Eileen's pulse, and suggested that she be put to bed as soon as possible.

"You can make other plans tomorrow, but what you need now is
rest."

Her eyes opened.

"That's kind of you, whoever you are," she said faintly. "If I could
have my old room for tonight—"

Unexpectedly Susie laughed.

"Not tonight, darling," she said. "Carlton sleeps there now, and
Carlton sleeps alone."

After that Carlton came down the stairs. He looked irritated, but he
was civil enough.

"Mother thinks you'd better stay here tonight," he said. "She sug-
gests that you take Marian's room. It's ready. She doesn't want the
servants disturbed at this hour."

Susie had giggled, but no one else smiled.

Then what? There had been the procession up the stairs, the doctor
supporting Eileen, Carlton carrying her suitcase, Susie following with
an amused smile on her face. Nothing unusual had happened then,
certainly, unless one remembered Jan. She was waiting outside her

mother's room, silent but resentful. She had switched on the lights, but that was all. The bed was not turned down.

Eileen stopped and looked at her.

"I'm sorry, Jan," she said. "I shouldn't have said what I did. I was excited."

"That's all right," Jan said awkwardly, and turning abruptly went back along the hall to her room and closed the door.

What else happened? Hilda tried to remember. Eileen unlocked her suitcase herself and got out a nightgown, but when Hilda offered to unpack for her she refused curtly.

"I'm leaving in the morning," she said. "Anyhow I hate anyone pawing over my things."

It was all over pretty quickly. Eileen settled, the doctor went back to speak to Jan. Susie went to bed, still smiling her cool smile. And going into Mrs. Fairbanks's room Hilda found her sitting up in bed, her eyes bright with excitement.

"So he's left her at last!"

"So she says."

"I hope it's true. But it wouldn't be like Frank to leave her. Now especially. Tell her I want to talk to her. I've got to get to the bottom of this."

Eileen did come, although not with any great rapidity. She sat on the side of her bed and thrust her feet into slippers, yawning widely. Then she put on a dressing-gown of Marian's from the closet and surveyed herself in the mirror.

"You needn't tell her I wore this," she said. "She'd burn it if she knew."

The idea seemed to amuse her. She tucked the gown around her— it was too long for her—and went into Mrs. Fairbanks's room. The old lady's voice was shrill.

"Come in and shut the door," she said. "Now what's all this nonsense?"

Eileen stayed for half an hour. Hilda could hear their voices, Eileen's soft, Mrs. Fairbanks's high and annoyed. And there was a brief silence, during which she heard the closet door creak. When Eileen came out she looked indignant. She closed the door and stood leaning against it.

"The old devil," she said, in a low voice. "She tried to buy me off! Look, may I have a little of that coffee? I need it."

"It will keep you awake."

"I don't expect to sleep anyhow. Not in that room."

Mrs. Fairbanks was excited when Hilda went in again, but she was certainly alive. She demanded to know why Eileen had told that cock-and-bull story about Frank being with Marian, and that she had told her she must leave in the morning. Hilda got her settled with difficulty. She was not sleepy, and she turned on the radio as the light was switched off.

"Get that woman out of the house in the morning," she said. "Get her out, or somebody will murder her."

That was at midnight. Eileen was quiet, the light out in her room. Courtney Brooke was still with Jan. Susie was reading in bed, her door open, and Carlton had gone back to the library, where he was presumably settling his nerves with the usual highballs.

At a quarter after twelve Mrs. Fairbanks turned off the radio, and soon after young Brooke, looking concerned, left Jan's room and came cautiously forward along the hall.

"She's taking this very hard," he said. "She says her father would never have left his wife, especially since she's going to have a child. She's afraid something has happened to him. I think I'll stay awhile. Where is Mr. Fairbanks?"

"He hasn't come up yet. In the library probably."

He did not go at once. He looked about him, at her tray, at the screen which shielded her from the draft, her easy chair. He thrust his hands in his pockets and took a turn or two across the hall and back.

"What about Jan's father?" he said abruptly. "Of course I know who he is. Who doesn't? Designed the courthouse, didn't he? But what sort is he? Jan's so damned loyal."

"I've only seen him for a minute or two."

"Still in love with his first wife?"

"I wouldn't know about that," Hilda said primly.

"Sort of fellow who'd get in a jam and jump out of a window? Or put a bullet through his head?"

She considered that carefully.

"I don't think so. He had a good war record, I believe. I wouldn't think he lacked courage."

"Oh, rats!" he said roughly. "It takes the hell of a nerve to kill yourself."

He went downstairs after that, his hands still in his pockets, his head bent in thought; a tall lanky worried young man, his hair on end as though he had been pushing his fingers through it. The picture, Hilda thought, of every intern she had ever known, but somehow likable. He reminded her of one in the hospital when she was a probationer. He had found her once in a linen closet and kissed her. It hadn't meant anything, of course. It had been spring, and the windows had been open. She had slapped him.

She drew a long breath and began to fill up her records.

The house was quiet after that. Below she could hear the two men's voices, faint and faraway. The radio was still at last. She looked at her watch. It was well after midnight. And then something happened which surprised and startled her.

The hall had a chandelier which was seldom used. It was an old-fashioned affair of brass and glass pendants, and now the pendants were tinkling. She looked up at them. They were moving, striking together like small bells, and she got cautiously to her feet. Someone was up there, moving stealthily about, and a moment later she had a considerable shock.

From the foot of the stairs she saw a vague figure. It disappeared almost instantly and without a sound, and when she reached the upper hall it was empty. She fumbled for a light, but she could not find it. The doors into the guest rooms were closed as usual. The long hall to the servants' quarters was a black tunnel, and at last she went down again, to find everything as she had left it. To her surprise she found that her knees were shaking. She sat down and poured herself a cup of coffee from the tray. One of the servants, she thought, curious about what was going on. Or maybe the house was haunted, after all. She remembered the opening and closing of the closet door, and found herself shaking again. Of all the absurd things! Maybe she needed glasses. But what about the chandelier?

Afterward she was to time that absence of hers; to do it with the police holding a stop watch on her. Three minutes, almost to the dot. Time to drive a knife into an old woman's thin chest, but hardly time to reach the room, commit the crime, and escape. And who could know that she would go upstairs at all? Eileen drowsy or asleep, her door closed and her light out. Susie and Jan far back along the hall, and the two men in the library below.

Yet then or later—

It was half past twelve when Eileen opened her door. She looked panicky.

"I've got a pain," she said. "Do you think anything's wrong?"

"What sort of pain?"

Eileen described it, and Hilda got up.

"The doctor's still here," she said. "I'll get him."

Eileen, however, was not listening. She was doubled over, holding herself, and Hilda put her back to bed. She lay there, softly moaning, while Hilda went downstairs. The two men were still in the library. Carlton, a highball in his hand, was looking strained, Courtney Brooke was at the telephone. He put it down when she told him about Eileen, and got briskly to his feet.

"I'd better look at her," he said. "We don't want her to abort. Not here, anyhow."

"No. For God's sake, get her out of the house before that happens. Or before Marian comes back." Carlton looked alarmed.

Eileen was watching the door as they came in. She was a pathetic figure as she lay there in her worn nightgown, her face contorted with pain.

"I'm sorry to be such a bother," she said. "I suppose it's the excitement. And my suitcase is heavy. I carried it to the bus."

He examined her briefly and straightened.

"You'll be all right. I'll give you a hypo," he said. "Do you mind boiling some water, Miss Adams?"

He followed her out into the hall. Carlton had come up the stairs. He asked briefly about Eileen and then went into his room. Hilda hesitated.

"I don't usually leave Mrs. Fairbanks alone," she said. "If I do I lock the door. But if you'll watch her—"

He grinned at her.

"Old Cerberus will have nothing on me," he said. "Do you think I want anything to happen to my best patient?"

"Something did happen. Once."

She left him with that, his bag open on the table, his hands fumbling in it for his hypodermic case and the tube of morphia sulphate. But his lightness had gone. He looked thoughtful, even grave.

Downstairs the house was dark, and the huge dingy kitchen eerie even when she had turned on the lights. It was a quarter to one, she saw by the kitchen clock. She was there for some time. The fire in the range was low, and it was perhaps fifteen minutes before she succeeded in boiling the water in a small aluminum pot and carried it up the stairs.

Courtney Brooke was where she had left him. He had poured himself a cup of coffee from her Thermos jug, and was holding it. But he was not drinking it. Some of the coffee had spilled into the saucer, and he was staring up at the landing on the third floor. He said nothing, however. He fixed the hypodermic and gave it to Eileen, still moaning in her bed.

"I don't think you'll lose your baby," he told her. "After all, it's only a month or so, isn't it? You're pretty safe. Just get some sleep. You'll be all right in a day or two."

"I can't stay here, doctor."

"You'll stay until you're able to leave."

He did not leave at once. He stood in the hall, looking uncertain and uneasy, but he merely finished his coffee. He was putting down the cup when without warning Mrs. Fairbanks's radio began to play. He started and almost dropped the cup.

"Does she do that often, at this hour?"

"She turns it on when she can't sleep. I suppose she's excited to-night."

"No good suggesting that it bothers the rest of the household, I suppose?"

"None whatsoever," she told him wryly.

He went back into Eileen's room before he left. She was still awake, but she said the pain was better. She thought she could sleep now. Hilda opened a window for her, the one over the porte-cochere, and tucked the bedclothes around her; Marian's monogrammed sheets, Marian's soft, luxurious blankets. Eileen's hand when she touched it was icy cold.

"I'll leave tomorrow," she said. "Tell them not to worry. I'll not bother them long."

Outside in the hall the radio could still be heard. Courtney Brooke picked up his bag and prepared to go. He looked young and tired.

"Tell Jan not to worry," he said. "I'll be on the job. But I'd give my neck to get her out of this madhouse."

11

Hilda was quite clear as to what followed. The doctor had hardly let himself out of the house when Carlton's door banged open. He came into the hall, tying his dressing-gown around him, his hair rumpled and his face scowling.

"Good God!" he said. "Why don't you turn that thing off?"

"Your mother likes it, when she can't sleep."

"Well, she might let the rest of us have a chance," he said, and pushed savagely past her.

With the door open the noise in the hall was appalling, and he closed it all but an inch or so. He said, "Mother," but Hilda heard no reply. The radio ceased abruptly, so that the silence was almost startling. But Carlton did not come out immediately. Later she was to be queried about that.

"How long did he stay? A minute? Two minutes?"

"Not more than two, at the most."

"But more than long enough to go around the bed and shut off the radio?"

She was miserably uncomfortable.

"I don't know. I heard something creak, and I thought he had opened the door to one of the closets. His mother's safe was in it. The door always creaked."

They timed her on that, too. One of the men walked into the room, turned the radio switch and came back.

"Longer than that?"

"Yes. I'm afraid—I think it was. I know I had time to uncork the Thermos jug and pour some coffee, and I had taken a sip or two before he came out."

"How did he look?"

"I didn't really look at him. He closed the door and said his mother was asleep. He must have gone to sleep himself soon after. I could hear him snoring."

It had commenced to rain after Carlton went back to his room, a summer storm, with rolling thunder and sharp lightning. The rain was heavy. It poured down in solid sheets, and with it came gusts of wind which set the trees outside into violent motion. Somewhere, too, something was banging. Not a door. The sound was too light for that. Hilda decided to look for it and then abandoned the idea.

She ate her supper mechanically. The radio was still silent, and her watch said two o'clock when, having finished, she carried her tray to the back stairs landing to be picked up in the morning.

The sound was still going on when she went back to her post. It would stop just long enough for her to hope that it was over. Then with a fresh gust of wind it would start again.

She was listening for it when there was a crash from the back stairs, followed by a startled "Damnation" in what was unmistakably a feminine voice. When she reached the landing she opened the door to find Susie standing there, a Susie with soaking hair and in a wet raincoat over a bedraggled nightdress. She was standing on one foot and anxiously examining the other.

"Why the hell did you leave that thing there?" she demanded furiously. "I've damned near cut a toe off."

In the light from the front hall Hilda grimly surveyed her, from her sodden blond hair to her slippers, one of which she held in her hands. One of her toes was bleeding, and a cup lay shattered on the tray.

"Better let me put some iodine on that," Hilda said. "Where on earth have you been?"

"I went out to the garage. I'd left my cigarettes in the car."

"It seems to be a family habit," Hilda observed dryly. "Mr. Fairbanks did that a night or two ago. When you locked him out."

Susie fixed a pair of sharp blue eyes on her.

"Oh," she said. "So Carl said that, did he?" Suddenly she giggled. "Not very original, are we?"

She limped forward, and Hilda put her in a chair and dressed her foot, with its pink-painted toenails. But she did not go to bed at once. Nor did she produce any cigarettes. Later Hilda was to know that Susie had done a superb piece of acting that night; that she had been frightened almost out of her senses when she came racing up the stairs. Now, however, she was herself again.

She glanced at Eileen's door and laughed.

"Good heavens," she said, "when I think what would happen if Marian found her there, in her bed!"

Hilda deliberately picked up her knitting. She had an idea that camouflage was not necessary with Susie, but it did no harm to try.

"I don't suppose she would like it," she said absently, counting stitches.

"Like it! Don't underestimate our Marian, Miss Adams. She's a tigress when she's roused. She'd do anything. What on earth is that noise?"

The slapping had started again. It seemed now to come from Eileen's room, and while Susie watched her Hilda opened the door cautiously. Eileen was asleep, her face relaxed and quiet, but one of the screens, the one of the window she had opened over the roof of the porte-cochere, was unhooked. It swung out, hesitated, and then came back with a small, sharp bang. The rain was coming in, wetting the curtains, and Hilda, having hooked the screen, closed the window carefully.

Susie had not moved. She was examining her foot.

"What was it?" she inquired.

"A window screen."

"That's funny. Marian always keeps them hooked. She's afraid of burglars. That roof outside—"

She stopped suddenly, as if she had just thought of something.

"What about Eileen? Is she asleep?"

"She's had a hypodermic. She's dead to the world."

"She couldn't have opened it herself?"

"Not for the last hour or so. Anyhow, why would she?"

But the open screen worried her. She took her flashlight and went back into Eileen's room. It was as she had left it, Eileen's suitcase on the floor, the window closed, and Eileen still sleeping. She went to the window and examined the screen. It could have been unhooked from the outside. A knife blade could have done it. But if there had been any marks on the roof beneath, the rain had washed them away. One thing struck her as curious, however. A thin light piece of rope was hanging down from one of the old-fashioned outside shutters. It swayed in the wind and one end of it now and then slapped against the window itself. But although it seemed to serve no useful purpose, it might have been there for years.

She left the window and opened the bathroom door. The bathroom was empty, and so, too, was Marian's closet, save for the row of garments hanging there. When she went back into the hall Susie was still there.

"Find anything?"

"No. How long has that rope been fastened to the shutter over the porte-cochere?"

"Rope?" said Susie blankly. "What rope?"

Hilda was worried. Useless to tell herself that nobody could have entered Mrs. Fairbanks's room that night. Useless to recall all the precautions she had taken. Her bland cherubic face was gone now. Instead she looked like an uneasy terrier.

"I'm going in to see Mrs. Fairbanks," she said. "She can't do any more than take my head off."

She opened the door and went in. The room was cool and dark, but outside the wind had veered and the curtains were blowing out into the room. She put down the window and then turned and looked at the bed. She only remembered dimly afterward that Susie was standing in the doorway; that there was a brilliant flash of lightning, and that all at once Susie was pointing at the bed and screaming. Loud piercing shrieks that could be heard all over the house.

She herself was only conscious of the small old figure on the bed, with the handle of a common kitchen knife sticking up from the thin chest.

Carlton was the first to arrive. He bolted out of his room in pajamas, and stopped Susie by the simple expedient of holding his hand over her mouth.

"Shut up," he said roughly. "Have you gone crazy? What's the matter?"

Susie stopped yelling. She began to cry instead, and he looked helplessly at Hilda, standing rigid at the foot of the bed.

"I'm sorry, Mr. Fairbanks," she said. "Your mother—"

"What's happened to her?"

"I'm afraid," she said, her voice sounding far away in her own ears. "I'm afraid she's been killed."

He shoved Susie aside, switched on the lights and went into the room. He did not say anything. He stood looking down at the bed, like a man paralyzed with horror. Not until he heard Jan's voice outside did he move.

"Don't let her in," he said thickly. "Keep everybody out. Get the police." And then suddenly: "Mother, *Mother!*"

He went down on his knees beside her bed and buried his face in the bed.

When he got up he was quieter. He looked what he was, an insignificant little man, looking shrunken in his pajamas, but capable, too, of dignity.

"I'd better look after my wife," he said. "She has had a shock. Will you—do you mind calling the police? And the doctor? Although I suppose—"

He did not finish. He went out into the hall, leaving Hilda in the room alone.

She did not go downstairs at once. She went to the bed and touched the thin old arm and hand. They were already cool. An hour, she thought. Maybe more. She had sat outside and eaten her supper, and already death had been in this room, in this body.

Automatically she looked at her wrist watch. It showed a quarter after two. Then her eyes, still dazed, surveyed the room. Nothing was changed. The card table and rocking chair were by the empty hearth. The door to the closet with the safe was open only an inch or two, and when she went to it, being careful not to touch the knob, the safe itself was closed. Nothing had disturbed the window screens. They were fastened tight. And yet, into this closed and guarded room, someone had entered that night and murdered the old woman.

She was very pale when she went out into the hall. The household was still gathering. William and Maggie in hastily donned clothing were coming along the back hall. Ida was halfway down the stairs to the third floor, clutching the banisters and staring, her mouth open. Jan was standing in a dressing-gown over her nightdress, her eyes wide and horrified, and Susie was in a chair, with Carlton beside her and tears rolling down her cheeks.

Hilda surveyed them. Then she closed the door behind her and turning the key in the lock, took it out.

"I'm sorry," she said. "Nobody is to go in until the police get here. I'll call them now."

But she did not call them at once. Eileen, roused from her drugged sleep, had opened her door. She stood there swaying, one hand against the frame.

"What is it?" she said dazedly. "Has something happened?"

It was Carlton who answered, looking at her without feeling, as if he could no longer feel anything, pity or love or even anger.

"Mother is dead," he said. "She has been murdered."

Eileen stood very still, as if her reactions were dulled by the drug she had had. She did not look at Carlton. It was as though she saw none of them. Then her hold on the door relaxed and she slid in a dead faint to the floor.

12

Hilda left her there with Jan and Ida bending over her. She felt very tired. For the first time in her sturdy self-reliant life she felt inadequate and useless. She had failed. They had trusted her and she had failed. Jan's shocked face, Carlton's dazed one, Susie's tears, even Eileen's fainting showed how terribly she had failed.

And it was too late to do anything. What use to call the doctor? Any doctor. Or even the police. The best they could do would be to exact justice. They could not bring back to life a little old lady who, whatever her faults, should not be lying upstairs with a kitchen knife in her heart.

She sat down wearily at the library desk and picked up the telephone. Even here things were wrong. It was some time before she got young Brooke's office. Then the girl she had seen there answered it indignantly.

"Give a person time to get some clothes on," she snapped. "What is it?"

"I want the doctor."

"You can't have him. He's out."

Eventually she learned that a woman had been knocked down at the corner by a bus, and Dr. Brooke had gone with her to a hospital. The girl did not know what hospital.

"Tell him when he comes back," Hilda said sharply, "that old Mrs. Fairbanks has been killed, and to come over at once."

"Jesus," said the girl. "There goes the rent."

Hilda hung up, feeling sick.

After that she called Inspector Fuller at his house. Her hands had stopped shaking by that time, but there was still a quaver in her voice. To her relief he answered at once.

"Yes?"

"This is Hilda Adams, Inspector."

"Hello, Pink. What's wrong? Don't tell me you've found some gold-fish!"

Hilda swallowed.

"Mrs. Fairbanks is dead," she said. "She's been stabbed with a knife. It couldn't have happened, but it did."

His voice changed. There was no reproach in it, but it was cold and businesslike.

"Pull yourself together, Hilda. Lock the room, and hold everything until I get there. Keep the family out."

"I've done that. I—"

But he had already hung up.

She went slowly up the stairs. Ida and Maggie had got Eileen into bed and were standing over her, the door to the room open. In the hall the group remained unchanged, save that Carlton was sitting down, his head in his hands.

"I've got the police," she said. "The doctor's out. If you'd like me to call another one—"

Carlton looked up.

"What's the good of a doctor?" he said. "She's gone, isn't she? And I want that key, Miss Adams. You're not on this case now. She's my mother, and she's alone. I'm going in to stay with her."

He got up, looking determined, and held out his hand.

"No one is to go in there," Hilda said. "Inspector Fuller said—"

"To hell with Inspector Fuller."

It might have been ugly. He was advancing on her when a siren wailed as a radio car turned into the driveway. Susie spoke then.

"Don't make a fool of yourself, Carl. That's the police."

William went down the stairs. He looked old and stooped, and his shabby bathrobe dragged about his bare ankles. When he came back two young officers in uniform were at his heels. They looked around, saw Eileen in her bed, and started for the room. Hilda stopped them.

"Not there," she said. "In here. The door's locked."

She gave them the key, and they unlocked it and went in, to come out almost immediately. One of them stayed outside the door, survey-ing the group in the hall with an impassive face. The other went down to the telephone. With his departure everything became static, frozen into immobility. Then Jan moved.

"I can't bear it," she said brokenly. "Why would anybody do that to her? She was old. She never hurt anyone. She—"

She began to cry, leaning against the screen and sobbing broken-heartedly, and with the sound the frozen silence ended. There was small but definite movement. Carlton lifted his head, showing a white face and blank eyes. Susie felt in her draggled dressing-gown for a cigarette and then thought better of it. And Hilda pulled herself together and went in to look at Eileen. She was conscious, but her pulse was thin and irregular, and Hilda mixed some aromatic ammonia with water and gave it to her.

"Let me out of here," she gasped. "I'm all right. I want to go home."

"Better wait until morning, Mrs. Garrison. You've had a shock. And anyhow you oughtn't to move about. You know that."

Eileen's eyes were wild. They moved from Maggie and Ida back to Hilda.

"I'm frightened," she gasped. "You can slip me out somehow." She tried to sit up in the bed, but Hilda held her down.

"I'm afraid that's impossible," she told her. "The police are here. They may want to talk to you."

"But I don't know anything about it," Eileen gasped. "I've been dead to the world. You know that."

"Of course I know it," Hilda said gently. "They'll not bother you much. I'll tell them."

Eileen relaxed. She lay back against her pillows, her eyes open but the pupils sharply contracted from the morphia.

"How was she killed?" she asked.

"Never mind about that. Try to be quiet."

The second policeman had come up the stairs, and from far away came the sound of another siren. Hilda walked to the window over the porte-cochere and looked out. The rain had almost ceased. It was dripping from the roof overhead, but the wind had dropped. The room was hot and moist. She raised the window and stood staring outside.

The screen she had fastened was open again. It hung loosely on its hinges, moving a little in the light breeze, but no longer banging.

She did not fasten it. She went back to the bed, where Eileen lay with her eyes closed, relaxed and half asleep.

"I'm sorry to bother you, Mrs. Garrison," she said. "Did you open a window tonight? Or a screen?"

"What screen?' " said Eileen drowsily. "I didn't open anything."

Ida got up. She had been sitting by the bed.

"Better let her sleep if she can, miss," she said. "Why would she open a screen?"

All at once the hall outside was filled with men, some of them in uniform. They came up the stairs quietly but inevitably, carrying the implements of their grisly trade, the cameramen, the fingerprint detail, the detectives in soft hats and with hard, shrewd eyes. A brisk young lieutenant was apparently in charge.

He nodded to Carlton.

"Bad business, sir," he said. "Sorry. Can you get these people downstairs? In one room, if that's convenient."

Carlton looked overwhelmed at the crowd.

"We'd like to get some clothes on," he said.

"Not yet, if you don't mind. The inspector will be here any time now. He'll want to see you all."

They shuffled down, accompanied by an officer, the three servants, Susie, Jan, and Carlton. Only Eileen remained, and Hilda, standing in her doorway. The lieutenant looked at her, at her uniform and at the room beyond her.

"Who is in there?"

"Mrs. Garrison. She can't be moved. I'm looking after her."

He nodded, and with a gesture to two of the detectives, went into the dead woman's room and closed the door. The others stood around, waiting. A cameraman lit a cigarette and put it out. One or two yawned. Hilda closed the door into Eileen's room and stood against it, but they showed no interest in her. Not at least until the inspector came up the stairs.

He took one look at her and turned to the uniformed man who had come with him.

"See if there's any brandy in the house," he said. "Sit down, Hilda. Bring a chair, somebody."

They looked at her then. The hall was filled with men staring at her. Their faces were blurred. She had felt this way her first day in the operating room. White masks staring at her, and someone saying, "Catch that probationer. She's going to faint." She roused herself with an effort, forcing her eyes to focus.

"I'm not going to faint," she said stubbornly.

"You're giving a darned good imitation, then," he said. "Sit down. Don't be a little fool. I need you."

The brandy helped her. When she could focus her eyes she found the inspector gone. But the phalanx of men was still in the hall, watching her with interest. She got up unsteadily and went into Eileen's room. To her surprise Eileen was up. She was trying to get into her clothes, and the face she turned on Hilda was colorless and desperate.

"I've got to go," she said. "If Frank goes home and finds I'm gone—I must have been out of my mind to come here."

"I can telephone, if you like. You can't leave, of course. They won't allow anyone to leave the house."

"You mean—we're prisoners?"

Hilda's nerves suddenly snapped.

"Listen," she said. "There's been a murder in this house. Of course you're not a prisoner. But you're getting back into that bed and staying there if I have to put a policeman on your chest."

That was the situation when there was a rap at the door. The inspector wanted her, and Hilda went out.

In the old lady's room nothing had yet been disturbed. Only the detectives were standing there, touching nothing. The inspector nodded at her.

"All right," he said. "Now look at this room. You know how you left it when Mrs. Fairbanks went to bed. Is anything changed? Has anything been moved? Take your time. There's no hurry."

She gazed around her. Everything was different, yet everything was the same. She shook her head.

"Try again," he insisted. "Anything moved on the table? Anything different about the curtains?"

She looked again, keeping her eyes from the quiet figure on the bed.

"I think Mrs. Fairbanks left that closet door closed," she said finally.

"You're not sure?"

"I'm sure she closed it. She always did. But there's a small safe in it. I think Mrs. Fairbanks opened it at night. I don't know why."

"A safe?"

He took out a handkerchief and pulled the door open. He examined the safe, but it was closed and locked.

"Anyone else in the house have access to it?"

"I don't think so. She was rather queer about it. She didn't really like anybody to go into the closet, and she locked it when she went out."

"I suppose this is the closet where—"

"Yes."

He showed her the knife, still in the dead woman's chest. She forced herself to look at it, but she was trembling.

"Ever seen it before?"

"I may. I wouldn't know. It looks like a common kitchen knife."

"There wasn't such a knife upstairs, for instance? Lying about."

She shook her head, and he let her go, saying he would talk to her later. As she went out the men in the hall crowded in, to take their pictures, to dust the furniture and the knife for prints, to violate—she thought miserably—the privacy of fifty years of living. And why? Who in this house would have killed an old woman? No one seeing the household that night could doubt that they were shocked, if not grieved. And who else could have done it?

Her mind was clearer now. The radio had been turned on before young Brooke left, so she was alive then. Who else? Carlton? He had gone in and shut off the machine. He could have carried the knife in his dressing-gown pocket. But—unless he was a great actor—he was almost broken by his mother's death. He had gone down on his knees by the bed. He—

Who else? Marian was away. Jan was out of the question. Eileen was sick and under the influence of the hypodermic. Susie? But how could Susie get into the room? How could anyone get into the room?

She went back carefully over the night. Eileen had left Mrs. Fairbanks at midnight and Hilda had put her to bed. At a quarter after twelve she had shut off her radio and apparently gone to sleep. It was almost half past twelve when Courtney Brooke had gone down to have a drink with Carlton in the library, and soon after that Eileen had complained of pain.

During all that time she—Hilda—had left the door unguarded only for the brief excursion to the head of the stairs to the third floor, along the back hall to carry her tray back, and much later when Susie crashed into it. True, she had been in the kitchen for some time, but Mrs. Fairbanks had been alive after that. Witness the radio.

Her mind was whirling. She had been in Eileen's room once or twice, but only for a matter of seconds. In any case she could have seen Mrs. Fairbanks's door, and any movement outside. Susie? But the old lady had been dead for some time before she left her in the hall to close Eileen's screen. An hour at least; maybe more.

She leaned her head back in her chair. On the table still lay her equipment for the night, the heavy textbook, her knitting bag, the thermometer in its case, the flashlight, her charts and records. She could see the last thing she had written, after Eileen's visit. *Patient nervous. Not sleepy. Refuses sedative.* She felt sick again.

From beyond the closed door came the muffled sounds of men moving about, and the soft *plop* of the cameramen's flash bulbs. A car drove in below, a bell rang, and a man with a bag came up the stairs. The medical examiner, she knew. But what could he find? A little old lady on her back, with her arms outstretched and a knife in her heart.

He was a brisk, youngish man with a mustache, and he was in a bad humor when the inspector came out to meet him.

"Pity you fellows can't move without a panzer division," he said. "I had the devil of a time getting my car in."

"Well, we won't keep you long," said the inspector. "Stab wound in the chest. That's all."

"How do you know that's all?"

"It seems to have been enough."

The medical examiner ignored Hilda. He went inside the room, followed by the inspector, and was there five minutes. He was still brisk when he came out, but his irritation was gone. He seemed depressed.

"So that's the end of old Eliza Fairbanks," he said, tugging at his mustache. "Who did it? You can bet your bottom dollar she didn't do it herself."

"No," said the inspector. "No, I don't think so. How long ago, do you think?"

The medical examiner looked at his watch.

"It's half past three now," he said. "I'd say two hours ago. Maybe more. Say between one and two o'clock, at a guess. Nearer one, perhaps, from the body temperature. Hard to tell, of course. *Rigor* sets in earlier in warm weather. I'll know better after the autopsy. What time did she eat last?"

He looked at Hilda.

"She had a tray at seven-thirty," she said. "She didn't go down to dinner. Poached eggs, a green salad, and some fruit. She was alive a little after one o'clock."

"How do you know that?" he asked sharply. "See her?"

"No. She turned on her radio."

He was still brisk as he went down the stairs. This was his job. When he went to bed he left his clothing ready to put on, the cuff links in his shirt, his shoes and socks beside the bed, his tie on the dresser. Even his car had a permit to stand out on the street all night. He lived like a fireman, he would say. But now he was slightly shocked. Mostly his work took him to the slums. Now there was a murder in the Fairbanks house. Somebody had jabbed a knife into old Eliza. Well, he'd be damned. He'd be doubly damned.

The inspector watched him down the stairs. Then he got a straight chair and sat down, confronting Hilda. There was no softness in his face. He looked angry and hard. Hard as nails.

"All right," he said. "Now let's have it. And it had better be good. No use saying it couldn't happen. It has."

She braced herself. She had failed, and he knew it. He wanted no excuses. He wanted the story, and she gave it as coherently as her tired mind would allow; Eileen's arrival, her story and subsequent collapse; Mrs. Fairbanks's demand to see her, and after that the unusual settling her for the night. Then came Eileen's pain, the two trips downstairs, one to speak to the doctor, the other to boil some water, leaving the doctor on guard, and the later discovery of Eileen's open screen slapping in the wind. But it was over Susie's appearance, wet and bedraggled, that he spent the most time.

"What about this Susie?" he asked. "Devoted to the old lady and all that?"

In spite of herself Hilda smiled.

"Not very. Mrs. Fairbanks disliked her, and Susie—well, I thought she tried to annoy her mother-in-law. But that's as far as it went."

"What about this excursion of hers? For cigarettes in the rain? Do you believe it?"

"It might have been. She smokes a good bit."

"But you don't think so?"

"I don't know. I don't think she's particularly scrupulous. But I doubt if she would kill anybody. She and her husband wanted to leave here and buy a farm. Mrs. Fairbanks objected. Still that's hardly a reason—"

"Any chance she could have unhooked this screen over the porte-cochere? Earlier in the night?"

"She didn't come upstairs after dinner. She and Mr. Fairbanks went to the movies."

"What about later? After the Garrison woman came?"

"She wasn't in the room at all. She hates Eileen Garrison like poison."

"What's she like? Strong? Muscular?"

"She looks pretty strong. She's a big woman."

He looked back along the hall. The screen which usually protected Hilda's chair had been folded against the wall, and he had an uninterrupted view.

"Where is her room?"

Hilda told him, and he went back and inspected it, including the door to the service staircase.

"You didn't see her leave?"

"No. The screen was in the way."

"So," he said thoughtfully, "she was outside for nobody knows how long. She's big enough to handle a ladder, and she had no reason for loving her mother-in-law. People have gone to the chair for less!"

All at once Hilda found herself defending Susie. She was too direct, too open. She was—well, she was simply Susie.

"Suppose she did get into Eileen's room? Eileen Garrison was there. She was awake until she had the hypodermic. And after that how could she get into Mrs. Fairbanks's room? I was here, in this chair. When we found the body at half past two it was already—cool."

Nevertheless, he sent an officer to locate a ladder, in the house or on the grounds, preferably wet. He did not sit down again after that. He stood still, frowning thoughtfully.

"What about this radio?" he asked abruptly. "Sure the old lady turned it on herself? Somebody might have used one of these remove control affairs. They operate as far as sixty feet."

"Don't they have cables, or something of the sort?"

"Not the new ones."

The men were coming out now. He let some of them go and detained two of the detectives.

"I want every room in the house searched," he told them. "Look for one of those remote radio controls. Look for a phonograph, too. And for anything suspicious, of course. Miss Adams will have to go into the room here in front. There's a sick woman there."

They moved off, quiet and businesslike. From the driveway below came the sounds of cars starting as the fingerprint and cameramen departed. No voices came from the library, and Hilda could imagine the group huddled there, stricken and dazed. She got up.

"Now?"

"If you please."

She went into Eileen's room. Eileen was asleep, but she roused at Hilda's entrance.

"What is it?" she said peevishly.

"I'm sorry. I'll have to search the room. All the house is being searched. I won't bother you."

"Go ahead. What are they looking for? Another knife?"

But the net result was nothing. The suitcase revealed a dress or two and some undergarments, most of them showing considerable wear. The closet, hung with Marian's luxurious wardrobe, provided a bitter contrast, but that was all. And Eileen, yawning, looked bored and indifferent.

"I wish you'd get out and let me sleep."

"How do you feel?"

"How do you expect me to feel?"

She was half asleep when Hilda left the room.

The search was still going on when she closed the door behind her. One of the detectives was on his way to the third floor, and she gathered nothing had been found. There was a uniformed guard outside Mrs. Fairbanks's door, and two men in white were inside by the bed with a long wicker basket.

So Eliza Fairbanks was leaving the home to which she had come as a bride, going in a basket, without the panoply of flowers and soft music, without even dignity or any overwhelming grief.

Standing in the hall Hilda swore a small and very private oath; to help the police to revenge this murder, and to send whoever had done it to death. "So help me God."

13

The family and servants were still in the library when she went downstairs. They paid no attention to her. It was as though the knife, now wrapped in cellophane and in the inspector's pocket, had cut them all away from their normal roots, their decent quiet habits of living. Only Jan looked up when Hilda entered, her eyes swollen, and clutching a moist handkerchief in her hand.

"Are they through?"

"Not quite."

"But this is dreadful. We're not prisoners. None of us would have hurt Granny."

"I don't see how it's possible for anyone to have done it."

Carlton turned his head and looked at her with blood-shot eyes. He was holding a highball, and it was evidently not his first.

"Where were you?" he demanded. "I thought your job was to protect her. What do we know about you? How do we know you didn't do it yourself?"

"Oh, shut up, Carl," Susie said wearily. "Why would she?"

Watch them all, the inspector had said. *They'll have the gloves off now. Watch Carlton. Watch his wife. Watch the servants, too. They may know something. Tell them about the ladder and the screen. That may make them sit up.*

She sat down. The servants were huddled in a corner, Maggie stiff and resentful, Ida staring at nothing, her hands folded in her lap, and William on the edge of a chair, his head shaking with an old man's palsy.

"Someone may have got in from outside," she said. "Mrs. Garrison's screen was open. They're looking now for a ladder."

She thought Carlton relaxed at that. He even took a sip of his drink.

"Plenty of ladders about," he said. "Police have some sense, after all."

Only Jan showed a sharp reaction. She sat up and stared at Hilda wildly.

"That's absurd," she said. "Who would want to do such a thing? And even if they did they couldn't get into Granny's room. Miss Adams was always in the hall."

Hilda watched her. She was not only terrified. She knew something. And Susie was watching her, too.

"Don't take it too hard, Jan," she drawled. "They've got to try everything. No use getting hysterical. That won't help."

It sounded like a warning. Again Hilda wondered if there was a conspiracy among them, a conspiracy of silence. As if, whatever had once divided them, they were now united. She got no further, however. Outside an ambulance drove away, and immediately after the inspector appeared at the door.

"I'd like to talk to you," he said to the room in general. "There are some things to be cleared up. If there's a place where I can see everybody, one at a time—"

Carlton got up. His truculence had returned, and he was feeling the whisky.

"I'd better tell you," he said thickly. "I suppose this Adams woman has already done it. I was in my mother's room tonight. I went in to turn off the radio. But I didn't touch her. I thought she was asleep. I—"

"We'll talk about that later. You're Mr. Fairbanks, I suppose?"

"Yes."

"And don't be a fool," said Susie unexpectedly. "He didn't kill her. He was fond of her, God knows why. Anyhow he hasn't got the guts for murder. Look at him!"

Her tone was half contemptuous, half fiercely protective. The inspector ignored her.

"If there is a room I'll talk to you there, Mr. Fairbanks. And I'll ask you to come along, Miss Adams, to check certain facts."

"I'm not talking before her," Carlton snapped.

"Miss Adams is one of my most able assistants, Mr. Fairbanks. If you prefer to go to my office—"

But the fight was out of Carlton. He looked at Hilda and shrugged.

"All right. God knows I have no secrets. Come in here."

He led the way to the small morning room behind the library, and the inspector closed the door.

Yet Carlton's story, as it was dug out of him, offered little or nothing new. He had been in bed when his mother's radio went on. It was very loud. It wakened him. He had gone in and shut it off. The room was dark. He had seen only her outline, but she had not moved.

"You came out immediately?"

"I did."

"Are you sure of that? Didn't you open a closet door while you were in the room?"

The question took him by surprise. He looked uncomfortable.

"I closed it," he said. "It was standing open."

"Wasn't that rather curious? I mean, why do a thing like that?"

"My mother liked it closed. Her safe was there."

"Did you stop to examine the safe?"

He hesitated.

"Well, I took a look." He glanced at Hilda. "I didn't know anything about Miss Adams. I just wondered—" He tried to smile and failed. "My mother was rather peculiar in some ways," he said. "I've never seen inside the safe. But if she had money there—"

His voice trailed off again.

"I thought she was crazy," he said heavily. "All this talk about bats and things. But I might have known better. Somebody tried to poison her this spring. I suppose you know about that?"

"She told me herself."

Carlton looked stunned.

"Are you telling me she went to the police?"

"I am. I saw her last Monday, and I sent Miss Adams at her request. She believed that someone in this house was trying to scare her into a heart attack—and death."

"That's absurd." He lit a cigarette with unsteady fingers. "Who would try a thing like that? It's silly on the face of it."

He looked profoundly shocked, however. Hilda, watching him, thought that for the first time he was really apprehensive. But the inspector shifted his questions.

"Do you know the combination of the safe?"

"No."

"Who benefits by her death?"

"That's the hell of it. We all do."

"Even the servants?"

"I'm not certain. I haven't seen her will. Her lawyer has it, Charles Willis. They may get a little. Not enough to matter."

"Have you any idea of the size of the estate?"

The shift had brought some color back to Carlton's face. He put out his cigarette and straightened.

"I don't know, and that's a fact," he said bitterly. "My father left about three million dollars. She must have quite a lot left. I wasn't in her confidence. I tried to talk to her, about her taxes and so on, but she wouldn't listen. She always thought I was a fool about money. But lately she's been cutting down expenses. I don't know why. She should have had a fair income."

"What do you mean by fair?"

"Oh, forty or fifty thousand a year."

The inspector smiled faintly. To him that amount represented capital, not income. There was a brief silence. Hilda looked at her wrist watch. It was half past four, and the early June dawn was already outlining the trees outside the windows. When the inspector spoke again his face was grave.

"The medical examiner sets the time of death as approximately between one and two o'clock. Nearer one, he thinks. He may be able to tell us more accurately after the autopsy. The only person known to have entered your mother's room during that time was yourself, Mr. Fairbanks."

Carlton leaped to his feet.

"I never touched her," he said shrilly. "I thought she was asleep. Ask Miss Adams. I wasn't in the room more than a minute or two."

He was in deadly earnest now, and cold sober. Hilda felt sorry for him. Of all the family, she thought, he was the only one outside of Jan who had had any affection for the old lady. Marian had resented her, had blamed her for the failure of her marriage. Susie had frankly flouted her. Even Eileen had called her an old devil.

"You went into the room, walked around the foot of the bed, turned off the radio, came back and closed the closet door. That right?"

"That's right."

He would not change his story, and at last he was allowed to go. The inspector looked at Hilda.

"True or false?" he said.

"Partly true, anyhow. If he closed the closet door, who opened it? He's keeping something back. Something he's not going to tell."

"Any idea what it is?"

"Not the slightest. Unless he knows his wife was outside in the rain. He's very much in love with her."

He got out the knife and laid it, still in its cellophane envelope, on the table beside him.

"Let's show this to Maggie," he said.

But Maggie, having worked herself into a fine state of indignation, repudiated it at once.

"It's none of mine," she said. "And I'd like to say that I've been in this house for twenty years and never before—"

"All right," said the inspector. "Get out and send in the butler and the other woman, Ida. And make some coffee. I've got some men who need it, too."

Maggie, considerably deflated, went out, and William and Ida came in. Neither of them recognized the knife, both had been in bed when Susie's shrieks wakened them, both were—according to the inspector's comment after they left—pure as the driven snow and innocent as unborn babes.

"But behaving according to rule," he said dryly. "Always more emotional than the family in a crisis. Watch it sometime."

Susie bore this out when she was sent for. She looked faintly amused as she wandered in, a cigarette in her fingers and her raincoat still covering her draggled dressing-gown.

"I suppose the dirty work begins now," she said, sitting on the edge of the table and ignoring the knife. "I didn't like her. I've had to take her charity and her insults ever since Carl's business failed. I thought she was an old bitch and I've said it. So I suppose I'm the leading suspect."

The inspector eyed her, the nightgown, the stained bedroom slippers, her hair still damp and straight.

"Not necessarily," he said dryly. "I'd like to know why you were out in the rain tonight."

"Your lady friend has told you, hasn't she? I went out to get some cigarettes from the car, and that damned storm caught me."

"There were cigarettes all over your room, Mrs. Fairbanks. I saw them there. I don't believe that was the reason you were outside."

Susie stared at him.

"So what?" she said defiantly. "I didn't kill her, if that's what you want to know."

"But you admit you didn't like her."

"Good God! I don't like you, but I don't intend to cut your throat."

"That's very reassuring," he told her gravely. "And I haven't accused you of killing your mother-in-law. I want to know if you were in Mrs. Garrison's room tonight?"

Susie's surprise was apparently genuine.

"Eileen's? I should say not. I sat in the hall while Miss Adams fastened her screen. She was asleep, thank God. That's as near as I came to her, and nearer than I wanted to be."

"You don't like her, either?"

"She's another bitch," said Susie with feeling.

But she was evasive after that. Hilda, watching her, was certain she was frightened, that her assurance covered something close to panic. She stuck to her story, however. She had gone out for cigarettes and the storm had caught her. The garage was locked, as was the door to the stairs leading to Amos's quarters. She had stood under the eaves of the building for a while. Then she had made a dash for the house.

"That's all?"

"That's all," she said defiantly.

The inspector took a piece of paper from his pocket and unfolded it.

" 'At five minutes before two,' " he read, " 'a woman yelped under my window. I raised it and looked out. She was standing still, but someone else was going out through the break in the fence. I think it was a man. The woman was Mrs. Carlton Fairbanks. She was rubbing her arm. I watched her until she went back to the house.' "

Susie's bravado was gone. She pushed back her heavy hair.

"Amos, the dirty skunk!" she said. "All right, I wasn't going to say anything, but I can't help you at that. There was a man there. I was trying the door to the stairs when he grabbed me by the arm. I yelled and he beat it. But I don't know who it was."

She stuck to that. He had been behind her when he caught her. He hadn't spoken, and the rain was like a cloudburst. All she knew was that he let go of her when she screamed, and disappeared. She hadn't said anything to Miss Adams. No use scaring a woman who had to be up all night. She had meant to tell Carl, but he was asleep and snoring. But she had had a shock. She hadn't felt like going to bed. She had sat in the hall, and then Mrs. Fairbanks had been killed.

She pulled back the sleeve of her raincoat and showed her forearm.

"Take a look at that if you don't believe me," she said.

There were two or three small bruises on her arm, as if made by fingers, and they were already turning purple.

"I bruise easy," she said.

Nothing shook her story. The sun had risen and birds were chirping outside when at last she was dismissed. With a warning, however.

"I think you know who the man was, Mrs. Fairbanks," the inspector said soberly. "I want you to think it over. It is bad business to keep anything back in a case of this sort."

She went out, and he looked at Hilda.

"All right, Miss Pinkerton," he said. "What about it?"

"She's a fine actress and a pretty fair liar," Hilda said. "She's protecting somebody." She hesitated. "It may be the doctor. He lives across Huston Street, and he uses that break in the fence. But it might have been innocent enough. He's in love with Jan Garrison. He may have meant to meet her. Or even"—she smiled faintly—"to look up at her window. I believe people in love do things like that."

The inspector, however, had jumped to his feet.

"The doctor!" he said. "He's in love with the girl, she inherits under the will, and he was alone outside Mrs. Fairbanks's door for fifteen or twenty minutes. Where the hell is he?"

"He took an injured woman to the hospital. He may be home now. But he couldn't have done it. The radio—"

"Oh, blast the radio," he said.

He went out into the hall and sent an officer to Courtney Brooke's house. After that he sent for Janice. She came in slowly, her eyes still red, and Hilda felt a wave of pity for her. Before going to bed she had wrapped the long ends of her hair in curlers, and they made her look childish and naïve. Even the inspector spoke gently.

"Sit down, Miss Garrison," he said. "You know we have to ask all sorts of questions in a case like this. You needn't be afraid. All we want is the truth."

"I don't know anything."

"I don't suppose you do. You were asleep when it happened, weren't you?"

"I don't know when it happened, but I wasn't asleep when Susie yelled. I wasn't sleepy, and Granny's radio had been turned on full."

"You hadn't expected to go out? Into the grounds, I mean."

Jan looked puzzled.

"Out? No. Why should I?"

"Let's say, to meet someone?"

It took her by surprise. She stared at him. Then a look of horror spread over her face. She looked wildly about the room, at Hilda, at the door. She even half rose from her chair.

"I don't know what you mean," she managed to gasp.

The inspector's voice was still quiet.

"Suppose you meant to meet someone by the garage. Then it

rained, and you didn't go. That would be understandable, wouldn't it? He came, but you didn't."

"Nobody came. I don't know what you're talking about."

"Would you swear on oath that you had no appointment to meet Doctor Brooke by the garage tonight?"

She only looked bewildered.

"Doctor Brooke!" she said. "Certainly not. He can see me whenever he wants to, here in the house."

He let her go, watching her out with a puzzled look on his face.

"Well, what *scared her?*" he demanded. "Do I look as formidable as all that, or— What about this Amos, anyhow? Think he's reliable?"

"He's a mischiefmaker. Stubborn and sly. He's probably honest enough."

"What is 'honest enough'?" he inquired quizzically.

But Hilda was thinking. She was remembering Jan's story that Courtney Brooke had seen her father outside the fence a night or two before. That, she was convinced, had been behind Jan's terror just now. Yet there were so many other things that she felt dizzy. The coldness for a day or so between Carlton and Susie, and Susie's fainting. Her idiotic story about going to the garage for cigarettes. Carlton, earlier in the week, carrying something from the stable and being locked out. The bats and so on in Mrs. Fairbanks's room, and the closet door which opened and closed itself.

They must make a pattern of some sort. Only what had they to do with an old woman dead of a knife thrust in a closed and guarded room?

It was just before young Brooke's arrival that one of the detectives from upstairs came down and stood in the doorway. He looked rather sheepish.

"There's a bat in that room where the old lady was," he said. "It was hanging to a curtain, and it acts like it's going crazy."

"It hasn't a thing on me," said the inspector, and sighed.

It was bright daylight when Courtney Brooke arrived. He looked tired and puzzled, and like Susie he showed evidence of having been caught in the storm. His collar was crumpled and his necktie a limp string.

"What's wrong?" he said. "I've just come back from the hospital. Is Mrs. Fairbanks—"

"Mrs. Fairbanks is dead," said the inspector dryly. "She was murdered last night."

The doctor stiffened and looked wildly at Hilda.

"Murdered! All I ordered for her was a sleeping tablet if she couldn't sleep. If she got anything else—"

"She was stabbed. Not poisoned."

The full impact seemed to strike him with that. He sat down, as though his legs would not hold him.

"I'd like an account of what you were doing last night, doctor," said the inspector smoothly. "Begin, if you please, with Mrs. Garrison's trouble, when you were sent for. You decided to give her a hypodermic. Then what?"

He made an effort to collect himself.

"I didn't notice the time. She was having pain. She was afraid of a miscarriage. I asked the nurse here to get me some sterile water. She went downstairs. It took some time, and I—"

"You remained outside Mrs. Fairbanks's door during all that time?"

He looked unhappy.

"Well, yes and no," he said. "I went back and spoke to Janice Garrison. She had been uneasy about her father. Her stepmother said he had left her, but she didn't believe it. She thought something had happened to him."

"Did you stay in the hall? Or did you go into Miss Garrison's room?"

"I went in. I was there only a minute or two. Long enough to reassure her."

Hilda spoke.

"You agreed to guard the door," she said. "Like Cerberus. You remember?"

"Well, look," he said reasonably. "Only the family was in the house. Nobody would have had time to get in from the outside. And it was poison she was afraid of. Not—being stabbed." He became suddenly conscious of his appearance. He put a hand to his collar. "Sorry I look like this," he said. "The fellow who brought me was on the steps. He wouldn't let me in the house."

The inspector eyed him.

"Never mind how you look. This isn't a party. It's a murder investigation." He cleared his throat. "That's all, is it? You stepped into Miss Garrison's room and out again. Right?"

"I might have been there five minutes," he admitted. "I'd been telephoning around for her, and—"

"You saw nothing whatever that might be useful? Nobody moving about?"

For an instant he seemed to hesitate, and Hilda remembered the coffee spilled in the saucer and his strange expression as she came up the stairs. But he shook his head.

"Nothing," he said.

He had gone home after giving Eileen the hypodermic, he said. It was raining a little, and he had taken the short cut by the stable and the break in the fence. He saw no one lurking there. And he was in bed asleep when a man from Joe's Market rang the bell and said a woman had had an accident at the corner.

"What time was that?"

About two, he thought. It was storming hard by that time. He had telephoned for an ambulance, taken his bag, and gone to the corner. The woman was lying on the pavement, with one or two people with her. She was pretty badly hurt. He had done what he could, and then gone with the ambulance to the hospital.

"I stayed while they operated," he said. "It's my old hospital, Mount Hope. They all knew me."

"At ten minutes to two you were in bed?"

"I was in bed when this fellow rang the bell. I opened a window and he called up to me."

"You were undressed?"

Brooke grinned.

"I'll say I was. I haven't got much on now, under this suit."

"You didn't run into Mrs. Susie Fairbanks, at the garage at five minutes to two, and catch hold of her?"

He looked astounded.

"Good God, no! Why should I?"

But he lost some of his spontaneity after that. He was wary. He answered the routine questions more carefully, and at last the inspector shrugged and let him go. He was irritable, however.

"What's the idea?" he said to Hilda grumpily. "That fellow knows something. Everybody around here knows something—except me. Even you, probably." He looked at her keenly. "I wouldn't put it past you, you know. You've held out on me before."

"Only when I thought it was necessary," she said, smiling up at him delicately.

But he had enough. He had had too much. He got up and banged the table.

"God damn it, Hilda," he roared. "If I thought you have any pets around here and are protecting them, I'd—I'd turn you over my knee."

14

It was eight o'clock in the morning before they could rouse Eileen enough to be interviewed. Carlton, unshaven and still only partially dressed, was at the telephone trying to locate his sister. Susie had brought him a cup of coffee, but it sat untouched beside him.

"Hello. That you, Blanche? Sorry to bother you. Did Marian happen to tell you where she was going to stop while she's away? It's rather urgent."

He would hang up after a minute or two, feverishly thumb the telephone book and commence all over again.

In the morning room Courtney Brooke was trying to comfort Jan, a Jan who lay face down on a long davenport and refused to be comforted. One of the curlers on the end of her long bob had come loose, and he sat turning the soft curl over a finger.

"Believe me, darling, it's all right. You mustn't go on like this. You break my heart, sweet."

"Granny's dead." Her voice was smothered. "Nothing can change that."

"It's a bad business, Jan. I know that. Only try to face it as it is, not as you're afraid it is. You're not being fair. Even the police don't condemn people until they have the facts."

"I saw him. I spoke to him." She turned over and sat up, her eyes wide with fear. "Now it will all come out, Court. She had it in the safe. She told me so. They'll open it, and—then they'll know."

"Whoever did it didn't open the safe. It's still there, sweet."

She got up, and as he steadied her he thought how thin she was, how badly life had treated her. His arm tightened around her.

"If it's still there," she said excitedly. "Do you think we could get it?

Oh, Court, can't we get it? She must have had the combination some-where. She never trusted her memory."

"We can make a try anyhow. Able to get upstairs?"

"I could fly, if I thought it would help."

They were a sorry-looking pair as they went up the long staircase, Jan's eyes still swollen, her rumpled nightgown under her bathrobe, her feet still bare. Young Brooke was not much better, a disreputable figure in a suit which had been soaked with rain, his hair standing wildly in all directions, and his collar melted around his neck. They did not notice the uniformed man in the lower hall, standing stolidly on guard, and there was hope in both of them until they reached the upper hall, to confront a policeman parked outside Mrs. Fairbanks's door, smoking a surreptitious cigarette.

He put it out quickly, so he did not see the dismay in their faces.

Brooke left soon after that. Eileen was still sleeping. The house was quiet. But outside in the grounds one or two men were quietly exam-ining the pillars and roof of the porte-cochere, and a detective in plain clothes and bent double was going carefully over the ground around the stable and near the fence.

He looked up as the doctor neared him.

"Got permission to leave the place?"

"I'm the doctor," Brooke said stiffly. "My office is across the street. Anything to say about that?"

He was in a fighting mood, but the detective only grinned.

"Not a word, brother. Not a word. Might like a look at your feet. That's all."

"What the hell are my feet to you?"

"Not a thing. You could lose 'em both and I wouldn't shed a tear. Lemme look at those shoes, doc."

Brooke was seething, but after a glance at the shoes, especially the soles, the detective only shrugged.

"Went out of here after the rain started, didn't you?" he said. "All right. That checks. I'll see you later. Those shoes could stand some work on them."

Brooke was still furious as he started across the street. For the first time he realized the excitement in the neighborhood. There was a large crowd around the entrance to the driveway on Grove Avenue, and the windows on both streets were filled with men in their shirt sleeves, and women hastily or only partially dressed. To add to his rage the slovenly girl from the house where he had his offices was on the steps, surrounded by a group of laughing boys.

He caught one of them and shook him.

"Get out of here," he said. "Get out and stay out, all of you." He jerked the girl to her feet. "Go inside and do some work, for once," he ordered. "If I catch you out here again—"

He knew it was useless. It was the ugly side of all tragedy, this morbid curiosity and avid interst which deprived even grief of privacy. But he could not fight it. He went upstairs and took a bath, as though to wash it away.

In the dining-room at the Fairbanks house the inspector was eating a substantial Sunday morning breakfast of sausages and pancakes, and a long rangy captain of the homicide squad was trying to keep up with him. Hilda, unable to eat, eyed them resentfully. Men were like that, she thought. They did not project themselves into other people's troubles as women did. All this was just a case, a case and a job. It did not matter that a family was being torn apart, or that some one member of it was probably headed for the chair.

William had brought in a fresh supply of pancakes when Amos came in. His small, sly eyes were gleaming.

"Fellow out in the yard says to tell you he's got a footprint," he said. "It's under the big oak, and he's got a soapbox over it."

The captain got up, eyeing his last pancake ruefully.

"I guess you win, inspector," he said. "Thirteen to my eleven. I suppose you'll want a cast."

He went out, and the inspector took a final sip of coffee and put down his napkin.

"I'm feeling stronger," he announced. "Nothing like food to take the place of sleep."

"I should think you could stay awake for the next month," said Hilda tartly.

He got up and lit a cigarette.

"Don't be crabbed," he said. "It doesn't suit you. You are the ministering angel, the lady who knits while people pour out their troubles to her. Which reminds me, how about the Garrison woman? I'll have to see her. What do you think of her?"

"As a suspect? All I can say is that women don't usually murder when they're threatened with a miscarriage and under the influence of morphia."

"Don't they?" He eyed her with interest. "How much you know! But you'd be surprised, my Hilda. You'd be surprised at what some women can do."

Eileen was still in her drugged sleep when Hilda, leaving him outside, went into her room. It was not easy to rouse her, and when she did waken she seemed not to know where she was. She sat up in bed, looking dazedly around her.

"How on earth did I get here?" she demanded, blinking in the light.

"You came last night. Don't you remember?"

She stretched and yawned. Then she smiled maliciously.

"My God, do I remember!" she said. "Did you see their faces?"

But she was not smiling when the inspector came in. She sat up and drawing the bedclothing around her stared at him suspiciously.

"Who are you?" she said. "I don't know you, do I?"

He looked down at her. A neurotic, he thought, and scared to death. Heaven keep him from neurotic women.

"I'm sorry, Mrs. Garrison. I am a police officer. I want to ask you a few questions."

But he did not ask her any questions just then. She seemed profoundly shocked as full recollection came back to her. She looked indeed as though she might faint again, and when at last she lay back, shivering under the bedclothes, she could tell him nothing at all.

"I remember Susie screaming. I got up and went to the door. Somebody said Mrs. Fairbanks was dead—murdered. I guess I fainted after that."

"Did you hear anyone in this room last night? Before it happened."

"I don't know when it happened," she said petulantly. "Ida was here, and the doctor. And the nurse, of course."

"Did you unhook the window screen over there, for any purpose?"

She went pale.

"My screen?" she said. "Do you mean—"

"It was open. Miss Adams heard it banging. She came in and closed it."

Suddenly she sat up in bed, wide-eyed and terrified.

"I want to get out of here," she said. "I'm sick, and I don't know anything about it. I wouldn't have come if I'd had any other place to go. They'd pin this murder on me if they could. They all hate me."

"Who hates you?"

"All of them," she said wildly, and burst into loud hysterical crying.

It was some time before he could question her further. But she protested that she had not even heard the radio, and that Mrs. Fairbanks had been as usual when she talked to her.

"She didn't seem nervous or apprehensive?"

"She seemed unpleasant. She never liked me. But she did promise to look after me when my—when my baby came."

She made no objection when he asked to take her fingerprints. "Part of the routine," he told her. She lay passive on her pillows while he rolled one finger after another on the card. But she did object when he asked her to stay in the house for a day or two longer.

"I'm better," she said. "I'm all right. The doctor said—"

"I'll let you go as soon as possible," he told her, and went out.

It was in the hall outside her door that Hilda remembered about the figure at the top of the third floor stairs. The inspector was about to light a cigarette. He blew out the match and stared at her.

"Why in God's name didn't you tell me that before?" he demanded furiously.

She flushed. "You might remember that I've had a murder on my hands, and a lot of hysterical people. I just forgot it."

He was still indignant, however. He went up the stairs, with Hilda following. But nothing was changed. The guest rooms with their drawn shades were as she had last seen them; the hall stretched back to the servants' quarters, empty and undisturbed. A brief examination showed all the windows closed and locked, and the inspector, wiping his dusty hands, looked skeptical.

"Sure you didn't dream it?"

"I came up and looked around. There wasn't time for anyone to have gone back to the servants' rooms. I thought it was Maggie or Ida, curious about Mrs. Garrison."

"When was all this?"

"Before I went down to boil the water for the hypodermic. I was gone only a minute or two. I hardly left the top of the stairs."

He was still ruffled as he went back along the hall. There were closets there, a cedar room, and a trunk room. All of them were neat and dustless, and none showed any signs of recent use as a hiding place. He lit matches, examined floors, and, still ignoring Hilda, went on back to the servants' quarters. Compared with the rest of the house they were musty, with the closeness of such places even in June, the closed windows, the faint odor of cooking from below, of long-worn clothing, and unmade beds.

Two of the rooms were empty, but Ida was in hers. She was sitting by a window, her hands folded in her lap and a queer look on her long thin face as Hilda went in.

"I was nervous and Maggie sent me up," she said. "But there's no use of my going to bed. I couldn't sleep."

It was the appearance of the inspector which definitely terrified her, however. She went white to the lips. She tried to get up and then sank back in her chair.

"What is it?" she asked. "I don't know anything. What do you want with me? Can't I get a little rest?"

Hilda tried to quiet her.

"It hasn't anything to do with Mrs. Fairbanks's death, Ida," she said. "I thought I saw someone in the upper hall last night, before— before it happened. If it was you it's all right. We're only checking up."

Ida shook her head.

"It wasn't me, miss."

"Would it have been William? Or Maggie?"

She was quieter now.

"I wouldn't know about that. They usually sleep like the dead."

But Hilda was remembering something. She was seeing the household gather after Susie screamed, and seeing Maggie and William come along the back hall on the second floor, while Ida was standing still, looking down from the front stairs to the third floor. She did not mention it. Quite possibly, Ida as the housemaid used those stairs habitually. She tucked it away in her memory, however, to wonder later if she should have told it. If it would have changed anything, or altered the inevitable course of events.

Neither of them could change Ida's story. She sat there, twisting her work-worn hands in her lap. She had been in bed. She had seen nobody, and she had liked the old lady. She had looked after her as well as she could. Tears welled in her eyes, and the inspector left her there and went out, muttering to himself.

"Damn all crying women," he said. "I'm fed up with them."

That was when he timed Hilda, making her leave her chair in the hall, go up, look around for a light switch, and come down again. He put his watch back in his pocket and looked at her grimly.

"Three minutes," he said. "A lot can happen in three minutes, my girl."

He left at nine o'clock, driving away with his uniformed chauffeur. The men who had been scattered over the grounds had disappeared, but one officer was on duty on Huston Street beside the break in the fence. Another was holding back the crowd at the gate, and two still remained in the house. Hilda watched the difficulty with which the car made its way through the crowd.

"It's disgusting," she said to the tall young policeman on duty in the lower hall. "They ought to be ashamed."

He smiled indulgently.

"They like a bit of excitement, miss." He smiled. "There's a lot of reporters out there, too. I caught one carrying in the milk bottles early this morning."

As she went up the stairs she could still hear Carlton at the library phone.

"Hello, George. I'm trying to locate Marian. She's out of town somewhere. I suppose you and Nell haven't heard from her?"

15

She was very tired. When she looked into Eileen's room Ida was running a carpet sweeper over the floor. Eileen's hair had been combed and fresh linen put on her bed. She looked better, although she was still pale.

"If you're all right I'll go to bed for an hour or two, Mrs. Garrison," Hilda said. "I haven't had much sleep lately."

"I'm perfectly all right. I told that fool of a policeman, but he wouldn't listen."

Hilda went back toward her room. But she did not go to bed. Maggie was carrying a tray into Jan's room, and she followed her. Jan was standing by a window, fully dressed. She looked at the tray and shook her head.

"I'm afraid I can't eat," she said. "Thanks, anyhow. I'll have the coffee."

Maggie put down the tray firmly.

"You'll eat," she said. "Somebody's got to keep going around here." Her voice softened. "Try it anyhow, dearie," she said. "Just remember she was old. She hadn't long anyhow."

Jan's chin quivered.

"She liked living."

"Well, so do we all," said Maggie, philosophically. "That don't mean we can go on forever."

She went out. Jan looked at Hilda.

"I've been trying to think. How are we to get word to Mother? I don't suppose it is in the papers, is it?"

"I hardly think so. There wasn't time."

"And there are no evening papers today," Jan said desperately. "She may not hear it until tomorrow. And she ought to be here. Uncle

Carl's no good at that sort of thing, and Susie's asleep. I went in and she was dead to the world. I wanted to talk to her. I—"

Her voice trailed off. Her hands shook as she tried to pour the coffee. Hilda took the miniature pot from her and poured it for her.

"Why not waken her?" she said quietly. "After all, if it's important—"

"Important!" Jan's voice was bitter. "You've seen her. You've heard her. You know she hated Granny. She hated living in the house with her. Uncle Carl wanted a farm, and she adores him. They can have it now," she added hopelessly. "They'll have her money. First she tried to scare Granny to death, and when that wasn't any good—"

"What do you mean by that?" Hilda demanded sharply. "Scaring her to death."

"Those bats and things. You don't think they got in by themselves!" Jan was scornful. "It was just the sort of thing she would think of. Scare Granny out of the house, or into a heart attack. What did she care?"

Hilda was thoughtful. In a way Jan was right. Susie was quite capable of it. It might even appeal to her macabre sense of humor. The murder, however, was different. She could not see Susie putting arsenic in the old lady's sugar or driving a knife into her heart.

"She had the chance last night, too," Jan went on. "She could have heard Courtney come back to talk to me while you were downstairs. She could have slipped through Uncle Carl's room and around the screen. Nobody would have seen her."

She stopped, looking startled. Susie was in the doorway, cigarette in hand and her sharp blue eyes blazing.

"So I did it!" she said. "You little idiot, didn't I lie my head off last night for you?" She threw back the sleeve of her dressing-gown and showed her arm. "You know who did that, don't you? Suppose I'd told the police your precious father was here in the grounds last night? And his wife inside the house with the screen over the porte-cochere open? Suppose I'd said that the whole thing was a plant to get Eileen into this house, so Frank Garrison could get in, too?"

Hilda watched them, her blue eyes shrewd. Neither of them seemed aware of her presence. She saw that Jan was on the verge of collapse.

"He wouldn't kill Granny. Never. You know it. Deep down in your heart you know it."

Susie eyed her. Then she shrugged.

"All right, kid," she said. "I didn't tell the police. I won't, either, unless you go around yelling that I did it. Or Carlton." Suddenly she sent a shocked look at Hilda. "Good, God, I forgot. You're police yourself, aren't you?"

"Not all the time. I'm a human being, too." Hilda smiled faintly.

"Well, forget it," said Susie. "I was just talking. The kid here made me mad. Maybe he thought Eileen was here. He might have come to find out."

She went back to her room, and Jan caught Hilda by the arm.

"That's why he came," she said desperately. "I swear it is. I'll swear it by anything holy. My window was up, and he called to me. He said, 'Jan, do you know where Eileen has gone? She's not in the apartment.' When I told him she was here and—and sick, he seemed worried. But he wouldn't come in. He went away again, in the rain. In the rain," she repeated, as though the fact hurt her. "I can't even telephone him," she went on. "Uncle Carl's still using it. And if the police find it out—"

"Why worry about that? He had no reason for wishing your grandmother—out of the way, had he?"

"Of course not." She lit a cigarette and smoked it feverishly. "He was devoted to her. But he doesn't know what's happened. He ought to know. He ought to be able to protect himself. Look," she said, putting down the cigarette, "would you be willing to tell him? To go there and tell him? It wouldn't do any harm. He can't run away. That's all I want, for him to know."

It was a long time before Hilda agreed, but the girl's sick face and passionate anxiety finally decided her. Also she was curious. There was something behind all this, something more than a distracted husband trying in the middle of the night to locate a missing wife. Why had he not come in when he learned that Eileen was sick? Surely that would have been the normal thing to do.

She knew she had very little time. The police had the cast of the footprint under the oak. They would be working on it now. They would have examined the shoes of the men in the house, measured them, perhaps photographed them. And if Amos knew more than he had told—

She hurried to her room to dress. As she opened the door she had the feeling that something had moved rapidly across the floor. Whatever it was she could not find it, and she dressed rapidly and went down the stairs. Evidently the officer there had no orders to hold her, for he smiled and opened the door.

"Out for a walk?"

"I need some air," she said blandly.

Under the porte-cochere, however, she stopped. The crowd was still on the pavement, held back by the guard, and a photographer was holding up his camera. She turned quickly toward the stable and the broken fence. Amos was not in sight, but the soapbox lay on its side under the oak tree, some fifty feet away. She hurried to the break in the fence, and straightened, to look into the lens of a camera. A grinning young man thanked her. She made a wild snatch at the camera, but he evaded it.

"Naughty, naughty," he said. "Papa slap. Now, what's your name, please?"

"I have no name," she told him furiously.

"Must be a disadvantage at times. How do they get you? Say, 'Here, you'?"

He took another flash of her indignant face before she could stop him, and she was moving rapidly toward the corner when she became aware that the crowd was coming toward her. It moved slowly but irresistibly, as though propelled by some unseen power from behind. A half-dozen small boys ran ahead of it.

"That's the nurse!" one of them yelled. "She's got her cap off, but I know her."

"Hey, nurse! What's happened in there?"

The reporters were in the lead now. In an instant she was surrounded by eager young faces. She could see her bus a block away, and she stood haughtily silent, like a small neat Pekinese among a throng of disorderly street dogs. "Have a heart, sister." "Come on, how was the old lady killed?" "Has anyone been arrested?"

She was driven to speech, in sheer desperation.

"I have nothing to say," she told them. "If you care to follow me while I get some fresh uniforms and look after my canary, that's all the good it will do you."

They laughed but persisted until the bus came and she got on. Looking back she could see them, returning discouraged to take up their stations again, to wait and hope for a break, to be able perhaps to get a new angle on the story and maybe a raise in salary. She felt unhappy and guilty, as though she had failed them. As, of course, she had.

She reached the Garrison apartment at ten o'clock. No one answered the bell, and at last she tried the door. It was unlocked, and she stepped inside, to find herself in a long gallery, paved with black-and-white marble, and with a fine old tapestry hung at the end. It surprised her, as did the drawing-room when she saw it; a handsome room carefully furnished, but with every sign of extreme neglect. The grand piano showed dust in the morning sun, the brocaded curtains were awry, the windows filthy, the rugs askew on the floor. Old magazines and papers lay about, and a vase of flowers on a table had been dead and dried for days.

Her tidy soul revolted. No wonder men left women who surrounded themselves with dirt and disorder. But there was no sign of Frank Garrison. The place was quiet and apparently empty. Not until she had investigated most of the apartment did she locate him, in a small room at the far end of the gallery. He was in a deep chair, and he was sound asleep.

Whatever she had expected it was not this. She inspected him carefully. He was in pajamas and bathrobe, and the Sunday papers were scattered around him. A cluttered ash tray and an empty coffee cup were beside him, and he had the exhausted, unshaven look of a man who had slept little or not at all the night before.

When she touched him on the shoulder he jerked awake. Not fully, however.

"Sorry," he mumbled. "Guess I dozed off." He looked up at her and blinked.

"Thought you were my wife," he said. "My apologies." He got up slowly, his big body still clumsy with sleep. Then he recognized her. He looked alarmed.

"Miss Adams! Has anything happened? Is Jan—"

"Jan's all right." She sat down. "I have other news for you, Mr. Garrison, unless you already know it. Jan wanted me to tell you. Mrs. Fairbanks is dead."

He looked surprised.

"Dead!" he said. "Just like that! Jan will take it hard. Still, I suppose it was to be expected." He looked down at his pajamas. "I'd better dress and go over. I didn't expect a visitor. What was it? Heart, I suppose."

"No," said Hilda.

"No? Then what—"

"She was murdered, Mr. Garrison."

He stared at her. He had been in the act of picking up a cigarette. Now his hand hung frozen over the box. The incredulity in his face gave way to sick horror.

"Murdered!" he said hoarsely. "I don't understand. Not poison again?"

"She was stabbed. With a knife."

He seemed still unable to take it in.

"I don't understand," he repeated. "Who would kill her? She hadn't very long to live. And nobody hated her. Even the servants—"

He did not finish. He got up and went to the window.

"Is Jan all right?" he asked without turning.

"She's worried, Mr. Garrison."

He swung around.

"Worried! What do you mean, worried?"

"You were outside the house last night, and Mrs. Carlton Fairbanks knows it."

"Susie! So it was Susie!" he said, and gave a short laugh. "She scared the insides out of me."

"Jan thought you ought to know," Hilda said patiently. "There may be trouble. The police have found a footprint. I imagine it's yours. I promised to tell you before they got here—if they come at all. Susie won't talk, but Amos might. He looked out the window. He may have recognized you."

He began to see the seriousness of his situation. Yet his story was coherent and straightforward. He had had what he called a difference with Eileen, on Wednesday night. He had packed a bag and gone to his club, and on Saturday morning he had taken a plane to Washington.

"Things haven't been very good," he said. "I needed a job, and I thought with all this government housing I might get something. I happen to be an architect. But it was a Saturday, and summer"—he smiled—"the government doesn't work on June week-ends."

He had got back to the apartment late the night before to find Eileen gone and her suitcase missing. They had had to let the maid go, and he didn't know what had happened to Eileen.

"I thought Jan might know," he said. "But I didn't want to telephone her and rouse the house. So I went over. It was one o'clock when I left there. I've done that before, talked to Jan at night, I mean. Her window was up, although it was raining cats and dogs, and I called to her. She said my wife was there, so I came back here."

"Meeting Susie on the way?"

"Meeting Susie on the way," he said, and smiled again. "She yelled like an Indian."

She considered that. It might be true. She had an idea, however, that it was not all the truth.

"You didn't go back again? To the house?"

He looked at her oddly.

"See here," he said. "What's all this about? They don't think *I* killed the old lady, do they?"

"Somebody killed her," Hilda said dryly, and got up.

He saw her out, apologizing for the dust, the evident disorder. He owned the place. He couldn't sell it, worse luck. Nobody could sell anything nowadays, even a tapestry. But she felt that behind all this, his confident manner, the composure on his good-looking face, his mind was far away, working hard and fast.

She was on a corner waiting for a bus when she saw the inspector's car drive up to the door of the apartment building and two or three men get out. So Amos had talked, after all.

She was not surprised, on her return to the Fairbanks house, to learn from William that the police had taken away the window screen from Eileen's room. But she was rather astonished to find Carlton, in a morning coat and striped trousers, and wearing a black tie, wandering around upstairs and carrying a hammer and an old cigar box filled with nails.

"Thought I'd nail up the other screens," he said vaguely. "Can't have people getting in and out of the house. Not safe."

He went into Eileen's room, a dapper, incongruous figure, and Hilda followed him. Eileen was sitting up in bed. She looked better, although she was still pale; and she managed an ironical smile when Carlton told her what he was doing.

"You're a little late with that, aren't you?" she said.

"Some of us still want to live, Eileen."

"You can do that now, can't you?" she said maliciously. "Live the way you like, get your Susie safe on a farm away from other men, raise pigs, do anything you damn well please."

He stiffened.

"That was entirely uncalled for. If you were not a sick woman—"

"If I were not a sick woman I wouldn't be here."

He finished his hammering, and later Hilda, remembering that day, was to hear the noise as he moved from room to room, and even to smell the putty and white paint with which he neatly covered the signs of his labors.

He finished at eleven-thirty, which was almost exactly the time Fuller and his henchmen were leaving Frank Garrison. He had told a straight story, but the inspector was not satisfied. He stood in the long marble-floored gallery and put his hat on with a jerk.

"I'll ask you not to leave town," he said. "Outside of that, of course, you're free. I suppose you have no idea where your first wife is? We'd like to locate her."

"I am not in her confidence," he said stiffly. "I would be the last person to know."

16

Police Department

From: *Commanding Officer, 17th Precinct*
To: *Medical Examiner*
Subject: *Death of Eliza Douglas Fairbanks, of Ten Grove Avenue.*
  1. *On June 15, 1941, at 2:15 a.m. a report was received from Inspector Harlan Fuller that a Mrs. Eliza Douglas Fairbanks, aged 72 years, had been found dead in her bed as a result of a stab wound in the chest.*
  2. *Case was reported at once by Inspector Fuller and usual steps taken. Inspector Fuller and Captain Henderson of homicide squad were assigned to case.*

The inspector had this document in front of him that noon. In such brief fashion, he thought, were the tragedies of life reported. Men and women died of violence. Tragedy wrecked homes. Hatred and greed and revenge took their toll. And each of them could be officially recorded in less than a hundred words.

Nor was the report of the autopsy more human. An old woman had died, cruelly and unnecessarily. Died in a closed room, with access to it almost impossible. And the autopsy, after recording her pathetic age, her shrunken weight, and the entirely useless examination of her head, abdomen, and thorax, merely reported the cause of death as an incised wound with a tract of two and one-half inches, which on being carefully dissected was shown to have reached the heart. And that the approximate time of death had been between twelve-thirty and one-thirty in the morning.

He put it down. After all, murder was an inhuman business, he thought, and began again to look over the reports and his own memoranda which had accumulated on the desk. Considering that the day was Sunday they covered considerable ground.

The house: *No sign of entrance by roof of porte-cochere. Blurred prints on window screen, one identified as belonging to Miss Adams, nurse. Three ladders on property, none showing signs of having been out in the rain. No indication pillars had been climbed. All doors and windows on lower floor closed and locked. No phonograph or remote control for radio found. Knife not belonging to kitchen. (Evidence of one Margaret O'Neil, cook.) At seat of crime fingerprints only of dead woman, servants and family, including those of Mrs. Eileen Garrison on back of chair. None of Mrs. Carlton Fairbanks. Prints of Carlton Fairbanks on foot of bed and closet door. Prints of dead woman on safe. No others.*

On the people in the house at the time of the crime his notes were brief, mostly written in his own hand.

Carlton Fairbanks: *Son of deceased. Member of prosperous brokerage house until 1930. Business gradually declined until 1938, when it was liquidated. Married in 1930 to Susan Mary Kelly. Came to live with mother in 1938. Wife disliked by Mrs. Fairbanks and daughter Marian. Both Carlton Fairbanks and wife anxious to leave and buy farm. Is supposed to inherit, along with sister and niece, Janice Garrison, under will. Admits entering room at or about 1:15 to turn off radio.*

Susan Mary Fairbanks: *See above. Reason for visit to stable-garage that night not known. Did not enter, as encountered Garrison and was scared away. No cigarettes in her car, although given as reason for night excursion. Does not conceal dislike of mother-in-law. Father contractor in small way. Family lives at 140 South Street in plain but respectable neighborhood. On good terms with them. Probably does not inherit under will but would share husband's portion.*

Marion Garrison: *Quarreled with mother and left home last Wednesday evening, June eleventh. Present address unknown. Thirty-eight years of age, thin, dark, usually dressed in black. Taxicab which called for her took her to Pennsylvania Station. No further information. According to servants, bitterly resentful over husband's second marriage. Has lived at Grove Avenue house since marriage in 1921, as mother refused to be left alone. Divorced in 1934 at Reno, Nevada.*

Janice Garrison: *Age 19. Probably inherits under will. Friendly with father and second wife. Apparently devoted to grandmother. No motive, unless money. Is supposed to be interested in Dr. Courtney Brooke.*

Courtney Allen Brooke, M.D.: *Age 28. Office and house at 13 Huston Street. Graduate Harvard Medical School. Interned two years Mount Hope Hospital. In private work one year. Small practice, barely earning expenses. First called to attend deceased March tenth, when treatment was given for arsenic poisoning. Has attended deceased at intervals since. Apparently in house during time of crime, in attendance on Mrs. Eileen Garrison, who was threatened with abortion. Alibi given by nurse Hilda Adams: the dead woman turned on her radio before his departure.*

Eileen Garrison: *Age 35. Married in 1934 to Francis J. Garrison, following divorce. Formerly governess to Janice Garrison Small, blond, nervous temperament. Born on farm near Templeton, thirty miles from city, where parents still live. Not liked by Fairbanks family, although Janice Garrison remained friendly. Could expect nothing under will. In house at time of crime, but sick and under influence of morphine administered at or about one o'clock.*

Francis Jarvis Garrison: *Well-known architect. Age 42. Inherited money. Supposed to be wealthy until 1929. Since then heavy losses. Pays ex-wife ten thousand a year alimony, tax free. Owns large apartment, but behind on maintenance charges. Divorced in 1934. Married daughter's governess soon after. Produces ticket stub to prove plane trip to Washington Saturday. Admits being in grounds night of crime and says he talked to daughter, to learn his wife's whereabouts. Uncertain of time. Thinks between 1:30 and 2:00 a.m. Encounter with Mrs. Fairbanks, Jr. purely accidental. Admits footprint his. Expects nothing under will.*

There were brief reports on the servants, but he glanced at them casually. Only Ida's he picked up and examined.

Ida Miller: *Country girl born in Lafayette County. Age 40. Ten years in Fairbanks house. Hysterical since murder. Possibly not telling all she knows.*

He was still looking at it when the commissioner came in. The commissioner had expected to play golf, and he was in a bad humor. The inspector offered him a chair, which he took, and a cigar, which he refused.

"Never smoke them," he said. "What's all this, anyhow? I thought you'd put that woman of yours to watch the Fairbanks house."

"Not the house," said the inspector politely. "Mrs. Fairbanks herself."

"So she lets her be killed! It's the hell of a note, Fuller. I may be new to this job, but when you guarantee to protect a woman—and a prominent woman at that—I want to know why the devil she wasn't protected."

"She was, as a matter of fact. It couldn't have happened. Only it did."

"Don't give me double talk," said the commissioner, the veins in his forehead swelling. "She's dead, isn't she?"

It was some time before the inspector could tell the story. He went back to the attempt to poison Mrs. Fairbanks, and to the mystery of the bats and so on in the room.

"They got in somehow," he said. "I've been over the place. I don't see how it was done. But it was."

"Carried in," said the commissioner. "That's easy. Carried in while she was out and left there. Room wasn't locked, was it?"

"Not during the day."

"All right. Get on with it."

He sat with his eyes closed while the inspector got on with it, reading now and then from his notes. At the end he sat up, eyeing the inspector with unexpected shrewdness.

"You've got only two suspects, Fuller. Frank Garrison's out. Why would he kill the old woman? He had nothing to gain. Anyhow, I know him. He's a damned decent fellow."

"I've known—"

"All right. Who have you got? This young doc and Carlton Fairbanks. The doctor's out. So Carlton's left. Know him, too. Always thought he was a stuffed shirt."

"That wouldn't go far with a jury." Fuller smiled unhappily. "Anyhow, he doesn't seem to me the type. Of course—"

"Type? Type! Any type will kill for a half of three million dollars. That's what old Henry Fairbanks left his widow when he died. In bonds, Fuller! No hanky-pank, no cats and dogs, no common stocks. Bonds!"

"It sounds like a lot of money," said the inspector. "Maybe you'd like to talk to Fairbanks yourself."

The commissioner got up hastily. "Not at all," he said. "I've got an engagement. And I guess you have your own methods. Better than mine, probably!"

With that he departed, and the inspector felt that he was left virtually with a rubber hose in his hand.

Back at the Fairbanks house Hilda had not gone to bed. She took off her shoes and rubbed her tired feet, but she was not sleepy. The sense of failure was bitter in her. Yet what had she done? She had left the door to go up to the third floor, a matter of three minutes or so. She had been fifteen minutes, maybe twenty, in the kitchen, but the doctor had agreed to stand guard. And Mrs. Fairbanks had been alive then. She had turned on the radio after that, turned it on loudly, as if the movements in the hall outside the door had exasperated her.

What else? She had taken her tray back, and later on Susie had stepped in it. She had gone back and found her there. How long had that taken?

She got up, and to the astonishment of the officer in the hall, paced it off in her stocking feet, carrying her watch in her hand. She could hardly believe it when the second hand showed only a minute and a half. Then what? She and Susie had sat in the hall, until the slamming screen in Eileen's room and taken her in to it. Eileen had been asleep, and she had closed and hooked the screen. And after that she had found Mrs. Fairbanks dead, and her hands were already cool.

It was Carlton, then, after all. It had to be Carlton.

She went back to her room and stood looking out the window. Amos, in his best clothes and with a smug look on his face, was coming toward his Sunday dinner. Birds were busy on the grass after the rain the night before. The crowd outside had diminished somewhat as the meal hour arrived, but it was still there.

Carlton, she thought wretchedly. She could see him now, dressed in his striped trousers and black coat and wearing a mourning tie, trying to fill in the time with a hammer and an old cigar box filled with nails. Did men kill their mothers and then go puttering around fastening screens? Decent, quiet little men who liked the country and growing things?

The unreality grew when she sat at the midday dinner table, watching him carve a roast of beef into delicate slices.

"Well done or rare, Miss Adams?"

"Medium, please."

Not Carlton, she thought, looking around the table. Not any of them. Not Susie, in a black dress with little or no make-up, and for once not smoking. Not Jan. Oh, certainly not Jan, looking young and tragic and not eating. Not even young Brooke, watching Jan and making such talk as there was. Certainly not Eileen, sick and hysterical in her room upstairs. Not William, his head still shaking as he passed the food. Not Ida, pale but efficient. Not any of them, she thought drearily. Then who?

The guards were taken out of the house that afternoon, but Mrs. Fairbanks's room was left locked and sealed. There was still no news of

Marian, and Jan, after a talk with her father on the telephone, had at last gone to bed and to sleep.

It was three o'clock in the afternoon when Carlton was taken to police headquarters for questioning.

Hilda was in the lower hall when it happened. He said nothing to anybody. When she saw him he was carefully selecting a stick from a stand, and he spoke to her quietly.

"If my wife asks for me," he said, "tell her I have some things to do downtown. I may be late, so ask her not to wait up for me."

She saw the car outside, with Captain Henderson and a detective waiting, and felt sorry for him, adjusting his hat in front of the mirror. When he turned she saw he was pale.

"I was fond of my mother, Miss Adams," he said strangely, and without looking back went out to the officers and the waiting car.

At four o'clock that same afternoon Marian Garrison came home.

17

She arrived apparently unwarned. Her first shock came when the taxi, violently honking its horn, tried to make its way through the crowd. The police officer drove it back, but when the driver stopped under the porte-cochere he found her collapsed in the seat and rang the doorbell.

"Lady here's in poor shape," he told William. "Want me to bring her in?"

William ran down the steps, to find her with her eyes shut and her face colorless.

"What is it? What's wrong, William?"

"I'm sorry, madam. Mrs. Fairbanks is dead."

"Dead? But the crowds! What's wrong? What happened to her?"

"It was quite painless. Or so they say. She was asleep when it took place. If—"

She reached out and caught him by the arm.

"Not poison, William? Not poison!"

He hesitated, his old head shaking violently.

"No, madam. I'm afraid—It was a knife."

She did not faint. She drew a long breath and got out of the car. The driver and William helped her into the house. But she could not walk far. She sat down on a chair inside the door snapping and unsnapping the fastening of her bag, her eyes on William.

"Who did it?" she asked, in a half-whisper.

"Nobody knows. Not yet. The police—"

She got up.

"I want to see Jan," she said wildly. "I must talk to her. I'd better try to go up to my room."

William caught her by the arm.

"Not right away, Miss Marian," he said in his quavering voice. "You see—"

She shook him off.

"What's the matter with you?" she demanded. "I'm going up to my room. Get Jan and tell her I'm here, and don't act the fool."

That was the situation when Jan ran down the stairs, Marian standing angry and bewildered, and William evidently at a loss to know what to do. She gave them one look and kissed her mother's cold face. But Marian did not return the caress.

"Why can't I go upstairs in my own home, Jan? What is all this?"

It was on this tableau that Hilda appeared, Marian's face flushed, Jan's pale, and her young body stiff.

"I'm sorry, Mother. We'll get her out as soon as we can. You see—"

"Get whom out?"

"Eileen. She's sick. She is in your room, Mother."

Marian's frail body stiffened.

"So that's it," she said. "You've brought her here and put her in my room. The woman who ruined my life, and you couldn't wait until I was gone to get her here!"

She would have gone on, but Hilda interfered. She took her into the library and gave her a stiff drink of Scotch. All the fire had gone out of her by that time. She seemed stunned. The liquor braced her, however, although she listened to Jan's story with closed eyes. But her first words when Jan finished her brief outline were addressed to Hilda.

"So you let it happen after all!" she said. "I left her in your care, and she was killed."

She was badly shaken, but she was frightened, too. Hilda was puzzled. She caught Marian watching Jan, as if the girl might know something she was not telling. She was more frightened than grieved, she thought. But she was coldly determined, too.

"Get that woman out of here," she said. "At once, Jan. Do you hear? If she can't walk, carry her. If she won't be carried, throw her out. And if none of you can do it I'll do it myself. Or strangle her," she added.

That was the situation when Hilda got the inspector on the telephone. He seemed annoyed, as though he resented the interruption, but he agreed to let Eileen go.

"She's hardly a suspect," he said. "Sure. Better get young Brooke's okay on it first."

She called the doctor, who agreed willingly, and went to Eileen's

room. To her surprise Eileen was already out of bed and partly
dressed. She was sitting in a chair while Ida drew on her stockings, and
she was smiling coldly.

"I heard the fuss and rang," she said. "Tell them not to worry. I'm
leaving. She can have her room. She can have the whole damned
house, so far as I am concerned." She slid her feet into her pumps and
stood up. "I suppose," she said, "that my loving husband has come
back, too."

"He came back last night. From Washington."

Eileen looked at her sharply.

"From Washington? How do you know?"

"I saw him this morning."

"Where? Here?"

"I went to the apartment. Jan asked me to. He had been here last
night and she was worried."

A flicker of alarm showed in Eileen's face.

"What do you mean, he was here? In the house?"

"In the grounds. He says he didn't know where you were, so he
came and called up to Jan's window to find out."

Eileen sat down on the bed, as though her knees would not hold
her.

"When—when was that?"

"Between one-thirty and two, I think," Hilda said. "His plane got in
at midnight, but he went home first. Then he walked here. It's quite a
distance."

Eileen's face had turned a grayish color. She seemed to have difficulty in breathing.

"Do the police know that?" she asked, her lips stiff.

"They know he was in the grounds. He admits it himself." And
then, because she was sorry for her, Hilda added, "I wouldn't worry
too much about it, Mrs. Garrison. Of course, they're suspecting everybody just now. I'd better order a taxi. I can go with you if you like."

Eileen, however, wished for no company. When Hilda came back
from the telephone she was looking better, or at least she was under
control. She was in front of Marian's table, eyeing herself in the mirror. Almost defiantly she put on some rouge and lipstick, and finished
her dressing. Ida had carried down her suitcase, and at the door she
turned and surveyed the room.

"Did you ever know what it is to pray for somebody to die?" she said
bitterly. "Did you ever see someone riding around in a car in the rain
while you walked, and wish there would be an accident? Did you ever

lie awake at night hating somebody so hard that you hit the pillow? Well, that's what Marian Garrison has done to me. And he still cares for her. After seven years he's still in love with her. He'd even go to the chair for her! The fool. The blind, stupid fool."

Carlton had not come home when Eileen left the house. He was still in the inspector's office, his dapper look gone, but his head still high.

"Just go over that again, Mr. Fairbanks. You went into the room, went around the foot of the bed, turned off the radio, and came directly out again. How could you see to turn off the radio? Did you light a match?"

"I didn't need to. It's an old one. We've had it for a long time. I knew where the switch was. And, of course, there was some light from the door into the hall."

"You still claim that you didn't speak to your mother?"

"I did not. She had a habit of going to sleep with the radio going. I've gone in and shut it off at times for the last ten years."

"You came out at once?"

"I did. Immediately. Ask the nurse. She was there."

But he was tired. He had eaten almost nothing that day, and although they gave him water when he asked for it and he was well supplied with cigarettes, he needed a drink badly. There was a cold sweat all over him and his mouth was dry. He moistened his lips.

"You had no reason, for instance, to investigate the closet where the safe is?"

"Why should I? It's been there for months."

"And the closet door?"

"Oh, for God's sake! How can I remember? What does it matter? Suppose it was open and I shoved it out of my way? What has that got to do with my mother's death?"

"Do you think anyone could have been hidden in the closet?"

"Who? My niece? My wife?"

"I'm asking the questions, Mr. Fairbanks," said the inspector. "You are the only person known to have entered your mother's room at or about the time she was—the time she died. I know this is painful, but we have to get on with it. If you had nothing to do with it you will want to be helpful. Nobody is trying to railroad you to the"—he coughed— "to jail. Now. You have said that you are one of the heirs to the estate."

A little of Carlton's dignity had returned. He was even slightly pompous.

"I presume so. My sister and myself. Probably there is something for my niece, Janice Garrison. I don't know, of course. My—my mother managed her own affairs."

"You must have some idea of the value of the estate."

But here he was on surer ground.

"It was a very large one at one time. Some values have shrunk, but it was carefully invested. Mostly in bonds."

"Did she keep those securities in the safe?"

"I don't know. I hope she didn't. She used to have several safe-deposit boxes at her bank. I suppose she still has them."

But always they went back to the night before. The knife. Had he seen it before? Had he bought it anywhere? Of course, knives and sales could be traced. He would understand that. And he didn't like the city, did he? He and his wife wanted a farm. Well, plenty of people wanted farms nowadays. He brightened over that.

"Certainly I wanted a farm," he said, his face brightening. "There's a living in it, if you work yourself. A man can keep his self-respect. I've studied it a good bit. These fellows who go out of town and play at it—they'll only lose their investments. They'll fix up the houses and build fancy chicken houses and pigpens, and in three or four years they'll be back in town again."

"The idea was to be independent of your mother, wasn't it?"

"Not entirely. But what if it was? There's nothing wrong about that."

They took him back, to the attempt to poison Mrs. Fairbanks on her return from Florida. He was indignant.

"I never believed she was poisoned. Not deliberately. Some kinds of food poisoning act the same way. I looked it up. She'd come back from Florida the day before. She might have eaten something on the train."

"The doctor doesn't think so."

"That young whippersnapper! What does he know?"

The inspector picked up a paper from his desk. "This is Doctor Brooke's statement," he said. He read: " 'Showed usual symptoms arsenical poisoning, heat and burning pain; was vomiting and very thirsty. When I saw her her pulse was feeble and she showed signs of collapse. Had severe cramps in legs. I gave her an emetic and washed out her stomach. Reinsch's test later showed arsenious acid, commonly known as white arsenic. I also found it in the sugar bowl on her tray. At request of family made no report to the police.' "

"Oh, my God!" said Carlton feebly.

He sat clutching the arms of his chair, hardly hearing what they

asked him. He looked smaller than ever, as though he had been deflated, and his replies were almost monosyllabic.

"Do you know anything about this campaign to terrify your
mother? The bats, I mean."

"No. Nothing."

"Nor how they were introduced into the room?"

"No."

"I'll ask that another way. Have you any suspicions as to how or why
they were being used?"

And at that he blew up.

"No. No!" he shouted. "What are you trying to do to me? Make me
confess to something I never did? I didn't poison my mother. I didn't
kill her with a knife. I don't know anything about your damned ani-
mals. I don't know anybody cruel enough to—"

His voice broke. Tears rolled down his cheeks. He mopped at them
helplessly with his handkerchief.

"I'm sorry, gentlemen," he said. "I didn't mean to make a fool of
myself. I was up all night, and I haven't eaten anything today."

They gave him a little time. He lit a cigarette and tried to smile.

"All right," he said. "I guess I can take it now."

But they got nothing of importance from him, except a pretty thorough idea that he was keeping something back. They did not hold
him, however. At eight o'clock that night the inspector drove him
home. They stopped and had something to eat on the way, and Carlton drank two neat whiskies. He looked better when they reached the
house.

There was no one in sight. Marian, after having her room cleaned
and aired, had retired to it and locked her door. Jan had gone with
Courtney Brooke to see Eileen, and Hilda was packing her suitcase,
preparatory to leaving, when she got the word. But Susie was waiting
in the library. When she heard the car she flew out at the inspector
like a wild creature.

"So *you've* had him!" she said. "The only one in this house who
loved his mother, and you pick on him! If you've done anything to
him you'll be sorry. Good and sorry."

"I'm all right, Susie," Carlton said mildly. But she was not to be
placated.

"Why didn't you take that nurse of yours? Or Frank Garrison? Or
me? I could have told you some of the things that have been going
on."

"Oh, shut up, Susie," Carlton said wearily. "There's been too much talking as it is."

They were in the house by that time. He gave her a warning look, and she subsided quickly.

"What's been going on?" the inspector inquired.

"Marian's back, if that interests you. She raised hell until Eileen got out." She lit a cigarette and grinned at him. "Nice place we've got here," she said airily. "Come and stay sometime, if you ever get bored."

He left them downstairs, Susie mixing a highball and Carlton lighting a pipe. It would have been quite a nice domestic picture, he thought, if he had not known the circumstances.

Hilda was in her room when he went up the stairs. She was standing by her window, looking out, and her suitcase was packed and closed on a chair. He scowled at it.

"You're not leaving," he said. "I need you here."

"I have no patient."

"You'll stay if I have to break a leg. Get young Brooke to put the girl to bed. Nervous exhaustion. Anything, but you're staying." He looked at her. "Anything attractive outside that window?"

"No. I was just thinking."

"About what?"

She had assumed again her cherubic look, and he eyed her with suspicion.

"Not much. Just a can of white paint."

"What?"

"A can of paint. Of course people do queer things when they're worried. They play solitaire, or bite their fingernails, or kick the dog. I knew one man who cut down a perfectly good tree while his wife was having a baby. But paint is different. It covers a lot of things."

"I see. Who's been painting around here?"

"Carlton Fairbanks. This morning. He nailed the screens shut and then painted over the marks he made."

"Very tidy," said the inspector.

"But he fastened his mother's screens weeks ago. I would like to know whether he painted them, too."

He laughed down at her indulgently.

"What you need is a night's sleep," he told her. "Go to bed and forget it. And remember, you're not leaving."

But she was stubborn. She wanted to see Mrs. Fairbanks's screens, and at last he unsealed and unlocked the door, and gave her the key.

The room was as it had been left, the bedding thrown back, print powder showing here and there on the furniture. She went straight to a window.

"You see, he didn't."

"I'm damned if I know why that's important."

"I don't know myself. Not yet."

"All right. Go to it," he told her, still indulgent, and left her there, a small intent figure in the ghostly room, still gazing at the screens.

He yawned as he got into his car. The crowd outside the fence had practically disappeared. Only a scant half-dozen men still stood there, the die-hards who would not give up until all hope of further excitement was over. He did not notice them. What on earth had Hilda meant about white paint? What had white paint to do with the murder? The thing nagged him all the way back to his office and later on even to his bed.

Back in Mrs. Fairbanks's room Hilda switched off the lights and prepared to leave. She knew death too well to be afraid, but the impress of Mrs. Fairbanks's small old body on the bed had revived her sense of failure. She stood still. What could she have done? What had she failed to do?

And then she heard it again, a faint scuffling noise from the closet.

18

She jerked the door open, but the closet was empty. The shoe bag still hung on the door, the safe was closed, and the sounds had ceased. Save for the low remote voice of Carlton and Susie from the library below the house was silent.

Out in the hall she felt better. The noise, whatever it was, had not been what she had heard before, and turning briskly she opened the door of Carlton's room and went in. She stopped abruptly.

There was a man in the closet. He was standing with his back to her, and fumbling among the clothes hanging there.

She felt for the light switch and turned it on, to see William emerging, blinking.

"Is anything wrong, miss?" he asked.

She was surprised to discover that she was trembling.

"No. I was in Mrs. Fairbanks's room and I heard a noise. I thought—"

He smiled, showing his excellent set of false teeth.

"It was me in the closet," he explained. "I look after Mr. Carl's clothes. He wants a suit pressed, and he's got paint on the toes of these shoes this morning. I'm sorry if I scared you. I am afraid we are all in a bad state of nerves. If you'll excuse me—"

She felt exceedingly foolish as he passed her with his usual impeccable dignity, but in doing so he dropped one of the shoes. She picked it up and looked at it. It was an old tan one, with a smear of white paint across the toe, and the ones Carlton had worn that morning had been black. There could be no doubt of it. She could see him now, his black shoes, his morning coat and striped trousers, as he moved from room to room, carrying his cigar box and hammer, and later the small can of white paint.

William had not noticed. He thanked her and went out, and she turned off the light behind him. She did not go out, however. She stood still until she heard him going down the back stairs. Then she closed the door, fumbled for a box of matches and getting down on her knees, began systematically to examine the row of neatly treed shoes on the closet floor.

She did not hear the door opening behind her. Only when the light went on did she realize that Carlton had come into the room. She turned, still on her knees, the smoldering match in her hand, to see him coming at her, his face contorted, the veins on his forehead swollen with fury.

For a moment she thought he was going to attack her. She got up quickly.

"I'm sorry," she said. "I was in your mother's room, and I heard a noise in here. I thought it might be another rat."

He did not believe her. She saw that. He took a step or two toward her and stopped.

"Aren't you through here? In this house?" he said, his voice thick with anger. "My mother doesn't need you anymore. Eileen Garrison has gone. Are you supposed to stay indefinitely, snooping around about what doesn't concern you?"

"Are you so sure it doesn't concern me?" she inquired. "The police sent me here, at your mother's request. And they haven't released me yet. I assure you I am more than willing to go."

He got himself under control with difficulty. He walked past her and closed the closet door. When he faced her again his voice was more normal.

"At least I can ask you to keep out of the family rooms," he said. "There are no rats in the house, and if anything of this sort happens again I advise you to notify the servants."

She left with such dignity as she could muster. As she opened the door of her room she heard again the soft slithering sound she had heard before, but she was too shaken to investigate it. She stood at her window for some time, trying to think. It was very black outside. With the disappearance of the crowd the guards had evidently been removed, for by the light of the lamp on Huston Street she could see no one there. The stable was dark, as though Amos was either out or asleep.

She was astonished when the luminous dial of her watch showed only ten o'clock.

She was still there a few minutes later when Marian rapped at her door and slipped inside.

"Don't turn on the light," she said. "It's too hot. Miss Adams, you were here. You saw it all. Who did it? Who killed my mother?"

Hilda could not see her. She was only a vague figure in the room, but her voice was hard and strained.

"I wish I knew, Mrs. Garrison."

"That woman—why did she come here?"

"I think Mrs. Fairbanks had told her—"

"Nonsense," Marian said sharply. "She had some purpose of her own. That statement that Frank was with me! I suppose she was after money. Did Mother give her any?"

"I wasn't in the room. She may have."

Marian took a case from the pocket of her housecoat and lit a cigarette. In the light from the match she looked more haggard than ever, but it was Jan's eyes, dark and tragic, that looked out from her raddled face.

"I don't understand anything," she said. "Why did they put her in my room? The whole third floor was empty. And why have the police taken the screen from one of my windows? They have it, haven't they?"

"There is a chance somebody got into the house last night through that window," Hilda said guardedly. "I found it open. It could have been done from the roof of the porte-cochere. It was only a hook, and the blade of a knife—Or, of course, it might have been opened from within, by someone in the room."

Marian dropped her cigarette.

"Oh, God!" she said. "Frank, of course. They think it was Frank, and she let him in! Have they arrested him yet?"

"No. They've talked to him. That's all."

"They will arrest him," she said in a flat voice. "Jan says he was outside. They will arrest him, and what defense has he? He could have climbed to the roof. He's very strong. I've seen him do it, on a bet. They'll say she let him into her room and hid him there. But he didn't do it, Miss Adams. He cared for my mother. He was the kindest man on earth. He's had the patience of God himself, and I ruined his life. I was a jealous fool. I let him go. I made him go. So now—"

Hilda let her talk. Mentally she was back at the window of Marian's room the night before, and something was whipping about in the wind outside. She looked at Marian.

"When I closed the screen in your room last night, before I found your mother, there was a light rope fastened to one of the outside shutters. Do you know anything about it?''

"A rope? Something that could be climbed? Good heavens, are you trying to say that Frank—''

"It wasn't strong enough for that. Or long enough. I just wondered about it.''

But Marian was vague.

"I wouldn't know,'' she said. "It might have been there for years. I don't remember it.''

Hilda went back with her to her room. It had changed, she thought, since Eileen was in it. The bed had a silk cover and small bright-colored pillows. The dressing—table where Eileen had so defiantly made up her face only a few hours ago still had the gold toilet set, but it was crowded now with creams and perfumes. A silver fox scarf had been tossed on a chair, and sheer undergarments, unpacked but not put away, lay on the chaise longue.

"Ida wasn't well,'' Marian said indifferently. "I sent her to bed.''

She had apparently forgotten the rope. But Hilda looked for it, raising the window to do so. It was gone.

Marian shrugged when she told her.

"Maybe you only imagined it.''

"I didn't imagine it,'' said Hilda dryly.

Back in her room she tried to fit the pieces of the puzzle together, but she got nowhere. The rope had been there. Now it was gone. It must be important, must mean something. Had Eileen taken it away, and if so why? Or had someone in the house removed it? Not Carlton. He had been away after Eileen left and Marian arrived. Not Jan. She had gone to see Eileen and had not come back. Susie? She was quite capable of it, if it was important. She would have no scruples, Susie. But why would it be important? A rope and a bit of white paint on a tan shoe. They must fit somehow. Or did they?

She felt the need of action. For days, she thought, things had been going on around her. Not only the murder; small stealthy movements, doors opening and closing, people talking and saying nothing, going out and coming in, and always she had been merely the watcher, seeing but not comprehending. The night Carlton had carried the bundle from the stable, the figure at the top of the stairs, the open screen in Eileen's room, and now—of all silly things—a missing rope.

She looked across. Susie's light was on. It showed over the transom, and she went over and knocked lightly at the door. But she did not go into the room. Standing there she could hear Susie crying, childish sobs that were as unrestrained as everything else about her.

She got her flashlight from her suitcase and went down the stairs. The doctor's car had just driven in. There was no mistaking its rattle, or the cough of its ancient engine. Young Brooke did not come into the house, however. Jan opened the door and stood there, her voice cool.

"I don't understand you. That's all," she said.

"I've told you. I'm not living off any woman. You're going to have money now, and I'm peculiar about money." His voice was stubborn. "I'll support my own wife, or I won't have one."

"I wouldn't use the money, Court."

"There's where you're wrong, my darling. You think you wouldn't. You think you'd go hungry and without shoes. You wouldn't. I watched you this afternoon and tonight, cleaning up the mess at your stepmother's. You didn't like it, did you? And that's luxury, my child. One week of boiled beef and cabbage—"

"You can't see anything but your perfectly sickening pride, can you?" said Jan, and closed the door on him.

Hilda went back to the kitchen. Unless the police had taken the rope it must be somewhere in the house, or in the yard. She tried the trash cans and the garbage pails outside without result. Then rather reluctantly she went down to the basement. It was enormous. She did not like to turn on the lights, and her flash made only a small pool of illumination in the darkness. There was rope there, a large coil of it for some reason in a preserve closet, but it was thick and heavy.

When she did find it it was in the furnace. A small fire had been built around it at some time, but it was only charred, not consumed. She pulled it out and turned the light on it, some eight feet of thin blackened rope, which must be important since someone had attempted to destroy it. She went back over the night before when she had seen it, Eileen asleep in her bed, the pouring rain, the slapping screen. And Susie in the hall, drenched to the skin.

She felt the ashes in the furnace. They were still faintly warm. Quite recently, then—within two or three hours—someone had tried to destroy it. She tried to think what it meant, but she was tired. She had slept a little that afternoon and since then she had been going around in circles.

Nobody saw her as she carried it upstairs. She wrapped it in a piece of newspaper and laid it in the top of her suitcase. Maybe tomorrow her mind would be clearer, or the inspector would fit it into his puzzle. All she wanted now was to go to bed.

She undressed by the open window, for the sake of the breeze. That was how she happened to see Jan when she left the house. Even in the darkness there was no mistaking her slim figure, the easy grace with which she moved. On her way to Courtney Brooke, she thought comfortably. To make it up, to say she was sorry, to effect a compromise between his pride and her own. Then she stared. Jan was not crossing Huston Street. There was no sign of her under the street light. She had gone into the stable.

Hilda never quite understood the fear which made her snatch up a dressing-gown and her flashlight and follow her. The lights were out in the lower hall, but the door to the porte-cochere was open. She was in her bare feet as she ran across the grass. Once at the stable, however, she began to feel foolish. The doors to the garage were closed and Amos's windows overhead were dark. There was no sound to be heard, and it was not until she turned on her light that she saw the door to the staircase standing open. She stepped inside and looked up. It seemed to her that there was a small flickering light above in the loft.

Then it came, a crash from overhead that sounded as though the roof had fallen in. She was too shocked to move at first. She stood still, staring up. Her voice when it came sounded thin and cracked.

"Jan!" she called. "Jan! Are you there?"

There was no answer, and she ran up the stairs. At the top she turned the flashlight into the loft.

Jan was lying without moving on the floor, blood streaming from a cut on her forehead, and the heavy ladder was lying beside her.

19

She was not dead. That was the first thing Hilda ascertained. Her pulse was rapid but strong, and she was breathing regularly; and Hilda's heart, which had been trying to choke her, settled back into its proper place. The cause of the accident seemed obvious. For some reason Jan had used the ladder to reach the cupola, and it had slipped. The cut was from an old birdcage on the floor beside her.

Hilda's first impulse was to go to the house for help. Amos was evidently out. His door was standing open and his rooms dark. But she felt an odd reluctance to leaving the girl there alone. She made her way across the small landing into Amos's rooms and turning on the lights, found the bathroom. There she got a clean towel and a basin of water, and was turning back when she heard the far door quietly closing.

At first she thought it had closed itself. She put down the basin and towel and pulled at it. It did not yield, however, and at last she realized that it was locked. Someone had reached in while the water was running, taken out the key and locked it from the outside.

Hilda was frantic. She beat on the door, but there was only silence beyond. Then her practical, rational mind began to assert itself. She opened a window and looked out. There was no one in sight save a woman whistling for a dog across Huston Street, and the distance was too great for her to drop. But there must be some method of communication with the house. She looked about, and found a house telephone beside Amos's bed. Even then she was not too hopeful. It probably rang in the kitchen or back hall, and the household was upstairs. To her relief, however, it was answered almost at once.

Carlton's voice, sounding resentful, came over the wire.

"What the hell's the matter, Amos?" he said. "Place on fire?"

"It's Hilda Adams, Mr. Fairbanks," she told him. "Jan's had an accident in the stable loft, and I'm locked in."

His reaction was slow.

"What do you mean, you're locked in?"

"Someone has locked me in Amos's rooms. And Jan's hurt. She's in the loft. I don't know what's happening, but hurry. I—"

He did not wait for her to finish. From the window she saw him emerge from the house and come running across the lawn, his dressing-gown flapping around his legs. She stood inside the door as he climbed the stairs, but he went on to the loft. There was a brief silence, while he scratched a match or two. Then his voice, outside the door.

"She must have fallen," he said. "I'll get Brooke."

"Don't leave her there," she said. "Not alone. I don't think she fell. There's someone around, Mr. Fairbanks. She's not badly hurt. Not yet anyhow. But don't leave her."

"What on earth am I do do?"

"Look around for the key. It may be out there, or on the stairs."

He found it finally. It had been dropped just outside the door. But he had used his last match. When Hilda emerged it was into darkness, and the loft also was dark.

"My flashlight," she said. "I left it here."

"No light when I got here. See if Amos has a candle, or matches. I'll get the doctor."

She felt her way to Jan. She was still unconscious, but when Hilda touched her she moved slightly. She sat down on the floor beside her in the dark, and she was still there when Carlton came back, bringing Courtney Brooke with him.

After that there was a good bit of confusion. The two men carried Jan to the house, the family was roused, and Susie, to everybody's discomfiture, went into violent hysterics. Hilda gave her a good whiff of household ammonia and Susie, choking for breath, came out of it. She looked up, tears streaming from her eyes.

"It's my fault," she said. "I knew I ought to tell. But Carl—"

"What should you have told?"

Susie did not say. She closed her eyes and went into a stubborn silence.

Across the hall Courtney was sitting beside Jan's bed, holding an ice pack to her head. Instead of a shirt he wore the coat of his pajamas, and his face was grim.

"Someone tried to kill her," he said. "She fell first. Then she was struck with the flashlight. There is blood on it."

Marian stared at him from across the bed, her face filled with horror.

"But who would do that to her?" she demanded. "Who would want to kill her?" She leaned over the bed. "Jan. Jan! Who hurt you? What happened to you?"

"I'd let her alone," he said. "She is coming out of it. The quieter she is the better. She'll be all right, Mrs. Garrison."

At midnight Frank Garrison arrived. Carlton, telephoning wildly, had finally located him at his club. He came into the room, his tall figure seeming to fill it, and Marian went pale when she saw him.

"What are *you* doing here?"

"She is my child, Marian," he said politely.

"You deserted her. You deserted us both."

He ignored that. He asked about Jan, and Courtney gave him his place beside the bed. Marian got up, her face a tortured mask.

"You are driving me out of this room. You know that, don't you? Why don't you go back to your woman? Jan is nothing to you. Less than nothing."

"Sit down, Marian," he said gravely. "This is our girl. We have at least that in common. And be quiet. I think she is coming out of it."

But Jan, coming out of it, was not much help. After her first wondering gaze around the room she simply said that her head ached, and after that she went to sleep. She was still sleeping when at three in the morning her father left the house, and the doctor sent Hilda to bed.

"She's all right," he said. "She'll have a day or two in bed, but that's all. You'd better get some sleep. You look as though you need it. I'm staying anyhow."

She slept for three hours. Then she got up and put on her uniform. In Jan's room Courtney Brooke was asleep, as was Jan herself, and she went downstairs and let herself out without disturbing anyone.

At the stable Amos had returned. Even before she climbed the stairs she heard him snoring. A dim light from the cupola showed her the loft as they had left it; the ladder lying across the floor, the trunks, the broken furniture. But lying where Jan's body had fallen was something she had not noticed the night before, a large piece of unbleached muslin some four feet square. She picked it up and examined it. It looked fairly new, and it had certainly not been there when Amos showed her the loft some days before.

She put it down and was stooping over the ladder when Amos appeared. He had pulled a pair of trousers over his nightshirt, and he was in a bad humor.

"What are you doing here?" he asked suspiciously. "If a man works all day and can't get his proper sleep—"

She cut him short.

"Lift this ladder, Amos. I want to look at the cupola."

"What for?"

"That's my business. Miss Jan was hurt here last night. I want to know why."

"Hurt? Not bad, is it?"

"Bad enough. She'll get over it."

The cupola, however, revealed nothing at first. It was floored, save for the square opening for the ladder. Such light as there was was admitted by slotted openings on the four sides. Except that in one place the dust of ages seemed to have been disturbed, it appeared empty. Then she saw something; an old pair of chauffeur's gloves. They had been shoved back into a corner, but she managed to reach them. She showed them to Amos when she climbed down again.

"Are these yours?"

He stared at them. Then he grinned.

"So that's where they went!" he said.

"You didn't put them up there?"

"Why would I put them up there?" he demanded truculently. "I lost them two or three months ago. I thought somebody stole them."

He wanted them back, but Hilda to his fury took them back to the house with her. One part of the mystery, she felt, was solved. But before she left she turned to him.

"I suppose you can account for your own movements last night?"

He took a step toward her, looking ugly.

"So I hurt her, did I?" he said harshly. "Like my own daughter, and I try to kill her! Sure I can account for where I was last night, if that's any of your business. You don't have to come out to the stable to find your murderer, Miss Police Nurse. Look in the house."

Jan was better that morning. Outside of a headache and some bruises she had suffered no ill effects. She even drank a cup of coffee and ate a piece of toast. But she had no idea what had happened to her, except that she thought the ladder had slipped.

She had not gone to bed. She had quarreled with Courtney and she could not sleep. She had decided to go over and see him. She had reached the stable when she heard a sound overhead. She thought it was Amos, and called to tell him that the door to the staircase was open. Amos, however, had not answered, so she had climbed the stairs.

She was not frightened. She had thought for some time that the bats in her grandmother's room might have come from the cupola.

"There were slits in the shutters," she said. "Pigeons couldn't get in, but bats might."

What she thought she heard, she said, might have been bats flying around. No, she couldn't describe it. It was just a sound. Not very loud, either. She knew the loft well. She had played there as a child. She didn't even light a match until she got there.

To her surprise the ladder was in place. She decided to investigate the cupola, and striking a match she climbed it. She was near the top when it gave way under her.

"I felt it going," she said. "I couldn't catch anything. I—well, I guess I just fell. I don't remember."

They let her think that. She was not told that it had probably been jerked from under her, or of the savage attack on her with the flashlight.

Hilda saw the inspector later that morning, sitting across from him, and placing on the desk between them the piece of muslin, the gloves, a small can of white paint, and the piece of charred rope. Fuller eyed them solemnly.

"You're slipping," he said. "No snakes? No guinea pigs?"

He lookd tired. He had slept badly, and it almost annoyed him to see Hilda, bland and fresh, her hands neatly folded in her lap.

"You're not human," he said. "And what in God's name does all this stuff mean?"

"Somebody tried to kill Janice Garrison last night."

He almost leaped out of his chair.

"What?" he yelled. "And you didn't call me? See here. I'll be damned if I'll have you running this case. You've let one murder happen, and now you tell me—"

He choked, and Hilda looked more bland than ever.

"I thought you needed your sleep," she said calmly. "And the family didn't want you." She smiled faintly. "They said they had had enough of you to last a long time."

"Who said that?"

"I think it was Carlton."

She told her story after that, the attack on Jan, her own discovery of the girl, being locked in Amos's rooms, and Carlton coming to the rescue.

"So he was downstairs, was he?"

"He was. Probably getting a drink."

Fuller leaned back in his chair.

"You don't think he is guilty, do you?"

"I think he was fond of his mother."

Their eyes clashed, the inspector's hard, Hilda's blue and childlike, and stubborn.

"He had the motive and the opportunity."

"You couldn't get an indictment on that, could you? No grand jury—"

"All right," he said resignedly. "Now what's all this stuff?"

Hilda smiled.

"I don't know about the rope. Not yet, anyhow. But suppose you wanted to scare an old lady, maybe bring on a heart attack. And suppose she's afraid of bats. Other things, too, like rats. You might get a supply of them, put them in an old birdcage covered with a piece of muslin and hide them where nobody ever went."

"The cupola?"

"The cupola. But bats—and other things—have teeth. At least I think so. So you use a pair of heavy gloves. You might look at those gloves. They have small holes in them."

"Where would you get the bats—and so forth?"

"Out of the cupola itself. I didn't see any. I probably scared them away. But there's a butterfly net in the loft. I suppose it would be possible."

He threw up his hands.

"All right. You win," he said. "But how did they get into the room?"

"I imagine that's where the paint comes in," she said tranquilly.

She was there for some time. When she got up the inspector went to the door with her. Always she amused him, often she delighted him, but that morning there was a new look of admiration in his eyes.

"You're a highly useful person, Miss Pinkerton," he said, smiling down at her. "If I didn't think you'd slap me I'd kiss you."

"It wouldn't be the first time."

"Which?" he said quizzically. "Slap or kiss?"

"Both," she said, and went out.

Ida was dusting the lower hall when she went back. She did not look up, and Hilda did not speak to her. She had no idea that it was to be the last time she was to see the girl alive.

20

The inquest was held at two o'clock that afternoon. It was very brief. Carlton Fairbanks identified his mother's body, and nothing new was developed. Susie came home looking sick and went to bed, but Marian stayed downtown to make arrangements for the funeral and to buy the conventional black.

She was still out when the inspector arrived at four that afternoon. Jan was better, sitting up in bed, with Courtney Brooke in and out of the room, but mostly in. They did not talk much. It seemed to content them merely to be together. And Carlton was in the library. He had had a drink or two, but he was entirely sober.

He did not seem surprised to see the inspector. He stood up stiffly.

"I rather expected you," he said. "Jan's accident, and all that. But I want to ask you not to judge us on what may seem unusual. If any one of us has been at fault—"

Here, however, his voice failed him. It was a moment or so before he pulled himself together.

"I know things look bad," he said. "When I saw the paint was gone— But it has nothing to do with my mother's death. Nothing. I am innocent, and so—God help her—is my wife."

He followed the inspector up the stairs. Hilda, watching them come, thought he would not make the top. He rallied, however, when she unlocked the door of the death room, although he did not look at the bed.

The inspector was brisk and businesslike. He went at once to the closet and ignoring the safe got down on his knees and examined the baseboard. He used a flashlight, and he rapped on it and listened, his head on one side, while Carlton stood mutely by. When he got up his voice was brisk.

"All right," he said. "Now I'd like to see your room, please."

This time Carlton led the way. He looked shrunken, incredibly aged. Once inside he closed the door to Susie's room, but when the inspector opened his closet door he spoke for the first time.

"I give you my word of honor," he said bleakly, "that I knew nothing about this until yesterday morning. I would have told you before, but it involved"—he swallowed—"it involved someone very dear to me."

He said nothing more. He stood silent while the inspector took out the row of neatly treed shoes. Even the tan ones were there, although the paint had been removed. The inspector picked up his flashlight and turned it on the baseboard.

"How does this open?"

"It slides—toward the fireplace. It's nailed now."

"Since yesterday?"

"Since yesterday. I nailed and painted it yesterday morning."

The white paint was dry. The inspector produced from his pocket one of those small arrangements where a number of tools are carried inside the handle. He fitted one and went to work. Carlton said nothing. A breeze from the open windows blew the curtains into the room. Outside the traffic of a busy Monday moved along the streets, and Joe's Market was filled with women, shopping and gossiping.

"That police car's back. Look, you can see it."

"Much good it will do. They don't arrest people like the Fairbankses for murder."

It took some time to slide the panel. The paint held it. But at last it moved and the inspector picked up his flashlight. He saw a small empty chamber, the thickness of the wall, and beyond it a flat wooden surface fastened to the floor with hooks and screw-eyes. He opened it, and saw as he had expected; that it was the baseboard of Mrs. Fairbanks's closet. On his right was the safe. He could touch it, but he could not reach the dial. The whole aperture was only seven inches high.

He got up, dusting his hand.

"I suppose that accounts for a number of things," he said. "Not only for the attempts to frighten your mother. It could account for something else, Mr. Fairbanks."

"For what?"

"A cable for a remote control to the radio in your mother's room. I suggest that your mother was killed earlier in the night, that you turned on the radio from here, that you later re-entered the room ostensibly to shut it off, but actually to disconnect the cable, and that when you went to the closet it was to place the cable there, so you could withdraw it quietly from this side.''

"Before God I never did.''

That was when Susie burst into the room. She came like fury, ready to spring at Fuller.

"You fool!'' she said. "You stupid fool! He never knew about it until yesterday.''

Carlton roused at that.

"Be still,'' he said. "Don't make things worse. They're bad enough. Go back to your room. I'll—''

She paid no attention to him. She was panting with anger and fear.

"Don't listen to him. I did it. I had it done. He'd never have found it if I'd had a chance to close it all the way. But if you think I put those creatures in his mother's room, I didn't.'' Her voice was shrill. She was trembling. "Someone else in this house did that. Not me. I wouldn't touch them with a ten-foot pole.''

She came out with her story. Nothing would have stopped her. Carlton had turned his back and was staring out the window. The inspector listened. Hilda watched.

It had started the winter before, she said. She had been in the bank, and she had seen Mrs. Fairbanks receive a large bundle of currency.

"She didn't see me,'' she said. "I saw her go down to her safe-deposit box, and I knew she was hoarding money. I told Carl, but he didn't believe me. Anyhow, he said it was his mother's business.''

Then came the matter of the safe. Why did she want a safe in her room? And she had changed in other ways, too. She became stingy with money. She had sent away the kitchenmaid and the second housemaid.

"I was scared,'' Susie said. "I knew damned well why she wanted a safe in her room. Maybe I was raised on the wrong side of the tracks, but I had a pretty good idea what she was doing; selling her securities and turning them into cash to save taxes. And now she was going to keep it in the house!

"I got my brother-in-law the job of doing the carpentry work,'' she said defiantly. "The safe was to be built into the wall, and I told him what I thought. Suppose she had two or three million dollars in cash in this house? A lot of people might know, her banks, her brokers. Things like that leak out. It wasn't safe. *We* weren't safe. Even if there was a fire—''

Her brother-in-law had suggested that she could at least keep an eye on things. "You can't change her," he said, "but you can watch her. Then if she's doing it you can get that son of hers to work on her. If she's trying to escape her taxes she ought to go to jail."

Mrs. Fairbanks and Marian were in Florida, Jan was visiting a school friend, and she and Carl were out of town for days at a time looking for a farm. He had no difficulty in doing the work. And when the old lady came back she—Susie—learned a good bit. Mostly by listening. Mrs. Fairbanks would drive out, come back and put something in the safe. After a time, as the money apparently accumulated, she developed a new habit. She would lock her door at night, set up a card table, and apparently count over her hoard.

"I didn't dare to open the baseboard all the way," Susie said, "but I'd push it out an inch or so. She kept her shoes in a shoe bag on the door, so they didn't bother me. She'd pretend to be playing solitaire, but she didn't fool me! But when I tried to tell Carl he wouldn't believe it. I didn't dare to tell him how I knew."

As to a possible cable to the radio and a remote control, she dismissed that with a gesture.

"That's crazy," she said. "He never knew the thing was there until after his mother was dead and he hunted out some black shoes yesterday morning to wear with his morning coat. Then he gave me hell, and yesterday he nailed it up." She went over and put a hand on Carlton's arm. "The one thing he suspected me of I didn't do," she said softly. "He thought I was keeping the bats in the stable. He found a birdcage up there wrapped in a cloth, and he was bringing it to me when the nurse saw him. He had to take it back!"

She eyed Hilda without rancor.

"You're pretty smart," she said, "but you missed that, didn't you? That's why I went out there in the rain that night. Carl had told me about it, and I wanted to see if it was still there, and what was in it."

"But you never got there?"

"I was scared off," said Susie, suddenly wary. "Somebody grabbed me. I don't know who."

Down in the kitchen Maggie was looking at the clock.

"I'd like to know what's keeping Ida," she observed. "She said she'd be gone only an hour, and it's five now." She poured William a cup of tea and took one for herself. "She's been queer lately," she said. "Ever since the old lady's death, and before."

"She'll be all right," said William. "Maybe she went to a movie."

But no one upstairs was thinking of Ida. Not then, certainly. Carlton did not know the combination to his mother's safe, and the inspector was anxious to open it.

"I think she would have written it down," Carlton said worriedly. "Her memory wasn't very good lately. Perhaps you have seen it, Miss Adams. It would be a combination of some sort, I suppose. Letters and numbers."

Hilda, however, had seen nothing of the sort. She had never seen Mrs. Fairbanks open the safe, and in the search of her room which followed nothing developed. They took the pictures from the walls, raised the rug at its edges, looked through the bed and under the paper lining the drawers of her table and bureau. They even examined the few books lying about, the vases on the mantel, the back of the clock and the radio, as well as the cards with which—according to Susie—she had merely pretended to play solitaire.

They were almost friendly, the four of them, during that interval. At least a common cause united them. When Maggie came to the door at a quarter to six, it was to see Mrs. Fairbanks's room completely dismantled, Susie on a chair examining the top of the draperies at the window, and an inspector of police lying under the bed, with only his legs protruding.

She looked apologetic.

"I didn't mean to disturb anybody," she said, highly embarrassed. "It's about Ida. She went out at one o'clock for an hour or so, and she hasn't come back yet."

The inspector had crawled out. He stood up and dusted his clothes.

"Does she often do that?"

"Never before, to my knowledge."

"Did she say where she was going?"

"She said she needed some darning silk. I wanted her to eat her lunch first. She looked sick. But she wouldn't wait."

The inspector looked at his watch.

"It's almost six now. Five hours. I wouldn't worry. She'll probably show up."

Ida did not show up, however. Marian came home from her shopping and her interview with the mortician looking exhausted and, refusing dinner, lay on her chaise longue, her eyes closed and her face bitter.

Carlton was closeted with Susie in her room, and Jan and Courtney had a double tray on the side of her bed, achieving the impossible of balancing it, holding hands, and still doing away with a considerable amount of food.

When Hilda carried it out he followed her.

"See here," he said. "What's been going on? What's this about Ida being missing?"

"I don't know that she is, doctor."

"Well, what's the row about? Maggie says you've practically torn up the old lady's room."

"We've been trying to locate the combination of her safe."

He whistled and looked back at Jan's door.

"I wouldn't tell her that, Miss Adams," he said. "It might upset her."

He declined to elaborate, and Hilda had that to puzzle over during the evening, as well as Ida's continued absence. At eight o'clock William had sent a wire to her people in the country, and he and Maggie were waiting in the kitchen for an answer. Young Brooke, having eaten his dinner, left for his office hours and came back at nine. Marian went to bed, and Carlton and Susie were in the library. Hilda, not needed anywhere, sat in her room and watched the twilight turn into night. She had gathered up a lot of odds and ends, but where did they take her? She was no nearer the solution of the crime than she had been before.

Ida? What about Ida? She could have discovered the opening into Mrs. Fairbanks's room; the panel not entirely closed, and Ida on her knees, washing the floor of the closet. She could even have slipped the bats into the room. She had been a country girl. She would not be afraid of such things. But why? What would be her motive?

She went back to the morning of the murder; Ida in her room by the window, her hands folded in her lap and a queer look on her long thin face as she and the inspector entered. She had been afraid, so afraid that she tried to rise and could not. And now she was missing.

In the next room the young people were talking. Hilda got up and moving carefully went to the front hall. Above her the third floor loomed dark and empty, and the long passage to Ida's room was ghostly. As the evening cooled the old house creaked, and Hilda, remembering the figure she had seen at the top of the stairs, felt small goose pimples on her flesh.

Once back in the girl's room, however, she felt better. She turned on the light and looked about her. There was no indication that she had intended to leave. A pair of washed stockings hung over the back of a chair, a discarded blue uniform lay on the bed, and a battered suitcase stood on the closet floor.

The wastebasket was empty, except for a newspaper, but under the pine dresser she found a scrap of paper. It was part of a letter, and it contained only two words. On one line was the word "sorry" and below it "harmless." Nowhere could she find any other bits, and at last she gave it up and put out the light.

She went quietly forward and down to the second floor. To her surprise the door into Mrs. Fairbanks's room was open, and she stepped inside. Young Brooke was there. He had opened the drawer of the table and had taken something out.

He started violently when he saw her. Then he grinned.

"Looking for cards," he said. "Jan and I want to play some gin-rummy."

He showed her the cards, but Hilda held out her hand for them.

"I'll take those," she said. "My orders are that nothing is to leave this room."

"Oh, have a heart. A pack of cards—"

"Give them to me, please. There are cards downstairs."

He gave them up reluctantly.

"And what will *you* do with them?" he inquired.

"Put them back where they belong," she said stiffly, "and lock this door."

She waited until he had gone out. Then she locked the door and took the key.

At midnight the telegram came. Ida had not gone home. And Hilda, getting Marian some hot milk to enable her to sleep, found the servants still there, Maggie and William and, smoking a pipe by the door, Amos. They were, she thought, both worried and watchful. And Maggie was convinced that Ida was dead.

"She was a good girl," she said tearfully. "A good Christian, too. And she minded her own business."

Amos shook the ahes out of his pipe.

"Did she now?" he said. "Sure of that, are you? Then what was she doing in my place yesterday, after the old lady was killed?"

"You're making that up."

"Am I? I found her in my bedroom, looking out of the window. She was a snooper. That's what she was. I never did trust her."

"You never trusted anybody," said Maggie scornfully. "What would she want in your room anyhow?"

"That's what I asked her. She said she had brought me some blankets. I've been here thirty years and she's been here ten. It's the first time she's been interested in my bed."

He seemed to think that was humorous. He grinned, but Maggie eyed him disdainfully.

"You might at least be grateful."

"Grateful? For blankets at the beginning of summer? Them blankets were an excuse to get in my room, and don't tell me different."

That night Hilda discovered why Susie had fainted a few days before.

Jan had sent her to bed, and she went gladly enough. All she wanted, she thought, was a hot bath and sleep, and tomorrow she could go home, to her bird and her sunny sitting-room. She had done all she could. She had not solved the murder, but she had solved one mystery. She locked the bit of paper from Ida's room in her suitcase, got out a fresh nightgown, and after some hesitation put the key to Mrs. Fairbanks's room under her pillow. Then she undressed and reached into the closet for her bedroom slippers. Curled up in one of them was something cold and clammy, and as she touched it it slithered out across her feet and under the bed.

She was too paralyzed to move for a moment. Then she put on her slippers and going across the hall rapped at Susie's door. Susie was in bed, the usual cigarette in one hand, the usual lurid magazine in the other.

"You might tell Mr. Fairbanks," Hilda said coldly, "that the thing that scared you into a faint the other night is under my bed. I believe it's harmless."

"Harmless!" Susie said. "I put my hand on it in that damned peephole, and it nearly scared me to death. It's a—"

"Yes," said Hilda calmly. "It's a snake. It would be nice to know who put it there."

21

OFFICE OF CHIEF MEDICAL EXAMINER REPORT OF DEATH

Name of deceased: *Unknown*
Last residence: *Unknown*
Date and time of death: *June 17, 1941. One a.m.*
Date and time examiner notified: *June 17, 1941. Two a.m.*
Body examined: *June 17, 1941. Eight a.m.*
Reported by: *City Hospital*
Body found: *At Morgue*
Pronounced dead by: *Dr. Cassidy*
Sex: *Female*
Age: *Approximately 40*
Color: *White*

Notes:
Woman reported discovered in great pain in rest room of Stern & Jones department store at 4 p.m. Store physician called and gave treatment for shock. When taken to City Hospital (see police report) was in state of collapse. Reached hospital 5:10 p.m., June 16th.

The body is that of a thin but sufficiently nourished female. From condition of hands believe worked at domestic service, office cleaning, or similar occupation. Clothing revealed nothing. There was no sign of violence on body.

There was no suicide note to be found. That the deceased was not anticipating death is possible, as a small paper bag containing darning silk was found in her purse. Also the report of the maid in said rest room, who states that the deceased was conscious when found, and said that she had been poisoned.

In view of the circumstances I am of the opinion that the cause of death was: Administration of arsenical poison by person or persons unknown: Homicide.

(Signed) S. J. Wardwell
Chief Medical Examiner

AUTOPSY

Approximate age: *40 years*
Approximate weight: *115 lbs.*
Height: *5' 3'*
Stenographer: *John T. Heron*
I hereby certify that on the 17th day of June, 1941, I, Richard M. Weaver, made an autopsy on this body eight hours after death, and said autopsy revealed:

No injury on body, which is that of a white female, apparently 40 years of age. Examination of viscera revealed characteristic symptoms of arsenical poisoning. Due to use of stomach pump impossible to tell time of last food taken. Possibly twelve hours before death.

Arsenic present in considerable amount in viscera.

(Signed) Richard M. Weaver
Assistant Medical Examiner

It was noon of the day after Ida disappeared before she was found at the morgue. The autopsy was over by that time, and Ida's tired hands were resting peacefully on a cold slab in the morgue when Carlton was taken there to identify her.

He gave one look and backed away.

"It's Ida, all right," he said hoarsely. "For God's sake, inspector! What's happening to us?"

"I imagine Ida knew too much," said the inspector, motioning the morgue master to push the body out of sight. "It's a pity. It's a cruel death."

He eyed Carlton thoughtfully.

"I've seen the reports," he said. "She went out yesterday without eating her lunch. At three o'clock or somewhat later she bought some darning silk at the notion counter of Stern and Jones. The saleswoman says she looked sick, and complained of cramps. The girl advised her to go to the rest room. She did. She sat in a chair at first. Then the maid got her to a couch, and called the store doctor. He says she didn't give her name or address, and by the time she got to the hospital she wasn't able to. It looks as though some time between the time she left the house and when she was found in the rest room she got the poison.''

With Carlton looking on, he examined the clothing Ida had worn when taken to the hospital. It revealed nothing. Her bag, however, provided a shock. It contained no lipstick or powder. The coin purse had only a dollar or two. But tucked in a pocket behind a mirror were five new one-hundred-dollar bills.

The two men stared at them incredulously.

"You don't pay her in money like that?"

"Good heavens, no. Where did she get it?"

The notes were in series, and the inspector made a record of their numbers. Then he sealed them in an envelope and ordered them put in the safe. Carlton was still unnerved when they reached the street. He lit a cigarette with shaking hands. But he was still fighting. He drew a long breath.

"At least this murder lets us out," he said. "None of us would kill the girl. And as for that money—"

"I suppose you were all at home yesterday afternoon after the inquest?"

Carlton flushed.

"You were there. You saw us. Except my sister. She was out shopping. But she would have no reason—You can't suspect *her* of this. She—"

The inspector cut in on him.

"Where does she usually shop?"

"At—I don't know. All over town, I imagine. What difference does it make? She was in Atlantic City when Mother died. And she was fond of Ida. You can't go on like this," he said, raising his voice. "You can't suspect all of us. It's damnable. It's crazy."

"We have had two murders," said the inspector stolidly. "There's a restaurant in Stern and Jones, isn't there?"

"I don't know. Marian ate her lunch after she left."

They parted there, Carlton stiffly to hail a taxi and go home, the inspector to go back to his office and call up certain banks. He found the one Carlton Fairbanks used, and asked them to check his account. After a brief wait he got the figures.

"Balance is three hundred and forty dollars. He drew out seventy-five in cash last week. That's all. Not suspecting him, are you, inspector?"

"No record of a withdrawal of five hundred in one-hundred-dollar bills in the last month or so?"

"No. He never has much of a balance."

It was one o'clock when he reached the Fairbanks house again. He interviewed the servants first. They were subdued and frightened. Even Amos had lost some of his surliness, and when they learned that Ida had been poisoned with arsenic there was a stricken silence. But they had nothing to tell him. Ida had taken Mrs. Fairbanks's death hard. She had eaten nothing in the house the day before after her breakfast, "and little enough of that." Asked where she kept her savings they agreed that she had an account at a downtown bank.

None of them believed for a moment that she had committed suicide.

"Why would she?" said Maggie practically. "She had a steady job and good pay. She wasn't the sort anyhow. She sent money every month to her people in the country. This will just about finish them," she added. "They're old, and farms don't pay any more. I suppose they've been notified?"

"Not yet. I want their address."

He took it down and asked for Hilda. William said she was in her room, and led him upstairs. She was sitting in a chair with her knitting in her lap, and he went in and closed the door behind him.

"I suppose you know?"

"Yes. There's a family conclave going on now in Marian's room."

"Overhear any of it?"

"I didn't try," she told him primly.

They went up the back stairs to Ida's room. Save for the preparations for lunch going on below the house was quiet, and Ida's room was as Hilda had seen it the day before. He searched it, but he found nothing of any importance. When he had finished Hilda handed him the piece of paper she had discovered.

" 'Sorry,' " he read, "and 'harmless.' Part of a letter, isn't it? What do you suppose was harmless?"

"I think," said Hilda mildly, "that it was a snake. You see, the bats and the other things hadn't worked, so she tried a snake."

"Who tried a snake?"

"Ida."

"What on earth are you talking about? If you can make a snake out of the word 'harmless'—"

Hilda smiled.

"I didn't. I found one in my closet last night."

He was startled.

"Good God! How do you know it was harmless?"

"Well, there was that piece of paper, of course. And I saw it myself. Just a small garden snake. I wanted to take it out to the yard, but Carlton Fairbanks killed it. With a golf club," she added.

He inspected her, standing there in her neat white uniform, her face sweet and tranquil, and he felt a terrific desire to shake her.

"So it's as simple as that," he said caustically. "Ida puts it in your closet and Carlton kills it with a golf club." His voice rose. "What the hell has a snake got to do with two murders? And stop grinning at me."

"I'm not grinning," said Hilda with dignity. "I don't think Ida put it in the closet. I think it escaped from that hole in the wall, and it nearly scared Susie to death. But I do think Ida brought it here; it and the other things."

"Why?"

"Well, she was a country girl. She lived only thirty miles out of town, and she went there once a month or so. I was wondering," she added, "if I could go there this afternoon. They may know of her death, but they are old. It will be hard on them."

He gave her a suspicious look.

"That's all, is it? You wouldn't by any chance have something else in your mind?"

"It wouldn't hurt to look about a little," she said cautiously. "I think Doctor Brooke would drive me out."

He went to the window and stood looking out.

"Why would she do it?" he asked. "She had little or nothing to gain by the will."

"Oh, I don't think she killed Mrs. Fairbanks," Hilda said quickly. "She hated the house. The work was too heavy, for one thing. She may have wanted to scare her into moving."

"But you don't believe that?"

"I don't believe she killed herself. No."

Before he left he saw Carlton.

"In view of what has happened," he said, "I'd like to keep Miss Adams here for a day or two longer. You need not pay her. I'll attend to that."

"So we're to have a spy in the house," Carlton said bitterly. "What can I do about it? Let her stay, and the hell with it."

22

Old Eliza Fairbanks was buried that afternoon from St. Luke's, with a cordon of police to hold back the crowd and photographers, holding cameras high, struggling for pictures of the family. Her small body in its heavy casket was carried into the church, and in due time out again. A long procession of cars drove up, filled, and drove away.

"What is it, a wedding?"

"Sh! It's a funeral. You know, the old woman who got stabbed."

Marian came out, her face bleak under her mourning. Carlton and Susie, Susie unashamedly crying. Jan, wan and lovely, but keeping her head high, and Courtney Brooke holding her arm. Nobody noticed Frank Garrison. He sat at the rear of the church, thinking God knows what; of his wedding perhaps in this same church, with Marian beside him; of Jan's christening at the font, a small, warm body in his arms; of Sunday mornings when he sat in the Fairbanks pew, and a little old lady sat beside him.

He got out quickly when it was over.

It was five o'clock when the family returned from the cemetery, and six before Hilda had got Marian to bed and was free. She went quietly out the side door and past the stable to Huston Street, to find Courtney waiting for her in his car.

"I hope we make it," he said. "The old bus does all right in town. When it stops I can have somebody fix it. But a trip like this—"

Hilda got in and settled herself.

"We'll make it," she said comfortably. "We've got to make it."

Yet at first there seemed nothing to discover. Two elderly people, stricken with grief, Ida's parents were only bewildered.

"Who would want to do that to her?" they asked. "She was a good girl. She minded her own business. And she was fond of the family, miss. Especially Mrs. Garrison, Mrs. Marian Garrison. That's her picture there." Hilda looked. On the mantel was a photograph of Marian taken some years ago. "She was pretty then," the mother said. "Ida used to help her dress. She—"

She checked herself abruptly, and Hilda thought the father had made a gesture. She got nothing further from them. They knew nothing of any bats or other creatures, and Hilda, watching their surprise, was sure that it was genuine. They sat in the old-fashioned parlor, with an organ in the corner and a fan of paper in the empty fireplace, and denied that Ida had ever carried anything of the sort into town. "Why would she?"

"Some laboratories buy such things," Hilda said mendaciously, and got up. "Someone had been keeping things in a birdcage in the Fairbanks stable. Never mind. I'm only sorry. If there is anything I can do—"

Courtney had not gone into the house. He was standing by the car when she came out.

"Funny thing," he said. "There was a boy over by the barn. I started over to him but he beat it. Well, how did they take it?"

"It's broken them," she said wearily. "I suppose it was the boy who did it."

"Did what?"

"Caught the bats and so on and gave them to Ida."

He almost put the car into a ditch.

"So that's it," he said. "It was Ida! But why, and who killed her?"

"Are you sure you don't know, doctor? On the night Mrs. Fairbanks died you saw someone on the third floor, didn't you? You were holding a cup of coffee. It spilled."

He passed a truck before he replied.

"That's as preposterous a deduction as I've ever heard," he said. "If that's the way the police work—"

"I'm not a policewoman," she told him patiently. "You saw someone, didn't you?"

"I've already said no."

He was lying, and he was not a good liar. She did not pursue the subject. She was very quiet the rest of the way back to town. Her face had no longer its bland cherubic expression. She looked dispirited and half sick. When young Brooke politely but coldly offered her dinner at a roadhouse she refused it.

"I'm not hungry," she said. "Thanks just the same. I want to get back as soon as possible."

Yet for a woman in a hurry she did nothing much when she reached the Fairbanks house again. She did not get into uniform. She merely took off her hat and sat down in her room. When Jan, on her way to bed, rapped at her door she was still there in the dark.

"Good gracious!" Jan said. "Don't you want a light? And did you have anything to eat?"

"I didn't want anything, Jan."

"Just what were you and Courtney cooking up this afternoon?" Jan asked curiously. "I saw you, you know. You were gone for hours."

"I was telling Ida's people about her," said Hilda. "It was rather sad. I hate to carry bad news."

She looked at the girl. How would she bear another blow? Suppose she was right and Ida had been put out of the way because she knew what Hilda thought she knew?

It was midnight before she made any move. The household was asleep. Even Amos's light in the stable was out, by that time. But she took the precaution of slipping off her shoes. Then, armed with her flashlight, she went up to the third floor. She did not go back to Ida's room, however. She went into the guest rooms, taking one after the other, examining the floors and the bathrooms, and removing the dust covers from the beds.

It was in the room over Carlton's that she found what she had been afraid to find.

She went to bed and to sleep after that, but she carried a sort of mental alarm clock in her head, and promptly at six she wakened. Nobody was stirring in the house when she went down to the library and called the inspector on the phone at his bachelor apartment. His voice was heavy with sleep when he answered.

"It's Hilda Adams," she said carefully. "I want you to do something. Now, if you will."

"At this hour? Good heavens, Hilda, don't you ever go to bed?"

"I do, but I get out of it. Will you have someone check the hotels in town for a woman who got there early Sunday morning and left that afternoon?"

"Sunday? Sure. But what's it all about?"

"I'll tell you later. I can't talk here."

She hung up and went upstairs again. She had been stupid, she thought. She should have known all this before. Yet she had also a sense of horror. It was still written all over her when she sat in the inspector's office that Wednesday morning.

"How did you guess it?" he said.

"Then it's correct?"

"Correct as hell. She checked in at five Sunday morning and left that afternoon. She left Atlantic City on Saturday."

She drew a long breath.

"I should have known it before," she said. "The figure at the top of the stairs and the chandelier shaking. I think young Brooke saw it, too, although he denies it. But the rooms looked the same. Only Ida had cleaned a bathroom, and she couldn't put back the dust. I suppose that cost her her life. If she had only raised a window and let the dirt in—"

In spite of himself Fuller smiled.

"The world lost a great criminal in you, Hilda," he said admiringly.

He looked over his notes. Marian had registered at one of the big Atlantic City hotels the night she had left home. She had remained most of the time in her room, having her meals served there, and she had left on a late train on Saturday.

"It checks," he said thoughtfully. "She came home late and Ida probably admitted her and told her Eileen was there. She smuggled her up the back stairs to the third floor and settled her there. Then what? Did she come down while young Brooke was with Jan, and stab her mother? It's—well, it's unnatural, to say the least."

Hilda sat very still.

"I'm not sure," she said at last. "She was there. I don't know where she hid while the house was searched. Maybe in the stable. Anyhow she got away, and after you let Ida go I suppose she made up the bed."

"What put you on the track?" he asked curiously.

"I don't know exactly." She got up to go. "Ida's parents said she was devoted to Marian. And then the doctor—I just wondered if Ida had seen Marian at Stern and Jones on Monday."

He looked at her with shocked surprise.

"You don't mean that, do you?"

"It could be," she said rather dismally, and went out.

He read over his notes carefully after she had gone. The waitresses in the restaurant at Stern & Jones did not remember Ida, But they did remember Marian, who was well known in the store. She had come in at three o'clock and had a cup of tea. But she had been alone. As to the will, in a long-distance call to Mrs. Fairbanks's lawyer, Charles Willis, in Canada for salmon, Willis said that the old lady had kept all three copies, but that Carlton was substantially correct. The estate was divided between Marian and Carlton, with Marian's share in trust for Janice.

"Although there was a hundred thousand dollars for the girl," he said.

The will had been made seven years ago. He did not think she had changed it.

After that the inspector went to Mrs. Fairbanks's bank, and had some difficulty in getting information. In the end, however, he learned that over the past year or two she had been selling bonds and converting the results into cash. This she apparently deposited in the safe-deposit boxes in the basement, of which she rented several. If she had removed this cash the bank had no knowledge of it. It was not an unusual procedure, especially where the customer was a woman. Women resented both income and inheritance taxes, always hoping to escape them. And here the bank added a human note. "As do most people," it said.

Back at his office he made a brief chronological chart:

In January, Susie had seen Mrs. Fairbanks remove cash from the bank and take it to her box.

In February, Mrs. Fairbanks and Marian had gone to Florida, while the safe was installed, and Susie's brother-in-law built the peephole.

On the ninth of March Mrs. Fairbanks came home, arriving that night. The next morning she was poisoned with arsenic. The arsenic was shown to have been in the sugar.

She was suspicious afterward of her household, making her own breakfast and at other meals eating only what they ate. But the attempt had not been repeated. From that day in March until the beginning of May everything had been as usual.

After that the so-called hauntings began. It was the first of May when she found the first bat in her room. Later there were two more bats, two sparrows, and a rat over a period of a month, and when another bat was discovered she had gone to the police.

"Someone is trying to kill me," she had said, sitting erect in her chair. "I have a bad heart, and they know it. But I'm pretty hard to scare."

He put his notes away and went thoughtfully out to lunch.

He saw Courtney Brooke that afternoon, and he laid all his cards on the table. He liked the boy, but he sensed a change in him when it came to the safe and the money possibly in it. He stiffened slightly.

"I don't care a damn for the money," he said. "As a matter of fact it bothers me. I'd rather marry a poor girl. I suppose you can open the safe, sooner or later?''

"It won't be easy. The makers will send somebody, if we don't find the combination. I'm putting a guard in the grounds tonight. If the money is there, it won't leave the house.''

But Brooke still looked uneasy, and Fuller changed the subject. He asked about arsenic. It could be obtained without much trouble, the doctor said; weed killers, of course, but also it could be soaked out of fly-paper, for instance, or even out of old wallpapers and some fabrics. But on the subject of the attack on Jan he waxed bitter.

"Who would want to kill her? The old lady and Ida, well, the old lady had the money and Ida probably knew something. But to try to kill Jan—''

"I don't think anyone tried to kill her.''

Brooke stared.

"Look at it,'' said the inspector. "She could have been killed. She was unconscious, and the nurse was locked up in Amos's rooms. But she wasn't killed. She probably began to come to, and she was struck to put her out again. Somebody was there who didn't want to be seen.''

Brooke said nothing. He gazed out the window, looking thoughtful, as though he was comparing all this with some private knowledge of his own. When he turned to the inspector it was with a faint smile.

"Funny,'' he said. "I've been scared to hell and gone. You've relieved me a lot. I've been hanging around under the window every night since it happened.''

But the smile died when he was asked about the night of Mrs. Fairbanks's death.

"I didn't see anybody on the third floor,'' he said flatly. "That's Miss Adams's idea. Just because I spilled some coffee—''

"I think you did,'' said the inspector, his face grave. "I think you saw Marian Fairbanks, and she saw you.''

"How could I? She wasn't there.''

"Just whom did you see, doctor?''

"Nobody,'' he asserted stubbornly. "Nobody at all.''

23

Ida had been poisoned on Monday, and Mrs. Fairbanks was buried on Tuesday. It was Wednesday morning when Hilda made her report, and it was the same night when Frank Garrison was arrested for murder.

Late on Wednesday afternoon Fuller went back to the Fairbanks house. He intended interviewing Marian, and he dreaded doing it. To believe that she had killed her mother and a servant and attacked her own child made her an inhuman monster. Unhappy and bitter as she was, he did not believe she was guilty. Nor, he thought, did Hilda.

He did not interview her, however. Marian was in bed, under the influence of a sedative, and he found Hilda back in uniform at her old post in the hall. An absorbed Hilda, who was not knitting or reading the *Practice of Nursing,* but instead had set up a card table and was patiently laying out a pack of cards.

"And people pay you money for this!" he said. "I wish my job was as easy."

She nodded absently, and he watched her as she gathered up the cards, closely inspected the edges, and then began to lay them out again. He sat down and watched her.

"What is all this?"

"I'll tell you in a minute." She was intensely serious. "It's the order," she said. "Clubs first don't do. Maybe it's the other way. Spades."

"Nothing has disturbed you, has it? You feel all right? No dizzy spells? Anything like that?"

She did not even hear him. She spread the cards again, gathered them up, looked at the edges, spread them slightly, and then handed him the pack.

There was something written on one side, and she looked rather smug.

"I think it's the combination to the safe," she said complacently.

Fuller examined the cards. Thus arranged they showed plainly written in ink a series of letters and numbers. Shuffled in the ordinary fashion they were not detectable, but in their present order they were perfectly clear. He gave her an odd look. Then he took out an old envelope and wrote them down.

"So that's the solitaire she played," he said thoughtfully. "Good girl, Hilda. How did you think of it?"

"Courtney Brooke thought of it first," she told him.

He eyed her sharply, but her face told him nothing.

He sent for Carlton before they opened the safe. He had little or nothing to say. He did not even ask how they had found the combination. Hilda unlocked the door, and he followed them in. The room was as it had been left after the search, and he carefully avoided looking at it. There was still daylight, but the closet was dark and Hilda brought a flashlight. Using it the inspector turned the dial, but he did not open the door.

"I'd rather you did this, Fairbanks," he said.

He stepped out of the closet, and Carlton stepped in. He pulled open the door and looked speechlessly inside. The safe was packed to the top with bundles of currency.

He made a little gesture and backed out of the closet. He looked small and singularly defenseless.

"All right. It's there," he said dully. "Do what you like with it. I don't want to look at it. It makes me sick."

It required some urging to send him back again.

"Look for your mother's will," Fuller said. "Bring out any papers you find. We may learn something."

The will was there, in a compartment of its own. It was in a brown envelope sealed with red wax, and it was marked *Last Will and Testament* in the old lady's thin hand. Carlton almost broke down when he read it. But there was another paper in the envelope, and he opened and read it, too. He stood, against the absurd background of hanging fusty dresses and shoes in the bag on the door, holding the paper and staring at it. But neither Hilda nor the inspector was prepared for his reaction to it.

"So that's why she was killed," he said thickly, and collapsed on the floor before they could reach him.

Frank Garrison was arrested late that night at his club. He was evidently living there. His clothes were in the closet, his brushes on the dresser, and he was in pajamas when they found him.

He said little or nothing. The inspector had sent the detectives out, and remained himself in the room while he dressed. Once he said he would better take his bag "as he might not be coming back soon." And again he spoke of Jan.

"Tell the poor kid to take it easy, will you?" he said. "She's had enough trouble, and she's—fond of me."

He puzzled the inspector. He offered no explanation of his being at the club. He offered nothing, in fact. He sat in the car, his fine profile etched against the street lights, and except once when he lit a cigarette he did not move. He seemed to be thinking profoundly. Nor was he more co-operative when they reached the inspector's office, with two or three detectives around, and a stenographer taking down questions and answers.

He was perfectly polite. He denied absolutely having been in the Fairbanks house the night Mrs. Fairbanks was killed, although he admitted having been in the grounds.

"I came home late from Washington. The apartment was empty—we had not had a maid for some time—and my wife was not there. I knew Jan was friendly with Eileen, so I went there to ask if she knew what had happened. We had quarreled, and I was afraid she—well, she's been pretty nervous lately. But Jan—my daughter—said she was there. I talked to Jan at her window. I did not enter the house."

"What did you do after that?"

"I walked around for a while. Then I went home."

"What time did you talk to your daughter?"

"After one. Perhaps half past. I didn't get back from Washington until twelve o'clock."

"Did your daughter tell you where your wife was? In what room?"

He colored.

"Yes. In my former wife's bedroom. I didn't like it, but what could I do?"

"She told you your wife was sick?"

"Yes."

"You didn't come in, to see how she was?"

"We had quarreled before I left. I didn't think she cared to see me. Anyhow, her light was out. I thought she was asleep."

"You have since separated?"

"Not exactly. Call it a difference."

"She is going to have a child."

He showed temper for the first time.

"What the hell has that got to do with this?"

But although he was guardedly frank about his movements the night of Mrs. Fairbanks's murder, he continued to deny having entered the house, through Eileen's window or in any other way. He had not climbed to the roof of the porte-cochere. He doubted if it was possible. And when he was shown the knife he stated flatly that he had never to his knowledge seen it before. He admitted, however, knowing that the safe was in Mrs. Fairbanks's room. "Jan told me about it." But he denied any knowledge whatever of its contents.

The mention of the safe, however, obviously disturbed him. He seemed relieved when the subject was changed to the attack on Jan in the loft of the stable; but he was clearly indignant about it, as well as puzzled.

"If I could lay my hands on whoever did it I—well, I might commit a murder of my own."

"You have no explanation of it?"

They thought he hesitated.

"None whatever. Unless she was mistaken for someone else. Or—" he added slowly—"unless someone was there who didn't want to be seen."

They shifted to Ida's death. He seemed puzzled.

"You knew her?"

"Of course. She had been in the Fairbanks house for years."

"She was attached to your first wife?"

"I don't know. I don't care to discuss my first wife."

"You are on good terms?"

"Good God, leave her out of this, can't you? I won't have her dragged in. What has she got to do with it, or my—feeling for her?"

He was excited, indignant. The inspector broke the tension.

"Mr. Garrison, did you at any time in the last few weeks supply this woman, Ida Miller, with certain creatures to introduce into Mrs. Fairbanks's room?" He picked up a memorandum and read from it. " 'Five bats, two sparrows, one or more rats, and a small garden snake.' "

The detective grinned. The stenographer dropped his pen. And Frank Garrison unexpectedly laughed. Only the inspector remained sober.

"Is that a serious question?"

"It is."

"The answer is no. I thought the old lady imagined all that."

"Have you at any time had in your possession a poison called arsenious acid? White arsenic?"

"Never."

"Can you account for your movements Monday afternoon? Say,
from one o'clock on."

The quick shifts seemed to bother him, but he managed to make a
fair statement. He had lunched at the club. After that he went to see a
man who was taking over some housing work in Washington. When he
went home his wife was still in bed. She had been "difficult." He had
told her he would send her a maid. After that he had packed a bag and
left. They had not been getting on for some time. Perhaps it was his
fault. He wasn't accustomed to being idle.

"Did you at any time Monday go to Stern and Jones? The department store?"

"I stopped in and bought a black tie. I was going to Mrs. Fairbanks's
funeral the next day."

"At what time?"

"After I saw the man I referred to. Maybe two-thirty or three o'-
clock."

"Did you see the girl, Ida, at that time?"

He looked puzzled.

"Where? Where would I see her?"

"In the store."

"No. Certainly not."

"Have you a key to the Fairbanks house?"

"I may have, somewhere. I lived there for a good many years. I don't
carry it."

It lasted until half past one. The questions were designed to confuse
him, but on the whole he kept his head. It was not until the inspector
lifted a paper from the desk and handed it to him that he apparently
gave up the fight. He glanced at it and handed it back, his face set.

"I see," he said quietly. "I was there that night. I could have got
into the house, by key or through my wife's window, and I had a motive. I suppose that's enough."

"You knew about this agreement?"

"Mrs. Fairbanks told me about it at the time."

"Who else knew about it?"

"My first wife. She signed it, as you see. Mrs. Fairbanks and myself."

"No one else knew about it?"

"Not unless Mrs. Fairbanks told about it. I don't think she did."

The inspector got up. He looked tired, and for once uncertain.

"I'm sorry about this, Garrison," he said. "We're not through, but I'll have to hold you. We'll see that you're not too uncomfortable."

Garrison forced a smile and stood.

"No rubber hose?" he said.

"No rubber hose," said the inspector.

There was a momentary silence. Garrison glanced around the room. He seemed on the point of saying something, something important. The hush was breathless, as if all the men were waiting and watching. But he decided against it, whatever it was.

"I suppose it's no use saying I didn't do it?"

"No man is guilty until he has been found guilty," said the inspector sententiously, and watched the prisoner out of the room.

Carlton broke the news to the family the next morning, a worried little man, telling Susie first, staying with Jan until she had stopped crying, and then going to Marian. He was there a long time. Hilda, shut out, could hear his voice and Marian's loud hysterical protests.

"He never did it. Never. Never."

When the inspector came she refused at first to see him, and he went in to find her sitting frozen in a chair and gazing ahead of her as though she was seeing something she did not want to face. She turned her head, however, at his crisp greeting.

"Good morning," he said. "Do you mind if we have a little talk?"

"I have no option, have I?"

"I can't force you, you know," he said matter-of-factly. "All I would like is a little co-operation."

"Co-operation!" she said, her face set and cold. "Why should I co-operate? You are holding Frank Garrison, aren't you? Of all the cruel absurd things! A man who loved my mother! The kindest man on earth! What possible reason could he have had to kill my mother?"

"There was a possible reason, and you know it' Mrs. Garrison," he said unsmilingly.

He drew up a chair and sat down, confronting her squarely.

"At what time did you reach here, the night your mother was killed?" he asked.

It was apparently the one question she had not expected. She opened her mouth to speak, but she could not. She tried to get out of her chair, and the inspector put his hand on her knee.

"Better sit still," he said quietly. "You had every right to be here. I am not accusing you of anything. Suppose I help you a little. You came home during or after the time your husband's present wife had arrived. Either you saw her, in the hall downstairs, or one of the servants told you she was here. However that was, you decided to stay. It was your house. Why let her drive you out? Is that right?"

"Yes," she said, with tight lips. "It was Ida. I opened the side door with my latchkey. There was no one around, so I went back to get William to carry up my bags. I met Ida in the back hall. She told me."

She went on. She seemed glad to talk. She had been angry and indignant. She didn't even want to see Jan. It was Jan who had brought it about. Jan had said that Eileen was going to have a baby, and had even brought her to the house. That was why she had gone away. To have her own mother and her own child against her! And now Eileen had invented some silly story and sought sanctuary here.

"I wasn't going to let her drive me away a second time," she said. "She had ruined my life, and now at my mother's orders they had put her in my room. I couldn't believe it at first, when Ida told me."

Ida, it appeared, had got her to the third floor by the back staircase, and made up the bed. They had to walk carefully, for fear Carlton would hear them in his room below. But she did not go to bed. How could she, with that woman below? She did manage to smoke, sitting by the open window. She was still sitting there when Susie began to scream.

"That was when Ida came to warn you?"

"She knew something was terribly wrong. Neither of us knew what. I thought at first the house was on fire. I sent her down, and listened over the stair rail. That's how I knew what had happened."

She sat back. Her color was better now, and the inspector, watching her, thought she looked like a woman who had passed a danger point safely.

"No one but Ida knew you were in the house?" he persisted.

"No one. Not even Jan."

"Are you sure of that? Didn't you come down the stairs while Doctor Brooke was in the hall?"

"Never."

But she looked shaken. Her thin hands were trembling.

"I think you did, Mrs. Garrison," he told her. "He was standing outside your mother's door. You spoke to him from the stairs. You told him to get Eileen away out of the house in the morning, didn't you?"

"No! I did nothing of the sort," said Marian frantically. There was complete despair in her face. She looked beaten. "I never spoke to him at all," she said in a dead voice. "When I saw him he was coming out of Mother's room."

The rest of her story was not important. She told it with dead eyes and in a flat hopeless voice. Brooke had not seen her, she thought, and Ida had helped her to get out of the house before the police had taken charge. She had used the back stairs and had gone out through the break in the fence. She had taken only the one bag which she could carry, Ida hiding the other, and she had spent what was left of the night at a hotel.

"I was afraid to stay," she told them. "After what I'd seen I didn't want to be questioned. I had Jan to think of. I still have Jan to think of," she added drearily. "Courtney Brooke killed my mother, and I've ruined Jan's life forever and ever."

24

Brooke was interrogated at police headquarters that afternoon. Inspector Fuller found him in his back office, dressing a small boy's hand.

"All right, Jimmy," he said. "And don't fool with knives after this."

The boy left, and Fuller went in. Young Brooke was putting away his dressings, his face sober.

"What's this about Mr. Garrison being held, inspector?" he said. "I was just going over to see Jan. She's taking it badly."

The inspector did not relax.

"You've been holding out on us, doctor," he said stiffly. "That's a dangerous thing to do in a murder case."

Brooke flushed. He still held a roll of bandage in his hand. He put it down on the table before he answered.

"All right. What's it all about?"

"You were in Mrs. Fairbanks's room at or about the time she was killed."

"Why not?" He looked defiant. "She was my patient. I had a right to look at her. She'd had a good bit of excitement that night, and I didn't go all the way in. I opened the door and listened. She was alive then. I'll swear to that. I could hear her breathing."

"Why didn't you tell about it?" said the inspector inexorably.

Brooke looked unhappy.

"Sheer funk, I suppose. I told Jan, after it all came out, and she didn't want me to. Not that I'm putting the blame on her," he added quickly. "I was in a cold sweat myself. In fact, I still am!"

He grinned and pulling out a handkerchief mopped his face.

"I thought I had as many guts as the other fellow," he said. "But this thing's got me."

He looked incredulous, however, when the inspector asked him to go with him to headquarters.

"What for? Are you trying to arrest me?" he asked suspiciously.

"Not necessarily. We'll want a statement from you."

"I've told you everything I know."

He went finally, calling to the slovenly girl that he would be back for dinner, and slamming the door furiously behind him as he left the house. He was still indignant when he reached the inspector's office. A look at the room, however, with the stenographer at his desk and Captain Henderson and the detectives filing in, rather subdued him.

"Third-degree stuff, I suppose," he said, and lit a cigarette. "All right. I'm a fool and a coward, but I'm no killer. You can put that down."

"No third degree, doctor. Just some facts. Sit down, please. We may be some time."

They were some time. Before they were through he was white and exhausted.

"Did Janice Garrison know of the document in the safe?"

"Yes. Why drag her in? She hasn't done anything."

"She was fond of her father?"

"Crazy about him."

"You knew that she was to inherit a considerable sum of money?"

"I did."

"What were your exact movements, the night Mrs. Fairbanks was killed? While the nurse was downstairs boiling water?"

"I cleaned the hypo with alcohol. After that I looked in at Mrs. Fairbanks. She was breathing all right, so I went back to see Jan. I was there about five minutes. I went back and poured some coffee. I was drinking it when the nurse came up with the water."

"At what time did you see Mrs. Garrison?"

He was startled.

"Mrs. Garrison! She wasn't there. She didn't come until the next day. Sunday."

"She was there, doctor. She saw you coming out of her mother's room."

"Oh, God," he said wretchedly. "So she was there, too. Poor Jan!"

But his story was straightforward. He had not seen Marian when he came out of Mrs. Fairbanks's room. Later, however, as he poured the coffee, he had felt that someone was overhead, on the third floor. The glass chandelier was shaking. He had looked up the staircase, but no one was in sight.

They showed him the knife, and he smiled thinly.

"Never saw it before," he said. He examined it. "Somebody did a rotten job of sharpening it," he said.

"It seems to have answered," the inspector observed dryly. "Have you ever done any surgery, doctor?"

"Plenty."

"You could find a heart without trouble? Even in the dark?"

"Anybody can find a heart. It's bigger than most people think. But if you mean did I stab Mrs. Fairbanks, certainly not."

He explained readily enough his search and Jan's for the combination of the safe.

"She knew the agreement was there. The old lady had told her. She was afraid it would incriminate her father. When nobody could open the safe I happened to think of the cards. Mrs. Fairbanks played solitaire at night. But maybe she didn't. Jan believed she locked herself in and then opened the safe, and we thought the cards might have the combination. I'd seen them with pictures painted on the edges. You arranged them a certain way and there was the picture."

"The idea being to get this document?"

"Well, yes. She was worrying herself sick. But the nurse was too smart for us. She locked the door."

It was five o'clock before he was released, with a warning not to leave town. He managed to grin at that. He got out his wallet and some silver from his pocket.

"I could travel—let's see—exactly five dollars and eighty cents' worth," he said. "I've just paid the rent."

The inspector looked at Henderson after he had gone.

"Well?" he said.

"Could have," said Henderson. "But my money's on the other fellow. Garrison was broke, too, but he wouldn't be without the alimony."

"Why didn't he have it reduced? It would have been easier than murder."

"Still in love with the first wife," said Henderson promptly. "Sticks out all over him."

"Oh," said the inspector. "So you got that, too!"

Alone in his office he got out the document he had shown to Garrison the night before, and studied it. Briefly it was an agreement written in the old lady's hand, signed by Marian and witnessed by Amos and Ida, by which Marian's alimony from her ex-husband was to cease on her mother's death. "Otherwise, as provided for in my will, she ceases to inherit any portion of my estate save the sum of one dollar, to be paid by my executors."

He had a picture of Mrs. Fairbanks writing that, all the resentment at Marian and the divorce and its terms in her small resolute body and trembling old hand. He put it back in his safe, along with the knife and Hilda's contributions—a can of white paint, a pair of worn chauffeur's driving gloves, a bit of charred rope, a largish square of unbleached muslin, and now a pack of playing cards. To that odd assortment he added the paper on which he had recorded the numbers of the new bills in Ida's purse, and surveyed the lot glumly.

"Looks like Bundles for Britain," he grunted.

He saw Eileen late that afternoon. She was in bed, untidy and tearful, and she turned on him like a wildcat.

"I always knew the police were fools," she shrieked. "What have you got on Frank Garrison? Nothing, and you know it. I didn't let him in through my window. I didn't let anybody in. I was sick. Why don't you ask the doctor? He knows."

He could get nothing from her. She turned sulky and then cried hysterically. She didn't know about Mrs. Fairbanks's will. She had never heard of any agreement. What sort of an agreement? And they'd better release Frank if they knew what was good for them. She'd get a lawyer. She'd get a dozen lawyers. She would take it to the President. She would take it to the Supreme Court. She would—

This new conception of the Supreme Court at least got him away. He left her still talking, and when the maid let him out he suggested a doctor.

"She's pretty nervous," he said. Which was by way of being a masterpiece of understatement.

On the way downtown he thought he saw Hilda in one of the shopping streets, but when he stopped his car and looked back she had disappeared.

He might have been surprised, had he followed her.

25

Hilda was at a loose end that afternoon. Courtney had recovered from his collapse and had gone out, still pale, to drive around in his car and think his own unhappy thoughts. Marian's door had been closed and locked since the inspector's visit. Jan wandered around the house, worried about her mother and ignorant of what was going on. And Susie, recovered from her fright about her husband, had settled down on her bed to a magazine.

"I'd better loaf while I can," she told Hilda. "It's me for the pig-pens from now on. If you think Carl will change his mind now that he gets some money you can think again."

Hilda was standing in the doorway, her face bland but her eyes alert.

"What do you think about the police holding Mr. Garrison?" she asked.

"Me? They're crazy. Carl says that paper they found will convict him, but I don't believe it. If you ask me—"

She stopped abruptly.

"If I asked you, what?"

"Nothing," said Susie airily. "If I were you I'd take a look at the radio by Mrs. Fairbanks's bed. Maybe you can make something out of it. I can't."

"What's wrong with it?"

"I don't know. It's set to a blank spot on the dial. That's all. Carl says he didn't move the needle."

She went back to her magazine, and Hilda went to the old lady's room. She closed the door and going to the radio switched it on. There was a faint roaring as the tubes warmed up, but nothing else. She was puzzled rather than excited. But she had already decided to go out, and now she had a double errand.

Her first errand was to the ladies' room of Stern & Jones. The attendant was the same woman who had looked after Ida, and she was immediately loquacious.

"A friend of hers, are you?" she said. "Wasn't it dreadful? And nobody knowing who she was all that time!"

"Was she very sick when she got here?"

"She looked terrible. I asked her if she had had anything that disagreed with her, and she said only a cup of tea. I called up the tearoom right away. Some of the girls had gone, but nobody remembered her. Anyhow, our tea is all right. It could not have been that, or a lot of other people would have been sick too."

"Is that all she said?"

"Well, she tried to tell me where she lived. She wanted to go home. Grove Avenue, I think she said. But after that she got so bad she couldn't talk at all."

Hilda was filled with cold anger when she left the store. The thought of Ida, dying and unable to tell who she was, enraged her. And now the radio assumed a new importance. If it had been turned to a blank spot on the dial and still played, the whole situation changed. Mrs. Fairbanks might have been already dead when it was turned on.

She visited a number of stores where radio sets were sold, including Stern & Jones. Some of them had remote controls. The boxes they showed her were only a foot long and four inches wide, and they operated as far as sixty feet from the instrument.

"You can set it out in the street," said one salesman, "and turn your radio on and off with it. Magic, ain't it?"

Sixty feet! That would include even Marian's room. But when she told the make and age of the machine the man shook his head.

"Sorry," he said. "It wouldn't work on one of those old ones. Not a chance."

It was the same everywhere. The machine in Mrs. Fairbanks's room was too old. And the remote controls which used cables were not only modern. They required considerable time for adjustment. But in the end she found something.

She was tired and her feet ached when at six o'clock she got back to the house, going directly to the kitchen. William was on the back porch, relaxing in the summer sun, and Maggie was baking a cake. She turned a red face from the oven when Hilda drew a chair to the kitchen table and sat down. But some of Maggie's suspicions had died in the last few days. She even offered her a cup of tea.

Hilda, however, was definitely off tea, at least for a time.

"I'd like a glass of water," she said. "Then I want to talk about Ida."

"I'm not talking about Ida," Maggie said stiffly. "If anyone thinks she got that stuff here in this house—"

"I'm not asking about her death. That's for the police. It's just this. Have you any idea why she carried those blankets out to Amos?"

"No. He didn't need them."

"Can you remember what happened that day? It was the day after Mrs. Fairbanks was killed, wasn't it?"

Maggie considered this.

"You know how she was that morning. She was so bad I sent her up to rest. She came down later, and that was when Amos says she carried out the blankets. I didn't see her myself. All I know is she didn't eat any lunch. She left when we were sitting down."

Hilda drank her water and went out to the stable. To her annoyance Amos, in his shirt sleeves, was smoking a pipe inside the garage. He was reading the paper, his chair tilted back. He looked up when he saw her.

"Anything I can do for you, miss?"

He grinned with his usual slyness, and Hilda regarded him with disfavor.

"You can come up to the loft with me," she said coldly. "And don't smirk at me, I don't like it."

Thus reduced, Amos followed her up the stairs. There was still light enough to see around, and to her shocked surprise she found the entire place had been swept and put in order.

"Who did this?" she said sharply.

He grinned.

"I did," he said. "Anything to say about it, Miss Policewoman? Any reason why I can't clean the place I live in?"

She ignored that, looking around her carefully. She had had very little hope at any time, but she disliked giving up. Amos was grinning again, pleased at her discomfiture.

"That isn't funny," she said. "I want some answers, and if I don't get them the police will. When you cleaned this place did you find anything that didn't belong? That you hadn't seen here before?"

The mention of the police sobered him.

"Nothing new. Only the birdcage was on the floor. It used to be in the cupola, when Ida kept her bats and things in it. Wrapped it in a cloth, she did. I threw it out."

"Oh!" she said blankly. "You knew it was Ida, did you?"

"Well, when a woman gets an old birdcage and a net and keeps climbing at night into that tower up there, I didn't think she was after butterflies, and that's a fact."

"Did you tell anybody, Amos?"

"Not me," he said negligently. "Bats don't hurt anybody. Let her have her fun, said I. She didn't have much."

She looked at him. He was incredible, this stocky individualist who had believed in letting Ida have what he called her fun, and who apparently knew far more than he had even indicated. It amused him to tell her so, leaning against one of the trunks and now and then sucking at his dead pipe. Indeed, once started it was hard to stop him. He said that one night Carlton came and, getting the cage, carried it to the house. It was empty, as he—Amos—happened to know. But he had brought it back before morning. He said it was Frank Garrison who had caught Susie by the garage the night Mrs. Fairbanks was murdered. He'd seen him. And he observed cheerfully that he knew Marian had been in the house that same night.

"Funniest sight I most ever saw," he said, his shrewd eyes on hers. "Her streaking across the grass in her nightgown when the police cars were coming in. I slid down and unlocked the door, but she never saw me. She hid in the loft until Ida brought her clothes and bags. Toward morning, it was."

"Why didn't you tell it at the time, Amos?"

"Nobody asked me."

She felt helpless before the vast indifference, the monumental ego of the man. But she had not finished with him.

"Why did Ida have those creatures, Amos? Was it to scare Mrs. Fairbanks away? After all, she had worked here for years."

He grinned at her slyly.

"Maybe she didn't like her," he said. "Or maybe she didn't like the stairs. Lots of climbing in the house. May have wanted her to move to an apartment. I've heard her say as much."

"I suppose you know how she got them into the room, too?"

"Sure," he said, and grinned again. "Through Mrs. Carlton Fairbanks's peephole in the closet."

She left him then. She felt that even now he might have certain reserves, certain suspicions. But he did not intend to tell them. She could see that in his face.

"So they've arrested Mr. Garrison," he said as she went down the stairs. "Mr. Garrison and the doc across the street. Don't let them fool you, Miss Policewoman. They'll have to eat crow before they're through." He seemed to think this was humorous. He laughed. "But I'd like to know how Ida felt when she got that snake," he said. "I'll bet she didn't like it."

"So there *is* something you don't know!" said Hilda coldly, and went back to the house.

Nevertheless, she had a curious feeling about Amos as she left him. As though he had been trying to tell her something. As though he was hoping that she would see what he could not tell her. And there had been something in his small sly eyes which looked like grief; a deep and tragic grief.

When she went upstairs she found Jan in the upper hall.

"She's still sleeping," she said. "I suppose she needs it, Miss Adams. They won't hold Father long, will they? They must know he didn't do it."

Evidently she did not know about Courtney, and Hilda said nothing. She tried the door to Marian's room and found it locked.

"How long has she been asleep, Jan?" she asked.

"I don't know. She's been in there since the inspector left. It's seven now."

Hilda rapped on the door. Then she pounded hard and called. There was no response, however. Jan was standing by, looking terrified.

"You don't think she's—"

"She's probably taken an overdose of sleeping medicine," Hilda said briskly. "Get a doctor. If you can't get Courtney Brooke get someone else. And hurry."

It was Brooke who came, running across the yard and reaching the house as Amos and William were lifting a ladder to the porte-cochère. He shoved them aside and climbed up. A moment later the screen gave way and he unlocked and opened the door into the hall.

"She's still breathing," he said. "Go away, Jan. I don't want you here. She'll be all right."

Hilda went in, and he closed the door behind her. Marian was lying on the bed, not moving. She looked peaceful and lovely, almost beautiful, as though that deep sleep of hers had erased the lines from her face and brought back some of her youth. But she was very far gone.

Brooke examined her and threw off his coat.

"Come on, Miss Adams," he said. "We've got to get busy if we're going to save her."

26

At nine o'clock that same night a young man carrying a parcel arrived at the house and asked for Hilda. William brought the message to Marian's door.

"Tell him to wait," she said briefly. "Put him in the morning room and close the door. Tell him he's to stay if it takes all night."

William hesitated, his old head shaking.

"How is she, miss?"

"A little better."

"Thank God for that," he said and tottered down the stairs.

It was ten o'clock when Courtney Brooke went out into the hall and, bending over, kissed Jan gently.

"It's all right, darling. You can see her for a minute. Don't talk to her."

When Jan came out he was waiting. He took her back to her room and put his arms around her.

"My girl," he said. "Always and ever my girl, sweet. Hold on to me, darling. You need somebody to hold on to, don't you? And I'm strong. I'll never let you down."

"I've had so much, Court!"

"You've had too much, sweet. But it's all over. There won't be any more."

She looked up into his eyes, steady and honest, and drew a long breath.

"Why did she do it, Court? Was it because Father—"

"Your father's all right. Take my word for it, darling."

"Then who—"

"Hush," he said, cradling her in his arms. "Hush, my sweet. Don't think. Don't worry. It's all over. You're to rest now. Just rest." He picked her up and laid her gently on the bed. "Sleep if you can. Think of me if you can't! Look out, darling. There's a moon. I ordered it for tonight, for you."

She lay still, after he had gone, looking at the moon. She felt very tired, but she was peaceful, too. It was over. Court had said so. She wrapped herself in his promise like a banket, and fell asleep. She was still asleep when, at eleven, the inspector drove in under the porte-cochere.

Susie and Carlton were in the library. Carlton's face was haggard, and even Susie looked stricken. She could accept murder, but she could not face suicide, or the attempt at it. Life was too important to her, the love of it too strong.

She sat beside Carl, his head drawn down on her shoulder, her eyes soft.

"Don't be a jackass," she said. "Of course she didn't do it."

"Then why would she try to kill herself?"

"Because she's the same kind of fool I am. Because she's a one-man woman." She sat up and lit a cigarette. "Let's forget it," she said. "Let's think about a farm. You can raise what you want, and I'll raise pigs. I rather like pigs," she said. "At least they're natural. They don't pretend to be anything but pigs."

"So long as you're around, old girl," he said huskily. "So long as you're around."

They did not hear the inspector as he went up the stairs and tiptoed into Mrs. Fairbanks's room, closing the door behind him. He did not turn on a light, or sit down. Instead, he went to a window and stood looking out. The whole thing was not to his taste. He had come at Hilda's request, and it was not like her to be dramatic. So Marian Garrison had tried to kill herself! It might be a confession, or the equivalent of one. And where the hell was Hilda, anyhow?

He was rapidly becoming indignant when suddenly without warning the radio behind him roared into action. he almost leaped into the air with the shock. It was playing the Habanera from *Carmen*, and the din was terrific. He was turning on the lights when Hilda came in.

For the first time in his experience she looked frightened. She shut off the machine and confronted him.

"That's how it was done," she said, and sat down weakly in a chair.

"What do you mean, that's how?"

She did not answer directly. She looked tired and unhappy.

"It's a phonograph. You set the radio dial on to a certain place and turn it on. It's a blank spot, where there's no station. Nothing happens, of course. But if you've got this machine plugged in on the same circuit, even in another room, it plays through the radio. As it did here.''

"There was no phonograph in the house that night," he said stubbornly.

"I think there was."

"Where was it? We searched this house for one. We didn't find it."

When she did not answer he looked at her. She was sitting still, her tired hands folded in her lap, her blue eyes sunken, the life gone out of her.

"I hate this job," she said. "I hate prying and spying. I'm through. I can't go on. I can't send a woman to the chair."

He knew her through long association. He realized that in her present mood he could not push her.

"It was a woman?" he said quietly.

She nodded.

"How was it done, Hilda?"

"It had to be done by someone who knew the house," she said slowly. "Someone who knew the light circuits. Someone who knew this radio and had a chance sometime to discover how to adjust the remote-control phonograph. It didn't need much. It could be done in a few minutes. After you find the blank spot on the radio, all you have to do after that is to turn the dial to that spot. Then you could start the record, and it would play here."

"Where was it played from just now?"

"There's a young man in Carlton's room," she said dully. "I promised him ten dollars to come tonight. I'd better pay him and let him go."

He gave her the ten dollars and she went out. She was gone a considerable time. When she returned she looked so pale that the inspector thought she was going to faint.

"He left the machine," she said. "He'll get it in the morning. If you want to see it—"

"See here, I think you need some whisky."

"No. I'm all right. If you'll come alone I'll show you."

She got up heavily and led the way. Carlton was still downstairs with Susie, but his room was lighted. Sitting on the floor by a base outlet was what looked like a small phonograph about a foot in diameter, with a record on it. It was plugged into the wall, and the inspector, picking up the record, saw that it was the Habanera from *Carmen*. He started it, and going to Mrs. Fairbanks's room switched on the radio.

Almost immediately the Habanera started. He switched it off, and went back to Hilda. She was still there, standing by a window.

"How long have you known about this?" he demanded.

"Only today. Something Susie said. I saw the radio set where it is, and—I wondered about it. You see, there are almost no stations on the air at one or later in the morning, and when they are it's dance music. I had just remembered it was something from *Carmen* that night. I should have thought about that sooner," she added, and tried to smile.

He had an idea that she was playing for time. He was wildly impatient, but he did not dare to hurry her.

"You see, it didn't take long," she went on. "I've tried it. Two minutes was enough to use the knife and turn the radio dial to the blank spot. And the doctor was in Jan's room for five minutes, maybe more. Even at that she took a chance. A dreadful chance," she said, and shivered. "She wasn't quite normal, of course. Those bats and things—"

"Listen," he said roughly. "Are you trying to tell me that Ida did all this?"

"Ida? No. She used them, of course. Amos saw her in the cupola. I suppose she was given a reason. Maybe to get Mrs. Fairbanks to leave the house. Maybe something worse, to scare her to death. And she hid the machine in the loft of the stable the next day. She carried it out in some blankets. That was why Jan was hurt, and I was locked in. The machine was hidden there, behind some trunks, or in one, I don't know. It had to be taken away, of course. She was in the loft when Jan got there. She had to get out."

She looked at her watch, and Fuller at last lost patience.

"Haven't we played around enough?" he said. "What is all this? Are you giving someone a chance to get away?"

She shook her head.

"I don't think so. No. I—" She closed her eyes. "Ida had to die, you see. She knew too much, so she got arsenic in a cup of tea. In the sugar, I suppose. The way Mrs. Fairbanks got it. If it hadn't been for Ida—"

Downstairs the telephone was ringing. Hilda got up and opened the door. Carlton was talking over it in the library. He sounded excited, and a moment later he slammed out the side door. Hilda was standing very still, listening while the inspector watched her. Her eyes were on the stairs when Susie came running up. She was gasping for breath, and her eyes were wide with shock.

"It's Eileen," she gasped. "She's killed herself with Frank's service revolver."

Then, for the first time in her life, Hilda fainted. The inspector caught her as she fell.

27

Two nights later Inspector Fuller was sitting in Hilda's small neat living-room. The canary was covered in his cage, and the lamplight was warm on the blue curtains at the windows and on the gay chintz-covered chairs. Hilda was knitting, looking—he thought—as she always did, blandly innocent. Only her eyes showed the strain of the past two weeks.

"Why did you do it, Hilda?" he said. "Why did you telephone her that night?"

"I was sorry for her," said Hilda. "I didn't want her to go to the chair."

"She wouldn't have done that. After all, a prospective mother—"

"But you see she wasn't," said Hilda. "That was her excuse to get into the house."

He stared at her.

"How on earth did you know?"

Hilda looked down at her knitting.

"There are signs," she said evasively. "And it's easy to say you have a pain. Nobody can say you haven't."

"But Garrison didn't deny it."

"What could he do? She was his wife, even if he hadn't lived with her for years. I suppose he had suspected her all along, after the arsenic. I knew he was watching her. He'd followed her there at night, maybe when she went to see Ida. In the grounds, perhaps."

"Then she knew about the agreement? That if Mrs. Fairbanks died the alimony ceased?"

She nodded.

"He must have told her. If they quarreled and she taunted him because he was hard up he might, you know."

"How did she get the arsenic into the sugar?"

"Maggie says she came to the house the day before Marian and her mother returned from Florida. Jan was home by that time. She came to see her. But Mrs. Fairanks's tray was in the pantry, and she went there for a glass of water. She could have done it then."

"But the poison didn't kill Mrs. Fairbanks. So then it was the terror. That's it, of course."

"The terror. Yes. Ida had told her about the hole in the wall, and—I think she had something on Ida. Maybe an illegitimate child. There was a boy at the farm, and Eileen's people lived near by. She'd have known."

"It was the boy who brought in the bats and the rest of the zoo, including the snake?"

"Well, I can't think of any other way," Hilda said meekly. "She may have told him she sold them, or something. Of course it was Ida who got Eileen the position as Jan's governess."

"And got a cup of poisoned tea as a reward!"

"She got the five hundred dollars, too. Don't forget that. In new bills that Mrs. Fairbanks gave Eileen the night before she was murdered. Maybe Eileen bought her off with them. Maybe she just kept them. I don't know. But she couldn't stand for the stabbing anyhow, poor thing. Remember how she looked the next morning? And she must have had the phonograph in her room while we were there. She must have been scared out of her wits. It wasn't until later that she took it to the loft, under the blankets, and hid it there."

"Where Eileen retrieved it the next night. And nearly killed Jan. That's right, isn't it?"

"Yes." Hilda looked thoughtful. "It's odd, but I saw her. I didn't know who it was, of course. I raised the window and she was across Huston Street. She pretended to be calling a dog."

He got up, and lifting a corner of the cover, looked at the bird. It gazed back at him with small bright eyes, and he dropped the cover again.

"You're a funny woman, Hilda," he said. "In your heart you're a purely domestic creature. And yet—well, let's get back to Eileen. How and when did she use this radio-phonograph? Have you any idea?"

"I knew she had it," she said modestly. "I found the man who sold it to her. She said it was to go to the country, so he showed her how to use it. As for the rest, I think she killed Mrs. Fairbanks and set the dial by her bed while the doctor was with Jan. Then he gave her the hypodermic and left her. That's when the music started. He was in the hall."

"Where did she have the thing?"

"Anywhere. Under the bed, probably. There's a baseboard outlet there. She let it play until Carlton went in and turned off his mother's radio. If he hadn't she would have stopped it herself. She didn't even have to get out of bed to do it. But of course things went wrong. I was there, in the hall. She hadn't counted on my staying there every minute. And Ida was busy with Marian. I suppose that's why she fainted when she did. She hadn't got rid of the machine, and I'd found the body. She had thought she had until morning."

"So it was there under the bed when you searched her room!"

"It was nothing of the sort," she said indignantly.

"All right, I'll bite. Where was it?"

"Hanging outside her window on a rope."

He looked at her with admiration, not unmixed with something else.

"As I may have said before, Hilda, you're a smart woman," he said, smiling. "My safe looks like a rummage sale. I'll present you with some of the stuff if you like. But I'd give a good bit to know why you interfered with the law and telephoned her."

"Because she hadn't killed Jan," Hilda said. "She could have, but she didn't."

"What did you say over the phone? That all was discovered?"

She went a little pale, but her voice was steady.

"I really didn't tell her anything," she said. "I merely asked her if she still had her remote-control radio-phonograph. She didn't say anything for a minute. Then she said no, she'd given it away."

There were tears in her eyes. He got up and going over to her, put his hand on her shoulder. "Oh, subtle little Miss Pinkerton," he said. "Lovable and clever and entirely terrible Miss Pinkerton! What am I to do about you? I'm afraid to take you, and I can't even leave you alone."

He looked down at her, her soft skin, her prematurely graying hair, her steady blue eyes.

"See here," he said awkwardly, "Jan and young Brooke are going to be married. Susie and Carlton Fairbanks are going on a second honeymoon, looking for a farm. And unless I miss my guess Frank Garrison and Marian will remarry eventually. I'd hate like hell to join that crew of lovebirds, but—you won't object if I come around now and then? Unprofessionally, of course, little Miss Pinkerton."

She smiled up at him.

"I'd prefer even that to being left alone," she said.

After he had gone she sat still for a long time. Then she determinedly took a long hot bath, using plenty of bath salts, and shampooed her short, slightly graying hair. Once more she looked rather a rosy thirty-eight-year-old cherub, and she was carefully rubbing lotion into her small but capable hands when the telephone rang. She looked desperately about her, at the books she wanted to read, at her soft bed, and through the door to her small cheerful sitting-room with the bird sleeping in its cage. Then she picked up the receiver.

"Miss Pinkerton speaking," she said, and on hearing the inspector's voice was instantly covered with confusion.

THE
YELLOW ROOM

1

As she sat in the train that June morning Carol Spencer did not look like a young woman facing anything unusual. She looked merely like an attractive and highly finished product of New York City, who was about to park her mother with her elder sister in Newport for a week or two, and who after said parking would then proceed to Maine, there to open a house which she had never wanted to see again.

Now she was trying to relax. Mrs. Spencer in the next chair was lying back with her eyes closed, as though exhausted. As she had done nothing but get herself into a taxi and out again, Carol felt not unnaturally resentful. Her own arms were still aching from carrying the bags and her brother Greg's golf clubs, which her mother had insisted on bringing.

"I wonder if I ought to take some digitalis," Mrs. Spencer said, without opening her eyes. "I feel rather faint."

"Not unless you have it with you," Carol said. "The other bags are piled at the end of the car, with about a ton of others."

Mrs. Spencer decided that a glass of water would answer, and Carol brought a paper cup of it, trying not to spill it as the car swayed. She did not return the cup. She crumpled it up and put it on the window sill. Her mother raised a pair of finely arched eyebrows in disapproval, and lay back again without comment. Carol eyed her, the handsome profile, the fretful mouth, the carefully tailored clothes, and the leather jewel case in her lap. Since George Spencer's death she had become a peevish semi-invalid, and Carol at twenty-four, her hopes killed by the war, found herself in the position of the unmarried daughter, left more or less to wither on the maternal stem. And now this idiotic idea of reopening the house at Bayside—

She stirred uneasily. She did not want to go back. What she wanted was to join the Wacs or the Waves or be a Nurse's Aide. She was young and strong. She could be useful somewhere. But the mere mention of such activity was enough to bring on what her mother called a heart attack. So here she was, with the newspapers in her lap still filled with the invasion a week before, and Greg's golf clubs digging into her legs. She kicked them away impatiently.

She did not come without protest, of course.

"Why Maine?" she had said. "Greg would much rather be in New York, or with Elinor at Newport. He'll want to be near Virginia. After all, he's engaged to her."

But Mrs. Spencer had set her chin, which was a determined one.

"Virginia can easily come up to Maine," she said. "After that jungle heat Greg needs bracing air. I do think you should be willing to do what you can after what he's been through."

Carol had agreed, although when she called Elinor in Newport her sister had said it was crazy.

"It's completely idiotic," she said. "That huge place and only three servants! Do show some sense, Carol."

"You don't have to live with Mother."

"No, thank God," said Elinor, and rang off after her abrupt fashion without saying good-bye. Elinor was like that.

Carol thought it over, as the train rumbled on. Of course she wanted to do what she could for Greg. After all, he deserved it. At thirty-four—he had been flying his own plane for years—he had become a captain and an ace in the South Pacific. Now he was home on a thirty-day furlough, and was about to be decorated by the President himself. But she was still edgy after the scene at Grand Central, the crowds of people, the masses of uniformed men, the noise and confusion, and the lack of porters.

Her mind, escaping the war, ranged over what had been done and what there was to do. The three servants, all they had left and all women, were finishing the Park Avenue apartment, sprinkling the carpets with moth flakes and covering the lamp shades against the city soot. Carol herself had worked feverishly. With no men to be had she had taken down the heavy hangings and done the meticulous packing away which had always preceded the summer hegira, and as if Mrs. Spencer had read her mind she opened her eyes and spoke.

"Did you ship the motor rugs?" she demanded.

"Yes. They're all right."

"And my furs went to storage?"

"You know they did, Mother. I gave you the receipt."

"What about Gregory's clothes?"

"He'll be in uniform, you know. He had left some slacks and sweaters at Crestview. I saw them last year."

The conversation lapsed. Mrs. Spencer dozed, her mouth slightly open, and Carol fought again the uneasiness she had felt ever since the plan had been broached. It had of course to do with Colonel Richardson. Even after more than a year he had never accepted Don's death. It was not normal, of course. All last summer he had come up the hill to see her and to sit watching her with anxious eyes.

"Don will have my cottage some day, Carol. You'll find it very comfortable. I've put in a new oil burner."

She put the thought away and began going over what was to be done. This was Thursday, June fifteenth. She was to stay at Elinor's in Newport until Sunday. Then, leaving her mother there for a few days, she would meet the three servants in Boston on Sunday and take the night train to Maine. Nothing would be ready, of course. The plan had been too sudden. She had wired Lucy Norton, the caretaker's wife, to drive over and open the house for them. But the place was large. Unless Lucy could get help—She knew that was improbable and abandoned the idea. The grounds too would be hopeless. Only George Smith remained of the gardeners, and as they had not meant to open the house he would hardly have had time to cut the grass.

The usual problems buzzed through her head. George had always refused to care for the coal furnace, or carry coal to the enormous kitchen range. Maybe Maggie would do this herself. She had been with them as cook for twenty years, and she was strong and willing. But the other two were young. She wondered if she could take them to the movies in the village now and then, and so keep them. Only there would be little or no gasoline.

She sighed.

The train went on. It was crowded, and it was hot. A boiling June sun shone through the windows, setting men to mopping their faces and giving to all the passengers a look of resignation that was almost despair. The only cheerful people were the men in uniform, roaming through the car on mysterious errands of their own and eyeing Carol as they did so.

She tried not to think about them and what they were facing. She went back determinedly to Bayside and the situation there. The heat had started early, so at least a part of the summer colony would have arrived. There had been no time to announce their coming, so she would have a day or two at least. But Colonel Richardson would know. He lived at the bottom of their hill, and he was always in his garden or sitting patiently on his porch watching for the postman.

She felt a little sick when she remembered that. All last summer, and the colonel saying: "When Don comes back." Or: "Don likes the peonies, so I'm keeping them." Puttering around his garden with a determined smile and haggard eyes, and Carol's heart aching for him, rather than for Don. For most of the pain had gone now, although she still wore Don's ring. They had been engaged since she was eighteen and he was twenty, but he had no money, so they had simply waited. Now he was gone. He had crashed in the South Pacific. There was no question about that. The other men of his squadron had seen his fighter go down, and his death had been officially recognized.

Mrs. Spencer opened her eyes.

"I left the Lowestoft tea set at Crestview, didn't I?" she inquired.

"Yes, Mother. You were afraid to have it shipped. It's in the pantry."

This promising to reopen a long discussion of what had or had not been left in Maine the year before, Carol took refuge in the women's lavatory. There she lit a cigarette and surveyed herself in the mirror. What she saw was an attractive face, rather smudged at the moment, a pair of candid gray eyes, heavily lashed, and a wide humorous mouth which had somehow lost its gaiety.

"Watch out, my girl," she said to it. "You're beginning to look like the family spinster."

She took off her gloves and used her lipstick. She had broken two fingernails getting ready to move, and she eyed them resentfully. Elinor would spot them at once, she thought. Elinor who was the family beauty, Elinor who had married what was wealth even in these days of heavy taxes, and Elinor who had definitely refused to look after her mother so that Carol could go into some sort of war work.

"One of us would end in a padded cell," had been Elinor's sharp comment. "And Howard would simply go and live at his club. You know Howard."

Yes, Carol reflected, she knew Howard, big and pompous and proud, of his money, of his houses at Palm Beach and Newport, his lodge in South Carolina for quail shooting, his vast apartment in New York, his dinner parties, his name in the Social Register, and of course of his wife. Carol had often wondered whether he loved Elinor, or whether he merely displayed her, as another evidence of his success.

She powdered her damp face and felt more able to face her sister and her entourage. But although the Hilliard limousine met them at

Providence, Elinor was not in it. Nor was she at the house when they finally reached it. There were no longer three men in the hall, but the elderly butler was still there. He seemed puzzled.

"I'm sorry," he explained. "Mrs. Hilliard expected to be here. She took her own car and went out some time ago. She—I think she had a long-distance call. Probably from Captain Spencer."

"I can see no reason why that should take her out of her house," said Mrs. Spencer coldly. "Very well, Caswell. We will go to our rooms."

Carol followed her mother. The house always chilled her. It was on too large a scale. And she was puzzled about Elinor too. Whatever her feelings, she kept her appointments. It was part of her social creed. Mrs. Spencer, however, was merely exasperated.

"I have learned not to expect much from my children," she said, "but when I come here so seldom—"

"She'll turn up, Mother," Carol said pacifically. "She always does, you know."

But it was a long time before Elinor, so to speak, turned up. She was even in the house almost an hour before they saw her at all. Carol, standing at the window, saw her drive in in the gay foreign car she affected, and smiled at her mother.

"She's here," she said. "Brace yourself, darling."

Only Elinor did not come. Mrs. Spencer's reproaches died on her lips. Her air of dignified injury began to weaken. And when at last the prodigal did appear there was obviously something wrong. Not that she did not give an excellent performance.

"Sorry, my dears," she said in her light voice. "Some awful man here about the blackout. Have you had lunch?"

"We had trays up here," her mother said, the injury returning. "I do think, Elinor—"

But Elinor was not listening. She glanced around the luxurious apartment, a boudoir and two bedrooms, and jerking off her hat, ran a hand over her shining blond hair. Carol, watching her and still puzzled, wondered how she had kept her beauty. Thirty-two, she thought, and she doesn't look as old as I do. Or does she? Certainly Elinor was looking tired and harassed, and perhaps—if such a thing were possible—rather frightened.

"I hope you will be comfortable," she was saying. "It's the most awful rotten luck, but I have to go to New York tomorrow. In this heat too. Isn't it dreadful?"

Mrs. Spencer stared at her.

"I do think, Elinor—" she began again.

"I know, my dear," Elinor said. "It's sickening. But I have to go. We're giving a dinner next week, and my dress has to be fitted on Saturday. I had to have one. I'm in rags."

Carol smiled faintly. Elinor in rags, with a dressing room lined with closets filled with exquisite clothes, was not even a figure of speech.

"Where will you stay?" she asked. "Your apartment's closed, isn't it? I thought Howard was at his club."

"I'll find some place," Elinor said, still airily. "Maybe the Colony Club. Howard's not coming out this weekend. He's playing golf on Saturday at Piping Rock."

Mrs. Spencer had lapsed into indignant silence. Elinor did not look at her. She was really not looking at anyone.

"I have a shocking headache," she said, putting her hand with its huge square-cut diamond to her head. "Do you mind if I lie down for a while? Do what you like, of course."

"Just what would you propose," Carol said, amused. "I can curl up with a book, but what about Mother?"

Once more, however, she realized that her words had not pentrated Elinor's mind. Behind her lovely face something was happening. It was as if her speech was following a pattern, already cut and prepared when she entered the room.

"Dinner's at eight," she said abruptly. "I'll see you then."

"I do think—" Mrs. Spencer began again. But Elinor had already gone, the door closing behind her. In spite of her bewilderment Carol laughed. Then, feeling repentant, she went over and kissed her mother's cheek.

"Well, we're here," she said cheerfully. "Don't bother about Elinor. Maybe she has something on her mind."

Mrs. Spencer caught her arm almost wildly.

"Carol, do you think Howard is being unfaithful?"

"He may have a pretty lady somewhere," Carol said. "But Elinor wouldn't mind, of course, unless it got out."

This picture of modern marriage proving too much for her, Mrs. Spencer closed her eyes.

"I think I'll have some digitalis," she said faintly.

Elinor left the next day, looking as though she had not slept, and piling her car with the numberless bags without which she never moved. She had not appeared at dinner the night before, sending word she still had a headache, and as she left shortly after lunch her mother's grievance continued.

Elinor's plan, it appeared, was to drive herself to Providence, leave her car there and take a train to New York.

"That leaves the limousine for you," she explained. "You can use it all you like. Howard laid in plenty of gas."

Mrs. Spencer said nothing resentfully, but Elinor did not notice. She talked on feverishly during lunch: Greg's citation, the probability of his marriage to Virginia Demarest before he went back, the dress for which she was to be fitted. And—which was unlike her—she smoked fairly steadily through the meal. Carol was uneasy, and when Elinor went upstairs for her coat and hat, she followed her.

Elinor was at the safe in her bedroom. She started somewhat.

"Money for the trip," she said lightly. "What's the matter with you, Carol? You look ghastly."

"I thought you did," Carol said bluntly.

"Nonsense. I'm all right. See here, Carol, why not stay here for a while? Greg won't go to Maine. He has other things on his mind, and it only reminds you of things you'd better forget."

"I can manage," Carol said rather dryly. "I can't change the plans now. It's too late."

"Let the servants go up alone. Lucy Norton will be there, won't she?" There seemed a certain insistence in Elinor's voice.

"I'm leaving Sunday," she said. "It's too late to change."

She watched Elinor at her dressing table, laden with the gold toilet things, the jars and perfume bottles which were as much a part of her as her carefully darkened eyebrows. She was running a brush over the eyebrows now, but the line was not too even.

Elinor's hands were shaking.

2

The trip to Boston was a nightmare. The train was jammed with a Sunday crowd, and stopped frequently with a jerk that almost broke her neck. It was still hot and her mind was filled with the events of the past three days.

Any attempt to locate Greg in Washington had met with failure, and Mrs. Spencer had taken refuge in her bedroom and a dignified silence. Then on Sunday she had openly rebelled.

"I think I'll go with you, Carol," she said. "I might as well. If all Elinor provides me with is a place to sleep and food to eat, I see no reason for staying."

It had taken Carol a half hour to persuade her to stay. June was often cold in Maine, and the house would be damp anyhow, she said. Also the girls would have all they could do. Her mother would certainly be uncomfortable. Better to wait a few days. At least she was well housed and well fed where she was.

And that crisis was barely over when she had a visit from Virginia Demarest. Virginia was a tall slim redheaded girl, very pretty and very young, and just now very indignant.

"I wish you'd tell me where Greg is," she said. "Or don't you know either? I haven't heard from him since he left San Francisco for Washington the first of the week."

She lit a cigarette and threw the match away almost violently.

"We only know he's in this country, Virginia. We are opening Crestview for him. Not my idea," Carol added hastily, seeing Virginia's face. "Mother thinks he needs to be cool after where he's been. He's somewhere in Washington probably. He was to get his medal or whatever it is this week. Of course he's busy."

"There are telephones in Washington," Virginia said stormily. "All the phones in the country seem to have been sent there. Also I presume they still sell three-cent stamps. What does Elinor say?"

"She's in New York. She hasn't heard either."

Virginia eyed her.

"She and Greg are a pretty close corporation, aren't they?"

Carol smiled.

"I came along later," she said. "Rather as an unpleasant surprise, I gather. Yes, they're fond of each other."

Virginia was not listening. She was looking at a photograph of Greg, tall and handsome in his flying clothes and helmet. Her truculence had gone now. She put out her cigarette and glanced rather helplessly at Carol.

"There's something wrong," she said. "Something's happened to him. Ever since he left after his last leave his letters have been different. I suppose men can fall out of love as well as in."

"That's ridiculous," Carol said, with spirit. "If ever I saw a man who had gone overboard completely it was Greg. Or course his letters are different. They had to be read by a censor. You know that."

But Virginia was not convinced.

"They have girls out there," she said. "Nurses, Wacs, all sorts. He may have found someone he likes. He's no child. He's thirty-four, and he's been around. You know him."

Carol knew him, she admitted to herself. She had always adored him, his good looks, his debonair manners, even the lightness with which he threw off his occasional lapses. It had been she, years ago, who had slipped to him the headache tablets or even the Scotch which braced him the morning after so that he could face the family. And she had understood him better than Elinor.

"You'd better grow up soon," she had told him one morning, standing long-legged and gawky by his bed. He grinned at her.

"Why?" he inquired. "God, what awful mess is this?" He took it, grimacing. "It's fun to be young, Carol. Or it was last night."

She roused herself when she reached Boston. She managed to get to the North Station in a taxi which threatened to break down at any moment, and she found there three tired and discouraged women servants who had had no dinner and were standing by the bags they had carried themselves. Only Maggie, the cook, gave her a thin smile.

"Well, we've got this far, Miss Carol," she said. "And if you know where we can get a cup of coffee—"

She got them fed after some difficulty, sitting with them at the table and trying to swallow a dry cheese sandwich. They cheered considerably after the food.

There were no porters to be had. They lugged their bags to the train and got aboard. It had taken on the aspects of adventure to the two younger girls, especially since Carol was with them. But when she tried to enter her drawing room the door was locked, and the porter said it was already occupied. It was useless to protest. If two tickets had been sold for the same room, you could blame the war and anyone who protested was unpatriotic.

She smoked a cigarette in the women's room before she crawled resignedly into her lower berth. She supposed everything was all right. Elinor would be at home by this time, and Virginia would have heard from Gregory. But her depression continued. Partly of course it was the thought of men fighting and dying all over the world. Partly it was the belonging to what her friends called the "new poor" and having a mother who refused to change her standard of living. And partly it was an odd sense of apprehension, compounded partly of her dislike for returning to Crestview, where before the war Don Richardson had courted her so gaily and won her so easily. To escape she tried to plan about the house. Lucy had had too short notice to have done much, but at least she would be there, small, brisk and efficient. In that hopeful mood she finally went to sleep, and it persisted even when at six the next morning they got out onto a chilly station platform and looked for the taxi Lucy was to send.

There was no taxi there, only a sleepy station agent who regarded the summer people as unavoidable nuisances and disappeared as soon as the train moved on. There was a small restaurant not far away, and after a wait they got some coffee. But no taxi arrived, and at last Carol managed to locate one for the ten-mile drive.

It was cold. The girls shivered in their summer coats, and Carol herself felt discouraged. She did her best to keep up their morale, pointing out the fresh green of the trees and when they reached it the beauty of the sea.

"Look," she said. "There's a seal. They're usually gone by this time. I suppose with no motorboats around—"

"It's awfully lonely," said Freda. Freda was the housemaid, young and rather timid. "I feel all cut off from everything."

"You feel cool too, don't you?" said Maggie briskly. "After the fuss you made about the heat. Just feel the air! Ain't it something?"

There was of course plenty of air, all of it icy, and Freda shivered.

"I'll be glad to get into a warm house," she said. "Where are we? At the North Pole?"

Nora, the parlormaid-waitress, had kept quiet. She was not much of a talker at any time, but she looked blue around the lips and Carol felt uneasy. If the girls didn't stay—

"Mrs. Norton will have breakfast ready," she said. "The house will be warm too. And the lilacs ought to be lovely still. They come out late here."

No one said anything. The taxi had passed Colonel Richardson's cottage and turning in at the drive was winding its way up the hill to the house. Carol began to have a feeling of home-coming as the familiar road unwound. They passed the garage and the old stable, unused for years; not, she remembered, since Gregory had kept a saddle mare there and she her pony. She took off her hat and let the air blow through her dark hair.

"Look, there are some lilacs," she said, hoping for a cheerful response. No one said anything. They made the last turn and before them lay the house, big and massive and white. It faced out over the harbor, but the entrance was at the rear, with the service wing to the left and what had been her father's study to the right. She saw the two younger women eying it.

"It looks big," Nora said, doubt in her voice.

"It's not as large as it looks," Carol said briskly. "It's built around an open court. I wonder what has happened to Lucy?"

Except that the winter storm doors and windows had been removed, the house looked strangely unoccupied. The front door was closed, and no small brisk figure rushed to greet them. They got out and Carol paid off the taxi, but there was still no sign of movement in the house. Also to her amazement she found the door locked, and while the women stood disconsolately among their bags and the car departed with a swish of gravel she got out her keys. The door opened, she stepped inside, to be greeted only by freezing air and a vague, rather unpleasant odor.

The women followed her in, looking sulky.

"I can't imagine what has happened," she said. "Mrs. Norton must be sick. If you get a fire started in the kitchen, Maggie, I'll telephone and find out."

She put her hat and bag on the console table in the hall. It was impossible to take off her coat, and except for Maggie, starting toward her kitchen, nobody had moved. The two girls stood as if poised for flight.

"What's the smell?" Freda said. "It's like something's been burned."

"Leave the door open," Carol said impatiently. "Mrs. Norton has been here. She may have scorched something. Go on back with Maggie."

She went along the passage around the patio to the library. The old study was untouched, and the covers were still on the hall chairs at the foot of the wide staircase at the side of the house. But the covering was off the shallow pool in the patio, and the shutters off the French doors and windows opening on it. To her relief she found that at least an attempt had been made to make the library livable. The rug was down, the dust covers were gone, some of the photographs and ornaments were in place, and a log fire had been laid, ready for lighting.

She put a match to it and straightened, feeling somewhat better as the dry logs caught. But the odor—whatever it was—had penetrated even here. She opened the French door onto the terrace and stood there looking out. The air was fresh, and the view had always rested her. The islands were green jewels in the blue water, and a mile or so away she could see the town of Bayside, small and prim among its trees. She drew a long breath and turned to the telephone.

It was not there. She gazed in dismay at the desk where it had stood. The silver cigarette box was there as always. The little Battersea patch case was in its place, as was the desk pad and the old Sheffield inkstand with the candles to melt the wax and the snuffers to extinguish them. But the telephone was gone.

Something else was there, however, which made her stop and stare. On the ash tray lay a partially smoked cigarette, and there was lipstick on it.

Lucy Norton neither smoked nor used lipstick, and Carol looked down at it increduously. Then she smiled. Of course someone had dropped in. Marcia Dalton perhaps, or Louise Stimson. Almost any of the women of the summer colony, climbing the hill and coming in to rest, could have left it. Nevertheless, her feeling of uneasiness returned. She moved swiftly through the adjoining living room and dining room to the pantry and kitchen. Maggie had taken an apron from her suitcase and was tying around her ample waist. The two girls were standing like a coroner's jury, reserving decision.

"I'm afraid some of the telephones have been taken out," she said with assumed brightness. "Is the one in the kitchen hall still there, Maggie?"

Maggie opened a door and glanced back.

"It's gone," she said. "Looks like they've taken them all."

"Good heavens," Carol said. "What on earth will we do?"

"Folks lived a long time without them," Maggie said philosophically. "I guess we'll manage. What do you think that smell is, Miss Carol? There's nothing been burned here."

It was not bad in the kitchen, although it was noticeable. Not unexpectedly, Freda, the youngest of the three, broke first.

"I'm not staying," she said hysterically. "I didn't plan to be sent to the end of the world, and frozen too. And that smell makes me sick. I'm giving you notice this minute, Miss Spencer."

Carol fought off the nightmare sensation that was beginning to paralyze her.

"Now look, Freda," she said reasonably, her face a little set, "you can't leave. Not right away, anyhow. I can't call a taxi. The cars in the garage have no gasoline and no batteries. They're jacked up anyhow. There's not even a train until tonight."

Maggie took hold then.

"Don't be a little fool, Freda," she said. "I expect Mrs. Norton's ordered the groceries. You take off your hat and coat, and I'll make hot coffee. We'll all feel better then."

A hasty inspection of the supply closet revealed no groceries, however. There was an empty coffee can and the heel of a loaf of bread. In the refrigerator were a couple of eggs, a partly used jar of marmalade, and a few slices of bacon on a plate. Maggie's face was grim. She looked up at the eight-day kitchen clock, which was still going.

"If that lazy George Smith's here we can send him into town," she said. "Go out and see if you can find him, Nora. He's the gardener—or he says he is."

She ordered Freda to the cellar for coal, and under protest Freda went. Carol sat down on a kitchen chair while Maggie looked at her with concern.

"You're too young to have all this wished on you," she said, with the familiarity of her twenty years of service. "Don't take it too hard. Somebody's sick at Lucy's, most likely. I don't know why your mother got this idea anyhow. Mr. Greg won't come. He'd got only thirty days and probably he'll want to get married. It's a pity," she added grimly, "that you and Mr. Don didn't get married before he left."

Because Carol was tired and worried, tears came into her eyes. She brushed them away impatiently.

"That's all over, Maggie," she said. "We have to carry on."

Then Freda came back, gingerly carrying a pail partly filled with coal, and Maggie started to light a fire. The odor—whatever it was— was not strong here, but when Maggie poured a little kerosene onto the coals and dropped a match onto it, Carol realized the odor was much the same. Perhaps Lucy had started the furnace fire that way.

Nora came back, shivering, from the grounds. "I don't see anybody," she reported. "The grass has been cut here and there, but there's nobody out there."

She huddled by the stove, and Carol got up abruptly.

"Something's happened to Lucy," she said. "Take over, Maggie, and get started. I'll go down to the village and find out what's wrong. I'll order some groceries too. The Miller market will be open now."

"One of the girls can do it," Maggie objected.

But Carol refused. She was worried about Lucy. Also she knew what was needed, and how to find it. And—although she did not say it—she wanted to get out of the house. Always before when she came it had been warm and welcoming, but that day it was different. It felt, she thought shiveringly, like a tomb.

3

She was still shivering as she got her bag from the entrance hall. She did not put on her hat. She left the front door open to let in more air, and stood outside looking about her.

There was no sign that George Smith had done much. Branches from the great pines littered the turnaround of the drive, and where the hill rose abruptly behind it the tool house appeared to be closed and locked. But the day was brilliantly bright, a bed of peonies by the grass terrace at the side of the house was beginning to show radiant pink and white blossoms, and a robin was sitting back on its tail and pulling vigorously at a worm. It was familiar and friendly, and she started briskly down the hill.

This was a mistake. She had not changed her shoes, and walking was not easy. The gravel had been raked into the center of the drive to avoid washing away in the winter rains and thaws, and the hard base underneath was rough. It was no use going to the garage, she knew. The cars had been put up for the winter. At the entrance gates, however, she hesitated. She could, she knew, telephone from the Richardson cottage, but she did not yet feel able to cope with the colonel and with his talk of Don. And the Ward place, separated from the Crestview by a narrow dirt lane, was as far up the hill as Crestview itself.

In the end she decided to walk the mile to the market. It was easier going on the streets, and besides she had always liked the town. Its white houses, neat and orderly, its strong sense of self-respect, its New England dignity, all appealed to her. It looked friendly, too, in the morning sun, and her anxieties seemed foolish and slightly ridiculous.

It was still early. Here and there, it being Monday, washing was already hanging out in the yards, but she saw no one she knew until she limped into the market. Fortunately it was open, and behind the counter Harry Miller was putting on a fresh white coat.

He looked rather odd when he saw her.

"How are you, Miss Carol?" he said, as they shook hands. "I heard you were coming. Early, aren't you, this morning?"

She smiled as she pulled up a stool and sat down.

"I had to walk," she explained. "No car, no telephone, no groceries, and no sense. I forgot to change my shoes."

"Sounds like a lot of misery," said Harry, eying her.

"It was. It is. Harry, do you know anything about Lucy Norton? She's not there, and even George Smith isn't around. I don't understand it."

Harry hesitated.

"Well," he said, "I guess you've run into a bit of hard luck, Miss Carol. Take George now. He's in the hospital. Had his appendix out last Thursday. Doing all right though. Kind of proud of it by this time."

"I'm sorry. He wasn't much good, but he was somebody. I'll go to see him as soon as I get things fixed a bit. What about Lucy?"

Harry still hesitated. He had always liked Carol. She was just folks like the rest, not like some he could mention. And that morning she was looking young and wind-blown and rather plaintive.

"About your telephone," he said evasively. "I guess your mother didn't pay any attention to the notice. You had to pay all winter even to keep one, and then you were lucky if you did."

"I suppose Mother got one," Carol said. "We didn't expect to come, of course. What about Lucy Norton? Is she sick too?"

"Well, I suppose I'd better tell you," he said, not too comfortably. "Lucy's had an accident. She fell down the big staircase at your place and broke her leg. In the middle of the night, too. She might be lying there still if that William who takes down the winter stuff hadn't come along. Seems like he wanted to borrow some coffee and the kitchen wing was locked. He went around to the front door and found it open. And found Lucy there. She's at the hospital too. Doing all right, I hear."

Carol looked startled.

"What on earth was Lucy doing on the stairs in the middle of the night? She always sleeps in the service wing."

He grinned.

"Well, that's a funny thing, Miss Carol. She says somebody was chasing her."

Carol stared at him.

"Chasing her? It doesn't sound like Lucy."

"Does sound foolish, doesn't it?" he said. "She's a sensible woman too, like you say. But that's what she claims. I only know what they're saying around here. Seems like she says it was cold that night, and she'd got up to get a blanket from some closet or other. The light company hadn't got around to turning on the electric current, so she took a candle. She got to the closet all right, but just as she was ready to open the door she says somebody reached out and knocked the candle out of her hand. Knocked her down too, and practically ran over her."

"It sounds fantastic."

"Doesn't it? They're calling it Lucy's ghost around here. Anyhow she was so scared that she picked herself up and made for the stairs. It was black dark, you see, so she fell right down them. It's a mercy she was found at all. Old William saw the front door wide open and went in, and Lucy Norton was at the foot of the stairs, about crazy with one thing and another. He got Dr. Harrison there and they took her to the hospital. She's in a plaster cast now," he added, almost with gusto.

Carol stared at him.

"It wasn't a ghost if it opened the front door," she said. "If the whole town knows about it, my maids will hear it sooner or later." She remembered Freda with a sense of helplessness. "It was a tramp, of course. Who else could it be? Unless she dreamed the whole business."

"Well, she sure enough broke her leg."

The market was still empty. She was aware that Harry was watching her with a mixture of curiosity and the deference he reserved for his summer people. She rallied herself.

"I'm terribly sorry," she said. "We're all fond of her. I'll see her as soon as I can. But a tramp—!"

"Anything missing from the place?" he inquired.

"I haven't really looked. I don't think so. We never leave much."

He cleared his throat.

"Might as well tell you," he said. "There was a light in the upper corner room of yours late that night. The one that looks this way. I was driving home, and I saw it myself. Looked like a candle, only Lucy says she wasn't in there."

"In the yellow room? Are you sure?"

"Sure as I'm standing here. After half past twelve it was."

She gave her order finally, and went out with her head whirling. But there was no time to see Lucy Norton then, or George either. She went to the office of the telephone company, only to find that there was less than no hope. As usual, she was told there was a war on and, in effect, what was she, a patriot or not? She was able to have the electric current turned on, and at the service station to find someone to put her small car in running order.

It seemed to her that everyone she saw looked at her with more than normal interest. Lucy's story had evidently spread and probably grown.

This was verified when she met the village chief of police at the corner. His name was Floyd, a big man with a sagging belt which carried the automatic he invariably wore as a badge of office, and with small shrewd deep-set eyes. He grinned as he shook hands with her.

"Glad you're back," he said. "We'd heard you weren't coming."

"Mother thought Gregory would like it."

"Bit quiet for him, I'd think. Unless Lucy Norton's ghost gets after him."

He laughed, his big body shaking. She had known him all her life, and the very fact that he could laugh was a relief. She found herself smiling.

"If there was anyone it may have been a tramp. Harry Miller says William found the front door of the house open."

He laughed again.

"No tramps around here, Miss Carol. Ten miles from a railroad! What would they be doing here? They'd starve to death."

She left him still grinning, and went on her way. She ordered coal, she bought some candy at the drugstore as a peace offering for the two recalcitrant girls, and at last she got a local taxi, picked up part of her order at the market, and drove home. She did not go to the house at once, however. She sent the taxi on with the groceries, and herself got out at the garage and unlocked the doors. The cars were there, mounted on blocks, her small car, her mother's limousine, and Gregory's old abandoned roadster. They looked strange under their dust sheets, but nothing had been disturbed.

She left the door open for the men from the service station, and went back to the drive, to find there what she had dreaded for so long.

Colonel Richardson was waiting for her. He was standing in the roadway, his tall figure erect, the wind blowing his heavy white hair. A veteran of two wars, he was colonel to every one, and—except for his obsession about his son—universally beloved. With his smile Carol's apprehensions left her.

"Hello," he said genially. "Come and greet an old man. I didn't know you were coming so soon."

She went over and kissed him, and he patted her shoulder.

"Look as though you could stand some good Maine air," he said, surveying her. "I only heard about Lucy Norton yesterday. Too bad. She's a fine woman. How are you getting along?"

"We'll manage. No telephone of course, and no cars or lights yet. Otherwise we're all right. How are you?"

"Fine. I find the waiting hard, of course, but I have to remember that I am not alone in that. Can I do anything now?"

She told him she could get along, and watched him going down the drive, swinging the stick he always carried, but with his back straight and his head held high. She looked after him, distressed for them both, that he should believe and she could not, that to him Don was still a living force and to her he was becoming only a memory. She was deeply depressed when she got back to the house.

She found Maggie at the stove, with a kettle boiling and her face smeared with soot.

"I got the furnace started," she said cheerfully. "Otherwise those fools of girls would still be hugging this fire. And I started Freda at your room. Soon as she's made the bed—"

Carol dumped her groceries on the table.

"Lucy Norton's broken her leg, Maggie. She's in the hospital."

Maggie turned, her face shocked.

"The poor thing! How did it happen?"

"Here in this house." Carol sat down and kicked off her pumps. "She fell down the stairs. There's a silly story going around that she found someone upstairs and tried to get away."

"When was all this?" Maggie, practical as ever, was opening the new pound of coffee.

"Last Friday night or early Saturday morning. The lights were off, of course." She looked at her feet. They were hurting, and she picked up one and began to rub it thoughtfully. "George is there too. He's had his appendix out."

"For God's sake!" said Maggie, her poise finally forsaking her. "Something scared *him* too?"

There was no time to answer.

There was a wild scream from somewhere upstairs, and a minute later Freda half ran, half fell toward the back staircase, and promptly fainted on the kitchen floor.

Later Carol was to remember that faint of Freda's as the beginning of the nightmare, to see herself bending over the girl, whose small face was ashy gray and the palm of one hand oddly blackened, of trying to prevent Nora from dousing her with a pan of water from the sink, and of catching Maggie's eyes as she straightened.

"Something's scared her too," said Maggie ominously. "Too much scaring around here, to my way of thinking."

Nora was still clutching the pan.

"Maybe she saw a mouse," she said. "She's deathly afraid of mice."

"We'd better leave her flat," Carol said. "Go up and get her a blanket, Nora. The floor's cold. You'll find them in the linen closet."

She bent over and felt the girl's pulse. It was rapid but strong, and a little color was coming back into her face. Carol herself felt rather dizzy. She stepped into her pumps and looked at Maggie.

"What's that on her head?"

Maggie bent over and looked.

"Seems like soot," she said. "Maybe she was lighting your fire. I'd better go and look. The place could burn up while we're standing here."

She did not go, however. Freda was stirring. She opened pale-blue eyes and looked around her uncertainly.

"What happened?" she said. "I must have fainted or something."

"If you didn't you gave a good imitation of it," said Maggie dryly. "You scared the insides out of us. Better lie still for a while. You're all right."

Freda was far from all right. With returning consciousness came memory, and without warning she burst into loud hysterical crying.

"I want to go home," she said between wails. "I never did want to come here."

"Shut up," Maggie said grimly. "Noise isn't going to help you. What scared you?"

Freda did not answer, and it was a part of the nightmare that Nora chose that moment to return. She came rather quietly down the back stairs and stopped, bracing herself against the frame of the kitchen door as if she needed support. There was no color in her face, but her voice was steady.

"There's somebody dead in the linen closet," she said, and shivered. "There's been a fire there too."

4

She did not say any more. She made for the door which led outside from the service hall, and they could hear her retching there. Carol made a move toward the stairs, but Maggie was ahead of her.

"They're both hysterical," she said. "Probably saw a blanket on the floor. Better let me go up, Miss Carol. You don't look so good yourself. You stay with Freda."

Freda was still crying, but she was sitting up now and fumbling for a handkerchief. Carol gave her one from her bag and she dried her eyes.

"I guess I flopped," she said. "So would you, if you seen what I did." She shuddered uncontrollably. "I opened the door where you said the linen closet was, and—"

She did not finish. Maggie came in, and one look at her face was enough.

"I guess you'll have to get the police," she said. "There's somebody there. Better not go up. I opened the windows in the hall, but I didn't touch anything else."

She went to the sink and washed her hands. Then she sat down abruptly, and began nervously pleating her apron.

"I don't feel so good," she said. "They're right about the fire. We'll never use them sheets and things again."

The nightmare feeling closed down on Carol. It had been growing since their arrival, with Lucy not there, and Harry Miller's story, and now this! She felt young and incapable, and the house itself had become horrible. She found she was shaking.

"Could you see who it was?" she asked.

Maggie shook her head.

"I told you. There's been a fire." She got up heavily and went to the stove. "I'd better make some coffee," she said, her voice flat. "It's a help. You'd better have a cup before you start for the village. Maybe you can get Colonel Richardson to drive you in. He's near."

"I ought to go up myself."

"You stay where you are," Maggie said forcefully. "Freda, you go up and lie down. Nothing's going to hurt you. Whatever it is it's over, and your room ain't near it."

Nora had come back by that time, but neither girl would go upstairs again. They looked shocked and helpless, but they looked, too, like a defiant combination against Maggie's common sense. Carol looked at them with what amounted to despair.

"I'm sorry, girls," she said. "Whatever has happened it has nothing to do with us. Mrs. Norton has broken her leg. She's in the hospital, and probably some tramp came in while the house was empty."

Nora was the first to recover.

"And burned himself to death!" she said, her voice high and shrill.

"That's for the police to find out."

"I'm staying for no police."

Maggie turned from the stove.

"That's where you're wrong, my girl," she said coldly. "You'll stay here as long as the police want you. Don't get any ideas about running away, either of you. You found the body, and here you're staying till they let you go."

It was subdued pair of young women that Carol took upstairs. The service wing was cut off from the main house by a heavy door, and after she had seen them to their rooms she opened it. From this angle she could see the door of the linen closet. It was next to that of the elevator which had been installed for her mother some years before, and it was standing open, its white paint blackened and blistered.

She stood still, almost unable to move. Soon she would have to get help, but first she must see for herself. The odor was very strong. It was a combination of scorched linen, burned paint, kerosene, and something else she did not care to identify.

The morning sun was flooding the closet. The house was built entirely around the patio, with a passage running around it on the second floor and the bedroom doors and that of the elevator and closet opening from it. The windows were open, and she was grateful for the air. She moved forward slowly, past Greg's old room, past the blue guest room and past the elevator door. Then she was at the closet, staring in.

The women had been right. There was a body inside, but it was not that of a tramp. It was that of a woman.

She did not go back to the kitchen. She went on rather blindly to the main staircase and huddled there on the top step. She was still wearing the black dress and fur-collared coat in which she had arrived, and she pulled the coat around her as if she were cold. She was not thinking yet. Her mind was too chaotic for that. She knew there were things she should do, but she was not ready to do them. Maggie found her there, her eyes wide and staring and her face chalk-white.

"I warned you," she said. "Maybe I'd better go for the police. It's nobody you know, is it?"

Carol looked up blankly.

"How can anyone tell?" Her voice was bleak, and Maggie was frightened.

"Now look, Miss Carol," she said, "it's not that bad. Maybe you couldn't recognize her, but she's—she's not really burned up. And the house is cold. If it's only been there since Saturday—"

Carol roused herself.

"Saturday? Why Saturday?"

"Because Lucy Norton was here Friday night," Maggie explained patiently. "You don't suppose this went on while she was in the house, do you?"

"It might have. I didn't tell you all the story. She says somebody reached out of the linen closet and knocked her down. That's how she got hurt. She was running down the stairs in the dark."

Carol got up slowly, holding to the stair rail, and Maggie caught her arm to steady her.

"I'd better get Floyd," she said. "Maybe I can telephone from Colonel Richardson's." And when Maggie protested, "I need the air," she said flatly, "I'm all right now. Let go of me. I'm only glad Mother isn't here."

Maggie nodded, and Carol went down the stairs. The sunlight on the white walls of the house made the patio dazzling, and she blinked in the glare. The blue pool needed paint, she thought distractedly, and some of the tiles had been cracked by the winter ice. It had been idiotic to build a house entirely around an open court. In winter any heavy snow had to be shoveled into a wheelbarrow and dumped on the drive, and when there was a rapid thaw the drainpipe in the pool was not adequate. More than once the plumber had had to come, have the current turned on, run a hose through the entry hall and pump the water out onto the drive.

She pulled herself together. All this was pure escapism, and she could not escape. There was a dead girl or woman upstairs, and she would have to notify the police. She was more normal when she left the house again, although her feet still bothered her. She had a pair of sandals in her bag upstairs, but she could not go back for them. Perhaps Colonel Richardson would telephone, or drive her into town. But as she stumbled down the drive once more, it was to see the Richardson garage doors open and the Colonel's car gone. This was the time, she remembered, when he drove his man, his only servant, into town to market, and the house would be closed and locked.

She stood still, shivering in the cold air. She could go up to the Wards' and get help there, but once again the long steep drive was more than she could face. She decided to walk, and some twenty minutes later she opened the door of the police station and went in.

Floyd was relaxing. He had taken off his belt and automatic, which lay on his desk, and was resting in a chair, with another drawn up for his legs. He looked up in astonishment when he saw her, and got to his feet.

"Anything wrong?" he inquired. "Here, maybe you'd better sit down."

She did not sit, however. She stood just inside the door, holding the knob as if to support her.

"There's somebody dead in the linen closet at Crestview," she said, her voice flat. "I thought maybe you'd better come up."

He looked astounded.

"Dead? Are you sure?"

"Yes. I think somebody tried to burn her. The house too, I suppose. Only the door was shut and the fire didn't spread."

"For God's sake," Floyd said softly. "So Lucy Norton wasn't crazy, after all."

He buckled on his heavy gun, his face set.

"My car's in the alley," he said. "I'll call Jim Mason. He's got the night job, so he's at home. I'd better call the doctor too. He's the coroner." He reached for the telephone and stopped, his hand on the receiver.

"You're sure of all this, are you?" he said. "Not mistaking something else for a body?"

"I saw it myself."

She sat down then and kicked off her shoes, and the next thing she knew Floyd was holding a glass of whisky to her lips and telling her to get it down somehow.

"I'm not the fainting sort," she protested. "I'm just tired."

"You gave a damn good imitation of passing out," he said gruffly. "Take the rest of this."

And she was still half strangled when he put her into his car.

The whisky helped. She felt less cold, and things were out of her hands now. The law was beside her, looking stern and capable. She was no longer alone. And the chief was a shrewd man. He asked genially about the family, her mother, and especially about Gregory.

"All mighty proud of him here," he said. "Hear he's being decorated by the President."

"He came home for that. They sent him. You know Greg. He didn't want to leave his men, or his plane."

She was looking better, he thought. He had always liked her. Had a rotten time, too, he considered, with that mother of hers and her hoity-toity sister. Then she'd been engaged to Don Richardson, and Don was dead, although his old man wouldn't believe it.

He turned into the drive and put his car into second gear. The engine promptly began to knock, and he apologized.

"Car's all right," he explained. "It's this rotten gas we're getting. Hello, there's the Dane fellow. Maybe we'd better get him."

He stopped the car. A man in slacks and yellow sweater had been slowly climbing the drive and limping slightly as he did so. He stopped when he heard the car behind him and turned, a tall figure with a lean, rather saturnine face and an aggressive jaw.

"Hello, major," said the chief. "Kind of early for a walk, isn't it?"

Dane grinned.

"My daily dozen," he explained. "When I can run up this hill I'll be ready to go back. Anyhow I saw smoke in this direction, and after the stories going round I thought I'd look into it."

The chief remembered his manners.

"Miss Spencer, meet Major Jerry Dane," he said. "The major had some trouble with the krauts a while ago in Italy, and he's here getting over it." He looked at the man again. "Miss Spencer's had some trouble too," he added. "Maybe you'd like to come along. She says there's a dead body in the house up here."

The major looked interested rather than astonished.

"A body?" he said. "Whose is it?"

He glanced at Carol.

"I have no idea," she said coldly. "If you want to discuss it I'll go on, if you don't mind."

"If it's dead there's no great hurry, is there?"

He was deliberately baiting her, and she felt her color rise. He saw it and grinned, showing excellent teeth in a sunburned face.

"Sorry," he said. "I'll hang onto the running board. Get going, Floyd. Let's see this corpse."

It was obvious that he did not believe her, and none of them spoke as the car climbed the rest of the hill. Carol promptly forgot Dane and braced herself for what was to come. And Dane himself simply lit a cigarette and from his precarious hold on the running board eyed her quizzically. Plenty of spunk, he thought, if what she said was true. Only—a body in the house! Whose body? Good God, he had walked up this hill daily for two weeks, and except for the Norton woman's accident the place had been merely an ostentatious survival of an era that was finished. In a way it had annoyed him, sitting smug on its hill while the rest of the world blazed and died.

He was relieved when Carol let them go upstairs alone, and he saw now why the house had looked so huge. The court around which it was built might be a lovely thing when it had been put in order, but was now neglected and ugly. But once upstairs he forgot the house. He was accustomed to death, as a man in his particular job knew death. But not the death of a woman. And what lay on the closet floor had been a woman.

It lay relaxed and face up, with the hands and arms close to the body, and the legs neatly outstretched toward the door. When Floyd tried to step inside Dane held him back.

"Better wait," he said. "Let's see what we can first. She wasn't burned to death of course. Look at the way she's lying. If she'd been burned—"

"I don't get it," Floyd said thickly. "Why kill her and then try to burn her?"

"That's a very nice question." Dane looked about him. "When was the Norton woman hurt?"

"Friday night. Saturday morning, maybe."

Dane began whistling softly to himself.

"No fingerprint people around, I suppose?" he asked, after a pause.

"Why would we be needing a fingerprint outfit?" the chief demanded belligerently. "We haven't had a crime here since one of the waiters at the hotel stole a watch, and that's twelve years ago."

Dane went back to his whistling, but his eyes were busy. The doorknobs were no good. Whoever had found the body had smeared them badly, both outside and in, and a thick layer of soot lay along the shelves and along the piles of neatly stacked scorched linen.

"Ever see her before?" he asked finally.

"How can I tell? Even her own mother—There's no local girl missing. That's all I know."

"How about a camera? There ought to be some pictures before she's moved."

Floyd's patience was rapidly going.

"Listen, son," he said. "There's a war on. I haven't seen a roll of film for the last year. And I don't own a camera anyhow. What do you think this is? The FBI in Washington?"

Dane did not reply. The doctor's car had chugged up the hill and now he was coming up the stairs, with Jim Mason, Floyd's assistant, at his heels. He stopped outside the closet and stared in.

"Good Godamighty!" he said. "How did this happen?"

"Maybe you can tell us," Dane said with his slightly sardonic smile. "I wouldn't touch anything but the body, doctor. Not that I think there's anything there. Just the usual procedure."

Floyd gave him a cold stare.

"We'll attend to that, Dane," he said. "Go ahead, doc. The major here says she was dead before the fire. How about it?"

The doctor went inside the closet and stooped over the body. He was there a couple of minutes before he backed out. He looked rather white.

"Hit on the head," he said. "Bad frontal fracture. Probably dead two or three days. No way to tell. Certainly dead before the fire."

"Then why any fire at all?" Floyd persisted.

The doctor was lighting a cigarette by the open window.

"How do I know?" he said irritably. "Maybe somebody didn't like her. Maybe somebody didn't want her recognized. Or maybe it was just a fire-bug. Remember the Elks' Club?" He sucked at his cigarette. "Better get her out of here," he said. "I want to look her over."

Dane left them then. He went downstairs, to find Carol in the library. She was curled up in a big chair by the fire, looking young and stricken. There was a tray with coffee on a small table beside her, but she had not touched it. His quick eyes took in the room before he spoke.

"I'm sorry to bother you," he said, "but have you got a camera in the house?"

"A camera?"

"They want to take her away, but I think there should be a picture or two first."

"My brother's camera is here. There are no films in it."

He shrugged his lean shoulders.

"Well, I suppose that's that," he said. "None in the town either, I understand. No telephone, I suppose?"

"No. They're all gone. Who is it up there, major? I mean—in the closet. Does anyone know her?"

He shook his head.

"Not yet. We'll find out later, of course. They don't think she's one of the local people. That's as far as they go."

She shivered, and he went to the tray and poured a cup of coffee. Her hand shook as she took it, but she tried to smile.

"The cook's cure for everything," she said. "I've been having it ever since I came. I have practically a coffee jag. Not to mention Floyd's whisky." She glanced up at him, standing beside her. Aside from his slight limp he appeared to be a strong, well-muscled man in his early thirties, and his face as he looked down at her was now friendly and smiling.

"Don't take this too hard," he said. "It has happened in this house, but it has nothing to do with you. A little paint and a little time, and you can forget it, Miss Spencer."

"I'll never forget it. Do you think it was this—this woman who scared Lucy Norton the night she fell?"

"Might be," he said lightly, and turned to go.

But she did not want him to go. She could not be alone again. Not then, with only the servants in the house and that horror upstairs.

"Would you like some coffee?" she asked, almost desperately.

"Is it strong?"

"It would float an egg."

"I'll be back for some in a minute."

He was longer than a minute. Mason had disappeared when he went back. He left Floyd and Dr. Harrison in the hall and went into the closet. There he stooped for some time over the body, touching nothing but inspecting everything. When he came out again his face was set.

"She was a young woman," he said. "And I don't think she was killed here. That's not certain, of course, but it doesn't look like it. The autopsy will tell a good bit more, probably. She wasn't wearing much when it happened. Apparently she'd slipped a fur jacket over not much else. Any girl around here have a silver fox coat?"

The chief snorted.

"A few, but mostly we leave them to the summer people. I'll ask around, of course. Taking a lot of interest, aren't you, Dane? Sure you didn't know her yourself?"

"Don't be a fool, Floyd. You brought me here. Why don't you get busy and look around for her clothes? If she didn't belong here she didn't arrive in what she's got on."

"I'll find them, all right."

But Dane was aware as he went down the stairs again that the chief's eyes, hard and suspicious, were following him.

5

He found Carol as he had left her. An extra cup and a pot of fresh coffee were waiting for him, and he sat down for the first time.

He nodded approval over the coffee.

"First real stuff I've had since I got here," he said. "Maybe I'd better explain myself. I know the Burtons well, and when I needed to fix up this leg before I went to France they offered me their house just along the hill from here. But of course you know it. And I've got a good man to look after me. He nurses me like a baby, but he can't make coffee."

He talked on quietly, about Alex, the man he had referred to, and who had lost an eye in Italy, about the war and his anxiety to get back into it.

"I've missed the invasion," he said with suppressed bitterness, "but there's still plenty to do. I want like hell to get back. I will too, if Alex and two hands like hams can fix me up."

He was lighting a cigarette for her when the screaming of a siren announced the arrival of the ambulance, and he was still talking against the sounds as the stretcher was carried down the stairs and out of the house and the other cars started their motors.

But she rebelled at last.

"I'm not a child, Major Dane," she said. "I'm twenty-four years old, and I'm perfectly strong. I want to talk about this murder. It is murder, isn't it?"

"Don't you think you'd better forget it? What's the use of discussing it? It's over."

"Over!" she said indignantly. "It has only started, and you know it. I suppose you've heard Lucy Norton's story. Everybody seems to know it. It was that closet she went to to get an extra blanket, and it was someone in that closet who rushed out and knocked her down. That's right, isn't it?"

"That's the story. I haven't seen Mrs. Norton."

"Do you think it was this—was this woman?"

He hesitated, but she had asked for it, he thought grimly.

"I think it unlikely, Miss Spencer. It is more likely to have been whoever killed her."

"Then it was murder?"

"It was murder. Yes. I don't need to tell you that a fire was set, after the crime. She wasn't burned to death."

"I don't understand it. The fire, I mean. When we came in this morning we all smelled something. If the house had burned it might have killed Lucy too. It's—horrible."

"That's one curious thing," he said thoughtfully. "Between Alex and myself I suppose we've heard every variation of the Norton story. She has not apparently mentioned any fire, or even smoke. I wonder—" He did not finish. "There may not have been much. By shutting the door the oxygen was cut off. Still, if you noticed it after two or three days she should have. It's curious. I've been around here every day. I watched the winter shutters being taken down, and on Friday morning I knew someone was working in the house. Mrs. Norton, of course. As a matter of fact—"

"Don't start and stop like that. What was a matter of fact?"

He smiled.

"Probably a mistake. I made a regular round, you see; up the drive, back to the house and over the grounds to that fountain of yours. From there I take the path through the woods to the Burtons'. That takes me past the kitchen. On Friday morning I thought I heard Mrs. Norton talking to someone."

"You didn't see anyone?"

"No. Nobody."

"It might have been William. He was taking down the shutters."

"Very likely. I just remembered it. It's probably not important. Mrs. Norton was late, wasn't she? I mean in opening the house."

"She got here only Friday morning. You see, we hadn't intended to come at all. Then my brother Gregory received thirty days' leave— he's been flying in the Pacific—and Mother thought he'd like to be cool." She smiled faintly. "He won't, you know. He will want New York and Newport. His fiancée is in Newport now."

He was thoughtful. The fire had burned down, and he got up and put a log on it.

"Let's reconstruct this thing," he said. "Just what would Mrs. Norton do when she got here Friday morning? She was alone, I suppose. That's the story as I get it."

"Yes. She couldn't get any help, and George Smith wasn't here. He'd had his appendix out. I suppose she'd light the furnace first. She'd probably light the stove in the kitchen too. After that—well, I think she came in here, so I would have a place to sit. I haven't been up in my room, but with so little time she probably did something there."

"Such as?"

"She would make the bed, I imagine. Or at least get out the sheets to air them. Oh, I see what you mean."

"Exactly," he said soberly. "The linen closet was probably all right then, on Friday morning."

Nora came in for the tray just then. She looked better, but she was still pale, and Dane smiled at her.

"Thanks for the coffee," he said. "And do you know if Miss Spencer's room is ready for her? She looks tired."

"The bed's made up, Freda says. That's about all, sir."

"So you see," he said when she had gone. "The linen closet *was* all right on Friday. Maybe someone was in the house talking to Mrs. Norton, maybe not. But there was no murder until that night."

He took up his cup and wandered about the room. The tissue paper had been taken off a jumble of vases, a plaster cast of one of her father's mares when people still kept horses, a Russian ikon, a Buddha or two, and the photograph of Elinor in her finery when she made her debut. But there was another photograph there, one of Gregory Spencer in uniform, and he stopped before it.

"Your brother, I suppose?"

"Yes. Can you see what I mean when I say he'd prefer New York?"

Dane inspected it carefully. A playboy, he thought, until war had sobered him. Or had it?

"Fine-looking chap," he said. "No wonder you're proud of him."

Carol did not answer. She was looking around the room, apparently puzzled.

"That's queer," she said. "I don't see my father's picture. It's always here. Mother wouldn't ship it to New York last fall, for fear something would happen to it. I wrapped it up myself and left it on top of that bookcase."

She got up and moved anxiously about the room. When she reached the desk she stopped.

"I've just remembered something else too," she said. "This morning I found a cigarette here, in this ash tray. It had lipstick on it. Lucy doesn't smoke, and as for lipstick—"

The stairs had made Dane's leg ache. His limp was more noticeable as he went to the desk.

"Any idea where it is now?"

"I suppose Nora threw it out."

"If that's true," he said, "the lipstick, I mean, it throws my first idea into the discard. What I thought was that, as the house was supposed still to be empty, anyone wanting to dispose of a body could bring it here, set fire to the house, and then escape. That whoever did it possibly had no idea Mrs. Norton was here. But if the dead woman was here, and smoking in this room—"

He left soon after. She went out to the terrace with him, and for a moment they stood together, looking down at the shore line and the roofs of the houses buried in foliage below.

"It looks peaceful," she said. "It's hard to believe that anyone here could do a thing like murder."

"There's murder all over the world," he said dryly. "Why think people like you are immune?"

She felt rebuffed as she went back into the house. It was obvious that Dane did not like what he called people like her. It had been in his face when he looked at Greg's picture. And she could not tell him that she loathed her own uselessness. Why should she? she thought resentfully. Just because he had been wounded in Italy did not give him the right to criticize those who could not fight.

In the library she resumed her search for her father's picture. It was not there, although she looked behind the books. It was not in the study either. When she went upstairs to continue the search she saw that the door to the linen closet had been sealed with strips of adhesive tape and blobs of red wax. They looked like blood, making her shiver. But the picture was not in her mother's room either, and at last she gave up and went downstairs again, to find an angry Maggie waiting for her.

"Did you tell that man he could look at my garbage can?" she demanded. "The tall one with the limp."

"You'll have to expect things like that, Maggie," she said wearily. "We've had a murder, you know."

"And what's happened to your mother's china tea set?" Maggie inquired, her arms akimbo. "It ain't here, and she sure thought a lot of it. If you're asking me, we've had a burglary as well as a murder."

"Who on earth would steal a tea set?"

"It was valuable, wasn't it?"

Carol felt completely confused as she went back to the library. There were things she would have to do. She would have to call Elinor at Newport and ask her to break the news to her mother as carefully as she could. But she dreaded doing it. She could see Elinor's lifted eyebrows and her angry reaction, as though she—Carol—was responsible. And of course she would have to see Lucy. If the girl had been in the house long enough to smoke a cigarette, Lucy must know about her.

She might even had admitted her. Only Joe Norton, the caretaker, had keys to the house, and Lucy would have used his, as she always did. Joe had the keys, so he could come in during the winter. So far as she remembered there were only two sets of keys.

But the real question was the identity of the body, and here she felt helpless. She would have to see Lucy as soon as possible, she thought. It would be only an hour or two before she had her car, and Lucy must know something. Only it was queer she had not said anything. According to Harry Miller, Lucy's story was merely that someone had come out of the closet and knocked her down.

She was starting for the garage to see what progress had been made when Freda stopped her.

The drive was empty. By this time the village certainly knew what had happened, but no crowd of thrill-seekers had gathered. The town, self-respecting as ever, was evidently going about its business as usual. Down at the garage someone was hammering, and the morning chill had gone. The sun was warm and heartening.

She had taken only a step or two when Freda called her. The girl still looked pale, but she was no longer hysterical. Carol stopped.

"What is it, Freda?"

"If you'll excuse me, miss," she said. "Maggie thought I'd better tell you. Somebody has been sleeping in the yellow room. There's sheets on the bed, and two or three blankets. The bathroom's been used too. The tub's still dirty."

Quite evidently she was enjoying the sensation she was making. For it was a sensation. Carol looked incredulous.

"I don't believe it," she said. "Mrs. Norton would never sleep there."

"No, ma'am," said Freda smugly. "She was using a room in our wing. Maybe you'd better come and look."

She followed Carol up the stairs, to find the other two women in the upper hall. The yellow room was at the front of the house, so she did not pass the closet to reach it, but she was acutely conscious of it behind her, its seared door and ruined contents. She was still certain Freda had made a mistake. The last person to use it the summer before had been Virginia, and some oversight—

But she knew as she reached the door that there had been no mistake.

The yellow room looked out over the bay, and had been one of her pet rooms. Its walls were yellow, its furniture painted gray, and the hangings and chair covers were a delicate mulberry. She saw none of that now, however. Freda had been right. The bed had been made up and slept in, there was powder on the glass top of the toilet table, and while the ash trays were empty there were cigarette ashes here and there on the floor. A candle on the table beside the bed had burned itself out. Only a shapeless blob of wax remained.

Maggie was the first to speak.

"Looks like she was sleeping here," she said. "She had her nerve, if you ask me."

Carol turned to Freda.

"You haven't touched anything in here, have you?" she asked.

"No, miss. I just opened the door and saw it. Then I looked at the bathroom. It's like I said."

Carol stepped inside the room. The nightmare feeling was returning, and there was something wrong. It was a minute before she realized what it was. There was no clothing in sight, and when she glanced in the closets they were empty.

"She must have had clothes," she said. "She wasn't wearing any. At least not a dress," she added. "They think she was wearing a kimono or something of the sort. There ought to be a bag too, and a hat. Unless the police took them."

"Plenty of girls don't wear hats nowadays." This was Freda, beginning to enjoy herself.

Carol turned to them.

"There mustn't be any talk about this," she said. "I'll tell the police, but nobody else is to know. Do please be careful. It may be very important."

She locked the door behind her and took the key. No use worrying about fingerprints, she thought. Freda's would be on the doorknob, and almost anywhere else. She waited until they had started down the stairs and then went into her own room. The bed had been made up with sheets from the servants' linen closet, and was turned down ready for use. Her dressing case had been unpacked, and Freda had placed on the toilet table the photograph of Don in his flying helmet which she always carried with her.

She did not look at it, beyond seeing that it was there. After all, one remembered the dead. One could not go on loving them. What concerned her now was a mystery which only Lucy Norton could solve, and she could not see Lucy until her car was ready.

She bathed and dressed, changing her traveling clothes for a knitted suit, but she did not go downstairs right away. She went to the window and stood there, looking out at the bay. The tide was low, and the sea gulls were busy hunting for clams, the white ones the adults, the gray ones of this spring's hatching. Even here back from the water she could hear them squawking. Over to the left, beyond the fountain her grandmother had sent from Italy, and hidden by the trees, was the Burton house. For a minute she was tempted to go there, to see Major Dane and tell him about the yellow room. But his final words had drawn a definite line between them. She decided against it. It would have to be the police.

When she went downstairs, however, it was to hear a male voice in the hall, and to find that the press had already discovered her. The press itself was in the shape of a rather engaging youth, who gave her a nice smile and looked apologetic.

"Name's Starr," he said. "Just happened on this. Came over from the big town to get a story on the new fish cannery here, and found this. I'm sure sorry about it, Miss Spencer. You're pretty young to run into murder."

"I'm old enough not to give any interviews to the press," Carol said sharply.

"I'm not asking for an interview. I was just thinking. You and this other girl. Only she got the raw deal. She's dead."

"How do you know she was only a girl, Mr. Starr?"

"Saw the body," he said, and reached into his pocket for some folded yellow paper. "Age approximately twenty to twenty-five," he read. "Bleached blonde. Possibly married, as wedding ring on finger. Feet small, bedroom slippers originally blue. Silver fox jacket, no maker's name. Clothing under body not burned. Looks like red silk negligee. Underwear handmade." He looked at her. "Make any sense to you?"

Carol shook her head.

"Doesn't sound like anyone you know?"

"It sounds like everyone I know."

He stood looking over his notes.

"Where's her dress?" he said. "She didn't come here in a thin silk negligee, did she?"

"I don't know anything about it," Carol said. "I suppose the police looked over the house. If she left any clothes, they would know it."

He thought that over. He looked young and rather shocked, for all his businesslike manner.

"Well, look," he said. "She's in a wrapper and she's got a fur coat on. So she's cold. So she looks around for a blanket. So she goes to the closet, and maybe she's smoking. So she faints—maybe something scares her—and that starts the fire. How about it?"

"Is that what they think in the town? The police and the doctor?"

"Hell, no. That's my own idea. Just thought of it, in fact. Anyhow, it's out. The doc says she's got a fractured skull. Sure you don't know who it is?"

"I haven't really seen her. All I saw was somebody lying there."

"You didn't miss anything," he said gruffly.

He put the paper back in his pocket and picked up a rather battered hat.

"No interview," he assured her. "Just a bit of local color. You know, big house, summer people, first murder in town's history. The doc says it was probably kerosene. Maybe gasoline. Any about the place?"

"Gasoline?" she said with some bitterness. "We were out of it before we left last year. Even the matches were left in a closed jar, for fear of field mice."

He departed finally, saying that he left his car at the gate, and promising not to quote her on anything. She rather liked him, engaging grin and all.

6

Back at the house Dane was met by a glum and scowling Alex. Even the black patch over the socket from which he had lost an eye looked peevish.

"What you been doing to that leg, sir?" he demanded.

"Nothing that a rest can't help. How about lunch?"

Alex refused to be conciliated.

"Maybe you don't want to go back to your job," he said, forgetting the "sir." "Just a smell of murder and you forget there's a war."

"Oh, go to hell," Dane said wearily. "Get me a drink and something to eat. How do you know there's a murder?"

"I buy our food in the town," Alex said, still sulky.

"Know any details?"

"Cracked on the head. Killer tried to burn the body." He added the "sir" here, and Dane grinned.

"Go on," he said. "Get me a highball, and don't be too stingy with the whisky."

He limped out to the porch and sat down. Alex was right, of course. He had a big job to go back to, and the stairs at Crestview hadn't helped his leg any. He put it up on a chair and fell into thought. He was still absorbed when Alex brought the Scotch. He roused, however.

"Sit down, Alex, and pour yourself a drink. I want to talk to you. We've got a case on our hands, and I'm damned if I know what it is. Except it's murder."

Alex fixed his drink and sat down, his one eye showing complete disapproval.

"If you'll excuse me, sir," he said, "I don't think it's any business of yours. Unless it's a spy case."

"No. I'm pretty sure it has nothing to do with the war. No spies. No escaped PW. Somebody wanted a girl out of the way, that's all. As far as they can tell, she wasn't local. Nobody is missing from around here. Now, how did she get into that house next door? And why? The family wasn't there. Only the Norton woman, and you know her story."

Alex stirred.

"I still don't see why you want to look into it, sir."

"I suppose it's because it's something to do. God knows I've been bored for months, hospitals, doctors, nurses and—What do you know about the Norton woman? Any family?"

"Only herself and Joe. That's her husband."

"No wealthy connections? Anyone likely to visit her dressed up in an expensive fur jacket? That sort of thing?"

Alex thought it more than improbable, and Dane shifted to the Spencers. Where Alex got his information he never knew. Perhaps it was because of his long job on the police force before the war. But Alex knew quite a bit: Carol's engagement to Don Richardson and the colonel's defiant refusal to believe in his son's death; Greg's fine record in the war in spite of his reputation as a souse, to use Alex's own words; and even Elinor's marriage to Hilliard, with all that it entailed.

Dane was thoughtful when he finished.

"So we wash out the Nortons," he said. "And apparently we wash out the village too. That seems to put it up to the family, doesn't it?"

Dane ate his lunch on the porch, as absent-mindedly as he regarded now and then the view of the bay below him. He was puzzled. Jim Mason had taken a hasty survey of the bedrooms at Crestview and reported no clothing anywhere. But if the girl had been staying at the house her clothes should have been there. That left two alternatives: she had not been staying in the house, or she had, in which case there had been probably three days to dispose of what she had worn.

When Alex came back for his tray he had lit his pipe, the cigarette he had found in Maggie's garbage can on the table in front of him.

"Suppose," he said, "you wanted to get rid of a girl's clothes and had plenty of time to do it. How would you go about it?"

Alex pondered.

"How about burning them? Plenty of furnaces around."

Dane shook his head.

"No good. Too much stuff in women's clothes that won't burn, zippers, hooks and eyes, God knows what. Nails from shoes, too. You ought to know that."

"Well, if it was me," Alex said, "and I had plenty of time I'd ship them somewhere. Hard to trace that way. I remember once—"

"I see. It's worth thinking about. You might check on that today. See if the express people sent something of the sort from any of the families around here the last of the week or today. The office is closed Saturday and today's truck doesn't leave until four o'clock. Try to get a look at what they have." He got up. "I'm going to the hospital. I'll drop you off in town."

While Alex cleaned up, Dane surveyed the possibilities. The nearest was Rockhill, the Ward property. But the Wards were elderly and lively largely in retirement, and Colonel Richardson, on the road below, was in the same category. The Dalton place was beyond the Richardson cottage facing the water, and with the Burton property, where he himself was staying, he had about completed the circuit.

None of them, he thought wryly, was likely to be involved in a cold-blooded crime. And the mystery was increased by the disappearance of the clothing. If she had been staying at Crestview, why in the name of all that was sensible hide it, since it had evidently been the intention to burn the house?

He climbed stiffly into the car when Alex brought it around, and that gentleman regarded him with a disapproving eye.

"You ought to be in bed, sir," he said. "What's the use my working on that leg if you don't take care of it?"

"I'll rest it later. I won't be long at the hospital."

Nor was he. Lucy Norton, according to the office there, was not so well and was allowed no visitors. If he suspected Floyd's large hand in this he said nothing. And Alex, picked up in the village, simply reported no soap.

"Nothing going out," he said. "Ladies in the town packed a barrel early last week for Greece. Nothing since."

Dane had been right about Floyd. By noon that day he had already traced the girl's arrival Friday morning, and after lunch he called a meeting of four men in his office: Dr. Harrison, Jim Mason, a lieutenant from the State Police, and Floyd himself. On the desk lay a bundle of partially burned clothing, and Floyd indicated it with a stubby finger.

"Well, there it is," he said. "No marks, no anything. You gentlemen got any ideas?"

Nobody apparently had, and leaning back in his chair Floyd told what he had learned of her movements after her arrival.

"One thing's sure," he said. "She set out for Crestview and she got there. She wasn't followed. She was the only passenger on the bus that got in at six-thirty that morning. So whoever killed her was around here somewhere already."

There was no dissenting voices, and he got up.

"I'm going to the hospital," he said. "Lucy Norton knows something, and she's going to talk or I'll know why."

But Lucy in her hospital bed, her leg in a cast and her hands clenched under the bedclothes, could apparently tell only of the hand that had extinguished her candle, and that someone had rushed past her and knocked her down. Her shock when she was told of the body in the closet was genuine to the point of terror.

"A body?" she said weakly. "I don't believe you. You mean somebody at Crestview was found dead?"

"That's what I'm telling you. A woman. A young woman. Somebody knocked her on the head and killed her, then tried to burn her body. Probably the night you fell down the stairs."

Put to her thus tactfully, Lucy went into a fit of convulsive weeping. The chief waited impatiently, but when he left he still knew nothing more. But he was satisfied at least that there had been no fire while she was lying at the foot of the stairs.

"I'd have smelled anything burning," she said, sniffling. "I didn't break my nose when I fell."

"Maybe you passed out."

"I guess I did for a while. But I'd have smelled it when I came to, wouldn't I?"

She was certain, too, that all the doors were locked that night. She accounted for the front door by the fact that whoever knocked her down must have left it open. But she was still semihysterical when he left her. After that she lay still for a long time, her eyes closed and her hands still clenched. When a nurse came in she roused herself. The story of the murder had reached the hospital, and Floyd's order as he left that Lucy was to see no one and communicate with no one had left it in a state of quivering excitement.

"I want to see Miss Spencer, Miss Carol Spencer," Lucy said feebly. "She hasn't any telephone. Maybe you'd send her a telegram."

"The doctor thought you ought to be quiet today, Mrs. Norton. I'm sure she'll be as soon as she can."

So that was it, Lucy thought helplessly. They wouldn't let her see Carol, she wouldn't know anything, and the police—

She lay still in her bed, her face desperate. She couldn't even warn Carol, and they probably would keep Joe out too. Not that Joe knew anything either, but she might have sent a message by him. Only—murder! She shivered and closed her eyes.

It was after that visit of Floyd's to the hospital that he sent for Carol to view the body and attempt to identify it. It was in the local mortuary, and lacking a morgue, it had been packed in ice and covered with rubber sheets. She took only one look, gasped and rushed into the air.

"That was cruel and unnecessary," she said when she got her breath. "You know I couldn't recognize her. Nobody could."

"Well," he said, "at least you can say that at the inquest. Sorry, Miss Carol. It had to be done."

He did not take her home at once. He drove around to his office and let her out there.

"One or two things we got might help," he said. "Won't hurt to look at them. They won't bother you any," when he saw her face. "Just some stuff she was wearing."

He sat down behind the desk and opening a drawer took out a small box which he emptied onto the blotter. There was a pair of artificial pearl earrings of the stud type, somewhat scorched and rather large, and a ring. He picked up the ring and held it out.

"Might be a wedding ring, eh?" he said, watching her with sharp eyes.

"Possibly. I wouldn't know."

He let her go then, still suspicious, still hoping to break the mystery through her. Then he got busy on the telephone.

"I want the phones put back in the Spencer house this afternoon," he said. "Get a jump on, you fellows. This is a hurry job."

"It will have to go to the War Production Board, chief. Make out your application and we'll send it in."

"The hell you will," Floyd shouted. "You get three or four instruments out of that shed behind the hotel where you've got them stored, or I'll arrest the bunch of you for obstructing justice."

The instruments went in that afternoon, and Floyd walked around to where Bessie Content sat before her switchboard.

"Listen, Bessie," he said. "I want you to do something for me, and keep your pretty mouth shut. Make a record of all calls from the Spencer place, and—you don't have to be deaf, do you?"

Bessie smiled with her pretty mouth.

"It gets awfully dull here sometimes," she said, "and my hearing's good, if I do say it."

After telling her to notify the night operator, Floyd went back to his office and again pored over the charred fragments on his desk. When he went home he took with him the fragment of red silk found under the body.

"Ever see a nightgown this color?" he asked his wife.

"No, and I never hope to."

She examined it carefully, going to a window to do so.

"It's good silk. That's hard to get these days. It used to come from China, you know. And it's sewed by hand," she said. "It's been expensive."

"From China, eh?" said Floyd, and lapsed into silence.

Carol in the meantime had not been able to go to the hospital. By the time her car was ready the news had spread, and to a summer colony shrunken by the war, it came as a welcome excitement in what had promised to be a dull summer. Telephones buzzed, where there were any. At the club, usually deserted in the afternoons, small groups of people gathered, and at teatime a few who had know the Spencers well drove or walked up the hill to commiserate with Carol and—if possible—to get a glimpse of the closet.

Carol received them as best she could, the elderly Wards, old-fashioned and solicitous, Louise Stimson, the attractive young widow who had built a smart white house near the club, Marcia Dalton, the Crowells, and so on. She managed tea and Scotch for them, looking young and tired as she did so, but she could tell them nothing.

Actually the first real information she got came from Peter Crowell, a burly red-faced man with a mouselike wife.

"Well," he said. "I guess they've traced that corpse of yours, Carol. Part of the way anyhow."

The Wards looked pained, and Carol startled.

"Got it from Floyd himself," Crowell went on, enjoying the sensation he was making. "She got off the Boston train at six-thirty Friday morning and took the bus for here. Quite a looker, I understand. Quite a dresser too. White hat, silver fox coat, an overnight bag, and a big pocketbook. The bus driver says she acted queer when she got off. Looked sort of lost, he said. She asked for the drugstore. Said she wanted to telephone. He told her it was still closed, but the last he saw of her she was going that way."

"Tell them about the bag, Pete," said Ida, his wife.

He took a sip of his Scotch and soda.

"That's funny," he said. "The bus driver saw initials on it, only he can't remember them. There were three, and I understand they didn't find it in the closet. You didn't see it, did you?"

Carol's voice was slightly unsteady.

"I didn't look, Peter. All I saw—"

The Wards got up abruptly, and old Mrs. Ward took Carol's hand and held it.

"I'm sure," she said, looking around the room, "that Carol would prefer not discussing what has happened." She turned back to her. "I'm sorry, my dear. If you can to stay with us for the next few days we'd be delighted to have you. That is really why we came."

Carol felt grateful to the point of tears. She managed to smile.

"You're both more than kind. I'd love to, but the servants wouldn't stay here alone. Not after what's happened."

She went out to the door with them. A graveled path connected the two properties, broken only by the lane leading up the hill. She walked to it with them, asking about Terry, their grandson who was flying in the Pacific, and telling them about Greg. They looked much older, she thought, and rather feeble. The war was hard on people like that. She felt saddened, and this was not helped when on her return she learned that the telephones were in again.

She would have to call Newport now. There was no longer any excuse.

The others drifted away slowly, until only Louise Stimson and Marcia Dalton were left. Peter Crowell's departing speech was characteristic.

"Any objection to my looking at that closet?" he said.

"The police have sealed it, Peter."

He looked annoyed.

"Well," he said, "soon as you can, get it opened and have it painted. Then just forget about it. What's it got to do with you anyhow? A strange girl gets herself killed in it. You don't know her. So what?"

She went back to Louise and Marcia. They were smoking, and she lit a cigarette and sat down. She had a definite impression that each was determined to outstay the other, Louise with an amused smile, Marcia's horselike face and tall thin body rather grim.

"So you've met Jerry Dane," Louise said. "Interesting type."

"I wouldn't know. Is he?"

"Definitely yes." She glanced at Marcia. "A wounded hero, isn't he? And good-looking too. Why on earth come here to recuperate?"

"There's no mystery about that," Marcia said tartly. "The Burtons offered him their house. At least," she added, glancing at Louise, "Carol has managed to meet him. That's more than you can say."

Louise got up.

"I didn't have a body around," she said cheerfully. "There's still hope, of course. Most things come in threes, don't they?"

She left on that, but Marcia stayed, planted solidly in her chair, with her thin legs stuck out in front of her. Carol knew her well, and she relaxed somewhat.

"What do you think of Jerry Dane?" Marcia asked abruptly.

"I haven't really thought of him at all. I haven't had time."

Marcia shrugged.

"Well, he's definitely a mystery. We've all asked him to dinner. We've asked him for bridge. We've even, God help us, asked him for backgammon and gin rummy. But nothing doing. He's still an invalid, and goes to bed early. An invalid! He climbs hills like a goat. I've seen him myself."

"Maybe he doesn't like games," Carol said indifferently. "I hope you don't mind, Marcia, but I've had a long day."

Marcia got up, but she did not leave. She stood looking into the patio.

"I suppose this house is an architectural bastard," she said, "but I've always liked it. It's queer Elinor never comes here, isn't it?" She fixed Carol with shrewd eyes.

"She likes Newport better. That's all. It's easier for Howard to get there for weekends."

But she realized that Marcia had dragged in Elinor's name for a purpose, and she felt herself stiffening.

"It's queer," Marcia said, still watching her. "I thought I saw her car about two o'clock last Saturday morning. I'd know that car anywhere."

"That's ridiculous, Marcia."

"I suppose it is. I just thought I'd better tell you. Someone else may have seen it too, or thought so. It was going toward the railroad, and making sixty miles at least. I didn't think there was another car like it in the world."

"There must be. She hasn't been here. I know that. She was in New York."

"Well, if you're sure of that—I'm a Nurse's Aide, and I worked late at the hospital Friday night. When I got home I let that damned dog of mine out. He didn't come back, so I went after him. That's how it happened."

"It's absurd, Marcia. You saw a car. You didn't see Elinor in it, and she wasn't in it. She couldn't have been."

But she was not so sure. She knew the deadly sharpness of Marcia's eyes. She knew, too, how the story would grow if Marcia told it. It was Marcia herself who reassured her.

"I suppose I was mistaken," she said. "Anyhow no use starting talk. You know this place. Any summer colony, for that matter. I'm not telling it, Carol. You can count on me."

It was some time after she left before Carol could control her hands sufficiently to light a cigarette.

7

She called Elinor that evening, shutting herself in the library to do it. There was something reassuring in Elinor's matter-of-fact voice.

"Hello, Carol," she said. "I hear you've had some trouble there."

"You know about it?"

"The gentlemen of the press," Elinor said lightly. "I've been trying to get you for some time, but you know what long-distance is nowadays. I hope it hasn't been too bad."

"It's been bad enough. Does Mother know?"

"Not yet. Of course when the papers get it— Have they any idea who it is?"

"Not yet."

"Her clothes ought to tell them something."

"They haven't found her clothes. Look here, Elinor. I called you up to tell you something. Marcia Dalton says she saw your car here last Friday night, or Saturday morning. She's just told me."

There was a brief pause. Then Elinor laughed.

"Marcia's seeing things," she said. "Tell her I have a perfect alibi, and that I don't go around murdering people in the middle of the night."

"You did go to New York?"

"I hope the telephone operators along the line are enjoying this," Elinor said coldly. "For their benefit I'll tell you that I left my car in Providence on Friday, took a train to New York, stayed in our apartment that night, shopped all day Saturday, had dinner with my husband that evening and went to the theater afterwards."

"You stayed in your apartment?"

"Why not? The club was jammed. So was every hotel. What's the matter with you anyhow? Do I have to have an alibi?"

Carol felt foolish as Elinor rang off with her customary abruptness. Of course Marcia had been mistaken. What possible connection could Elinor in New York have with a murder on the Maine coast? Or, granting there was one, would she possibly have risked everything she prized so highly on such an excursion? Yet there remained the puzzling question of why the dead girl had come to Crestview, and why Lucy—if she knew about it—had let her stay.

Elinor *could* have made it. She could have come by car, arriving that night, gone back to Providence the same way, left her car there, and taken an early morning train to New York. Only why? Had the girl been Howard's mistress? His money laid him open to that sort of thing. But even then she could see Elinor's sheer disdain of a dirty business. She might leave him, demanding an enormous settlement, or she might choose to stay on and ignore the situation. But to connect her with a crime of passion was impossible.

Carol was still in the library when Jerry Dane tapped at the terrace door. She admitted him, and he looked down at her gravely.

"I'm afraid I was rude to you today," he said. "My leg was hurting damnably, and—well, I'm sorry. I won't do it again."

"It's all right," she told him. "I don't blame you for calling me one of the cumberers of the earth. I just can't help it, that's all. I have to look after my mother."

"Don't make me more abject than I am. I came to tell you I couldn't see Mrs. Norton. Did you?"

"No." She recited her day while he listened, about being compelled to look at the body and the things on Floyd's desk, and the fact that by the time her car was ready she could not go to the hospital. He had taken out a pipe and filled it, and as she talked she watched him. He was hard, she thought, the sort of man who in a war killed without scruple. But he was honest too. Honest and dependable, and she had to talk to someone or go mad.

"There's something else I ought to tell you," she said. "It happened here this afternoon, and it has bothered me a lot. There's no truth in it, of course, but it could cause trouble. Marcia Dalton claims to have seen my sister's car here the night Lucy was hurt and this girl was murdered."

"Have you called your sister?"

"Of course. She has an alibi. She was in New York that night. It's ridiculous, isn't it?"

"Naturally." His face remained impassive. "Is there anything else? Might as well clear the slate, you know."

"Well," she said, her voice doubtful. "I suppose I should have told the police before this, but I couldn't see Lucy, and the place has been full of people this afternoon." She looked at him apologetically. "I don't even like telling you, but I suppose I must."

"I see," he said patiently. "Just what is all this about?"

"It's about the yellow room, the room over this. Somebody had been staying there, and taken a bath."

His voice sharpened.

"Didn't the police look over the house?"

"I suppose they glanced in. They were looking for her clothes, weren't they? They wouldn't notice anything else. They probably thought Lucy Norton slept there. But the bed's been used, there's powder on the toilet table, and there are cigarette ashes on the floor. Lucy doesn't smoke, of course, and she slept in the service wing."

"And her clothes?"

"There were no clothes there when I saw it."

There was a longish pause. His pipe was dead, and he did not re-light it.

"They didn't find her clothes," he said at last. "I was here, you know. Mason came back empty-handed. But if she slept here she undressed here. The simplest answer is that whoever killed her took her clothes away so she wouldn't be identified. That and the fire— See here, Miss Spencer, do you still maintain that you have no idea who she was? Or why she was here?"

She shook her head.

"No to both," she said. "So far as I know I've never seen her before, or heard of her."

"Well, let's put it another way. Who knew you were coming back, and when?"

"Quite a lot of people. It was no secret."

"Isn't is possible she was waiting here to see you?"

"Why on earth would she? There's a hotel in town. Lots of people rent rooms, too. To come here, with the house cold and empty—"

"She did come, you see," he said, still patiently. "She came, or she was brought here after her death. What you say about the yellow room seems to indicate that she came. When she came is another matter. If she slipped in at night after Mrs. Norton had gone to bed it might explain some things."

"Explain what?"

"Explain why Mrs. Norton apparently knew nothing about her

being here." He got up. "Mind if I look at the yellow room? Unless you've had it cleaned."

"It's the way I found it. The door's locked."

He nodded his approval, and they went up the stairs together.

The yellow room was as she had left it. She noticed that he touched nothing when he went in. He inspected the bed, where a spot of lipstick showed on one of the sheets. He bent over and looked at the cigarette ash on the floor. And he stood for some time at the bathroom door.

"Was this left as it is?" he asked rather sharply. "Soap and towels, and so on, when you left last year?"

"Soap? I hadn't noticed. I suppose Lucy puts such things away when she closes the house."

"Then this girl seems to have known her way around pretty well," he said grimly. "Either that, or Mrs. Norton knew she was here. What about these towels? Are they from the servants' rooms?"

"They're guest towels. That's queer. Lucy must have given them to her."

He turned to a window and stood there, looking out. There was still some light, and a breeze was covering the bay with small white-capped waves. Except for a few fishing boats the harbor was empty, and overhead an army plane was making its way to some inland field. He was not thinking of the harbor, however, or even of the war at that moment.

"Floyd is going to trace her further, if he can," he said, without turning. "Whether anyone in the town saw her. Whether she made any inquiries to find this place. He's a small-town policeman, but he's nobody's fool."

He was still at the window when they heard a car chugging up the hill. He put out the light quickly.

"Sounds like his car," he said. "Better get downstairs. And let me do the talking if you can."

They were in the library and Dane was filling his pipe when Nora announced the callers. They came in rather portentously, Floyd, Dr. Harrison, the state trooper, and still another man in plain clothes. Floyd was carrying a bundle under his arm.

The chief introduced the strangers, Lieutenant Wylie and Mr. Campbell.

"Mr. Campbell is the district attorney," he said impressively. "Seems like we're getting famous all at once."

"That's hardly the word," said Mr. Campbell dryly, as Floyd placed his package on the center table. "We don't like to disturb you, Miss Spencer, but we're trying to identify the—this woman. It seems likely that she had a reason for coming here. After all"—he cleared his throat—"there are a good many houses here not being opened for the summer. It seems strange her body was found in this one."

It was Dane who answered that. He was standing by the fire, looking interested but nothing more.

"Probably most of them are boarded up," he said. "This one happened to be open."

"With a caretaker in it," said Mr. Campbell. "Why take a chance on a thing like that?"

Carol asked them to sit down, and offered them cigarettes. Lieutenant Wylie produced a pipe and asked if she objected. Then Mr. Campbell cleared his throat.

"I need not stress the need of identification of this woman, Miss Spencer," he said. "I believe you have said you don't know her."

"I didn't say that," she protested. "How can I tell? I hardly saw her, and when I did—I can't think of anyone who would come here, or why they would be killed here. All I know is that she *was* here."

Her voice sounded strained, and the doctor smiled at her.

"No need to worry, Carol," he said. "It's only a matter of identification. She may have been killed outside and her body brought here."

"But it wasn't," she said, half hysterically. "She had slept here. Go up and see for yourselves. She had slept in the yellow room."

If she had tossed a bomb into the room, the reaction could hardly have been greater. They poured out into the hall and up the stairs, and Carol found Dane's hand on her arm.

"Better not say I've been up there," he said cautiously. "Let them look for themselves."

She nodded. Dr. Harrison knew the yellow room, and the others were already inside when they got there. The place spoke for itself, the bed, the toilet table, the tub in the bathroom, and the district attorney looked at Floyd.

"Missed this this morning, didn't you?" he said unpleasantly.

"How the hell could I know Jim Mason hasn't the sense of a louse?" Floyd said. "I had my hands full as it was." He turned to Carol. "When did you find out she'd slept here?"

"One of the maids saw it."

"When was that?" he asked.

"Around noon, I think."

"And you didn't report it?"

"I thought someone would be back. I had no telephone, and the house was full of people all afternoon. I locked the door so it wouldn't be disturbed."

He eyed her suspiciously.

"It wasn't locked just now, Miss Spencer."

The lieutenant had opened the closet door.

"Nothing here," he said laconically. "Unless—"

He was a tall man. He ran an exploratory hand over the closet shelf, and when he brought it out it was holding a small white hat. It was a gay little hat, crisp and new, and all the eyes in the room were turned on Carol.

"Belong to you?" the lieutenant inquired.

"No," she said faintly. "I never saw it before."

She sat down on a chair inside the door. More than anything else the little hat had brought the real tragedy of the murder home to her. She felt dizzy and her heart was pounding furiously. She did not realize that Floyd was standing over her until he spoke.

"You missed it, didn't you, Miss Spencer?"

"Missed it? I never saw it."

He looked triumphantly around the room.

"I'm wondering," he said, "just what became of the rest of her clothes. She came here in a black dress and a pair of pumps, and she had a purse and an overnight bag. She undressed in this room. Look at that hat. Now what I want to know is who disposed of them, and how?"

Carol stared at him.

"Why would I do it? When she was killed I was at my sister's in Newport. I didn't come into this room until Freda reported it to me. And I didn't even need to tell you about it. I did. Isn't that enough?"

"Somebody got those clothes," he said doggedly.

Sheer indignation brought her to her feet.

"Why don't you go down and look in the furnace?" she said indignantly. "That's where I would burn them, isn't it? Go on down, all of you, sift the ashes—that's what you do, isn't it? And I hope you get good and dirty!"

"Don't you worry about me getting dirty," Floyd said grimly, and after locking the door led the way downstairs again.

In the library once more the state trooper placed the hat beside the package on the table, and Floyd went over what he had so far discovered. The girl had got off the bus at half past six or thereabouts on Friday morning, June the sixteenth. She had asked the driver for the drugstore, but he had told her it would not be open yet. After that nobody saw her in the town that early morning until at seven-thirty or so Mr. Allison, who owned the local Five-&-Ten, saw a girl in a white hat, a fur jacket and a black dress sitting in a public park near the bandstand. When he looked again, she was gone.

After that the trail picked up somewhat. She had had a cup of coffee at Sam's hamburger stand when it opened at eight, and asked for a telephone book. Apparently she did not find what she wanted, and Sam had told her half the telephones in town had been taken out. She had not seemed worried, however. She had merely said a walk would do her good, and asked the direction of Shore Drive, which led to Crestview.

Sam had said she was pretty, about twenty-five or so, and very well dressed. What he actually said, Carol learned later, was that she "looked like some of the summer crowd," and that he didn't think she would walk far "in them spike-heeled shoes she wore."

None of the taxi men in town had seen her. Apparently she had walked to her destination, whatever that was.

Dane did not interrupt. He listened intently, but when the district attorney made a gesture toward the package he made a protest.

"Is that necessary?" he asked. "Miss Spencer has had a bad day. She looks exhausted."

"We have to do what we can, major. There may be something here she will recognize."

It was Floyd who opened the bundle, carefully saving the string, his big fingers working at the knots. Opened and spread out on the table was what was left of the short fur jacket, badly burned, the scorched pair of bedroom slippers, and a few scraps of cloth, one of them red silk or rayon. Over all was the odor of burned fur, and Dane quickly lit a cigarette and gave it to Carol.

It helped somewhat. She was able to face the table, even to go to it. Floyd was holding up the scrap of red material and once more all the faces were turned to her.

"What's this, Miss Spencer?" Floyd asked.

"I wouldn't know. It looks—it might be part of a kimono or a dressing gown. It wouldn't be a slip."

"That's what my wife says." He looked around the room. "So what? So she was undressed. She wasn't expecting any trouble. She undressed and went to bed in that room upstairs, and what happened to her happened to her in this house."

Dane spoke for the first time.

"That doesn't follow," he said. "She might have gone outside, for some purpose."

"What difference does it make?" said Floyd belligerently. "She's dead, isn't she?"

"It might change things somewhat." Dane picked up one of the slippers and shook it. A pine needle slipped out and lay on the desk, and Floyd flushed angrily. "Whether she was killed in this house or not," Dane said casually, "she was outside that night. What does Mrs. Norton say?"

"That's my business," Floyd said gruffly, and proceeded to tie up the package again, crushing the white hat in with the rest and fastening it carefully with the string he had saved. They left after that, all except Dane, but following a colloquy at the front door the state trooper came back to the library.

"I'm afraid I'm going to bother you some more, Miss Spencer," he said apologetically. "I'd like to look over the house, if you don't mind, and . . ." He hesitated, then smiled. "The district attorney thinks it would be a good idea to clean out the furnace. It's lighted, I suppose."

Carol had rallied. She even managed to smile at him.

"Of course," she said, "I had to burn up the evidence somehow. It's been going all day."

He grinned back at her.

"Some things don't burn, you know," he said cheerfully. "You'd be surprised how many. Nails out of high-heeled pumps, snaps off clothes, buttons, initials off bags, all sorts of things. You sift them out of the ashes and there you are."

The last they saw of him he was going lightly up the stairs, and for some time they heard him moving about in the yellow room overhead.

Dane was thoughtful.

"Just remember this," he said. "Even if they find those things have been burned in the furnace, it doesn't connect you with the case."

"You think they will?"

"It's possible, if not particularly intelligent. Of course Mrs. Norton's accident may have prevented it. Whoever did it couldn't know she'd broken her leg. They might have expected her to run screaming out of the house."

He left soon after that, telling her to lock her door but that otherwise she was safe enough. "There will be troopers in the basement all night," he said. "Better get all the sleep you can. I may need you to-morrow."

With which cryptic statement he departed, going out through the door to the terrace and motioning her to lock it behind him.

8

Carol did not sleep much, although she felt relaxed. Through the old-fashioned register in the floor came the muffled sound of men's voices from the furnace cellar, and she learned in the morning that the lieutenant and one of his men had spent most of the night there. They had made a thorough job of it, emptying the furnace itself and coming up to wash looking as if a bomb had burned them. But all they found was the melted remains of what looked like a teaspoon, which Maggie had reported as missing since the year before.

The word had gone out by that time. Floyd may have lacked a camera, but he knew police procedure. He had sent out a description of the girl to the Missing Persons Bureau and by teletype all over the country. The newspapers had been busy too, and evidently Elinor had been unable to keep them from her mother. Carol, still keeping up largely on coffee, was called to the telephone to hear Mrs. Spencer's voice, shaken and hysterical:

"What sort of a mess have you got yourself into? The papers are dreadful."

Carol controlled herself with difficulty.

"It was done before I got here, mother. Please don't worry."

"It's easy for you to say that. When I think of the notoriety, the disgrace of the whole thing—I'll never live in that house again. Never. And I want you to leave, Carol. Do you hear me? Come back here at once."

"I'll have to wait for the inquest, mother."

"Good heavens, are they having an inquest? Why?"

Carol finally lost her patience.

"Because it's a murder," she said. "Because they think we have something to do with it. And I'm not so sure but what we had."

She rang off, feeling ashamed for her outburst but somewhat relieved by it.

There was a new development that day, one which seemed to justify her last statement to her mother, although it was some time before she learned about it. On that same morning, Tuesday, June twentieth, a caller appeared at the East Sixty-seventh Precinct station in New York City. He looked uneasy, and he carried a morning paper in his hand. The desk sergeant was reading a paper, too. He looked up over it.

"Anything I can do for you?"

"I'm not sure. It's about this murder up in Maine. I think maybe I saw the girl, right here in town."

"Plenty of people think that. Had five or six already."

But later the visitor's story proved interesting, to say the least.

He was the doorman at the apartment house on Park Avenue where the Spencers lived, and on the morning the family had left for the country, a girl had called. She had asked for Miss Carol Spencer, and seemed greatly disappointed when told she had gone. What had taken him to the station house was that the description fitted this girl, white hat, fur jacket and all.

"She acted like she didn't know just what to do," the police reported his statement. "I thought maybe she'd just got off a train. She had a little bag with her, as well as a pocketbook. I don't know what she did do, either. The elevator man was off, and just then the bell rang. When I came down again she was gone."

That, he said, had been about ten o'clock the previous Thursday.

Carol did not learn this until later. She was worried and upset that morning. She had called the hospital, to learn that Lucy Norton was allowed no visitors, and to suspect that the police were keeping her incommunicado until the inquest. Also both the younger girls were threatening to leave, Freda declaring that she had seen a man in the grounds from her window after she had put out the light the night before. Only dire threats by Maggie that the police would follow and bring them back kept them at all.

She was unpacking her trunk when Nora came up to tell her Colonel Richardson was downstairs, and she went down reluctantly. He was standing by the library fire, and looking shocked.

"My dear girl!" he said. "I just heard, or I'd have come before. How dreadful for you."

"It's all rather horrible. We don't even know who she was."

"So I understand. I learned only just now, when I went to the village. But surely Lucy Norton would know. I saw her husband bring her that morning."

"The police aren't letting her see anyone."

He considered that. She thought he looked very tired, and his lips had a bluish tinge. His heart was not too good, and he had probably walked up the hill.

"Well, thank God it doesn't concern you," he said. "I'll not keep you, my dear. And don't worry too much. Floyd is an excellent man."

He left soon after. She went with him to the door and watched him start down the drive, leaning rather heavily on his stick. When she turned to go in she saw Dane. He was still in slacks and sweater, and he was carefully surveying the shape of the hill behind the house. When the colonel had disappeared he walked over to the drive and, stopping, examined the grass border beside it.

He straightened and grinned at her.

"Hello," he said. "Colonel know anything?"

"No. He'd just heard."

He lit a cigarette and limped over to her.

"How about helping me with a little job this morning?" he inquired. "I'm no bird dog, with this leg. I could use an assistant."

"What sort of job?"

"Oh, just hither and yon," he said vaguely. "Know if anybody tramped around this drive lately?"

"Outside of a half dozen men I don't think of anybody."

"Up the hill, I mean."

"Oh, that?" She looked up the hill. It was heavily overgrown with shrubbery, and on the crest was an abandoned house, gray and forlorn in the morning light. "I wouldn't know. I don't think so."

"How about the tool house? That's it up there, isn't it?"

"There's a path to it. Anyhow George Smith is in the hospital. He hasn't been around lately."

"Well, someone's been up that hill lately. The ground's dry. There hasn't been any rain for weeks. But the faucet for the garden hose has dripped in one place, and somebody stepped in it."

"That doesn't mean a thing," she said. "The deer sometimes come down at night."

"The deer don't wear flat rubber-heeled shoes," he said shortly.

"I'm afraid I don't know what you mean."

"Well, look," he said rather impatiently. "According to Alex, those troopers didn't find anything in the furnace last night. So there are several alternatives. Her clothes were burned elsewhere, they were shipped out of town—which they weren't—or they're hidden some-place."

"And you think they are hidden?"

"Hidden. Possibly buried. Look back, Miss Spencer. Things didn't go according to schedule. Lucy Norton wakened. That was a bad break. Then she fell down the stairs. That gave whoever did it a bit of time, but not much. And there was a lot of stuff to dispose of, the woman's clothes, her pocketbook, and her overnight bag. How far could the killer travel with all that? With air wardens patrolling for lights, the fire watchers looking for fires ever since the drought? Not to mention lovers on back lanes like the one over there."

"I see. You think the things are on the hill."

"I think it's possible. That's all."

"But if they meant to burn the house, why bother with them at all?"

"Remember what I said about Lucy. There wasn't a chance to set a fire that night. It was done later. It had to be."

They started slowly up the hill, beginning at the leaking pipe and being careful not to step on the mark he had discovered. It was small, either from a woman's flat shoe or from that of a rather undersized man. There were no prints beyond it. The hill stretched up, dry and dusty, and before long Carol's slacks were covered with sandburs and her stockings ruined. Dane did not move directly. He circled right and left, but when they reached the deserted house above neither of them had found anything. Dane sat down abruptly and rubbed his leg.

"Damn the thing," he said irritably. "I'll get hell from Alex for this."

He gave her a cigarette and lit one himself.

"You might call this a preliminary search," he said. "They're not on top of the ground. They may be under it."

"Buried?"

"Maybe. It's been done, you know. The idea is to lift a shrub, say, and dig a hole. After that you replant the shrub and pray for rain." He gave his slightly bitter smile. "Someone around here may be watching the sky this very minute, hoping for rain," he said. "Pleasant thought, isn't it?"

He got up and dusted off his slacks.

"I don't like your being in that house alone," he said abruptly. "Oh, I know. It's all over, and you're a damned attractive girl and nobody would want to hurt you. So was that other girl, remember. But I was a fool to bring you up on this hill. If anybody gets the idea that you're looking for something here—There's one thing to remember about murder. It's the first one that's hard.''

"I ought to be safe enough. We haven't found anything."

"That's not what I said."

They went down the hill, this time by way of the tool house, and outside it he stopped.

"Mind if I go in?" he asked.

"It's probably locked."

It was not locked, however, George's appendicitis attack had probably been sudden. Dane opened the door and went inside. It was orderly in the extreme, a table with an old oilcloth covering, a chair, a shelf with a hit-or-miss collection of dishes, and around the walls garden implements in tidy rows, an electric lawn mower, rakes, spades, wicker brooms, and coils of hose.

"Neat fellow, George," he said, and looked around him. "About the way he left it last fall. Except—" He stopped over something, but did not touch it. "Come in," he said. "It looks as though we may be right, after all."

What he had found was a spade. It was deeply encrusted with clay, and a few dried leaves were still stuck to it. Carol stared down at it.

"You think they were buried with this?"

"There's a good chance, isn't there? In that case whoever buried them knew about this tool house. Knew where it was and what was in it. Interesting, isn't it? Don't touch it. There may be prints on it."

Carol did not hear him. She was standing in the doorway, looking at the shelf, her eyes incredulous.

"There's Mother's Lowestoft tea set," she said slowly. "And Father's picture, and the sampler Granny did when she was a little girl."

"Maybe George liked them!"

"You don't understand." She was fairly drugged with amazement. "There were all in the house last fall. I don't understand. George wouldn't touch them, or Lucy. It looks as though someone meant to save them."

She reached up for the china, and Dane slapped her hands smartly.

"Don't touch," he said. "You've got to learn this game, my girl, and it isn't a pretty one."

She was still bewildered.

"I wonder," she said. "Freda says she saw a man in the grounds last night. Do you think he was after these? It sounds silly, doesn't it?"

He did not think it sounded silly. He thought it sounded rather sinister, in fact. But he said nothing. He found a battered tin tray and using his handkerchief to move them he placed the china, the photograph, and the framed sampler on it. Then, tucking the spade under his arm and remarking that he felt like a moving van, he left her, taking a short cut through the trees to the Burton house and grinning when he saw Alex's face. He put the tray down on the living-room table and eyed it lovingly.

"What's Tim Murphy doing these days?" he inquired.

Alex rallied.

"Not so much, sir. You know the private detective business. It's kind of up and down."

"Good," Dane said cheerfully. "Let's hope it's down. I think we need him here, Alex. Better see if you can locate him. And don't call from the village. I have an idea Floyd has the telephones pretty well tied up."

Alex looked rebellious, but Dane ignored it.

"Tell him to take the night train from Boston if he can make it," he said. "You can meet him tomorrow morning with the car. And have him bring a camera. I want the prints on this stuff."

"Isn't that Floyd's business?"

Dane's strong thin face hardened.

"Listen," he said harshly. "I'm making it my business, and I'm working fast. There's a girl over there who may not be safe, and I can't bother with small-town police just now. Get that, and keep your mouth shut. Tell Tim to bring some old clothes too, the worse the better. He may have to do some gardening."

This idea cheered Alex so enormously that he made an excellent imitation of an omelet for lunch, singing over his frying pan as he did so.

Carol did not tell Maggie about her discovery in the tool house. She felt tired and discouraged. The mystery was deepening, and a second attempt to see Lucy brought no results. The hospital reported over the telephone that she was still not allowed visitors.

Because she was weary she did something she had not done since she came. She used the elevator to go upstairs, and it was in the elevator that she found something. She had not turned on the light, but she felt something under her foot as it slowly climbed, and reaching down felt for it. It was only a bobby pin, so she held it indifferently until she reached her room.

There she glanced at it. It was a pale color, and there was a long hair caught in it. She felt rather sick as she looked at it, for the hair was blond, and she was certain it had belonged to the murdered girl.

She put it on her toilet table, and lay down on the chaise longue. She did not realize that it had any significance, except that the girl had at one time or another been in the elevator. And she had not much time to think about it. Nora reported a message that the inquest would be held on Thursday, and that she was to attend. But there was a second message, which filled her with dread. Colonel Richardson hoped she would dine with him that night.

She had known it must happen. Ever since Don's plane had crashed into the sea she had had these solitary meals with his father, here in Maine last summer, once or twice in New York when he was on his way to Florida or coming back from there. Always she dreaded them, his obstinate refusal to accept his son's death, his determined cheerfulness and plans for her future—and Don's.

Nevertheless, she sent word that she would go, and getting up drearily hunted out a dinner dress and sent it down to be pressed. She did not lie down again. She pulled a chair to the window and sat there looking out.

Could Elinor have been in Bayside when Marcia claimed to have seen her? And if so, why? She went over Elinor's conduct at Newport. She had certainly been unlike herself. She did not often have headaches, yet she had spent one whole afternoon and evening shut away with one. And there was the time when Carol had found her at the safe in her bedroom. She had been surprised, not too pleasantly.

She knew Elinor through and through. Behind her lovely face was determination and a certain hardness. If she cared for anyone it was for Greg. But if Howard was threatening her position and security she might go to any length to preserve them. Still, Elinor and murder!

She tried to think clearly. If the girl had come deliberately to the house it had been to see someone. Not Lucy. Surely not Lucy. Then it was either her mother or herself, or both. But what story had she told, that Lucy Norton had put her in the yellow room? It must have been good, for Lucy to accept a stranger. For a moment she wondered about Greg, then she dismissed him. He had been away for a year, and he was deeply in love with Virginia. Turn things about as she would she came back to Elinor, Elinor who would have known how her mother valued the tea set and the other things now in the tool house.

Having reached that point she picked up the telephone and called long-distance; and Bessie at her switchboard in the village pricked up her ears.

She got Elinor without trouble.

"I want you to come up here," she said without preamble. "I'm not taking this thing alone, and the inquest is on Thursday."

"Don't be ridiculous." Elinor's voice was sharp. "Why on earth should I come? Anyhow, we're giving a dinner that night. I couldn't possibly get away."

"A dinner? Who for? Greg?"

"Greg's in New York, and Mother's having a fit. But he has no idea of going to Maine. I know that. Why don't you close the house and go back home? Mother won't go to Crestview now, and she loathes it here."

"Aren't you forgetting something?" Carol said tartly. "We've had a murder here. I can't leave. You'd better come, Elinor. Your name may be dragged into this yet."

"If you mean that story of Marcia's, don't be a fool. You know Marcia."

"I do. And I know you could have been here. You'd better bring your alibi with you."

Elinor laughed, without mirth.

"I suppose you know that that girl was asking for you in New York. The doorman reported it to the police this morning. That leaves us all involved, doesn't it?"

"The more reason for you to come."

There was a brief silence. Carol could almost see Elinor, her active mind weighing the pros and cons of the situation. When she spoke again she had evidently decided.

"I dare say the telephone operator will testify if Marcia doesn't," she said. "You've certainly given her plenty to think about. I suppose I'll have to come. It's absurd, of course. I can take the train Wednesday night. You'd better meet me."

"I'll send a taxi," Carol said shortly. "And listen, Elinor. Don't bring your maid. I can't take care of her, and it's quiet here anyhow. She'd be bored to death."

"Quiet!" said Elinor. "You don't sound quiet." She rang off, and Carol went back to her chair. Her room usually quieted her, with its picture window looking out over the water, its dusty rose walls, its French blue furniture and white rug. It had been an oasis of peace, too, after the shock of Don's death. Now she glanced at his picture. Incredible that he was gone, she thought, and that she was here alone. He had been so alive; he and Terry Ward tramping in and out of the house, raiding the kitchen together, golfing and swimming together, with her tagging along. They had all been too young for Greg and

Elinor, of course. And Don had never liked Greg. She didn't know why, unless he was jealous of him, his plane, his good looks, the big house and the money.

Greg had only laughed about her engagement.

Nevertheless, she felt better now that Elinor was coming. They were not particularly congenial, but Elinor had brains. She was far more intelligent than Greg, who was in some ways still the little boy who never grew up. And Elinor's hard common sense was what she needed now. She had put her head back and closed her eyes when Dane found her there, late in the afternoon.

He had had a busy time. He had called Floyd at the police station, but he was out, and Jim Mason innocently gave him a piece of news; that the doorman at the Spencer apartment house had notified his precinct station house that somebody answering the dead girl's description had called there last Thursday morning.

"They'd gone," Jim said. "She must have followed them."

"Not here," Dane said shortly. "They weren't here. Who did she ask for?"

"Carol Spencer, he says. Wait a minute. It's here somewhere."

Dane could hear shuffling among some papers. When he spoke again he was evidently reading.

"Stated that she asked for Miss Spencer, and that he told her the Spencer family had left for the summer," he read. "Did not say where they had gone."

"Thanks, Mason."

He rang off. It was another thread, he thought, pointing in the same direction. The dead girl had known where to find Carol Spencer. But that had been on Thursday, and she had reached the village Friday morning. She had evidently not known about the Newport visit.

Out on the porch he wondered why the case was interesting him so much. He had had worse ones, many of them. And he knew he was not helping his leg any. Alex's disapproval followed him wherever he went. He sat there for some time, feeling tired and uncertain. The breeze was ruffling the surface of the bay, and a great sea eagle was drifting with the wind. A navy dirigible was moving oceanward, and he watched it, scowling. For the climb up the hill had told him something. He was not ready to go back to his work. If he did, they would put him on a desk job. He had missed so much, he thought savagely, and now here he sat like an old dog, licking his wounds.

His inertia did not last long. When he heard Alex snoring after the lunch dishes had been washed he tackled the hillside once more.

This time he did not go by way of Crestview. He went up through the woods from the Burton place and, concealed by the trees and heavy undergrowth, began to work down the slope. The air was cooler by that time, although the light was not so good, and it was by pure chance that he stumbled on something which proved his theory correct.

He had thrown away his cigarette and ground it out with his heel. Within five inches of his foot something partly hidden by dead leaves was shining. He stooped and picked it up.

After dropping it in his pocket he turned and retraced his steps, taking a line from the tool house to where he had found it and going on from there. The growth was particularly heavy. There were times when he had to crawl, and other times when an outcropping of rock forced him to detour. But he found nothing more, and at last, dirty and discouraged, he went down to the Spencer house and to follow an astounded Nora up the stairs.

"That Major Dane is here, miss," she said. "I told him you were resting, but he said it was important. He said not to get up. He'll take only a minute."

"I'll go down. Ask him to wait."

Dane was behind Nora, however, and he came without ceremony into the room. Distracted as she was, Carol smiled when she saw him. His slacks were stained, his sweater was snagged, and there was a long scratch along one cheek. He grinned sheepishly.

"You'd never guess they're after me for the movies, would you?" he said. He pulled up a chair and sat down. "Sorry to barge in like this. You look as though you needed a rest. Delayed shock, probably."

She turned wide candid eyes on him.

"Not delayed shock. Just one shock after another. I don't believe that girl was killed in the house, Major Dane. I think she was brought in later. That's why the front door was open."

"That doesn't necessarily follow. Who opened it in the first place?"

"Perhaps she did it herself." She got up and going to her toilet table picked up the bobby pin.

"I found it in the elevator," she told him. "It's a bobby pin, if you know what that is."

He took it and went to the window with it.

"In the elevator?" he said, after a minute. "Where's that? I haven't seen an elevator."

"You can't tell it's there unless you know about it. The doors are solid. There are two large closets, one on each floor, and Mother had it put there.''

"Where is it?''

"The upper door opens next to the linen closet. I just happened to use it today. I was tired.''

"It hasn't been used since you came?''

"I suppose the bags were brought up in it. They usually are. But that pin is for light hair, and the hair in it is blond. None of us here is a blond, and—she was, wasn't she?''

He nodded absently. Of course the elevator had been used, he thought. If there had been any prints they would be gone now. Like the linen closet. Probably like the spade handle. Probably like everything in the whole damned case. But if the elevator was concealed it meant that someone who knew about it had used it to carry the girl's body to where it had been found.

"I suppose it was well known? The elevator, I mean?''

"Mother always used it. It wasn't any secret.''

He said nothing. He folded the bobby pin in a clean handkerchief and put it back into his pocket. Then he opened his hand and placed something on the chaise longue beside her. She raised up to see it better. It was a large metal initial, such as is fastened on a woman's handbag. It was an *M*, and she looked from it to his impassive face.

"Where did you find it?'' she asked.

"I went up the hill again this afternoon. It wasn't far from the top.''

"Anyone could have lost it, couldn't they?''

"Not where I found it,'' he said grimly. "No woman ever carried a handbag through that brush. It hadn't been there long either. It's not even tarnished.''

She began to feel frightened. It had nothing to do with the metal initial on the couch. It concerned the man beside her. Elinor could laugh at Marcia. She could and probably would wrap Floyd and the district attorney and all the rest of them around her delicate finger tips. But this man was different. He had a bulldog tenacity, an unsmiling determination that began to alarm her. He must have seen it in her face, for he got up impatiently.

"I wonder what you're worrying about,'' he said. "You know this is part of that dead woman's outfit. You know her clothes are somewhere about, or at least you did this morning. What happened since? What are you afraid of? Your sister?''

He didn't wait for an answer. He stalked to the window and stood there, looking out.

"Nice view from here," he said, in a different voice. "Better than mine, I think." He turned then, came back, and picked up the gadget from the couch. "I'll let you rest now. I have to bathe and shave. I'm dining out tonight."

She was definitely uneasy now. If he was dining out, he must have a reason. But she tried to make her voice light.

"Don't tell me you've succumbed at last. Who succeeded in getting you?"

"Miss Dalton. She likes to talk, I gather, and I need some information. This working in the dark—" He saw her expression, and his voice changed. "I'm sorry," he said. "I've hurt my leg again, and this thing's getting me down. Don't mind if I'm rough. I've been living a rough life."

He was ready to leave when he saw Don's picture. He went over and looked at it, the helmet, the haggard eyes, the boyish face.

"This is not your brother."

"No. It's Donald Richardson. He was lost more than a year ago, in the Pacific. I—was engaged to him."

"Sorry," he said. "A lot of fine fellows gone."

He went soon after, telling her before he left that Alex had found a man to cut the grass for her. "Not a gardener," he said, "but a useful person to have around. Name's Tim. Tim Murphy, I think. If you like he can sleep in the house. You'll be less nervous with a man around. And so will I."

9

The colonel looked better that night. He wore the dinner clothes without which he was never seen after six o'clock, alone or not, and for once he did not talk about Don immediately.

He made her a cocktail, admired her summer evening dress, and served her an excellent small dinner, with some fine old claret. He did not even discuss the murder, except to say that he hoped the police were not troubling her. He rambled on. Old Nathaniel Ward was not looking well. There was a barmaid at the club, doing nicely too. This idea that women couldn't mix drinks—

He came at last and deviously to Elinor.

"She hasn't been here lately, I suppose?"

"She doesn't like it. No. She's at Newport."

"And you were with her last week?"

She felt herself stiffening. There was something coming, she knew. It came, almost immediately.

"I was quite sure of that, of course," he said, in his courtly manner. "It just happens that Mrs. Ward said something about somebody seeing a car like Elinor's here one night last week. I'm glad you can say where she was."

She took a hasty sip of claret.

"There are a number of cars like Elinor's in the country," she managed to say. "Of course it's absurd. What night was it?"

"I think it was Friday. Don't worry about it, Carol. You know how stories spread here."

He did talk of Don after dinner, and she found it for once a relief. Not that he said much. There was a map pinned on the wall, but he did not refer to it. However, she sensed in him a concealed resentment and fear of Dane.

"Who is the fellow anyhow?" he asked. "Just because the Burtons loaned him their house doesn't mean anything. I've looked him up in the *Army and Navy register*. He's not there."

"I suppose, with all the new officers . . ."

"I'd be just a little careful, my dear. All sorts in the service now, and he's a bit of a mystery. I remember in the last war we got a lot of good men, but we got a lot of bounders too."

She had walked down, and he took her back home up the hill. Neither of them saw Alex, on guard among the trees and burning a hole in his pocket with the cigarette he had hastily stuffed there.

He remained on duty until two o'clock, when Dane relieved him, a Dane in a dark outfit and with a revolver in his pocket. They wasted no words.

"Okay?"

"Okay."

Then Alex went home, and Dane began his cautious circuit of the house. Nothing happened, and at dawn he disappeared. But not to sleep. What he had learned from Marcia Dalton that night looked as though Carol's family was involved in the murder, and he did not like the idea.

He had driven down to the Dalton place. Two or three cars were already parked in the drive, and he cursed himself for letting down the bar he had so carefully erected. But he had at least a chance to see a dozen or so of the summer people, the Wards, the Peter Crowells, Louise Stimson, a few others. He stood, stiff in his uniform, through several rounds of cocktails, watching and listening, but he learned nothing from any of them except the prospects of the approaching election and the cost of living. Then at the table Marcia, beside him, had abruptly turned to him.

"You're interested in our murder, aren't you?" she asked, her sharp eyes on his.

"Merely as an observer," he said lightly.

"Well, I don't think Carol Spencer ought to be alone in the house. She's a nice child. Where's her family?"

"I understand her sister is coming."

Marcia looked surprised.

"Elinor!"

"Why?"

She gave him a long look, then turned abruptly to speak to Peter Crowell on her left. She talked to him through the lobster and up to the saddle of mutton. Then, as though she had made up her mind, she turned back.

"I'm going to tell you something I've promised not to tell," she said in a low voice. "I've known Elinor Hilliard all my life. I don't like her much. I know her car. It's a foreign job you can't mistake, and I'm pretty sure I saw it the night that girl was killed."

He duly registered surprise.

"That's hard to believe," he said.

"Carol doesn't believe it. I told her, and she said Elinor couldn't have been here. But there's nothing wrong with my eyes, and if you're interested you ought to know. I haven't told anyone else," she added. "And don't let Carol know I spoke to you, will you? I'm fond of her, and I think she's in a jam."

He played a rubber or two of bridge after dinner. His mind was not on the game, but he won ten dollars from Peter Crowell and that gentleman was not pleased. He got out his wallet and eyed the scratch on Dane's face.

"Saw you on the hill above the Spencer place this afternoon," he said. "What are you looking for? More bodies?"

"You never know your luck," Dane replied indifferently, and was to remember that later with what amounted to horror.

He had gone home, relieved Alex, and was in bed at six o'clock the next morning when a highly disreputable-looking individual with a battered suitcase got off the train ten miles away. He looked around, saw a car at a distance, and after the crowd dispersed moved casually toward it. Once inside he grinned.

"What goes on?" he inquired. "Don't tell me he's on the old job again. I don't believe it. Not in this neck of the woods."

Alex shrugged as he started the car.

"He'll tell you himself," he said, his one eye on the road.

"I thought he was resting that leg of his."

"Not him," Alex said disgustedly. "He's been working his head off to get well so he can go back. Bored stiff, too. He was fit to be tied until this happened. Now his leg—"

"Well, what happened, for God's sake? Why the fingerprint stuff? Is it this Spencer murder?"

"I'd rather the major told you himself."

It was Tim's turn to stare. Then he burst into raucous laughter.

"The major!" he said. "When did he get to be a major?"

"They move them up fast these days," Alex said imperturbably.

"Yeah, but they don't move them from a sergeant in the army to a majority in six months. The last time I saw him he was lugging a pack, and don't think I'm fooling. What are you doing? Kidding me? He's in some special branch of intelligence, isn't he?"

Alex slowed the car for a curve. His one eye was wary.

"Look, Tim," he said. "A lot of fellows got queer jobs in this man's army. Now they're there, now they're here. Maybe they're in Japan or the Philippines. Then before you know it they're somewhere else. He was a major when he got shot in Italy. I was there."

"That where you lost your eye?"

"I got off easy," Alex said comfortably.

Tim was silent. He was a typical Brooklyn Irishman who had fought his way from the police force to a business of his own, and just now his expression was one of amusement.

"Okay," he said. "So he's a major, and what am I? A tramp?"

"I imagine you're to be a gardener."

Tim stared.

"Well, I'll be God-damned," he said, suddenly sour. "A gardener! What the hell does that mean? I never saw a blade of grass until I was thirty."

"You can run a lawn mower," Alex said, enjoying himself hugely. "You know. You just push the thing. It cuts the grass. Then you rake it up."

Indignation kept Tim quiet for a time, but his curiosity was too much for him.

"All right. I cut somebody's grass. Then what?"

"I expect you're to keep an eye on the Spencer girl. The major thinks she may be in danger."

It was Tim's turn to enjoy himself.

"So he's fallen for a girl at last," he said. "Always said he'd fall hard when he did. What's she like?"

"Just a girl. You'll be seeing her when you're digging in the garden."

"I'm doing no digging," Tim said firmly, and relapsed again into silence.

He cheered over his breakfast, however, and he was loading his camera when Dane appeared at noon. Tim grinned.

"Morning, major," he said. "Hear you've been promoted."

"Temporarily, Tim. Don't bother about the rank stuff unless there are people around." He glanced at the camera. "I see you're ready."

"All set."

For the next hour or so they worked, as they had worked together before. They ate lunch while Tim's films were being developed, and inspected them later. There were prints on all the china, and on the photograph frame as well. Tim looked up.

"Looks like a dame's," he said. "Kind of long and tapering. You take a man's, even if he's got a small hand, the prints are broader."

Dane nodded. He had no longer any doubt that they were Elinor Hilliard's, and the whole picture looked clear. She had been in Bayside the night of the murder, and she had somehow managed to save her mother's treasures before she set fire to the house. He halted there. She had not set fire to the house. That had been done later, Saturday or Sunday night. So what?

But it was the spade that added to the confusion. There were smudged prints on the handle, but one or two were clear enough to prove that they did not resemble the others. They were not large, but Tim was confident they were a man's. Without much hope Dane sent them to Washington, using the post office at the railroad for reasons of his, and going to the hospital that afternoon.

He did not ask for Lucy. He found George Smith sitting up in bed, and took a chair beside him.

"Doing all right, are you?" he inquired.

"Be better when they take me off this pap they're feeding me," George said sullenly. He surveyed Dane's uniform. "You're the fellow at the Burton place, aren't you?"

"Yes. I thought I'd better see you. I can get a man to do your work until you're able to carry on, if that's all right with you."

"Sure is," George said more cheerfully. "All I got done was a bit of mowing. Then this pain hit me."

"You hadn't done any work in the garden, I suppose?"

"Nothing but the grass, and not much of that. You tell the other fellow he'll find everything nice and tidy in the tool house, and to keep it that way. I'm particular about my tools."

Before he left Dane resorted to the old device of offering George his cigarette case, and carried away with him excellent impression of five large and calloused fingers. He did not even need to compare them with the ones on the spade handle.

Tim spent an hour or two that afternoon sauntering over the hillside. To any observer he was merely hunting a dog, whistling now and then, and occasionally calling an imaginary Roger. But he covered considerable ground and found nothing. He spent the evening with Dane going over the case, but in the end he gave it up.

"Sounds like the sister," he said. "Only she didn't work it alone. Who helped her?"

"That's what I'd like to know," Dane said soberly, and went back over his notes again.

10

Elinor arrived early the morning of the inquest, Thursday. She came by taxi, surrounded by luggage and irritable at the hour, the trip, at Carol's insistence that she come at all, that she had had to abandon her dinner party, and been obliged to leave her maid behind.

If there was anything else, her manner did not show it. She went up to Carol's room and surveyed her as she lay in bed.

"You look like the wrath of God," she said. "Don't tell me the story now. I've read it in the papers. That's a hellish train. I need a bath and some food."

But she did not bathe at once. When Carol had dressed and gone downstairs she found her in the library, her breakfast tray almost untouched and she herself with a cigarette, staring down through the French door at the harbor.

"I can't see why you wanted me," she said fretfully. "As to that car business, there are hundreds of cars like mine. Marcia only wants to make trouble. She's always hated me. I don't have to testify today, do I?"

"Not unless you know something. If you do, I advise you to tell it."

Carol's voice was dry, and Elinor looked at her sharply. Then she laughed.

"It was you she asked for in New York, not me," she said.

She went upstairs after that, and Carol heard her bell ringing in the pantry. She knew what that meant. Without her own maid Freda would be pressed into service, to draw her bath, to press her clothes, to help her dress and fix her hair. But Elinor had had to come, if only to confront Marcia if necessary.

When she herself went up later it was to find Elinor in bed, with the odor of bath salts heavy in the air and Freda opening a half dozen bags. An elaborate traveling toilet set was already on the dressing table, and Freda was looking sulky. Elinor's voice was sharp when she saw her.

"I don't see why you leave the linen closet like that, Carol. Surely you can have it cleaned and painted. Those red seals on it make me sick. They look like blood."

"The police want it that way."

"And these sheets!" Elinor said crossly. "Why in the name of heaven sheets like these?"

Carol kept her temper, although she flushed.

"You might remember our own are scorched. I wouldn't use them anyhow, Elinor. And I can't buy sheets. There are none in town."

She sent Freda out, for the house was still only partially livable, and did the rest of the unpacking herself under Elinor's watchful eyes. But her heart sank when, on the toilet table, she saw a number of pale bobby pins, the color of Elinor's hair. She finished however before she began to talk. Then she sat down on the edge of the bed and smiled at her sister.

"I wish you'd trust me, Elinor," she said. "I don't think you killed anybody. That would be idiotic. But if you were here that night—"

"What on earth would bring me here?"

"I haven't an idea," Carol said candidly. "But you see I found a bobby pin in the elevator, and it looks like yours."

Elinor astonishment was real. She sat up in bed, staring. Then she laughed.

"A bobby pin! My God, Carol! And in the elevator! I haven't been in it for years. I'd forgotten there was one."

There was the ring of truth in her voice, and Carol drew a long breath. She felt a vast sense of relief. She was even able to laugh a little herself.

"Well, that's that," she said, and slid off the bed. "It had me scared, you know. Marcia was so certain."

"Tell Marcia where she can go," Elinor said vindictively. "And now get out and let me sleep. What time is this inquest? And why do I have to go?"

"It's this afternoon. You don't have to go. I just think you'd better."

They were more amicable by that time. Elinor asked about Lucy Norton and if she could see her. But when she was told about the yellow room her expression changed.

"Will that have to come out at the inquest?" she asked.

"Why not? She was staying here."

"And you don't know why? What did she tell Lucy, Carol? She must have had some sort of story for Lucy to put her up here. What does Lucy say?"

"I don't know. The police won't let her see anybody."

She was certain now that Elinor had learned something which had terrified her. Lying there in her bed, with no makeup on and her face heavily cramed, she looked white and drawn. Beyond asking to have the shades lowered and saying she would try to sleep she did not speak, however. Carol went downstairs, somewhat dazed and highly apprehensive.

Below, the house was gradually becoming livable again. The long drawing-room rug was down, the covers off the furniture, and as Carol went forward she saw a man carrying chairs and tables onto the terrace. He looked up and grinned at her.

"I'm the new man," he said. "Tim Murphy. Just call me Tim. Major Dane said to go right ahead, and do anything I could."

She smiled in return.

"We're glad to have you, Tim. We needed help badly."

"I'm no gardener, miss. I can cut the grass. That's about as far as I go."

"That's about as far as you need to go."

He nodded and went back to work, but Carol was aware that behind his grin he had inspected her sharply. She dismissed the thought, and getting her car drove into the village for suppliers. Elinor had not brought her ration book, of course, and Carol, struggling over butter and bacon and buying the chickens she was beginning to loathe, wondered if her sister even knew about rationing. But she was more cheerful, now that she was out of the house. She had only imagined the fright in Elinor's face, she thought, and this was borne out when she found Elinor downstairs on her return. She was as carefully dressed as usual, but she was looking perplexed.

"What's wrong on the hill?" she inquired. "There's a man wandering around up there. I saw him while I was dressing."

"I didn't see him. What did he look like?"

"I don't know. He kept stooping over, as though he was looking for something."

Carol put down her bag and confronted her.

"There are some things you ought to know, Elinor," she said. "You know how they found the—how they found the body. She was in a nightdress and a dressing gown, with a fur jacket over them, and she had been sleeping in the yellow room. At least she'd gone to bed there. But we've never found her clothes. They have to be some-where."

"So they think they're on the hill?"

"Maybe not on it. Buried in it."

She repeated what Dane had told her, about the possibility of such a method, the digging of a hole and the replanting over it. But Elinor thought the idea farfetched.

"Why not burn them?" she said lightly. "Why go to all that trouble, if they had to be got rid of? And why are they so essential? After all, she's dead."

"They want to know who she was," Carol said patiently. "It's almost a week, and they still don't know."

Dane was gone—if it had been Dane—when she saw the hillside again. She viewed it from the servants' dining room, with an upset Maggie at her elbow.

"I don't mind Miss Elinor," she said. "I know her ways. But if Freda's to spend all her time with her I'll have to have more help, Miss Carol."

She conciliated Maggie as best she could, and she and Elinor ate lunch almost in silence. With Elinor there the days of trays was over, and lunch was served in the dining room, at a small table near the window. A Coast Guard boat was taking a practice run up the bay, and beyond one of the islands they could see the white sails of a yawl. Carol had always loved the view, but this day the approaching inquest hung heavy over her. Elinor, too, was absorbed and silent. She smoked steadily and only looked up once to ask a question.

"Do you think Lucy Norton will be able to testify?"

"I don't know. I shouldn't think so."

But she was wrong. Lucy did testify that day.

The inquest was held at the town hall. Long before two o'clock the street was lined with cars, and half a dozen reporters and cameramen were on the pavement. Elinor faced them with stony calm, but Carol was less lucky. She sneezed just as one shutter clicked, and later she was to see that picture, her face contorted in agony.

"Miss Spencer showed great distress" was what it said beneath.

The hall was jammed. The coroner, Dr. Harrison, sat at a small table below and in front of the stage, with certain articles covered by a sheet; and the six jurymen sat at one side. They had been shown the body, and looked rather unhappy. Over all was the noise of chairs scraping and people moving and talking. Elinor looked around her distaste-fully.

"It sounds like the zoo at feeding time," she said. "And smells worse."

Nevertheless, she put on a good act, smiling and nodding to the people she knew, and ignoring the others. She had dressed carefully in a white sports suit and a small white hat, painfully reminiscent of the one which probably lay under the sheet on the table, and she looked calm and detached. Carol, watching her smile at Marcia Dalton, felt a reluctant admiration for her.

With the first thump of the gavel the noise subsided, and the silence was almost startling. The coroner's voice was quiet when he began. There had been no identification of the body. Under the circumstances that had been impossible. Later they hoped to learn just who the young woman was who had been done to death in such a tragic manner. In the meantime an inquest was simply an inquiry, to get such information as they could. The witnesses would be under oath to tell the truth. Any failure to do so would be considered as perjury, and the person guilty under the law.

After that introduction came the report on the autopsy. The medical examiner from the county seat had conducted it, and he read his report. The body was one of a young woman, between twenty and thirty probably. There had been no assault. The internal organs were normal, and there were indications that she had borne a child.

The crowd stirred at this. Heretofore she had been merely a girl, dropping, so to speak, out of the blue to be killed mysteriously in the vicinity. Now she became a young mother, and suddenly pitiful.

The medical examiner went on. Deceased had eaten her last meal probably six hours before death, as the process of digestion was well established. Said deceased had been a blonde, and very little work had been done on the teeth. In spite of the situation in which she had been found she had been killed by a blow that had fractured her skull.

The fire which had burned her hair and clothing had been started after death. There was no smoke or soot in the lungs, or any indication from the effect of the burns that she had been dead for some time before the attempt had been made to incinerate the body.

He paused here, for the coroner's questions.

"Would it be possible to state how long this interval might have been?"

"No. Except that death was already well established."

Chief Floyd was the next witness. He told of Carol's arrival at his office, and of going back with her to Crestview. He had found the body in the closet and had it removed after Dr. Harrison had examined it. No, he had taken no pictures. No one had a camera; or if they had, there were no films.

Asked about the position of the body, he said it was on the floor of the linen closet, with the head toward the rear, and what he called the limbs neatly arranged. Most of the clothing, he said, had been burned, but it was there in that bundle if the jury cared to see it.

They jury did care. It came forward solemnly and stared at what lay on the table. None of them touched anything, and they filed back, more sober than ever and somewhat shocked. Elinor Hilliard, too, had lost some of her poise. She was pale and evidently shaken.

"It's horrible," she said suddenly. "I want to get out, Carol. I'm going to be sick."

But Carol caught her arm.

"Be careful," she said. "You have to stick it, Elinor. It will be over in a minute."

Dane, standing at the rear of the hall, saw the bit of byplay; Elinor's attempt to rise, and Carol restraining her. He had, as a matter of fact, been watching Elinor from the beginning. She knew something, he was convinced, but what or how much he was not sure. Now as the exhibits were re-covered he saw her relax, and puzzled over that too.

There followed an interval while a blueprint of the house was circulated among the jury, and this was still going on when there was some movement at the rear entrance doors. People were craning their heads, and to Carol's surprise she saw that Lucy Norton was being brought in. She was in a wheel chair, and her leg in its cast was carefully propped in front of her. A nurse in uniform was pushing the chair, and Lucy was staring straight ahead, looking pale and nervous.

Her arrival, Dane saw, was a shock to Elinor. He could not see her face, but she sagged in her chair and Carol looked at her anxiously. The audience, however, did not notice this. It was absorbed in Lucy, in her wheel chair now beside the table, with the nurse bending over her.

They did not call her at once. Freda was the next witness, and a nervous one. She had gone upstairs to fix Miss Spencer's room for her, and had gone to the linen closet for sheets. There were black smears all around the door, and she rubbed at one with her finger. "It came off like soot." After that she opened the door and saw somebody lying on the floor inside. That was all she knew. She had run down the back stairs and fainted in the kitchen. "I was sick to my stomach," she said.

They did not keep her long, nor Nora, nor Maggie, who followed them. Even Carol was asked only perfunctory questions, about verifying the fact and notifying the police. Asked if she knew the identity of the deceased she said she did not, nor had she any idea why she was in the house.

So far there had been no mention of the yellow room. Evidently that was waiting for Lucy. The bus driver testified as to the arrival at six-thirty on Friday morning of the week before of a young woman dressed as the deceased was supposed to have been dressed. Sam of the hamburger stand stated that such a young woman had had coffee in his place early that morning and looked at the telephone book, but did not call anybody. And some of the interval between arrival and that time was bridged by Mr. Allison of the Five-&-Ten. He told of seeing such a young woman sitting in the public park opposite his store.

"It was early, a little after seven o'clock," he said, "And I'd just opened the place. She was on a bench by the bandstand, looking as though she was waiting. She wasn't in any trouble that I could see. There was a squirrel there, and she was trying to coax it to her. Then I went away. When I looked again, about ten minutes later, she was gone."

Lucy was better now. Dane saw that she was listening carefully. She was slightly deaf, and her chair had been wheeled well forward. But Carol, closer to her, saw her holding her hand behind one ear, and was certain that the hand was trembling.

When at last she was called, Dr. Harrison treated her with considerable gentleness.

"We appreciate the willingness of this witness to appear," he said to the audience. "As you all know, she has had a serious injury. But her testimony is important. Now, Mrs. Norton—"

She took the oath without looking at the crowd. There was no noise now. Some of the people at the rear of the hall were standing up, to see or hear better. But the early part of her testimony was disappointing. The girl had arrived at Crestview about half past eight on Friday morning. She had asked for Miss Carol Spencer, and had seemed disappointed that she had not arrived.

"She kind of hung around for some time," Lucy said. "She claimed to be a friend of Miss Spencer's, and she said Miss Spencer was expecting her. I didn't know what to do. I had plenty of work on my hands, but she didn't go away. She just sat in the hall and waited. It was cold there, so I asked her back to the kitchen. I'd lit the stove.

"I told her nobody was coming until the first of the week, and I said she'd better go down to the village and telephone to Mrs. Hilliard's at Newport, where Miss Carol was staying. But she said her feet hurt her, and couldn't she at least clean up after the train trip. That's how she came to be in the yellow room. I didn't see any objection to that. She was well dressed and looked like a lady. But I thought she was kind of nervous.''

She went on. She had got soap and towels, and the girl took a bath and came down in a red kimono. She talked pleasantly, and she offered to pay Lucy five dollars to let her stay the night. Her railroad ticket back was for the next day. She had showed it. And with travel the way it was now she would have to stay somewhere.

Apparently she had won Lucy, although she refused the money "except for enough to get some food for her. All I had was what I'd brought for myself.''

She had gone to the village for some groceries, and she cooked a nice lunch and carried it up on a tray. The girl stayed in her room all afternoon. She thought she had slept. But when she carried up her supper the door to the yellow room was locked, and she wouldn't open it until she told her who she was.

"She tried to laugh. She said it was just habit. She'd been staying in hotels. But I wasn't comfortable after that, although she seemed to know the family all right. She asked about Mrs. Hilliard and Captain Spencer, and how Mrs. Spencer was. She'd asked for cigarettes and I brought her some, but she didn't leave the room again, so far as I know.''

She had given Lucy the name of Barbour, Marguerite Barbour, and the initials on her bag were M.D.B. That seemed all right, and there wasn't much in the house to steal anyway, Lucy said. Nevertheless, she was uneasy. She slept badly that night, and when it turned cold she had got up for an extra blanket. As the electric current had not been turned on she took a candle and went to the main linen closet, since the servants' blankets had not yet been unpacked.

Her voice grew higher at this point, as she relived the terror of that night.

"I'd just got to the closet—the door was open an inch or so—when something reached out and knocked the candle out of my hand. I was too scared to move, and the next minute the closet door flew open and knocked me down. I—''

"Take a minute,'' said the coroner kindly. "I know this is painful. Take your time, Mrs. Norton.''

She drew a long breath.

"That's about all anyhow," she said, more quietly. "When I got up I guess I was screaming. Anyhow I wanted to get out of the house. But it was black-dark, and that's how I came to fall down the stairs."

"Did anyone pass you after that happened?"

"I don't know. I must have fainted. I don't know how long I was out. I don't remember anything until I heard the birds. That was at daylight."

"When you came to, did you notice anything burning?"

"No, sir. There was nothing burning, or I'd have known it."

They asked her very few questions. She had not really seen the hand that knocked over her candle. As to what ran over her after the door knocked her down, she didn't remember any skirts. But who would, with dresses only to the knees anyhow, and women wearing slacks half the time?

They wheeled her out after that, and Carol was recalled. She knew no one named Barbour, certainly no Marguerite Barbour. And she had no idea who could have been using that name.

"You wouldn't recognize the description of her clothing?"

"They are practically uniform for spring or summer. No, I don't."

"It is possible of course that she gave a name not her own. Would that help any?"

Carol shook her head.

"No one I know is missing," she said. "I have no idea who she was, or why she wanted to see me." She looked around the room. It was a sea of faces, curious, some of them skeptical, and not all of them friendly. She stiffened slightly. "If she was frightened to lock her door she was certainly not afraid of Lucy Norton. But she might have been afraid of someone else."

"You are not accusing anybody?"

"Certainly not," she said, her color rising. "I know nothing about this girl. I don't even believe she came to see me. That was an excuse for some purpose of her own. But there may be someone who does know why she came. That's all."

They excused her then, and the coroner made a brief summary. It was hoped that the identity of the deceased would soon be established. She was evidently in good circumstances. The face powder she used had been analyzed and was of a fine quality. Her feet and hands had apparently been well cared for. And young women of that walk of life did not disappear easily. It was, of course, one of their difficulties that her purse as well as her clothing had not been found. They hoped to do that eventually, unless it had been destroyed, and all over the country authorities were trying to discover if a young woman of this description was missing.

In the meantime this inquest was an inquiry into the cause, whether it had been accidental, suicide or murder. He felt he should say here that it was considered impossible that she could have so injured herself, or—as had been suggested—that a cigarette could have caused the fire. However the jury had heard all the evidence, and must make its own decision.

And they did, without leaving the room. It was murder, by a person or persons unknown.

11

Dane had left his car in an alley some blocks away from the hall. He slipped away to it quietly as soon as the verdict was in, and sat thoughtfully smoking until Tim Murphy joined him, when he took a back road home.

"Well," he said, "what did you think of it, Tim?"

"Phony," said Tim, biting off a piece of cigar and lodging it in his cheek.

"The Norton woman's story?"

"Sure. Look at her! She's nobody's easy mark. None of these New Englanders are, especially the women. So what? She gives the girl a room, she buys groceries for her, and she carries trays up to her. It doesn't make sense."

"No," Dane said, still thoughtful. "She didn't perjure herself, but she didn't tell the whole story. Find anything on the hill this morning?"

"That's the hell of a place to search. I picked up a bushel of burs. That's all."

Dane glanced at the sky.

"There's one thing," he said. "If this dry spell keeps on we may get a hint. It's no weather to replant anything, and if you see some shrubbery wilting—Did you notice Miss Spencer's sister, Mrs. Hilliard?"

"Who could help it?" said Tim, with appreciation. "Not so young, but a looker all right."

"She's supposed to have been seen here—or, rather, her car was—the night of the murder."

Tim whistled.

"Think it's true?" he inquired.

"I think it's possible. She married Howard Hilliard. You know who he is. Money to burn. She's not going to let anything interfere with that. Place at Newport, house at Palm Beach, apartment in New York, a yacht when there were such things. The whole bag of tricks."

"I see. Think this dead girl was Hilliard's mistress?"

"It's possible. Only why come here?"

Tim spat over the side of the car.

"Well, you sure bought yourself a job," he said philosophically. "You can have it. How long have I got to search that hill or push that lawn mower? I got blisters already."

Dane did not reply at once. He was in uniform, and he ran his finger around the band of his collar as though it bothered him.

"We got one thing there," he said. "The girl's name, or the name she gave. Marguerite D. Barbour. The police will go all out on that. Me . . ." He hesitated. "The initials are probably right. They were on her bag. How about calling up your people in New York, Tim? If she spent a night there at a hotel she's used those initials, but maybe another name."

Tim demurred.

"Know how many hotels there are in New York?"

"You can get help. I'm paying for it."

"It's a damn good thing you don't have to live on your service pay, whatever that is, or whatever your service is for that matter," Tim said resignedly. "All right. My best men are gone, but I can cover this, I suppose."

"Not from here. Drop me at the house and drive over to the railroad. There's a booth in the station there."

"What about dinner? I have to eat sometime."

"Get it over there," said Dane heartlessly. "I've never known you to starve yet. And listen, Tim. If you don't pick up anything by midnight take the train yourself. I want to beat the police to it."

"Why, for God's sake?"

"Call it a hunch. Say I don't trust this bunch up here. It's a big case, and they're likely to go off on a tangent that may damage innocent people."

"Such as the Spencer girl?"

"She's out of it," Dane said dryly. "Go and get your toothbrush. Alex will take you over, and you can get a taxi back."

He rested until dinner. He had found that he could still do only a certain amount before the old trouble asserted itself and Alex began to baby him again. It annoyed him that night to find his dinner coming up on a tray.

"Damn it," he said irritably. "I can walk, can't I? And where's the coffee?"

"Drink the milk?" Alex said firmly. "Coffee keeps you awake, and you know it."

"No word from Tim?"

"He's probably eating a beefsteak somewhere."

Dane smiled. The matter of ration points was a sore one with Alex. But he dutifully drank his milk, and as a result he was sound asleep when the fire started on the hill above Crestview.

Tim had telephoned. The only one of his assistants he had been able to locate had found nothing so far, and he was taking the night train to New York.

"On his hunch!" he told Alex with some bitterness. "And in an upper. I'll do it, but I don't have to like it, do I?"

The fire started late. Carol and Elinor had dined at the Wards' that night. It was Elinor who accepted over the phone.

"If we bury ourselves it will make talk," she told Carol. "There's too much of it now, after that story of Lucy's today."

"Lucy isn't a liar."

"Oh, for heaven's sake!" said Elinor impatiently. "That's the point. She *was* telling the truth. But now everybody knows that awful girl had some reason for coming here. She wasn't using this house as a hotel."

In the end Carol agreed. They walked over to the Wards', using the gravel path that connected the two properties, and lifting their long skirts as they crossed the dusty lane. In the summer twilight they both looked young and lovely in their light dresses, Elinor's hair piled high—with Freda's assistance, of course—and Carol's brushed back smoothly from her forehead. When they went in they found the colonel there, rather guiltily trying to hide a map.

Mrs. Ward put down her knitting and got up.

"How nice to see you," she said, "and how beautiful you both look. How are you managing, Carol?"

Carol said she was getting along, but inwardly she was shocked. Mrs. Ward looked ill. She had changed since the preceding Monday when she had been at Crestview. So had Nathaniel, for all his smiling hospitality. Only the colonel seemed himself, defiantly hopeful, as though he were daring fate to deal him its ultimate blow.

No one mentioned the inquest, or that strange story of Lucy's. Mrs. Ward had picked up her knitting again but her eyes were on Carol with an odd intentness.

"When do you expect Gregory?" she asked.

"We don't know. I suppose he's still in Washington or maybe New York. He may not come at all, of course. He's going to be married. And the way things are now . . ."

Mrs. Ward inspected her work. Their grandson, Terry, had been flying in the South Pacific, and she was knitting socks for him.

"Even there their feet get cold, poor dears," she said. "They fly so high, you know. How frightful this war is!"

The other three were talking together over their cocktails, and Mrs. Ward lowered her voice.

"I don't think Gregory ought to come up, Carol," she said. "After all, why should he? It will only spoil his leave. He has seen enough of death where he has been. I might as well tell you. Floyd was here today after the inquest."

"Floyd? What did he want?"

"Just to know if we had seen or heard anything that Friday night. But he asked about Gregory."

There was no mistake about it. Mrs. Ward's veined old hands were shaking. She gave up all pretense of knitting.

"But that's absurd," Carol said stormily. "Greg was in Washington. Floyd's crazy. He has only to use the telephone to learn that."

Dinner was announced then, and they went out to the vast baronial hall that was the dining room. Carol's color was still high, but Elinor was her usual self. She talked about Greg's decoration, and his approaching marriage, and she inquired about Terry Ward, who it seemed was either on his way back on furlough or about to be.

Nevertheless there was constraint at the table. They ate the usual soup, fish and chicken, and there was the inevitable discussion of ration points and thin cream. But neither of the Wards ate much, and Carol was glad when the meal was over and old Nathaniel took Elinor out to his garden.

They left early, Elinor pleading fatigue after her journey, and Nathaniel seeing them home and then returning for what he called his nightly game of chess with the colonel.

"He can't do much else," he said. "His heart's not too good. Fine fellow, the colonel. We're very fond of him."

He left them at the door, saying a rather abrupt good night, and turned back, his small figure almost immediately lost in the shadows. Carol had the feeling that he was relieved to get rid of them, and wondered why. It was not until they were inside the house that its possible meaning began to dawn on her. Elinor had started up the stairs when she stopped her.

"Wait a minute," she said. "Elinor, when Marcia saw your car that night was Greg in it?"

The hall was dark. She could not see Elinor's face, but her sister turned and stared down at her.

"How often," she said, "do I have to tell you Marcia did not see my car?"

"Have you seen Greg at all?"

"How could I? He's been in Washington and New York. What's the matter with you, Carol? If you start suspecting your own family—"

"It's only because old Mr. Ward has insomnia," Carol said, rather wildly. "He gets up and takes walks at night. And tonight Mrs. Ward said Greg oughtn't to come here. She looked queer, too. Elinor, I can't take much more. If you know anything, tell me. I won't run to the police, but at least I'll know where I am. Major Dane—"

"What about Major Dane?" Elinor said sharply.

"I don't know. I think he's Intelligence or something. I saw him at the inquest today. I don't think he believed Lucy."

"He'd better mind his own business," Elinor said inelegantly, and went up the stairs.

It was one o'clock that morning when Carol heard the fire siren. She roused from a deep dream, in which Greg was hiding from her and she was following him, to hear the noise and sit bolt upright in bed. She got up, feeling for her slippers in the dark, and went to the window. The village seemed to be all right, but there was a reddish glare reflected on the clouds above the house, and the siren kept on. It was calling the volunteers now, and the engine was already on its way, its own shrill clamor adding to the din. She was still in her night clothes when she ran to Elinor's room, to find her standing at the window in a pale negligee, gazing out.

"It's the hill," she said. "I think that empty house up there is going. It's lucky the wind is in the other direction, or we'd go too."

Carol looked out. The fire had already roared up the hillside. It had escaped the tool house, but as she looked the dried shingles of the roof of the abandoned house above began to catch, and the hill itself was a roaring inferno. The engine had gone to the fire hydrant up the lane, but she could hear the cars of the volunteer firemen as they began to roar up the Crestview drive.

She realized that it was hopeless, although men were shouting and running, and she even saw Maggie rushing out with a broom. The lane would probably keep it from Rockhill, and a cement road beyond the burning house would stop it there. But the hillside was gone. Even its trees were burning. Her first thought was the trees.

"I can't bear it," she said. "They've been growing there for years. Greg built me a swing there once. Remember?"

Elinor nodded. She looked somber in the red glare, but she said nothing. It was some time before Carol remembered that the firemen would want coffee. She dressed rapidly and went to the kitchen, to find the two maids huddled there and a bedraggled Maggie standing over the stove, with the coffee under way.

"They turned the hose on me," Maggie said calmly. "Who started that fire, Miss Carol? Don't tell me somebody dropped a cigarette. I saw it before it had gone very far. It looked like it began all over the place." She turned to the other women. "One of you girls run out and tell those men to come in for coffee when they're ready."

But it was three in the morning before they wanted coffee. They straggled in then, tired and dirty and some of them with small burns. Maggie used some precious butter on them, lacking anything else. Most of the men of the summer colony had turned out, and they were as dirty as the rest. The house above was gone, and the hillside was burned, wiped out completely. They had saved a few of the trees, however.

They stood around, eating sandwiches and drinking coffee. A bewildered lot. The air warden who had turned in the alarm was Sam Thompson, who ran the hamburger stand in the village, and he told his story to an interested audience.

"I went up the lane just before one o'clock. It was all right then, but five mintues later I saw the glare and ran back. Looked like there were five or six fires, all going like mad. I raced over to the Wards'. There was a light on there, and it was the nearest house from where I was. Mr. Ward was still up, and he telephoned the fire department. When I got back the whole hill was one solid blaze."

"Think somebody set it?"

"Maybe. Maybe not. With the wind the way it is, and everything dried up, it could spread itself."

That was when Carol saw Jerry Dane. He was in his pajamas with a dressing gown over them, and he was as dirty as the rest. She took him a cup of coffee, and he regarded her coolly.

"Nice work!" he said. "How many people besides you know I was looking for something up on that hill?"

"You're not invisible," she said, her voice as cold as his. "And don't look at me like that. I didn't do it."

"Well, somebody did." He put down his cup and his face softened. "Listen, Carol," he said. "Someday you may decide to tell me what's behind all this. You may save a life or two if you do. Perhaps your own. So don't wait too long."

She did not reply, and she did not see him again. By four o'clock in the morning the house was empty. The girls were washing up, and she found Elinor in the library making herself a drink from the small portable bar table there. At some interval she had gone upstairs to do her face; but she looked tired and irritable.

"What was that Dane man saying to you?" she asked. "He looked nasty."

"Only asking me why I started the fire," Carol said ironically. "And what I was keeping from him. He thinks I know something."

"And do you?"

"What do you think?"

There was a rather pregnant silence. Elinor said nothing. She sipped at her drink, and Carol lit a cigarette and watched her. Which was the precise moment which Captain Gregory Spencer chose to return to his summer home.

He came in from the terrace, a tall blond man in uniform with Elinor's good looks in masculine mold, but with Carol's candid eyes and Carol's smile. He was smiling then as he dropped a bag and straightened to look at them.

"Well," he said. "Here's the sailor home from the sea, and the hunter—"

Elinor looked stunned.

"Greg!" she said. "What are you doing here?"

He did not reply. He held out his arms and Carol went into them. He held her close.

"Poor little girl!" he said. "Been going through hell, haven't you? I couldn't get away any sooner."

Out of sheer relief she began to cry. She stood in the shelter of Greg's arms and felt safe and protected again. And Greg held her off and gave her a little shake.

"Stop that," he ordered. "Didn't you know I'd come? Where's your hanky? Here, use mine." He wiped her eyes, and over her head looked at Elinor. "What's the matter with you? Why shouldn't I come? I thought that was the big idea in opening the house."

He released Carol and poured himself a drink.

"Quite a fire, wasn't it?" he said. "I've been hiding out for the last couple of hours. It looked as though they had plenty of help, and this is my best uniform. I thought it was this house at first. What on earth happened?"

"Probably someone dropped a cigarette," Elinor said calmly. "There hasn't been any rain for ages."

He seemed satisfied. He finished his drink and yawned.

"What about bed?" he suggested. "Plenty of time to talk tomorrow. I drove up, and I'm tired. You look as though you could stand some sleep, Carol." He inspected her closely. "Taken quite a beating, haven't you?"

Suddenly Elinor got up.

"Everybody has taken a beating," she said furiously. "It's not over, either. Why should you come here to be dragged into it? I thought you were going to be married right away?"

"So I am," he said, "God willing." He looked at Elinor. "But I'm not letting Carol take this mess alone. It's got her down already. Look at her."

"Then I think you're crazy," said Elinor, her voice sullen.

Carol went up to see his room, which was still closed, but the first excitement and relief of seeing Greg was gone. There was something behind Elinor's semihysteria, and the look Greg had given her. It had almost been as if he was warning her, and alone upstairs, fumbling in the dark back hall for sheets from the service linen closet, she felt once more the old closeness of the two downstairs. They might quarrel—they had always quarreled—but they would stand together, against her, against the world.

By the time she had made the bed and seen to towels and soap Greg had come up. He stopped in front of the sealed closet door and inspected it.

"Why all this stuff?" he inquired. "I thought the thing was more or less over. It's horrible, right here in the house."

"Maybe you can get them to take it off."

"I'll do my damnedest," he said. "It makes me sick to look at it. I suppose they have no idea who did it?"

She looked up at him, and at once she felt that she had to talk to him, to tell him what was driving her into a nervous collapse. He looked big and reliable, and he was Greg, whom she had always adored. She lowered her voice.

"I hate to tell you, Greg," she said, "but I'm frightfully worried. Marcia Dalton says she saw Elinor's car here the night it happened."

She had been prepared for surprise, perhaps for indignation. She was not prepared for the stricken look he gave her.

"Oh, my God!" he said. "What was she doing here?"

He tired to pass it off, of course, said the whole thing was preposterous and to forget it. But he had had a shock, and she knew it.

It was faintly daylight before she went to bed. She left a note on the kitchen table saying that Greg had arrived and not to disturb him, and before she went up to her room she glanced out the kitchen window. There were still men around, watching for fires like that had a way of eating for hours under the leaves and then flaring again. But in the gray of the dawn the blackened hillside stretched up to the skeleton of what had been a house above, its green beauty destroyed and small patches here and there still smoking.

Her car was still in the drive where she had left it. It looked shabby in the morning light, but at least the fire had not touched it. And already the birds were singing, although some were fluttering about with small frightened chirps. Their nests were gone, she thought tiredly. Their nests and their babies. Even the old orchard where in the autumn the deer came at night to stand on their slim legs and eat the apples.

In her room she undressed slowly. The patio was gray with the dawn, and across it she could see faintly the outline of Elinor's door. As she looked she saw it open and close, and realized that Elinor had gone to waken Greg and talk to him.

She was too exhausted to wonder why.

12

Dane slept late the next morning. He did not waken until noon, when Alex called him to the telephone. It was Tim in New York.

"Think I've struck oil," he said. "Registered as Mary D. Breed." He gave the name of a hotel. "Answers description. Gave residence as St. Louis. May be phony, of course. Only arrived Wednesday evening. Checked out the next morning."

Dane was making notes on a pad.

"Seen the room?" he asked.

"Look, Dane, you know what hotels are like. There have been half a dozen in that room since. Yeah. I looked at it. Seven dollars a day. Worth about three. Paid in cash."

"Anybody remember her?"

"The porter thinks he does. Says he carried down her suitcase. Gave him fifty cents. Remembers the fur coat and white hat."

"A suitcase? She didn't bring it with her. Probably checked it at the railroad station."

"With the stub in her bag. Sure," Tim agreed. "New Haven Railroad to Boston. From Boston to Maine. Could have left it anywhere."

"It may have her initials on it."

"Yeah, and it may not. Have a heart, chief. Have you seen the checkroom at any of the railroad stations lately? Anyhow, I can't get hold of it if I do locate it. Unless you want the police in on this. Maybe they could get it. I can't."

"Keep the police out. That's why you're there, Tim."

"I'm damned if I know why," Tim grumbled. But Dane was not listening.

"Better take a plane and go to St. Louis," he said. "We'll have to try. How about money? Got enough?"

"I get airsick," Tim protested. "Besides, I hate flying."

"I'm sorry, Tim. I haven't much time, you know. I'll soon be back in service. Make it on a plane, and go to the police there. Give both her names. Chances are they don't know any details about the murder. It's just a hope, but it's all we've got."

Tim was still protesting when Dane put down the receiver. He went to the window and looked out toward the hillside which had burned the night before. Somebody had been smart, he thought. Alex had been down by the stable when it started, and he had seen nobody. The first warning he had had was the glare, and by the time he reached it it was too late.

"Started in half a dozen places," he had reported, his voice sulky. "Gasoline, probably."

Dane was worried, too, about Tim's call over the telephone. If Floyd was as smart as he thought he was it had been unfortunate, to say the least. And from his point of view it had indeed. At that moment Bessie at her switchboard had plugged into the chief's office.

"I've got something for you," she said excitedly.

"Good girl. What is it?"

"A man named Tim called Dane from New York. Said she spent the night at a hotel there, and registered from St. Louis. Name Mary D. Breed. He's gone on to St. Louis. Tim, I mean."

"Fine work, Bessie. Get the chief of police in St. Louis and call me back, will you? We're getting hot. Who's this Tim? Did he say?"

"No, he didn't. But he called Major Dane 'chief,' if that means anything."

If Dane did not hear this conversation he was fairly sure it had taken place. He was still annoyed when Alex brought his lunch to the porch. Alex's eye was bloodshot and his eyebrows singed, and Dane found himself grinning in spite of his irritation.

"Good place we chose for a rest, isn't it?" he observed.

"It might be, if we'd mind our own business," said Alex, and added a "sir" with some reluctance.

"At least we know we were on the right track. The stuff is buried there, or was."

"Much good that does," Alex grumbled. "I went over it this morning. It's burned, and burned good. You couldn't find your grandmother in it."

Dane disclaimed any intention of looking for that aristocratic old lady in such surroundings, and ate a good lunch. After that he inspected the hillside. As Alex had said, it was hopeless. It was covered inches deep with charred wood and ashes, and the skeletons of blackened trees towered over it.

It was the border that interested him, however. It was irregular, as the though the fire had started in several places at once, and he was inspecting it when someone spoke behind him. He turned sharply, to find a youngish man eying him.

"Quite a fire, wasn't it?" he said amiably. "Spoils the place, rather. I always liked that hill. Used to play on it when I was a kid."

Dane inspected him. He saw a big good-looking man in slacks and sweater, rather than like his own outfit, who was smiling as he offered a cigarette.

"I'm Greg Spencer," he explained. "Only got here last night after the show was about over. Drove up. My sisters were pretty much upset."

"They've had a good bit to be upset about. Especially Miss Carol."

Dane was not certain, but he thought Gregory Spencer's pleasant face became rather wary.

"Yeah. Terrible thing," he said. "She's a courageous child, or she'd have got out before this. How she kept the servants—I came as soon as I could. Iv'e been in the South Pacific, and I'm trying to get married before I go back."

Dane introduced himself. They had been in different theaters of war, but the service was a common bond between them. Also Dane found himself unwillingly liking the other man. They went in together for a drink, to find Elinor there alone.

"Carol's gone to see Lucy Norton," she said. "We've had Floyd and his outfit here all morning. To hear the way they talked to the servants you'd think we had set that fire last night."

"Why think that?" Dane asked.

"I don't know," she said pettishly. "It's silly, of course. It spoils the place dreadfully."

She did not look well. She was as carefully dressed as usual, but she looked her age and more. Dane took his highball and went to the fireplace, where he could face her.

"I was looking at it. I think it was deliberately set."

If she knew anything about it she was good, he thought. She lifted her carefully penciled eyebrows in surprise.

"But why?" she asked.

"The dead girl's clothes were never found. They might have been hidden there."

"That's rather farfetched, isn't it?"

Gregory put down his glass.

"Oh, come now, major," he said. "Why go looking for trouble? The place was dry, and probably somebody dropped a cigarette."

"Dropped six cigarettes, in that case. It started in half a dozen places."

There was an uneasy silence. Greg picked up his drink again.

"What you're saying is that it was set to burn the—to burn the girl's clothes. Is that it?"

"It looks like it. That's why the police have been here. They're used to forest fires, you know. I expect they had a ranger with them, didn't they?"

Elinor didn't know. She had slept late, and they had not come into the house. The servants had told her. And for goodness' sake let her forget it. She was giving a dinner that night at the club. She went back to her list, using the telephone now and then while the two men talked, about the war, about their respective services, even about the political situation. Carol found all three of them there when she came. She came in tumultuously, flinging off her hat and ignoring Dane completely. Greg looked at her.

"Well, did you see Lucy?" he asked.

"If you can call it that. They kept a nurse in the room every minute. I tried to get rid of her, but she said she had orders. I think Lucy knows something, but she doesn't intend to tell it."

Dane, conscious of tension when Carol came in, now sensed relief in both Elinor Hilliard and Greg. Especially in Elinor.

"What makes you think she knows anything?" she inquired.

"The way she looked at me. The way she tried to send the nurse on an errand. She wouldn't go, of course."

"Rather highhanded of Floyd, eh?" said Greg. "Have a drink and forget it, Carol. So long as the old girl minds her own business, why worry?"

Carol refused the drink. She picked up her hat and prepared to leave and Dane, seeing her almost for the first time—except for a glimpse at the inquest—without the slacks and sweater which had made her look young and boyish, realized now that she was neither; that she was indeed a highly attractive if indignant young woman, and that she was still angry with him. In fact, at the door she turned on him sharply.

"I suppose all this pleases you," she said. "You think I started the fire last night, don't you? You told Floyd to keep Lucy from talking, too. He'd never think of it himself."

"Perhaps you underestimate Floyd," he said gravely. "I didn't advise him about anything. I rather think we have different ideas about the whole business."

She did not leave, after all. She was still in the doorway, looking uncertain, when Floyd accompanied by Mason, came along the hall. Mason was carrying a largish package wrapped in newspaper, which he held onto even after he sat down. Floyd did not sit at all. His big face showed excitement and something else.

"Sorry to bother you all again," he said. "Hello, Greg. Didn't know you were back."

"Got back this morning. Drove up."

"After the fire?"

"After the fire. Yes."

The chief looked around the room.

"Well, folks," he said, "that's what I came to talk about. Seemed queer to me, that fire. It spread too fast. It looked like it had started all over the place. So I got one of the forest rangers here this morning. He thinks the same as I do. Somebody set it."

No one spoke. He braced himself on his sturdy legs.

"Now it isn't as though things were just as usual around here. Maybe we've got a firebug. Maybe we haven't. What we know we've got is a murderer, and that ain't common. Not here it isn't. So I begin to think. That girl's clothes were never found, but she was staying in this house, and she didn't come in a red wrapper. So—well, there's the hill. Lots of places to hide clothes there." He glanced at Dane. "I reckon Major Dane had the same idea. He's been snooping around some. So the hill gets burned and the clothes with it. That's the general idea."

He fished in his pocket and brought out something which he held in his hand.

"It's still burning in places up there," he said. "Likely to go on some time. So I put a man to watch it. This is what he found." He opened his hand and held it out. On his broad palm lay another metal initial letter, this time a B. It was blackened by fire, but it had not melted. "Off the bag she carried," she said, and looked around the room. "Anybody recognize it?" he inquired.

No one spoke until Elinor rose abruptly.

"This is all very interesting," she said, "but I can't see how it concerns us. None of us were here at the time this girl was killed, and I object strongly to your attempt to involve us. It's ridiculous."

"Whoever set that fire knew the girl's stuff was on the hill," he said stubbornly.

"How do you know who set the fire?"

"Sit down, Miss Elinor," he said. "I'm not through yet. Give me that package, Jim."

Mason placed it on the table. This time it was not fastened, and he simply unrolled it and exposed its contents. What lay there was an old-fashioned pitcher, of the sort that belonged with a washbowl in the days before modern plumbing. It was chipped here and there, but the pattern was clear and distinct. Floyd stood off and let them see it.

"No prints on it," he said. "The gardener over at the Ward place, Rockhill, found it in the shrubbery near the lane there this morning. It might have been hidden there a year or so ago, but old Nat Ward took a notion to clean out that corner today. So here it is."

Dane glanced at Carol. She was staring incredulously at the pitcher, and her color had faded.

"Maybe some of you remember it," Floyd said. "Probably not you, Miss Carol. You're too young. But you might, Greg. Miss Elinor too."

Elinor shook her head, and Greg looked puzzled. Dane pursued his policy of watchful waiting.

"It looks familiar," Greg said slowly. "It's years since I saw a thing like that, but the pattern—"

His voice trailed off, and Floyd smiled.

"It just happens," he said, "that I know where it came from. I took it to old Annie Holden at the China Shop, and she remembered it all right. It was a special order. She got out her books and showed it to me. Your grandmother bought it thirty-odd years ago before your father built in the extra bathrooms."

"But what has it got to do with the fire?" Carol asked, looking bewildered. "I don't see—"

"Only that it's had gasoline in it," Floyd said. "That fire was set with gasoline, Miss Carol, and it was poured out of this."

There was a stricken silence. Dane, watching all the faces, realized that the difference between surprise and fear was very small. They all looked shocked. In a way, they all looked guilty.

"Of course," he said quietly, "you have to show that it came from this house. Things like that can be given or thrown away. Unless the rest of the set is here—"

"You needn't bother," Carol said, her voice flat and expressionless. "It's been in the attic for years. I saw it there the other day. You can go up and look if you like. One of the maids can show you the way."

Floyd nodded to Mason, and he went out. No one said anything. Floyd replaced the monogram letter in his pocket and looked at Carol.

"Your car was in the drive last night. I saw it there when we were working on the fire."

She nodded.

"It's too far down to the garage. I've been leaving it there at night. The weather was all right."

"All right for a fire too," he said. "Got any rubber hose around?"

"Rubber hose? There is plenty in the tool house."

"Narrow hose, I mean. Tubing."

She tried to think.

"I suppose there is," she said. "For shampooing hair. We usually leave such things here. Why?"

"Siphon out the gas. You can't turn a tap and let gas out of a car, you know, Miss Carol. You have to siphon it." His voice was milder when he spoke to her, almost apologetic. "Miss any gas today? That thing there"—he indicated the pitcher—"holds quite a bit."

"I didn't notice," she told him, and fell silent again.

There was a rattle of crockery from the stairs and Jim Mason came in. He was carrying an assortment of heavy porcelain, a washbowl, soap dish, tooth mug and so on, and his manner was triumphant as he placed it on the table.

"There's another piece up there, but I didn't bring it," he said, wiping his face with a dusty hand. "Ladies present. Guess this is enough anyhow."

There was no argument about it. Except that it had been wiped, the pitcher was obviously a part of the set, and Floyd's face was uneasy as he looked at Carol.

"Now," he said, his voice still mild, "why did you hide that girl's clothes, and set fire to the hill, Miss Carol? Who are you trying to protect?"

13

An hour or two later Dane left the house, as did Floyd and Mason, the latter still carrying the crockery and putting it carefully in the chief's car. Floyd looked disgruntled. His questions had got him nowhere. Carol had simply looked confused.

"I don't know," she said over and over. "Yes, I did go with Major Dane to the hill, but I never thought of burning it. Why should I?"

People were already coming to call by that time. The news that Greg was in town had got around, and the summer colony came in numbers to see its returned hero. Also of course to look at the burned hillside, and to conjecture once more about the murder.

The chief in disgust had wrapped his pitcher and escaped, with his satellite trailing him. And Dane had had to admire the three Spencers. Blood always told, he thought; Elinor delicately pouring tea, Carol seeing that the men—and most of the women—had drinks, and Greg hearty and cheerful, apologizing for his impromptu costume and shrugging off his new honors.

He did not stay long after Floyd's departure. The pitcher was a solid if chipped piece of evidence, and Carol had known about the metal initial he had found on the hill. On the other hand, she had looked, he thought grimly, as confused and guilty as the innocent often did look.

He stopped by the fountain, a monstrosity of yellow marble with a tall bronze figure on top, and around the basin a row of grinning satyrs, some holding goblets aloft, some playing on pipes or cymbals. He lit a cigarette and sat down on the rim of the basin. Only two or three days earlier he and Carol had sat here, after a futile search of the hill. His leg had hurt damnably, and she had asked him how he got it.

"In Italy," he had told her. "Old Alex got me back, or I wouldn't be sitting here. That's how he lost his eye."

And later that day Freda had walked across with a beefsteak and kidney pie, not for him but for Alex, with a card which said: "For Alex, with thanks." Alex had blushed with embarrassment.

"What the hell you been telling?" he demanded. "I'm no bloody hero. If that gets around—"

Dane had laughed.

"I don't think it will," he said pacifically. "Calm yourself, old boy. If ever a man deserved a steak and kidney pie you do."

And now Floyd suspected her of burning the hill. He was not fooling himself. She could have done it, have learned something that made it imperative to destroy the dead girl's identity. But she was not under arrest. There had been time before the first callers were announced and had traveled the long hall around the patio for Floyd to tell her so.

"I'll just ask you not to leave this town," he had said. "I think you'd better stay too, Greg. As for you, Miss Elinor—well, I wouldn't be in a hurry if I were you."

"Why should I stay here?" Elinor had demanded. "I'm needed at home. I have a husband there, and a mother."

"From what I hear they won't suffer any," Floyd said dryly. "You got plenty of help, haven't you?"

Greg's protest had been violent. He was about to be married, and part of his leave was gone already. But his real resentment had been at the accusation against Carol.

"Preposterous," he said. "Why would she do it? Ruin a place she's loved all her life? And you can't connect her with the murder. Don't try to push us too far, Floyd."

"All right," Floyd said. "Explain that pitcher. That ought to be easy."

Dane went over that in his mind. The chief was shrewd. Only perhaps he was beginning at the wrong end. What was the motive for the murder? Who was the girl? Why had she come to the Spencer place, claiming to know Carol? And why had she got up late at night, left her room and gone outside. For sometime that night she had been outside. There was the pine needle in her slipper to prove it. Why had she gone out, clad only as she was with her fur jacket to keep her warm? Whom had she met that June night? A woman?

He thought it possible. Could it have been Elinor Hilliard? There was that story of the Dalton girl's about seeing Elinor's car. But Elinor had an alibi, or so she claimed. Gregory? He considered Greg Spencer carefully. He might have used his sister's car, and he was the kind to be tied up with women. Dane knew the type well. Yet there were one or two things against the theory. The dead girl had been small and light, but her body had almost certainly been taken up in the elevator. Gregory, in a hurry as he must have been, would not have needed to use it, not with Lucy in the house.

The bobby pin had belonged to her. He knew that, if Carol did not. The hair caught in it had been bleached and showed dark at the root, whereas Elinor Hilliard was a natural blonde.

All right. Go on from there. Greg would not have used the elevator, even allowing for Lucy's slight deafness. He had investigated it after Carol had given him the bobby pin, and it made an unmistakable rumbling sound. But Elinor Hilliard could have, taking the desperate chance it must have been.

He considered that carefully. She had presumably been seen that night, or her car had. Also no sooner had she arrived yesterday than the hillside had been burned that night. There was a resemblance here too, he thought. In both cases fires had been set. But once again he found himself up against Lucy's definite and, he believed, truthful statement that there had been no fire while she was still in the house.

He lit another cigarette and straightened his leg.

Was it possible, he wondered, that the girl had not been killed on Friday night, after all? That she had stayed on for another day, living in the yellow room and eating what she could find? He thought it unlikely. Not only had the postmortem fixed the approximate time as Friday. There was also Lucy's story of the hand reaching out from the closet door. That had been real enough for her to break a leg, trying to escape from it.

He got up rather drearily and limped home. There was no news from Tim, but he had not expected any. Tim had only had time to reach St. Louis. But Alex found him irritable and without appetite that night.

"For a man who's trying to get back in this war," Alex said somberly, "you act like you never heard of a kraut. You eat that custard. It's good for you—sir."

He did not eat the custard. He pushed it away and lit a cigarette.

"The police think Carol Spencer set the fire last night, Alex."

"That girl? I don't believe it, sir."

"Nor do I. Just the same she's in real trouble. A little more and they'll arrest her for arson, and possibly for concealing evidence of a crime."

Alex fixed his one eye on the view.

"I've been thinking, sir," he said. "Maybe somebody chased that girl outside."

"In a fur coat?"

"We don't know she had it on, do we? It was easy enough to put it on later. As I get it, the idea was to make it look as though she was killed in the house."

"Why?"

"Well, to let the murderer get away. The Norton woman mightn't have found her right off. She had a lot to do before she made the beds. Take her two or three days, likely, before she needed to get into the linen closet."

"And how would you get in the house?"

Alex was thoughtful. His big body tensed with the effort of thinking.

"Well, if you didn't have a game leg you could shinny up the pillars of that little porch off the kitchen. You can break the lock of a window easy enough, and maybe nobody would notice it up there."

"Any other way you can think of? As I recall, one window in the yellow room was open when I saw it. That's where the girl was staying. How about a ladder?"

"There's a pruning ladder down by the stable. I seen it myself. It's close up. You don't notice it unless you're going by. I use that way for a short cut."

"You might look at it sometime and see if it's been moved."

He sat still for a long time, smoking one cigarette after another. It was useless to try to see Lucy Norton, who was, he was confident, holding in her stubborn head the key to the mystery. He knew, too, that it was possible Carol Spencer had set the fire after all. She would so it if she was trying to protect someone. But whom was she trying to protect? Elinor Hilliard? Her brother? Then again he gave her credit for too much intelligence to have left the pitcher where it was found. It would have been easy to bring it back to the house, wash it and return it to the attic.

Or would it? The fire must have caught fast, and the drive been brilliantly lighted almost at once. Had she found herself more or less cut off, unable to get back with the incriminating pitcher in her hand? He considered that. An air warden on his rounds had seen the blaze and run to the Wards' to telephone. He would have used the path that led to the Spencer place. In that case she could have been cut off, have heard the warden running, taken refuge in the Ward property, and in panic had dropped the thing where it had been found.

The same applied to Elinor, of course. Either one of them could have hidden until the warden had entered the Ward house and then by way of the lower garden and the trees have worked her way back. Gregory was eliminated. It was unlikely that he had known what was in the attic. Unlikely, too, that his surprise when he saw what Mason had carried down could have been assumed.

He looked at his watch. It was almost nine. If Marcia Dalton was at home she would have finished her dinner, and it was time he had a further talk with her.

He said nothing to Alex, except that he was to keep an eye on the Spencer place until he got back, and he did not take his car. He walked down the drive and toward the beach to the Dalton house. A big dog came running at him, but let him alone when spoken to. And he found Marcia alone, playing solitaire in the living room. Her long face lighted when she saw him.

"Well!" she said. "Don't tell me this is a dinner call. I don't believe it."

She was obviously flustered. She insisted on getting him the highball he did not want, informed him that the servants had gone to the movies, and ordered him into a comfortable chair without giving him a chance to speak. Then she sat down, eying him shrewdly.

"So you're not asked to the party either!"

He looked surprised.

"What party?"

"Elinor Hilliard's giving one at the club. She left me out too. I suppose Carol told her I'd seen her car, so here I am, *sur le branche.* I can't say I mind. I'm a Nurse's Aide and I've been at the hospital all day." She gave him a sharp glance. "Still on the trail, major?"

His lean face did not change.

"On what trail, Miss Dalton?"

She made an impatient gesture.

"I'm not an idiot. Maybe you're in love with Carol, I wouldn't know. But you're interested in this case. You won't get far with it, of course."

"That's rather an interesting statement."

"Sure it is. I mean it, too. We're pretty much of a clan here. We stick together. We have our differences, but when it comes to trouble— You'll find Carol and Greg Spencer are part of us. Not Elinor."

"So, granting that I am puzzled by this, I can expect no help. Is that it?"

She did not answer directly.

"You're up against something more than that," she told him. "Greg and Elinor will stick together through wind and high water. They're like twins, only she's bossed him for years. If Greg set that fire last night, Elinor knows about it. I think he did."

"I see. And the murder?"

"I never claimed to see anybody in Elinor's car that night. All I know is that the car was here. I'll swear to that on a stack of Bibles. But go down to the club some morning and watch them there. I haven't told them anything, but someone else has. If Elinor was here that night, Greg was with her. At least some man was. He comes back this time, and the hill is burned. Think about that, Major Dane. If this Barbour girl's clothes were hidden there—"

"Who saw Greg in the car?"

"I didn't say it was Greg. That's not only what I think, but what a lot of other people think too."

"All right," he said patiently. "Who saw this man in the car?"

"Old Mrs. Ward. Mr. Ward's a bad sleeper. He walks around sometimes at night, and this night he was gone so long she got worried. She went after him, but she didn't find him. She saw a car that looked like Elinor's going down the drive at Crestview, only there was a man in it. He wasn't driving it. Somebody else was, and that puzzled her. There hadn't been a murder then, so far as anybody knew, and she happened to speak about it to someone the next day. She thought if it was Greg it was odd he hadn't stopped to see them. He was a friend of Terry, their grandson."

Dane sat upright in his chair, staring at her.

"Good God!" he said. "Are you telling me that this summer colony knows a thing like that and won't tell it?"

"I warned you," she said comfortably. "We stick together. I'm furious at Elinor tonight, or I'd probably still not be sticking my neck out. Then of course old Mrs. Ward doesn't see very well. There's one school that believes she was mistaken. The other school thinks Greg was here; but he's the local hero, so what the hell?"

He was still astounded. He got up and took a turn or two around the room before he spoke.

"I wonder why you're telling me this, Miss Dalton. It's not just because you're left out of the party."

For a minute her mask dropped.

"No," she said. "It's because Greg needs a friend. I'm fond of him, you see. I never had a chance, of course. But this crowd has got him tried and convicted, and someday Floyd and his bunch will hear it. Maybe Greg did it, I don't know. But he never planned to do it. He's not that sort. Only remember this. Lucy Norton had a better reason to let that girl stay in the house than she told at the inquest. And Greg likes women. I guess he's had his share of them."

Dane looked undecided. He looked at his watch.

"Maybe I'd better see Mr. Ward," he said. "If he's a bad sleeper he may still be up."

But, although he found Mr. Ward awake and reading in his library, he left at the end of a half hour completely baffled. Mr. Ward was courteous, even affable. He offered a chair and a drink, only the first of which Dane accepted, and he brought up at once the matter of the fire.

"Bad thing," he said. "I always liked that hill. Of course we'll all a little overgrown. Too much enthusiastic planting in the early days. But a fire . . ."

When Dane broached the murder however he became reticent.

"Horrible thing," he said. "Terrible for Carol Spencer, too. I'm glad some of the family are with her. It was no place for her to stay alone."

That gave Dane his opening. He was quick to take it.

"I understand your wife saw a car leaving the Spencer place the night of the murder. Can you tell me anything about it?"

Mr. Ward frowned.

"I see you've heard that story," he said. "There's nothing to it. Absolutely. She saw a car, certainly, but it may have backed into the drive to turn around. That's all I know, sir, or my wife either. The amount of gossip here in the summer is outrageous."

"She didn't see who was in it?" Dane persisted.

"She thought it was a man, but she can't even be sure of that. Her eyes are not what they were, and it was a dark night."

He rose, and Dane saw he was expected to go. He waited a moment, however.

"You yourself didn't see this car, Mr. Ward?"

"Certainly not," the old gentleman said testily.

But Dane persisted.

"The police might like to know all this, Mr. Ward."

"Neither my wife nor I run to the police with all the tittle-tattle of a place like this. As for the car, it was a car. It might have been anybody's."

He himself showed Dane out, but he did not offer to shake hands.

He stood in the doorway, small and wiry and watchful, until he could no longer hear Dane's footsteps on the drive. After that he locked the door, put out the lights and went upstairs to his wife.

"I wish to God," he said, "that you'd learn to curb your tongue. They've learned about Elinor Hilliard's car. Major Dane has just been here."

Mrs. Ward sat up in bed. She had lost color, and she wrung her thin old hands.

"Oh, Nat," she said. "What are we to do? What *can* we do?"

He was still upset, but he went over and patted her on the shoulder.

"I'll have to go out," he said. "Try and sleep, my dear. I'll not be long."

She protested almost wildly, but he did not listen. His small neat body was erect and purposeful as he left her, and he stopped long enough in his dressing room to slip a revolver into his pocket.

14

Lucy Norton died that same night.

It happened either during or some time after Elinor Hilliard's dinner at the club. Characteristically, Elinor's reaction to Floyd's visit had been to insist on going on with the party. Greg had protested.

"Don't be a jackass," he said. "Whom are you trying to fool? The police? What do they care? If it's the summer people, I imagine there's plenty of talk already without your trying to show you don't give a damn. Call it off. Have a headache. You've done that before when it suited you."

"And let everybody know something new has happened? Let me alone, Greg. We've got to carry on."

Carol felt helpless between the two of them. When Greg appealed to her, however, she sided with Elinor.

"I don't see what else we can do," she said. "You can't ask twenty people to dinner, let their cooks have the evening off and then tell them to eat scrambled eggs at home. What about that pitcher? It got out of the house somehow. It didn't have legs."

"Why worry?" Elinor said lightly, and looked at her watch. "Good gracious, I have to get my hair done. I'm taking your car, Carol. Greg's going to the barber. He needs his."

"Why can't you walk? If I'm to fix your tables and take the champagne—"

"I'll be back in plenty of time."

She was not, of course. Carol dressed early, putting on a white dress which made her look gayer than she felt, and getting to the club just in time to palce the cards on the table before the first guest arrived. It was Colonel Richardson, imposing as ever in dinner clothes, and bringing his own contribution of a bottle of old brandy.

"Nothing in the club like it," he told her, handing it over carefully. "I laid up some for Don years ago, but there's plenty left. You're looking very lovely, my dear."

He wanted to talk about the fire.

"Most puzzling," he said. "Of course the weather is dry, but to spread as fast as it did! Who raised the alarm?"

"One of the air wardens saw it first."

"I was wondering," he said. "I saw that man of Dane's around your place late last night. You remember I stayed at the Wards', playing chess. I certainly saw him—Alex, I think they call him. Rather odd, don't you think? Being out at that hour?"

Her nerves were none too good. She put down the last place card and looked at him.

"If you mean he set the fire, I think you're wrong, colonel. Both he and Major Dane worked hard to put it out."

But Henry Richardson had something to say, and proceeded to say it.

"I've been coming here for a good many years," he said with dignity. "We've never had anything worse than a burglary, and that was by a waiter at the hotel. Then this Dane arrives, with a servant who looks like a thug, and we have both a murder with an attempted fire—in your house, my dear—and another fire last night."

Carol flushed.

"Isn't that rather ridiculous? After all, he's an officer in the army. Even if you can't find his record."

"There have been bad hats in the services as well as everywhere else."

Good gracious, she thought wildly, I'm quarreling with Don's father, and Don is dead. She forced a smile.

"I'm sorry," she told him. "I haven't had much sleep lately, and I'm certainly not interested in Major Dane. Now do go and help receive the people. Elinor's late, as usual."

He was not entirely reassured, however. He put his hand on her arm before he left.

"Just don't see too much of this fellow," he said. "He's hard, my dear. Not the sort I like to see with you."

The party was a success, at least at first. Elinor's parties always were. She had skimmed the cream of the bridge-playing crowd, the food was good, the drinks plentiful. The noise rose over the cocktails until Carol felt her head buzzing. She drank two herself, and Greg had more than were good for him. But looking around the table Carol wondered why Marcia Dalton was not there. Pete Crowell was being the life of the party, so far as noise was concerned. Louise Stimson was wearing all her pearls over a black dress that was a trifle low for wartime, and watching that Greg's wineglass was kept full. But Marcia was not there.

It was a deliberate affront, she realized, because Marcia had claimed to have seen Elinor's car the night of the murder. It was stupid of Elinor, she thought. Marcia had a bitter tongue.

She was roused by seeing Greg, his voice slightly thick, lifting his glass. She tried desperately to catch his eye, but he did not look at her. He was on his feet, his eyes slightly glazed, but with his usual beaming cheerfulness.

"To Floyd, our remarkable chief of police!" he said. "Who suspects the Spencer family of both arson and murder!"

There was an appalled silence, but there was nothing to do about it. Elinor had heard him, and was forcing a smile.

"Don't try to be funny, Greg," she said, across the round table. "People might misunderstand you."

He shut up then. But the damage had been done, and those who had not heard him were being informed by the ones who had. Perhaps Carol imagined it, but the gaiety seemed to have gone out of the party. There was low-voiced conversation, a hint of caution, and now and then a face turned curiously toward herself. She was relieved when Elinor got up, and the men drifted into the smoking room for cigars and brandy. Carol herself managed to get away from the women, and outside to the pool.

There was a fog coming in. It crept along like thick white fingers among the islands, bringing a chill with it, and already the village lights had practically disappeared. She heard a car starting up somewhere close by, but paid no attention. It was twenty minutes later when Elinor called sharply from the porch of the club.

"Greg! Where are you, Greg?"

"He's not here," Carol answered. "Perhaps he's gone home."

She went back into the club. Elinor was almost in tears with rage.

"It wasn't enough for him to get tight and say what he did," she said furiously. "He's walked out on a bridge game. You'll have to take his place, Carol."

Afterwards she remembered that night with horror: Greg gone in the fog, herself at the bridge table, bidding, doubling, winning or being set; and sometime, perhaps as she sat there, Lucy mysteriously dying on the floor of her hospital room.

That was where they found her, on the floor and without a mark on her. She had gone to sleep around ten o'clock, a hysterical nurse reported the next morning, and she had been all right then. She had been nervous since the inquest, and she had taken a sleeping tablet at nine.

"I didn't look in after that," the nurse said, sniffling. "I was busy, and she wasn't sick. Then when I carried in the basin to wash her for breakfast—She would never have tried to get out of bed. Never."

Floyd and Dr. Harrison reached the room almost simultaneously. There was nothing to be done, of course. The doctor said she had been dead for hours. Rigor had already set in. And Floyd looked infuriated.

"Mark or no mark," he said, "she's been murdered. She knew something she wasn't telling, so this is what she got."

The doctor got up from his knees.

"Looks like heart, Floyd."

"Heart! With her on the floor like that?"

Both men surveyed the body. It lay beside the bed, in its cotton nightgown, the small face relaxed and peaceful. On the bed itself the covers had been thrown back, as if Lucy herself had done it. The only indication that anything was wrong was that the cord of the pushbutton, which had been fastened to the lower sheet with a safety pin, had been torn away and lay on the floor. Floyd pointed to it.

"Who did that?" he demanded, his face red with anger.

"It happens," the doctor said, still calm. "It slipped and when she felt the heart attack coming on she got out of bed to get it. You've got murder on the brain."

Floyd was still suspicious. He went out into the hall, where an uneasy intern was waiting.

"Any way anybody could have got in here last night?"

"The doors are locked at ten o'clock, chief, when the watchman takes over. She—wasn't killed, was she?"

"That remains to be seen," Floyd said loftily. "Any empty rooms around here?"

"Eleven. Patient went out late yesterday afternoon."

The chief grunted and looked around. Eleven was across the hall. He strode in there and looked around him. The bed had been stripped and not yet made up, and a window was open. The intern had followed.

"Who was in here?"

"The Crowells' little girl. She had her tonsils out a couple of days ago."

Floyd examined the window. The fire escape was just outside, and he grunted again. There were scratches on the rusty edge of the ladderlike steps, and some of the paint had been scraped off.

"Come in here," he said, almost cheerfully. "Bring the doc over, will you?"

But the doctor was not convinced. Someone might have come in. He didn't dispute that. Lucy however had not been killed. "She might have been frightened," he said. "Nobody laid a hand on her, Floyd. Take it or leave it."

"What about these Crowells? Know anything?"

"They're all right, so far as I know. I operated on the girl. I don't know much about them. Get her down to the mortuary, Floyd. I'd better do a post-mortem."

It was the doctor who notified Joe Norton, Lucy's husband, and after a brief hesitation called Carol Spencer. She did not understand at first.

"Dead?" she said. "Lucy! But she was all right yesterday. She was getting better."

"She died suddenly."

"You mean her heart?"

"I think so. She tried to get out of bed alone."

"But she'd never do that," Carol protested. "I can't believe it."

She put down the receiver and wondered what to do. It was still early. The servants had had their breakfast, but Elinor and Greg were not yet awake. She decided to drive to the hospital, and found Joe Norton already there when she arrived. He was sitting on a bench in the lower hall, his face in his hands and his whole attitude one of hopeless grief. She sat down beside him and put a hand on his knee.

"I'm sorry, Joe. Terribly sorry."

He raised his head and looked at her with red-rimmed eyes.

"They say it was her heart," he said bitterly. "Wasn't anything wrong with her heart. That's their way of getting out of it."

"Getting out of what?"

"They killed her. That's what. Somebody gave her the wrong medicine. Or maybe she knew something she wasn't meant to tell."

She had not seen Lucy, and she supposed they were making a post-mortem examination. She herself still felt stunned, and to add to the tension Joe suddenly decided to locate Lucy and was restrained only with difficulty. She quieted him finally. She even succeeded at last in taking him back to Crestview, where he sat in the kitchen, not talking, while a horrified Maggie fried him some eggs and forced him to eat. When Carol went back, however, he had gone.

So great had been her own surprise that it was not until she was in her own room after his departure that she began to wonder why Lucy had been found on the floor, or if heart trouble was really the answer. There had been something in the doctor's voice which puzzled her.

The doctor, to tell the truth, also was puzzled. There was no question that Lucy had died because her heart had stopped, abruptly and finally. But it should not have stopped at all. It was a fairly sound and healthy organ, as was all the rest of what had been Lucy Norton. Shock, he thought, as he put down his scalpel. Shock and fright? He wondered. He reported to Floyd, who was content to take his post-mortem *in absentia.*

"Nothing," he said. "Slight bruise on elbow as she fell. Nothing else, inside or out."

"Maybe *she* climbed that fire escape?" Floyd jeered. "Look again, doc. Maybe poison."

"The laboratory's doing that now. I think it unlikely."

It was more than unlikely. It was impossible. The lab reported that Lucy had eaten a light hospital supper of creamed chicken and gelatine at five-thirty, and that she had died sometime after midnight, the process of digestion being far along.

Carol knew nothing of all this. She was grieved for Lucy, and slightly annoyed when at eleven o'clock she looked across the patio to see Elinor getting into a taxi on her way to the club. Freda had certainly told her about Lucy, but she was going anyhow, to sit poised and smiling and slightly defiant under one of the big umbrellas by the pool, to gather around her such men as were available, and to drink her before-lunch cocktail as though she had never heard of the death.

It was not normal behavior, even for Elinor. Carol found herself recalling Marcia's story about the car, and the fire which had happened so opportunely. For the first time she began to suspect that her sister was involved, not in Lucy's death but in what had preceded it.

She had to know. It was no use drifting along, with murder and sudden death all around them; with Elinor at the club and Greg still asleep. She had to find out.

Elinor's room was already cleaned when she got there. Freda had gone, and the bottles and jars of cosmetics were in neat rows on the toilet table. The elaborate comb and brushes and mirror without which Elinor never traveled were in place, as well as her jewel case on a small stand beside her bed. Carol only glanced at them, however. She closed the door to the hall and went to the closet.

Considering that she had come merely for the inquest, Elinor had brought a surprising amount of clothes. There were floor-length dinner dresses, high-necked in deference to the war. There were elaborate negligees and sports dresses. On the shelf above, carefully placed on trees, was a row of hats, one of them small and white, and her shoes and slippers were neatly treed on the slanting shelf near the floor.

She examined them all, feeling guilty as she did so. Once Freda alarmed her. She came into the room, saw the closet door ajar and closed it without seeing her. Not until she had been gone for some time did Carol resume her search, moving the dresses along the rod that supported the hangers and inspecting them one by one. She paid particular attention to the dinner gown Elinor had worn to the Wards' the night of the fire, but it told her nothing. She had almost finished when she saw the warm woolen dressing gown hung on a hook behind the rest.

She had not seen it before. It was a practical tailored affair, dark blue, with neat pockets and a cord to fasten around Elinor's slim waist, and she took it down and examined it, her heart pounding in her ears.

It was not only dusty around the hem. There were two or three sandburs caught in it. She stood still, holding it, and trying not to see the picture it painted: Elinor in the attic, getting Granny's old pitcher, Elinor on the drive, siphoning gasoline from the car, and Elinor setting fire to the hillside and then coming back to the house and hanging up the garment, as casually as she did everything else.

When she heard Greg's voice speaking to Freda, she hurriedly replaced the dressing gown where she had found it. But Greg did not come in. She was relieved, although she knew it was only a respite. She had to go on. She found nothing more, however. Among the shoes were bedroom slippers to match the negligees and one practical pair of soft tan leather. Except that these last showed a scratch or two, there was no indication that they had been outside the house.

Greg was on the terrace when she went downstairs. He was staring out at the bay, smoking and depressed.

"I'm sorry about last night, Carol," he said. "Made a fool of myself, of course. What's this about Lucy Norton?"

She lit a cigarette before she could trust herself to speak.

"She's dead, Greg. That's all I know."

"Queer," he said moodily. "Always thought she was a sturdy little thing. Heart, Maggie says. It will be hard on Joe." He put out his cigarette. "I just talked to Virginia on the phone. She's pretty badly upset. Everything's ready, church engaged, bridesmaids ready, presents coming in, and here I sit. *I* didn't set that fire."

She summoned all her courage.

"Are you sure you don't know why it was set, Greg?"

He stared at her incredulously.

"Why it was set? Good God, Carol, I don't understand you. Why should I know a thing like that?"

"I'm not sure," she said wearily. "I only know it was started from this house. There's no other explanation. And at some time or other Elinor has been outside in the grounds at night. I found some sandburs in the hem of her dressing gown. She knew about that pitcher too, and my car was there. She could have got the gasoline from it."

To her surprise he laughed, although rather grimly.

"I can suspect Elinor of a number of things," he said dryly. "I know her. But the last thing in the world she would do would be to soil her pretty hands with gasoline, or go out in the night alone in a dressing gown and carrying Granny's old pitcher to start a fire. That's out, Carol. Don't be a little fool."

Perhaps he was right, she thought. It wasn't like Elinor, none of it, and when Elinor herself arrived soon after, bringing a half dozen people for a drink before lunch she felt still more doubtful. This was Elinor at her best, the perfect hostess, the fastidious, immaculate person she had always been.

They sat around, well dressed and prosperous appearing. Some of them had been on the links. The talk was idle, of golf, of the party the night before, of the war, of politics. It was some time before Lucy was mentioned. Then someone said that Floyd was still clinging to the idea she had been murdered, that he had found where the fire escape had been used.

Louise Simpson looked up at Greg with her faintly malicious smile.

"And Greg with no alibi for last night!" she said. "Where did you vanish to, Greg?"

"Me?" He grinned at her. "I wasn't climbing any fire escapes. I had a lot to drink. I drove it off."

She persisted, still apparently only mischievous. "There's a story you were here the night of the murder, you know. You'd better get busy on a couple of alibis."

Greg looked astonished. He put down his glass and glanced around the group.

"I don't get it. What story? I haven't heard it."

"Just that you were seen here, coming out of the drive in Elinor's car," Louise said pertly.

"In Elinor's car? For God's sake, what would I be doing here in Elinor's car?"

She laughed. "That's the question, of course," she said, and finished her cocktail.

It was Peter Crowell who broke the startled silence that followed.

"Why don't you mind your own business, Louise?" he demanded. "Of course there are stories, Greg. There always are. That's only one of them. Don't let it worry you. Nobody believes it." He got out of his chair. "It's time to go," he said. "More than time, if you ask me."

15

The news of Lucy's death did not reach Dane until Alex returned from his marketing that morning. There was still no word from Tim in St. Louis, and Dane was restless. He had walked again over to the hillside. Most of the watchers had left and the last vestige of fire had gone, but he knew the uselessness of further search. When he went back he had determined to see Lucy Norton, police or no police. There was still the question as to why she had allowed the dead girl to stay in the house, had fixed her bed, even carried soap and towels to her. What sort of story had she put up that Lucy would agree to let her stay there? He felt the whole answer lay there.

He considered that, ruffling through such notes as he had made. He had always believed in following the essential clue, and so far he had considered the dead girl's identity as probably providing that. Now he wondered if her story to Lucy was not more important. These New England women, he knew, were not soft. They were as hard and firm as the soil that bred them. They had character and a certain skepticism, especially about strangers. Yet Lucy had accepted her. Why? What proof had she had? What, for instance, had she shown? A card? A letter?

Some identification she had certainly produced. Something she had carried with her in her bag, something now either buried or in the murderer's possession.

The news of Lucy's death was therefore a shock to him.

"Found her on the floor, sir," Alex reported. "Floyd's running around in circles. According to all I can find out, he thinks somebody climbed up the fire escape and knocked her down."

Dane ate a hasty lunch and drove into the village. He found the police chief grim and not inclined to be communicative.

"She's dead. That's all I'm going to say, Dane. The district attorney's coming over. I wish to God he'd keep out of this. I've got enough trouble of my own."

"What brings him?" Dane inquired. "If it was her heart—"

"Well," Floyd said grudgingly, "there are one or two more things I don't like. Somebody jerked the pushbutton off the bed, for one thing. Then about one A.M. one or two of the patients report somebody opening their doors and looking in. Searching for her, probably. Didn't know what room she was in."

"That ought to let out some of your prize suspects."

"Yeah? Just who? None of the Spencers except Carol knew where she was. And Greg Spencer says he was driving all over the map when it happened."

He did not mention the fire escape, nor did Dane. He blustered about these tight-mouthed women who wouldn't tell all they knew; that he was sorry as hell about Lucy, but if she'd only talked—However he was on the trail of something. That dead girl, now.

"She probably came from somewhere in the Middle West," he said. "Say somewhere about St. Louis, eh?"

He grinned at Dane, and Dane gave him an amused smile in return.

"I imagine we'll both know before long," he said, and went out.

The hospital was quiet when he got there. It was inured to death. It did the best it could. After that things were either up to God or to the patient, depending on your view of things. It was busy, though. No one paid any attention to Dane as he wandered around, first outside and then through the halls. Floyd was right about the fire escape. It showed fresh scratches on the rusty iron. And upstairs he had no trouble locating Lucy's empty room. But he was disappointed in finding it had been stripped and Lucy's small possessions gone.

He was tired and exasperated as he drove home. If something had frightened Lucy into the heart attack that had killed her, what was it? Or who was it?

All along Lucy's attitude had bothered him. So far as he knew she had not mentioned the presence of the girl in the house when she was found and taken to the hospital. All she had told was of a hand reaching out of the closet. Yet at the inquest she had come out flat-footed with the fact.

Had that caused her death? Sent her midnight visitor up the fire escape, to hunt her out and so terrify her that she died of shock? But why such a visitor, unless she either knew or possessed something that might be incriminating?

It was this possibility which had sent him to the hospital; to find if possible what clue to the girl's identity Lucy had in her possession. He was still working on this idea when Tim called him late in the afternoon from St. Louis.

"No soap," he said, "and hotter than the hinges of hell here. What do I do now?"

"Better catch a plane back. I may need you."

Tim protested the plane violently.

"I was airsick all the way out, and how!" he said. "Have a heart! Lemme come on my back, in a good old sleeper. I'm apt to be shoved off the plane anyhow. Any fellow with a brief case under his arm can claim priority."

Dane grinned and agreed. Nevertheless, he was uneasy. There was only one explanation of Lucy's getting out of her bed, and that was fear. If this sort of thing was to go on—

He walked worriedly about the room. His limp was almost gone, and he realized that he had not much time left. Yet if Carol was in danger—and he began to think she might be—the mystery ought to be solved soon. Not that it was a personal matter, he told himself. No man with this type of job had any business falling for a girl. Any girl. But the thing had to be stopped.

That night he drove out to the Norton place, a small frame house on a back road some miles away. A number of cars parked around it showed that Joe was not alone in his trouble. As Dane got out of the car he realized that the drought had broken at last. A fine drizzling rain was falling, making the place look bleak and forlorn. He felt like an intruder as he rapped at the door.

A woman opened it, looking at him suspiciously. She agreed to call Joe, however, and he appeared, haggard and resentful.

"If you're from the police I wish you'd let me alone," he said roughly. "She's dead. That's enough, ain't it?"

"It's not enough if somebody terrified her last night," Dane said. "Better think that over, Mr. Norton. She had a broken leg, but she got out of bed. Why did she do that?"

Joe doubled his hard fists.

"Just let me know who scared her," he said. "He'll never know what struck him."

It was some time before Dane could persuade Joe to let him see what of Lucy's effect he had brought from the hospital. They were disappointing, at that. Joe had cleared the kitchen of people, and under his suspicious eyes Dane examined what he laid out on the table; a few cotton nightgowns, some handkerchiefs, the clothing she had worn to the inquest, and last of all her shabby pocketbook.

There were only two or three dollars in it, proving that the murdered girl had not bribed her way into the house. These, a used handkerchief, and a slip containing a list of groceries bought from Miller's market the day of the girl's arrival merely bore out her story as she had told it at the inquest. And Joe knew nothing more than Lucy had told him, which was substantially what she had testified.

However, when Dane pressed him, he admitted that Lucy had been unlike herself when he saw her at the hospital.

"Seemed like she had something on her mind," he said. "I asked her, but she wouldn't tell me. Said she'd tell Miss Carol when she came. Only thing I got out of her, she said she thought the girl was scared of something the night she was killed. She didn't know what."

So it was back to the Spencer family again, Dane reflected glumly as he drove home. But how? Which one of them was involved? Gregory could have burned the hillside. His easy statement that he had arrived after the fire meant nothing. And so far they had all taken his alibi for granted. But a man could not be in Washington receiving the Medal of Honor for bravery and committing a murder at the same time. Nor could the sight of Greg, knowing him as she did, have alarmed Lucy Norton to her death.

Nevertheless, he called Washington that night, driving over to the railroad station to do so. He asked that no name be used in the return telegram or telephone message, and felt he had done all he could as he drove back.

It was his turn to keep an eye on the Spencer place. Alex was to relieve him at four in the morning, and was already snoring stertorously in his bed when Dane went out. It was still raining, a thin drizzle which would do little to help the crops but was enough to wet him pretty thoroughly as he went through the trees. It was very dark. His landmark was the light marble of the fountain, and he found it and stopped there. From where he stood the house was a dark mass, looming a hundred yards ahead. Its very darkness and stillness reassured him. He moved, limping slightly, toward it.

There was a clap of thunder then, and somewhere not far off a car backfired. Or was it a backfire? He was not certain. The rain had suddenly increased to a roar and made all sound uncertain.

He finally decided it had been a car, and began as usual quietly to circle the house. He moved first along the side toward the sea, where the terrace was empty, the chairs and tables taken in against the rain, and he went on noiselessly, until he had reached the entrance at the rear.

Each night he or Alex had watched the windows and tried the doors. Now, as he felt for the one on the drive, it was open. What confronted him was only the empty darkness of the hall. It startled him by its very unexpectedness, and it was a moment or two before he stepped warily inside. Except for the splashing of the wall fountain in the patio everything was quiet, and he was uncertain what to do. Either one of the household had left the house for some purpose, or someone had been admitted. The door had surely been locked before the family went to bed. But the total darkness made it unlikely anyone had come in. Then who was missing?

He stood for a second or two before he decided to make a move. He knew the house fairly well by that time, and he found the stairs without trouble. Still groping, he passed the door to the yellow room and went on to Carol's. It was closed and locked. He began to feel rather absurd, but he knocked finally, and felt an enormous relief when he heard her voice inside.

"Yes? What is it?"

"It's Jerry Dane," he said. "Don't be frightened. I found the front door open and the house dark. I was afraid someone might have come in."

"Just a minute."

He heard her light snap on, heard her closet door open and knew she was putting on something hastily over her night clothes. She looked very young and startled when she opened the door, her hair loose about her face and her eyes wide.

"Did you say the front door was open?"

"Yes."

"I don't understand. I locked it myself tonight. What time is it?"

"After one o'clock. Perhaps you'd better check up and see if anyone has gone out. I'll look around myself. Somebody may have come in, but I doubt it."

He turned on the lights in the yellow room while she hurried on. It was empty, and the windows were closed. He was still there, remembering it as he had first seen it, when Carol came back.

"It's Elinor," she told him. "I can't understand it. Why would she got out on a night like this? And Greg's asleep. I heard him snoring. She must have gone alone."

He glanced into Elinor's room before they went downstairs. The bed had been used. The book she had been reading was on the table beside it, and a breeze from the open window was ruffling its pages and sending in a thin spray of rain. A pair of sheer stockings hung over the back of a chair, one or two silk undergarments were strewn about, and her evening slippers were on the floor.

"You see," Carol said, her lips stiff. "She had undressed for the night. She had gone to bed too. Why would she go out? Or where?"

"There's a chance she's in the house. I didn't look in the service wing downstairs."

But Elinor was not in the house. Five minutes after he had discovered the open door Dane turned his flashlight up the hill and saw something lying there among the burned and sodden bushes near the lane.

It was Elinor, and she had been shot.

She was not dead. She had been shot through the thigh, and she was bleeding so profusely that Dane was afraid to move her. She was unconscious, and she remained unconscious through much that followed: the rousing of the household, Dr. Harrison on his knees in the rain and mud beside her, the arrival of the ambulance, and Carol's departure in it while Greg dressed and got his car.

Dane was glad to have a few minutes to himself, but he learned little. There had been footprints both in the lane and on the hillside, but either the rain had obliterated them or the ambulance had destroyed them. He did find a small pool of what looked like bloody water in the lane itself, and within a foot or two of it a small shell comb, like those Elinor wore in her hair. She had been shot there, he decided, shot and then carried a few yards up the hill.

He was still there when Greg called him to the car. Greg was badly shocked. His hands were shaking, and after a look at him Dane told him to move over and took the driver's seat himself.

"That shot," he said as they started. "It was fired pretty close to the house. Didn't you hear it?"

Greg shook his head.

"No. I don't hear much once I'm asleep. It was an accident, of course."

"Why?"

Greg stared at him.

"Don't tell me you think somebody tried to kill her," he protested. "Why would they? She doesn't even belong here. It was someone after a deer. They come down from the hills at night, you know."

"Rather early for deer, I imagine," Dane said dryly.

"I've seen them as early as this."

"It was no deer who carried her from the lane to where we found her. And it's a pretty stormy night for hunters, you know. Why don't you face it, Spencer? Someone tried to kill your sister tonight."

"Oh, for God's sake!" Greg moaned, and lapsed into bewildered silence.

16

Elinor was in the operating room when they reached the hospital, Carol, white-faced and quiet, was waiting outside in the hall. Dane thought she looked heart-breakingly anxious, when Greg went to her and took her hand.

"She'll be all right, kid. You know that, don't you?"

She roused and tried to smile at him.

"You'd better call Howard, Greg. It's Saturday. He may be in Newport."

He seemed relieved to have something to do. He went down to the telephone, leaving Dane awkward and tongue-tied. When Greg came back he reported that he had failed to locate Hilliard, he was neither at his apartment in New York nor at the Newport house.

"Probably at one of the golf clubs," Greg said, "but I can't chase him all night. I left word at both places to have him call. It's all we can do."

Dane listened glumly. He was restless. In his slacks and rubber-soled shoes he had been pacing the hall, feeling that somewhere he had fumbled. He was convinced that all these people, Elinor and Gregory and even Carol, had known something they had not told anyone. Had Gregory actually been here in Elinor's car the night the girl was murdered? Was that what they were hiding? Yet looking at Carol, clinging to Greg as if she found him a tower of strength, it seemed impossible to believe that she knew or even suspected such a thing.

Greg's distress, too, was evident. Always Dane had realized that the tie between Elinor and Greg was very close. He would never have shot her. But he was conscious of a faint stir of jealousy when Greg put his arm around Carol and she rested her head on his shoulder.

"You've helped me weather a lot of storms, kid. We'll weather this all right." He beamed down at her, his pleasant face strained and tired. "She'll be all right. Lost a lot of blood, that's all. And blood's what I ain't got anything but!"

It was three o'clock in the morning by that time. Somewhat belatedly Floyd had been notified, and he stamped out of the elevator in a bad humor, followed by Mason, who looked only half awake. Dane took advantage of his arrival to slip downstairs and telephone Alex.

"Get the car down to the hospital as fast as you can," Dane told him. "Don't ask any questions. Just get here."

He did not leave at once, though. Floyd had followed him down. He had to tell his story, and to realize that the chief of police was regarding him stonily.

"It's a queer thing, Dane," he said, "but you've been mixed up with this funny business from the start."

"What do you mean by that?"

"You walked up the drive to the Spencer place every morning, didn't you? Maybe you were there when this girl arrived."

"So I killed her!"

"So maybe you knew who she was," said Floyd, still cold.

"Oh, for God's sake!" said Dane wearily. "I didn't know her. I never even saw her before. And I'd never seen Mrs. Hilliard until she came here."

"So you say. What were you doing out at Joe Norton's last night looking over Lucy's things? Did she have something you wanted?"

Dane laughed mirthlessly.

"I'll tell you someday," he said dryly. "And I'll tell you this now. Either Mrs. Hilliard was knocked out on the lane, or she was shot there. In any event she was dragged or carried to where she was found. And I didn't do it."

Floyd was still watching him with cold unblinking eyes.

"All right," he said. "Then maybe you'll explain why you were around the Spencer place tonight in the rain. Carol says you came in and wakened her. That might be damned smart of you, Dane, if you knew what you were going to find."

"I'll tell you that right now," Dane said sharply. "I was doing what you ought to have been doing. I was keeping an eye on Crestview. Somebody around here is dangerous, Floyd. Maybe you'll get that into your dumb head someday."

But Floyd was not dumb, and Dane knew it. As he waited for the car he went over what he knew. Elinor had not been taken out of the house. She had gone out for some purpose of her own and, unlike the murdered girl, she had been fully dressed, even to the heavy shoes on her small feet and the light raincoat which had enabled him to find her.

Where had she been going? To the Wards? There was the story that Mrs. Ward had seen a man in her car the night the girl was killed. It might have worried her. But at such an hour? And in a storm?

He dismissed the Wards for what he was beginning to call X, the unknown. X, he thought grimly, would solve the equation, only he had none of the other factors.

He got away finally, irritated and taciturn. The rain was still heavy, and the night air cold. In the car he told Alex nothing except that Elinor Hilliard had been shot, and left that individual in a state of smoldering resentment. And at the entrance to the Spencer place Dane told him to turn in, without explanation.

"You might hang around," he said. "I may be some little time."

"And what will I be doing hanging around?" Alex demanded, his voice sulky.

"Try taking a nap," Dane said halfheartedly, and got out as the car stopped.

The house was still brightly lighted. He found the front door locked, rang the bell without results, and going around to the kitchen saw through a window the women inside, gathered in a close group and obviously terrified. He knocked on the glass and heard one of them scream.

"It's only Dane," he called reassuringly. "I've come from the hospital."

The noise subsided and Maggie admitted him, looking relieved.

"I'm sorry," she explained, "but we decided not to let anyone in. There's a coldhearted murderer around, major."

"You're probably right," he told her gravely. "That's how I happened to be here tonight. I was afraid something would happen."

The girls looked panicky again, and he hastened to reassure them. He felt that it was over now, and Mrs. Hilliard would certainly live. In that case she might tell them who had shot her. There was no mystery about her being out. She had gone out, perhaps for a breath of fresh air, and had probably been attacked in the lane and carried—he did not say dragged—to the hillside.

Maggie gave him some coffee, her consistent remedy for all emergencies, and only after he drank it did he tell her he would like to go up to Elinor Hilliard's room.

"There may be something there to indicate why she went out," he said. "Anyhow I'd like to look at it. Did Mrs. Hilliard get a telephone call tonight?"

If she had they did not know it. They let him go up alone, and after a brief survey which showed him nothing he wanted to know he went on to the yellow room. The lights were turned off, although he did not remember that either Carol or he himself had done so, and when he switched them on he stared around him in astonishment. The room had been hastily searched. One window was open, the edges of the rug had been turned back, the mattresses on the twin beds displaced, and a loose baseboard had been pried away from the wall near the mantel.

Dane stood looking at this last for some time. It had been a good hiding place if she had used it, he thought sourly. And either someone who had known it was there or who had better eyes than his had seen it.

He went back over the night's events. Carol had had no chance. She was in the house only long enough to notify Gregory and call the doctor. Gregory himself? He had come on the run, still pulling on his dressing gown as he came. Anyhow why should he? He had several days in which to search the house. After that, with the exception of the servants, the house had been empty. But the lights had all been on, and it seemed unlikely that anyone could have entered the front door while they were on the hillside. He was certain, too, that the windows of the yellow room were all closed when he saw it last.

Alex's ladder, he thought, his mouth tight. He had slipped up badly there. He should have seen that it was taken away.

Before he went downstairs he examined Gregory's room. It was furnished as it probably had been since his boyhood holidays there: his college photographs on the wall, a snapshot of a grinning youth who might have been himself at sixteen holding a string of trout, a shelf of books, and a glass-topped box of slowly desiccating moths.

The room was kept with military tidiness. Greg's uniforms were hung up, the drawers in the bureau neatly in order. The closet door was open as Greg had left it, and Dane looked at the suitcase on the floor. It was closed but not locked. He opened it, to find a service automatic. It had not been fired recently, however, and he put it back and shut the case.

There was no sign of any intruder downstairs until he reached the side door. This, more or less under the staircase, opened on to a grass terrace, and the door was unlocked. Careful not to disturb any possible prints he went outside and found what he had expected. The ladder was lying on the ground under the windows of the yellow room.

The picture was clear now, so far as it went. Whoever had entered the house had used the ladder, but had left by the side door.

Once more he cursed Tim for his refusal to fly back. He left the ladder where it was, and going back to the car found Alex asleep in it, which added to his irritation.

"No hope you saw anybody around, I suppose?" he said, taking the wheel himself.

"You told me to take a nap." Alex was aggrieved. "Who'd be hanging around a night like this anyhow?"

Dane drove home, to call the hospital and learn from Carol that Elinor was out of the operating room, and that lacking a blood bank they had typed Greg and were giving her an infusion.

"They think she has a good chance. She's stronger than she looks, you know."

"Good. What about you?"

She seemed surprised.

"Me? I'm all right. Anxious, of course. I'd better come back and get dressed."

"Listen," he said earnestly. "I want you to stay there until full daylight. If you won't I'll come for you myself. I'm not taking any chances on you."

There was something new in his voice, a sort of protective tenderness she had not heard in it before. It made her feel a little happier. She had not had much affection since Don's death, and even Don himself had been a casual, debonair lover. After a moment's silence, she said, "You think it's a homicidal maniac, don't you?"

"I told you once, the first murder is the hard one."

After some argument she agreed to stay, and at last he relaxed and went to bed. Not to sleep at once, however. He was puzzling over the yellow room and what—if anything—had been hidden in it. And for some reason he was seeing Mr. Ward, small and elderly and wary, saying that he did not run to the police with what he called tittle-tattle, and rather abruptly ending the interview and not shaking hands when he left.

He would have been greatly surprised had he known that at that same moment Mr. Ward was putting his car away with as little noise as possible, and stealthily entering his stately house. Or that when he went up to his dressing room he took a revolver out of his pocket and placed it carefully in a drawer, under a tidy pile of the stiff-bosomed dress shirts he so seldom used these days.

Dane was up and out again at eight that Sunday morning. The rain had stopped, and except for Maggie returning from early Mass there was no one in sight at Crestview. He waited until she was safely in the house, then going through the woods to the crest of the hill he began to work his way down. No one had traveled in that direction, however. He crunched and slid through the debris of the fire, watching the ground intently, and was brought up suddenly by a small shallow hole.

It was freshly dug. A pool of rain water lay at the bottom, and a garden trowel had been dropped a few feet away. Dane examined the hole carefully. It was only a foot or so deep and as much across. The ground around it was trampled, and he thought the digging had been hasty.

He picked up the trowel with a handkerchief. The handle was fairly clean, and he wrapped it in the fresh linen. He was still carrying it when, having followed down to where he had found Elinor, he came out on the lane once more. The road was muddy, and the heavy rain had washed away all traces of the bloody water he had seen the night before, as well as any possible footprints. There was one, however, which remained fairly intact. He measured it beside his own, and decided that it had been made by a fairly tall man. He was still stooping over it when he heard someone behind him. It was Mr. Ward.

He wore an overcoat against the cold morning air, but he was bareheaded. Instinctively Dane glanced at his feet. Even in galoshes they were small, and Mr. Ward saw the look and smiled frostily.

"It might have been mine," he said. "I'm often here. I don't think it is, do you?"

"Doesn't look like it." Dane straightened. "There was some blood here last night. It's been washed away. Did you hear the shot, Mr. Ward? It was fired about here."

"Who hears a shot these days?" Mr. Ward countered. "A shot and a backfire sound much alike. No. I heard nothing. I was asleep, I suppose. I don't even know when it happened. In fact, I've only just heard about it. The milkman is our local paper."

He did not look as though he had been asleep. In fact, he looked old and exhausted, his face a yellow-white and his veined hands unsteady. He looked at the handkerchief-wrapped trowel.

"I see you've found something, major."

Its shape betrayed it. Dane opened it carefully, and Mr. Ward took a step nearer to look at it with nearsighted eyes.

"A trowel!" he said. "What does that mean? We all have them. Where did you find it?"

"It was on the hillside," Dane said carefully. "I wondered about it. That's all."

He did not mention the hole, nor did he have occasion to, for at that moment Nathaniel Ward staggered. He caught Dane by the arm, and the trowel fell to the muddy ground. Days later Dane was to wonder whether that action was intentional or not, but certainly the old man's color was definitely worse. He looked like a man who had received an unexpected blow. He did not even speak for a moment. Then:

"I'm sorry," he muttered. "I'm too old for all this, I suppose. Just a moment. I'll be all right."

Dane held him now with both arms. His body felt small under his heavy coat. Dane managed to reach his pulse, and found it stringy and faint.

"I'd better get you to the house," he said. "Or if you'll sit here on the bank I'll get someone to help you back."

But Ward held up a protesting hand.

"Don't alarm my wife," he said. "I'll be all right. I'll sit down, if you'll assist me."

The trowel was still on the ground. Dane seated Mr. Ward on the bank and then picked it up. Part of the handle was covered with mud, and he swore under his breath. Nevertheless, he rewrapped it. Mr. Ward did not seem to notice. He was sitting with his eyes shut, but his color was slowly coming back.

"I'm most apologetic," he said. "I don't often come out before breakfast, but when I heard about Elinor I decided to walk over to see if I could do anything."

It could have been true. He had come along the graveled path that connected the two properties. But Dane believed that the old man had been shocked to find him there, although the attack, whatever it was, had been real.

"Have you spells often?" he asked.

"I get dizzy now and then. Nothing to do with my heart. Middle-ear trouble probably." He was much better now. He pulled out a clean handkerchief and wiped his forehead. "Don't let me keep you. I'll sit here for a minute. I'm perfectly all right."

Thus dismissed, Dane moved back toward Crestview. He was still suspicious, although he hardly knew why, and halfway along the path he turned and looked back. The immaculate Nathaniel Ward was picking something from the mud near his feet. Even at that distance it gleamed dully, and Dane was certain it had been the shell from the gun with which Elinor had been shot.

He hesitated. He could go back and demand to see it, in which case Nathaniel would certainly deny he had it, or he could go on and pretend he had seen nothing. He decided to go on.

17

Breakfast was ready when he got back to the house. When Alex brought in the bacon and eggs he found Dane examining the trowel, and looked astonished.

"What's that, sir?"

"I imagine it was intended to dig up the clothes on the hill. Look here, Alex. What do you know about the Wards? And I wish to God you'd learn how to make coffee."

"I'm no cook, sir. I never pretended to be a cook. If you don't like the way I do things—"

"All right," Dane said impatiently. "What about the Wards?"

Alex scratched his head.

"Well, they're very highly thought of here," he said. "Very rich, but the townspeople like them. They give to the churches and the hospital, all the local stuff. Their son was killed in the last war. They've got a grandson in this one. They've been coming for forty years or so."

"Their grandson been back lately?"

"They expected him, but he didn't turn up."

Dane called the hospital after breakfast. Elinor Hilliard was somewhat better and was conscious. Greg was still there, but Carol was at home, and he went over to Crestview after he had hung up. He had expected to learn she was in bed, but he found her in the library beside the fire. She was looking exhausted, her hands lying limp in her lap, and her eyes lifeless. But she smiled at him.

"I've just had a telephone battle with Mother," she told him. "You would think I had shot Elinor myself. Either I'm to go home, or she will come up."

"And you don't want her?"

"She can't help, and she doesn't understand," she said wearily.

"She's used to this house with seven or eight servants in it. And the way things are . . . Howard will be coming, but he can stay at the hotel."

"Then you've located Mr. Hilliard?"

"Not yet. It's Sunday, so his office is closed. He may be weekending anywhere. Mother didn't know."

He gave her a cigarette and took one himself as he sat down.

"Do you mind a little family talk?" he asked.

"I'm used to them. What about?"

"Your sister. Are she and her husband happy together?"

She thought that over, as if she were uncertain.

"It depends on what you call happy, I suppose. They're congenial. They like the same things; you know, parties and bridge and plenty of money. He's frightfully proud of her." She roused then and stared at him. "You aren't thinking Howard shot her, are you? That—well, that would be ridiculous."

"All right," he said. "Cancel Howard. Why did she dress and go out last night, Carol? It was raining, you know."

She gave him the candid glance that always touched him.

"She was after her clothes, wasn't she?" she said. "At least I'm afraid she was. I don't know, of course."

Anyhow that bar was down between them, thank God, he thought. She had been so pitifully alone, with no one to turn to. If she would lose him—

"I don't pretend to understand it," she said, closing her eyes. "My brain doesn't seem to work. She's had time enough to look for them, and last night it rained. She's like a cat. She hates rain. Yet she—I don't think she killed that girl, you know. And she liked Lucy. She'd never have bothered her."

"But you think she knows more than she's telling?"

"Yes. That's what frightens me. If she's protecting someone . . ."

He knew what she meant. Carol thought Elinor was protecting Greg. He changed the subject abruptly.

"Have you been upstairs since you came back?"

"Only to dress. Why?"

"You didn't look in the yellow room?"

"No. What about it?"

She was sitting erect now, and looking frightened.

"It's all right," he told her quickly. "Nothing to worry about. I saw it on my way home. I'd come in to see everything was all right. Somebody had searched it pretty thoroughly."

She relaxed at that, as though the mere searching of a room was nothing compared with the welter of blood and mystery that surrounded her.

"I don't understand," she said slowly. "It's been carefully cleaned. Unless the police . . ."

"I don't think it was the police. It may tie in with your sister's being shot. Suppose she heard someone in the house and followed outside—"

She shook her head.

"She'd never do that," she said and got up. "I'll have to see the room, I suppose. I'm glad Freda hasn't seen it first."

He had prepared her as well as he could, but the first sight of the yellow room certainly shocked her. He had to restrain himself from putting his arms around her.

"Look, my dear," he said, "It's not so bad as all that. Someone was looking for something. That's all."

"So we're just to go on, two people dead, Elinor shot and the hill burned. I can't take much more, Jerry."

She cried a little then, and after a while he held her head against his shoulder and felt for a handkerchief.

"Blow for papa," he said, and was pleased to see her lift her head and smile.

"I'm not really a baby," she told him. "I play golf and tennis and swim and ride a horse. Usually I'm just average. But this has got me down. It's—as Greg would say—it's pretty rugged."

She insisted on straightening the room before the servants saw it, and the next few minutes they spent repairing the damage as best they could. Dane even managed to get the baseboard back in palce, somewhat tottery but still, so to speak, on its own. The church bells were ringing when they finished, and she stopped to listen, as though it was strange that people should be going quietly to morning service while her own world was so chaotic. He felt that in her, and he kissed her lightly before he left.

"For being a good girl," he said cheerfully, and limped down the stairs to find Colonel Richardson, breathing hard from his climb, in the hall.

"What damnable thing is going on?" he demanded. "Nobody tells me anything. I have to hear it from my servants or from someone who happens by. A girl murdered and burned! Lucy Norton dead! Now Elinor Hilliard is shot, and I'm not so much as notified."

"I'm sorry, colonel," Dane said pacifically. "Things have happened pretty fast. Mrs. Hilliard was shot only last night, and it may have been an accident."

He snorted and looked at Dane suspiciously.

"What was she doing outside in the rain?" he demanded. "I know Elinor. I never liked her much, but she wouldn't go out alone at night in the rain for a million dollars. And she likes money at that. What happened? Does she know?"

"She's not allowed to talk. She's barely conscious, I believe. She lost a lot of blood. But she's going to be all right."

Dane got the impression that the colonel had more to say. He stood still for a moment, as though debating something with himself. But evidently he decided against it, for he saluted stiffly, turned on his heel and departed. Dane, watching him as he left, thought that aside from his almost defiant head he was not a well man. His lips after the climb up the hill had been slightly blue. And he was leaning rather heavily on his stick. He was certain too that the colonel had not been entirely frank with him.

There was a car climbing the hill as he was leaving. It came with difficulty, gasping and roaring, and when at last it came into sight he saw an ancient vehicle, driven by a grinning young man who brought it to a stop and then mopped his face with a handkerchief, as though he had been pushing the car himself.

"Got here," he said triumphantly. "She's a good old bus, only a bit on the asthma side."

He got out and looked around him, at the burned hillside, at the house and then at Dane himself.

"Say, what goes on?" he inquired. "Another death and a shooting since I was here last! That's going some. That the hill where the Hilliard woman was attacked?"

"Attacked? Who said she was attacked?"

"Don't tell me she was shot by accident, or that she tried to kill herself by shooting herself in the leg. Who shot her, and why?"

His smile, in spite of Dane's resentment, was engaging.

"Mind telling me who you are?" he inquired. He eyed Dane's slacks. "Are you the brother, Captain Spencer? I'm Starr from the paper over at the county seat. I was here before."

"I live next door," said Dane, somewhat diverted by all this. "I don't know anything. If you want a story go to Floyd, the police chief here."

"Old sourpuss?" Starr laughed. "He'd clap me in the clink as soon as he saw me." He viewed Dane with keen young eyes. "Say, I've seen you before, haven't I?"

"Hardly likely," Dane said dryly. "I've been here only a few weeks."

But the boy grinned and then whistled.

"I've got you! Starr with the eagle eye. Starr the boy reporter who never forgets a face. Remember the time that gang blew into the county seat to order machine guns, and you came up from Washington?"

Dane was annoyed.

"Now listen, son," he said. "I'm in the army, now and until the war is over. I'm getting over a shot in the leg, and if you know what's good for you that's all you know."

"But hell, sir—"

"That's an order," Dane snapped.

Starr subsided. Dane felt repentant as he watched his crestfallen young face, and told him briefly what had happened, the shot followed by the finding of Elinor Hilliard wounded. He intimated, however, that she had heard someone outside and been shot while investigating. And the boy—he was little more—gave him something in return.

"Funny thing," he said. "I saw the body of the girl they found in the closet. She sure as hell was wearing a wedding ring. Floyd never gave that out, did he?"

"It's the first I've heard of it."

He was thoughtful after the reporter left. Did Floyd have the ring and was he deliberately keeping quiet about it? Or had this youngster been mistaken? After all, it had not been a pleasant sight.

His leg was better. It had been improving for some time, he realized as he walked home, and the thought cheered him considerably. His voice was almost gay when he was called to the long-distance phone. Nevertheless, the message, couched in careful language, gave him furiously to think. The subject of the inquiry, it said, had received his "what you may call it" in Washington on Wednesday, June fourteenth. He had had a room at a hotel and had stayed there Wednesday night. At some time on Thursday he had packed a bag hastily and said he was taking a plane to New York, giving no address there, and not returning at all.

"Not back yet," said the voice. "Hotel has had no word. Drinking pretty hard before he left. No other details. Corroboration by letter."

Dane thought a minute after he hung up. Then he got in touch with Tim Murphy, who had reported from New York and was waiting for train accommodation north. He knew that Bessie would be listening in, but there was no time to waste.

"About the C.M.O.H., Tim," he said. "Find out if the holder was registered there in New York at a hotel between these dates. It's important. Probably one of the big places, but I'm not sure. And get a move on. We've had more trouble here."

He gave the dates and Tim took them down. He had some trouble with the Congressional Medal of Honor, but finally understood. He had not finished, however.

"I located that suitcase here," he said. "Initials M.D.B. Sounds all right, doesn't it?"

"Sounds fine."

"Railroad company won't let it go. But they can get it opened, or a friend of mine there can. What are they to look for?"

"How the hell do I know?" Dane said irritably. "Papers, documents, photographs—you know as well as I do."

"No panties?"

"No panties," said Dane grimly. "And you'd better come back here as soon as you can. I need you."

Dane rang off, confident that Bessie at least would be puzzled. He was not so sure about Floyd, nor indeed about the whole business. After all, Greg was not only a nation-wide hero, with his picture in all the papers. He was Carol's brother, and Dane was not fooling himself any longer about Carol. Not that it was any use, he knew. This was a long war, in spite of the idiots who were betting it would soon be over. And Carol had waited for Don Richardson. He was not going to ask her to wait for him.

As for Greg he was puzzled. He could have come here by plane, killed the girl and got away. Nevertheless, there was the fact that he had come back, rather cheerfully than otherwise. Murderers did not return to the scene of their crimes, unless they were psychopathic. They got as far away as they could, and stayed there.

He was thoughtful when he called Alex, who came from his kitchen without removing the apron tied around his broad body.

"What about this grandson of the Wards?" he asked. "You say he hasn't come home lately."

"No, sir. They were expecting him a while ago, but he couldn't get away. They'd planned some sort of party for him, but he had to go back to the Pacific. Old lady went to bed over it. Kinda hard on her."

"That the one they call Terry?"

"Yeah. Not short for Terence. Mother's name was Terry. He's a flier in the Pacific. Good guy, by all accounts. Father and mother both dead. Lived with the old folks.''

As usual Dane ate his lunch outside. The weather had cleared, and a plane had ventured out, flying low. He ate at the corner of the porch, so that by turning his head he could see either the bay or the ridge of hills above him. He could see the skeleton of the burned house, a chimney of the gardener's house at Rockhill, and above and beyond them all two or three abandoned summer properties.

He had driven or walked around most of them, with their neglected gardens and their blank closed windows. Now, returning to the X of his earlier equation, it occurred to him that someone could hide almost indefinitely in any of them. He did not admit even to himself that he preferred an unidentified criminal to Greg Spencer. It was merely a part of his system to explore all possibilities. He said nothing to Alex when he took his car that afternoon and drove around over the hill. Owing to the gasoline shortage, the roads back there were completely deserted, and the first two empty houses were closed so entirely that he gave them up after a brief examination. The third was different.

It was also closed, of course. It was almost buried in vegetation, and no tire marks showed on the ragged drive. But a winter shutter was loose, and underneath it in the soft ground he found a footprint or two. He took his automatic from a compartment in the car, and going back to the building managed to raise the window.

It creaked badly. He waited for a while; then, nothing happening, he put a leg over the sill and crawled inside.

The building, shut in as it was, was almost entirely dark. It smelled moldy and dank. But it also smelled faintly of tobacco smoke. It was not fresh. It might have been there for a week or more. Nevertheless, someone had been in the house recently, and might still be there.

The darkness bothered him. He had forgotten to bring a flashlight, and after he left the room by which he had entered only the hall showed a faint illumination from the window he had opened. Using matches he more or less felt his way along, until a blank space indicated a door.

He stepped inside and almost fell over a pile of blankets. They were lying there, abandoned in a heap, as if they had been dropped casually. Otherwise the room was undisturbed. It had been a dining room and some of the old-fashioned furniture still remained. Outside of the two blankets, however, he found nothing. The kitchen, too, was neat and empty. Apparently no one had cooked there for years. But the few dishes in the closet he found remarkably clean, and he was whistling softly to himself as he lit a cigarette and went up the stairs. Here were the usual bedrooms, the beds with ancient mattresses on them and everything else of value gone.

On one bed, however, was a pillow, somewhat indented as though it had been slept on. That the house had been occupied by someone, and that recently, he did not doubt. But he did not doubt either the care with which all evidence of each occupation had been eliminated. The blankets were a curious oversight. He puzzled over them, leaving the house as he had found it and drove slowly home.

18

Carol Spencer was not the same girl who only ten days or so before had kicked Greg's golf clubs out of her way in the train and worried about opening Crestview. That sheltered, carefully set-up young woman had vanished. She was as neatly dressed as ever, her eyes as frank, her smile—when it came—as spontaneous. But there were lines of strain in her face, and she looked very tired. Maggie, coming in after Dane had gone that morning, surveyed her with disfavor.

"Are you planning to stay up all day?" she inquired truculently. "What good will you be to anybody if you get sick?"

"I don't suppose I can sleep. What about the girls, Maggie?"

"Scared of their shadows. That man who was going to help hasn't showed up again, and I'm having to fix the furnace myself."

"That's ridiculous. I'll tell Greg to do it." Carol got up, but Maggie caught her arm.

"There's that newspaper fellow snooping around," she hissed. "Up with you, Miss Carol. I'll tell him you're sick. And sick you look," she added. "I'll bring you some coffee right off."

She whisked Carol up the stairs and stood by until she got into bed. For a second or so she paused indecisively by Don Richardson's picture. Then she faced Carol, her honest Irish face troubled.

"I've got something to tell you, Carol," she said, reverting to years ago when Carol was a child, running in from play to ransack the refrigerator or to find sanctuary from her governess. "I don't like to say it, especially just now, but you'll have to know it sooner or later."

Carol smiled. Maggie's troubles usually referred to her department of the house. This proved to be different, however.

She had been out the night before, Maggie said. At the Daltons' with the maids there playing hearts. She was surprised when she found how late it was. It was around one o'clock when she put on her galoshes and got her umbrella and started home, and before she reached the main road she heard a shot.

"It could have been a backfire," she said, "but I didn't think it was. I didn't hear any car. I just stood still, kinda scared. I guess I was there five minutes or so. It was raining cats and dogs. And then I heard somebody running. He was splashing down the lane, and—now mind, I don't say he shot Miss Elinor; why would he?—but it was Colonel Richardson."

Carol sat upright in her bed, her face a mask of astonishment.

"It couldn't have been, Maggie. Not the colonel! He never—"

"I seen him plain enough," Maggie said stubbornly. "White hair and all. He looked as though he was wearing a bathrobe or something, and he went into his house and slammed the door as though the devil was after him. Believe me, I got up to the house fast by the short cut from the road. I was plenty scared."

Carol dismissed all this with a gesture.

"He's been queer lately," she said. "And don't tell me he'd leave the Wards' in that storm and in what he was wearing. I been going over it in my mind ever since. Seems to me he'd had just time to come from the hill where they found Miss Elinor, but I didn't see any gun. Why else was he running like that, with the heart he's got?"

"I'm sure there's some perfectly ordinary explanation, Maggie."

"Well, it's off my mind anyhow, miss." Maggie returned with dignity to her role of cook to a respected family. "I'd rather you didn't mention it to the police, if you please. I don't want that Floyd poking around. The way he went up to the attic where he had no business to be, and carried away your grandmother's washstand set . . ."

This grievance being an old and safe one, Carol let her go on. After Maggie had gone, however, she lay back and thought with some anxiety over the story. Had the shot alarmed the colonel, so that he had run back to his house? Had he already told the police the story? And why had he been in the lane at all, unprotected from the rain? She came back to Maggie's statement that he had been what she called queer. Outside of his obsession about Don, which was largely wishful thinking, he had seemed much as usual to her, courtly and kind.

Greg came in to interrupt her thoughts. He had had breakfast and some sleep at the hospital, and although his handsome face looked weary the news he brought was good.

"She'll be all right," he told her. "Lost a lot of blood, but it missed the big artery. She hasn't any idea who did it. They won't let her talk much, of course, but it's a puzzler, isn't it?''

He wandered about the room, said he needed a bath and shave, and wondered if they could have lunch up there.

"Think the staff will run to a couple of trays?" he asked boyishly.

She thought it would, and they had cocktails and ate the usual Sunday dinner of chicken and ice cream together in her room. It was characteristic of Greg that he threw off Maggie's story about the colonel as easily as he threw off everything which did not immediately concern him. She marveled at that ability of his. He was the old Greg, for all his war record, saying life was fun, even when he had a headache the morning after.

"The Irish are an imaginative lot," he said, amused. "The old boy runs to get out of the rain, so he's mixed up in this mess. Or maybe Maggie shot Elinor herself and makes this up! She isn't fond of Elinor, you know. Never was."

He clung to the theory that the shooting was the result of an accident. Carol found herself accepting it, as the simplest way out. But after he had gone, to bathe and shave and take a nap, she made a decision. She took off Don's engagement ring for the first time since he had put it on her finger, and put it away in her jewel case. She felt freer without it, as though she had finally laid a ghost.

In the meantime Dane took his car and drove down to Floyd's office. He had decided to tell the chief about the empty house. It would at least keep him busy, he thought derisively, and off his own neck. But Floyd was not alone when he got there; he was in angry consultation with Campbell. The district attorney was cold and unsmiling, chewing on an unlighted cigar, his hat on the floor beside him and his expression one of annoyance mixed with contempt.

"What did you expect me to do?" Floyd was demanding savagely. "I'm here alone except for Mason and a traffic man. I can't put guards around the whole town. I haven't got them. If I ask for more help it raises the taxes, and watch the people howl."

"You knew Lucy Norton didn't tell all she knew at the inquest," Campbell said, scowling.

"So what? So I'm to put an intern at the hospital outside her door as a guard? They've got more than they can manage there now. Look at this town, only one doctor left, no men available, no nothing. As for the Hilliard woman, if she wants to wander around at night in the rain and get shot that's her business. I can't keep her in her bed, can I?"

Neither of them paid any attention at first to Dane. He walked to the desk and stood waiting until the argument ceased, Then:

"I was driving around the back roads today," he said to Floyd. "Know a place called Pine Hill?"

"Been empty for years," Floyd said sulkily. "What about it?"

"I have an idea someone's been sleeping there lately. Maybe a tramp, maybe not. Couple of blankets on the floor. Bed upstairs may have been used."

Floyd blew up.

"That's all I need," he roared. "It's an unknown now, is it? That saves your friends at Crestview, I suppose. I may be only a hick policeman, but I haven't lost my senses."

"You might go up and look." Dane's voice was mild.

"You bet I'll go up and look, and if this is a plant, Dane—"

"It's not a plant."

Campbell spoke then.

"What's your idea, major? How did you happen on this house?"

Dane sat down and got out a cigarette.

"I don't exactly know," he admitted. "There are a good many imponderables in the case. You can't leave out X, you know."

"Who's *X?*" Floyd snorted.

"It's just a symbol I use for myself. Meaning the unknown factor, of course. Has Mrs. Hilliard talked yet?"

"If you can call it talking! Says she doesn't know who shot her. Says she wasn't on the hill at all. Couldn't sleep and went out as far as the dirt lane there. Knows she was shot and remembers falling. That's all."

Dane was thoughtful. Elinor's story did not hold water, of course, except that she had not been on the hill. That was true enough. He looked at Floyd.

"Was the girl who was murdered wearing a wedding ring when you found her?"

"What's that got to do with it?" Floyd was still surly.

"Well, was she?"

Reluctantly Floyd opened the drawer of his desk and took out the box Carol had seen earlier. He shook its contents out onto the desk blotter. "The jury saw these," he said resentfully. "I don't know what right you have to look at them."

Dane surveyed them, the scorched imitation pearl earrings and a narrow gold band. He picked up the latter and weighted it in his hand, then he carried it to the window and examined it. There was a poorly engraved inscription inside it.

"C to M," the chief said grudgingly, "if that's any help to you."

"Mind if I borrow it for five minutes?"

"What for?"

"Just an idea I have. Make it ten. I'll be right back."

He did not wait for consent. As he left he heard the chief's voice raised in protest, and Campbell's milder one.

"If he's got any ideas we need them," he was saying. "So far as I can see—"

Dane was longer than ten minutes. It was a half hour before he had wakened the local jeweler from his Sunday nap, induced him to open his shop and produce his watchmaker's glass. With this screwed in his eye, Dane examined the ring carefully. It was, as he had thought, of the light and inexpensive kind, but he focused his attention on the engraving.

His face was sober as he thanked the watchmaker and returned the ring to Floyd. He made no comments as he put it back on the desk. Floyd was less truculent now. He put the ring back into the box, and the box into the drawer again.

"Sorry if I've been kind of rough with you, major," he mumbled. "Fact is this thing's got me. I don't sleep. I don't eat. This is a resort town, and things like these in the papers don't help any."

"Maybe we can clean up some of it."

Floyd eyed him.

"If you've got anything you ought to tell me," he said resentfully.

"I've found Pine Hill."

"Still after X, are you?"

"I think it's worth looking into. You might find some prints, for one thing."

"And then what? I can't fingerprint everybody in this town. Or any tramp who chooses to break into an empty house and sleep there."

Dane drove to the hospital after he left the police station. Elinor Hilliard was still allowed no visitors, but her husband had been located and was expected at any time. He had somehow managed to get a plane and was flying up.

In spite of his new knowledge Dane found himself wondering about Hilliard. So far he had been only a name, but he could not afford to eliminate anybody. And this was corroborated when, on reaching Crestview, he found Carol still in bed and Marcia Dalton and Louise Stimson snugly settled in the library. They had walked up, they said, and finding Carol and Greg both asleep had come in for a rest and a drink.

"How's the sleuthing going?" Louise asked, her smile faintly impertinent.

"Sleuthing? If you mean finding Mrs. Hilliard—"

"The talk is that you were watching this house when you found her."

"Then you'll have to admit I failed pretty completely," he said gravely.

It was obvious that they meant to stay, and he groaned inwardly. They gave him the local gossip, however. According to it, Greg was out. He would never shoot Elinor. And someone, coming home by the back road, had seen a car driving madly along the main road at two o'clock that morning. They had no authority for it. It was being told, that was all.

"What sort of car?" he asked.

"Not Elinor's this time," Marcia said. "A long dark one. I wish I knew how people get the gas they do. I can't."

"It sounds like Elinor Hilliard's husband," Louis drawled. "They seem to have all they want, don't they? And Howard always drove like the devil. Maybe the girl they found here was living with him, and Elinor put her out of the way. She might, you know. She's a pretty cool proposition."

He got rid of them at last, and went back to the kitchen. Greg was still asleep, Maggie said, and the two girls, Freda and Nora, were upstairs packing to leave.

"I can't hold them," she said. "Not any longer. They're scared. So am I, but I'm staying. I can't leave Miss Carol like this. Maybe I can get somebody from the village. Only the town's scared too. It's as much as I can do to get the groceries delivered."

"I might be able to locate the man Alex got you for a day or two. Tim Murphy, wasn't it?"

"A fat lot of good he'd be! He walked off without notice."

"He could wash the dishes."

In spite of what was waiting for him upstairs he smiled to himself. The thought of Tim washing the dishes and scouring pans was almost too much for him. But he needed a man in this house, and Tim had done worse things in his time.

"I'll try to find him," he said. "He may have a perfectly valid reason for not showing up."

The two girls were lugging suitcases down the back staircase as he went toward the front of the house. One look at their determined faces showed him the uselessness of protest, and he went forward and up to Gregory Spencer's room.

Greg was awake. His shower was running, and he did not hear the knock at the door. When he came out of the bathroom, clad only in a pair of shorts, he found Dane settled in a chair calmly smoking, and stared at him in amazement.

"Sorry," Dane said. "I rapped, but you didn't hear me. I had a question to ask, and it couldn't wait."

"What sort of question?"

The very fact that Greg's face was suddenly wary convinced Dane he was right. At least he had to take a chance. He took it.

"I was wondering," he said quietly, "just when and where you married the girl who was killed in this house ten days ago."

19

If he had depended on surprise he succeeded. Greg did not even protest. He stood still, his fine big body moist from the shower, a bit of shaving lather on the lobe of one ear, and threw out his hands in a gesture of resignation.

"I suppose it had to come out," he said. "How did you know it?"

"A number of things turned up. For one, she wore a wedding ring. It said 'G to M' inside it."

"A ring? I never gave her a ring."

It was Dane's turn to be surprised.

"She had it. Floyd has it now. His eyes aren't too good. He thinks the G is a C. He may know better by this time."

But Greg was still bewildered.

"I give you my word of honor, Dane, I never gave her a ring." Then the full meaning of the situation began to dawn on him. He sat down abruptly on the edge of the bed. "I didn't kill her, either," he said heavily. "You probably don't believe that, but it's true."

"You must have wanted to get rid of her," Dane said inexorably. "You were engaged to another girl. She was planning to marry you on this leave. And I'm telling you now, you haven't an alibi worth a cent, unless you can prove you were in New York when it was done."

Greg shook his head confusedly.

"I didn't do it. I don't even know who did."

"But you knew she was dead, didn't you? You went ahead with your plans for being married again. How did you know all that, Spencer? Who told you?"

"I'd rather not answer that," Greg said slowly. "I knew it. That will have to do." He drew a long breath. "I'd had a year of hell, Dane. It was a relief."

He dropped his head in his hands. It was some time before he looked up, and his eyes were dull and hopeless.

"Let me tell you the story, Dane," he said. "God knows I'll be glad to get it off my chest. I came back on a special mission last May a year ago. I guess you know how these things are. I did the job—it was in Los Angeles—but I had to wait for a plane to take me back. I fell in with a lot of fellows, and they found some girls somewhere.

"We were drinking pretty hard, and one of the girls seemed to like me. I remember that, and by God that's about all I do remember, except that I woke up a morning or two later below the border in Mexico with this girl in a room with me, and she said I'd married her."

Dane nodded. He knew better than most the strain of the war, and the drinking that was so often an escape from it. He was no moralist, either. He offered Greg a cigarette and took one himself.

"Go on," he said. "It's a dirty trick, of course. It's been done before."

Greg looked grateful.

"Well, figure it out for yourself," he said. "It was true enough. She had a certificate. And until I saw it I didn't even know her name!

"I went back to the Pacific, and I tried my damnedest to get killed. That's why I got that decoration. Believe me, I was sick at my stomach when they pinned it on me. I'm still sick. I'd tried all year to break off with Virginia. Imagine how I felt when I came home and found she had planned our wedding! I couldn't marry her. I couldn't marry anybody. I tried to prime myself to tell her by taking a few drinks, and that turned out as you might expect.

"That's the story, Dane. I didn't kill Marguerite, but I knew she was coming east. She wrote me at Washington. I haven't seen her since I left, more than a year ago, but I sent her a thousand dollars then to keep her quiet. I thought maybe she'd let me divorce her. But she didn't want a divorce. She was coming east to see Carol and my mother. I tried to stop her. I flew to New York, but I was too late. She'd left her hotel. The next thing I knew she was dead."

"You didn't know she was coming here?"

"How could I? Mother and Carol were in Newport. But she must have told poor old Lucy who she was, or she wouldn't have let her in the house. That's what gets me, Dane. I can't pretend I'm sorry about Marguerite, but Lucy—what on earth happened to Lucy?"

He got up. He looked rather better, as though telling the story had given him relief.

"I've wondered," he said. "Lucy was fond of us. She might have killed herself. She was a little thing—Lucy, I mean—but these New Englanders are capable of violence. The way their boys are fighting in this war—But of course that's crazy, isn't it? Who shot Elinor? Who burned the hill? What's it all about anyhow?"

The contrast between the two men was very marked at that moment, Greg's bewildered, not too clever face against Dane's keen determined one. Dane lit a cigarette.

"I can tell you about the fire," he said casually. "At least I'm morally certain. Your sister, Mrs. Hilliard, set it."

Greg's expression changed, hardened. He flushed angrily.

"You'd better have good reason for an accusation of that sort," he said stiffly. "My sister is not mixed up in this. It's my story, not hers."

"You're sure of that, are you?"

"Absolutely."

"She knew you married this girl, didn't she?"

For the first time Greg's frankness deserted him.

"She didn't know it until recently."

"How recently?"

"I don't remember."

He was definitely on guard now, and Dane got up.

"About that ring," he said, "How do you account for it?"

"She must have bought it herself. I never gave her one. I never even saw her, after Mexico."

"Any letters of yours?"

"Only one with the check in it. The check had my name on it. I didn't sign the letter. Only my initials."

"Do you think she brought the letter with her?" Dane persisted. "She brought something, I am sure of that, and something somebody wants. I don't know what it is. I don't even know who wants it. If it wasn't your sister who was shot last night I would think you were that person. Look here, do you remember any of the men in Los Angeles who were in that party?"

Greg shook his head.

"They came and went, the way those things are. I expect some of them are gone by this time. Anyhow I'd had plenty to drink before that. I was pretty well under before the party—if you can call it a party."

"Was young Ward part of the crowd?"

"Ward? You mean Terry? He may have been. I didn't see him."

There was a long silence. Then Greg returned to Elinor.

"What about Elinor and the brush fire on the hill?" he asked. "That's the hell of a thing to accuse her of."

"Her car was seen here the night of the murder, captain. Now wait a minute—" as Greg made a move toward him. "I don't think she killed the girl. It seems unlikely under the circumstances," he added dryly. "The fact remains that she may have known more than she's ever told. For instance, there was a definite attempt to conceal Marguerite's identity. Her clothes haven't been found, not even her overnight bag. Perhaps Carol has told you why we believed her things were buried on the hillside, about the spade we found and so on.

"But she may not have told you that Mrs. Hilliard was pretty badly scared when Lucy testified at the inquest. I watched her. I know. But Lucy Norton was careful. She told only a part of the truth, and Mrs. Hilliard knew it."

"She didn't kill her," Gregory said thickly. "I'll stake my oath on that."

"Then why did she set fire to the hill?" Dane demanded. "I think you'll find she did exactly that. She knew the pitcher was in this attic and Carol's car was in the drive. She even had a rubber hose to siphon off the gasoline. I saw it in her bathroom, part of a shampoo arrangment. It still smelled of gasoline, although I imagine she had tried to clean it."

"I don't believe it," Gregory said stubbornly. "I don't believe she was here when Marguerite was killed. Why don't you ask her?"

"Because she had an alibi of sorts." Dane's voice was bland. "She claims to have spent that night in her empty apartment in New York. She certainly was in New York Saturday. She says she had dinner with her husband that night and went to the theater. She probably did, unless he is involved in this too. But she could have been here, you know; have driven the rest of Friday night to Providence and taken an early train to New York. In fact, that's almost certainly what she did."

"So she shot herself!" Greg said roughly. "She went out in the rain, climbed the hill and shot herself in the thigh! For God's sake, Dane, make sense."

"All right," Dane agreed. "Let's try something else. She didn't kill the girl. She came after her, because she knew she was coming here. When she got here the girl was already dead, so she did the only thing she could think of. She took the body upstairs in the elevator and put it in the closet."

"It sounds crazy."

"It does indeed, but something of the sort happened. The body was hidden to gain time, of course."

"So Elinor could get to New York and go to the theater!"

"So she could protect you, captain. And her own position too. Want me to go on?"

"I'll have to hear it sometime," Greg grunted.

"All right. Let's say Lucy's still at the foot of the stairs. She's unconscious, but she might recover any minute. Mrs. Hilliard didn't know Lucy had broken her leg, but she had to get rid of the girl's clothes. She found them in the yellow room, along with her bags. Lucy was stirring by that time, and probably moaning. What could she do? Take them with her? She was going to New York, remember, and Lucy might raise the alarm any minute."

"Can you imagine Elinor burying them in the middle of the night? She could have got rid of them in a hundred places on her way to New York." Greg was openly defiant now. "She has her faults, but she's not an idiot."

Dane nodded, still imperturbable.

"Precisely. That's where I stop. I've been stopped there for ten days; bridges, rivers, empty fields, and those clothes buried up on the hill! Unless she had help, of course."

There was another silence. Greg broke it.

"Who claims to have seen her car?"

"Old Mrs. Ward, for one. She was out looking for her husband. It seems he sleeps badly. She told it quite innocently. But the Dalton girl saw it too. She was out with her dog."

He had commenced to dress. Dane watched him idly, his mind busy with what he had learned. He roused as Greg shrugged into his blouse.

"What about your alibi when your wife was murdered?" he asked. "You left Washington on Thursday of that week, I know that. You'd better be sure you can fill in that interval, Spencer, and don't tell me you don't remember. You'll have to remember."

Greg laughed, unexpectedly and without mirth.

"All right," he said. "I registered at the Gotham on Thursday. You can check that. And I called Elinor at Newport that day. You can check that too. You can check that I got my car out of storage also, to drive to Newport to see Virginia and the rest of the family. But you can't check me for Friday or most of Saturday, because I can't check myself. I'd got that letter from Marguerite, and I told you how I was," he added dryly. "I can drink like any other man most of the time. Then when things get too strong for me I drink myself blind. I came to somewhere in lower New York. I'd been slipped a Micky Finn and robbed. That was at noon on Saturday, and you can ask the hotel how I looked when I got back."

"That's no alibi, and you know it," Dane said sharply. "What was too strong for you? Not that letter, was it? What did Mrs. Hilliard tell you over the long-distance telephone on Thursday? That was it, wasn't it? And who do you think your sister thought she was protecting when she got here that Friday night? You, wasn't it?"

There was another long silence. Greg was obviously trying to think the thing out. When he spoke he did not answer Dane's questions.

"I can't see Elinor in it at all," he said. "I can't see her killing any-one or—you know, digging a hole and burying those clothes. I've done my share of digging since the war began. So have you probably. It isn't easy."

"No," Dane agreed. "And the ground was hard that night. No rain for a long time. How did she know the girl was coming here, Spencer? She did know, didn't she?"

But here again Greg was evasive. He hadn't known it himself, he said. She might have learned it some other way. Dane realized that he was on guard now and got up, looking tired.

"All right, Spencer," he said wearily. "You've got the story now. Where do we go from here?"

"To see Elinor," Greg replied gruffly. "Damn it, Dane, she'll have to talk now, or I'll find myself at the end of a rope."

20

Elinor did not talk that day, however, or for several days thereafter. She had developed a fever, and no visitors were allowed, not even her family.

Hilliard arrived on Monday, bringing extra nurses and a consulting surgeon on the plane with him. Dane saw him at the hospital, a heavy florid man, on the shortish side, inclined to be pompous, and to regard Elinor's shooting both as an accident and a personal affront.

"These damned hunters!" he said, red with indignation. "Shooting deer out of season, of course. When a woman like my wife can't even leave her house safely—!"

He succeeded in isolating Elinor completely, although the consulting surgeon seemed undisturbed about her.

"She's all right," he said privately to Dr. Harrison. "A little fever, that's all." He smiled faintly. "Three nurses," he said, "and the country short of them! Well, she's his wife. If he's willing to pay for it, I suppose it's not my business." He glanced at Harrison. "What's she afraid of, anyhow?"

Dr. Harrison looked surprised.

"Afraid? What makes you think she is?"

"Looks it. Acts it. Jumps every time the door's opened. Probably causes her temperature too. Does she know who shot her? Think that's it?"

"I haven't any idea. She doesn't talk about it."

"Maybe she'd better," said the consultant, and took off his mask and white coat. "Well, I guess that's all, doctor. Congratulations and thanks."

Tim had arrived the day of Greg's confession, but he brought little or nothing Dane did not already know, which annoyed him greatly.

"For God's sake," he said, "why send me all over the country risking my neck when you know it all?"

Nor had he discovered much from the suitcase. It had revealed underwear and a dress or two, all of good quality, and a snapshot of a baby a few weeks old.

"You know the sort," Tim said. "No clothes. Legs in air. Kind of a nice kid. Boy."

"She'd had a child."

"Had, eh? Well, that explains it."

Tim's good humor died quickly, however, when he learned that his next assignment was to watch Carol at the Spencer house, and to help Maggie, now alone there. He stalked back to Alex in the kitchen.

"What's wrong with him?" he demanded, indicating Dane in the front of the house. "Is he crazy? Or is he just crazy about that girl next door? It'll cost him the hell of a lot to pay me for washing dishes."

"Money don't worry him," Alex said calmly. "Got plenty, or his old lady has. Father was a senator."

Which ambiguous statement kept Tim silent for a moment. Then:

"What's this about the Hilliard woman getting shot? Papers are full of it. Somebody after deer?"

"Sure," Alex said, patting a hamburger neatly into shape. "In June, on a rainy night at one A.M."

Tim whistled.

"Another, eh?" he said. "Well, maybe Dane's right about the girl friend. How about lending me one of those pretty aprons you wear? If I'm to wash dishes all day and stay up all night I won't need anything to sleep in."

Dane himself was at a loose end, with Elinor shut away and no possibility of seeing her. He was confident now that she had not been alone the night Marguerite was killed. Yet his telegram from Washington saying the answer was no, had left him without any specific suspect. And Floyd was still digging. In spite of his skepticism he had investigated Pine Hill. He might already know that the letter inside the wedding ring was a G and be keeping the wires hot about a possible marriage. And in the center of the mystery was Carol, growing thinner and more confused each day.

He went over his notes the day of Tim's return, changing and elaborating them, and after his custom numbering them.

(1) The body in the closet. Laid out carefully, and with the fur jacket not fully on. It had covered only one arm. Had this been done after death?

(2) The wedding ring on body. In spite of the engraving, Greg claimed he had never seen it. (Can probably be checked in Los Angeles.)

(3) Fire in closet. Set sometime after death. In that case improbable either Greg or Elinor had set it. Lucy Norton's statement at inquest. No smoke or odor of burning that night.

(4) The bobby pin found by Carol. Someone not strong enough to carry the body had taken it up in the elevator. Hair obviously bleached, indicating it belonged to dead girl.

(5) The curious discovery in the tool house. Not only the spade, but the Lowestoft tea set, and so on.

(6) Burning of hillside. Pitcher taken from Crestview attic. Almost certainly done by Elinor Hiliard to cover evidence.

(7) Strange death of Lucy Norton.

He sat for some time over that. Someone had climbed the fire escape and found Lucy in her room. She had been sufficiently alarmed to get out of her bed, and to fall dead with a heart attack. Would she have been murdered otherwise? Had only the noise of her fall driven the intruder away? But why? He was convinced now that what she had learned from the dead girl had been that she was Greg's wife. But she had not told it at the inquest. After some thought he put an X after that entry and went on.

(8) Shooting of Elinor Hilliard and moving of her body from the lane. Why had she dressed and gone out in the rain? To meet someone, and if so, who was it? Another X here.

(9) Why had Mr. Ward stealthily retrieved shell from mud in lane? Where did the Wards figure in the mystery? The grandson, Terry?

(10) Attempt, the night Elinor was shot, to discover and probably remove girl's clothing if buried on hillside. Elinor? X?

(11) Search of yellow room same night, while entire Spencer family at hospital. X again?

(12) Deserted house, Pine Hill. Who had been staying there? Blankets left after all other clues carefully removed. Probably overlooked in darkness and forgotten. X?

After some thought he added another note, thinking grimly that it was the thirteenth.

(13) Terry Ward expected back on leave. Did not apparently arrive.

He put away his notes and began to check the movements of the murdered girl. She had reached New York on Wednesday, June fourteenth, and gone to a hotel. On Thursday, shortly after Carol and Mrs. Spencer had left, she had inquired for them at their apartment house. That left her plenty of time to go to Boston and take the night train for Maine, arriving at the village by bus the next morning.

He sat for some time gazing at this last item. He had missed something here. Boston was only five hours from New York, but suppose she had not gone directly to Boston? Suppose she had stopped off at Newport and seen Elinor Hilliard?

The more he considered it the more certain he was she had done exactly that. If she intended blackmail she would naturally go to Elinor. He leaned back and closed his eyes. He could almost see what happened. The girl, pretty in a common way, in the fur jacket and white hat. Admitted under protests, unless she had said she was Mrs. Spencer. And Elinor sweeping into the room.

"Mrs. Spencer? Which Mrs. Spencer?"

"I'm Greg's wife."

Elinor staring at her, dazed and incredulous.

"I don't believe you. And you're getting out of this house. At once."

"You can put me out right enough. But you can't change things, you know. I've got my certificate."

"I wouldn't believe it if I saw it."

"You're not going to see it. I'm taking care of that. All right, Mrs. Hilliard. If you feel this way about it, maybe your mother and sister won't. I've looked them up. In Maine, aren't they?"

Leaving, and Elinor rushing to the telephone, telling Greg what had happened, and Greg unable to face it and taking the usual way out. Going to New York, on his way to Newport, and starting to drink himself blind on the way.

It had to be something like that, if Greg's story was true and if Elinor had been at Crestview the night of the murder. Why had she come? To buy the girl off, to urge a divorce and promise some considerable sum in return? Or to kill her? Everything else aside, she was capable of going to almost any length to avoid scandal and to save her social position. Even Hilliard would not have taken it well. But if she had killed Marguerite Spencer he was certain she had not done it alone.

He realized that he was going stale on the case, and that afternoon he asked Carol to go for a drive.

"I need exercise," he told her. "Why not leave the car somewhere and do a bit of climbing?"

"I'd love it. How about your leg?"

"I've forgotten I have it!"

They had a happy afternoon. From the top of a low mountain they could see the open ocean, and the bay sprinkled with its low green islands, like emeralds set in blue. Far below, the women on the golf course were bright bits of color, and the town itself picturesque and gay.

Sitting on a rock there he told her a little about himself; about his enlistment in the army, about his having been detached to a special job, and his anxiety to get back to it.

"It takes me around a lot," he said casually. "Trouble is, a man in my position has no business having ties. My mother worries as it is."

"All women have to accept it, don't they? I mean, almost everyone has somebody."

He reached out and took her hand.

"Look, darling," he said, "I'm pretty badly in love with you. I've been fighting it for days, but you might as well know it. I know you still remember Don Richardson, for one thing. The other is—" He threw away his cigarette. "How does any man know he's coming back these days? Or he won't be mutilated, or blind?"

"Would that matter so much?" she asked quietly. "If the woman cared—"

"It would," he said fiercely, and got up. "It would matter my dear. All right. Let's go."

He flew to Washington that night. With Elinor still shut off he felt he had reached a dead end, but there were things he could learn there he could not learn elsewhere. He was not too happy. He had done an idiotic thing, he felt. He had told Carol he was in love with her and in the same breath had said he had no intention of marrying her. Only a damned fool would do a thing like that, he reflected, as the plane roared south.

He did not go to a hotel. He had kept a small apartment there, and he admitted himself, mixing a good strong drink before he turned in. But he slept badly. He bathed and shaved, dressed, got some breakfast at a restaurant, and then reported to an office tucked away among the innumerable War Department buildings. He was not limping at all as he went in, and the man behind the desk surveyed him with a smile as he thrust out his hand.

"Hello, Dane," he said. "How's the Eagle Scout?"

Dane grinned.

"I'm fine. Hard luck, missing the invasion."

"Well, you've had plenty—Dieppe, Africa, Sicily, Anzio beachhead, Cassino. That's a record for any man."

Dane shrugged and sat down.

"I'm reporting for duty," he said, "but I'd like a few days first. Maybe a couple of weeks. There's a case in Maine I'd like to look into."

"That murder at Bayside?"

"Yes." He grinned. "I see you read the papers."

"Greg Spencer's apparently mixed up in it somehow. That puts it up to us in a way. Not our business, of course, but after all a fellow with a record like his—Better tell me what it's about, Dane."

Sitting there, referring to his notes, Dane related what had happened. It was not an uninterrupted narrative. Telephones rang. People came in and went out, quick important decisions were made. But he finished at last, and the man behind the desk made some notes.

"I wired you before," he said. "So far as we can check Terry Ward did not come east on his present furlough. He's still somewhere on the Coast now. Be leaving soon. Of course, all that's not positive. When you can cross the continent in seven or eight hours, and you're a flier with friends in the service, you can get places pretty fast."

"Any way to check on his past? Say the last year to two?"

"What sort of check?"

"Women. Did he play around with anyone like the Barbour girl?"

"My God, Dane, what do you think he is? Just because he flies doesn't mean he has wings like an angel."

It was the best Dane could do. He stayed in Washington for a day or two, learning nothing of any importance, meeting fellow officers, drinking at this bar and that, even going out to dinner once. But he was increasingly restless. On Thursday he flew back to Maine. It was still daylight when he arrived, and Alex met him at the field, and Alex with a long face and his one eye anxious and unhappy.

"I'm glad you're here, sir," he said. "Floyd arrested Captain Spencer for murder this afternoon."

21

Carol had had a rather difficult time during Dane's absence. Greg was taciturn and worried. Tim—the man who was to assist Maggie—had a habit of turning up at unexpected places, particularly at night. And Colonel Richardson had taken it upon himself to see that she was not lonely or downhearted.

It was difficult to see Maggie's picture of him running in the rain in the dignified elderly man who daily brought her flowers from his garden, and who talked garrulously the small gossip of the community. On Tuesday he noticed that she was no longer wearing Don's ring. He picked up her hand and looked at it.

"Have you no faith, no loyalty, my dear?" he asked gently.

"It's so long," she said, afraid of hurting him. "It's over a year. I have tried, but . . ."

"They've been found after longer periods than that," he insisted, and the next time he came he brought a clipping about such a case, and a map.

"Now look, my dear," he said. "You see what I mean. I've drawn in the new routes, ship and plane. This is where he was seen last. That doesn't mean his plane went down there. It might still have gone quite a way, and here's this island."

He pointed at it, his eyes full of hope, his lips slightly blue, and his veined elderly hand tremulous. She quivered with pity for him, but why couldn't he accept it? she thought. Other people did. There were people near-by, among the townspeople and the summer colony, who had had similar losses. They did not talk about them. They went around with quiet faces, or with the forced smiles that made one ache for them.

The situation was complicated by his continued jealousy of Jerry

Dane. Not that he spoke about him. It was just there, behind his faded blue eyes as he watched her. In a way it was like a silent battle between them, one of strategy rather than the firing line. But she did not put on Don's ring again.

Greg watched the situation morosely.

"Why don't you get rid of the old buzzard?" he said. "I'm sorry for him. I'm sorry for a lot of other people too. Only they bury their dead decently. He won't."

Tim did not add to her comfort. He was watching her carefully. At night, after she had gone to bed, he prowled around, trying her door to be sure it was locked, watching all doors and windows. At two in the morning Alex took over, but outside the house, and Tim got some sleep. Carol knew nothing of the arrangement, although Greg, coming home late Tuesday night from a dinner and taking a short cut to the house, found himself confronted with a flashlight which blinded him. He was indignant.

"What the devil's all this?" he demanded.

"It's all right, captain. Sorry. Just happened to be passing and saw you."

He had a vision of a big body and a face with a patch over one eye, and went on, still surprised and affronted.

It was almost a relief to Carol when on Wednesday afternoon a sort of inquest on Lucy Norton's death was held. There was no need of an inquiry, Dr. Harrison insisted. He even doubted if it was legal. But Floyd set his heavy jaw and demanded one.

"What's the difference whether she was hit on the head or scared to death?" he shouted. "All right. All right. We won't have a jury. We'll conduct an inquiry, and we'll let the public in if it wants to come. What's wrong with that?"

It was held in Floyd's office, which was jammed to the doors, but it brought out nothing new. Even Joe Norton's statement told nothing fresh.

"She was all right when I seen her last," he said. "Only she had something on her mind. I don't say she was scared. She just wasn't talking. If you ask me, that girl told her something before she got killed and somebody got in her room at the hospital to find out what she knew."

Asked if he had any idea what this knowledge could have been, he had not. "Except that the girl said she was a friend of Carol Spencer's," he said after some thought. "It might have been something about the Spencers."

As having possible bearing on the case, a statement from Elinor Hilliard was read. She had not seen the person who shot her. She had been unable to sleep and had gone out. The rain was not heavy at that time. She had been in the lane when she had heard someone running toward her; in fact, she had thought there were two people, one behind the other. She was not sure, however. It was very dark. But she had not been on the hillside and had no idea how she got there. She had been conscious when she fell, but she must have fainted almost at once. Someone must have carried her to where she was found.

There was no verdict, of course, and the press went away dissatisfied. There was only one angle the reporters had not already known. This was the fact that several patients in private rooms had had their doors opened the night of Lucy's death, opened and then closed again.

Floyd, realizing that things had fallen rather flat, made a small speech, standing behind his desk to do so.

"I think," he said, "in view of one murder and a shooting, not to mention the death of Lucy Norton, this town should take certain precautions; such as an early curfew for the children and the careful locking of houses at night. Without wanting to cause undue alarm, there seems to be someone around who doesn't hesitate to kill, and I shall inform the state troopers and forest rangers to that effect."

That had been the situation until Thursday afternoon, when Greg was arrested. Alex at the airport, having thrown his bomb, produced a bottle of Scotch from beside him in the car.

"Better take a drink, sir," he said. "There's a fog coming in. It's cold."

Dane drank the liquor straight. It burned his throat, but he felt better after it.

"All right," he said, as Alex put the car in gear. "Let's have the story."

Alex did not know a great deal. What he had had come from Tim, and that gentleman, liking Greg and considering Floyd too big for his pants, had resented the highhandedness of the procedure.

"As I get it, sir," Alex said, "Captain Spencer and Miss Carol were having lunch when Floyd drove up. He had Mason and a state trooper with him, but only Floyd went into the dining room. Tim was in the pantry, and the door has a little glass window in it, so he saw it all.

"That girl got up, but Spencer didn't move. The girl said 'Is there anything wrong, chief?' and Floyd didn't answer her. He walked over to Spencer and said he was arresting him for the murder of his wife.

Wife! I haven't got that straight yet. But so far as I know Spencer didn't say much. He told his sister not to worry, he hadn't done it, and he asked if he could pack a bag. Floyd sent the trooper up with him, but he didn't make any trouble. Last Tim saw of him he was getting into Floyd's car. He's in jail at the county seat now, and they're going to call a special session of the Grand Jury."

It was a long speech for Alex, so long that he lapsed into complete silence after it. Dane was grateful for it. Floyd must have his case, he considered, to have gone so far. And he knew a good case could be made.

His chief worry was Carol. He looked at his wrist watch when he got home. It showed only nine o'clock, so without stopping he walked over to Crestview. She was standing on the terrace gazing forlornly out at the bay, now misty with fog, and his heart contracted with pity when he saw her. Evidently she recognized his step, for she turned quietly and waited for him.

He was astounded to find her face frozen into a stiff, resentful mask.

"Haven't you a good bit of courage to come here?" she demanded.

"Courage? What do you mean?"

"You've got what you wanted, haven't you? Greg's under arrest. That's what you've been working for, isn't it?"

He lit a cigarette and studied her, not speaking.

"I keep asking myself why," she went on, her voice flat. "Why? He knows Greg didn't do it. He was here when it happened. Maybe he did it himself." And when he still said nothing: "What do I know about you, Jerry Dane? Nothing. Not who you are or what you do. You put a man in this house to watch us, everything we do. Then you get poor Greg's story out of him. He was married to that tart, and that's luck for you, isn't it?"

"You're excited, my dear."

She gave a small hollow laugh.

"That's funny, coming from you," she said, her voice still bleak. "Why wouldn't I be excited? My brother's under arrest for murder. My mother's in bed with a heart attack. My sister's been shot—did you do that too? And Greg's fiancée's driving me crazy over the telephone wires."

"See here," he said authoritatively. "You're not excited. You're hysterical. Sit down and listen to me or I'll carry you up to bed and get a doctor."

He waited until she sat before he spoke. Then his voice was as cold as hers.

"In the first place, I didn't kill the girl. In the second place, your brother didn't do it either. Now stop being a little fool and listen to me. I've been doing my damnedest to keep Greg from being arrested. I couldn't do it in time. But an indictment—if it comes to that—is not a trial, and I'm not through," he added grimly. "Now—did you eat any dinner?"

She was quieter. She was even apologetic.

"I'm sorry," she said in a small voice. "I've been here alone all afternoon, and thinking about Greg . . ."

He smiled at her.

"That's better," he told her. "Now, once again—did you eat any dinner?"

"I wasn't hungry."

"You're going to eat now," he said firmly. "Half of that attack on me was empty tummy. And after I've got some food in you I'm going to see Floyd. I think he's slipped up. At least I hope he has. How is Mrs. Hilliard?"

She looked at him, surprised.

"Elinor? She's doing all right. Howard's going home. Or he was until this happened. He's sent for his lawyer now."

"And your sister is still not talking?"

"What do you mean, talking?"

He eyed her gravely. She could take it, he thought. She had plenty of guts. Nevertheless, he told her as gently as he could.

"I'm afraid she knows some things, my dear. I think she knew of this marriage, which was hardly a marriage at all. Greg was on leave and drinking when it happened, and this girl more or less kidnaped him. But I think she knows something else, or suspects it."

"What? Don't treat me like a baby, Jerry. I'll have to know sooner or later, won't I?"

"I think she knows either who shot her or at least why she was shot, Carol."

She took it well. "Does that mean—do you think she knows anything else?"

"I'm afraid she does, darling."

She was silent when he called Tim and asked for some food for her. And Tim, in a white coat too small for him, took the order stolidly, as if he had never seen Dane before.

"Certainly, sir," he said, in an outrageous imitation of an English butler. "And may I offer the major a cup of coffee, sir? Or perhaps you would favor a ham sandwich."

Dane was not amused. He managed to get her to eat a little, and he saw her go to bed before he called Alex to bring the car. It was almost ten o'clock by that time, but he counted on Floyd's being still in his office. He had not expected to find Campbell there, however. Both men eyed him with disapproval and resentment.

"I've a damned good idea to arrest you, Dane," Floyd said explosively. "You've known all along this girl was Spencer's wife. You've been covering for him—for the whole family, for that matter—and you know it."

Dane sat down. He was still in uniform, and he put his service cap carefully on a table beside him.

"I suppose it was the wedding ring," he said casually.

"You suppose right. I'm no fool. I got Hodge Hopkins's glass on it myself after you brought it back. That C was a G. How many men's names begin with G?"

"George, Gilbert—" Dane began easily. But Floyd held up a ham-like fist.

"And Gregory," he said. "Not that I was sure. Not then anyhow. In fact we had a bit of luck. The Coast turned up a young woman who had been reported missing by the people who were keeping her baby. Lived outside Los Angeles. She answered the description, clothes and all, and Doc Harrison said the girl here had had a kid. Didn't know that, did you?"

"I did."

"Oh, you knew that too," Floyd said nastily. "Two years old. A boy."

"Not Greg Spencer's child, of course," Dane said, still evently. "Never saw her until a year ago. Only spent a day or two with her. Very drunk at the time."

Floyd passed that off with a gesture. He was evidently feeling jubilant, although the district attorney was less happy.

"Well, then I got busy," Floyd went on. "The Los Angeles force had no record of a marriage, but they said some parties went to Mexico. It was easy there. No Wassermans, no trouble. Just get married. And there it was, Gregory Spencer and Marguerite Barbour."

"And the date?"

Floyd looked at a telegram in front of him. "May seventeenth of last year. And to save you trouble I'll tell you Spencer was in Los Angeles at that time. *Also* he can't account for his whereabouts the day the girl was killed here." He sat back, looking complacent. "How do you like it? Even you fellows can slip up now and then, eh?"

"What do you mean by 'you fellows'?" Dane asked dryly.

"FBI man, aren't you? Were before the war, anyhow."

Dane neither denied nor assented. He lit a cigarette and blew out the match.

"We all slip. I suppose he frightened Lucy Norton to death and shot his sister, too?"

"We're not trying him for either of those. We don't have to."

"You can't very well leave them out."

"He may have done them both. I'm not saying. The Norton woman, yes. I expect she saw him that night when she fell down the stairs. His sister, probably no. Somebody took her for a deer."

"And the person who was hiding up at Pine Hill? What about him?"

"I've been up," said Floyd comfortably. "So have the State Police. So had Mr. Campbell here. Know what? Those blankets came from the Ward place. Had the cleaner's tag on them. Nathaniel Ward says his wife gave them last fall to a fellow who helped their gardener. He's in the Marines now. Nice fellow too. Name's Arthur Scott. Used to go hunting and stay out all night."

Dane got up.

"So Arthur Scott came back from the South Pacific or wherever he is now and slept at Pine Hill within the last week or two. Is that what you're saying?"

The district attorney roused at last. He spoke gravely.

"I understand your disappointment, major," he said. "The family is well known, and Greg Spencer has a fine war record. I'm only sorry this has happened. But there is no use dragging red herrings across Floyd's trail. He's done a great piece of work."

"All but finding the guilty man," Dane said curtly, and went out into the fog and dim-out of the night.

22

He drove slowly back to his house. As he passed the club he could hear the laughter inside and the sound of the jukebox in the bar. He remembered how strange it had felt when he was first brought back from the war, to find people living normal lives. It had been a long time before a plane over the hospital had not caused him to flinch.

Perhaps no man was unchanged after he had been in this war; could take safety for granted, or even the ordinary human happinesses. Had he been wrong, and had this happened to Greg Spencer? At least twice he had admitted to prolonged and heavy bouts of drinking, that usual attempt on the part of exhausted nerves to relieve strain or achieve forgetfulness. And drunken men do strange things, as he knew well.

But again there arose the question of his sister. Guns could be fired and cleaned, of course. Also, people were sometimes shot by mistake. Had Greg meant to kill someone else and shot Elinor Hilliard instead? He tried again to reconstruct the night it had happened, Carol's drowsy response when he knocked at her door, and Greg—

He thought that over, the search of the house and Carol reporting Elinor missing. "And Greg's asleep. I heard him snoring. She must have gone alone."

He remembered Elinor's room, the bed used, the book left as she had put it down, with the wind from the open window ruffling its pages, and her sheer stockings on a chair. If Greg was asleep, who or what had roused Elinor? Had someone seen her light and called through the open window? If so, who had it been?

His mind turned again to the Wards, their blankets in the empty house, the old man's odd behavior the morning after Elinor had been shot, and even further back, to the evening he himself had left Marcia Dalton's and gone to Rockhill. What was it Mr. Ward had said? Something about not running to the police with every bit of tittle-tattle he heard. And his own impression that the old man had wanted to get rid of him that night.

He was not greatly surprised the next morning to learn from Alex that a dozen men or so were working on the hillside.

"Digging all over the place," Alex reported. "Tim called me up to tell you."

Dane dressed and went over. The hill was crowded with men who looked like a hastily assorted group of gardeners from various estates. They had pegged it out, each man with a definite area, and he was still watching them when one of them near the burned house suddenly let out a yell and Floyd hurried across to him.

They had found the cache. Floyd was holding up a small overnight bag, using a bandanna handkerchief to do so, and peering down at something at his feet.

"That's all, men," he shouted. "We've found them. You can quit work. And thanks."

He was still there when Dane made his way over to him. Except for the bag Floyd had touched nothing. He was probably waiting for a photographer, Dane thought, and was not surprised when the reporter, young Starr, came loping across, camera in hand, from his old jalopy. He did not even see Dane. He waved the man back and stood over the hole, focusing carefully.

"Gee, chief," he said. "That's the stuff all right. Bad news for somebody."

Dane could see the pit now, not far from the small shallow one he had seen before. It was wide rather than deep, and the clothing in it had been dropped carelessly. A small black shoe, what looked like a black dress, and edge or two of peach-colored underwear, and the corner of a flat pocketbook were in sight. They made him faintly sick. Good or bad, the girl they had belonged to had lived and liked living. Now—

He went down to break the news to Carol, only to find that she was not alone. He heard a sonorous voice as he walked along the hall.

"But, my dear girl," it was saying pontifically, "I never touch criminal cases. Why Mr. Hilliard sent for me I don't know. As for this fellow Dane you refer to, I've never heard of him."

Thus disposed of with neatness and dispatch, Dane reached the door. The speaker was standing in front of the fire, a short tubby elderly man exuding displeasure from every pore, while Carol was looking crushed. Evidently this was Hilliard's lawyer.

"If—as seems entirely probable—Gregory Spencer has committed—" Hart began. Then he saw Dane and stopped.

"What if he hasn't committed a murder?" Dane said aggressively. "And what about remembering that Miss Spencer has had a shock and ought to be in bed?"

"Who the hell are you?" said Mr. Hart, pomposity lost in indignation.

All the last two weeks of anxiety and frustration came suddenly to the surface in Dane's retort.

"My name's Dane, sir. I gather that means nothing to you. But if you're starting by accepting the fact that Spencer's guilty, I suggest that you take the next plane back. He's better off without you."

Mr. Hart was apparently stunned. He reached for his pince-nez and surveyed Dane through it, uniform and all.

"I see," he said. "Brother officers. The services take care of their own."

Dane took a step toward him, and Hart retreated abruptly.

"All right, all right," he said, the unction gone out of his voice. "I take that back. I'm rather upset. I had no sleep last night. I hate planes, and to be confronted with murder—"

"By a person or persons unknown," Dane said softly. *"Still* unknown, sir."

The learned counsel left after that, presumably headed for the hotel and Hilliard, and Dane, rather ashamed, broke the news about the hill to Carol. She took it stony-faced and unflinching.

"It doesn't prove anything against Greg, does it? After all, since he wasn't here—"

"No, but there are other things not so good."

He could not hold off any longer. He put her in a comfortable chair and then told her the whole story as he knew it. He omitted nothing, but he gave her only facts, not theories. And her wide intelligent eyes never left his face.

When he had finished she nodded.

"I can see why they arrested him, Jerry. I can't see why you think he didn't do it."

"Do you?"

"No. Of course not." She looked startled.

"All right, darling. Now I want you to think, and think hard. What about Terry Ward? He was expected here but he didn't come. Is that right?"

"Yes. But if you're trying to make a case against Terry—"

"He's involved somehow, darling. Pretty seriously, I think. He's on the coast now, for one thing, although I can't find out if he's been east. He may have been in the crowd last year when Greg met this girl. He may even have been in love with her himself. That's possible, you know. And what's wrong with the Wards? Greg's arrest has upset them pretty badly, or something has. I saw the doctor going in there a while ago."

But her mind was still on Terry. He was young and gay. He adored the old people. He had been Don Richardson's friend, and there was some story of the two of them taking up Greg's plane years before, and that Greg in a white fury had threatened them both with jail. Of course that meant nothing, she said. It was just kid stuff, and certainly Terry would never murder anybody.

Dane made no comment. He did not say that this Terry was a different man, one who had been taught to kill. He sat back, watching her and thinking what it would mean to get her away from here, from the neurotic mother, from Elinor's selfishness—if nothing more—and Greg's ability to get himself into trouble.

The mention of Don Richardson had reminded her of Maggie's story about the colonel. She repeated it now.

"So much has happened since," she said, "I simply forgot it. But Maggie's quite positive. It was only a few minutes after she heard the shot. Of course the colonel may merely have been hurrying home from the Wards'. They play chess very late."

He did not ask her for further details. He persuaded her to try to get some rest, and went around to see Maggie herself. Maggie's story was even more dramatic, the running, the hatless head with its white hair, the dressing gown, the slamming of the colonel's front door. "It was him all right," she said, "and I'm going to that potbellied Floyd to-morrow and tell him so."

He advised against this. He told her he had some ideas of his own, and to keep quiet until it was time for her to speak. But Maggie was still suspicious. She was convinced that the colonel had lost his mind since Don's death. "The way he pesters Miss Carol, poor child." And he lived close enough to Crestview for what she called any sort of monkey business. In the end, however, she promised and he left, puzzled by the incident but also aware of the Irish tendency toward exaggeration. Any man might run if he had heard a shot near him. Only it was rather curious that the colonel apparently had not spoken of it.

He went home, feeling more in the dark than ever. If Floyd had found anything of importance in the girl's pocketbook that morning, he did not know it, would not know it until the trial probably. But there was one angle of the case which, he realized he had neglected, and after some hesitation he added it to his notes.

(14) If Marguerite had been married before she married Greg Spencer, who was the man?

He could not do anything about it that day. He might indeed have to go to the Coast himself to trace it down. But one thing was obvious. He would have to see Elinor Hilliard, regardless of hospital rules or the small army that supposedly surrounded her.

In the end he found this surprisingly easy. Apparently with Greg's arrest Floyd had taken away the troopers, and the nurse on duty was probably somewhere smoking a cigarette. Because the day was hot the doors were open, and he found Elinor's room without difficulty.

She was more or less lying in state, wearing an elaborate bed jacket, and with her hair freshly done. There was a silk blanket cover on the bed, and a mass of delicately colored small pillows around her. Evidently reinforcements had come from Newport, he thought grimly.

Elinor herself still showed the effects of shock and pain. Even the touch of artificial color on her face and lips did not hide the fact that she was a desperately frightened woman. She almost leaped out of the bed when she saw him.

"I'm sorry," he said, smiling at her reassuringly. "I didn't mean to scare you. Do you mind if I sit down? I want to talk about your brother."

It was the right opening. She looked at him angrily.

"These fools!" she said. "Arresting Greg! He never killed that girl. Never."

He drew a chair beside the bed.

"No," he said. "I don't think he did. But he may go to trial, Mrs. Hilliard. Too many people are not telling what they know."

"What people?"

He watched her carefully.

"The Ward family, possibly including Terry, their grandson," he told her. "And you yourself, Mrs. Hilliard. I think you were here the night your brother's wife was killed. I think you know who killed her."

"You're crazy," she said defiantly, although she visibly paled. "Why would I come here? If you believe that malicious story of Marcia Dalton's—"

"I'll tell you what I believe, Mrs. Hilliard. After you hear it you can decide whether you will let your brother be tried for murder or not. I can easily verify some of it. This girl, Marguerite Barbour—or Spencer—learned of your brother's presence in the country, and followed him east. She may have gone to Washington first. If she did, he did not see her there. I know she spent one night at a New York hotel. I know she tried to see your sister or mother at their apartment, and missed them there. I know she checked her suitcase at Grand Central the next morning, and I think as soon as possible after that she got in touch with you."

"Don't be ridiculous. I won't listen to any more. I don't have to." She reached for the button which would call the nurse, but he took her hand and held it.

"Do you want me to tell you this? Or shall I go to Floyd with it? I don't think Mr. Hilliard would care for that. Do you?"

She said nothing, and he went on.

"I believe she went to Newport and saw you there, probably at your own house. She told her story. She had her marriage certificate, didn't she? You pretended to need time to think things over, or perhaps to raise money for her. But you did not tell her your mother and sister were there at the time. She said she was coming here, and you let her come. Why did you do that, Mrs. Hilliard? To get her out of the way? Or to kill her that night?"

"I didn't kill her," Elinor said hysterically. "She was dead when I got there. She was lying on the upper steps outside the front door, in a wrapper over her nightdress. I—I got away as fast as I could."

"Alone?"

"Certainly I was alone."

"You didn't telephone your brother to meet you here?"

"He was never here at all."

"Now look, Mrs. Hilliard," he said patiently. "Part of the truth is not enough. Who carried her body up in the elevator and left it in the closet, so that it would not be found and you would have time to get away? Who took her clothing and buried it? And who later on set fire to the closet? I need those answers if I'm to save Greg."

"I don't know," she said, despair in her voice. "I never buried her clothes. I never touched—her. And why would I try to burn her? It's terrible. It's sickening to think of."

"You left her where she was?"

"Yes. I thought she was dead. I didn't know. I hoped she was dead. She was dreadful, a common tart and after money, of course. I drove up that night, and I brought most of my valuables with me. I wanted to buy her off, to get a divorce, anything, and I couldn't get my hands on much money without telling Howard."

"And that's all?"

"That's all," she said, and closed her eyes.

Dane felt a momentary pity for her. If she was telling the truth she was only innocently involved. But he had not finished.

"If that's really all," he said, "I wonder why you set fire to the hill? You must have known what was there."

She shrugged slightly. He felt she was on guard once more.

"What else could I do?" she demanded, her former defiant self again. "Her clothes hadn't been found, and you and Carol were searching the place. You believed they were there, and she had had that dreadful marriage certificate with her in her handbag. I didn't want it found."

"Does Greg know you did it?"

"I never told him. He still doesn't know anything, except that she had written him she was coming east—to blow the lid off, she said."

"You know he had no alibi."

She lay back exhausted on her pillows.

"If you know Greg," she said weakly, "you'd understand. He loathed her. He couldn't even face her. When he got my telephone message that I had seen her he simply went on a binge. He didn't even know she was dead until he saw the papers in New York. Even then he wasn't sure it was the same girl. He didn't really know anything until he got here."

Her voice trailed off, and he got up hastily.

"I'll get your nurse," he said. "Maybe things aren't so bad, Mrs. Hilliard. If you have anything more to tell me let me know."

She did not open her eyes.

"Does all this have to come out?" she asked weakly.

"Perhaps not. I can't promise, of course."

But it was his final question that roused her to genuine surprise.

"Is Terry Ward concerned in all this?" he inquired.

"Terry! Good heavens, what has he got to do with it?"

He stood up, looking down at her. He had not liked her. To him she was the epitome of all grasping self-indulgent women. Now, however, she looked really exhausted.

"Just one thing more," he said. "Your mother's china tea set. How did it get to the tool house?"

She did not even move.

"I can't imagine," she said wearily. "It sounds like one of Mother's better ideas. She hides things, you know. And who cares anyhow?"

He was only partially convinced as he drove home. He believed that she had told the truth, so far as she knew it. The girl had been dead when she got there on that futile frantic excursion of hers. But he still felt that she was holding something back; that if she did not know she at least suspected the identity of the man who killed the girl and frightened Lucy to death, and later shot her.

On the way out he met Dr. Harrison. He had come from the Wards', and was trying desperately to get a nurse, for the night at least.

"I may have one tomorrow," he said worriedly. "But I need one tonight. Mrs. Ward had a stroke this morning, and old Nat is useless. There's only a maid with her."

"Why not ask Marcia Dalton?" Dane said idly. "She's had some training."

And was only aware after he got into his car that he had had a really brilliant idea.

23

Marcia arrived at the Ward house at nine o'clock that night, looking efficient and calm. Old Mr. Ward himself let her in, and took both her hands.

"My dear girl," he said, "how kind of you. She is—she is quite helpless, you know." To his own embarrassment his eyes filled with tears. He released her hands and got out a meticulously folded handkerchief. "After more than fifty years," he said unsteadily. "It's hard."

"It won't do her any good if you yourself get sick," Marcia said practically. "I'll take over now. You go to bed."

He put the handkerchief away.

"She's been a wonderful wife," he said, still shakily. "I've wired Terry, but you know how it is these days. He may be anywhere. They come and go, these boys of ours—I think she was worried about him, although she was so brave. To say good-bye, and not know if it's the last one or not . . ."

"I didn't know he had been here."

"Not here, my dear. The last time we saw him. That was some months ago. Now, if you care to go up—The housemaid, Alice, is with her, but she has never had any contact with illness. We have sent for nurses, of course, but they are very hard to find."

In spite of her long talk with Dane that afternoon Marcia felt reassured as she followed him up the stairs. Everything looked normal, a quiet house, a little old man grieving for his wife. How could there by any danger in this staid establishment? Yet Dane's last words were ringing in her ears.

"Watch everything," he said. "Talk to the servants if you can. Find out if Terry was here this summer, even for a night. If you can find a way to do it, see if Mr. Ward gave a couple of blankets to an assistant gardener last fall. And look around for a rifle or a revolver. Only for God's sake be careful.''

Mr. Ward left her at the top of the stairs. She went into the sickroom, to find Alice, the elderly housemaid, sitting beside the bed. She got up when she saw Marcia, looking greatly relieved.

"I'm glad you're here," she whispered. "I'm no hand at this kind of thing. She can't talk, you know."

Marcia did not whisper. She had been taught never to whisper in a sickroom, and she saw, too, that the woman on the bed was not asleep. She was looking at her with intelligent, despairing eyes.

"What orders did the doctor leave?" she asked in her normal voice.

"Just to keep her quiet. As if she isn't quiet, poor dear thing! He's coming back tonight. She was took this morning. No warning, either. I think she's been worried about Captain Spencer. She was a great friend of Mrs. Spencer's. Then with all those men digging on the hill over there . . .''

When Marcia got rid of her she went over to the bed, where the small thin body of an old woman barely raised the covers.

"I'm going to stay here," she said, looking down. "I won't bother you, Mrs. Ward. I'll just be here. Is that all right?"

The eyelids blinked, whether by accident or design she could not tell.

"I'm to stay until you get some nurses," Marcia went on. "I'll try to get Mr. Ward to go to bed. That's what you want, isn't it?"

There was no doubt now. The blinking was fast and definite.

"I'd better tell you about Greg Spencer, too, so you won't worry. I know you're fond of him. He isn't guilty, Mrs. Ward. Major Dane has been working on the case. He knows a lot the police don't know, so Greg's all right."

There was no blinking this time. The eyes gazed at her steadily and then abruptly closed. There was no expression at all on the wrinkled face, and Marcia found herself as deliberately cut off as though a door had been shut in her face. When Mr. Ward came in she was shading the lights, and his wife was apparently asleep.

She motioned him out into the hall and followed him.

"She's conscious," she said. "I suppose you know that."

"I had thought so. I wasn't certain."

"She seemed pleased when I told her you were going to bed. So please do, Mr. Ward. Show me the linen closet, in case I have to change the bed, and then I'll put on a dressing gown and take over."

"Alice and I did change the bed once," he said awkwardly. "There is a certain incontinence. I'm afraid we were clumsy. I'll wait for the doctor, Marcia. Then I may lie down for a while. It's been a bad day.''

He did not go to bed, however. He went into an upper sitting room, and as she moved around she could see him there not reading, just waiting, his hands on the arms of his chair and his eyes gazing at nothing, with all hope dimmed out of them.

After the doctor's visit there was nothing left to do. She managed to get Mr. Ward to bed, and sat down by her patient, apparently still sleeping. The utter silence of the house bothered her. She had a suspicion, too, that her patient was not asleep; that when she moved around the room she was being watched. She was not a nervous woman, however. Even when at midnight the front doorbell rang it was only the wild blinking of the old lady's eyelids that surprised her.

Marcia got up.

"Water?'' she inquired, and picked up the cup.

Mrs. Ward refused it. She continued to signal with her lids, however, and when the bell rang a second time it was almost wildly so.

"What is it? The doorbell?''

"Yes,'' the eyes signaled.

"Mr. Ward's going down. I hear him moving about in his room.''

This was clearly wrong. With a look of complete despair the eyes closed, and Marcia went out into the hall. She was in time to see Mr. Ward in a dark dressing gown going down the stairs, and that he was holding a revolver in his hand as he did so.

She was prepared for anything by that time. If she had seen the old man level the gun and fire it she could hardly have been surprised. What she did not expect was to hear the friendly excited voice of Colonel Richardson, and to see Nathaniel quickly hide the gun in his pocket.

"I've just heard, Nat. Why in God's name didn't you send for me? You know I'd do anything I could.''

"I know that, Henry. There isn't anything anyone can do. But come in. Marcia Dalton's with her now, until we can locate a nurse. She offered to stay.''

"Sounds like her,'' said Henry approvingly. "Good girl, Marcia. Sound as a bell.''

They went into a downstairs room and Marcia found herself still clutching the stair rail. Whom had Nathaniel Ward expected when the doorbell rang? Or before it rang? Why had Dane cautioned her? Did he suspect either of these elderly men of murder? The whole thing was preposterous. Yet she was not sure. Certainly Mrs. Ward had quieted, and not long after, Marcia heard the colonel leaving and old Nathaniel coming upstairs once more.

She dozed a little that night, and when at seven o'clock she heard Bertha, the cook, in her kitchen she let Alice relieve her and went down for some coffee. Bertha was red-eyed but talkative.

"Such a good woman, Miss Dalton," she said as she put the percolator on the stove. "And now to have this happen to her! First Mr. Terry goes to war. That almost finished her. And now this. Alice says she can't talk, or move herself around at all."

"People get over these things," Marcia said consolingly. "She may have some paralysis left, but she may live for quite a while."

She drank her coffee, standing by the kitchen stove, while Bertha talked.

"It happened all at once yesterday morning," she said. "She was watching those men digging up the hill. Then suddenly somebody over there yelled, and I heard Mr. Ward calling. When I got in there she was on the floor, and the poor old man bending over her and looking like death. You know," she said, turning honest eyes on Marcia, "there's been something funny going on lately. You know how honest this place is. Nobody locks anything up, or didn't until that girl was murdered. Well, we lost a couple of old blankets not so long ago. The madam told Alice to air them before she sent them to the Red Cross in the village and Alice forgot them. The next day they were gone. First time that's happened, and I've been coming here with the family for twenty years."

That would interest Dane, Marcia thought, although she had no idea why. But before she left the kitchen she had learned that Terry had not been there at all that summer, or if he had, the servants did not know it.

She had learned one more thing to report before she left. She had carried her second cup of coffee into the living room, when the telephone rang. She picked it up and answered it. It was a long-distance call from San Francisco. A man's voice speaking.

"Hello," it said. "I'd like to speak to Mr. Ward, please."

"I'm sorry. He's asleep, but I'll get him. Is that you, Terry?"

"I beg your pardon?"

"Is that Terry? Terry Ward?"

"Lieutenant Ward is not here. I am simply giving a message from him. If Mr. Ward's asleep don't bother to wake him. Just tell him everything is all right. Got that? Everything is okay. He's not to worry."

"Everything is all right," she repeated. "Is that message from Terry?"

"Sorry. Time's up," said a voice, and the connection was broken.

Nathaniel Ward was still asleep under the influence of the barbiturate the doctor had given him when the nurse arrived that morning. Marcia wrote the message and carried it into his dressing room, to find him on the couch there, the weight of the weapon in his pocket dragging his robe to the floor. Next door, in the big double bed they had shared for so long, Mrs. Ward seemed to sleep fitfully. The strained look had gone out of her face.

Marcia reported to Dane that morning on her way home, her own long face tired and rather bleak.

"For what it's worth," she said when she finished, "they're both scared. She is, at least. She didn't want him to answer the doorbell."

She was rather surprised to find the emphasis Dane laid on the blankets, however.

"Did she say when this was?" he asked.

"Not long ago. That's all."

But it was his final question that left her in open-mouthed astonishment.

"How good are Mr. Ward's eyes?" he asked. "You know him. Does he have to wear glasses all the time?"

"He's practically blind without them."

He did not explain further. He let her go after that, telling her she was the fine person he had always suspected, and that she had done more than her one good deed that night. What the rest was he did not say, but she drove away that morning in a glow of self-satisfaction slightly modified by bewilderment.

24

That was on Saturday. For two days Greg had been in a police cell at the county seat. It was not too bad. He had a narrow bed, a chair, and a chest of drawers. He could order food brought in, but he ate very little. He had no knowledge of the excitement his arrest had caused, of the consultations in Washington, or of the reporters milling about the town. One of them even managed to be arrested, to find himself no nearer Greg than before.

He found the lack of action hard to bear. He spent hours smoking and pacing the brief bit of floor space, and in trying to think things out. Thinking, however, was not his long suit. That they were calling a special session of the Grand Jury he knew. Hart had gone, and a famous criminal lawyer was on his way up.

But his real longing was to get out of the mess and join his squadron again. He never doubted that he would, and even his love for Virginia faded beside that. He had wanted to marry her. God, yes. But more even than that he wanted the air again, to be with his own gang, to go out and give the dirty bastards hell, and then to come back, report, eat, and sleep, so as to be ready for the next mission.

He had no idea that Virginia had arrived at Bayside. Nor for that matter had Dane, drinking his before-lunch highball at the desk in what he called his study, and waiting for Alex to return from an errand. The first warning he had was a sort of volcanic eruption, when one of the porch chairs fell over and the front door slammed. The next moment he was confronted by a young and pretty redheaded girl.

"So that's the way you work to help Greg!" she said. "Sitting here and sopping up liquor while these damned fools try to send him to the chair!"

"Not the chair. No chair in this State."

His calmness and his grin stopped her cold. She stared at him.

"I see. It's not your neck, is that it?"

"Why not sit down? How much do you think you help by acting like a ten-year-old, Miss Demarist? I suppose that's who you are."

She subsided into a chair, but she still looked like a frightened willful child. Dane grinned at her.

"That's better," he said, "and just for you enlightenment, more crimes are solved at desks—with or without liquor—than by leg work. It takes both, of course. I might add that Carol Spencer has had enough to bear, without hysteria added to it."

"I'm not hysterical."

"Then behave like it."

He gave her a cigarette, and taking one himself, told her the essential facts; his own belief in Greg's innocence, the fact that he still had a few things up his sleeve, without explaining, and also the fact that if the Grand Jury brought in an indictment it was not fatal or even final.

"The cards are stacked against him at the hearing, of course," he said. "The district attorney calls his witnesses. The defense hasn't a chance. But, as I say, that means nothing."

She herself, completely subdued by that time, could tell him nothing. She knew Greg drank "when he was unhappy." She knew there were girls who married soldiers to get their allotments. But she was in the hell of a mess, to use her own words. She wasn't sending back her wedding presents. She still loved Greg, and she meant to marry him if it had to be in a prison cell. Whereupon she began to cry, produced a handkerchief, said tearfully that she had been an idiot, and departed more quietly than she had arrived.

He went back to his desk and his drink, thinking over the widening circle of every crime, the emotions involved, the people who were hurt, the lives that were blasted. War was different. You killed or were killed, but you left behind you only clean grief, without shame.

After some thought he added to his notes Marcia's report on the telephone call from San Francisco.

(15) Everything is okay. Mr. Ward is not to worry.

Alex found him still there, the ash tray filled with cigarette stubs, one of them stained with lipstick which he saw immediately and ignored.

"I got Hank Miller alone all right, sir," he said. "Not easy on Saturday morning. I don't think he suspected anything."

"Extra canned goods, eh?"

"Plenty. All sorts. Cheese, sardines when Hank could get them, baked beans, anything that didn't have to be cooked. I said I'd heard it was black market stuff, and Hank showed me his slips."

"Still doing it?"

"Not for a week or so, sir."

"Well, it ought to be easy to find out where it went."

Dane took Carol with him for a drive that afternoon, both to get her away from Virginia and to have a little time with her himself. He had not yet retrieved his error on the mountain. She was too distressed about Greg, and he told himself philosophically that it could wait. But he did not take her to the mountain again. Instead, he circled around until he reached Pine Hill. Here he stopped the car and looked at her, smiling.

"How would you like to look for clues?" he inquired.

"What sort? I'm no good at that kind of thing, Jerry."

"Well, you have good eyes, as well as very lovely ones. Let's see what you can find. Suppose you wanted to hide a lot of tin cans somewhere. How would you go about it?"

"Hide them? You mean bury them?"

"I hardly think so, with all this undergrowth. Still, they might shine, I suppose. Maybe they're covered. Let's look, shall we?"

"Wait a minute," she said, as he started to get out of the car. "Do you mean someone's been living here?"

"There's a chance. That's what we're here to find out."

He did not need to explain further, and it was Carol herself who found them, hidden neatly under an old box near the deserted stable. She stood looking down at them, with Dane beside her.

"Then this means—"

"It may be one thing to help Greg," he told her. "Don't count on it too much, my darling. There's still a lot to be done, but this is the first real step. And it's yours."

When they got back into the car his face was set and so absent that she thought he had already forgotten her.

"I'm going to see Floyd," he told her. "I'll drop you off in the lane. And don't speak of what we've found. Not to anyone. It might be dangerous."

After he left her he drove smartly into the village, to find Colonel Richardson entering Floyd's office, with Floyd at his usual place and

Mason with his chair tilted back in a corner. Neither man rose, and the colonel remained standing before the desk. None of them noticed Dane.

"Well, colonel," Floyd said, "anything I can do for you?"

"I have something to tell you," said the colonel, standing with his hat in his hand and his white hair blowing softly in the breeze from an open window. "It will, I hope, save Captain Spencer from an indictment next week. He is innocent, but these things stick, sir."

The chief gave Dane a quick glance but did not greet him.

"You'll be good if you can save Spencer, colonel," he observed casually. "We have enough to convict him two or three times. He was married to the Barbour woman, he was engaged to a redhead—she's here, and a good excuse for murder any time—and he has no alibi for the night the girl was killed. I think he was here and we can prove it. What more do you want?"

The colonel sat down, carefully placing his hat on his knee.

"I can prove he did not shoot his sister, sir," he said stiffly.

"What's that got to do with it? We've never claimed he did."

The colonel flushed.

"You think that we have more than one murderer in this vicinity? That's nonsense, Floyd."

"Why more than one?"

"I'm not alone in the conviction that Gregory Spencer has committed no crime," he said slowly. "Perhaps I should have spoken sooner, but things have been moving fast. But with Mrs. Ward having a stroke, and Nathaniel carrying a gun even last night when I distinctly saw it in his dressing gown pocket—"

Floyd was looking astonished.

"See here," he said, "you're not accusing old Mr. Ward of shooting anybody, are you?"

"Certainly not. The man who shot Elinor Hilliard was taller than Nathaniel."

"For God's sweet sake!" Floyd shouted. "Are you saying you saw him?"

"I did. Not close enough to recognize him, but I certainly saw him."

Sheer amazement kept Floyd silent. Mason's jaw had dropped. Neither one paid any attention to Dane or interrupted as the colonel told his story.

On the night Elinor had been shot, he said, he had unfortunately taken coffee after dinner, with the result that he could not sleep. He had gone downstairs about one o'clock to get a magazine, and was at the table in the center of the room when he saw a face at the window. It was raining hard. The pane was wet, and it was merely a flash, but there was no mistake about it.

He had put out the light at once and gone outside. There was no one there, but he heard someone running. He could see that it was a man, fairly tall and in a dark overcoat or raincoat, but that was all.

However, several suspicious things had been happening, the colonel explained, including Dane now in his glance, "so I thought it best to follow him. He went up the lane between Rockhill, the Ward place, and Crestview. I tried to follow him to see who it was, but I was in bedroom slippers and I'm not so young as I was. That was when I heard the shot."

"Why haven't you reported this sooner?" Floyd asked angrily.

"I would not be here at all," the colonel said simply, "but an old and dear friend passed away an hour ago. Mrs. Ward is dead. This cannot hurt her now."

"What does that mean?"

The colonel drew a long breath. His color was bad, Dane noticed.

"The fellow turned in at the Ward place," he said, and was silent.

It was a moment before Floyd spoke.

"And that's all? You didn't investigate further?"

Colonel Richardson looked at him bleakly.

"I found Elinor Hilliard," he said. "I pulled her up on the hillside, away from where some late car might run over her. She was lying in the lane. Then I ran back to my house and telephoned the doctor. His line was busy, and I was trying to get the hospital when I heard people running about and calling. I knew then she had been found. After that I—well, I just kept quiet. If she had been killed I'd have had to tell what I know, of course."

Floyd was watching him intently, his eyes hard and suspicious.

"Why are you telling it now?" he inquired.

"Because it was not Gregory Spencer. I've know Greg all his life, and this man was not so tall. I've a hard decision to make, but I can't allow an innocent man to be tried for his life."

"Who was it? You know, don't you?"

"I'm not sure, but I'm afraid it was Terry Ward." He drew a long breath. "Remember, I'm making no accusation. And I don't think the shooting was deliberate. I was after him and Mrs. Hilliard got in his way. But he's had a long, grueling experience as a fighter pilot. He may be suffering from combat fatigue. I don't know."

Dane spoke for the first time.

"Does Mrs. Hilliard know you moved her?" he asked.

"I don't think so. She was completely unconscious. Shock, of course."

"Have you any idea why she was out in the rain that night?"

The colonel stirred unhappily.

"She must have been on her way to the Wards'," he said. "That's obvious. She had followed the path to the lane and was crossing it. He may not have meant to kill her or even shoot her. He wanted to scare her, probably."

"And have you told the Wards this story?" Floyd demanded curiously.

"No. I would not have come at all, but I cannot allow Carol Spencer's brother to be crucified without a protest."

He turned quietly and went out, closing the door behind him.

25

Dane remained behind when the colonel left. Floyd sat staring at the door, his mouth partly open, and Jim Mason let his chair down with a thump. Floyd's eyes turned to Dane.

"What brings you here?" he inquired. "Were you in that lane too when the Hilliard woman was shot? Looks like the whole summer colony gets around in the middle of the night. Maybe you did the shooting," he added. "You are quite a shot, aren't you?"

"I haven't been camping out at Pine Hill for two weeks or so."

"And who has? We searched that place. Nothing there but the blankets."

"If you'll look again you'll find a number of fresh tin cans there, by the garage."

"And what would that mean?" Floyd roared. "What's the idea anyhow. Are you all in cahoots to try to save Greg Spencer. Some hobo camps out in an empty house, and all at once he kills a girl, shoots a woman, and scares Lucy Norton to death! The colonel says he sees him, you find where he's been staying, and there's your killer!"

Having done his duty, Dane drove slowly home. One part of the colonel's story had struck him as distinctly odd. He was still thinking it over when he saw him on the street ahead, walking slowly and dejectedly home. He stopped the car.

"Care for a lift?" he asked.

The colonel roused himself.

"Thanks. Yes, I would, I'm not as young as I like to think I am, major."

When they started again Dane reverted at once to the colonel's experience the night Elinor was shot.

"I can see you were in a difficult position," he said. "You're not sure it was Terry Ward, are you?"

"What am I to think? It was someone who knew his way around, and war does strange things to men. I know that."

"Would Mr. Ward go armed against his own grandson?"

The colonel's color rose. He looked goaded and unhappy.

"I'm afraid he's going armed against me. He hasn't been the same for some time. He may have seen me moving Elinor, you know. May have heard the shot and come out." He tried to light a cigarette with uncertain hands. "He's been different since then. We used to play a good bit of chess together. We haven't for some time."

The picture of the two elderly men, each suspecting the other, was rather pathetic. It was the old story, Dane thought, no one being entirely frank. It was the same with every crime.

"Just what do you know about Terry Ward, Colonel Richardson? Known him a long time?"

"Since he was born. Knew his father before him. Fine Boston family, you know. His grandmother's death will be a blow to the boy. Only thing is"—the colonel cleared his throat—"he'd never shoot Elinor. There may have been some reason for the other. God knows I judge nobody. But why Elinor?"

"It was raining hard. He may not have seen who it was. You yourself said something like that, sir."

The colonel looked uncertain. He even looked shaken.

"I can't help, I'm afraid," he said thickly. "Nat won't see me. He won't see anybody today. He's a broken man."

"Have you any idea where Terry is now?"

"Gone, I suppose. They move fast these days. Hop a plane and are back on some God-forsaken island before you know it. I shouldn't say that perhaps. My own son may be on just such an island. You know, I'm considered something of a crackpot around here." He smiled faintly.

"Really? About what?"

"About my son. We were very close. After my wife's death I had only the boy, and—well, let that go. Only I've always felt that I would know if anything had happened to him. Maybe you think that's foolish."

"Not at all," Dane said gravely.

"For instance, I knew when he had pneumonia in college. I wakened out of a sound sleep, and I was so sure that I telephoned at once. He had it, you see. It's—well, I suppose it's psychic, although I don't like the word."

He got a clipping from his wallet. It was the story of a flier found after months on a Pacific island, where the natives had kept him alive. He had been badly injured, but had returned to duty. Dane read it gravely.

"Am I to understand that you think this may be your son?" he inquired.

Henry's face fell.

"That would be too much to hope, I expect. But it shows it can happen, doesn't it? There are so many islands," he added, almost wistfully, "and I've never felt that Don was gone."

"There's always hope," Dane said. "That's what keeps most of us ticking, isn't it?"

The colonel got out stiffly at his gate. He had aged even in the last day or so, and it seemed absurd that Nathaniel could suspect him of anything. Or was it? Dane pondered that on his way home. The story could be true, or it could be a cleverly concocted one, made up after all the evidence was in. The colonel had been a military man. He was used to firearms, and his story of having found Elinor in the lane was as incredible as Floyd had evidently regarded it.

He wanted badly to talk to Mr. Ward, but this was not the time for it, with Terry flying back to the blue inferno of the Pacific, with Mrs. Ward lying dead, and Nathaniel himself wandering around like an ancient distracted ghost. Time was growing short too. He still had no alibi for Greg in New York. Tim had had men working on it from his own agency, but with the plethora of army officers in the city and the definite percentage of them who drank to excess after prolonged battle strain, they had failed utterly.

In the end he decided to see Elinor again. He found her looking better, the room full of flowers, and a nurse reading a book by a window. Elinor looked frightened when she saw him. He went over to the bed.

"I would like to talk to you, Mrs. Hilliard," he said. "If you want the nurse to stay it is all right with me."

Certainly she did not want the nurse. She sent her out quickly. Dane closed the door and went back to the bed.

"I'm wondering," he said, "if you are really willing to let your brother be found guilty of a murder you know he didn't commit?"

She looked terrified. She cowered back among her pillows, as though she feared actual bodily violence.

"I can't talk," she said wildly. "I can't say I was here that night. It would wreck my life. Howard's too, all he has built for himself."

"So that's all you are thinking of?"

She had recovered somewhat by this time.

"I told you before. I don't know who did it. I don't know anything about it. I found her on the doorstep, and I left her there."

"Will you swear to that in court? Because I'm going to see that you are called at the trial."

"I won't go to court," she said obstinately. "I'll leave the country first." She was sullen now. "Maybe Greg did it. How do I know? She was already dead, I tell you."

"Was it Greg you drove away that night, Mrs. Hilliard?"

She collapsed then. He got no more out of her. The nurse, returning, found her alone and weeping noisily, and when Dr. Harrison arrived he gave her a sedative.

"Tragic about her brother," he said as he left. "She's devoted to him."

In a way Dane had played his last card. The solution, in view of Elinor's silence, had to lie elsewhere, and he decided to fly to the Coast. He told Carol his plan that evening, sitting on the terrace in the warm darkness, with Virginia in bed and only the sleepy call of a gull now and then to break the silence.

"The story's out there," he said, "and my leave is over soon. There's no time to waste."

"But you'll come back here?"

Something in her voice made him reach over and take her hand, now bare of Don's ring. He touched that finger gently.

"Before I go I want to ask you something," he said. "Are you still remembering Don Richardson? Do you still think he may come back? And if he ever does will you marry him?"

"He will never come back, Jerry," she said positively. "I know that."

"But if he does?"

"No," she said simply.

He let go her hand.

"I've never thought of myself as a marrying man," he said soberly. "In a way I have no right to ask any girl to marry me. My work is pretty important. Don't get any false ideas about it. It's not sensational, but it cuts me off from normal living. It takes all I've got, and sometimes more."

She stirred in the dark.

"Are you proposing to me? Or are you giving me up?" she inquired.

"Both," he said promptly. "I want you to wait for me, my darling. I want you to come back to. Good God, Carol, I wonder if you know what that would mean?"

"I will wait," she said. "No matter what happens, I will always wait, Jerry."

Then and only then he took her in his arms.

He left for the Coast the next day, Sunday, and he was still there when the Grand Jury met on Wednesday. The county seat was jammed with reporters and cameramen. Carol found herself in a small hotel room, with only a bed, a dresser and a chair or two, and with a group of newspapermen next door who banged things about, talked all night, and apparently drank when they were not talking.

Evidently Campbell and Floyd had built their case carefully. There was an air of assurance about the district attorney as he made his opening speech to the twenty-three men who sat in a semicircle around the room.

"It becomes my duty, as the representative of this sovereign state," he began pompously, "to bring to your attention one of the most cruel crimes in our history. On the night of Friday, June sixteenth last, a summer night when our citizenry slept or worked to further a disastrous war, a young woman was done to death in the village of Bayside, in this county.

"Not only was she murdered by a heavy blow on the head, but an attempt was made to destroy her body. Her effects were taken to conceal her identity, and a quantity of inflammable liquid was poured over her and subsequently ignited."

He went into details here, of the discovery of the body, the failure to locate the missing clothing, and the fatal identification. "A young woman, not yet thirty, and so far as we have discovered without family, except for a child which had been born some time previously.

"This woman came from Los Angeles, where she had given her child to a family with the idea of adoption soon after its birth. She had continued to see this boy, now two years old, at intervals, and we have the statement of the foster mother that on her last visit she was in a cheerful frame of mind.

"Yet she came to Bayside, in this state, to a large summer estate known as Crestview, and there she was done to death."

He elaborated on the size of Crestview, "an establishment of so many rooms they had to be referred to by name;" that she had been assigned by the caretaker to what was known as the yellow room, and from this yellow room she had gone to meet her death.

"We know now what she told the caretaker, to obtain admission to the house. She told her that she was married, and to whom, and we will later present the certificate of this marriage discovered—along with her other effects—through the acumen of Samuel Floyd, the chief of police in Bayside.

"Unfortunately this caretaker, one Lucy Norton, is now herself dead, under circumstances which I shall not ask you to consider. But you will learn that every effort was made to conceal and destroy not only this young woman herself, but her personal effects.

"However, we now have certain facts which point to a certain individual as guilty of this heinous crime. These facts will be presented to you by various witnesses, and you will then decide whether or not to bring in a true bill against this prisoner.

"Shall we proceed, Mr. Foreman?"

Carol was the first witness. She had made her way through the curious crowd outside on her arrival with her head high, paying no attention to the cameramen as they shot her, but in the Grand Jury room she felt as though she was before a medieval inquisition. As she sat down she sensed that the men gazing at her were unfriendly; that she represented to most of them the idle rich, who lived on the bent backs of the rest of the world. Nevertheless, she told her story clearly, the finding of the house locked and Lucy gone, the discovery by Freda— now unfortunately departed into the limbo of domestic service elsewhere—and her own brief sight of the body.

She was shown the crushed white hat, the burned fur jacket, slippers, and the piece of the red negligee. But she refused to identify them. "They were brought to me later," she said. "I did not see them on the—on the body. I only saw there was someone there."

When they let her go she was relieved to find young Starr waiting for her outside, his old car at the curb and his grin as engaging as ever.

"How about a drink?" he inquired cheerfully. "Don't mind those old bozos in there. It's not a trial, you know."

"They looked as though they hated me."

"So what?" he said, pushing her through the crowd. "I wouldn't trust one of them in the dark with you. That ain't hate."

He took her to a small bar and ordered her a brandy. He took beer himself, and when they were settled at a small table he watched her color come back. When she seemed all right again he leaned forward confidentially.

"I'm in kind of a jam myself," he told her. "Haven't known whether to talk or not. You see I was around your place right after they took Mrs. Hilliard to the hospital."

"How does that put you in a jam?"

"Well, it's like this," he said, lowering his voice. "I'd been hanging around the town all day. Mrs. Norton had been found dead, and it looked queer as all hell. On the floor, with a broken leg and so on. Then when I started back about one o'clock that night I saw the ambulance coming out of your drive, and another car after it. That looked funny, so I left my car and walked up to your place.

"I was just looking around, you know. It was raining hard, but I kinda like rain. And there was a ladder under what you call the yellow room. I guess I hadn't any business to do it, but I suppose you know what I found. Somebody had been there before me. Maybe I ought to tell the police about it. I don't know. I damn near told Dane about it. I guess I funked it. He scares me, that guy."

"I don't see why. He's very kind."

He stared at her.

"Kind!" he said. "I wouldn't like to go up against him. That's all I can say. He was in the FBI before the war. I saw him kill a man myself."

Carol caught her breath.

"What sort of a man?" she asked, her voice uncertain.

"Gangster, right here in this town. Don't let that worry you. He needed killing. I guess Dane's been doing special work since the war. Secret stuff, you know. The way those fellows are trained—!" He smiled at her again. "I kind of suspected Dane of murdering that girl. Looked like spy stuff. That's out now."

Seeing that this new picture of Dane had disturbed her, he reverted to the yellow room. Had the police noticed the loose baseboard in it? Had she any idea what the girl might have hidden behind it? And who did she think had torn the room apart?

When he found she knew nothing he took her back to the hotel; to the bleak room with its bed and bureau and chair, and its silence, since the press was still waiting outside the Grand Jury room. It stood there, watching the faces of witnesses, dropping endless cigarette butts on the wooden floor, and making bets on the outcome, with the odds in favor of indictment.

26

The session was still going on, in secrecy and under oaths of silence. Impressed witnesses came and went. Floyd, Dr. Harrison, Marcia Dalton, tearful and not certain now she had seen Elinor's car the night of the murder; making a bad impression too, as though she were shielding someone. The bus driver who had brought the girl, and Sam Thompson, with his story of her looking through his telephone directory.

The list of exhibits grew. It now included the ring, the marriage certificate with a sworn statement by a Mexican magistrate that he had married Marguerite Barbour and one Gregory Spencer a year before, the dead girl's clothing and bags, uncovered on the hill, and the pitiful fragments of what she had worn the night of her death.

Except for the marriage certificate her handbag had contained little of importance, a hundred-odd dollars in bills and currency, the usual powder, rouge and lipstick, some cleansing tissue, a receipt from the hotel in New York, a return railroad ticket to New York, and a check for her suitcase at Grand Central. The suitcase itself was added to the list of exhibits, with the baby's picture shown for its psychological effect on the jurors. Thereafter Campbell referred to her as "this mother," with due effect.

The table became loaded. There was even the pitcher from the attic, with a laboratory report that it had contained gasoline, and the State's contention that it had been used to prevent the discovery of the buried effects.

But the State also added one exhibit which explained what had been a mystery to Maggie. It produced a large oilcan which had disappeared from her kitchen, and Hank Williams to testify that he had sent Lucy Norton a gallon of the fluid on the morning of the murder.

Maggie, brought over by Floyd under protest and put on oath, was obliged to state that it was almost empty when she had first seen it at Crestview on her arrival.

The foreman of the jury put on his glasses and inspected it.

"Is it the State's contention that the contents of this—er—holder were used in an attempt to destroy the body?"

"It is."

The oilcan had its proper effect on the jury. It was a familiar thing. They used ones like it in their own kitchens, yet here was one which had been debased to a sickening purpose. The district attorney saw this and was contented, and because Greg's attorneys knew fairly well what was going on, that—in effect—no holds were barred, they at last took an unusual step. They requested that Greg himself be allowed to appear.

Campbell stood for some time, the formal application in his hand. Then, sure of what he had, he agreed.

"The defendant has applied for permission to appear here," he said to the jury. "If it is the will of this body to hear him we will produce him."

The Grand Jury agreed, and Greg was duly warned by the foreman.

"This jury is willing to hear what you have to say. You have come here of your own free will. What you say will be at your own instance. Remember this, however. Everything you say will be recorded here, and may be used as evidence against you if we so decide."

But Campbell was not so sure when Greg appeared. He impressed them, there was no doubt about it. His size, his good looks, his uniform and the ribbons he wore. He acknowledged at once that he had married the girl, under the influence of liquor and what he now thought might have been marijuana. When shown the ring, however, he denied ever buying it. He left the country after the marriage, sending her a thousand dollars and hoping never to see her again. Asked about the child, he said he understood there was one two years old. If so, it was not his. He had never known her until the night he met her, when she was introduced to him by somebody. "But there was a crowd. I dodn't remember who it was."

He stated flatly that he had been in New York the night of the murder. Unfortunately he had no alibi, but his attorneys were working on that. He had had a letter from the girl saying she was coming east to see his family. He had tried to head her off, but was too late. He had not come to Bayside at all until the Thursday after her death.

Asked if he had gone to see Lucy Norton at the hospital he denied it absolutely. As for why he had come to Crestview the night of the fire, he had come because his two sisters were alone there. No, he had not set fire to the hill. He had not known there was anything buried there.

He was pale and sweating when they finished with him. They took him back under guard to his police cell, and a kindly officer brought him some whisky.

"Understand those fellows ripped the guts right out of you," he said.

"They made me look like a fool," Greg said. "And act like a murderer," he added bitterly.

Campbell was cheerful at the end, although his face was grave.

"Remember this," he said impressively. "This woman—this mother—stood in his way. He was engaged to a young and lovely girl, of his own class. The preparations were made for this marriage, and then what happened? This woman who is now dead wrote to him. She intended to see his family, to claim what was rightfully hers. She was on her way east.

"He knew this would be fatal to his hopes. It is the State's contention that, having missed her in New York, he went to Newport and there in all probability obtained his sister's car; that in it he drove to Bayside, in some manner induced her to admit him to the house there, and there with intention and premeditation did her to death."

There was more. Campbell gave himself a free rein, and when at last he stated that he had done his duty and depended on the jury to do the same, there was not much question as to the issue. Two hours after he had finished they brought in a true bill, and the next day Gregory Spencer was taken to court and arraigned for first-degree murder. He listened to the indictment as it was read, said "Not guilty" in a clear voice, and gazed still with the hurt look in his eyes to where Carol and Virginia were sitting in the courtroom.

Virginia gave him a brilliant smile . . .

Dane read all this in a Los Angeles paper. He had reached the Coast on Monday morning, having changed into civilian clothes on the way. Now it was Thursday, and so far he had drawn almost a complete blank. There was no chance of learning anything about the party at which Greg had met Marguerite, or who had constituted it. The town was filled with officers, coming and going.

Nor did his search for a previous marriage of the murdered girl help him any. He went to Tia Juana, without result. She could have married anyone, anywhere. Neither Arizona nor Nevada required tests or delays for licenses. And when he attempted in San Francisco to trace the telephone call which had notified the Wards that everything was okay, he found after long investigation that it had been made from a pay booth.

Two things he did get, through the Los Angeles police. The first was where Marguerite had bought her wedding ring and had it engraved. It was a small shop, and the jeweler was repairing a watch when he entered. He worked for a few minutes before he took the glass from his eye.

"Anything I can do for you?"

"I understand you sold a wedding ring to a young woman, and engraved it. The letters were 'G to M'."

The jeweler eyed him.

"Well, that's my business," he said shortly.

"I'd be glad if you could tell me the details."

"Details? There weren't any. She wanted it engraved while she waited. I don't do things that way, but she had to catch a train. I did it. She paid me. That's all."

The other information was more valuable. Again through the police he located the young woman who was caring for Marguerite's child.

On the Thursday he read that Greg had been indicted he took a taxi to an unfashionable part of town, and saw a neat white bungalow, with a small child, a boy, in a play pen in the yard. There was no one else in sight, and he walked over to the child.

"Hello, there," he said. "What's your name?"

The boy grinned, showing a partly toothless mouth, and holding out a toy to Dane.

"All alone, are you, son? Where's your mother?"

She came out then, a pleasant-looking young woman. The police had given him her name, Mrs. Gates, and he smiled at her over the baby's play pen.

"Fine child you have here," he said pleasantly.

"Yes, isn't he? And good, too."

"You're Mrs. Gates?"

"Mrs. Jarvis Gates. Yes."

"I'd like to talk to you about—what's the boy's name?"

She stiffened.

"It's Pete," she said defiantly. "And I've been told not to talk to anybody."

"I'm working on this case, Mrs. Gates. After all, since his mother had been killed—"

"I'm not talking. I may have to go east to the trial. I didn't like her much, but all I can say is that if that man killed her I hope he gets what's coming to him."

It was sometime before he could persuade her into the house. She took the boy with her and held him, as if Dane might have designs on him. The bungalow was small but neat. The front door opened into a diminutive living room, and beyond that was a bedroom. Behind he surmised was a kitchen and not much else. Evidently there was no money to waste here, he decided, and produced fifty dollars in tens and fives from his wallet.

He did not give them to her, however. He placed them on a mission oak table at his elbow.

"I want to ask you some questions, Mrs. Gates. If you don't care to answer them you don't have to, of course. And I assure you Pete is safe, so long as you want to keep him."

"I've had him for two years." Her eyes filled with sudden tears. "If they try to take him away—"

"I'm sure nobody has any such intention."

"We want to adopt him, my husband and I. We wanted to right along, but she wouldn't let us. She said he was her ace in the hole, whatever that means."

"I see," Dane said. "How did you get him in the first place?"

Either the money or his assurance that she could keep the child loosened her tongue.

"I was in the hospital when he was born," she said. "I had just lost my own baby, and she heard about it. Maybe you know what she was like. She didn't want a baby around. She liked men and parties. She— well, she didn't want to be bothered. Anyhow she said I could have the baby. She would pay a little to help take care of him, and she promised that someday we could adopt him."

"She didn't mention the boy's father?"

"No. That's why I thought—well, I thought maybe she wasn't married. She'd used the name Barbour at the hospital, Marguerite Barbour. She didn't care for the baby, you know." She looked at Dane. "I mean, she was keeping him for some reason or other, but she didn't pay any real attention to him. She didn't even pay for him regularly.

"Then one day in the spring she came here. She was all dressed up, and she said she was going east before long. I remember what she wore, a black dress and a white hat, and a fox jacket. She said she'd paid five hundred dollars for it. And she had a bag with her initials on it, M.D.B. I asked her where she'd got all the money, but she just laughed at me.

"She said she wouldn't be gone long, and that I'd hear from her soon. She was going to New York. She didn't say why, but she owed me a lot for the baby's keep, and she promised to send it as soon as she got there. But I didn't get the money, and Jarvis had flu and was out of work. Then I saw about this murder, and the clothes and so on, so one day I just went to the police. I was afraid it might be her."

That was all. He left the fifty dollars on the table, smiled at the baby, and having got the name of the hospital concerned, took his waiting taxi and drove to it. Here at first he met with disappointment. The hospital did not disclose such information as he required. He would understand that now and then they had unmarried mothers. They had no right to disclose their names.

It required his calling the FBI before they permitted him to see their files, and the FBI in the shape of a cheerful ex-associate of his chose to be funny.

"Maternity hospital!" he said. "For God's sake, Dane, what are you doing there? Having a baby?"

In the end he got the authority, however. The cards for two years before were placed at his disposal, and he ran rapidly through them. He found Elizabeth Gates, white, Protestant, age twenty-seven. Female infant dead on birth. And he found Marguerite Barbour, also Protestant, age twenty-six, Male child, weight seven and a half pounds.

He went back to his hotel. The day was hot, and he took a cool bath before he looked at the papers. Greg had been indicted. He even rated the first page, along with the war news. Murder Charged Against Medal Holder. Grand Jury Finds True Bill Against Spencer. War Ace Indicted. It was not unexpected, but the headlines gave him a shock.

He obtained Marguerite's former address from Mrs. Gates before he left. Now, because he felt that action—any action—was imperative, he drove there. It was a typical boardinghouse, with a pleasant little rotund woman in charge.

"Yes, she lived here," she said. "I told the police all I knew. There's no use going up to her room either. They searched it, and I have a nice schoolteacher in it now."

"I don't want to look at the room," he said, to her evident relief. "I'd like to talk about Marguerite Barbour herself."

She led him into a small neat parlor and sat down opposite him.

"I'll tell you all I know," she said. "I didn't like her. I keep a respectable house, and she—well, I had my doubts about her. But when she came she was going to have a baby. The town was crowded already. I had a room, and I couldn't turn her away. Anyhow she paid her rent regularly, which is more than I can say for some of them.''

"How did she pay the rent?''

She seemed surprised.

"On the first of the month.''

"How? In cash?''

"She paid by check.''

"Didn't that strike you as unusual? If she was earning her living the way you think she was, she'd be likely to pay cash, wouldn't she?''

The landlady flushed delicately.

"She's dead,'' she said. "I'm not saying any evil about her. Anyhow she had money of her own. She said it was an allowance from an uncle, but when I think of it that's queer. No uncle has turned up since.''

"I see,'' Dane said thoughtfully. "How did she get this allowance?''

"Every month, by mail. It was a postal money order. I know that, because she had to take her driver's license for identification to get it cashed. She had a car, you know.''

"This uncle—did she ever say anything about him?''

"No. I think he came to see her once about two years ago. I wasn't here, but the maid told me. She's gone now—the maid, I mean—but she said he was a gentleman. Not the sort she mostly ran around with. Of course, I never let any of my girls take men to their rooms.''

Dane considered that.

"Old or young?'' he asked.

"She didn't say.''

"This sum of money every month—she might have been blackmailing somebody,'' he suggested.

The landlady had never thought of that, although she "wouldn't put it past her.'' Asked as to where the letters came from she said she hadn't noticed, but the last one had arrived about the first week of June. She thought it came from Maine. There had been none since.

As Dane limped out to his waiting cab he realized that his leg was bothering him again. He wondered if excitement did not make it worse, for under his veneer of cool impassivity he realized that he was excited. The dates, the clues all fitted. He needed only one fact to complete his evidence, and he got it by long-distance that night. But he was not happy. As the cab started he was more depressed than he had thought was possible when he began to see his way through a case.

27

It was Monday night when he got out of the plane and saw Alex's disapproving eye in the glare of the car's headlights. The heat even at that hour was appalling, New England going through its brief but annual hot spell. It was like being plunged into a Turkish bath, and he said so as Alex stowed away his bag.

"Better over by the sea, sir," Alex said dryly. "What you been doing to that leg?"

"The leg's all right. I'm tired, that's all."

Alex glanced at him. Dane's lean stern face looked tired and there were new lines in it, but Alex thought it best to ignore them. In answer to questions he made his usual brief replies. Nobody had been seen around Crestview. The redhead had gone home. Mrs. Hilliard was still in the hospital, but he'd heard she was up and around. Hilliard himself had gone. As for Floyd, he was strutting around so puffed up he'd had to let his belt out.

It was too late to see Carol. But Alex's statement about the heat had proved erroneous. He did not go to bed. Instead, he changed into slacks and a thin sleeveless jersey and went out of the house. For some reason he felt uneasy. He lit a cigarette, and wandering over to Crestview found Tim near the lane. He was standing there gazing up the road, and Dane's silent approach made him jump and grab for his gun. He smiled sheepishly when he saw in the starlight who it was.

"Hell!" he said disgustedly. "My nerves are about shot. How long am I to keep this up?"

"Anything new?"

"I think we've located Greg Spencer in New York the night of the murder. Not sure yet, but it looks like it."

Dane nodded.

"That's a big help," he said. "What were you watching when I came up?"

"I don't know. Where does this road go anyhow?"

"It joins a paved one up above. Why?"

"There was somebody on it a few minutes ago. Went up the hill. Anybody live up there?"

Dane was thoughtful.

"Maybe somebody who lives back in the country. Only empty summer places near. How long ago was it, Tim?"

"Ten minutes or so. I didn't see who it was. It's kind of rough walking. Heard him stumble."

"Stay here. I'll go up a bit. It's too hot to sleep anyhow."

The lane *was* rough walking. Dane had no particular reason for climbing it. There were a dozen possible reasons for someone to be out at one o'clock in the morning. But the exercise was good after his long trip in the plane, and there was a slight breeze now coming down from the hills. He went on, without any attempt at caution, cheerful because his leg responded well and his muscles had not lost their tone. When he reached the upper road he turned left, by a sort of automatism. The deserted house lay there, shielded by its overgrowing shrubbery and trees and faintly outlined in the starlight. It had no interest for him. It had served its purpose. And he had walked far enough.

It was when he turned to go back that he saw the light by the stable, low down and moving slowly. It was swinging around, forming small circles, then going on, as if searching for something on the ground. He watched it for some time before he started cautiously toward it. He was badly dressed for working his way through the underbrush. His slacks caught on briers and his slippers did little to protect his bare feet and ankles. His long training helped him, however. He was within fifty feet of the stooping figure when a branch caught his sleeve and broke with a loud snap.

He never heard the shot. Something hit him on the head and he felt himself falling. He lost consciousness at once.

Carol was awakened that night by the telephone beside her bed. Out of sheer exhaustion she was sleeping heavily. The radium dial of her clock as she fumbled for the instrument showed it was two o'clock, and her voice was thick as she answered it.

Dr. Harrison was on the wire. He sounded apologetic.

"Is that you, Carol?" he asked. "I thought I'd better call you up.

We've had another accident, if you can call it that. Nothing to frighten you," he added hastily, "but Major Dane's been hurt."

The room swirled around her. By a great effort she controlled her voice.

"Now badly?"

"It's not very serious. He's still out. We're taking pictures, but apparently there is no fracture. He'll do nicely, but I thought I'd better let you know."

She was trembling now.

"What happened to him, doctor? Don't tell me it's another—" Her voice broke. "Someone attacked him. That's it, isn't it?"

"He was shot. Just a crease along the head, but he's had a narrow escape. He probably fell heavily, and that didn't help things."

She was out of bed by that time, still holding the receiver.

"I'm coming down," she told him. "I'll be there in fifteen minutes."

She heard him saying urgently that she was to stay in the house, that apparently nobody was safe. But she put down the receiver while he was still talking. She dressed frantically, although some remnant of caution remained in her. She went to find Tim, but Tim was not in his room. She found him in the hospital when she got there, pacing the hall downstairs like a wild man. "Goddammit, I let him go up that hill myself! Me, Tim Murphy!" Then, seeing her face, he made an effort at control. "He'll be all right, Miss Carol. He's been through worse than this. Has more lives than a cat. Just remember that."

She sat down, because her knees would not hold her. The hospital was wide awake and active, nurses hastily roused and busy, and an intern coming out of the X-ray room with plates in his hand. He gave Carol a nod.

"Looks all right," he said reassuringly. "Had the hell of a wallop, of course."

Tim thrust himself forward.

"We're seeing him," he said aggressively. "I want to know who shot at him. Then I'm going out and get the—" Here his language became unprintable. He used a few army words not common in polite society, and added some of his own invention.

The intern looked amused, Tim's costume and language both being on the lurid side.

"No objection to your going up, I imagine," he said genially. "Dr. Harrison's expecting Miss Spencer anyhow. Only"—he added with a grin—"I'd advise you to do your talking now. I can take it. Dane can't."

They followed him to the elevator, Tim indignant but silent, Carol beyond speech. Dr. Harrison was in an upper hall, and he examined the plates by the light of a nurse's desk lamp before he spoke to them. He looked up cheerfully.

"No fracture," he said genially. "Just a scalp wound. He'll come around pretty soon, I imagine."

Some of Tim's fury abated. As for Carol, she drew her first full breath since she had heard the news, although Tim's story did not help much. He told about Dane's appearance, his decision to walk up the lane, and then of hearing the shot. When Dane did not come back he had started up the hill. He saw nobody, heard nothing. He had a flashlight, but "all those places are grown up like nobody's business." Anyhow, he was still searching when he heard the siren of Floyd's car. It had stopped near him and Floyd and Mason got out. Floyd had pointed a gun at him.

"Like to scared the life out of me," Tim said. "Thought I'd shot somebody. Wanted to know what I was doing there, and where was the man who'd been killed. I almost burst out crying. 'I'm looking for Major Dane,' I said. 'He came up here and he hasn't come back.' He didn't trust me even then. He took my gun and saw it hadn't been fired. Then he led the way back to the stable."

Carol was trying to make a coherent pattern of all this.

"But—Floyd?" she said. "How did he know?"

"Got a telephone message. It said somebody was dead by the stable at Pine Hill. Can you beat it? How many people were up there to-night?"

It was some little time before they were allowed in to see Dane. He was not alone. Alex was standing like an infuriated guardian angel over the bed. Nobody spoke. Dane's eyes were closed, but as Carol moved to him he looked up.

"Hello, darling," he said. Then something strange about the situation roused him. "What the hell happened?" he said. "Where am I?"

"You're all right, Jerry."

He gave her his old sardonic grin.

"That's what you say," he said, and closed his eyes again, his mind was slowly clearing. When he looked up a few minutes later only Alex was in the room. Dane motioned to him, and he came over to the bed.

"Soon as it's daylight," he said cautiously, "go up to Pine Hill. Take Tim if you can. Anyhow, get there before Floyd wakes up to it." He paused. Talking was still an effort. "Whoever shot me was hunting something on the ground by the stable there. Better bring everything you find."

It was still dark when he was left alone to sleep if he could. Alex went unwillingly, leaving Dane's gun on the table beside the bed, and carefully locking the window which opened on a fire escape. But Dane did not sleep. His head ached and his mind was working overtime. He lay still, his eyes closed, and carefully put together what he knew and what he suspected.

The bandage interfered with his hearing, however, and he was not aware that his door had opened softly. Only a sort of sixth sense told him he was not alone in the room. He did not open his eyes at once. Whoever it was came nearer, and then paused beside him.

He looked up then and reaching out a muscular hand grabbed the arm poised above him. His own automatic dropped on the bed, and Elinor Hilliard gave a faint scream and would have fallen had he not held onto her. In the faint light she looked paralyzed with terror.

"Just what were you trying to do?" he said. "Kill me?"

She shook her head.

"What are you going to do with me?" she said faintly.

"Send for Floyd, I imagine." His voice was hard. "You've got away with a good bit, Mrs. Hilliard. You're not getting away with this."

He released her. She dropped into a chair, her face chalkwhite and her teeth chattering.

"I wasn't going to shoot you," she said. "You said I'd have to go to court, I just thought—if you'd keep out of things until it's all over—"

"Until Greg's convicted?"

"They'll never convict him. His record's too good. It was all circumstantial evidence anyhow."

Her color was slowly coming back. He was holding the gun, and she made no attempt to escape. He could see her better now, the thin scum of cold cream still on her face, the silk negligee, but he was pitiless and scornful.

"All along," he said, "you've been playing a game to save your own skin. I'm sick of you. If you didn't know certain things I'd hand you over to Floyd at once. I may yet. Now I want the truth. Who killed Marguerite Barbour?"

"I don't know," she moaned. "That's the truth. You can arrest me if you like. I still can't tell you."

He believed her. He did not like her. He wanted to take her lovely cold-creamed throat and choke her to death, for her heartlessness and selfishness. But this was the truth and he knew it. His head was aching damnably. He lay back for a minute and closed his eyes.

"What do you know about Greg's marriage?" he asked. "Had he any enemies?"

She seemed surprised.

"I wouldn't know. I suppose so."

He looked at her.

"Could it have been a trap?"

"Of course it was a trap. That little bitch—"

"I don't mean that," he said, his voice tired. "Suppose someone wanted to get rid of the girl, and Greg was drunk. It would have been easy, wouldn't it? Greg had money. If she was told that—"

But she didn't know even that. He took her again, slowly and painfully, through the night of the murder. She answered him as though she was sleepwalking, but at one question she roused.

"Did you see anyone in the lane when you arrived that night? At or near the lane?"

"Near it, yes," she said. "But it couldn't have been important, could it?"

It was daylight when he let her go back to her room and her bed, with a warning.

"Even money can't buy you out of some things," he told her. "And I'm not forgetting tonight. I don't forget easily. You're coming out with all you know when the time comes—unless you want your husband to learn about this."

She crept out like a whipped dog, and he managed to get up and lock the door behind her.

He was wide awake and much improved the next morning when a nurse brought him a shoe box, closely tied with string. She was curious. She stood holding it in her hands, weighing it tentatively.

"Not flowers," she said smiling. "Not food. Maybe tobacco. You're not supposed to smoke, you know."

"I doubt very much if it's tobacco," he told her, and put it aside until she had gone.

Tim and Alex had taken him literally. He eyed with extreme distaste the collection of old horseshoe nails, dingy buttons, the eroded leather handle of a riding crop, and a rusted shoe horn. In the bottom, however, he came upon treasure. He covered the box and put it on the table beside him.

By afternoon he was sitting up in bed, resenting the skullcap bandage on his head and demanding his trousers and some food. But about the shooting he was oddly reticent. He had walked up the lane, thought he heard someone moving at Pine Hill, and had gone in to investigate. Floyd, puzzled and annoyed, looked at him shrewdly.

"You didn't only hear someone moving, Dane," he said. "You saw whoever it was, didn't you?"

"Absolutely not."

"But you've got a damned good idea who it was, haven't you?"

"What makes you say that? How much can you see of a man behind a flashlight?"

Floyd got up out of his chair, his face flushed with anger.

"I don't want to go after a man in your condition," he said, "but all along, Dane, you've been holding out on me. Either you're coming clean now or I'll arrest you as an accessory to murder. Greg Spencer wasn't alone when he killed that girl. If you know who helped him—"

"I'm sorry, Floyd," Dane said soberly. "Maybe I underestimated you at the beginning. You've done a smart job, and it isn't your fault you've been off on the wrong foot all along."

"You're crazy," Floyd shouted furiously. "I've got Spencer, and you know it. He'll go to trial, and he'll be convicted."

Dane only lay back and closed his eyes, leaving Floyd to depart in helpless rage. The chief went back to his office and sitting at his desk went over his case against Greg. It was fool-proof, he thought: the motive, his engagement to marry again, his lack of any alibi in New York, the accurate knowledge by the killer of the house where the body was found, and Greg's presence in the town when Lucy Norton died. Even the child, he thought. It all fitted. Why the merry hell had Dane said he was off on the wrong foot?

After a time he called the district attorney on the phone.

"What do you make of this attack on Dane?" he said. "Fit in anywhere?"

Campbell was in a bad humor.

"Not unless he did it himself!" he snapped. "It's playing the devil with the case. The governor's been on the wire. Seen the papers?"

"Don't want to see them," Floyd said curtly, and hung up.

Late that night Dane, still nursing a bad headache and a considerable grouch, was roused by cautious footsteps on the fire escape outside his room. Alex had at last gone home, after locking the window and drawing the shade.

"Bad room to give you, sir," he said. "Don't trust that fire escape. Someone's gunning for you, and no mistake."

Dane laughed.

"Go home and go to sleep, Alex," he said. "That shot wasn't meant to kill me. It was meant to scare somebody off. Or anybody."

Alex stalked out, but not before he had once more placed Dane's automatic on the table beside him. It was still there when, shortly after midnight, Dane heard cautious footsteps on the fire escape outside. He took the gun and sliding out of bed, stood beyond range beside the window. He was there when the steps reached the top and someone rapped carefully on the windowpane.

Whoever he had expected—and he had expected someone—it was not the young voice which answered his challenge.

"It's Starr," it said. "From the press. I have some news for you."

Dane unlocked the window, and Starr crawled in. He looked excited, and as Dane stood by he drew a piece of paper from his pocket. Dane read it without expression.

"Came through two hours ago on the teletype," he said, grinning. "See it in the paper in the morning! Queer story, isn't it?"

Dane looked tired.

"It happens, you know. It's a queer war. May I keep this?"

"Sure. I copied it for you. That's not what I came for, anyhow. I guess I'll have to plead guilty to entering and stealing. I was in the yellow room at Crestview the night the Hilliard woman was shot. I wasn't the first," he said defensively, seeing Dane's face. "I was over here late. The night telephone operator is a friend of mine." He flushed slightly. "I was on the main road when I saw the ambulance come out, and then another car. Well, I'm a newspaperman. What would you have done?"

He waited until Dane got back into bed, then he repeated the story he had told Carol in the bar. At the end, however, he grinned sheepishly. He pulled another paper out of his pocket and laid it in front of Dane.

"Found it behind the baseboard," he said. "It sort of came loose in my hand. It's the kid's birth certificate. I thought you might be interested in the name she gave him. For his father, of course."

Dane read it, then laid it down.

"I'd like to know why you held this out," he said coldly. "You might have saved me a lot of trouble.

Starr smiled sheepishly.

"Have a heart, major. It promised to be a story. When I got around to it you were on the Coast. What was I to do? He couldn't have killed her anyhow. But that's not what brought me tonight," he said, brightening. "I know from the telephone operator who it was who called the police last night to say you'd been shot."

He looked expectant, but Dane's face did not change.

"Thanks," he said dryly, "I know that already."

Late as it was—or early in the morning—Dane made two calls as soon as Starr had gone. One was to Dr. Harrison. The doctor was naturally annoyed but alert when he heard Dane's voice.

"Sorry to disturb you at this hour," Dane said, "but it's rather important. Going back to the way the Barbour girl was killed, she was struck more than once, wasn't she?"

"Two or three times. One blow did most of the damage. The skull was pretty thin."

"You thought of a poker, didn't you?"

"Or a golf club, yes. What's it all about, Dane?"

"Just one thing more. Have you had any inquiry lately as to the exact nature of the injury which caused death?"

"Well, yes. Of course it was quite casual. I was making a professional call yesterday on—"

"Never mind," Dane said sharply. "No names, please. And thanks."

28

Mr. Ward reached the hospital early the next morning, to find a flustered nurse coming out of Dane's room carrying a washbasin and Dane's voice raised in fury.

"You get me a pair of pants," he bellowed. "If Alex took mine snatch some off one of the doctors. I'll be damned if I go around like this, draped in a blanket! Where the hell are my slacks?"

Nathaniel found him in the center of the room, his face red with indignation and a blanket held around him, over the short hospital shirt. He had the grace to look embarrassed.

"These institutions," he said as he got into bed. "Trying to wash my face for me and refusing to get me my clothes. I'm all right. It was only a graze."

He smiled, his tanned face under the white turban of bandage looking rather odd, but the old gentleman apparently did not notice. He stood inside the door as though uncertain. Then he advanced to the side of the bed and laid the morning paper on the covers.

"I take it you've seen what's here," he said. "I've come to you, major, instead of going to the police. I need some advice."

His voice was steady, the thin reedy pipe of a very old man, but he looked shaken.

"I imagine I know what it is," Dane said. "Sit down, sir, won't you?"

He glanced at the paper. Starr's story was there. He read it quickly, then he put it down.

"He has courage," he said. "The whole story is incredible, isn't it? And four Jap planes shot down!"

Mr. Ward sat very still for a moment.

"I think he wanted to die," he said finally. "Is that courage or desperation?"

"They're often the same," Dane said quietly. "At least it's no longer necessary to try an innocent man for a murder he did not commit."

Mr. Ward stiffened.

"I would never have allowed Greg Spencer to suffer, Major Dane," he said with dignity. "Since my wife's death the necessity for silence is over. I did what I could. Now of course it is out of my hands. That is why I have come to you in spite of what has happened. You're a military man. Where does justice lie, major? A quarrel, a blow, and against that the story there in the paper."

"That's what happened, is it?"

"So he told me. He was desperate. He came back to the library where I was waiting for him, and he acted like a madman. I went over to Crestview at once, hoping she was only unconscious. But she was dead, lying half in and half out the doorway, and Elinor Hilliard was bending over her body.

"I'd never seen her before. I didn't know who she was until Elinor told me she was Greg's wife. I think she thought then Greg might have done it. But she was frantic that night. She wanted time to get away, and she wouldn't let me call Lucy Norton, or anybody.

"I don't suppose I can tell you the horror I felt. It was Elinor's idea to hide the body. She didn't care where, so she herself could escape. You know Elinor," he said wryly. "She didn't care about the girl at all. Her whole idea was to gain a few hours.

"She wanted me to carry her up to the linen closet, but I'm not young. Later I did get her up in the elevator. I laid her out as decently as I could. And that's what I was doing when Lucy came along the hall. It was the worst minute of my life when she stopped at the door of the closet, major. I did the only thing I could think of, I reached out and knocked the candle out of her hand. Then in the dark I tried to get away, and I'm afraid I bumped against her and knocked her down.

"She wasn't hurt. She got up screaming and made for the stairs, and I heard her fall. When I found her in the hall below she had fainted. I didn't know she was injured, of course. My only idea at first was to get Elinor safely away. And I had to work fast. Elinor was still outside—she hadn't come in at all—and she wanted the girl's clothing. She was anxious not to have her identified, at least not for a time. We didn't expect to have more than a few minutes, until Lucy Norton came to, but even that would give her time to get away.

"Maybe I should have called the police, but look at my position. I had a half-crazy boy on my hands, and the shock might have killed someone I cared for. There was Elinor to consider, too. I had got the girl's clothing from the yellow room, and she was in a hurry to go. I suppose you can guess the rest. We had to get him away and Elinor agreed to drive him to Boston, where he could get a plane. He wasn't in uniform, you know.

"Well, I am a pretty old man, and I was in bad shape when they left. Elinor didn't help me, either. At the last minute she thrust the girl's clothes at me and told me to burn them. But I couldn't burn them." He smiled thinly. "We have an oil furnace."

"So that's why you buried them?"

"Yes, I did it that night. I couldn't get into my own tool house. The gardener keeps the key. I got a spade from the one at Crestview. I didn't do a very good job, I'm afraid, but I lifted a plant or two and replaced them. It wasn't easy in the dark, and I didn't know about her fur jacket. It was in the powder room downstairs. I found it when I went back to see if Lucy was badly hurt. One of the worst things I had to do was to go back to the closet with it and try . . ."

He seemed unable to go on. Dane, watching him closely, asked him if he needed brandy. He refused.

"I'm glad to talk," he said. "It helps a little. I've carried a burden for a long time, and a sense of guilt too. When I told my wife the next night she almost lost her mind, and when later on she saw them digging up the hillside she—it killed her." He stopped again. "I have that to add to my sins," he said heavily. "After more than fifty years, major. My dear wife . . ."

He managed to go on, although it was obviously a struggle.

"It was unfortunate that I had not told her the night it happened," he said. "She had been out looking for me, and she had seen Elinor's car. It was too bad, for she mentioned it later to a caller, and as it turned out Marcia Dalton had seen the car too and recognized it as Elinor's."

He sat back in his chair, as if he had finished, and as if the telling of the story had exhausted him. Dane could not let it stop at that, however.

"How did he get to your house that night?" he asked.

"Quite openly. By plane and then taxicab. And I assure you there was no murder in him when he came. I was alone downstairs. My wife and the servants had gone to bed. I let him in. You can imagine how I felt when I saw him, in civilian clothes and with a scar on his face. He was excited, but perfectly normal. I would have said he was a happy man that night. Of course we had to take certain precautions. You understand that. To avoid shock."

"He didn't mention the girl?"

"No. I don't think he knew she was at Crestview. He was too excited to go to bed, he said, and he went out for a walk. I suppose he saw her then, at Crestview. I didn't know she was there myself, or who she was."

"He'd been fond of her?"

"Long ago. Not lately. Later on he told me he had been keeping her while he was in training, and that she had had a child by him. He said she'd been a damned nuisance ever since."

"And that night?" Dane prompted him.

"I don't know. I never asked him. She may have gone downstairs for something, a book or a cigarette, and he saw her through a window. He must have attracted her attention somehow, but she couldn't very well bring him into the house. She went outside, just as she was. Certainly she wasn't afraid of him."

"He admitted that he'd killed her?"

"He said it was an accident. He had hit her with his fist, and her head struck the stone step. Later he said he'd introduced her to Greg Spencer last year, while Greg was drinking. Said he told her to marry him. He had plenty of money. He wanted to get rid of her, of course."

There was a long silence. Dane was trying to coordinate the story with what he already knew. Some parts of it fitted, some did not. He stirred.

"I'm sorry, Mr. Ward," he said. "This next question will be painful, but I have to know. Did he try to burn the body? You see, I know he was staying at Pine Hill."

The old man looked sick. His face was a waxy yellow and his hands were shaking. Dane was about to ring for a nurse, but he made a gesture of protest.

"It's all right," he said unevenly. "It can do no harm now. God forgive, major. I think my wife did it."

"Your wife!"

"I had told her the story, you see. All of it, and she was a woman of strong loyalties and deep affections. She knew the body was there, and that Lucy was in the hospital. And she had a key to Crestview. We have stayed through the winter once or twice, and she would go in occasionally to see that everything was all right.

"I imagine Lucy had left some kerosene in the kitchen. There was no electric light on, and she was using a lamp there. From the first my wife was certain the dead girl would be identified and we would be involved. But also she could not endure the thought of her being

here she was. She wanted me to take her back into the country and
bury her. But I was not strong enough to dig a grave."

Dane had suppressed his astonishment, but he found himself rigid
with pity.

"I see," he said. "After all, who can blame her? The girl was dead."

"She had been dead for two days. I think she did it on Sunday night
after I had gone to church. It was a dreadful thing to do, but the
weather was warm, and Carol was coming the next day. My wife never
told me, of course, but I remember little things now, the tea set in the
tool house and one or two other things Mrs. Spencer valued. I remember, too, that she had asked me if the house was insured."

He got out a neat handkerchief and dried the palms of his hands.

"She looked very ill that night, but she wouldn't let me call a doctor. I remember she didn't go to sleep. She sat by a window, looking
out at Crestview. But of course the house didn't burn."

Dane gave him a minute or two to recover before he spoke again.

"When did you know he had come back?"

"He never went very far. Certainly not to Boston. He was afraid of
what the girl might have told Lucy Norton. Elinor says he went only a
few miles that night. The next thing I knew he was hiding up at Pine
Hill, hoping to see Lucy and keep her quiet. Both of us—my wife and
I—were nervous about him by that time, but we managed to feed him,
and I took a couple of blankets to him. I suppose he did see Lucy," he
added grimly, "and the shock killed her."

"What about Elinor Hilliard?" Dane inquired. "Why was she shot?"

"She was badly worried. You can understand that. I suppose she
meant to see me that night. Lucy's death had frightened her. Or she
may have meant to look for the clothes I'd buried. But he was not a
killer, major. I hope you realize that. She may only have been in his
way. Colonel Richardson was after him, you know. He may only have
fired a shot to stop Henry and it struck Elinor. I don't know. I never
saw him after that night. As a matter of fact I drove him to the railroad
myself. But he would not talk."

Dane was thoughtful for some time. The old man was fumbling in a
pocket.

"You slipped up about the blankets at Pine Hill," Dane said finally.
"Why did you leave them there? You'd made a good job of the rest of
it."

The old man produced a letter and laid it on his knee. He took off
his pince-nez and wiped them.

"When you reach my age," he said wryly, "You forget things. When

I remembered them it was too late. You'd already found them and told Floyd. And I'd lost my glasses when I was carrying out the empty cans he'd left. That is why—"

He got up, the letter in his hand.

"That is why I shot you, major," he said. "You knew I did it, of course?"

"I knew it, yes," Dane said soberly.

Nathaniel stood, looking down awkwardly at the man in the bed.

"I don't know what is proper under such circumstances," he said. "I can't apologize. I can only explain. I had missed my glasses some time before, and that night I went to look for them. When I heard you—my nerves aren't what they were. But I never meant to shoot you, only to frighten you off. I beg you to believe that."

"I'm glad you're not a better shot," Dane said cheerfully. "I thought it was like that when I was able to think at all. You see, I understand a great deal, Mr. Ward. More than you think, perhaps." He reached for the shoe box. "You'll find your glasses in here," he said, "but they're broken. Don't pay any attention to the other stuff. Just throw it away. Only"—he added with a smile—"I suggest you don't bury it."

Mr. Ward took the box awkwardly.

"What about the police?" he asked. "Should I go to them? Before he left he sent me a statement, to be opened after his death, or in case Gregory Spencer was convicted. I am keeping it at home."

"Let's wait a bit," Dane suggested. "Greg Spencer won't be tried for some time. And things sometimes work out. After all you may be wrong, you know."

The letter was on his bed when Nathaniel went out, and Dane marveled at the strength which had carried the old man through the last few weeks, and which might have to carry him even further. It was some little time when at last he picked up the letter and began to read it.

29

He knew at once when Carol came in that morning that she had seen the newspapers. She was very quiet, but she went to his arms at once.

"I don't want to talk about it, Jerry," she said. "Later, perhaps. Not now."

"Just so it doesn't change things between us, darling."

"Nothing is changed," she said steadily.

"Have you seen the colonel?"

"I stopped there. I didn't see him. His man said he wasn't feeling very well." She stopped, and withdrew herself from his arms. "What am I to do, Jerry? It seems so brutal somehow."

"I think that it will settle itself, Carol," he said, his steady eyes on her.

He put her in a chair—he was dressed by that time, and a small dressing had replaced the bandage—and sat down near her.

"This is not going to be easy, darling," he told her. "And I'll ask you to withhold judgment for a while. I want to read you a letter. Mr. Ward brought it in this morning."

He offered her a cigarette, but she refused, and he read the letter through to the end. Now and then he looked up, but she made no comment. She sat with her clear candid eyes on him, her face rather pale but otherwise calm.

He left off the salutation, and a following unimportant paragraph or two. He began:

"I have some news for you both, but I want you to keep it to yourselves for a while. I've found Don Richardson."

Dane glanced at Carol. She had not moved, and he went on: "I was visiting one of our fellows in a hospital, and Don was in a convalescent ward. He was playing dominoes with a sergeant, and at first he didn't see me. When he did he only looked puzzled.

" 'I think I've met you somewhere,' he said.

" 'Why you old son of a so-and-so!' I told him. 'I'll say you have. What's the matter with you?'

"Then the fellow with him said he'd lost his memory. He'd been for months on an island somewhere. The natives had looked after him, but he'd had a fractured skull. 'Got a silver plate there now,' the sergeant said. 'Been here for a good while. But things are coming back, aren't they?' he said to Don. 'You knew this guy all right.'

"Well, he didn't. Not at first anyhow. He was not in an officers' ward, for nobody knew who he was. He was just part of the flotsam and jetsam of a war, brought back and dumped. I had to hurry, but I went back the next day, and he was definitely on the up-and-up.

" 'You're Terry Ward,' he said. 'I know you now.'

"He didn't remember his crash or the island, either, but he asked about his father. He didn't want him to know until he could get back to see him. Old Richardson has a bad heart, you know. And when I'd seen him several times he said I was to write you this, that he would come to you first, and then you could arrange how to break it to his dad so it wouldn't be a shock.

"I suppose I've been a help. They call him Jay here, because he was naked as a jay bird when they found him, and the natives had probably taken his identification tags. I agreed to keep his identity a secret until his father had learned it. To avoid shock. And I gave him a couple of hundred dollars. The reason I'm writing is that you may see him soon. He went AWOL from the hospital last week, and as I'll be leaving before long it will be up to you. Just remember this. He's changed a lot. Got a beard for one thing, although he's promised to shave it off. And they've done some plastic work on him. Not bad, but not good either. He's pretty much depressed. The boys say he talked about a Marguerite and somebody named Greg—maybe Greg Spencer— while he was delirious after the either. And I'm sure he's got something on his mind he won't talk about.

"All I know is that he said he had some things to see to, then he was going back to the Pacific again to fly if he had to stow away to get there. He'll do it too, silver plate and all. It's the whale of a story, isn't it? Be good to him—but of course you will. He's had a rotten time. All my love to you both. Terry.

"P.S. I'll send you some sort of word if he comes back here, or manages to get back to his squadron. Just an okay."

When Dane looked up Carol was sitting with her eyes closed, as though to shut out something she could not bear. It was some time before she spoke. She was very pale.

"Marguerite!" she said. "Are you telling me that Don killed her? That Don came here and killed her? And shot Elinor. I don't believe it, Jerry. He wasn't like that."

His voice was gentle.

"I've told you this before, my darling. War changes men. They're not quite the same after it. And there are always designing women waiting around for them."

"But—murder!"

"I've asked you to withhold judgment, for a few hours anyhow. And don't forget this either, Carol darling. You've read the story in the paper. He wasn't only saved from that island. He got back to his squadron and has been fighting hard ever since."

"You think that condones what he did?" she asked. "He killed that girl because she had married Greg. And he's allowed Greg to be indicted, to sit in a cell and wait for trial. Is that courage? It's despicable, and you know it."

Dane glanced at his wrist watch. Something had to happen, and happen soon, unless he himself was crazy. Sitting on the edge of his bed—there was only one chair in the room—he began carefully to tell her Nathaniel Ward's story as he had heard it; softening nothing, making it as clear as he could. To this he added his own visit to the Coast, the Gates family, and finally the birth certificate.

Carol read it with only a slight rise of color.

"That only makes it worse," she said. "She bore him a child. She even named it for him! And then—"

She did not finish. Someone was coming along the hall. When the door opened Dr. Harrison came in. He looked grave and unhappy when he saw Carol.

"I'm afraid I have bad news for you, my dear."

She got up quickly.

"Not Greg!"

"No. Colonel Richardson died at his desk an hour ago. It was painless, of course. He was writing a letter at the time, and—well, it's understandable. He had taken bad news for two years like a man and a soldier. But good news—"

Dane drew a long breath. There were tears in Carol's eyes.

"He was one of the finest men I ever knew," she said quietly. "I'd better go there. He was all alone, except for his man. Perhaps I can do something."

Dane got Alex on the phone the moment she was out of the room. He gave him some brief instructions and hung up. His mind was already busy with what was to be done to quash the indictment against Gregory Spencer. They would reconvene the Grand Jury, he thought, and present the new evidence, and for once he was grateful for the secrecy of such a proceeding. When Alex called all he said was a laconic "Okay," and Dane relaxed as though a terrific burden had been lifted from his mind.

Some time later Floyd was sitting across from him, his legs spread out and his face sulky.

"So you've make a monkey out of me," he said. "How the hell did you know?"

"I didn't. I worked on Terry Ward for some time. There had to be an X somewhere. Who was hiding out up at Pine Hill? Who got into the hospital, trying to talk to Lucy Norton, and scared her literally to death? Who ran into Elinor Hilliard at night and shot her in order to avoid recognition. Washington reported Terry was on the Coast and hadn't left there.

"Maybe I began to believe in miracles myself! But I was pretty well stymied. Washington had no record of Don's being alive. I couldn't discover anything on the Coast. Yet here were the Wards protecting somebody. Not Terry. He hadn't been east. All along they'd been in it. They—"

"Are you telling me old Nat Ward buried those clothes?" Floyd demanded.

"You'd better ask him," Dane said smoothly.

"All right. You've dug a lot of worms to get a fish," Floyd said resignedly. "So you pick on another hero for your fish! Don Richardson's guilty. How are you going to prove it?"

Dane settled back in his chair.

"I haven't said Don killed that girl, Floyd."

The chief sat forward, his face purple.

"Stop playing games with me," he bellowed. "First Don did it. He says he did. Then he didn't. Who the hell did?"

"The colonel," said Dane, lighting a cigarette. "The colonel, Floyd. And he never knew he had done it."

When Floyd said nothing, speech being beyond him, Dane went on.

"Figure it out for yourself. There was always X, you know. And X didn't behave like a guilty man. He hung around after it was over. He waited for the inquest. He tried to see Lucy Norton, to find out what she knew and hadn't told. Wouldn't a guilty man have escaped as soon as he could?''

"Pretty smart, aren't you?" Floyd said. "You got most of that from old Ward himself this morning!"

"All right," Dane said amiably. "I had two guesses, Don or the colonel. And if it was Don it didn't make sense. Why didn't he see his father? The colonel would have died to protect him. Instead of that Don took a farewell look at him through a window. The colonel didn't like the idea, so he tried to follow him. I don't think he even knew it was his own son. He really thought it was Terry Ward."

Floyd got out a bandanna handkerchief and wiped his face. He was sweating profusely.

"Go ahead," he said. "Go on and dream, Dane. So the colonel killed the girl and went home and had a good night's sleep. Go on. I can take it."

"Well, think it out for yourself," Dane said reasonably. "The colonel had been paying for the support of his grandson ever since he was born. He'd gone to the Coast and seen Marguerite—if that was really her name. I suspect she was born Margaret—and he knew her. Imagine his feelings when he saw her, the morning she arrived, on her way to Crestview. He was an early riser. He had to have seen her, to account for what happened. Maybe she saw him too.

"Anyhow he went up to the house that night, after Lucy had gone to bed. She couldn't take him into the house. She put on a negligee and went to the door to talk to him. I think she told him she had married Greg, and that she offered to bribe him. If he'd keep quiet about Don's baby he needn't pay any more hush money, or whatever you choose to call it.

"He must have been in a towering rage. Not only about the trade she suggested. Here she was, a little tramp, married to Carol's brother and capable of telling her she had been Don's mistress. Not that he thought it out, I imagine. I think he simply lost his head and attacked her. He didn't know he'd killed her, of course. He left at once, and from that Friday night until her body was found in the linen closet he must have thought she had got away. I saw him myself once, walking around the house, to be sure she had gone.

"The next thing he learned was that she was dead in the linen closet.

"He hadn't put her there. So far as he knew he hadn't killed her. I think all he felt was relief. She was out of the way, and someday he would locate the child and provide for him. The Wards believed Don Richardson had done it. Don had told them so. But his story didn't hold water. He said he'd knocked her down with his fist and she'd struck her head on the stone step. You saw that wound. It hadn't been made that way. I thought of a poker or a golf club. I didn't think of a thin skull and a heavy walking stick.

"After I found someone had been hiding out at Pine Hill I still had to do some guessing. I knew by that time it wasn't Terry Ward. I had the Wards looked up. Terry was the only relative they had. Whom were they protecting, and why? Whom were they feeding? And whom were they afraid of? They were afraid of someone. Old Nathaniel was carrying a gun. And when you dug up the clothes on the hillside Mrs. Ward had a stroke.

"But as I said before there was one thing I kept thinking about. Whoever shot Elinor Hilliard had been trying to escape from Colonel Richardson. That was out of the picture entirely. Why in a pouring rain did X stand outside the colonel's window, peering in?

"Think that over, Floyd. Don Richardson was a happy man the night of the murder. He had got rid of the girl by marrying her to Greg Spencer while Greg was drunk. He'd always hated Greg, I imagine; the big house on the hill and the small one below. Greg's good looks, his money, even his plane. And he was on leave in Los Angeles the night of the party. I knew that from Washington.

"Then he gets here and takes a walk to quiet down. He goes over to Crestview. Why not? He's engaged to Carol, isn't he. He doesn't know the girl's there. He goes over by the path in the dark, and what he sees is his own father slashing at someone with his cane! When his father's gone he goes over and strikes a match. It's Marguerite, and she's dead.

"Whatever his faults, he was a good son. He loved his father, and his father was a sick man. What was he to do?

"Well, after all, he's presumed to be dead. What does it matter? He goes back to the Wards' with a fool tale that he's killed her, that he's knocked her down with his fist and she's hit her head on the stone doorstep. She wasn't lying on any stone doorstep when she was found. She was in the doorway of the house. That step is wood.

"My own idea is that she *had* been out that night. Remember the pine needle in her slipper. She may even have gone down to the colonel's and he took her back, probably growing angrier all the way. It must have taken a lot to make him strike her. But he never knew he had killed her. The hall was dark—no electric current. He may not even have heard her fall. Nor even that Lucy Norton, seeing Don in the hospital that night, thought she was seeing a ghost and died of it.

"All along the colonel thought it was Terry Ward, and he was devoted to the Wards. He was sure it was Terry who had shot Elinor Hilliard. He did his best, got her out of the road and tried to call the doctor. But he wasn't the same after that. I saw him the next day. He put up a good show, but he was in poor shape."

Floyd stirred.

"Why was the Hilliard woman out that night anyhow?"

"I found a small hole on the hillside the next day. You see, she was covering up as well as she could. Nathaniel had told her he had buried the clothes, and she'd burned the hill. But she was still frightened. She had tried to save Don to save herself, but too much was going on. She was scared of him. So were they all, for that matter."

"She burned the hill!"

"Certainly. Who else? Carol Spencer knew it."

"Giving me the runaround again," Floyd grunted uneasily.

"As a matter of fact," Dane said, "you've got all the Spencers suspecting each other. That threw me off for a while. I suppose I've got a bias in favor of our fighting men, but I never thought Greg Spencer was guilty. I got Tim Murphy on the job—"

"Who's Murphy?"

"One of the best private operatives in New York. Got his own agency." And when Floyd relapsed into speechless fury, Dane smiled.

"So," he said, "I began to believe in miracles myself. Don Richardson hadn't liked Greg, and it looked too much like coincidence that Greg had married his girl. She *was* his girl. She'd named the boy for him. I found that out on the Coast, from his birth registration. And Terry Ward hadn't left the coast. So what? So maybe Don was alive after all.

"But, if it was Don, he wasn't acting like a man with a crime on his soul. He was hiding out at Pine Hill. Why?

"Well, I'd learned somebody else had a motive, had been paying a sort of blackmail since the boy was born. But I was still guessing until last night, when I learned that Colonel Richardson had been inquiring of the nature of the wound which killed the girl.

"Mr. Ward had mixed things up by shooting at me, and Elinor Hilliard was keeping her mouth shut. I only learned within the last few hours, for instance, that as she turned into the drive the night of the murder she saw the colonel going into his house, and he was carrying a stick."

"He always carried a stick," Floyd said belligerently. "I liked the old boy. Everybody liked him. If you're trying to say he killed that girl in cold blood—"

Dane's face looked very tired.

"Not at all," he said. "I'm saying that for the first time in his life Colonel Richardson struck a woman, and she died of it."

There was a prolonged silence. Then Floyd got up.

"I suppose you're sure of all this," he said heavily. "It's going to make a stink, Dane. That's bad for the town."

"Not necessarily. I want to say this. Don Richardson would never have allowed Spencer to suffer, or his father either. He went back to the Pacific to fight, but he left Mr. Ward a statement to be opened in case Spencer was convicted or he himself was killed."

"Saying he didn't?"

"Probably," Dane said dryly.

"Then where the hell are we?"

"Nowhere." He gave Floyd a grim smile. "Except that Greg Spencer will never go to trial."

"That's what you say," Floyd said, still truculent. "You've been doing a lot of guessing, Dane, but where's your proof? All you've done is lug in a dead man who can't defend himself. Who didn't even know he'd done it! I gave you credit for better sense."

"I think he did know it, the last day or so. Remember, he thought Mr. Ward was going armed against him. He said so. Then why? Had Nathaniel found the body and tried to dispose of it, to protect him? Did they know he had done it, and think he had lost his mind? He himself told me he was considered something of a crackpot around here.

"There's something else too, Floyd. It's just possible he thought he recognized Don at the window that rainy night. He wasn't sure, of course. That might have been the reason he followed him. In that case he must have been badly worried. Why hadn't Don come to see him? Why had he done none of the normal things? Had Don found the girl unconscious and killed her himself?"

"I'm betting on Don this minute," Floyd said. "Always was a wild kid. If that girl had two-timed him—"

"Let me go on," Dane said tiredly. "The colonel was in bad shape. He had to know. So yesterday he saw Dr. Harrison. The girl had died of one blow, by a poker or something similar. He knew then that he had killed her.

"I don't suppose he slept at all last night. Part of the time he spent writing out a confession. Then when he got the newspaper, with the news that Don was alive and fighting again, he collapsed.''

Floyd's face was ugly.

"What's all this about a confession?''

"I have it here.''

Floyd jerked it angrily from his hand and glanced at it. He looked apoplectic.

"How did you get hold of this?'' he snarled. "Damn it all, Dane, you've been messing in where you didn't belong ever since this case started.''

"As soon as I'd heard from the doctor last night I called the colonel up and suggested it,'' Dane said coolly. "At its worst it was manslaughter, and he knew he hadn't long to live. Greg Spencer had to be saved somehow. You had too good a case, Floyd, and I hadn't any. Don't blame the night telephone operator. I'm a friend of a friend of hers.''

"How'd you get hold of it?''

"Oh, that! I sent Alex there this morning. Good man, Alex.''

"He's a dirty snooper,'' Floyd bellowed, but Dane merely smiled.

"All right. Have it your own way. You'll find the colonel admits an excess of rage, during which he struck her with a heavy stick he was carrying, and seeing her fall. He admits leaving her there, but not knowing she was dead. He admits he'd been paying her what amounted to blackmail. He even admits to searching the yellow room later for the child's birth certificate and some evidence of where she had hidden him with the idea of collecting on him later. He didn't finish it, of course. His heart went back on him, or he would probably have claimed he tried to burn the body!''

"And who did?''

"Does that matter now?''

The two men stared at each other, the one shrewd and angry, the other hard and inflexible. Floyd got up.

"By God, Dane,'' he said, "I'm still not sure you didn't do it yourself!''

He stamped out, and Dane laughed quietly as the door slammed.

30

He left the hospital that afternoon. Alex had stood by while he dressed, his one eye watching every movement.

"I'll bet that leg's bad again, sir," he said. "You aren't fooling me any."

"Leg! I wouldn't know I had a leg. I'll be going back soon, Alex. I have a little business to transact first. Then I'm off."

"What sort of business?" Alex inquired suspiciously. "Any more murders around?"

"This is different," Dane said, carefully knotting his tie. "Very, very different."

He was sober enough when he reached Crestview. Tim admitted him, a grinning Tim who reached for his cap with a differential air, and spoiled it by clutching him by the arm.

"What the hell's cooking?" he said. "You're a tightmouthed son of a so-and-so, but if you're letting me scrub pots while you have the time of your life running over the country and getting shot—"

Dane smiled.

"The pot scrubbing's over, Tim."

"Well, well! I suppose Floyd killed the girl. He's the only one I haven't suspected."

"I'll tell you later. Where's Miss Spencer?"

"Locked in her room. Maggie's been up half a dozen times with coffee. She won't let her in."

"I'll go up. She may see me."

He went up the stairs. He wasn't limping at all. In the upper hall he stopped at the door to the yellow room and looked in. It was a pretty room, he thought. The baseboard had been nailed back in place, the mulberry curtains were in neat folds, and the fragment of candle had been replaced by a fresh one, in case a storm shut off the electric current.

He glanced back along the hall. The linen closet had been repainted. It gleamed fresh and white in the light from the patio, and in the patio itself the pool had been repainted and filled. It shone like a bit of the sky overhead, where a bomber was droning along, as if to remind him that there was still a war, and he had a place in it.

He moved along to Carol's door and rapped.

"It's Jerry," he said, "I have to see you."

He thought she hesitated. Then the key turned and she confronted him. She looked exhausted, but she was not crying. She stood aside to let him enter, but she made no movement toward him.

"I have to thank you for a great deal," she said quietly. "You've saved Greg, even if you had to kill Colonel Richardson to do it."

He looked puzzled.

"You told him about Don, didn't you? People don't die of joy. You called him from the hospital, and told him."

"I couldn't tell him anything he didn't know, Carol," he said gravely.

"What does that mean? If Don came here and killed that girl—"

"Listen, my dear," he said. "I'm feeling pretty low just now. I've made a mess of a lot of things, and I don't like the way the case has turned out. But remember this. I asked you today to withhold judgment. I needed something I didn't have at that time. Now I'm asking a question. Suppose Don is innocent, Carol?"

"You don't mean that Greg—"

"Not Greg. No. I'm wondering how you feel about Don, now that he is alive. You cared for him once. Now he is more than alive. He is fighting like a man. You can be proud of him. And the affair with Marguerite—can't you understand that? The hunger a man feels for a woman when he's been cut off from them for months, or years. He was young, and he'd been in training for a long time when he met her. He didn't know she was a—well, what she was."

"Are you defending him?"

"I am. He is even braver than you know, my dear. You see, he confessed to a murder he didn't commit. That takes courage. Perhaps that changes things with you—and him."

"I'm not in love with him, if that's what you mean. But I don't understand," she said steadily. She sat down, looking lost and unhappy. "Why would he do such a thing?"

He told her then, moving around the room as he did so. Sometimes stopping in front of her, again looking out the window, where the bomber was circling lazily overhead and the empty harbor with its emerald islands lay below. Once he stopped and offered her a cigarette, but she shook her head.

"Go on," she said steadily. "I want to know it all. It's time I did, isn't it?"

When he had finished she sat very still. Nevertheless, except that she had lost color, she had taken it better than he had even hoped.

"It's hard to realize," she said, rather bleakly. "If it was anyone but the colonel. He was so kind, Jerry, so—gentle."

"He was a man," he reminded her. "Very much a man, my dear. When that little tramp tried to bribe him he struck at her. I'm afraid I'd have done more than that."

She was trying to think things out, from this new angle.

"Then it was the colonel who scared Lucy, and shot Elinor. I—I don't believe it."

"Not the colonel, my dear. Don shot Elinor. I don't think he meant to, any more than Mr. Ward intended to hit me. It was an accident. He was trying to get away."

But he did not tell her, would never tell her, what he knew now was the real tragedy of that night; of Don, anxious for a last sight of his father, slipping down from Pine Hill in the rain to peer through a window and see the colonel, standing in full view in that lighted room. Or of the heartbreaking thing that had followed, the colonel starting up the lane after him and Don desperately trying to escape.

"What would happen if his father saw him? Can you imagine the Colonel keeping that news to himself. And what became of Don's statement to the Wards that he had killed the girl? Was he to tell his father that? The man who had done it without knowing it, and who had a bad heart anyhow. What did Elinor Hilliard matter, in a situation like that?

"He probably came across her unexpectedly," he said, "and he was pretty jumpy. Don't ask me where he got the gun, my darling. I don't know. It may have been Nathaniel Ward's. Don never meant to be taken alive. Be sure of that."

He sat down near her, watching her, wondering at the fortitude she had shown for the past month. Perhaps it was the same courage which had won Greg his decoration. Whatever it was he knew that he loved her more than he loved anything else in the world. It was not time to tell her so, however. Not so long as the bewildered look was still in her eyes.

"I still don't know why she went out at all that night, Jerry."

"I rather imagine," he said quietly, "she had decided to do away with the things on the hill. Too much was happening; Lucy's death the night before, for instance."

"Why did he come back, Jerry? It seems so strange. To hide out, up there on the hill—"

"Well, look, my dear. He was trying to protect his father. He waited for the inquest, but if Lucy knew anything she didn't tell it. Nevertheless he knew Marguerite too well to trust her. If she had told Lucy she was to see the colonel that night Lucy might break down, under pressure.

"So he saw Lucy that night at the hospital, and because she thought he meant to kill her, or perhaps because she thought he was a ghost, she—well, she died of fright. That's all I know, and it doesn't matter now. What does matter, my darling, is that it's over. All over."

She cried a little then, not for the colonel, at peace at last, not even—he realized gratefully—for Don, doing his man's work in a man's war. Some of it was relief, but there was grief, too; for the colonel, for Lucy, and for Joe now sitting alone in his empty house. For Mrs. Ward. And even, he thought wryly, for Marguerite herself, because she, too, had been young and had wanted to live. He let her alone, beyond giving her what he termed a perfectly good shoulder to weep on.

"More beautiful women than you have sobbed on it," he said. "But to hell with them. You're my girl now. Or are you?"

She smiled after a minute or two her old smile, which had so endeared her to him from the beginning.

"I'll be good to you, darling," he said gravely. "I've got a job to do, but I'll be coming back. I'd like to know I was coming back to you. Men have lived because of that, you know," he added. "Because they had someone to come back to."

"Why do I have to wait?" she asked. "I'm tired of being the spinster in the family. Or are you really asking me to marry you at last?"

He drew her into his arms, the muscular arms which had been trained to kill in many wartime ways, but which could also be gentle and protective.

"I'm asking you to marry me," he said. "Here and now. Before I go. Will you?"

"Tim gives you excellent references."

"Never mind Tim. Or Alex either. I'm not marrying them. Will you, darling?"

"Of course," she said. "I thought you'd never really say it."

There was nothing saturnine about his smile as he held her ever closer. He had forgotten his job. He had even forgotten his leg, which was fine. He put his full weight on it, and without warning it gave a jump and began to ache furiously. He released her with a grunt.

"Hell!" he said. "We may even have a little time for a honeymoon, sweetheart." And sat down abruptly on the nearest chair.